I0761879

THE DATING GAMES SERIES

VOLUME 1

INCLUDES:

DATING GAMES
WICKED GAMES
MIND GAMES

USA TODAY BESTSELLING AUTHOR
T.K. LEIGH

DATING GAMES

Published by Carpe Per Diem, Inc. / Tracy Kellam, 25852 McBean Parkway # 806, Santa Clarita, CA 91355

Edited by: Kim Young, Kim's Editing Services

Cover Image Elements:

Vectorovich © 2020

designer_things © 2020

Used under license from Adobe

BOOKS BY T.K LEIGH

CONTEMPORARY ROMANCE
The Dating Games Series
Dating Games
Wicked Games
Mind Games
Dangerous Games
Royal Games
Tangled Games

The Redemption Series
Promise: A Redemption Duet Prologue
Commitment (Redemption Duet #1)
Redemption (Redemption Duet #2)
Possession (Possession Duet #1)
Atonement (Possession Duet #2)

ROMANTIC COMEDY
The Book Boyfriend Chronicles
The Other Side of Someday
Writing Mr. Right

ROMANTIC SUSPENSE
The Vault
Inferno

The Beautiful Mess Series
A Beautiful Mess
A Tragic Wreck
Gorgeous Chaos

The Deception Duet
Chasing the Dragon
Slaying the Dragon

Beautiful Mess World Standalones
Heart of Light
Heart of Marley
Vanished

For more information on any of these titles and upcoming releases, please visit T.K.'s website:
www.tkleighauthor.com

USA TODAY BESTSELLING AUTHOR

T.K. LEIGH

CHAPTER ONE

I'VE ALWAYS HAD an affinity for the number three.

Third time's a charm.

Past, present, future.

Beginning, middle, end.

Three is considered the perfect number, and not just by me. Many religions view it as a sacred number, a holy number. Even Plato recognized the idealism in it, dividing his Utopian city into three populations — Laborers, Guardians, and Philosophers.

Three is also the "magic" number in fairy tales. A hero or heroine is often given three choices, or they overcome the obstacle on the third try. Think back to the beloved tale of *Cinderella*. When the prince searches for his perfect match, with the aid of a glass slipper, Cinderella's is the third foot he tries after unsuccessfully attempting to shove it onto her darling step-sisters' feet. There's a tension inherently built into this number that has always spoken to me on an ethereal level. Throughout my life, everything always happened in threes, perhaps due to my own insistence.

I graduated third in my high school class. Granted, there were only a whopping ten people in my graduating class, but that made it even more significant, considering I was in the top 33.33%. I kept my circle of best friends small, only three of us. And up until now, I've only had sex with three people.

The first was my neighbor, Brent. There was no romantic attraction. I was almost eighteen and thought it best to have a practice round so I'd be fully prepared when it counted. Plus, we both felt like we were the last two virgins our age in all of Nebraska. Years later, I found out Brent was gay. I hope it wasn't his experience with me that made him realize this.

My second sexual encounter was with Christian Murphy. He was the one I wanted to practice for. (Thank you, Brent.) Handsome. Popular. Smart, without having to try. I thought he was the man I would spend the rest of my life with, which concerned me, because he was only my second.

But when Trevor Channing walked into my History 101 class freshman year of college, it was suddenly goodbye, Christian, and hello, Trevor!

You know those scenes in movies where the heroine locks eyes with the leading man the first time and an explosion of orchestral music fills the background? That's what happened with Trevor. Without saying a word,

I knew he'd forever be my number three. My perfect match.

Which is why it feels like all the wind has been sucked from my lungs as I stare at him incredulously. I must not have heard him correctly. There's no way those words came out of his mouth, not when we're celebrating my thirtieth birthday at the sushi place where we shared our third meal after moving to New York.

All day, I'd been confident this was the night he would pop the question. After all, we've been together over ten years. Not to mention the fact I often said I wanted to wait until I was thirty before I got married. Surely, Trevor would have taken the hint that this meant he should propose on a birthday of such significance. Every sign pointed to me screeching "yes" after he got down on one knee in front of a restaurant full of strangers and poured his heart out. Hell, in my fantasy, he even shed a few tears because of how overwhelmed he was.

As is typically the case, my fantasy was so far from reality.

Perhaps Chloe brought the wrong batch of brownies to the office and this is the result of having mistakenly consumed one of her "special treats", as she refers to them. Perhaps it's the lack of sleep from pulling an all-nighter to rewrite my article for the magazine. Perhaps it's due to the shot of Jameson I threw back to settle my nerves before heading here. But as I stare into Trevor's deep-set hazel eyes, his expression filled with pity and something else I can't quite put my finger on, I know none of those circumstances are true.

The truth is my boyfriend just broke up with me.

The man I moved my world for so I'd be near him during law school.

The man I supported by working two jobs while he studied for the bar exam.

The man I imagined for myself when all other girls were dreaming of marrying that year's boy band lead singer.

"Evie?" He cuts into my thoughts, snapping me back to the present. I used to enjoy listening to him talk. Now it oozes with betrayal. "Please, say something."

I place my hands on the small wooden table, bracing myself as I draw in a deep breath. "Are you seriously breaking up with me?" My voice rises in pitch, unable to reel in my disbelief at this turn of events. My jaw tenses as I peer at him with an unfocused gaze. I'm convinced I'm in some alternate universe, like when Alice daydreamed about a world of pure nonsense, then ended up in Wonderland where everything wasn't as it seemed. That's got to be what's going on here, too. Any minute, the White Rabbit will come scurrying in front of me. Right? *Right?*

Trevor leans closer, hushing me, not wanting to make a scene. He's always been this way. He's not boring, per se, but he can be quite…serious, perpetually worried about even the most subtle hint of impropriety. After all, he is a lawyer. His maturity was one of the many things I found attractive about him.

Until Trevor, I was convinced the entire male species was the same. That they only cared about when the next *Call of Duty* would be released, despite my naïve hope they'd eventually outgrow that kind of thing when they sprouted hair on their balls. It was a rude awakening when I went away to college and walked through the hallways of my dorm to see my male counterparts huddled in front of a screen, their fingers glued to game controllers in a way that solidified my suspicion they'd probably never touched a clitoris with such excitement. Hell, they probably couldn't even *find* a clitoris. At least I'd never let them near mine.

Then I met Trevor.

Handsome.

Intelligent.

Mature.

I thought this was it. *He* was it. The person I was meant to be with. My Bogart, my Grant, my Gable.

"Please, Evie," he implores. My stare only becomes more harsh as I recall everything I've done for him, everything I've sacrificed for him...just so he can walk away after twelve years. "You have to understand how difficult this is for me."

"For you?" I blink repeatedly. "You think this is only difficult for...*you*?"

He glances over his shoulder, anxious about anyone overhearing. If he wanted to avoid a scene, he should have considered that before breaking up with me in public. The restaurant isn't too busy yet, considering it's only a little after five. I'd originally thought it odd he asked me to meet him for dinner so early, but I figured he wanted to devote as much time as he could to celebrate my birthday.

Apparently, he forgot about that, too.

"I gave you over a decade of my life, Trevor. I did everything to support you, to make you happy, to make this relationship work. I sacrificed my own dreams so you could pursue yours. I worked two jobs while you went to law school so you wouldn't have to worry about working and could focus on your studies. I've done *everything* for you. Every decision I've made over the past twelve years has been for *you*, for *us*."

"But that's the thing..." He blows out a breath, running a hand through his dark hair. "We started dating when we were eighteen, too young to experience life."

"We've experienced life. Together." I reach across the table and cover his hand with mine. The familiar warmth of his smooth skin comforts me. But it's fleeting. Too soon, he pulls his hand away. The corner of his mouth twitches, a nervous tick I've grown accustomed to over the years.

"We're not the same people anymore."

"People change all the time. It's part of being in a relationship. We all grow, regardless of how long we're together. The important thing is that you love the person you're with. I loved you back then. I still love you now. And I know you love me. That's why this is so hard for you. Because you know you're making a mistake."

He shakes his head, slowly, deliberately. "I'm not, Evie. We've grown apart. We no longer want the same things."

"All I want is you," I say, grasping at straws.

Standing, he re-secures the button on his suit jacket. Then he retrieves his wallet, throwing several bills onto the table to cover the tab. At least he didn't break up with me and expect me to pick up the check.

"But I no longer want you. I need to think about my future. I work for one of the top firms in the state, if not the country. If I want to be taken seriously for partner, I need to consider the type of woman they'd want me to be with."

His words are like a knife to the heart, yet he manages to hold his head high, acting as if he hadn't inferred he was choosing his job over me.

"And you don't think they'll take you seriously dating me." The truth leaves a sour taste in my mouth, one even the aroma of ginger in the air can't alleviate.

"Can you blame me, Evie? This is a very conservative firm with a client list that includes direct descendants of the Vanderbilt's, Rockefeller's, and Kennedy's…to name a few." He lowers his head, avoiding my gaze. "Didn't you ever wonder why I never asked you to come to any of the firm's events?" He glances up, chewing on his lower lip. "I can't exactly tell them what you do for a living, not when it entails doling out ridiculous dating advice or recommending vibrators."

I blanch, my mouth growing slack, my eyes wide. "You always knew I wanted to be a writer. I was an English major when we met. The fact I'm doing what I set out to do shouldn't come as a huge shock to you, Trevor."

"It's not. It's *what* you're writing. You were one of the few girls I'd met who seemed to know precisely what she wanted and had a plan to achieve it. I knew you wanted to work in the magazine industry. I thought you'd want to do more than pen fluff pieces about how a woman could tell if a guy's really into her. Maybe your parents are right. Maybe you'd be better off if you got your teaching certificate. Then you'd have a more respectable profession."

He holds my gaze for a moment longer, then steps back. "You can stay in the apartment until you find a place of your own. I'll be working long hours over the next month anyway. I'll sleep on the couch for the time being. You'll barely notice I'm even there."

"You're kicking me out?" I practically screech.

"Don't say it like that. Technically, it *is* my place. I pay the mortgage. My name's on the title. But there's no rush. We can be roommates until you're able to find your own place."

"Roommates?" I ask, still unable to wrap my head around this.

"I don't want this to ruin our friendship. We started out as friends. I hope that doesn't change."

I shake my head, at a complete loss for words. How can we be friends after this? I'm pretty sure we crossed that line, oh, about eleven years ago when he told me he couldn't imagine his life without me. I still can't imagine my life without him. Why did he suddenly change his mind?

"I've got to get back to the office," he says after stealing a glimpse at his watch. "I'll see you..." He stops short of saying anything more than that. Then he turns from me, everything about his stride confident, as if he didn't just end a twelve-year relationship.

CHAPTER TWO

HEART POUNDING AND fists clenching, I burst through the doors of a bar a few blocks from Columbus Circle, finding Chloe, Nora, and Izzy sitting at the bar, a drink in front of each of them. Chloe's about to take a sip of her martini when I plop into the empty chair to her left.

"I need tequila." I wave down the bartender, Aiden, ignoring the inquisitive stares coming from the women who've become my best friends since I uprooted my life and moved to New York for Trevor. And for what? For him to break up with me because I may not be as stuffy as the other wives and girlfriends of the people he works with?

"The usual?" Aiden's brows furrow as he assesses my appearance. There's a benefit to being a regular at your weekly happy hour watering hole. However, right now, that benefit allows Aiden to realize something's off. I'm not sure how to explain the events of the past hour. It still seems surreal, like I'll wake up and all of this will be a nightmare.

"Yes. And a shot of tequila."

He eyes me skeptically at first, then fills my order, placing my manhattan in front of me, followed by the shot glass filled with a clear liquid. Thankfully, he remembers I like the silver stuff best.

Without offering a single word of explanation, I grab the shot and raise it, meeting my friends' confused expressions. They *should* be confused. I'm supposed to be out celebrating my engagement to my fiancé, possibly drinking ridiculously expensive Champagne in a suite at the Ritz he booked for the occasion. Instead, I'm sitting at the bar I go to every Thursday night, trying to reconcile the drastic turn my life's taken.

"Here's to wasting nearly twelve years on a man who no longer wants to be with me because I'm not *serious* enough." Rolling my eyes, I down the liquid, grimacing as it burns my throat. I bang the glass back onto the bar, asking Aiden for another shot. The only thing that will make tonight better in comparison is waking up tomorrow with a hangover that will leave me cursing the gods who invented alcohol.

"He *broke* up with you?" Chloe asks, aghast, her nose scrunched up in repulsion. Her medium-length, gray and lilac ombre-colored locks still hold the perfect beach wave, her makeup freshly applied. There isn't a single wrinkle on her black pencil skirt or silk blouse, despite having worn it all day at work.

I met Chloe when I started working at the magazine several years ago. Her cubicle is next to mine, and we became fast friends. She's the go-to on all things involving every celebrity out there. Hell, I haven't even heard of some of the people I hear her discussing. Thanks to our friendship, I also grew close to Nora, Chloe's college roommate, who now runs a yoga and meditation studio in the Village, and Izzy, Chloe's childhood best friend.

"Happy fucking birthday to me!" I lift my next shot, throwing it back, this one burning a little less.

"Why?" Nora inquires, her doe-eyes wide, strawberry blonde hair perfectly coifed.

"I thought you were happy," Izzy adds. I'm thankful she's here, so I'm not the only one who looks like she didn't just step off the runway, like Nora and Chloe do. She's still dressed in her scrubs, evidence that she must have come here straight from the hospital, where she works as a pediatric oncology nurse. Her long, dark hair is pulled back into a tight ponytail. She doesn't wear much makeup, but she doesn't need it, her Latina heritage giving her a naturally tanned complexion.

I face my friends, offering them a tight smile as I smooth my frazzled red hair. "I guess I'm not serious enough for him." I roll my eyes.

"What do you mean?" Chloe presses, her lips formed into a tight line.

"Start at the beginning," Nora instructs. "I want to know everything."

The last thing I want is to rehash what just happened. I'm surprised I made it out of that sushi restaurant without having a complete breakdown. There's no telling how much longer I'll be able to keep it together. At least I'm in a place with an endless supply of alcohol.

"When I got there, he was sitting at a table in the corner. His legs were bouncing as he chewed on his nails. I thought he was nervous about popping the question. I guess the first clue should have been when I leaned in to kiss him and he turned so I kissed his cheek instead."

"He did not!" With wide eyes, Nora slams her hands on the bar, drawing the attention of several people.

"He's working on a huge case and the trial starts next week. I figured he might be worried about getting sick. I didn't even think twice about it. He always turns into a germaphobe right before trial. When I sat down, he was still visibly anxious, which was absolutely adorable. I mean, he was about to propose. At least that's what I thought." I take another long sip of my manhattan, the effects of the alcohol loosening my lips.

"Then he grabbed my hand and toyed with my ring finger. Or maybe I imagined he did because, in retrospect, there's no way he'd do that. It doesn't make sense. Anyway, he went on and on about how he'd been thinking about doing this for a while but didn't know how I'd react, blah blah blah. I mean, the entire lead-up…the way he held my hand, the way he was so excitable, the way he made it sound like this was a monumental time in our relationship…made me think this was it. He was finally going to pop the question."

The more I speak, the louder my voice becomes. Gone is the heartbreak that consumed me when I watched Trevor walk out of my life without a single glance back. Now I'm annoyed. Annoyed that I gave twelve years to a man who tossed it aside because he didn't think I was serious enough to be the wife of a partner at some stuffy law firm. Annoyed that I put so much effort into being the perfect girlfriend I believed he deserved. Annoyed I didn't see the signs he wasn't happy.

"What did he say next?" Nora pulls her left hand away, hiding the engagement ring on her finger. When she first told us she was getting married, we were all shocked. She'd only been dating her fiancé for three months, not to mention he started as a Tinder hookup that turned into more than a one-time thing. Although I doubt I'd personally be able to overlook the idea that my partner had been a player before me, he makes Nora happy. That's all I care about.

"What do you think? I was so wrapped up in the moment, it didn't register he broke up with me at first. I was about to squeal 'yes' at the top of my lungs, but as I opened my mouth, I replayed his words in my mind. That's when I realized he wasn't reaching into his jacket for some ridiculously expensive ring. Instead, he said it was time we both went our separate ways. That if he wants to be partner, he needs to be more 'serious'," I explain, using air quotes.

"More serious?" Chloe's voice is laden with disgust. As far as friends go, she's the cynical one. Nora's the romantic one. Izzy's the career-driven one. And me… Well, I'm not sure what I am. They'd probably say I'm a mixture of all three.

"Apparently, he doesn't consider a woman who writes about sex and dating for a living as serious, at least not to his standards. But that's complete bullshit! I'm serious! Look at me." I gesture at my business attire. Then I raise my martini glass. "I'm drinking alcohol out of a glass with a stem. If that doesn't say maturity, I don't know what does. If I were immature, you three would be holding my legs in the air while I did a keg stand or something like that."

"I don't think he means you're immature," Izzy assures me with all the sympathy and compassion I've come to expect from her. "You're sophisticated, motivated, not to mention talented. Don't mistake immaturity as having a sense of humor. You have the latter in spades. Regardless, you're also driven. How many other people can claim to be doing exactly what they set their mind to when they were just a teenager?"

I shrug, brushing it off.

"You made your own way in this industry," Chloe adds. "The only reason I got the job I did was because my dad works for the *Times* and made phone calls. Not you. You didn't know a soul. You got in on talent and drive alone. So don't let Trevor make you think you lack motivation."

"Oh, but I do." My voice oozes sarcasm. "Obviously, since I have a degree in English, I should be doing something more than writing articles about sex. But I *like* having a sex and dating column."

"He's a prick for not supporting you, especially if you enjoy what you do. I don't see you giving him a hard time for not making partner yet."

I scoff. "Well, according to him, at least he has a *real* job." I dig my fingers through my hair, yanking at it, groaning in frustration. "Couldn't he have chosen a different day? *Any* other day? Now I'll forever equate my thirtieth birthday with the day he broke up with me."

I reach for my drink, about to take another sip, when I spy a handsome man in a suit walking past the bar, his hand on the lower back of a beautiful woman wearing a cocktail dress. The alcohol loosening my inhibitions, I call out to him. "Hey! You!"

Surprisingly, he pauses, both he and who I assume to be his date looking at me. They probably stopped here to grab a drink before heading off to the theater or some romantic dinner. Hell, he may even be proposing tonight.

"You look like a person with good judgment, someone who's not a complete moron."

"Thank…you?" he replies with a wavering smile, unsure what to make of my statement.

"Would you ever break up with your girlfriend on an important date, say… I don't know. I'll just pull something out of thin air. Her birthday?"

"God no." He laughs, peering down at the woman beside him. There's a warmth and affection between them. I had that. At least I thought I did. Now what am I supposed to do?

I don't know life without Trevor in it. I've never imagined the possibility. Am I supposed to pretend I'll be okay, that I can fall out of love as quickly as he did? We were together longer than most married couples. At least longer than Brittany Spears' marriages.

He looks back to me. "I'd never live to see another day if I did that."

"Thank you, sir!" I lift my glass, toasting him. "You are a gentleman. My boyfriend, well…ex-boyfriend is not. It's my thirtieth birthday today."

The bar erupts in applause and congratulatory shouts of happy birthday. I'm not sure why, but something about the combination of their applause and the alcohol flowing through me has me standing and curtseying to my new friends.

"Thank you. Thank you. And do you know what my boyfriend of twelve years gave me as a birthday present?"

I scan the bar area. Now that it's close to seven on a Thursday night, the booths and tables in the remodeled industrial space are filled with a mixture of locals and tourists. Despite that, the background chatter has become almost non-existent, everyone interested in what I have to say. I suppose learning about a stranger's pathetic heartbreak is infinitely more interesting than discussing the unstable markets.

A woman calls out from the opposite end of the bar. "It better have been a ring!"

I point at her. "After this long, I thought it would be. I earned that much. We met during my freshman year of college. The instant I saw him walk into my history class, I no longer cared about the Battle of Bunker Hill. I just wanted him to bunk my hill."

A roar of laughter tears through the space, causing me to smile for the first time all evening. I look at my friends, who wear amused expressions on their faces. Maybe this is what Trevor referred to when he said he needed to be with someone more serious. I thought he liked the fact I'm on the eccentric side, that I don't mind being the center of attention. After all, I minored in theater. Hell, my bold personality is what caught his attention all those years ago.

"When he smiled at me that day…" I trail off, placing my hand over my heart, sighing. "I swore I heard music. I know what you're thinking," I add quickly, hoisting myself up onto the bartop so I can address the crowd.

Aiden doesn't stop me. A smirk forms on his lips as he crosses his arms over his chest. Too bad he's gay. He would be a great rebound, if I were into that kind of thing.

"That I had probably just come from a meeting of what we called the 420 Club." I lock eyes with a table full of twenty-something men, who nod in understanding. "You guys know what I'm talking about, don't you?" They lift their beers, laughing, as I address the rest of the bar once more. "But honestly, I heard music. If hearing music in your head doesn't mean you've just found your fucking soul mate, I probably belong in a straitjacket. Which may be the case anyway, but I digress." Grabbing my glass, I take another sip of my drink, before continuing.

"I've always been a planner. My mother claims I was the one who put her on a schedule for my feedings as a baby, not the other way around. So even when I was a little girl, I knew the type of man I wanted to spend the rest of my life with. Just my luck that man went to the University of Nebraska, too."

"Go Huskers!" a voice shouts, and I look in its direction.

"You're from Nebraska?" I ask a man I estimate to be in his mid-fifties. His skin is pale, gray hair thinning.

He nods. "Kearney."

"Ah, so you had electricity."

Chuckling, he nods once more. "Most days."

"Well, I grew up in a little town called Hickman." I pause for emphasis, which I learned in some of my acting classes. "Let me repeat that for you. Hick…man, Nebraska. I mean, if that doesn't scream we marry our cousins, I don't know what does."

Laughter fills the space once more. I glance behind me, meeting Aiden's eyes as he leans against the back counter and winks. He probably didn't expect there to be an opening act for the band scheduled to play later. I hand him my glass, an unspoken request for him to fill it. Two manhattans and two tequila shots in the span of less than an hour isn't a smart idea, but being smart isn't in the cards for me tonight.

"Now, something I should mention is that I have a slight affinity for the number three." I hold up a hand. "Don't ask. And no, I'm not OCD and have to lock and unlock the door three times. Except on the third day of the third week of the third month of the year."

There's another burst of laughter and applause. Once it dies down, I continue. "I like to think it was a sign when Trevor walked into my history class at exactly 3 PM on September third and proceeded to sit in the third row of the lecture hall… Which also so happened to be the row I sat in because, well, it was the third row. I *always* sat in the third row."

I feel a tap on my back and glance behind me to see Aiden handing me a fresh drink. I thank him with a smile, then take a sip before placing the glass beside me on the bar.

"Our relationship began like all good relationships do… By me pretending to be inept at U.S. history so he'd tutor me." I bat my eyelashes, passing everyone a demure look. "But after our first test and he saw I got the top grade in the class, he realized it was all a ploy. So he asked me out, and the rest is history.

"Fast forward four years. Trevor graduated with a degree in finance. I graduated with a degree in English and a minor in theater, which is probably why I have absolutely no problem telling a bar of complete strangers about my breakup. And my mother said theater would be useless." I roll my eyes, my expression oozing sarcasm. "I'm proving her wrong this very second. Anyway, after graduation, Trevor was accepted into Columbia Law here in New York. There wasn't even a question in my mind. I would move to New York with him."

A nostalgic smile lights up my face as I recall those early days of living in the city. For the longest time, I thought I made a mistake, especially when I was forced to take a cold shower in the middle of winter because the building superintendent hadn't fixed the hot water heater. Or when the smoke alarm went off anytime I tried to cook because it was placed right above the stove. Or when we lost power on Christmas and had to order Chinese takeout because the meal I'd planned was a lost cause without electricity. At the time, all the disasters made me long for the comfort and space of Nebraska. I now look back on everything and laugh.

"I worked as a bridal assistant for a wedding planner during the day. Honestly, it was the perfect job for someone as obsessed with planning and organization as I am. Essentially, I was the bride's bitch. 'You need Voss water instead of Evian? At your service.' 'You don't want your maid of honor to look better than you, even though she's prettier on the inside and out? That can be arranged. We'll be sure to pick a dress style that doesn't complement her body type.' 'Don't want the groom to find out you had one last fling with his best man the night before the wedding? There's the morning-after pill for that.'

"However, being a wedding planner's assistant didn't pay enough to cover all our bills, not to mention my student loans, so I got a second job as a bartender. All to support Trevor so the only thing he had to worry about was studying. I figured he'd return the favor down the road. I suppose he did, in his own way. After he passed the bar and got a job at an incredible firm, we eventually moved into a great apartment in Brooklyn. One he paid for, which he reminds me regularly." I pinch my lips, shaking my head at how blind I've been. "My support of his dreams has been nothing short of unwavering. I don't think he's ever truly supported me in mine."

I jump off the bartop and grab my glass, pacing as I attempt to come to terms with how Trevor could be so callous as to break up with me without even a hint of remorse or regret.

"I was the perfect girlfriend. I kept our place clean, despite working long hours. On those nights he worked late, I often dropped by the firm to bring him dinner. I was so convinced if I did everything right, we'd fly off into the sunset like Danny and Sandy and live happily ever after. Hell, I even *waxed* for him." I gesture to my crotch area. "Do you have any idea how much that hurts? That shit feels like someone just doused gasoline all over your nether regions, then lit a match and tossed it, forcing you to wallow in agony for hours with no relief in sight." I pause, allowing the laughter to swell, then die down. "But I did it for him. Because that's what people do when they're in love, isn't it? They do everything to keep the other person happy."

Everyone seems to nod in agreement.

"What they *don't* do is break up with them on their thirtieth…*fucking*…birthday because they no longer think their partner of twelve years is serious enough."

"Fuck him," a man shouts above the silence, his New York accent thick. I look in his direction as he raises his beer toward me. "He doesn't deserve you anyway."

I nod, smiling in appreciation. "You're probably right. Because everything he's done tells me I deserve someone so much better than what I allowed myself to settle for, all because he checked off every box the teenage version of myself said she wanted in a potential husband."

I blow out a long breath, blinking back the tears forming. "But how do you tell your heart to stop loving someone?"

My expression turns pleading, inwardly wishing someone has the secret to this. The atmosphere shifts, becoming more solemn. I hate ending my story on such a sour note, so I force a smile, although it doesn't reach my eyes.

"I'll tell you what you do, Evie." My voice wavers. "You take a page from Scarlett 'Fuck All Men' O'Hara. A lovely Irish lass, much like myself. You worry about it tomorrow." I lift my glass and practically the entire bar follows suit. "Because tomorrow is another day," I finish in my best Scarlett O'Hara impression.

In an instant, the deafening sound of cheers and applause surrounds me. By morning, I may regret consuming the amount of alcohol that provided me the loose lips to share my heartache with a room of strangers. Based on the phones that have been pointed at me the past several minutes, I'm sure I'll be a viral sensation by tomorrow. Right now, none of that matters. All that does is trying to salvage what I can of my thirtieth birthday.

With a smile, I curtsey once more, slowly turning to each corner of the bar to offer my thanks for their rapt attention.

And that's when I notice *him*.

Outwardly, there's nothing unique about him.

Except for the disheveled light brown hair that curls over the collar of his perfectly tailored suit.

Except for the penetrating blue eyes that remain locked on me, the heat in his gaze making me think he can read my innermost secrets.

Except for the way he's the only one not clapping, simply assessing everything about me.

He's sitting by himself at a table in the corner, away from the regular Thursday evening revelry. While this isn't a complete dive bar, he still seems out of place with his Armani suit and Tag Heuer watch. Needless to say, I'm intrigued. Who is he? Why is he peering at me in a way that makes me feel like he can see straight through the mask?

"What are you going to do about your living situation?" Izzy asks once the laughter and applause die down.

I snap out of my daze and lower myself back to my chair. My limbs are jittery as I take a deep breath, unable to shake the heat of a pair of blue eyes staring at me.

"I'm not sure." My voice is distant. "He said I didn't have to move out right away. And maybe I shouldn't. Maybe Trevor needs some time to realize what a mistake this is."

"You honestly think it's a mistake?" Chloe presses, obviously annoyed.

"He *is* under a lot of pressure with that big trial coming up. If this one goes well, he could be on a fast track for junior partner. I think..." I toy with the stem of my glass. "I'm *sure* he'll eventually come to his senses. I mean, if he didn't want to be with me, why wouldn't he insist I immediately find somewhere else to live? He knows I could crash on the pullout in your den. Instead, he told me to stay as long as I need." I'm probably grasping at straws, but I'm not ready to give up on Trevor yet. Maybe he needs to know that. "Perhaps if I'm still living there, he'll be reminded of exactly what he's throwing away."

"Oh, I know what you should do!" Nora exclaims, her eyes brightening as if having an epiphany.

"What's that?" I ask. "And no. I am *not* putting up a profile on Tinder."

She laughs. "No. I wasn't going to suggest that, although there is nothing wrong with meeting someone on Tinder. I was going to suggest you hire August Laurent."

I pinch my brows together, shaking my head. "August Laurent? Who's that?"

"He's this guy…" She looks at Chloe. "I'm not sure how to explain. He provides a…boyfriend experience, so to speak."

"Boyfriend experience?"

"Yeah," Chloe answers. "Women pay him to pretend to be their boyfriend for however short or long a time as necessary."

"So…an escort," I scoff.

"Not just any escort." Nora smirks, her eyes dancing with excitement. "He's, like, the most sought-after escort on the East Coast, if not the country. And he lives right here in Manhattan. Women line up to hire him."

"Sorry, but I don't need an escort. Or to pay someone for a 'boyfriend experience'. I have an *actual* boyfriend."

Chloe lifts a finger. "Had."

"Yes. Had. But like I said, my situation with Trevor is just temporary."

"This guy specializes in that kind of thing."

"What do you mean?"

"What's one of the biggest motivators out there?" Chloe narrows her gaze.

I stare blankly at her.

"Jealousy, Evie." Nora looks at me like I'm a complete idiot. I've just been out of the dating world for so long. True, my job entails doling out relationship and dating advice on a regular basis, but I've never had to play any of these games myself. The mere thought exhausts me. "I'm sure hiring a ridiculously hot guy to pretend to be your boyfriend would have Trevor banging down your door in no time."

"So he takes advantage of women who've had their hearts broken?" I bring my glass back to my lips, inhaling the oaky aroma of the whiskey before taking a sip. "Real stand-up guy."

"People swear by him." Chloe arches her brow. "For what it's worth. They say he helped them realize their true value. Helped them feel worthy of being loved again, whether it be by their ex or someone new."

"He must have a magical penis." I laugh, wavering a little in my chair. "Super penis." I snort, amused at the image I've concocted in my head of a penis wearing a cape. "Faster than a premature ejaculation," I joke, coming up with his superhero tagline. Ideas for a feature in my column swirl in my head.

Martini spews out of Izzy's mouth as she chokes on the sip she had just taken. I swipe at my face, removing a few droplets.

"Didn't that super model hire him?" she asks Chloe once her coughing settles down.

She nods. "Holly Turner."

"Holly Turner?" I repeat. "Why would she have to hire an escort? The woman's stunning! You'd think she'd have a line of men vying to take her ex's place."

"She refused to confirm she did, in fact, use this guy's services," Chloe explains, "but she did admit that had it not been for the help of a 'dear friend' during her separation and eventual divorce, she never would have realized how unhappy she'd been. This 'dear friend' made her feel beautiful again."

I straighten my spine, finishing my drink. "I don't need someone to help me feel beautiful again. And I certainly don't need to hire some escort to pretend to be my boyfriend. I'll handle Trevor on my own. I just need..."

"Yeah?"

"I just need to celebrate my thirtieth birthday and forget that Trevor ruined the day for me."

The girls pass a devious grin amongst each other. I have a feeling I'll regret this tomorrow, but for now, I need a night with my two best friends.

"You got it, Evie." Chloe signals Aiden. A line of shots appears in front of us within a few seconds.

"Here's to thirty." Izzy raises her shot, Chloe, Nora, and me mirroring her, gulping down the liquor.

Just as I take a sip of the water Aiden's thankfully placed in front of me, a body brushes against mine. A shiver rolls down my spine, making me breathless. I glance behind me to see Mr. Armani Suit walk toward the door. Everything tells me to look away, to return my attention to my friends, but the tipsy version of Evie doesn't listen, keeping her eyes glued to his tall physique instead. This is the best suit porn I've seen in a while and I can't get enough.

As he's about to walk out the door, he stops. My heart skyrockets to my throat when his gaze locks with mine. A blush builds on my cheeks as I snap my eyes forward, doing everything to pretend he didn't catch me ogling him. But he did. And the smirk on his full lips confirms this fact.

Bastard.

Chapter Three

SUN STREAMS THROUGH the windows, bathing the room in light, rousing me from unconsciousness. I squint, having difficulty adjusting to the brightness. I don't remember my bedroom being this bright, considering it faces west. Then again, the last thing I probably thought about last night when I stumbled back to the apartment was closing the drapes.

Rubbing my eyes, I try to shake off the cobwebs, my tongue feeling like sandpaper. Thankfully, drunk Evie must have predicted I'd wake up with a hangover to rival all hangovers and left a water bottle and a couple aspirin on the nightstand. Drunk Evie really is thoughtful.

I reach for the pills, pop them into my mouth, and chase them with a huge gulp of water, practically downing the entire bottle to dull the fire. After returning the bottle to the table, I collapse back onto the bed, the cool, silky sheets comforting against my skin.

As I stare at the ceiling, I exhale a long breath, the reality of yesterday slowly trickling back. Trevor really did break up with me. On my thirtieth birthday. Because I'm not serious enough. I'll show him how wrong he is. I just need to nurse this hangover, then I'll begin Operation Prove Trevor Wrong. If he wants a serious girlfriend, I can be that. I can tone down the jokes. I can stop making snarky comments. I can even write some different articles for the magazine. Less raunchy, more smart humor. What I can't do is throw away over a decade of our relationship because he doesn't think I'm the type of girl he can be with if he wants to make partner. I've always been a problem solver. Right now, this issue with Trevor is simply a problem I vow to fix.

Closing my eyes, I wrap the comforter around my body. I expect the remnants of Trevor's scent to infiltrate my senses. But it doesn't. One night and his aroma has already faded from the bed we once shared.

As I try not to think about that, my foot brushes against another body. I still, inhaling sharply. Did Trevor forget he broke up with me? Was he so exhausted after working all night he was on autopilot and climbed into bed? Better yet, did he already realize what a mistake he made and changed his mind, but I was in too much of an alcohol-induced coma to remember him telling me as much?

Hope building, I glance beside me, expecting to see Trevor's impeccable dark hair. Everything about him is always perfect, right down to the lack of bedhead when he gets up in the morning. He makes me feel like Cousin It next to him.

When I see a full head of disheveled, sandy brown hair instead of Trevor's pristine locks, I bolt up. The duvet falls around my waist, revealing my underwear-clad body. Then I look up, realizing I'm not in my bedroom.

"Shit, shit, shit," I whisper shout, wracking my brain for a clue as to how I went from having a girls' night to sharing a bed with a stranger. Maybe it's not that bad. Maybe I told him my sob story about what happened earlier in the night and he offered me a place to sleep so I didn't have to go back to a home full of memories.

But practically naked?

Nice try, Evie. There's a better chance of it snowing in Florida than that being true. There's only one explanation why I'm scantily dressed and in another man's bed after a night of drinking.

I had a one-night stand.

With a stranger.

Hours after the man I thought I'd marry dumped me.

No wonder it seems like the world's out of balance this morning, aside from the dizziness consuming me due to the alcohol I'm sure still flows through my bloodstream. I've now slept with four men.

Surely this can be excused as a result of some relationship-related PTSD. I'm not trying to make light of the severity of actual PTSD, but I need something, *anything* to make me feel better about the situation. I don't have one-night stands. I just...don't. Especially with someone I met at a bar. What kind of man takes home a drunk girl and sleeps with her anyway? No one worth sticking around to find out about.

Mumbling a silent prayer that I can escape unnoticed, I carefully lift the duvet off me and step onto the chilly hardwood floor. As I tiptoe around the large room, every muscle in my body aches, probably due to the previous night's calisthenics. I search for my dress, expecting to find it crumpled on the floor, along with a trail of his clothes leading to the bed. Instead, it's neatly slung over a chair in the corner. Maybe he's a neat freak.

When I tug the dress over my head, a whiff of a powder-fresh scent filters into my nostrils. I'd anticipated it to smell like alcohol and sweat, not as if it had been recently laundered.

Curiosity piqued, I glance at the bed to get a better look at the man I found irresistible in my alcohol-induced fog. When I see his chiseled face, I release what I hope is a noiseless gasp, my hand flying to cover my mouth.

It's him. The man I noticed sitting across the bar after telling the entire place about my breakup. The man who caused a jolt of electricity to course through my veins when he brushed against me. The man whose blue eyes

I couldn't get out of my mind all night, even after he left. How the hell did I end up here?

Cautious, I step closer to the bed, hoping something will trigger a memory. If nothing else, at least I went home with an attractive guy. Well, attractive isn't an accurate descriptor of this man's beauty. The way he looks so peaceful, yet still incredibly masculine as he sleeps causes a tingle to spread through me at the thought of what we did last night. I can almost hear his deep voice whispering his most carnal desires into my ear. I imagine he was a sensual lover, one who put my needs first, making sure I was taken care of. Maybe it's a good thing I can't remember. Then I can pretend it never happened. Pretend I've still only slept with three people.

My eyes rake down his naked torso, confirming what I'd imagined last night as I ogled his physique. Broad shoulders. Sculpted pecs. Chiseled abs. And the cherry on top… An intricate tribal tattoo of a phoenix covering his back. This is a man who obviously takes care of himself. He's not one of those guys who's too muscular that it's unattractive. His muscles are firm and defined, but not overly so. He's pure perfection, making it nearly impossible to look away.

That's when I notice the triangle of scars on his abdomen near his hipbone, an imperfection on an otherwise flawless physique. They're pink and faded from the obvious passing of years, but I'm intrigued by the story behind them.

Instantly, my mystery man shifts, letting out a raspy groan. It hits me deep in my core, a heightened desire filling me. It almost makes me want to crawl back into bed to see if we can recreate what happened last night in the hopes of jumpstarting my memory. But I can't do that to Trevor. Not now that I'm coherent and thinking clearly again.

Hastily collecting my shoes and purse, I hurry from the bedroom, praying I'm able to escape before he wakes up. I have no desire to face him, not when whatever happened last night was a giant mistake. I need to get out of…wherever I am before whoever he is notices I'm no longer in his bed and comes looking for me. Then I can pretend this never happened. New York is an enormous city. The likelihood of our paths crossing again is nonexistent.

Quietly shutting the bedroom door behind me, I pause, holding my breath, listening for any movement from within. Thankfully, all I hear is silence. I blow out a slow exhale and continue down a long corridor, wondering where I am. Whoever this man is, he must do pretty well for himself. His place is bright and modern, sleek wood flooring coupled with immaculate walls containing well-appointed black-and-white framed prints of famous landmarks in New York. The Brooklyn Bridge. The Empire State Building. Ellis Island.

As I emerge into the luxurious living room, I'm caught breathless at the view from the expansive windows filling the far wall. The sun shines through them, the breathtaking sight of Central Park several dozen stories below us.

"Wow." I can only imagine what a place like this cost. The mortgage on the apartment I shared with Trevor in Brooklyn was over $3,000 a month. A place overlooking Central Park in Columbus Circle? It must cost several million.

Even more intrigued as to who this mystery man is, I consider snooping to see what else I can find out. Hell, I can't even remember his name. I wonder if I asked for it, or if I agreed to sleep with him regardless of whether I knew it. I'd like to say I'd never do such a thing, but all bets are off.

I shift my attention to the enormous kitchen island and spy a stack of mail on the corner. When I start toward it for no other reason than to learn his name, I discern the faint echo of footsteps from down the hallway.

My pulse soaring, I spin around, hurrying out of the apartment, leaving my one-night stand where it belongs… Behind me.

CHAPTER FOUR

WHEN I EMERGE onto the street, I'm enveloped by the fevered pace of midtown Manhattan, the sidewalks moving with the energy of this place I've grown to love. Sirens blare, horns honk, truck brakes squeak and moan. But as I revel in the mass of people walking in every direction possible, coupled with the strength of the sun on this summer day, the panic of waking up in a strange man's bed is overshadowed with a new reason to panic… It's Friday. And I'm most likely late for work.

Reaching into my purse, I retrieve my cell, thankful it still has a little battery life left, and spy the time. 9:35.

"Crap," I mutter, dashing through the crowd of men and women in suits, as well as the occasional tourist snapping photos, not paying attention to the people trying to skirt around them. At least I had the wherewithal to have a one-night stand with someone who lives only a few blocks from the office. As much as I hate showing up in the dress I wore yesterday, I don't have enough time to go back to Brooklyn and change if I want to be on time for the weekly check-in with the magazine's editor. Thankfully, I have extra clothes at work.

I reach the building in record time and run through the lobby, my heels clicking on the marble tile. After scanning my ID badge, permitting me entry through the turnstiles, I join the mob of people waiting for an elevator. When one arrives, we all pile in, everyone glued to their phones as we ride up to our respective floors.

Having no idea how I must look this morning, I pull out the compact I keep in my purse, checking my reflection. I cringe, the bloodshot eyes staring back evidencing a night of overindulgence and lack of sleep.

I do my best to adjust my appearance with the few tools I have. I secure my wavy red hair into a fashionable messy bun on the top of my head, then pull out a few ringlets to frame my face, making it appear the haphazard style is intentional. After I put a little powder on my fair skin and line my lips with gloss, I pop a mint into my mouth to rid myself of rank morning breath, hoping it will be sufficient until I can get to the toothbrush I keep in my desk.

The instant I'm done readjusting my appearance, the elevator comes to a stop on my floor. I straighten my spine, holding my head high as I emerge into the magazine's busy newsroom, smiling as I pass the chipper receptionist who, just like the rest of the entry-level staff, is waiting for her big break in the modeling industry. The place is bright and buzzing with energy, phones ringing off the hook, nails tapping against keyboards, music playing from a few desks.

As I continue through the rows of cubicles, I exude all the confidence I can muster in the hopes no one realizes I dragged myself out of a stranger's bed and am wearing the same dress I had on yesterday. What am I thinking? Of course they'll notice. This is a women's fashion magazine. For many of these people, fashion is their life. They could probably tell me what I wore on a certain date better than I can.

Bypassing my cubicle, I head straight for the break room, needing caffeine before I face what I imagine will be a day from hell. I enter the space, the aroma of coffee making my mouth water. As I pour myself a cup, I hear a familiar whistle, followed by the sound of drawn-out clapping. I groan silently. There's only one person it could be.

"Did you just slow clap my walk of shame?" I slowly turn around, stirring sweetener and creamer into my coffee.

"You bet your ass I did, sweet cheeks," Chloe retorts, annoyingly chipper for what seems like an early hour.

Her hair is sleek and lustrous, her outfit stylish, her gray eyes bold and refreshed. I hate her for not suffering from the same hangover as me. Then again, she exhibited something called self-control last night, whereas I fired for effect. I didn't drink to take the edge off. I drank to forget. It worked...a little too well.

"Based on your appearance..." She gestures to my dress, more than aware it's the same one I wore yesterday, "it looks like you never made it home last night."

I take a sip of coffee, briefly closing my eyes as I savor the nutty flavor.

"So if you didn't go home, where did you have your Uber take you?"

I arch a brow, looking over my mug at her. "Uber?"

"Yeah. Uber." She peers at me as if I'm a complete idiot. "You tried to take the subway, but we convinced you that you were too drunk, so you called for an Uber."

"Of course! I took an Uber!" I place my coffee on the counter and withdraw my phone from my purse. Ignoring the multiple texts from my mother, I bring up the app and search my latest trip.

Chloe grabs my arm, tugging me from the break room. Thankfully, my reflexes are quick enough that I grab my coffee before she drags me through the offices.

"Do you not remember what happened between leaving the bar and waking up this morning?" she asks softly so no one can overhear.

"I vaguely recall wanting to go home and sleep off the alcohol..." I suck in a breath, my eyes flinging to my phone. "But when the Uber driver pulled up in front of our place, I couldn't go inside." I shove my cell at her.

She takes it, looking at the map of my trip, which appears to be one large circle. "I must have had him take me back to the bar."

"Why?"

"All I know is I couldn't go into that apartment and be surrounded by memories of Trevor. Maybe I went back to find you and crash at your place for the night."

"Instead of having the Uber driver *take* you to my place?"

I shake my head. "I can't attempt to rationalize what went through my brain last night, other than way too much alcohol."

"I guess I can understand that. And I said you could crash with me as long as you need to, not just one night. I'm barely there anyway."

"That's unnecessary." Once we reach my cubicle, I place my mug on the desk, then open the storage cabinet in the corner, pulling out a fresh bra, panties, and wrap dress, as well as my toothbrush and toothpaste. "Like I said yesterday…" My steps are quick as I walk toward the ladies' room, Chloe following. "I'm sure once this trial is over and Trevor is less stressed, he'll realize what a mistake he made."

I lock myself in one of the stalls and rip my dress over my head. I almost want to keep it on since it smells like my mystery man.

"Evie, wh—"

"I don't remember making it back to the bar," I interrupt, knowing all too well she's about to ask what my plan is if Trevor doesn't believe he made a mistake. I'm not going to think about that right now. It's not an option. Everything about my relationship with Trevor had gone according to plan…until now. We've gotten derailed. I need to get us back on track. That's all.

"Then where did you go, because the Uber dropped you back off at the bar." She pauses. "Or at least close to the bar." I imagine her scrutinizing the trip map on the app. "Actually, he dropped you off in Columbus Circle."

I gasp, straightening my spine.

"What is it?"

I hastily pull the wrap dress over my body, tying it around the waist. "That's where I woke up this morning." I collect my things and step out of the stall.

"Where?"

"Columbus Circle. More specifically, on the seventy-something floor in an apartment overlooking Central Park that had to cost millions." Finding my toothbrush, I squeeze some toothpaste on it.

Her eyes widen as she gapes at me. "Who the hell did you sleep with last night? A goddamn Rockefeller?"

"I have no idea, but he was at the bar," I say as I brush my teeth.

"He was?"

I nod, then spit into the sink, wiping the residue from around my mouth.

"Sitting alone at a table in the corner. I noticed him after I did my little…act."

"You did, did you?" She waggles her brows, crossing her arms as she leans against the counter.

"Not like that." I turn my attention to the mirror, fixing my appearance the best I can. "But he wore this gorgeous designer suit and had even more gorgeous eyes. Any female with an interest in the male population would notice this guy."

"*I* never noticed him."

"Well, you're missing out, because this guy…" I peer at my reflection, recalling the electricity that filled me when his body breezed by mine. The touch was so subtle, but hit me deeper than anything had in recent memory, even when Trevor and I were intimate. I blame it on the combination of the alcohol and my heartbreak, refusing to consider the possibility there's a different reason for my reaction.

"Yes?" Chloe presses.

"Beautiful. Absolutely beautiful, Chloe."

She places her hand on her hip, analyzing me. "Okay. So he's gorgeous. That doesn't explain how you ended up in his apartment in Columbus Circle."

"I don't know how I ended up there." I snatch my phone out of Chloe's hand and stare at the map of my Uber trip, seeing it wasn't a complete round trip. The car dropped me a few blocks shy of the bar. I lean against the tile wall, wishing something would trigger a memory. As I rest my head on the cool tile, I inhale a breath, blinking repeatedly.

"What? What is it?"

"All the stop and go of the car. He was a typical New York driver, gunning the gas before coming to a screeching stop at a light." I snap my eyes to Chloe. "It made me sick, so before I threw up in his car, I had him let me out by the Time Warner Center."

"And did you throw up in his car?"

"I don't think so." I pinch my lips together, thinking. "No. I definitely didn't." I squint, pieces of the previous night trickling back like raindrops. "I remember feeling dizzy after getting out of the car, so I grasped a bus bench to steady myself, but it didn't help. The world kept spinning. I think I mumbled something about never drinking again." My eyes widen as his voice fills my mind. "That's when I heard someone say, 'That's probably a good idea', or something like that."

"Who?"

"Him. Mr. Armani Suit." I smile dreamily at the memory of looking up to see my knight in shining armor standing before me, his blue eyes emblazoned in my mind. Noticing Chloe smirking, I quickly wipe the smile off my face, pretending not to be affected. "After that, I don't remember much."

"You like him," she comments after a brief silence.

"What?" I step back, aghast. "No. Absolutely not. I don't even know his name."

"That's never stopped me before," she answers dismissively.

"I was under duress. I drank far too much, made the mistake of going home with some random guy, then woke up practically naked in his bed. Just goes to show you what kind of slimeball this guy truly is, sleeping with someone who's obviously drunk. So not only did my boyfriend dump me, I get to end my week with a visit to the clinic to get tested because who knows if this guy put on a condom."

"How do you know you slept with him? You said yourself you don't remember much."

"I woke up in my bra and panties."

"All the more evidence you *didn't* sleep together. Who in their right mind puts their bra and panties back on after sex? Especially drunken sex. Who sleeps with a bra on anyway?"

"Again, I can't attempt to rationalize what I was thinking last night. And trust me. I know how I get when I've had too much to drink. I'm sure once I saw this guy without his shirt on, all thoughts of Trevor went out the window and I only cared about one thing…getting laid. Or maybe I did it to spite Trevor…a revenge screw, so to speak…which I must have thought was a *brilliant* idea with all the alcohol I drank last night."

She smirks, amused by my misfortune. I guess I deserve it. I've repeatedly claimed I would never have a one-night stand. That I would only sleep with someone I felt a strong connection to. I'm not a prude. While I enjoy sex as much as any other woman, I don't feel the need to sleep around.

Then again, when most people are at the age where they're exploring their sexuality, I was already dating Trevor. We explored our sexuality together. Is this what my life will be like without Trevor? Having to sleep around and hope to find someone I connect with? God, I don't even want to think about having to date, especially in New York City.

"So…" She grins deviously. "What *did* he look like without his shirt on?"

"An Adonis," I answer before my brain can tell my mouth to shut it. "Fuck, Chloe. Male perfection. Broad shoulders. Sculpted chest. Abs you want to lick. With a body like that, I'm sure I was all over him. Which makes me feel even more guilty."

"Why? Trevor broke up with you."

"Yes, but—"

"Oh, there you two are," a voice interrupts. We whip our heads toward the door. Maggie, the editor-in-chief's assistant, stands there, a self-important expression on her face. Sometimes she forgets she's the editor's assistant, not assistant editor. Big difference. "The meeting's about to start. Viv's waiting on you guys."

"Sorry, Mags. We're coming." Grateful for the reprieve, I smile at Chloe as I follow Maggie, drop ping off my clothes from yesterday at my cubicle on the way.

As I'm about to walk into the conference room, a hand covers my arm. I look at Chloe, her slate-gray eyes narrowed on me. "Listen, Evie. I get that you're hurting over what happened with Trevor, and you have every right to be. Maybe this is the opportunity you need to have a little fun and figure out who you are."

"I already know—"

"Who you are?" Her voice is low, her expression filled with skepticism. "If you do, why are you willing to change that just so Trevor will want to be with you? I get you have a history. I can't even imagine how difficult the next few weeks...hell, months will be trying to adjust to a new normal. I'm the last person you should take relationship advice from, considering I avoid them like the plague. But instead of wasting time concocting a plan to win Trevor back by becoming the type of person he wants to date, you should focus on finding someone who wants to date you as you are right now."

She places her hands on my biceps, her eyebrows pulled down. "Because the Evie I know is a complete badass. And any guy who doesn't see that doesn't deserve you."

CHAPTER FIVE

CHLOE'S WORDS LEAVE me questioning whether salvaging my relationship with Trevor is the right move. How could it not be? Like she said, she's the last person I should take relationship advice from. In the five years I've known her, she hasn't been in a single committed relationship. She doesn't understand the dynamic of a real relationship. It's all about give and take, being in a partnership. Sometimes one person has to shoulder more of the weight. Right now, I need to do the heavy lifting. I refuse to give up so easily.

Resolved, I step into the conference room, coming to an immediate stop when my eyes fall on the spread of flowers covering the table, cards and chocolate interspersed among the extravagant display.

"What's going on?"

I want to believe this is merely a birthday celebration for me. It probably started that way, but as I spy the sympathy covering my coworkers' faces, coupled with the balloons that say "I'm sorry" and "Get Well Soon", I'm positive that's not the case.

"It appears condolences are in order."

Vivian Wood, Editor-in-Chief of *Blush* magazine, is the picture of sophistication. Then again, I'm fairly certain she could make a paper sack look like this year's latest fashion trend. Not a single strand of her platinum hair is out of place. She's in her sixties, but her youthful complexion, devoid of wrinkles, makes it appear as if she's not a day over forty. She's slender, dressed in skinny jeans, gorgeous heels, and a suit jacket. I consider myself on the tall side at five feet, nine inches, but that's no match for Viv. That's probably one of the reasons she's remained single most of her life. Her six-foot height must intimidate most potential partners. Let's face it. The majority of men would feel emasculated standing next to a woman who's taller than them…especially a woman as confident and successful as Viv.

"Sorry about the breakup, Evie." There's an air of authority about her as she strides toward me, a devilish smirk crawling across her thin, pink lips. "Or I should be sorry, but the opportunist in me looks forward to how this will affect your perspective in some of your articles."

"It won't."

Her smile widens. "We'll see about that. For the past five years, you've been writing about sex and dating from the safety of what you thought to be a secure relationship. That's not the case anymore. Trust me. I've been single in this city for thirty years. It's a jungle out there. I'm looking forward to what new and exciting things you'll bring to the table now."

"I'm sure it's not that bad."

Chloe snorts a laugh and I shift my gaze to her. "The men in this city are a different breed altogether."

"She's right," Lenora, the editor for health and beauty, offers. I head toward Chloe, sitting beside her on the couch. "Most of them are glued to their phones."

"And forget about being chivalrous," Dawn, one of our graphic designers, adds. "I can't tell you how many dates I've been on with a guy who didn't even open the door or pick up the check."

Chloe turns to me. "So if you come across a man who takes care of you, go after that." She winks, an unspoken reminder in her gaze about last night's mystery man.

"I'll keep that in mind," I say. "And thank you all for your kind thoughts. But honestly, I'm okay. I have a plan."

"Of course you do," Viv quips as several other people snicker or groan, accustomed to my quirks. "Evie Fitzgerald, the girl with a plan."

I suppose after working here this long, she's gotten accustomed to my idiosyncrasies, particularly my love for plans and itineraries. I've always preferred structure. Whereas Chloe loves waiting until the last minute to get her work done, often sending her final piece to Viv mere seconds before it's due, I work ahead, not rushing anything. Hell, I have pieces I intend to write for the magazine and blog planned out for the next six months. My planner is a work of art, and my lifeline. Structure keeps me grounded, focused.

"Speaking of which, let's hear what you have planned for the August issue."

I blow out a relieved breath, happy to concentrate on work instead of my breakup for a moment. With a smile, I discuss my idea of exploring the world of dating in five major cities across the country. An idea that just came to me, thanks to Chloe. Viv thinks it's brilliant, since she's under the impression I'll be rejoining the ranks of single people.

Once she gives me the go-ahead, she continues going around the room, everyone pitching different story ideas for the next issue. She nixes a few, approves others, or reworks some to make them more compelling. Her ability to know a brilliant idea when she hears one has kept her at the helm of this magazine for over a decade.

When I was a teenager, I scrambled to the shelves for my monthly copy of *Blush* magazine. I always knew I wanted to work in this industry, so I did what anyone with a dream would do. I studied. Working for *Blush* was the end goal. One I didn't think I'd ever achieve. It's continually been the top women's magazine in the country, always on the cutting edge. While I didn't see myself offering dating tips, it's a stepping stone to being able to write things I really want to, things of interest to all women. Reproductive rights, equality, economic justice… Just to name a few.

Once the meeting ends and we have our assignments for next month's issue, about half of which will never make it to print, we disperse. I hang back to collect the gifts my irreverent coworkers bestowed on me. As I read one of the cards that went along with a bouquet of roses, Chloe sidles up next to me.

"'Sorry for your loss. Wishing you moments of peace and comfort as you remember all the good times you had together.'"

She snort-laughs at the ridiculousness of it all.

"Did I just get a bereavement card for getting dumped?" I muse as I toss it back onto the pile.

"It appears so."

This shouldn't surprise me. Since accepting Viv's offer to work here, I've come to learn many of the employees have a rather dark and cynical sense of humor. When the mouse that roamed the office, evading all the traps the exterminators set out for it, had finally been outsmarted, one of the fashion columnists declared a day of mourning. He even went so far as to plan a memorial for our fallen friend. There's no such thing as a normal day at *Blush* magazine.

"How did everyone find out?"

She shrugs as she helps me gather everything. "News travels fast around here. You should know that by now. It's a miracle you didn't find out Trevor was breaking up with you *before* he told you. That happened to Maureen over in beauty."

Arms full, we head out of the conference room with what we manage to carry.

"At least I get chocolate out of it. Like a parting gift after picking the wrong door on *Let's Make a Deal*." I imitate my best announcer's voice. "Instead of a beautiful diamond or a lifetime of security, we'll be sending you home with a box of drugstore chocolates. Better luck next time!" We turn into my cubicle and I deposit the first batch of flowers, cards, and chocolates onto my desk.

"Oh, come on. You got a lot more than just a crappy box of chocolates."

"You're right. I got sympathy cards meant for the death of a loved one, flowers, and a few balloons."

"Don't forget the sausage."

I frown. "Sausage?"

"Yeah." She waggles her brows, making an obscene gesture with her hand. "Mr. Armani's sausage, on the off-chance I'm wrong and you *did* sleep with him. Regardless, I'd take that consolation prize any day over some schmuck who didn't realize what he had."

"Trevor's under a great deal of stress." I repeat the same argument, although my words lack the conviction they had earlier. "He knows what he had." I avoid what I can only assume to be Chloe's annoyed stare. "I just need to remind him of that."

I step out of my cubicle to get the rest of my breakup gifts when I almost run straight into Viv. I inhale a sharp breath, stopping in my tracks.

"Sorry, Viv. I wasn't looking."

"That much is clear, Evie. I'd like a word."

"Of course." I force a smile, pass Chloe a nervous look, then follow Viv, curious as to her sudden need to speak to me. Normally, all magazine-related problems are addressed at our weekly meetings. Then again, Viv's known to use her employees' real-life issues in concocting new, edgy story ideas. I worry she's about to ask me to do something crazy, like sign up for online dating apps and journal my experience. Or apply to *The Bachelor.* Or something that would rival the premise of *How to Lose a Guy in Ten Days.*

Once we're in her office, she closes the door, putting me even more on edge. "Have a seat, Evie." Her voice is even as she gestures across the desk.

"Is everything okay?" Tentative, I sit down in the bright orange chair. Her workspace is decorated in a stunning mid-century modern design. Vibrant colors. Sleek lines. Uncluttered shelves. Every time I step into this room, I feel like I've just walked onto the set of *Mad Men.* In fact, Viv bought many of the items here in a prop auction.

"Everything's great. I wanted to speak with you in private about an…opportunity."

She opens one of the desk drawers and withdraws a file. Placing a pair of dark-rimmed glasses over her eyes, she scans the papers in the folder.

"Since we hired you, our readership has seen a steady increase. These days, every other magazine similar to ours struggles to capture the market's attention. But your wit, coupled with your love of social media, has helped us stay modern. Prior to bringing you onboard, our sex and dating column was the least popular. Most people overlooked it as being the same stale advice women have received for decades. But you gave it a fresh coat of paint, so to speak. You write stories real women can relate to, although I've yet to be the lucky recipient of a penis picture over the Internet."

I laugh, recalling my most recent blog post that garnered hundreds of thousands of shares on social media. "That's all I wanted when I took over the column. To make dating and relationships more relatable. To help people realize relationships don't have to be as hard as we make them."

"And you've done an incredible job. We all know this industry can be tough, having wide swings from quarter to quarter. But it hasn't been that way lately, and I think a lot of it has to do with your ingenuity. You bring a fresh perspective to a platform we all feared would soon die."

She removes her glasses and places them on the desk, pinching her lips together. "As you know, Grace is pregnant and will be leaving at the end of the year. She's decided not to return to work, which means I'm now looking for a new assistant editor. You interested?"

My eyes fling wide open as I sit in shock. I thought I'd have to work here much longer and gradually move up the ladder. I'd be more than happy if she offered me a transfer to the current events desk, with Margo being promoted to assistant editor. But to consider me for the position? This would be a huge promotion for me, not to mention the exact thing that could show Trevor I can be the serious, professional type. What's more professional than working as assistant editor at the top women's magazine in the country? For someone with a degree in English, there's not much higher I can go.

"Vivian," I breathe, shaking my head, covering my mouth with my hand. "I don't know what to say."

"Say you're interested."

"Of course I am. This is… This is amazing. I promise I won't let you down." I make a move to get up, but her voice stops me.

"Well, the job isn't yours yet."

I cock my head.

"Grace will be staying through December, but we'd like to start exploring our options now. So we're prepared. I'm sure you can appreciate that."

"I can." My shoulders fall. The likelihood of me getting chosen over people with more experience and seniority is slim to none. "And who are your other options?"

"Judy from celebrity news."

I nod. That doesn't come as a shock. She's been in the magazine industry for nearly twenty years. I'm surprised she wasn't promoted the last time an assistant editor left.

"Margo from current events."

Another obvious choice. Another woman who's made a career out of working in magazines. A woman whose job I've coveted for years.

"And you."

"Okay. So what do you need me to do?"

"Show me you can fulfill the duties of this role — conceptualizing and pitching stories for all sections of the magazine, as well as researching, interviewing, writing and editing the copy. You'll also oversee all the social media accounts and develop a content calendar for those."

I place my hands in my lap, wishing I hadn't gotten as drunk as I did last night. I would have much preferred having this conversation with a clear mind and a full night's sleep.

"I'm more than ready to take on all those responsibilities. I may not have the experience Judy and Margo do, but I'm a damn hard worker and won't be satisfied until I've perfected my craft. Not to mention the idea of planning content for our social media accounts gets me all sorts of excited."

"I knew it would. That's why I'm considering you. Now I need you to prove you're up for the job." She grins, sitting back in her chair, tenting her fingers in front of her. "Pitch me a story. Something no other magazine has written about. Something we can blast all over the cover and people will be lining up to grab their copies."

"Right now?" I fidget with the silky material of my dress, toying with the hem.

"Yes, right now. As my assistant editor, you'll need to be on your toes. Show me you can pitch something without advance warning. There are times a story doesn't pan out at the eleventh hour and you'll have to scramble to put something together, perhaps even a featured story, in little time."

"Okay." I look around her office, doing everything to get my creative juices flowing. I'm a writer. This is what I do. I find inspiration in the most obscure places and turn it into a story. Maybe if I weren't still nursing the mother of all hangovers, I'd be able to come up with an idea, but my brain is still cloudy. Then again, maybe something from last night could be my source of inspiration.

I flash my eyes back to Viv. "August Laurent."

Intrigued, Viv narrows her gaze on me. "Excuse me?"

"August Laurent," I repeat. "From what I understand, he's the most sought-after escort on the East Coast, possibly even the country."

Her lips turn into a conniving smile. "I'm more than aware of who August Laurent is. I'm also very aware he values his anonymity and privacy. He's never agreed to an interview. And despite repeated attempts by other reporters to unmask this mystery man, no one's been successful. What makes you think he'll allow you to interview him?"

"I don't know." My voice wavers, a sinking feeling forming in the pit of my stomach that I've just pitched Viv an impossible story. I don't want her to pick up on that, though. "Isn't part of being assistant editor seeking out those difficult stories? Imagine having a man dressed in a beautiful suit on the front page, not showing his face, with the headline 'August Laurent: Unrobed', or something like that. This guy is like Keyser Söze."

"Who?"

"Keyser Söze. The mystery man behind all the shit that goes down in *The Usual Suspects*."

Viv looks at me with quizzical eyes. Apparently, she's never seen one of my all-time favorite movies.

I shake my head. "It doesn't matter. All that does is this guy is a legend, but also a ghost. Imagine being the first magazine to get the inside scoop or, better yet…reveal his true identity."

Viv studies me for another long moment, then says, "Okay, Evie. Run with it. Let's see what you can do. Treat it as if it *will* be a feature, because whoever turns in the best article gets the feature story *and* the job. I'm giving you plenty of time, so I expect nothing less than absolute perfection. Don't let me down."

"I won't, Viv." I raise myself to my feet. "Thank you again for even considering me." I head toward the door.

"Oh, and Evie?"

I glance over my shoulder, meeting her eyes.

"Just a reminder. We deal with real facts, not sensationalized falsehoods." She gives me a knowing look. "Make sure you only write the true story. I won't accept anything less."

CHAPTER SIX

MY FEET CAN'T carry me as quickly as I need them to as I hurry from Viv's office. All I do is pray I didn't just set myself up for failure by pitching Viv an impossible story. How is it everyone seems to know the name August Laurent, yet I've been blissfully unaware my entire life? Now I'm even more intrigued.

Out of breath, I round the corner into Chloe's cubicle, her peachy perfume wafting in the air. Her space is much more cluttered than mine. A celebrity news columnist, she always has various tips she's received scattered across her desk, hoping to be the first to report on whatever this month's big story will be, usually a pregnancy or new birth. Our audience loves reading about the children of the rich and famous. I can't blame them. I like reading about it, too. It normalizes them, apart from them having enough money to hire a nanny to help with midnight feedings, dirty diapers, and meltdowns.

"Evie, are you okay?" Her brow wrinkles in concern when she sees me.

I sit in her spare chair, my eyes zeroed in on her. I grab a notepad sitting on her desk and flip to a blank page, pulling out the pen I perpetually keep in the bun in my hair, readying myself to scratch down every word Chloe says. So many of my colleagues have forgone notepads for the ease of digital recorders. There's something about putting pen to paper that energizes me, makes me feel like I'm a participant in the story instead of a casual observer.

"I need you to tell me everything you know about August Laurent. Don't leave out a single thing." My firm voice relays the seriousness of the situation.

"Reconsidering Nora's idea from last night?" She winks.

"What? No," I answer quickly. "I don't need to pay someone to date me."

"Then why are you interested in August Laurent?"

I roll my chair closer to hers so no one can overhear, needing her to understand the depth of the hole I just dug for myself. "Because Viv is considering me for the assistant editor position when Grace leaves."

She releases a shriek of excitement, and I hush her, unsure if I'm supposed to discuss it.

"I'm as surprised as you. I honestly never gave it much thought."

"But Viv's giving it to you?"

"Not exactly. She wants to make sure I can handle a wider range of assignments first."

Chloe arches a brow. "Meaning?"

"Meaning she kind of put me on the spot and asked me to pitch her a story that would sell hundreds of thousands of copies." I fight a yawn. I don't know how I'll make it to five o'clock. All I want is to crawl into bed and sleep all weekend. Then the reminder I don't really have a bed anymore hits me, depressing me even more. If this is a sign for what awaits me in my thirties, I'd like to return them for a refund. Or maybe just skip straight to forty. "She's also considering Judy and Margo. Whoever produces the best story gets the job."

"So you pitched August Laurent?" Chloe's voice is a mixture of surprise and superiority, almost like she knew I'd eventually want to know more about this guy. The concept is appealing, particularly from a sex and dating standpoint. What pushes a woman to such extremes that she doesn't think she has any other option but to hire someone to date her, or give her a "boyfriend experience", as they referred to it last night? I don't care how bad things get. I'd never stoop to that level.

"It was the first thing that popped into my head. To be honest, my brain isn't exactly firing on all cylinders today. I'm lucky I was able to come up with anything at all."

"You honestly think you'll get him to agree to this story?"

"Why not?" I shrug, trying not to feel dejected by the constant uncertainty facing me. "Why wouldn't he want to set the record straight on why he does what he does? I know I would. Unless he really is just a sleaze."

"He's remained anonymous for years," Chloe repeats the same warning Viv offered. "He's like the Keyser Söze of the escort world. A name you say that forces a certain reaction."

"See!" I exclaim, slamming my hands on the notepad, causing Chloe to startle. "I told Viv the same thing! But she never saw *The Usual Suspects,* so the analogy was lost on her."

"Instead of being some scary spook story you tell your kids so they eat their vegetables, it's more a threat to your spouse. 'Take me on vacation or I'll hire August Laurent to do it.'"

"'If you don't go down on me, August Laurent will!'" I offer, getting in on the game.

"'Let me use a strap-on with you, or I'm calling August Laurent!'"

I laugh, then stop, her words registering with me. "Wait. A strap-on?" My forehead creases.

"Too far?"

"Yeah, a little. Weirdo," I joke before fixing my expression. "So, tell me what you know."

She sighs, leaning back in her chair. "I don't know much more than what you'll find online, which is next to nothing."

"But you know everything about everyone! And didn't you say Holly Turner hired him when she went through her divorce?"

"She never came right out and said she did, but she insinuated she spent a month in Fiji with him to escape reporters when news of her separation hit the papers."

"That's all? Nothing else? She must have said more than that. Anything to help me track down this guy."

"She was pretty tight-lipped about the entire thing." She pulls her bottom lip between her teeth, sucking on it.

"What is it?" I ask urgently.

"Nothing. It's probably nothing."

"Or it could be something."

Turmoil covers her expression.

"Come on, Chloe. You're the gossip queen! You must know something!"

She sighs in resignation. "Fine, but there's no guarantee there's truth to any of this. All I get are bits and pieces from people."

"Yes, but you get *lots* of bits and pieces, all of which could eventually fit into one puzzle."

Rolling her chair closer to mine, her voice becomes practically inaudible. "He's careful not to give out too much personal information to any of his clients. He makes it all about them, which I suppose is what they're paying him for. The guy's interested me for a few years, but with my column the way it is, I can't stop to hunt down a ghost. Still, you hear rumors."

"And did you hear a rumor about this mystery man sharing a piece of personal information with one of his clients that could potentially help me?" I grin wide, to which she nods.

"When Holly was here for a shoot a few months ago, we got to talking. Of course, she never mentioned *who* helped her through her divorce, but I read between the lines. It had to be August Laurent. She said he told her the importance of establishing a routine, some sort of normalcy in her life when it feels like it'll never be normal again."

I pinch my lips together, his advice resonating with me. I like having a routine when my life hasn't been uprooted. Now, after Trevor, I crave it even more. In fact, the thought of spending a few hours updating my planner has me more excited than I've been in a while.

"I'd mentioned how I prefer to be spontaneous, that I doubt I could ever do the same thing every single day. She said he claimed you could find normalcy in something small. Then she shared the example he gave her."

"And what was that?" I scribble down a few notes on my pad before looking back up at her.

"He apparently lost someone very close to him and had trouble coping with the loss. What helped was starting his day by going to the same coffee shop and ordering the same pastry. It gave him something to look forward to. To this very day, when he's in town, he still goes to the same coffee shop and orders the same chocolate hazelnut pastry."

She shifts her attention to her laptop, scrolling through a folder that must contain thousands upon thousands of images. Finding one, she turns the screen toward me. It's a blurry photo of a woman in a sleek pink dress, dark sunglasses covering her eyes, her face downturned.

"Who's that?"

"Carly Jensen. She's rumored to have hired August Laurent." She points to a man walking a few feet behind her, his eyes also obscured by dark sunglasses. "That man."

I squint, trying to make out his features, but it's impossible. Nothing about him stands out, not to mention he's walking several feet behind Carly.

"Chloe, I—"

"Wait. There's more." Keeping the photo on the screen, she searches for another one. When she finds it, she clicks on it, the image similar to the previous one. Another celebrity walking on the street wearing sunglasses. Another man in a dark suit trailing behind.

"This proves nothing."

"It may not, but it's a start."

I shake my head. "I don't see how. "There's nothing—"

"Because you aren't looking close enough," she interrupts. "Part of getting the scoop before anyone is being attuned to the details everyone else overlooks. Like this."

She zooms in on the man's hand. I squint again, faintly able to make out the familiar logo of Manhattan's famous Steam Room etched on the coffee cup. Then she does the same to the other photo.

"Isn't the Steam Room famous for their chocolate hazelnut pastries?" she asks, a smirk on her face.

"They are."

"Bit of a coincidence, don't you think?" She sits back and folds her arms in front of her chest.

I stare at the two photos. It could be nothing, but it could be everything.

"I guess I know where I'll be spending my time now."

Chapter Seven

OVER THE NEXT few weeks, I make myself a cozy little home at a corner table in the Steam Room on Fifth Avenue. Based on the sheer number of people who frequent this place, it seems to be a popular spot among locals and tourists. I'm not surprised, considering it's located across from Central Park.

When I first concocted this plan, I didn't think it would be too difficult to figure out who August Laurent was — note whoever ordered a chocolate hazelnut pastry every morning, then see who was a repeat offender. I underestimated how popular that particular danish is. August Laurent probably knows this, too, which was why he didn't mind sharing this piece of personal information with his client. The entire population of Manhattan orders these damn pastries, which has made my job even more difficult. I've resorted to focusing on men without wedding bands whom I consider attractive enough to be a male escort. Shallow? Perhaps. But I have to narrow down the pool somehow.

On the last Thursday in June, as I sit in what's become my satellite office, I hear a deep voice order an Americano and the chocolate hazelnut pastry. I tear my eyes away from my laptop, hope building inside me that this may be the man I've been looking for.

The instant I do, I inhale a sharp breath, understanding why the timbre of the man's voice made my thighs involuntarily squeeze together. There he is… Mr. Armani Suit.

Dumbfounded at my horrible luck, all I can do is stare, although all reason tells me to look away, to hide, to pretend I have no idea who he is. What are the freaking chances? Of all the coffee shops in this city, the one person I hoped to never see again walks into this one. Then, in confirmation of my belief that the universe is out to get me, a pair of vibrant blue eyes shifts to mine, a sly smile curling his lips.

"Shit." I lower my head and stare at my laptop screen, wishing I could disappear into the background. I've always loved the unique shade of my red hair…until this moment when I'd give anything to blend into a sea of blondes and brunettes.

As I pretend to read the words I've written over the past hour, the aroma of citrus mixed with spice invades my senses, reminiscent of the morning I woke up in a strange man's bed. I pinch my lips together, concentrating even harder, as if it will make him disappear. Then I hear his voice — low, deep, hypnotizing.

"I thought it was you. But maybe you should get up and run away so I can be certain." There's dry amusement in his tone.

I reluctantly look up, about to reply with a snarky comment when I'm rendered speechless. I'd forgotten how captivating this man is. At least drunk Evie doesn't skimp on good looks, even when she's had a few too many. Sandy, disheveled hair. Vibrant azure eyes framed with lashes any woman would kill for. Olive skin that appears to have been kissed by the sun. Strong face with angular cheekbones. Broad nose. Two-day scruff along his jaw. And full, lush lips surrounding gleaming white teeth.

I lick my lips as I scan the rest of his frame, the navy blue suit he's wearing just as impeccable as the one he wore the night we first saw each other. But that's not what has my mouth salivating. It's the memory of what lies beneath — firm muscles, intricate tattoo, and mysterious scars on his otherwise flawless physique.

"Evie?"

I snap my eyes back to his, pretending I hadn't been ogling his body. The smirk pulling on his mouth is all the evidence I need to know he caught me in my mental undressing of him. Again.

"Hello," I say, exuding all the confidence I can, not wanting him to realize I can't remember his name…if he even told me. The cocky, self-assured way he carries himself gives off the impression it's not a stretch to think he *didn't* tell me his name. That he saw some drunk girl nearly passed out by his apartment and brought her up to take advantage of her.

But something about the way he gazes at me with heat and a hint of relief gives me pause. Perhaps Chloe was right when she suggested we may not have slept together. Now would be the perfect time to ask him, but I'm too embarrassed to admit I can't remember much of that night.

"It's good to see you again."

He narrows his eyes, unnerving me. "Is that so? From where I'm standing, you seem…flustered."

"Honestly, when I walked in here earlier this morning, the last thing I expected was to run into someone I made the mistake of going home with after drinking far too much. So, as much as I've enjoyed this awkward little reunion, you'll have to excuse me. I have work to do."

I return my eyes to my laptop, pretending to look incredibly busy and important. My muscles tense as I wait for him to walk away. Instead, he takes the seat across from me.

I stare at him, annoyed by his rashness. "What part of 'get lost' did you not understand?"

"I didn't exactly hear you say 'get lost'."

"No." I glower at him, then check over his shoulder to make sure I haven't missed anyone who looks like he might be an escort ordering a chocolate hazelnut pastry. "I was trying to be polite. It seems manners aren't your thing."

"Hmm… Manners. Like saying goodbye?" He arches a brow.

"Yes."

"It seems we both have a lesson to learn in manners then. Where I'm from, we say goodbye when we leave. Is that not customary where you grew up?"

He leans back, brushing his thumb against his lower lip. My eyes float to his mouth and I salivate at the idea of how they might taste. I squirm in my seat, hoping he doesn't pick up on what a tangled bundle of hormones I am.

"What did you say the name of your hometown is? Hickman? Do you not say goodbye in Hickman?"

"We do," I answer sheepishly.

He rests his elbows on the table, inching toward me. "Then why did you leave without saying goodbye?"

I open my mouth to respond, but he cuts me off.

"And don't say because you didn't want to wake me."

I snap my jaw shut. His formerly arrogant expression now carries a hint of vulnerability, at complete odds with the image I'd painted of him in my mind. "Maybe because I was embarrassed."

"Embarrassed?" He cocks his head at me. "Embarrassed about what?"

"Oh, I don't know," I shoot back sarcastically. "Because I got raging drunk and woke up in a stranger's bed."

He parts his lips to say something, but I hold up my hand. Now it's my turn to interrupt him.

"I'm sure you have no qualms about picking up drunk girls at a club or a bar and taking them home with you. What happened a few weeks ago… That's an isolated incident. I was drunk and dealing with some personal stuff, which caused me to make the horrible decision of going home with someone I don't even know."

"You know who I am. I told you. My name's Julian."

I blink repeatedly, something about that name sparking a memory. I snap my fingers. "That's right! Julian! Now I remember. I kept calling you Julius Caesar." I laugh, recalling the numerous times I'd slurred "*Et tu, Brute*", to which he responded that his name was "Juli*an* not Juli*us*".

"You didn't remember my name?" He appears genuinely hurt.

I shrink into myself, a momentary feeling of guilt washing over me before I brush it off.

"Listen, Julian, I appreciate you taking the time to come over to say hi and not ignore me. If I were in your shoes, I would have done just that. Hell, I *tried* to do that. But I'm here to work on a story that could land me a promotion." Agitated by his presence, I fidget with my hands. "As you overheard at the bar, my boyfriend broke up with me because I'm not serious enough. So this promotion can certainly prove otherwise."

"A story?" He gives me a wry smile, causing his dimples to pop. If he weren't irresistible enough to begin with, he has to have dimples, too? It's like the big guy upstairs put together everything I find attractive about a man, then gave him the opposite personality I need. And as much as looks are important, personality trumps all.

"Yes. I'm the sex and dating editor for *Blush* magazine."

"But you're up for a promotion?"

"Assistant editor of the entire magazine. As long as I nail this story."

He peeks over my laptop at my notepad, squinting to decipher my chicken scratch. "August Laurent?"

Indignant, I cover my notepad with my hand, pulling it toward me and flipping it over so he can't see. "He's the subject of my story."

He doesn't react. I take his silence for confusion.

"He's the most sought-after escort in the country. Apparently, he lives right here in Manhattan," I explain. "No one's been able to nail down this guy for an interview, so that's what I'm trying to do. My sources say he frequents this place, so if you'll excuse me…" I lock eyes with him, hoping he gets the hint that I have no desire to continue this conversation.

Finally, after a stare down that feels like it lasts hours, he reluctantly gets up. "Well, I'll leave you to your work."

"Thank you." I reach for my coffee, taking a long sip, trying to calm my overwrought nerves. The last thing I need is to be distracted and miss spotting the man who could be the mysterious August Laurent.

"For the record…" When I hear Julian speak, I lift my head, meeting his sincere eyes. "It was nice to see you again, Evie." His lips curve up at the corners. "Really nice." Then he disappears into another section of the coffee shop.

CHAPTER EIGHT

I CAN'T GET Julian out of my mind the rest of the morning, despite a valiant effort on my part to do so. Every time I think of his sapphire eyes and the earnestness in his voice when he confessed he was happy to see me, my body heats as my stomach erupts in flutters I haven't experienced in too long now.

Whenever I consider the possibility that maybe there's something more there, I remind myself it's all part of his game. Men like Julian crave the chase. Once they've captured their prey, they'll either destroy it in a way that makes it unrecognizable, or release it back into the wild with the hope of finding something tastier, perkier, younger. I'm too smart to allow Julian to capture me again.

Since my focus is essentially nonexistent, thanks to one Julian…whatever his last name is, I decide to call today a loss and return tomorrow, refreshed and rejuvenated. After collecting my things and shoving them into my laptop bag, I do like all New Yorkers do and check my social media on my phone to avoid eye contact as I head out of the coffee shop, paying no attention to the couple walking in.

"Evie." It's not a question. More like a statement of surprise.

I lift my head, admiring the long, sleek lines of the suit-clad body, sucking in a breath when I peer into a pair of familiar hazel eyes. Eyes that once looked at me with such devotion as the owner declared his love. I swallow hard through the lump in my throat at the comfort I once felt whenever I peered into them. Now I only feel inadequate.

"Trevor…," I breathe, unsure what else to say.

"Hey." He looks as uneasy about our unexpected meeting as I do.

I've been living in our apartment the past few weeks, but we haven't seen each other. Every night, I prepared a dinner plate for him, thinking he'd be hungry whenever he got home from the office, yet I was always asleep when that happened. By the time I woke up in the morning, Trevor would already be gone, his plate in the dishwasher. It probably sounds like nothing, but the gesture fills me with hope that this separation won't last. That he'll see how much he needs me in his life.

Until I see the woman clinging to his arm, their hands intertwined. If seeing him for the first time since he broke up with me isn't hard enough, now I have to look at him while another woman holds his hand, feels his skin, enjoys his warmth. That's supposed to be *my* hand, *my* skin, *my* warmth.

When a throat clearing sounds, Trevor tears his eyes from mine, looking at the petite woman at his side. She can't be more than five-foot-two, and probably a perfect size two. She's pretty, I suppose, but nothing stands out that makes her remarkable.

Her dark hair is pin straight, not a single strand out of place, as opposed to my wild red locks I have trouble taming. It fits my personality — bold and a bit reckless. Her clothing choice is a complete juxtaposition to my love of color, her conservative charcoal suit something I wouldn't even wear to a funeral. Her makeup is simple. Not over the top, but enough to add color in all the right places. I like making a statement with my makeup. My mother once told me a great red lipstick could make everything better, advice I've carried into adulthood. She doesn't seem to have a single curve on her body, compared to my shapely hips and ample chest. The combination of my physique and red hair causes many people to comment that I resemble the character Joan from *Mad Men*.

Is this *really* what Trevor wants? Someone boring and…ordinary? It's almost like he purposely found someone who's the polar opposite of me. I'm not sure if I should find satisfaction or sadness in that fact.

"Sorry." He licks his lips as he tugs at his tie, a nervous tick of his. I wonder if his new friend even knows that yet. "Evie, this is Theresa. Theresa…" His Adam's apple bobs up and down, "this is Evie."

She stares me down, her mouth forming a tight line. Her lukewarm reception gives the impression that Trevor must have mentioned me. I can almost hear her disapproving thoughts, wondering what he could have seen in someone like me.

Likewise, girlfriend. Likewise.

In an attempt to be the bigger person, I reach my hand toward her. "Theresa. So wonderful to meet you."

She plasters a fake smile on her face, although she can't fake it like I can. She better practice because she'll need to fake some orgasms if she plans on staying with him. Sex is...okay, but she'll need some extra assistance if she wants to get off on a regular basis.

"I've heard so much about you."

I look from Theresa to Trevor. Even their names are similar. It's creepy. "I wish I could say the same." I keep my tone upbeat, not wanting anyone to catch on to how hard it is for me to see him with another woman, especially mere weeks after he broke up with me. "I didn't realize you liked this place. It's out of the way from your office. What is it? Fifteen blocks from Thirty-Fourth and Fifth?"

"Actually, it's closer to twenty. But Theresa's never had one of their chocolate hazelnut pastries. I stop by every morning for one before heading into the office."

"You do?" I try to hide the hurt in my voice over the fact that I didn't know this about him. And that I haven't noticed him during the weeks I've been camped out here. Who else haven't I noticed? What if my propensity to be easily distracted by cute puppy videos on the Internet caused me to miss August Laurent?

"Yeah. But I haven't been able to get here recently because of the trial."

"Right," I breathe in a drawn-out voice, relieved. "The trial."

I don't even bother to ask how it went as we stare at each other in uncomfortable silence. I do my best to pretend the idea of him sharing a chocolate hazelnut pastry with Theresa doesn't break me even more. He's supposed to want to share these things with me. Hell, my office is only a few blocks away, yet not once did he ask me to meet him here.

"Well…," I say, my tone upbeat. We had the spark once. I have to figure out how to get it back. Then he'll come to his senses, and I'll be there waiting. "I need to get back to work."

I'd normally make a joke about having to take a few vibrators for a test drive for an article I'm working on, but I don't, choosing the mature route. Although it's hard… *Really* hard.

"It was nice seeing you." I skirt past them and push my way through the glass doors. The instant I'm outside, I lean against the brick wall of the building, exhaling a breath. People move along this busy section of New York as if I don't matter, don't exist. Like Trevor just made me feel, despite our lengthy history.

"That's him then, is it? Your ex?"

I whip my eyes to my left, watching with a furtive stare as Julian strolls toward me.

Great. Just what I need. Sometimes I wish my life had background music so I can understand what the hell is going on. Right now, I'm at a complete loss. All I know is it seems like the universe is conspiring against me.

"So what if it is?" I cross my arms in front of my chest, acting as if seeing Trevor had no effect on me.

"Hope you don't think it rude of me to say—"

"The fact you lead off with that statement means whatever's about to follow is rude."

He closes the distance between us, his gaze searing my flesh, causing it to prickle. Trevor never stared at me with this much heat, this much want, this much raw need. When I first met Julian, I figured I imagined the connection. But it's here. And I'm sober, despite my burning need for a drink after running into Trevor, then Julian again. Both within minutes of each other.

"He doesn't seem your type."

"Great." I roll my eyes. "Yet another person who thinks Trevor's too good for me." I push past him, but stop in my tracks, the Irish temper I'm normally able to keep under wraps exploding from me. Whirling around,

I narrow my fiery stare on him, my jaw tense, my fists clenched. "Who do you think you are anyway? You know nothing about me, other than how I am in bed, which you shouldn't have found out in the first place. I can't do anything to change that now, though. So while I appreciate your little pep talk, I am *so* not in the mood today."

I turn from him, my hair nearly smacking me in the face with the force as I walk in the opposite direction of the magazine's office.

"I can help you!" he calls after me.

"With another romp in the sack?" I shout over my shoulder as I cross the street, swept up in the sea of people heading toward Central Park. "Thanks for the offer, but I'd rather keep our one-night stand to just that. One night. Goodbye, *Julius*."

CHAPTER NINE

THERE ARE TIMES I've often longed for the simple and sparsely populated life I lived back in Nebraska. The sheer amount of people who live, work, or play in New York City can be suffocating. Right now, I use that to my advantage, allowing everyone heading into the park to shield me from Julian.

Once I'm certain I've evaded him, I break off from the crowd and walk down one of the meandering paths, mature trees shading me from the hot June sun. The sound of runners' feet hitting the pavement is coupled with birds and the background noise of Manhattan, but there's still a tranquility here you can't find anywhere else.

Dogs pull their walkers along the trails, tourists stop for a picnic on a grassy area. A few locals on their lunch break sit on a bench and read. I even spy a couple having their engagement photos taken. It causes me to slow my steps, unable to look away. I had planned this very thing for Trevor and me.

I even had a list of shots I wanted our photographer to capture. Thanks to my time working for a wedding planner, I knew exactly what I wanted. Now, I stare at this couple with longing, faced with the possibility that I've truly lost Trevor, that this breakup may not be due to stress, as I tried to claim it was.

My legs seeming to give out as I confront this new reality, I fall onto a bench, recalling the distance that seemed to stretch between us, even when we had first moved here. I always excused his behavior, considering he was in law school. Maybe we fell out of love all those years ago, but neither of us would admit it, not wanting to prove our parents right when they warned us moving to New York together was crazy. But I remember all the happy moments we shared, too.

Like when we'd order a pizza and sit out on the fire escape to eat it, the view of the city more mesmerizing and exhilarating than any movie could be.

Like the time we got lost when trying to figure out the subway system and ended up somewhere in the Bronx. Instead of asking someone for help finding our way back, Trevor insisted we figure it out on our own. Together. And we did.

Like the way all the tension slowly rolled off his body when he'd climb into bed beside me after a long day of studying. He'd wrap his arms around me and fall asleep. In those moments, everything was worth it.

I have to believe it still is.

"You're giving me a complex, ya know," a voice startles me from my quiet reflection.

I snap my head to my right to see Julian helping himself to the vacant space beside me. He drapes his long arms along the back of the park bench, resting the calf of one leg on the other thigh.

"How many times are you going to run away from me, Evie?"

"Not used to a woman telling you no?"

He narrows his steely gaze on me. "I'm not used to *anyone* telling me no."

Rolling my eyes, I stand. "Well, get used to it because the only answer you'll ever get out of me is no. Have a nice day, Julian." When I spin from him, I almost run into a group of cyclists flying by. Thankfully, their reflexes are quick and swerve out of my way, allowing me to avoid any additional embarrassment today.

"Even if I said I may have a way to help you with your predicament with your ex?" he calls out.

I halt, gradually turning to face him, tilting my head to the side. A voice in my head reminds me that I barely know this guy, so there's only one reason he'd want to help me. But there's something about the way he looks at me that keeps me here. A genuine affection that's been missing from Trevor in recent days.

I place a hand on my hip, pinching my lips into a tight line. "Well, are you going to share how? Or do you hope I pick it up telepathically?"

With a smile that can only be described as panty-dropping, he gestures back to the park bench, an unspoken request for me to sit. I hesitate, but eventually acquiesce, ignoring the buzz of energy that sparks in my body as I pass him, inhaling a hint of his aroma.

Once we're both situated, he glances at me. "You're serious about getting back with your ex?"

"Of course!" I exclaim, indignant. "We were together twelve years. You don't throw away twelve years overnight. He probably didn't think he had any other option if he wanted to be taken seriously as a possible candidate for partner. All the other partners' spouses have more serious jobs. I get that giving sex advice isn't something to be proud of."

He rests his forearms on his thighs, considering my words. "I believe it shows you have no problem talking about uncomfortable topics, a trait Trevor should find valuable."

I struggle not to react to his compliment, failing miserably as heat covers my cheeks.

"So let me help you prove that to him."

"How?"

"Date me."

I straighten my spine, leaning farther away from him. "What?"

The expression on my face is probably akin to that of a child who prematurely learns Mommy or Daddy is actually Santa Claus. Nothing could have prepared me to hear Julian suggest we date to help me win back Trevor.

"Sorry if I sound blunt, but are you fucking crazy? I just told you I want to get back together with my ex and you ask me to date you?"

"It won't be real." He laughs, causing his eyes to sparkle. It's the first time I've heard him laugh, and it's just as hypnotic and seductive as I imagined it would be. "Just for show. To make him jealous. He's moved on. You should make him think you've done the same."

I shake my head, thinking the entire idea absurd. It reminds me of my conversation with Chloe and Nora that night at the bar when I first heard the name August Laurent. They suggested I hunt him down to do the very same thing. I was against it then. I'm still against it now.

"It would never work. The chance of running into Trevor in a city this size is slim to none. Hell, I haven't even moved out of our apartment yet and today was the first time I've seen him since we broke up two weeks ago."

He whips his head toward me, his brows pulled in. "Wait a minute. You're *still* living with him?"

"Yeah." Chewing on my lower lip, I shrug. "I figure if I don't move out, he'll realize how much he needs me in his life, how big of a mistake it was to walk away from me."

Julian shakes his head, pinching the bridge of his nose before returning his impassioned gaze to me. "That's exactly *why* you should have moved out by now. Don't give him the satisfaction of knowing you'll always be waiting for him." He shoots to his feet and grabs my hand, tugging me off the park bench. I'm too off balance from the sudden movement to fight him. "Come with me. This appears to be a bigger task than I originally thought."

I fight to keep up with his long strides as he leads me through the park. "Oh, really? And what makes you an expert in how to win back a boyfriend? Forgive me if I don't see you as the romantic type."

"You don't think I'm romantic?"

"This shouldn't come as a shock to you," I argue, but am quickly cut off when he stops walking and yanks me against his hard body. Initially, I struggle in his arms, but when he leans toward me, his breath warming my neck, I melt, becoming a ball of clay in his rather capable hands. That spark is back, that unyielding rush of need filling me, urging me forward.

"You may not think I'm romantic," he begins, his tone low and seductive. I exhale a shaky breath as my eyes roll into the back of my head, my nerve endings firing. "But if that's the case, do you think I would have cared that you were no longer in my bed when I woke up the morning after our chance meeting?"

I stiffen, shooting my gaze to him.

"Because I did," he continues, barely pausing for a beat. "For days, all I could think was I should have gotten your number. So I did what anyone would do in this digital age. I scoured Facebook to find you. I searched for anyone with every variation of the name Evie. Evelyn. Yvonne. Yvette. Everything remotely close to Evie, hoping I could track you down and see if…"

"If what?" Floating my eyes to his, I lose myself in deep pools of blue.

"If you feel this, too."

His mouth inches closer to mine, the anticipation of feeling his lips on my tender flesh unhinging me in a way that erases all sense of what's right. I've reverted to pure animalistic desire. No emotions. No reason. Just the urge to be satisfied.

"Feel what?" My heart pounds violently against the walls of my chest as I brace for his kiss, praying it will be as incredible as I imagine.

"How much you want to say yes to my little proposal." Before I have a chance to react, he pulls away, straightening his jacket, acting as if he weren't just about to kiss me.

I'm wound tight, a bundle of sensation in desperate need of release. It doesn't help I've been celibate for two weeks. It's the longest I've gone without sex since I met Trevor. That's got to be why I'm ready to agree to anything. It's desperation. That's it. Nothing more.

Recovering quickly, I run my hands along my dress, fixing my expression. "Your proposal is ridiculous. In order for it to work, Trevor needs to see us together."

He passes me a sly grin. "You really have no idea who I am, do you?"

"I know who you are." I square my shoulders. "Your name's Julian. *Not* Julius."

Bemused, he smirks. "Do you know anything else?"

"Just the fact you must have a shit-ton of money, or at least a really wealthy sugar mommy…or daddy. I'm not one to judge."

He chuckles, the corners of his eyes creasing. "Definitely no sugar mommy…or daddy. I can assure you of that." When his laughter wanes, he narrows his gaze on me. "Suffice it to say, Trevor *will* hear about us. A lot of people will. They'll all wonder about the mystery woman on my arm. It's summer. Party season is under way in the Hamptons."

"The Hamptons?" I swallow hard. I'd heard stories about those parties, mostly from Chloe, but you have to know someone to get an invitation. Hell, I've never even been north of Jones Beach on Long Island. The Hamptons is like a different world than what I know.

"Precisely. Men are protective and territorial by nature. In his mind, he can still stake a claim over you because you haven't moved on. Attend enough of these parties on my arm, he'll come to believe you have moved on. If his so-called 'ownership' over you is threatened, he'll realize his mistake. He'll never do that as long as you remain in his apartment, cook and clean for him, do his laundry like the status quo hasn't changed. It *has* changed. And he needs to feel that change or he'll never admit he fucked up. Trust me on this."

I ponder his words for a moment, something not adding up. Maybe living in New York has made me more cynical. "I find it hard to believe any guy like you would proactively want to help a woman he's slept with get back with her ex unless he wants a repeat. So, as enlightening as this entire conversation has been, it's over. I'm not interested in a replay." I turn from him, my legs not moving as fast as I wish they could.

"Evie, wait!" he calls, but I ignore him, continuing down the path. Then I hear him bellow, "We never slept together!"

I come to an abrupt stop, my pulse quickening. Passersby look in our direction, a few snickers and gasps ripping through the air, but I don't pay them much attention, too shocked by his admission.

"What did you say?" I ask over my shoulder.

He advances toward me. "We never slept together."

"But—" I square my shoulders, fully facing him.

"But then why would you wake up in a strange man's bed in just your bra and panties?"

I nod, still shell-shocked by this revelation.

"Because you threw up all over your damn dress... And my shoes."

Embarrassment fills me as I close my eyes, cringing. "I did?"

"Sure did."

"But how—"

"When I headed up to my place, I saw someone who looked alarmingly like this beautiful, charismatic woman I'd witnessed tell an entire bar about her breakup that evening. So, out of curiosity, I walked up to her. That's when I overheard you say you were never going to drink again."

"To which you said, 'That's probably a good idea.'"

He smiles. "I did. To which you responded by emptying the contents of your stomach."

I bury my head in my hands. "Oh god. I really am never drinking again. I'm so sorry."

His arms wrap around me...unexpected, yet comforting. I inhale a breath, my muscles relaxing at his familiar aroma. "It's okay. We all have those nights where the only cure is bourbon or tequila. Nothing to be embarrassed about. Not the first time I've had someone throw up on me. And it probably won't be the last."

"Unless you have some sick fetish, it should be." I tilt my head up at him. "You don't have some weird fetish where you pay people to puke on you, do you? That's not why you want to do this, is it?"

He chuckles as he drops his hold on me. "Certainly not. No sick fetishes here." He raises his hand. "Scout's honor."

I pinch my lips. "Why do I get the feeling you were never a Boy Scout?"

"Very observant of you. I wasn't."

There's a brief silence before I speak again. "So you saw me drunk on the street, then what? You decided to take care of me when the rest of the city just walked right by?"

"What can I say? I know how it feels to be overlooked, to think no one notices you. Plus, you'd just had a horrible night. The last thing you should do on your thirtieth birthday is spend it in the drunk tank at the local police precinct. I brought you back to my place to make sure you were okay, that you weren't about to pass out and choke on your own vomit."

"You washed my dress," I breathe. It's not a question.

"You probably thought the worst of me when you woke up in my bed. I considered sleeping in one of the guest rooms, but the reason I brought you to my place was to keep an eye on you. I couldn't do that if I slept in a different room. When I woke up and you weren't there, I panicked. I could only imagine what you must have thought, and I hated the idea of you walking around thinking we slept together. I needed to track you down and explain. That's why I searched for every name close to Evie on Facebook. I even went to the bar I first saw you at in the hopes I could find you."

"I haven't been in the drinking mood after that night. Plus, once my boss told me about the possible promotion, that's been my focus."

"I don't take advantage of women," he states with determination, his jaw firm. "Particularly drunk women. I just…" He blows out a breath. "I just wanted you to know the truth."

I stare into the distance, reflecting on this new information. No one in the city cares about each other. It's always every man for himself. The idea that Julian took it upon himself to make sure I was okay has me rethinking my original assumption.

"You really are a good guy," I murmur, more to myself than anyone else.

"I'm no saint, but I try to be a decent human being. Okay?"

"Okay." It's all I can manage to say as relief fills me. Trevor's still my number three. There's no number four. But now the idea of there being a number four doesn't seem to be the apocalyptic event I once believed it to be. For two weeks, I'd carried on like there was a number four. There were no flooding rains requiring me to build an arc. No swarm of locusts. No great famine, apart from that between my legs. Life went on. And I get the feeling it will continue to go on even if there were to be a number four.

"So, what do you say?" He runs a hand through his hair, drawing my attention back to him. "Want to be my fake girlfriend?"

To anyone else, I'm sure it sounds like a great offer. Pretend to date some ridiculously good-looking, presumably wealthy man who looks incredible in a suit. But it's not that easy for me. Even though Trevor's moved on, there's still a level of guilt.

"I apologize if I appear skeptical, but I just don't see what *you* get out of this."

"Simple. I get a seat at the table."

I scrunch my brows together. "Excuse me?"

"Listen…" He licks his lips. "I didn't always have money. Because of that, there are a few prominent people in my circle who are bitter about my windfall. I'm typically relegated to the 'kid's table', so to speak. Old money versus found money kind of thing. A dear friend who's been around this life for more years than she cares to admit suggested a girlfriend might help. Showing up at many of these events as a bachelor could be working against me. I'm in the middle of a few huge projects for my company, but there's a lot of bureaucratic red tape I need to cut through to get them off the ground. Some of the nation's most powerful people summer in the Hamptons."

"And if they see you're in a committed relationship and aren't just some bachelor playboy pissing away his fortune, they'll take you more seriously."

He nods. "Like I said, it'll be a win-win. I can conduct some much-needed business. You can make Trevor so jealous that he'll come crawling back to you."

I chew on my bottom lip, considering his offer. Julian certainly makes it sound appealing. But he doesn't know Trevor like I do. He's always had an uncanny ability to weed through the bullshit, which is why he's one hell of an attorney, even for only being thirty. He'll see through this bullshit, too. When he does, it will only reaffirm his reasons for breaking up with me in the first place — that I don't take anything in life seriously enough.

"I really do appreciate the offer, but Trevor will see right through our game in a flash. It will never work. I'm sorry. But I'm sure you can find someone else to help you." I lock eyes with him, feeling a twinge of guilt at the disappointment crossing his brow. "Goodbye, Julian."

When I turn from him, a part of me hopes he'll call my name once more. He never does.

CHAPTER TEN

"I CAN'T BELIEVE you're actually trying to figure out who August Laurent is," Nora says Friday afternoon as we unpack all the boxes containing possessions from my former life.

After my run-in with Julian in Central Park yesterday, I went back to the apartment I shared with Trevor instead of heading to the office. All I heard was Julian's warning that if I kept living with him, I'd only give him the satisfaction of knowing I'll always be around and waiting. I refuse to do that any longer. He needs to know I'm ready to walk away, too. A part of me hoped Trevor would reach out to talk when he walked into the apartment last night and saw the stacks of boxes containing my things. He never did. So, after our weekly meeting at the magazine earlier today, I convinced Chloe to play hooky. When I told Nora of my plans, she volunteered to help, as well. The only one missing from our circle is Izzy, but treating kids with cancer is more important than helping me move.

"Yeah," I groan. "And it's proving to be impossible. The man's a ghost."

"Like Keyser Söze."

"Exactly!" This is why we get along so well. We all think the same thing. It can be a little scary at times, but being able to anticipate what each other is thinking and feeling makes things easier.

"I wonder what he looks like." She grabs a magazine off the stack of back issues of *Blush* and flips through it.

I've kept a copy of every single issue since I started there. I remember holding the very first one in my hands and seeing my name in print. The feeling was indescribable. I even slept with it on my nightstand that night. Trevor never even asked to read the article.

"Maybe he appears differently for everyone who hires him. You know, like the Mirror of Erised in *Harry Potter*." She stops flipping through the pages, turning the magazine around to show us an image of Brad Pitt and Angelina Jolie when they were still "Brangelina". "Brad Pitt would be *my* August Laurent."

Chloe laughs. "I don't think it works that way, Nora. I don't think he changes his appearance based on what the person who hires him wants to see."

With a frown, Nora returns the magazine to the pile, then places them on a small bookshelf. "Pity. Wouldn't that be nice?"

"Sure," I say with an eye roll.

"How did you figure out he frequents the Steam Room anyway?" she presses.

I avoid her speculative gaze as I remove a few of my favorite coffee mugs from bubble wrap. Trevor always hated my affinity for mugs with snarky sayings on them. He drank out of the same boring black mug, said most adults don't drink out of mugs with profanity. I guess I'm not like most adults.

"Just a hunch based on a few tips."

"Hmm…" Her lips form a tight line. "Those tips wouldn't have come from our very own gossip queen, would they?" She waggles her brows, nodding toward Chloe.

I open my mouth to respond just as my phone rings. I glance at the screen, my breath hitching when I see Trevor's face smiling back.

"Who is it?" Chloe asks, noticing my reaction.

"Trevor," I answer hesitantly.

"What do you think *he* wants?" Nora sneers.

It took my friends no time at all to go from Team Trevor to Team No One, especially after I told them about seeing him yesterday. Of course, I left out any mention of bumping into Julian and his little proposition.

"Maybe to tell me he realized he made a mistake."

"You're not going back to him after this, are you?" Chloe presses.

Unsure how to respond to her, I shrug. I should just write him off. If we'd only been together a few months, I'd do just that. But it's been twelve years. There's a certain level of patience, understanding, and forgiveness that increases over time.

"Trevor," I say when I answer. It's strange to greet him this way. Normally, I'd say "Hey, baby" or "Hiya, sweetie". I hate I can't do that anymore.

"Oh, Evie. Hey," he responds, like he's surprised to hear my voice, even though he was the one who called.

"Is there something you need, or was this a butt dial?" I quip in a sarcastic tone when he doesn't say anything more.

"Right…" There's a pause and I hold my breath. Something's different in the timbre of his voice. Regret? Remorse? Sorrow? "I stopped by the apartment to change suits for tonight." Hope builds inside me that my plan has already had the intended effect. "There was a delivery for you."

"A delivery?" I can't remember the last order I placed. I normally have everything sent to the office, unless it's a big item.

"Yeah. It's… Well, someone sent you flowers."

I roll my eyes, thinking it's someone else from the magazine who decided to send me flowers in condolence for my breakup. Most likely one of the contributors who doesn't regularly come into the office.

I'm about to explain what my coworkers do during a breakup, when he cuts me off. "Who's Julian?"

My jaw falls open, a rush of adrenaline causing my skin to tingle from the name alone. "Julian?" I swallow hard.

In an instant, Chloe and Nora kneel directly in front of my position on the floor, their curious eyes trained on me. *Who's Julian?* Nora mouths. I hold up a finger, hushing them. This is as much a mystery to me as it is to them. Why would he send me flowers after I turned him down yesterday?

"I didn't mean to read the card, but it wasn't in an envelope. It was kind of hard to miss. Are you already seeing someone else?" His voice is low with a hint of jealousy. I shouldn't smile at the pain I hear, but it gives me a taste of vindication. Now he knows how it feels. Even if I'm *not* seeing Julian, he doesn't need to know that.

"You've already moved on. You can't expect me to sit around and wait for you, can you?"

"Well… No. I guess not." He blows out a long breath. "I just thought—"

"Actually, you didn't, Trevor. That's the problem. You didn't think. You didn't think I'd ever get over you. Well, maybe I have."

"Is that the only reason you're dating him?" His voice becomes strained, turning into almost a growl. I picture him pacing in front of the entryway table, tugging at his hair, sneering at the flowers Julian sent. "To piss me off? To make me jealous?"

"Do you really think so little of me that I'd stoop to such levels?" I keep my tone calm, refusing to show any hint of emotion. "Maybe I'm with Julian because he makes me laugh, makes me smile, makes me feel like I matter." I stand, pacing in the little free space between all my boxes. "And you know what? He likes that I'm a bit eccentric. He likes that I don't fit into the cookie-cutter mold it appears you want. He likes I don't have a size two body. Not to mention he *really* likes that I have more than a handful up top."

Nora snort-laughs, her wide eyes sparkling with amusement. I may have dug the knife a little deeper than necessary, but it feels good. Who knew? Apparently, Julian did.

"So am I doing this to make you jealous? No. I'm doing this to give me the happiness I deserve." I draw in a deep breath, my own words surprising me. I think they surprise my friends, too. They gape at me for a moment, then they both jump to their feet as they give me a silent standing ovation.

I glare and wave my hands at them, warning them not to make me laugh as I return my attention to my phone. "As you probably already noticed, I've packed up my things and brought them over to Chloe's. You shouldn't receive any additional deliveries for me over there, but text me if you do and I'll swing by to pick them up. There are a few more things I need to get out of the apartment this weekend. After that, you'll finally have me out of your life. I'm sorry it's taken so long."

A lump builds in my throat at the double meaning. I want him to beg me not to go, to tell me he doesn't want to come home to an apartment without tripping over my shoes, or seeing my collection of coffee mugs that haven't yet made their way into the dishwasher. But he doesn't. He doesn't say anything.

"Goodbye, Trevor."

I stay on the line a moment longer, praying he'll admit he made a mistake. But he doesn't. I go to end the call to see he already has. I remain motionless for a moment, simply staring at the phone as I try to process what just happened. Is this officially the end of Trevor and Evie? Trevi? I'd even planned for us to honeymoon in Rome just to go to the fountain bearing the same name as our couple name. Will I ever find someone I'll have an awesome couple name with again?

"Want to tell us what the hell is going on?" Chloe's voice pulls me out of my thoughts.

I glance to see her standing beside me, her arms crossed.

"Who's Julian?" Nora adds. "Why didn't you say anything about a new suitor?"

I shake my head, unsure where to even begin with this. I still can't wrap my head around it myself. "Julian isn't a suitor," I begin, then my phone rings once more.

"Is it Trevor telling you there's another delivery of flowers from yet another gentleman caller?" Nora giggles.

Rolling my eyes, I look at the phone to see my office line number, indicating it's a call forwarded from there, something I do whenever I'm away from my desk during normal business hours.

"It's a work call." I grit a smile. "Just a second." I bring the phone back up to my ear, squaring my shoulders and plastering on as professional an expression as I can, even though whoever's calling can't see me. "Evie Fitzgerald."

"Hello, Evie," a deep baritone responds.

The instant that voice comes over the line, my core clenches, my breath quickening as desire builds inside me, low and deep. My cheeks heat, so I look away from Chloe and Nora, hoping they don't notice the sudden change in my demeanor.

"Good afternoon, Julian."

Nora squeals and I glare at her. She quickly silences herself, but that doesn't stop her and Chloe from making obscene gestures, the occasional moan of "Oh, Julian" thrown in for added emphasis.

"Is it?" There's a hint of amusement in his voice, leading me to believe this was all part of his plan to begin with.

"It is now." I walk away from my two best friends, who seem to be acting like they're in middle school instead of professional adults, and head to the bay windows in Chloe's living room, looking out at the streets of Greenwich Village.

"And why's that?"

"Oh, I don't know." I lower myself to the window seat. "Maybe because my ex-boyfriend just called me in a jealous rage because someone happened to send me flowers."

He chuckles, the sound still having the same effect as it did yesterday. "Is that right?"

"That's right."

"I told you I can help, did I not?"

"All you did was send flowers," I retort. The last thing I want is to sound overly eager to agree to his proposition. I'm still not convinced it's the right way to go about this. "You were lucky Trevor was even home when they were delivered. He's been practically sleeping at the office these days."

"You call it luck. I call it due diligence."

"Due diligence?"

"Precisely. I promised that if you agreed to help me, I'd do everything to help *you*. Randomly sending you flowers doesn't cut it. If I simply wanted to send you flowers, I would have sent them to your office. I wanted *him* to know I sent you flowers. Which is why I paid the delivery person to sit outside your building and wait until he saw Trevor walk in."

I'm momentarily speechless by the length it appears Julian went in order to make Trevor jealous. I have to hand it to him. It certainly worked.

"Do I want to know how long the delivery man was sitting outside?" I'm unsure if I should consider this a creepy form of stalking or if it is simply a demonstration that he's a talented manipulator.

"Probably not. So, what do you say, Evie? Did I prove you wrong?"

I brush my hair behind my ear, ignoring the questioning stare of my two friends, who are now squeezed on the opposite side of the window seat, their gazes seemingly glued to my every move.

"What do you mean?"

"You said Trevor was too smart to buy into the idea of us being a real couple."

"And he is."

"You still believe that?"

"I do. He asked if I was only dating you to make him jealous, so he's certainly skeptical."

"But he *did* think you were dating me." His voice is light and playful. "I think my column deserves points for that alone."

"This isn't a game, Julian."

"Of course it is. Life is merely a game. So are relationships. It's all about strategy."

"Is that what this is? Your strategy to get me to agree to your proposition?"

"And if it is?"

I pinch my lips together, carefully considering my words. "Then it seems you're going to awful lengths when I'm sure you have your choice of women who'd gladly agree to be your arm candy at a few parties in the Hamptons."

Nora shrieks again, but Chloe jabs her in the side, silencing her. Still, they both stare at me like I'm the three-headed dog from *Harry Potter*.

"But I don't want any of them. I want a stunning, irresistible woman who can hold her own in a room full of stuffy businessmen and their stuck-up wives."

"You're barking up the wrong tree because I—"

"Don't think you fit that description?" he interrupts, finishing the thought on the tip of my tongue. "Well, you're wrong. Maybe in your ex-boyfriend's opinion you don't, but from what I've seen, you're the perfect person for the job. I'm not looking for someone who can't form an intelligent thought if her life depended on it, or someone who will only speak when spoken to. I'm looking for someone with edge. Someone who has confidence in spades. That's you. So let's do this. I help you. You help me. Tit for tat."

I chew on my bottom lip, torn. On one hand, I don't have anything to lose by agreeing. It could work, considering how jealous Trevor sounded just from the idea of me receiving flowers from another man. But on the other hand, there are too many variables, too many ways for this to turn from a strictly business relationship into something…more.

"It's unwise to agree to this without ironing out all the details. Despite what you may think you know about me, I prefer when there's a concrete plan."

"I couldn't agree more. I'll make dinner reservations for seven o'clock tonight. Shall I pick you up from your place or the office?"

"Tonight?" I look to Chloe and Nora for guidance. Their eyes are bright with excitement over the prospect of me having dinner with a guy tonight.

Chloe mouths, *My place*, then winks.

"How about you tell me where and I'll meet you there."

"I had a feeling you'd be a challenge." I can hear the smile in his voice. "If this is to work, we need to give off the appearance of being a real couple."

"Real couples meet at restaurants all the time, especially in this city. I met Trevor constantly. In fact, I can't remember the last time we went out when I *didn't* meet him there." The second the words leave my mouth, a pang squeezes my heart.

"And that's precisely why I'll always pick you up for every single one of our outings," he responds, not allowing me to dwell too long on my realization. I wonder if he knows this. "No exceptions. So, again, your place or the office?"

"How about my friend Chloe's?"

"Is there a reason you don't want me to pick you up at your place?"

"I moved out."

"Good girl." The way he caresses those two words forces me to squeeze my legs together, an ache building as my overactive imagination goes to places it shouldn't, not when I'm still supposed to be pining for Trevor. "Program this number into your phone. Let me know when you're ready."

"Hold on." Jumping off the bench, I head into the bathroom, wanting some privacy. I put him on speaker, then switch to my contacts. "Ready."

He rattles off his number and I input his information into my phone. "That's my cell. Text me her address."

"I will." I save his number and take him off speaker, bringing my phone back up to my ear.

"No. Right now."

I groan. "Seriously? Been stood up too many times?" I open the door, stepping back into the living room, only to be met by my friends' scowls.

"Never, but you're different from the usual women I find in my company."

"Fine." Continuing past Chloe and Nora, I pull the phone away and switch to the message app. After typing out a quick text with Chloe's address, I hit send, then return my cell to my ear. "Is that a good or bad thing?"

"Only time with tell." I hear the ping of an incoming message in the background. When he speaks again, his tone is low, almost seductive. "I'll see you at seven, Evie."

"I look forward to it." I stare blankly ahead, about to hang up when I think of something. "Julian, wait!"

"Yes?"

"What's your last name?"

"My last name?"

"Yeah. In case you turn out to be a serial killer, I'd like Chloe and Nora to know the full name of the man I was last seen with. That way, the police have a head start on tracking down my body to some old, abandoned warehouse in Jersey City you've re-purposed as a kill room."

"Dammit. You've figured me out."

I laugh, a lightness in my chest at how effortless it is to joke with him. I almost don't want to hang up.

"Gage," he says finally. "My last name is Gage."

"Okay."

"Okay," he says.

It's silent for a moment. Then I blurt out, "Guinevere."

"Excuse me?"

"My real name's Guinevere. That's why you couldn't find me online. Evie's a nickname. I had trouble pronouncing my name when I was a little girl and called myself Evie. It just kind of stuck."

"Guinevere… I like that." He pauses, then says, "See you in a few hours, Guinevere."

CHAPTER ELEVEN

"WHAT THE HELL is going on?" Chloe asks once the line goes silent.

I clutch the phone for a moment longer while I attempt to recover my composure enough to face my friends.

"And who is Julian?" Nora teases.

I turn around, meeting their curious eyes, at a loss for words.

"Based on your conversation, he sent you flowers, which made Trevor jealous, and now you're going to dinner with him. Who is he and where did you meet?" Chloe presses.

I worry my bottom lip, rubbing my hands along my jeans. What do I tell them? What *can* I tell them? If I'm supposed to pretend to date Julian, won't we have to keep up appearances? But this is Chloe and Nora, my two best friends. We're the three amigas. Three musketeers. Sisters from another mister. Am I expected to keep up the charade in front of *everyone*?

"Okay." I blow out a long breath. "But you can *not* tell a soul. No one else can know about this." I narrow my gaze on Chloe, my stare harsh, trying to relay the severity of the situation. "This is so far off the record, it would be akin to career suicide if you were to print it."

"You have my word." Her light eyes are bright and filled with all the sincerity I've come to expect from her, especially when discussing private matters. There are few people I believe when they make me a promise. Chloe's one of them. "This will stay between us. No one else."

Secure in her assurance, I walk to the couch and sit down. Chloe and Nora follow, sitting next to each other on the opposite end. Once they're situated, I face them.

"I spent yesterday morning in the Steam Room, like I have been all week."

"Yeah, I know," Chloe says.

"What you don't know is that as I was trying to figure out who August Laurent is, Mr. Armani Suit came in."

"Shut up!" Nora playfully jabs me. "He did not! What are the chances?" She bounces with excitement.

Ever since I'd shared the story of waking up in a strange man's bed and struggling to remember what happened, she made it her mission to get to the bottom of who he was. She'd even asked Aiden, the bartender, if he knew, to no avail.

"Apparently pretty good." I roll my eyes, feigning annoyance with the idea of seeing the man I swore I had no desire to cross paths with again.

"What did you do?" Chloe inquires, not as excitable as Nora.

"I did what any self-respecting thirty-year-old woman in my shoes would do when facing a man whose bed she woke up in after a night of drinking."

"You tried to hide, didn't you?"

"Do you blame me? I hoped to never see the guy again. So I did my best to act disinterested, although… Holy hell, girls." Warmth radiates through me as I melt into the couch, unable to contain my smile. "On a scale of ten, this guy is, like, a solid eleven. He was even hotter than I remember. Usually, it's the other way around. And bonus, I learned his name is Julian, so there's that."

"What did he say?"

I stare into space, recalling our conversation in the coffee house. One thing stands out above all others. "He wanted to know why I left without saying goodbye. He appeared genuinely upset by it."

"Aww…," Nora and Chloe say in unison, passing each other an endearing look.

"No. Not *aww*. This is not an *aww* moment."

"It is," Chloe insists.

"No."

"It's destiny, Evie!" Nora beams as she clutches my hand, squeezing. "You get wasted and sleep with who I can only imagine to be God's gift to the male form, can't remember a thing, then cross paths with him two weeks later. I'm not sure the odds of something like that happening, especially in a city the size of New York, but it's got to be unheard of!"

"It's not destiny." I brush off the idea, even though I'd briefly considered it. "And…" I trail off.

"And…what?" Chloe leans in, clinging to my every word.

I expect them to break out the popcorn as they take in the story I've kept from them for twenty-four hours. I'm not sure why I thought I could keep it from them forever. Maybe because I assumed yesterday was the last time I'd see Julian. Boy, was I wrong. Maybe it *is* destiny.

Returning my attention to them, I admit, "You were right."

"Right?" Confused, Chloe's brows pull in.

"We *didn't* sleep together."

"I knew it!" She pumps her fist in the air. "I mean, who in their right mind would have the wherewithal to put her bra back on after having sexy times? Hell, what woman would fall asleep with her bra on in the first place, unless they were completely incapable of taking it off? And there's no way he wouldn't take it off to get a look at those girls." With a laugh, she gestures to my chest. "You have fantastic boobs."

"Thank…you?"

"Start at the beginning," Nora orders. "And don't leave out a single detail."

With a grin, I run them through yesterday's unexpected events. Seeing Julian and learning his name. Dismissing him so I could work on finding August Laurent. Being unable to focus after our encounter. Running into Trevor with another woman as I left the coffee shop. Bumping into Julian again. Him telling me what happened the night of my birthday, then proposing a little arrangement.

"An arrangement?" Chloe waggles her brows deviously.

"Like a friends with benefits thing?" Nora smirks. "No strings, but you still get treated to a rocking orgasm when needed? Trust me. Those are a lot of fun." She looks to Chloe, who nods in agreement.

"No… Well, I don't think so. We still have to iron out the details, but if I agree to be his date to a bunch of stuffy dinner parties and events he has coming up, he'll help me win back Trevor. I turned him down, claiming Trevor was too smart to believe I'd be dating someone like Julian, especially so soon after our own breakup, but then…"

"Julian sent flowers to you at Trevor's while he was conveniently present," Chloe sings, filling in the blanks.

"Exactly."

"And it made him jealous."

"Sure did."

"So Julian wanted to prove you were wrong about Trevor being too smart. Now you're considering his proposal."

"You hit the nail on the head. But I haven't agreed yet. I still have my doubts—"

"Despite the fact that Trevor was jealous after only a bouquet of flowers?" Chloe tilts her head at me. "Imagine if he caught you guys doing it? He'd come crawling back to you in a flash."

"I don't know about that. Even if he *is* jealous, there's no guarantee it'll make him want to be with me."

Chloe and Nora share a look, shrugging.

"The reason Trevor broke up with me is because he doesn't think I'm serious. Lying to him and pretending to date someone else?" I grab one of Chloe's colorful throw pillows and hug it to my body. "That will most likely only solidify his original opinion."

Squinting, Nora considers my words for a moment. "Then why didn't you tell Trevor you *weren't* dating Julian? And why didn't you refuse to meet Julian for dinner tonight?"

I stare forward, shaking my head as I give the only answer that seems fitting. "I couldn't say no to him."

Chloe jumps to her feet, tugging me off the couch and into the den, which has become my bedroom, Nora following close on our heels. "Well, what are you going to wear?" She proceeds toward a hanging rack, shifting through all my clothes.

"I have no idea. I don't even know where he's taking me tonight." I plop down onto the bed.

"Ask him." She nods at my hand, which still clutches my cell.

"What? I can't do that."

"Sure you can," Nora encourages.

"Then he'll think I'm excited about tonight, and I can't be excited about tonight. It's strictly a business dinner. A glorified negotiation, so to speak."

With a groan, Chloe steps toward me, taking the phone from my hand. "Then I'll text him. While I'm at it, I'll ask him what kind of panties he prefers. Briefs, thongs, or commando. Ya know... So you can dress appropriately...in all respects."

My reflexes have never been so quick as I rip my cell out of Chloe's hands. "Fine. I'll text him." I open my messages to see he responded to the one I'd sent with her address.

Julian: *The Village? My mother always warned me about dating a village girl.*

A smile builds on my face as I respond.

Me: *Well then, it's a good thing I'm a Nebraska girl. Is there a dress code for dinner?*

Julian: *She warned me about Midwest girls, too. And wear something nice. A dress. Nothing too formal, but nothing too casual, either.*

Me: *What will you be wearing?*

Julian: *Are you sexting with me?*

I blush at his comment, drawing a blank as I try to come up with a witty response. Normally, I'd have an entire arsenal of possibilities. But something about Julian unnerves me, like I'm not myself.

Me: *If I were sexting, you'd be squirming in your seat, itching to drive over here and see me. I'm simply asking as a point of reference. And so I don't pick out the same Brooks Brothers' suit. It's happened before, and it was the embarrassment of the century. So I made Trevor go home and change.*

Chloe bursts out laughing. I glance over my shoulder to see her and Nora peering at the screen.

"You're horrible," Nora comments.

"Everyone uses comedy in awkward situations."

"But you use it in *all* situations."

"What can I say? I live an awkward life."

When my phone buzzes, we all fling our eyes back to the screen.

Julian: *Oh, Guinevere. I do enjoy your wit. No need to worry about us wearing* *the same Brooks Brothers suit. I don't own any. Most of mine are Tom Ford, which I'll be wearing tonight. I think slate gray. I'll see you at seven.*

I'm about to type a response when Nora snatches the phone from me. "Don't."

"What? Why?"

She blows out a breath, pinching the bridge of her nose. "You've been out of the dating world for too long."

"No, I haven't," I protest. "I've been working in it for years."

"Working in it and living it are two different things." Chloe gives me a knowing look.

"I—"

"You need to make him want you."

I stand up from the bed, heading to my rack of clothes to find something suitable for tonight. "This isn't a real relationship. It's not even a relationship. Plus, I haven't agreed to his proposal yet. I'm not sure I *want* to. Using someone to make Trevor jealous? It's definitely a bit juvenile, if you ask me."

"Fuck Trevor," Chloe interjects harshly. "Don't do this for Trevor. Do this for you. Have some fun this summer instead of moping around with a broken heart. And maybe this Julian is just the person to help you do that and get over Trevor."

"I doubt that." I stare ahead, avoiding her eyes. "We have absolutely no interest in each other."

Nora stands, walking toward me. "I find that hard to believe. For both of you. You blushed the entire time you spoke to him. And Julian? He digs you. Mentioning sexting? He's flirting with you. I told you not to respond to his text because he *wants* you to. By leaving him hanging, you'll have him thinking about you all afternoon until he sees you tonight. He'll be so on edge, he won't be able to contain himself."

I pull a yellow polka-dot dress from the rack, holding it up to my body. It's a fun, flirty, summer dress, reminiscent of a pinup girl style. Both my friends simultaneously shake their heads, grimacing. I groan. I want to go for something that screams just friends. I have a feeling they want me to wear something that makes me look like a temptress.

"Like I told you…," I begin with a sigh.

"Yeah, yeah. It isn't real." Nora does her best imitation of my voice.

"It's not.

"Trust me." She narrows her gaze on me. "He's into you. If he weren't, he would never have proposed this arrangement. I have a knack for picking up on these things. It's, like, my superpower or something."

I scoff, averting my gaze so my friends can't see the twinge of hope building over the idea of someone like Julian Gage being interested in me. He's so mature, so mysterious, so…sophisticated.

"In fact, I can prove it to you." She jumps up, shifting through my dresses.

"How?" I place a hand on my hip, arching my brows.

"I guarantee, before we've all agreed on a dress for you to wear tonight, he'll text again. He's probably staring at his phone, waiting for you to respond. Eventually, it'll be too much, so he'll message you something he hopes you won't be able to ignore. But you'll do just that. When you see him tonight, *you'll* have the upper hand. *You'll* be the one in control."

She returns her attention to my clothes, stopping to look at a few dresses before moving on. I'm about to argue, yet again, that her experience on Tinder doesn't make her a dating expert when a loud chiming rips through the quiet space.

We stop moving, all eyes zeroing in on the phone on the bed. Nora faces me, wearing a self-satisfied smirk. She crosses her arms over her chest.

"Did someone text you, *Guinevere*?"

My mouth growing dry, I slowly walk toward the bed and grab the phone. "Sorcery," I murmur as I unlock the screen.

"Who's it from?" she asks in faux curiosity.

"Julian."

"And what does it say?"

I'll never hear the end of it after I read this to her. "'And as far as your earlier comment that I'd be itching to see you if you were sexting… I already am.'"

Her expression is smug as she turns from me, looking through my dresses once more. "Dating is one strategic game. Even fake dating."

On a hard swallow, I remain silent, her words mirroring what Julian said. How all of life is simply a game.

"Play your cards right, you might just end up with a royal flush."

CHAPTER TWELVE

"HOLY CRAP, EVIE!" Nora squeals when I walk out of Chloe's bedroom and into the open living area.

The two girls took it upon themselves to give me a makeover as we opened a bottle of chardonnay. It was reminiscent of adolescent slumber parties, apart from the wine. We gushed over the prospect of a date with a ridiculously attractive man while they perfected my hair and makeup. And, of course, being the list-maker I am, I jotted down a list of pros and cons for Julian and Trevor, hoping it would help sway my decision. It didn't.

"You're smoking hot. I barely recognize you." She gets up from the couch, bringing her half-filled wine glass with her.

"Thanks… I think."

"It reminds me of my first date with Jeremy," she gushes as she leads me over to the full-length mirror hanging on the far wall, checking her handiwork.

"How?" I turn to her. "You met him on Tinder. Your first 'date' was a no-strings hookup. This is nothing like that."

"Whatever you say, Evie." She squares my shoulders, forcing me to face the mirror once more as she smooths a few of my flyaways. "Unlike what you think, you can't plan for everything. I wasn't looking for anything serious. Neither was Jeremy. You can't deny chemistry. Now look at us." With bright eyes and a brilliant smile, she holds out her left hand where a stunning diamond sits on her ring finger. "I'd say that's a pretty damn big string. All because I stepped out of my comfort zone, veered away from my *plan*, and allowed life to take the wheel."

"I'm happy for you, Nora." Despite their unconventional beginning, they are perfect for each other, not to mention Jeremy treats her like a queen. That's all any woman wants. Too bad there appears to be a lack of kings around these days.

I return my eyes to the mirror to do one last check. Nora was right. I don't look like myself. I wear makeup on a regular basis, but don't spend this amount of time on all the shading and contouring. The pallet Nora used makes the green of my eyes pop even more. Couple that with my red hair, the pouty, red lips, and the slim-fit black dress that hugs all my curves in the right places, which Chloe insisted I wear, and I've never felt so glamorous, so...beautiful.

"You don't think it looks like I'm trying too hard?" I spin around to face my friends. "I mean, this isn't a date."

"We know," Chloe groans. "You've only reminded us every minute since you hung up with this guy. And it's not about trying too hard. It's about using your natural…assets to come out on top in your negotiation. With a dress like that and your fantastic curves…" She gestures down my frame, "this guy will be eating out of the palm of your hand. Trust me."

"I don't—"

The buzzer rips through the apartment, interrupting me, and we all jump. My pulse skyrockets as I fling my wide eyes to the door, my breath quickening. I've never wanted to run away and hide as much as I do right now. I don't remember being this on edge when Trevor picked me up for our first date. Then again, we were friends first. Not to mention, all he had to do was take the elevator down a few floors in our dorm.

"Evie…" Nora places her hands on my arms, soothing me. "Relax. You remember all the conditions we discussed earlier?"

I nod quickly. "I made a list in my phone."

"Good. Remain firm. Keep the ball in your court."

"How do I even do that? I haven't been on a date, real or fake, in over a decade. Not like you guys."

"Well, then…" Chloe approaches and slings an arm along my shoulders. "If you ever find yourself in an uncomfortable situation and aren't sure what to do, ask yourself, 'What would Chloe do?'"

My two best friends burst out laughing. It's no secret what Chloe would do. It's what she always does.

With a groan, I push away from them. "That would end with me beneath him. And we are *not* going there. It's on my list." I hold up my phone before dropping it into my clutch. "No sex."

"It wouldn't end with me beneath him," she argues, then winks. "I much prefer being on top." With that, she spins, heading toward the door.

When her hand touches the doorknob, about to turn it, she glances over her shoulder, her brow arched, giving me one last chance to call it off. This is why I love her. No matter what, she'll always have my back. As much as she's exhibited her excitement over the idea of me going to dinner with Julian, she'll support me if I decide to cancel. Friends like Chloe and Nora are nearly impossible to find. I'm grateful I did. Navigating the stormy waters of my break up with Trevor would have been infinitely more difficult had it not been for them.

On a deep inhale, I nod. Time seems to stand still as she opens the door, revealing Julian on her front stoop. The instant my eyes lock with his, all the breath leaves me. He parts his lips slightly, his gaze darkening as he takes in my appearance, scanning me from head to toe. He doesn't even pay attention to Chloe, which is different. Whenever the three of us go out, Chloe seems to get the majority of the attention, what with her slender physique and unique shade of hair. It's difficult *not* to notice Chloe. But Julian doesn't even give her a second glance. I *like* that he notices me.

"Hi," his voice cuts through the silence.

I'm not sure how long we've been staring at each other. All I know is I can stare at this man all night and not be tired of the way he looks. A pair of dark jeans hang from his waist. Not too tight, but not too baggy, either. A beige jacket is slung over a white button-down shirt, the top two buttons undone, revealing a few tufts of chest hair. The previous times I've seen him, he's been in business attire — perfectly tailored suit, tie, shoes that cost more than I make in a year…including the ones I threw up on. While I like him in a suit, I love this dressy, yet casual look.

Nora nudges me and I snap out of my stupor. "Hi."

He bites his lower lip, reluctant to rip his eyes away from me, but he eventually does, addressing Chloe. "You must be Chloe." He holds out his hand.

"And you're Julian Gage." Her tone is borderline accusatory. I furrow my brow. I don't remember telling her his last name. Then again, the entire afternoon is a whirlwind. It probably slipped out while they helped me get ready.

"Guilty as charged." He laughs politely as Chloe steps back, allowing him to enter the apartment, but keeping her furtive stare trained on his every move.

As he walks toward me, his eyes rake over me in a way that makes me think he's seeing me for the first time. Or maybe, thanks to my impromptu makeover, he's seeing me in a different light. During our previous encounters, I was dressed well, but not like this. Not in a dress that clung to my curves. Not with my hair styled. Not with my makeup impeccable. I don't even feel like that same woman anymore. Maybe that's a good thing.

"Guinevere," he murmurs as he leans in, kissing my cheek, his lips lingering on my skin, turning the exchange from a friendly one into something more sensual. My heart seems to do backflips in my chest, his proximity overwhelming me. "You're stunning." He inhales deeply, a subtle moan escaping his throat on the exhale. "And you smell even better, if that's possible." He pulls back, his delectable smile disarming me. "I get the feeling with you, *anything* is possible."

The innuendo in his tone sends a shiver down my spine. I remind myself of the list I'd made of conditions that must be in place for me to agree to this. No sex is right at the top. Perhaps I should add no sexual innuendos to that list.

Remembering my friends' advice that I keep the ball in my court, I smile coyly, increasing the distance between us. "I thought you said you'd be wearing a suit. That's more of a blazer and jeans."

When he flashes a devious grin, I have to fight the urge not to jump on him and ride him until he erases every last trace of Trevor from my life. The old Evie would never think such a thing, but the energy buzzing between Julian and me is electrifying. Add in my sudden ability to only get off with the assistance of inanimate objects, and I'm on edge.

"Would you hold it against me if I admitted I lied just so you'd wear a dress?"

I pass him a demure look, batting my lashes. "You *wanted* me to wear a dress? Any reason for that?"

My breathy voice surprises me. Is this how people act in relationships? Like whoever they think the other person wants them to be? How will that work? Won't they get tired of pretending to be someone else, causing the relationship to go up in flames?

Isn't that what I'm doing with Trevor? Aren't I trying to convince him I can be serious instead of wanting him just to love me for me?

"I'm staring at the reason for that." Julian leans even closer, his breath dancing on my skin, intense, warm, thrilling. "You're exquisite, Guinevere. And any man who couldn't see what he had doesn't deserve you."

I meet his heated gaze, losing myself in the darkening blue. For a second, I almost believe his endearing words. Then I remember it's all an act. He's putting on a show, making my friends think this is a real date. He has no idea they know the truth. Stepping back before I do something I'll regret, I glance to my right, Nora grinning at me.

"Julian… This is my other friend, Nora."

"Pleasure to meet you," he says, reaching for her hand and taking it in his. "Do you live here, too?"

"No. I live in Queens with my fiancé, but when Evie said she was moving out of her old place and needed our help, we were more than happy to take time off and lend a hand. It's a worthy cause."

"I couldn't agree more." He shifts his gaze from Nora, looking between the three of us.

"Well, we should get going then, shouldn't we?" I look to Julian.

"Where are you going?" Chloe demands, her tone surprising me.

"Chloe," I hiss, furrowing my brow, an unspoken question as to the origins of the stick that now seems to be firmly shoved up her ass.

"It's a fair question," Julian responds with authority, not even batting an eye. "I'm sure you're both skeptical about her going out with a guy she barely knows, but I promise, you have nothing to be worried about." He adjusts his posture, the smile gone from his face. Now his expression appears all business. "I'm taking Evie to dinner at Maison Noir in Hell's Kitchen. After that, I'll bring her straight back here."

"Or maybe you should take her back to your place," Nora interjects, waggling her brows.

"Okay then!" I interrupt, nudging Julian toward the door. This is officially becoming more awkward than when I brought Trevor home to meet my parents. "Time to go! See you girls later."

I hurry onto the stoop, wanting to get out of here before it gets even worse. However, I'm not used to the three-inch heels Chloe dressed me in and my ankle catches. Everything happens in slow motion as I try to right myself, but my weight is already crashing forward. Suddenly, I'm stopped mid-collapse, a pair of strong arms wrapping around me and pulling me upright. My heart is caught in my throat as I stand chest-to-chest with Julian, peering up into his eyes.

"Got ya." His smooth voice sends a shiver through me.

"Thanks." The safety of his embrace and passion in his gaze turns me into a blubbering fool, unable to form a coherent thought.

"I have a feeling you're going to keep me on my toes."

"Me, too," I whimper.

He holds me a moment longer until he's confident I have my footing, then releases me. I don't say anything as he helps me inside an idling town car, a driver standing next to it. Once the door closes, giving me a moment to myself as he runs around to get in beside me, I blow out a breath.

I'm in deep trouble.

CHAPTER THIRTEEN

"AM I OVERDRESSED?" I ask as the car pulls up in front of a building in Hell's Kitchen, Maison Noir etched on a gold plate next to a nondescript wooden door. The nearly thirty-minute drive through the typical Manhattan traffic was unnerving as I attempted to ignore the sizzling electricity between us.

"Are you kidding me?" Julian leans toward me when the driver steps out. "I haven't been able to keep my eyes off you yet. You look incredible."

"We're alone," I remind him with a trite smile. "You can drop the act."

My door opens, allowing me a brief reprieve from Julian's intensity before he rushes out of the car himself, hurrying to catch up.

"What makes you think it's all an act?" His hand rests on the small of my back as he leads me toward the building.

Now that we're on display, I pass him an enamored look, doing my best to give off the impression I'm head over heels in love with him. I can play his game just as well as he. A minor in theater not a wise choice, Mom? Well, I'm about to put all those acting classes to use.

"Let's not pretend this is anything other than what it is, Julian." My voice is sickly sweet, a complete contradiction to the words I speak. Facing him, I stand on my toes, my lips hovering near his. I sense his composure crack when I exhale, my breath ghosting over his mouth. His grip on me tightens, his jaw clenching. His reaction gives me an added boost of confidence.

"And what *is* this, Guinevere?"

"Two people who agreed to have dinner to discuss the potential of entering into a business arrangement." I move my lips along his jawline, every inch of him seeming to harden as I lean into the crook of his neck. "Nothing more."

I linger for a moment longer, then abruptly pull back, swaying my hips as I head into the restaurant without waiting for him. I can sense the heat of his gaze on me and silently thank Chloe and Nora for their dating advice. I still have the upper hand. That's exactly what I need if I'm to get through tonight without this guy becoming number four. Officially.

When Julian finally joins me, he acts as if he weren't about to slam me against the wall and kiss me in a way Trevor never did. I hoped he'd be on edge and out of sorts, just like I felt when I first saw him stroll into Chloe's apartment. Instead, he's as collected as I remember him from our first meeting, an air of authority in his voice when he gives the *maître d'* his name.

"Of course, Monsieur Gage," he says in a thick French accent, winking. There's a hint of familiarity between the two. I wonder if Julian brings all his dates here. Worse, I wonder if he's proposed this sort of arrangement to other women in the past. I have no reason to believe he hasn't. Why does my chest tighten at the idea of me being another one in what I can only assume to be a long list of women?

"Guinevere?" Julian's voice cuts through. I dart my gaze to his, his brow wrinkled in concern. "Are you okay?"

"Certainly, darling." I grit a smile and step toward him.

As we follow the *maître d'* into the dining area, I focus my attention on the décor in an effort to ignore the warmth emanating from Julian's hand resting just above my waist. The place is all dim lighting, intimate tables, and mirrored walls, making the room appear bigger than it actually is. With it being New York, space is at a premium, but we're tucked away in a corner, giving us privacy, which will prove useful for our discussions.

Once we each have a glass of wine in front of us and have placed our orders, I pull my phone from my clutch and open the "notes" application, scanning the points I'd typed out earlier.

I look at him, my expression serious. "First, if I'm to agree to this, I'd like to establish boundaries. Obviously, there will have to be a certain level of physical contact, but there needs to be a line. Sex is absolutely out of the question." I look down, my face heating, the confidence I'd felt earlier dissipating now that we're getting into the nitty-gritty of what will and won't be permitted in our fake relationship. "I'd prefer we not—"

"Guinevere," Julian's soft voice interrupts as his hand grabs mine. I snap my eyes to his, an innate response my brain has somehow learned in only a few days' time. "Put the phone away."

"But—"

He brings my hand up to his lips, his gaze unwavering. The seconds stretch as he nuzzles against my knuckles, but doesn't kiss them. Regardless, the roughness of his unshaven jaw against my flesh causes a tingle to trickle down my spine. Then he looks out of the corner of his eye, as if trying to tell me something.

As cautiously as possible, I shift my gaze toward the entrance of the restaurant, my breath hitching when I see Trevor walk in with Theresa, his hand on the small of her back as they're led toward a table. He holds out the chair for her, something he's never done for me, at least not that I can remember.

"How—"

"Don't you want him to think we're together? Considering he appears to have moved on, as well."

"I suppose, but—"

"Then you need to put the phone away. People who are into each other don't spend dinner on their cells. We'll have this discussion, which appears to be extremely important to you, but we'll do so without the talking points you've already made notes of. Like I said, dating is simply a game. The ref just blew the first whistle."

Doing my best not to look at Trevor to see if he's noticed me sitting here with Julian, I pull my hand away, discreetly pushing my phone back into my purse before reaching for my wine glass, swirling it.

"I still haven't agreed to anything," I remind him.

"I think you just did, baby doll." He winks.

"I—"

"You could have easily ignored my request. But you didn't. So that tells me there's a part of you, however small, that *wants* Trevor to think we're together."

I raise my glass, taking a sip of the full-bodied red, allowing it to warm my stomach. It's robust with a hint of spice, the perfect pairing for the filet mignon I ordered. If Julian's treating me to dinner, I may as well take advantage and go for the gold.

"What I *want* Trevor to think and what he actually *does* are two different things. Yes, he was jealous when he intercepted the flowers you sent. However, as I pointed out during our conversation, he did accuse me of only dating you to make him jealous. So, regardless of what I agree to, that will always be in the back of his mind. That we're only together for a juvenile purpose."

"Juvenile?"

"Yes. Juvenile." I lean closer, lowering my voice. My expression remains amorous, as if I'm murmuring my deepest desires to this intriguing man. "Even you must admit it's something you'd do in high school. Your smart, studious, perfect boyfriend breaks up with you, so you get back at him by dating the school flirt. The one who seems to go through women like toilet paper. The one who could get any girl he wants, but he somehow decides to clean up his act with the theater geek. I've already seen that movie. Hell, I *lived* that movie in high school. I'm not sure I'm interested in a sequel."

Julian's gaze remains resolute, unaffected by my outburst. When he brings his hands in front of his face, he tents them, his fingers brushing against his lips in quiet contemplation.

"Then perhaps we should forget about my original proposal altogether."

My mouth grows slack as I cock my head at him. "Forget about it?"

I'm not sure what my end game was, but I didn't expect him to call it quits before our meals even arrived. And I was really looking forward to that steak. Did I overplay my hand? I wish Chloe and Nora were here to tell me what to do.

I've spent the past five years dishing out relationship advice, but I never took any of it seriously. It was more a comedic outlet for my writing, a way for me to poke fun at how crazy and stressful dating could be. No one would think I'd actually advocate starting a collection of your date's toenail trimmings and present it to them on your first anniversary. At least I hope they wouldn't.

"Yes, Guinevere. No matter what I say or do, I fear I'll never be able to convince you this idea is anything but juvenile. And maybe it is. I simply saw it as a way to solve *both* our problems. I was already on the lookout for someone who might be interested in posing as my girlfriend. When I heard you share your troubles that night at the bar, I thought you'd be perfect. And I still think you'd be perfect for what I need."

I worry my bottom lip, absorbing his words. "Why me?"

"Why *not* you?"

"I can list a thousand reasons. I'm sure there are plenty of women who would gladly agree to pretend to be your girlfriend. Hell, you might even get laid, which one would argue would be a nice bonus. You won't get that with me."

He leans closer, gazing thoughtfully at me with his penetrating blue eyes. It almost feels like he's able to peer into my soul.

"Did you ever stop to think that's exactly why I asked you?"

"Because I *won't* sleep with you?" I push out a laugh, then sip my wine. "Most men would probably expect sex from this kind of arrangement. Unless, of course, they were gay…" My breath hitches, wide eyes darting to Julian. "Oh, my god!" I whisper-shout, glancing around the restaurant, ensuring no one's paying attention. Apart from Trevor's occasional wandering gaze, no one seems to care about our conversation. "You're gay, aren't you? You need me to pretend to date you to keep your sexual orientation a secret so some conservative politician will back whatever project you're working on. That's why you didn't take advantage of me when I was drunk and in your bed."

He chuckles, his expression brightening with amusement. "I've been called a lot of things in my life, but I've yet to be accused of being gay."

"It's okay if you are. There's nothing wrong with it. No one cares these days, especially in New York. Are you from a religious family? Is that why—"

"I am *not* gay. That's *not* why I'm looking for someone to pose as my girlfriend. And that's *not* why I didn't take advantage of you. I didn't take advantage of you because I'm not an asshole. I don't take advantage of women. Period." His voice is determined, his eyes steadfast.

At that moment, the waiter approaches with our meals, cutting through the tension. The aroma of garlic and meat invades my senses as my mouth waters from the beautifully prepared steak in front of me. I pick up my knife and slice into it, meeting Julian's eyes as he cuts into his lamb, the meat falling off the bone.

"*Bon appetite*," he says in a perfect French accent, which piques my curiosity, but not enough to press him about it. Not with my steak inches from my mouth.

I take a bite, moaning at the buttery flavor of the impeccably prepared filet.

"You really know how to tease a man, don't you?"

"Why? Am I teasing you?" I bat my lashes, thankful for the flirtatious atmosphere between us once more.

"You have no fucking idea."

The tone of his voice hits me deep in my core. As much as I want to tear my eyes from his, I'm unable to, the tension cracking and sizzling. Why don't I remember it being like this with Trevor?

"So…" I clear my throat, my brain finally communicating with the rest of my body to look away from Julian before I throw myself at him without a single regard for the fact we're in public. "Getting back to why we're here."

"Yes?"

"Why me? Especially considering you know I'm not exactly over my ex."

"That's one of the reasons," Julian answers nonchalantly. "Less drama. Less headache. I get the pleasure of the company of a woman who's familiar with what it takes to be in a committed relationship and will be able to sell the idea that we're in one. And I won't have to worry about you wanting more than I'm willing to give."

"This begs the question of why you need to pretend to be in a committed relationship. Why aren't you in one? You're not one of those guys who thinks it's his civic duty to screw as many women as possible, yet refuses to commit to anyone, are you?"

"Certainly not," he answers with a chuckle. "I'm just not interested in a relationship."

"At all?" I arch a brow. It reminds me of Chloe's take on relationships. Maybe I should suggest they get together since it seems he has more in common with her. "Life is full of relationships," I continue, pushing down the jealousy bubbling at the idea of Chloe and Julian hooking up, "even if they're not the intimate type. You appear to be rather successful in whatever it is you do. You don't get there unless you build business relationships."

"That's different. We leave all emotions out of things to get the job done. It's not personal."

"So you're just not interested in a relationship that requires you to get too personal."

His expression pensive, he considers my statement for a moment before nodding. "Yes. I suppose that's correct." He brings his fork to his mouth, taking another bite of his lamb.

"May I ask why?"

"I'd rather you didn't."

I sigh, lifting my glass. "Then I suppose you'll have to find someone else to be your fake girlfriend."

His gaze turns steely, his jaw tightening. I've hit a nerve. "Suffice it to say, I don't buy into the requirement that in order to be happy, you have to be in a relationship with someone. Some people aren't cut out for that."

"And you think you're one of them?" My voice is timid as I press on. The more I do, the greater the chance he'll walk away.

"I know I am. And that's all I'll say on the matter."

Silence falls between us, awkward and stiff. It's the most distant I've felt around him since we met. In an attempt to ignore it, I push my food around my plate, my appetite disappearing.

"As far as the other reason…"

When I hear him speak again, I lift my eyes to meet his. "Pardon?"

"I said one of the reasons you're perfect for this is that I don't have to worry about you falling for me. But there's more."

"And what's that?" My heart drums in my chest, his tone a stark contrast to the anger with which he spoke mere seconds earlier. I marvel at his ability to flip the switch so quickly.

With extreme grace, he swirls his wine before bringing it to his mouth. My eyes instantly focus on his lips. I'm mesmerized by everything this man does. I should find comfort in the fact nothing will ever happen between us. Hell, these were my conditions, after all. Regardless, a twinge of disappointment settles in my heart at never knowing him on a more intimate level.

"There was something in your voice as you informed the entire bar of your breakup. I can't quite explain it. After twelve years, you'd think there would be anger, sadness, disappointment. But there was something else instead."

"Sarcasm?" I offer, recalling the bitterness that prompted me to share my heartache with complete strangers. I'm sure the alcohol didn't hurt in that regard, either. No need to give me a truth serum. Give me a shot of tequila and I'd tell you the location of Jimmy Hoffa…if I knew it.

"That's not it." He shakes his head. "I heard hope."

"Hope?"

"Yes. And determination. Your ability to find humor about what could only be described as one of the most heartbreaking events of your life shows your strength of character. You didn't go home, watch *When Harry Met Sally*, and gorge on Ben & Jerry's."

I scoff, "Not by choice."

He studies me for a moment before speaking again. "I think it was. I may not know you as well as Chloe or Nora, but I've picked up on a few things. One of those is you only do what you want. If you didn't want to spend time with me, you wouldn't be here."

I lower my eyes, not wanting to acknowledge his statement bears a hint of truth. Two days ago, I never would have expected to be sitting here with him in this restaurant while Trevor looms a few tables away. Now I've barely thought of Trevor, all my focus on Julian. Maybe that's how it's supposed to be.

"Have I answered all your questions?" Julian asks when I remain silent. "Is there anything else you need to know before you agree to my proposal?"

Lifting my head, I do my best to appear collected, as if he hadn't weaseled his way under my skin throughout the evening by simply being honest and upfront with me. It's more than I can say for Trevor as of late.

"If I agree, I don't want you to think it's an open invitation to make out with me whenever it suits you.

"I'll be escorting you to fundraisers, charity dinners, galas, things like that. Not to a sex club."

"Well, that's a shame. I'll need to return my flogger and ball gag."

After momentarily scrutinizing me, Julian breaks into a hearty laugh, attracting the attention of a few of our fellow diners, Trevor included. There's a hint of jealousy mixed with longing in his gaze. It makes me feel somewhat vindicated. A frazzled aura surrounds him, like he's having trouble focusing on whatever Theresa's saying because I'm sitting a few tables away with a very handsome, successful man. Then, not paying attention, he knocks his wine glass over, the red liquid spilling all over Theresa's white blouse. Waiters rush to help clean up the mess, but the damage is already done.

I turn my eyes back to Julian, struggling to reel in my smile. Maybe we *can* kill two birds with one stone.

"In all seriousness, I promise not to do anything you're uncomfortable with."

"Even if I say no kissing?"

He blinks repeatedly, taken aback. "No kissing?"

"Yes. At least on the mouth. I'm agreeable to a kiss on the cheek or forehead, but I'd rather we draw the line there."

He recovers his composure. "Any reason for that?"

"It's too…personal." I fidget with my napkin in my lap, the soft texture comforting. "It seems I'm not built like you. I do get attached to people. As long as we have the line drawn at no kissing, I won't forget what this is…a business arrangement."

"Okay." He nods curtly after a moment of contemplation. "You have my word. No kissing on the lips."

"Really?" I cock my head.

"You sound surprised. Why wouldn't I agree?"

"Oh, I don't know. Won't people think there's something amiss if they don't see us kiss?"

"Trust me, Guinevere." His voice is smooth and confident. "There are other ways to demonstrate your desire. Kissing is the easy way out. There's nothing suggestive about one mouth pressing against the other. No. Desire is in the way your bodies find each other, the way your eyes darken with unmatched hunger, the way a shiver runs through you at the promise of what's to come."

I swallow hard, doing my best to make it appear as if I'm not slowly losing my composure at his sensual words, to pretend I don't already react that way whenever I'm in his presence. "Says the man who avoids committed relationships."

"I never said I was perfect." He dabs his napkin against his mouth, making me incredibly jealous of a piece of fabric. "So no sex, no kissing. What are your other conditions?"

"Right." I square my shoulders. "An itinerary."

"An itinerary?"

"Yes. I don't like the unexpected. I've been a bit of a planner my entire life. Hell, I'd already planned my wedding to Trevor before we even met." I laugh under my breath. "I tweaked a few things once we *did* meet, but that's beside the point." I return my gaze to Julian. "I like having a plan, knowing what's expected of me so I can anticipate…things."

"Things?"

"Yes. I'd like to know precisely the type of event and when I'll be required to be…at your service."

"You'll never be 'at my service', Guinevere," he responds quickly. "But if a list of events makes you less on edge, I'm happy to provide one. I understand your job is important to you, so I'll limit the events to weekends and holidays. I just ask you set aside Fridays through Sundays."

"We have our weekly staff meeting Friday mornings."

"Then you'll leave right after. Is that agreeable?"

"Yes. That's fine. Viv is flexible with us working out of the office."

"Any other conditions?"

I chew on my lower lip, recalling the list I'd come up with earlier in the evening. "A firm end date."

He nods. "No sense dragging this out longer than necessary. Come Labor Day, you're free to return to your normal life. Anything else?"

"No." Those were my non-negotiable conditions. I thought he'd put up more of a fight over no sex or kissing. I guess I was wrong.

"Okay then. Agreed on all points. Now I have a few conditions of my own."

"Such as?"

"First, you'll be staying in my beach house with me." He leans closer, lowering his voice. "Don't worry. You'll have your own room and space. Anytime we're not scheduled to be somewhere, you can do whatever you'd like. You won't need to spend extra time with me. You can sit by the pool, go to the beach, whatever you like. Your free time is just that...yours."

"And your other conditions?"

"It's more of a...request."

I arch a brow. "And that is?"

"I'd appreciate your word that you'll commit to me for the duration of the summer and not end this arrangement early. I need a woman by my side for all the social events that fill the summer season in the Hamptons. So in the event Trevor has a change of heart and wants you back, I'd request you hold him off until the end of summer. After that, we walk away and never have to see each other again. By then, I'm hoping this project will be underway. I'll make up a story about how you're still in love with your ex, which isn't a stretch, and we'll go our separate ways.

"So... What'll it be, Guinevere? Will you be my fake girlfriend?"

I stare into space, considering his proposition. Out of the corner of my eye, I catch a glimpse of Trevor. Instead of the frantic energy that surrounded him before, he's calm, he and Theresa seeming to laugh off the mishap. He brings her hand up to his mouth, peppering soft kisses against it. I don't remember the last time he looked at me that way.

Resolute, I return my attention to Julian. What do I have to lose? Trevor's already moved on. Why should I torture myself by waiting for him to come to his senses? After twelve years, maybe I deserve to have some fun myself. A summer in the Hamptons at what I can only imagine to be a luxurious beach house may be exactly what the doctor ordered to mend my broken heart. What could possibly go wrong?

"Yes, Julian. I'll be your fake girlfriend."

CHAPTER FOURTEEN

"DO I WANT to know whether tonight was just a coincidence?" I ask once we're in the back seat of the town car and on the way to Chloe's apartment.

"Whatever do you mean, Guinevere?" Julian flashes a conniving smile.

I blow out a breath, crossing my arms. "You know *exactly* what I mean, Julian. Trevor showing up at the same restaurant we happened to be dining at is a bit suspicious, wouldn't you agree?"

"New York's not as big as people think."

Not saying a word, I narrow my gaze at him like my mother always did when she knew I was being purposely evasive.

"And what would you say if I *did* plan it?"

"First, I'd say you have impeccable stalker abilities. Perhaps that's your true calling."

He curves his body toward me, grinning deviously. "Who said it's not? You did figure out I have a secret kill room in Jersey City. You don't lure people to a kill room without properly doing your research…or, as you referred to it, stalking." He winks before leaning back against the seat.

"That's right. How could I forget about the kill room? Okay then, Dexter…"

He laughs at my nickname for him, a twinkle visible in his eyes, even in the darkened car.

"Care to share how you knew Trevor would be dining there tonight?"

"Simple." He rests his elbow on the center console, drumming his fingertips against the leather. "Theresa is actually a close friend of my neighbor in Southampton. They went to prep school together or something. I just so happened to see her post on Instagram yesterday that she'd bought a new dress for a dinner date with her beau. Friends asked where she was going, and she spilled. No information is too difficult to find out these days. Not with social media."

"So you *did* stalk her."

"Again, I prefer to call it research."

"Okay. So you knew where they'd be. How did you get a reservation? From what I know of that place, they have a waiting list a mile long. You need to book months in advance."

"That's true, unless you know someone."

"And you know someone."

"I know a lot of people."

"But does Trevor know people?" My voice is low and wavers slightly. "Or did Theresa just go in my place?" I suck in a breath, another possibility crossing my mind. A more heartbreaking possibility. "Or was it Theresa's date all along?"

I never even considered that Trevor had cheated on me. He didn't seem the type. Plus, we lived together. I would have noticed if he came home smelling of another woman's perfume. Then again, there were plenty of nights he never came home at all. Was he lying to me the whole time?

"Does it matter?"

"What?" I shift my gaze to Julian.

"Does it matter?" he repeats, this time more forcefully. "At this moment, right here, right now…" He brings his hands to cup my face, an intensity in his eyes causing a surge of desire to pool in my stomach. "Does…it…matter?"

I swallow hard, trying to calm my racing heart, on the brink of insisting it does. Whether Trevor made that reservation for me or Theresa is the difference between me opening my heart to him again or constructing a wall and never allowing him in. But Julian has a point. All evening, I barely thought of Trevor and Theresa, despite them sitting mere feet away. Every ounce of my attention was devoted to Julian. I was in the moment with him. He was all that mattered.

"No," I say softly. "It doesn't." My words come out sounding surprised, and I am a little. Regardless, they're true. Right now, there is no Trevor or Theresa. It's just Julian and me.

"Good." He keeps my face in his hands for another moment before pulling away. The sudden lack of contact leaves me longing for more.

Not wanting to let on, I clear my throat, pulling my cell out of my clutch. "Are there any pressing dates I should be made aware of now? Like within the next week? I don't have any vacation planned, and am able to work from out of the office, but I have a few big projects going on."

I shift my eyes to him when he doesn't say anything right away. His brows are pulled in, an analytical gaze on his face as he seems to assess me. I'm not sure what to make of it. Then he sighs, relaxing into the seat.

"This coming Thursday is July Fourth. The celebrations go all week, starting tomorrow."

"Tomorrow?" My mouth becomes slack. "I have things I need to get done this weekend. I need to have a life outside of our arrangement."

"And I understand that. I'm not asking you to attend every single party with me. Just the important ones."

"And July Fourth is important."

He nods. "The annual Red, White, and Blue Gala."

"Gala?" I arch a brow. "Am I going to need a dress?"

He laughs, his eyes dancing in amusement. "You're going to need a lot of dresses, swimsuits, stuff like that. Some of these events will be formal, like Fourth of July. Others will be less so. There will be charity auctions, boat christenings, perhaps even some Ladies' Tea luncheons you'll most likely be invited to once word gets around you're my girlfriend."

My stomach suddenly feels weighted down. Lowering my head, I fiddle with the hem of the dress I bought at a discount clothing store, inadequacy washing over me.

"Do you honestly think this will work, Julian? This lifestyle you lead is vastly different from mine. Hell, for all intents and purposes, I'm homeless right now. The only reason I'm not on a street corner holding up a cardboard sign is because Chloe's letting me sleep on the pullout couch in her den. The idea of anyone in your social circle accepting me is ridiculous. Don't you think you'd be better off finding someone who knows the difference between the salad and fish fork?"

With a smirk, he grabs my hand, stopping me from fidgeting. "The fact that you know some settings have both a salad and fish fork shows you're not as inexperienced as you'd like me to believe. We may not know each other well, but the instant I saw you, I knew you were the only person who could do this with me. The only woman I'd *want* to do this with." He brings my hand to his lips, treating my skin to a delicious kiss. "So bury your doubt. Your unabashed confidence is what caught my attention. Don't let the idea that you're not good enough, like Trevor made you think, take it away. You *are* good enough. Hell, you're better than most people can ever dream to be. Don't forget that. Okay?"

I slowly turn my eyes from his, breathless from the passion and genuine affection in his words. "Okay." It's all I can manage.

After a few silent moments, the car comes to a stop. I glance out the window to see we're already at Chloe's building. Julian and his driver step out at the same time. When my door opens, I smile in thanks at his driver before turning to Julian. He places his hand on my lower back, leading me toward the brownstone.

The closer we get to the front door, the more my heart rate increases. What's the proper protocol for saying goodnight to the man you're pretending to date? I doubt I'd find the answer in any rule book. Perhaps this entire experience will give me more material for the column. Instead of just giving advice on normal relationships, I can give tips for fake relationships, too. I'm already writing it in my head...*Fifty Rules for Pretending to Date an Undateable Man.*

Not wanting to endure any more awkwardness than I already have, I take control of the situation, facing Julian and extending my hand toward him. "Thanks for dinner. I thoroughly enjoyed it."

Squinting, he eyes my hand, a bemused smirk forming on his lips. "A handshake?"

"Yes. Your driver obviously knows about our arrangement, as does Chloe, since she and Nora were sitting next to me when you called. There's no need to put on an act right now. So, thank you for dinner." I extend my hand even farther, making it clear that I'm serious about the handshake. When he lifts his hand, I exhale a small breath of relief, only to let out a surprised squeak when he grabs my hip instead, pulling me against him.

In an instant, the desire I'd struggled to suppress all evening flickers back to life as my body fuses into his. He brings a hand to my face, tilting my head back, forcing my eyes to his. They're so intense. So consuming. So vivid. The hair on my nape stands on end, every inch of me aching with raw need.

"Do you honestly believe the only reason I touch you is to put on a show? To keep up an act?" His voice is deep and lustful as he lowers his mouth toward my neck. A slave to his unspoken command, I crane my head, this dance between us feeling like one we've done dozens of times over. Instead, we're two strangers.

"The thought's crossed my mind."

"Well, get the thought *out* of your mind. Yes, I had certain criteria I was looking for in approaching someone about the prospect of this little arrangement. Smart, funny, confident. Most importantly, *attractive*." He nuzzles against my skin, the roughness of his scruff jarring, exciting, and everything I need but didn't realize it.

"Even though you want to keep emotions out of it?" I murmur, my eyes rolling into the back of my head as his breath tortures my skin. It's pure agony, but in the most addicting way.

"That doesn't mean I don't want to be attracted to the person." He lightly runs a finger down the curve of my neck, his breath following the same path, so close yet still not crossing any line. "And I am *profoundly* attracted to you." His hands cup my cheeks and my eyes flutter open, staring into his enamored gaze once more. "You're one of the most alluring women I've seen in a very long time. You have a classic beauty to you. One women would pay thousands of dollars to have, but it's natural for you."

I part my lips, my breath coming in pants the longer his body remains pressed against mine.

"And you're confident in your own skin. Skin thousands of men would love to taste." He smooths my hair behind my shoulder, his hand brushing the exposed flesh. "But what had me absolutely mesmerized was this mouth." He shifts his eyes from mine, focusing on my mouth.

When he brings his lips within a breath of mine, my knees weaken. Desperate for some sort of release, I squeeze my thighs together. Mr. Winky, as I've named my battery-operated boyfriend, will definitely be getting a workout tonight.

"The things that came out of it were witty, charming, and full of hope. With each word you spoke, I was hungry for more. More of your words. More of your mouth. More of you."

He leans even closer, his lips hovering so near to mine I can practically taste them. Wine. Spice. And a hint of chocolate from the soufflé we shared.

"No kissing," I murmur, my teeth chattering. "You agreed."

I sense his mouth curve into a smile. Then he drops his hold on me. I open my eyes to see him retreating down the stairs.

I'm unable to move, to breathe, to think, a statue frozen in time as I watch him walk toward the car. Before he ducks inside, he glances back at me, a mischievous grin on those lips I was a whisper away from kissing, despite insisting we not.

"Kissing is for amateurs, Guinevere. You're in the big leagues now." He holds my gaze a moment longer, then winks before disappearing into the car.

As his car drives off into the night, I lean against the door, placing my hand over my racing heart, trying to calm it down.

One thing is abundantly clear… I am royally fucked.

CHAPTER FIFTEEN

"HOW DID THE date go?" Chloe asks the following morning when I emerge from my makeshift bedroom. I head toward the one-cup brewer in the tiny kitchen and pop a pod into it. Instantly, the aroma of coffee fills the air. Just the smell of this magic potion helps erase the cobwebs from my restless and frustrated night, thanks to one Julian Gage.

"It wasn't a date, Chloe." I avoid her eyes as I answer. "Just dinner to discuss a mutually beneficial arrangement."

"So you said yesterday." She looks up from her laptop where she's probably working on a story about some celebrity gossip that hit the wires within the past few hours. Chloe typically pulls all-nighters on Fridays and Saturdays, since that tends to be when all the juicy stories happen. "Have you come to a decision about this 'arrangement'?"

After adding a bit of milk and sweetener to my coffee, I join her on the couch, keeping my head held high. "I have. And I've agreed to help."

"Hmm." Her lips press together.

"What?"

"Nothing." She waves a hand dismissively, returning her attention to her laptop.

"No. It's not nothing. You don't *hmm* unless you want to say something but are holding back. What is it? Why did you go from wanting me to jump Julian's bones to giving him the stink eye the instant he showed up at the door last night? Is it because he's ridiculously good-looking and you don't think it makes sense for someone like me to be with him?" With each word, my voice gets louder. "Because I'm more than aware I don't fit the mold of the cookie-cutter, waif-like model a guy like him would normally be with. But I—"

"Evie, no. It's not that. It's just…" She blows out a breath as she pulls her gray and lilac locks into a messy bun on top her head. "Why didn't you tell me it was Julian Gage?"

I furrow my brow. "Why does it matter? And how do you know his last name? I don't think I told you."

"You didn't."

"Then how—"

"You don't know who he is, do you?"

I shrug, feeling like an idiot for not Googling him before going out with him. Last time I was single, Myspace was still a thing. That's how long it's been.

Pushing out an exasperated sigh, Chloe types on her laptop before turning it toward me. Heat rushes through me when Julian's vibrant blue eyes stare back from a Wikipedia article. The ache I'd momentarily relieved with the use of my battery-operated boyfriend is back and more intense than it was last night.

"Evie?"

I refocus on Chloe, discreetly wiping at my lip in the hopes that I'm not drooling. Thankfully, I'm not.

"Should I leave you and the laptop alone for a minute?" She giggles.

Rolling my eyes, I zero in on the screen and read a rather lengthy biography of the man who left me a quivering pile of hormones last night.

Julian Gage was completely unknown until Theodore Price, a distant relative of the Vanderbilt family, passed away, leaving the majority of his vast fortune to him. This prompted a fierce contest over the will by Mr. Price's children, who assumed they'd inherit everything. While Mr. Price didn't disinherit them altogether, providing each of his three children a rather generous testamentary gift…in most people's standards…it was nothing compared to the billions of dollars he'd gifted Julian.

Mr. Price's children tried to allege the will was invalid and that Julian exerted undue influence over an old man who wasn't of sound mind. However, the court found that his children wouldn't know whether he were of sound mind, considering they'd rarely spoken to him over the past few decades. Mr. Price's housekeeper testified to that fact. She also stated that Mr. Price and Julian become acquainted when Mr. Price saw him in a local park and offered to teach him how to play chess, since he seemed interested in the game. I can't help but smile at the image in my mind of a sixteen-year-old Julian befriending an older man over a game of chess. When I was sixteen, most boys only cared about video games. I can't see Julian as someone who was ever interested in video games.

Upon Mr. Price's death, Julian took the helm of the Price-Young empire. Hotels. Restaurants. Commercial buildings. There are hundreds of properties in New York City alone. It's all incredibly impressive, but what catches my eye is the mention of a non-profit he's tied to. An organization aimed at helping victims of domestic violence. It certainly piques my interest, another puzzle piece of who Julian truly is sliding into place.

I should have stopped reading there, but the section labeled "Personal Life" grabs my attention and I scroll down. Labeled one of the most eligible bachelors in the country, there are various photos of him posing with beautiful woman after beautiful woman. Models. Actresses. Heiresses. Every single one of them is all legs with barely an ounce of fat, a complete one-eighty from my ample chest and curvy hips. It again begs the question

I posed last night… *Why me?*

"Are you thinking what I'm thinking?" Chloe asks when I push away from the laptop, a sickness forming in my stomach.

"Why would he pursue me if he has his pick of any number of gorgeous women?"

She shrugs, silently agreeing. "I just don't want to see you get hurt, Evie. That's all."

"What do you know about him?" I meet her eyes, unsure if I want to hear her answer.

"No more than what you read about in that Wiki article. There's no information at all about his younger years. He's an extremely private guy. People try to get details about him from those he's closest to, but they all stay tightlipped. There's a great deal of speculation about why he's never had a serious relationship, although he's been photographed with plenty of gorgeous women, as you see. My vote is he's gay."

I choke on my coffee. "I accused him of the same thing," I say through a fit of coughing.

"You *did*?"

The tense atmosphere slowly wanes. Now we're just two friends dishing about my date last night. Who cares if Julian has a Wikipedia page? Hell, even I have one because of my position at the magazine, although there's not much information on it. That doesn't make me someone worth knowing. Granted, Julian probably has a few billion reasons why he's worth knowing, but that doesn't make a difference to me. I'd still find him endearing, regardless of the size of his bank account.

"Trust me. There is absolutely no way that man is gay."

This catches Chloe's attention and she smirks. "Is that so?" She crosses her arms over her chest. "I thought you weren't going to sleep with him. Hell, you said even kissing was off the table."

"I didn't sleep with him. We didn't even kiss." I waggle my brows.

"You didn't? Then—"

"I told him my conditions, and he agreed to all of them. I thought for sure he'd insist on kissing me if we're pretending to date."

"It *is* a bit of a challenge, isn't it?"

"Not to him, apparently. He said kissing's for amateurs. And after the goodnight kiss that wasn't last night, I'd say he's right. Kissing *is* for amateurs." I bite my lower lip, reeling in my smile. "And Julian Gage is certainly no amateur." I fan myself, causing both of us to break out into a fit of giggles.

When our laughter fades, her expression turns serious once more. "So you're going to do it? You're going to be his fake girlfriend?"

"I am," I respond thoughtfully before my eyes harden. "But you can *not* tell a soul the truth, that it's just for show. You can't use this in any of your articles. This is incredibly off the record."

She reaches across the couch and clutches my hand. "You have my word. If you say it's off the record, it's off the record. I like my job."

I laugh slightly, knowing how seriously Viv takes this kind of thing.

"But I value our friendship even more. I just don't want you to get hurt."

"I won't—"

She quickly holds up her hand. "I know you, Evie. You get attached to people. Hell, you were with Trevor for twelve years."

"That's different."

"Still, you're not the type of girl who does random hookups. You're either all in or all out. There's no in-between with you. I just…" She blows out a breath. "I don't want you to fall for this guy and end up getting hurt because this is only a business deal for him."

"It's nothing more than a business deal for me, too. Weren't you saying I deserved to have some fun this summer?"

"That is true. And Trevor certainly does deserve to have the fact that you're dating one of the most eligible men in New York shoved in his face." Her eyes focus on me. "And it will be shoved in his face. Not by me, but Hamptons' parties are a hotbed for gossip columnists. Gossip websites *will* publish photos of you together. You won't be able to keep it quiet for long."

"Julian doesn't want it to be kept quiet. He wants us to act as if it's real."

"And there's no part of you that wishes it were?"

"Of course not," I respond quickly. "I'm not interested in him." I straighten my spine, exuding all the confidence I can muster just as the sound of my phone ringing rips through the space. I dart my eyes to the screen, a warmth filling me when Julian's name pops up.

"Not interested, you say?" Chloe teases, getting up from the couch. "Your wide smile and increased breathing indicate otherwise, Evie." She narrows her eyes on me. "Just be careful."

With that, she disappears into her bedroom, allowing me to speak with Julian in private.

Not wanting to sound overly eager, I blow out a long breath, then bring the phone to my ear, answering in a sultry tone.

"Good morning."

"Good morning, Guinevere. As requested, I've emailed you an itinerary for the next two months."

His tone is clipped, formal, almost as if I'm merely another call he has to make in conducting business. It's like he's a different person than the man who left me a panting mess on Chloe's front stoop last night. Did I imagine it all?

"Please check your calendar and let me know what conflicts you may have. I prefer to know in advance. Like you, I'm not fond of surprises."

"All I have planned this summer is work," I answer in a tone matching his own.

"There are some events that may occur during the week, so I'll need you to take the time off, if it can be arranged."

"I don't foresee a problem. Like I said last night, my boss doesn't mind if I work out of the office, as long as all my work is turned in by my deadline."

"Also, my personal stylist needs your measurements to pull things for you. She'll be reaching out to you sometime today. She's located in Midtown. You can either go to her or she can come to you."

"Personal stylist?"

"If you're to act the part of my girlfriend, you need to dress the part. Don't worry. You can keep the clothes when the summer is over. My stylist has a list of things you'll need. I'll see you Wednesday."

"Wednesday?" I ask, feeling overwhelmed as I not only attempt to absorb the difference in demeanor, but the reality of what pretending to be this man's girlfriend will entail. "But—"

"Take a look at the itinerary. I'm sure it will answer all your questions. If not, the number for my assistant is included. Goodbye, Guinevere."

"Goodbye, Julian."

But the line's already dead.

CHAPTER SIXTEEN

THE STEAM ROOM is particularly busy Monday morning as I sit at my usual table with the perfect view of the counter and dining area. The murmur of low conversation competes to be heard over coffee beans being ground and employees shouting orders to each other. I've yet to indulge in any of their pastries, but I feel my hips getting bigger simply from sitting here these past few weeks… Calories by osmosis or something like that.

I do everything I can to focus on how to determine which of the men on my list of possibilities is the real August Laurent, like I'm playing my own version of *To Tell the Truth*. Instead, all I can think of is Julian. How sweet and charming he was Friday night, then how cold and distant he seemed during our brief phone call. All weekend, I reminded myself it shouldn't matter, that it's only a business relationship, that it's not real. But I *felt* something. Was he really that good of an actor?

The itinerary he sent is quite extensive. There's something requiring my presence every weekend. It boggles my mind to think people live this way. Galas. Fundraisers. Art auctions. Pool parties. Bonfires. And this is a normal summer. I already feel like I don't belong, and I haven't even stepped foot in the Hamptons yet.

I try not to think too much about it, concentrating instead on the copious notes I'd made the previous week. As I flip through them, I'm unable to shake the feeling I missed something. None of the men on my list scream escort. Maybe August Laurent isn't in town. Maybe something came up and he had to take some bored housewife off to a remote island in exchange for a ridiculously obscene amount of money.

As I'm about to pull up the web browser on my laptop to sort through another one of the dozens of articles I found online theorizing about who he could be, my cell rings, the number to my work line popping up, indicating it's a forwarded call.

"Evie Fitzgerald," I answer. There's no immediate response. When I'm about to speak again, a voice interrupts.

"A little birdie said you've been looking for me." The deep baritone hits me in my core. Gravelly. Mysterious. Bemused. There's a hint of an accent. French maybe? It's not obvious. Just enough to make me believe he's not American-born.

"And does this little birdie have a name?" I ask coyly as I scan the coffee shop. It could have been someone else, maybe a wrong number, but it's too much of a coincidence. My gut says this is *him*, that he somehow heard I've been sitting in this café every morning on a quest to figure out who he is.

There's a chuckle on the other end, a low rumble. I picture him in a perfectly tailored suit, leaning back in the chair of his office, the beautiful cityscape of New York in the background, the brilliant summer sun beaming through the windows. Or maybe he's like the rest of wealthy Manhattan society and spends his summer in the Hamptons, which would account for why I haven't seen him. Perhaps he's just now waking up at ten in the morning with a view of the Atlantic Ocean and is calling me from the balcony of a luxurious beach house he purchased with the proceeds of taking advantage of women.

"I never reveal my sources. But I'm intrigued to know how you found out about my little secret."

I smile, lifting my coffee to my lips. "Like you, I never reveal my sources. Your story caught my attention, and I'd like to learn more. As would my readers."

"I'm sure they would. Do you realize how many people have been where you are? Sitting in that very café at a table close to the counter, yet still with a great view of the dining area, notebook out, scribbling down notes about every man who's come in to order a chocolate hazelnut pastry?"

I swallow hard. I don't know why I assumed I could outsmart this man who appears to take his privacy to a level I've never seen. It hadn't even crossed my mind that other people had done this very thing. And where are they now? Did they give up because the man truly is a ghost? Did he call them and tell them it's a lost cause?

"You're not the first, Miss Fitzgerald, although I will say you're the first who doesn't scream 'reporter'."

"No?"

"Trust me. That's a good thing, considering the editor at your fine magazine doesn't want her staff to be like normal reporters, which is why her publication's kept circulation high, despite the changed environment."

"You've done your research."

"I always do."

"Well, since I don't scream reporter, what do you say to sitting down for a one-on-one interview?" I waggle my brows, even though he can't see.

"So you can write an article cheapening what I do, claiming something ridiculous, such as I take advantage of women?" There's a teasing quality to his tone.

"*Do* you take advantage of women?"

"Absolutely not."

Excitement bubbles in my veins as I flip to a blank page in my notepad, jotting down the date. "You answered a question. Does this mean you agree to be interviewed?" There's no masking the hope in my voice.

"Not yet. I'm sure you've realized by now the importance of anonymity in my line of work."

"I do… To an extent. But I'd like to understand better. That could be more effectively accomplished face-to-face. Perhaps an interview and a photo shoot."

He laughs once more, the sound light and natural. Not forced, like you hear so often during initial meetings. "I have to give you credit, Miss Fitzgerald. You certainly are persistent."

"No. Just stubborn. I am Irish, after all."

"I had a feeling you were."

"What gave it away? The last name?"

"No. Your fiery personality."

"You don't even know me," I quip back.

"Ah, but I do. You familiar with the old saying, 'You write what you know'?"

I chew on the inside of my cheek, not answering.

"Well, I've read your column. In fact, I've read everything you've ever published at that magazine…print *and* online."

My jaw drops. "I've been there over five years now," I say, dumbstruck. "I've written hundreds of articles."

"Just like I'm sure you've been scouring the Internet for information on me, the instant I learned a woman named Evie Fitzgerald from *Blush* magazine was looking for me, I did some research of my own."

"Is that right? And what did you find out?"

"That you, Miss Fitzgerald, are extremely talented. Actually, I was able to skip a few days of ab exercises from the workout I got laughing at your work. You have a gift."

I blow out a laugh. "Sure. Tell my ex that."

"Your ex?" His voice rises in pitch, curious about my statement. I hadn't meant to say anything like that. It just kind of slipped out.

"It's nothing. I shouldn't have said that. I didn't—"

"It's obviously not nothing. Tell me."

"Thanks for the offer, but it's okay."

"You want to understand what it is I do, why I do what I do, this is part of it. What I do isn't as black and white as accompanying a beautiful woman to one event or another. It's giving them the confidence they need, for whatever reason, to help them see what any man with half a brain should. So if you want greater insight into August Laurent, tell me about your ex."

"Are you *bribing* me?"

"Not a bribe. But if I'm to agree to an interview, I'd like to know we're on an even playing field. If you expect me to share personal information about myself with you, and the rest of the world, I'd ask you do the same in return…minus the rest of the world. So, if you tell me why your ex doesn't think you're talented, I'll answer one of your questions."

I hesitate, considering his offer for a moment. I could tell him I'm not comfortable with this, but I really want this promotion. I want to finally write something with meaning, something people will talk about for weeks.

"Because he doesn't think what I do is something to be proud of. I suppose that's why this interview is so important. This story can get me promoted to assistant editor…of the entire magazine. That will show him I *am* good at what I do, that I *am* a talented writer."

"Why does it matter?" August asks after a brief silence. "If he's your ex, why do you care what he thinks?"

"It's not just proving it to my ex," I respond, not wanting to admit I'm holding out hope that Trevor and I still have a chance. "It's proving it to everyone who ever told me I should use my English degree to become a teacher instead of writing."

"Let me guess. Your parents perhaps?"

I exhale a long breath. "You have to understand. Mom was an English teacher and shared her love for the written word with me. When most parents read their children *Green Eggs and Ham*, she read *Pride and Prejudice*. My father's a former English teacher, but is now the principal of the high school. Even my older brother's an English teacher. They thought I was crazy for wanting to use my degree in English to be a writer. They *still* don't think I'm a real writer, since all I write is sex and dating advice. So the opportunity to write an article like this, then getting promoted where I can write more interesting and compelling articles… I finally *will* prove them wrong."

"Okay then," he says after a protracted pause. "What would you like to know about me?"

"Where to start?" I laugh, lightening the tension.

"I find the beginning is usually best."

"I agree. So, Mr. Laurent—"

"Please, call me August."

"Okay. August… How did you start doing…" I wave a hand around, "whatever it is you do?"

"The local Escorts R Us was hiring, and I seemed to be what they were looking for."

My eyes widen. "Really?"

"Certainly not." He chuckles, something about it causing a shiver to roll down my spine.

It's an unexpected response and I adjust my posture, squeezing my legs together. He does have a smooth, pacifying voice. I could picture him as a sex phone operator, if that were even still a thing. *Is* that still a thing?

"I hope you're not always this gullible."

"Not usually, but there isn't much reliable information on the Internet on how to become a high-priced and extremely sought-after escort."

"Why? Looking for a career change? In case the promotion doesn't work out?"

"I'd rather not sell my body for money."

"Ah, but that's where you have it wrong, Miss Fitzgerald. Yes, men are typically only interested in one thing when they hire an escort."

"Sex."

"Precisely, although that's technically illegal in most states. Escort services get around it by claiming the client is simply paying for the company of the employee."

"And why do women hire an escort, if not for sex?"

"Companionship. That's it. Women just want to feel something. They want to be romanced, feel adored. That's what I do. On the record, I never set out to be in this profession."

"Is that right?" I jot down notes as he continues telling his story.

"I doubt anyone says they want to be an escort when they grow up," he jokes. "It just…happened. It was never about taking advantage of women when they're feeling unguarded. I understand how it looks, especially when I'm selective to whom I offer my services."

"So you agree you specifically only choose women who are vulnerable?"

"Their vulnerability means they need my services more than someone else. I come in not simply as a piece of 'arm candy', but to empower women who are at a time in their lives when they need to feel like they have value. At the end of the day, my goal is to make every single woman who hires me feel beautiful, like they're worthy of being loved. That's it."

"And it works?"

"I like to believe it does. I help these women realize their worth. Realize they're meant to be more than just something nice to look at while accompanying their powerful husbands to whatever society event is going on that week. Many of my clients grew up in wealth. From their earliest days, they were raised to believe their only role in life was to marry someone of equivalent social standing. It sounds antiquated, especially in these modern days, but trust me when I say the caste system is still alive and well, even here in the land of the free and home of the brave. The haves of this country want to keep the have-nots out of their circle. They're the equivalent of American royalty. They marry their daughters off to people in their circle, and the cycle is repeated through the generations.

"These women are strong, resilient, and highly educated, but they've been mentally — and sometimes physically — abused for so long, they truly believe their only worth in life is offering a nice smile and making sure their bodies are in top physical condition so their husbands don't stray to something younger…which I know for a fact they do anyway. Hell, I've even had some of my clients tell me their husbands offered them up to their associates in order to make a deal on a valuable piece of real estate or something else, viewing them as a piece of property. Nothing more."

"And you think what you do helps break the cycle?"

"I hope so. Before many of these women sought my services, they believed their only option was to stay in a loveless, often abusive relationship. Their husbands made them feel like they were disposable. Some of them have never worked a day in their lives. Their husbands made them believe if they left the marriage, they'd have nothing. So they stayed, resigning themselves to a life of unhappiness. I give them the strength and confidence they've never felt, which helps them with the next step, whether it be filing for divorce or trying to make things work with their spouse."

"How do you claim to not take advantage of these women then? It sounds like they've been taken advantage of their entire lives. Now you come in and use their vulnerability to sleep with them."

"Who says I've slept with them?"

"Have you?"

"I believe that may be a question for another day, Miss Fitzgerald."

"Okay, but you didn't answer my question about how you started doing this. Obviously, something must have happened in your life that made you become the Keyser Söze of the escort industry."

The line's silent for a moment. Then he breaks into a throaty laugh. It's deep, intense, and all-consuming. Everything I get the feeling this man is in real life.

"The Keyser Söze of the escort industry?"

"You *do* know who that is, don't you?"

His laughing gradually dies down. "Yes. I have seen *The Usual Suspects*."

"Then you know why I call you that. You're like an enigma, a ghost story wives can threaten their husbands with if they act like assholes. 'Better treat me well, or August Laurent will come to my rescue.' So how does one become August Laurent? Or is it a combination of Keyser Söze and the Dread Pirate Roberts?"

"The what?"

"The Dread Pirate Roberts," I repeat. "Please tell me you know what that's from; otherwise, I'll have to question my faith in the human race."

He laughs again, and I find myself melting into my chair from the sound. "*The Princess Bride*. One of my absolute favorite movies. But the book is better."

"It always is. So, did you get taught the ropes from the August Laurent who came before you? Like in *The Princess Bride*?"

"No. It's just me. But you do give me an idea for when I'm ready to hang up my hat."

"Hang up your hat?"

"I can't do this forever. Unfortunately, what I do has a time limit. Or an age limit."

"And that's the only reason you'd walk away? When you age out, so to speak?"

He considers my question for a moment, then answers, "Yes."

"But what about finding a wife? Settling down to have a family of your own?"

"You assume I don't already have one," he jests, bemused. I picture him leaning back in a chair, brushing his masculine fingers against his lips, much like Julian does when I say something amusing.

"I think it's a valid assumption. Not sure how practical it is to do what you do *and* be married. I doubt any woman would put up with that. I wouldn't."

"And you're right. Which is why I'm not involved. Nor do I plan to become involved with anyone in the near future."

"Don't you want that?"

"Want what?"

"A real relationship."

"I'm happy with my current situation. It satisfies me in a way you'd only be able to scratch the surface of."

"I understand that," I say quickly. "Obviously, you enjoy…whatever it is you do. Otherwise, I doubt you'd be doing it. But aren't you lonely?"

"How can I be lonely when I have the pleasure of keeping beautiful women company?"

"You keep them company. But who keeps you company?" I press. When he doesn't immediately respond, I continue. "Everyone wants to find love. Real love. True love. It's what wars are fought over. That and religion, but I suppose one could argue love would enter into that equation, too. Throughout our adult life, every decision we make is generally for the purpose of love. What is so important about remaining on this path that you're willing to sacrifice finding love?"

There's a pause on the line. When he finally speaks again, his voice is a bit softer than it was mere seconds ago. "I'll tell you what, Miss Fitzgerald, since you seem to believe so strongly in the concept of love… If I ever find someone worth giving this all up for, I'll gladly grant your magazine an exclusive photo shoot and you can plaster my face from here to kingdom come."

"Really?"

"Yes. Really." I remain silent as I absorb his words. Then he clears his throat. "I believe we've gotten off track again."

"Right." I snap out of my daze. "We were talking about how you became August Laurent." I bring my pen back to my notepad.

When he speaks again, he sounds different, less emotional, more business-like. "As I mentioned earlier, it just kind of happened."

"There must have been some propelling event that made you stop and say, 'I'm going to be a male escort for a living. I'd be damn good at it.' What was yours?"

"I promised a friend I'd take her to her brother's wedding."

"A wedding date turned you into an escort?"

"She'd recently broken up with her boyfriend, who also happened to be the best man. She was the maid of honor. To say it was awkward is an understatement. Since she was still upset, she was anxious about seeing him. I offered to go as her date and do everything to make her ex regret leaving her. I did just that."

"You pretended to date her? And no one caught on?" This has my curiosity piqued, considering the agreement I'd made with Julian.

"I suppose you could say I'm a good actor. But I was a good actor because I knew how important this was to her. And it worked. During the entire ceremony and reception, he couldn't keep his eyes off her. He even suggested they give the relationship another shot. But after one weekend with me, after I spent the time to treat her the way I believed she deserved to be treated, she realized what she felt for her ex wasn't love. That she deserved so much more from a relationship than a guy who refused to support her dreams."

There's something in his tone, almost like he's silently asking if his story sounds familiar. And it does. Then again, he could be making it up to get me to sympathize with what he does for a living.

"So how did one wedding date turn into a career of empowering women, as you like to put it?" I ask, not wanting to dwell on my recent breakup with Trevor.

"Not long after that weekend, I started getting other requests to accompany more women to important events, mostly weddings. Now, over fifteen years later, it's evolved into more than accompanying them for a weekend wedding. Some women hire me for a month at a time to help them through a difficult time in their lives. As you've found out, you can't run an Internet search and book me. It's all by referral. My clients require a certain level of privacy, as do I. What keeps me in business is the fact that the only people who know who I am are my clients. To everyone else, I'm simply an old friend of the family or wealthy donor to whatever cause the family is championing at the moment."

"And no one's put the pieces together?"

"I do believe that's another question, Miss Fitzgerald."

"No. Simply a necessary follow-up."

There's a lightness in his tone when he answers. "I like you. I have a feeling I'm going to enjoy talking to you."

"So you agree to do the story?"

"I swore I'd never do this, but there's something about you that intrigues me, so yes, I'll agree."

"And I can publish what you tell me?"

"Unless I tell you it's off the record. And I'll require strict approval before it's printed. This is non-negotiable. Under no circumstances are you to reveal any information that may allow people to figure out my true identity. My anonymity is all I have, the only thing that keeps me doing this."

"Absolutely. Not a problem." I can't help but beam, my eyes lighting up. I want to dance, shout, tell the world I was somehow able to get August Laurent to agree to have a story written about him. I have no idea what angle this will take, but from this brief conversation, I get the feeling he's interesting enough that any angle will have women flocking to read the article.

"On that, I'll let you get on with your day. I always say to leave on a high note. And I'm not sure I've ever seen anything as beautiful as the smile on your face right now."

A warmth spreads through me at his words. It takes me a minute to grasp the hidden meaning. When I do, I shoot up, my heart racing as I feverishly scan the crowded coffee shop for any man on his phone.

"Have a good day, Buttercup."

"Wait!" I beg, but my plea is met with silence. I look at my screen to see the call's been disconnected. I hastily gather my things, shoving them into my bag, when a woman wearing the café's uniform approaches.

"For you, miss." With a smile, she places a white plate containing a chocolate hazelnut pastry on my table. "Enjoy. It's our most popular item."

I frown. "I didn't order this."

"A gentleman did. Requested it be sent to you."

"Who?" I ask frantically, my voice bordering on desperation.

She stands on her toes, trying to peer over the heads filling the busy coffee shop. Then she inhales a breath, pointing toward the doors.

"That's him. Right there. Brown hair. Sunglasses. Gorgeous suit."

"Thank you!" Adrenaline pumping through me, I sling my bag over my shoulder, dashing through the coffee shop, trying to keep him in my line of vision. When I step onto the sidewalk, a body slams into me, causing me to lose my balance, propelling me forward onto my hands and knees.

"Watch where you're going next time, lady. Fucking tourists."

"I'm not a tourist, asshole!" I shout, getting back on my feet, no thanks to anyone walking by. Dusting myself off, grateful the only injury is to my ego, I scan the bodies passing, not one of them matching that of the man I observed leaving the café.

Frustration fills me. I was so close to unmasking *the* August Laurent. Still, I know more about him than I did an hour ago. But now I'm desperate for even more information, to find out what makes him tick, why he feels the need to hire himself out as a companion. He says he empowers women. That's a reason *they* hire *him*. I want to know his reasons, too.

As I'm about to head toward Central Park to see if he went in that direction, even though I know it's probably futile, my phone pings with an alert. It's not unusual. I get dozens of emails every hour. But something makes me pull my phone out of my bag and open my email.

To: Evie Fitzgerald
From: August Laurent
Subject: Special Place in Hell

Dear Miss Fitzgerald,

You do realize there's a special place in hell for people who walk away from the Steam Room's famous chocolate hazelnut pastries. They are quite...sinful.

Kindest regards,

A

Smiling, I type a reply as I walk, no longer frantic about finding him now that I have his email address.

To: August Laurent
From: Evie Fitzgerald
Subject: Already Going

Dear August,

I'm already going to hell. I figure either go big or go home. So I'm going big, starting with leaving that pastry on the table. In my experience, delayed gratification only heightens that first taste.

E

I hit send, unsure what came over me to act so bold. I suppose we all feel a level of power behind the safety of a computer or, in my case, a phone, which pings again.

To: Evie Fitzgerald
From: August Laurent
Subject: Deal with the Devil

Dear Miss Fitzgerald,

Now I'm intrigued as to what you've done to have earned a ticket on the proverbial Highway to Hell. And even more intrigued by your interest in delayed gratification.

I hope you have a productive Monday. I'll be in touch soon and we can continue our conversation...speaking of delayed gratification.

Damn. He's smooth.

Chapter Seventeen

My eyes are transfixed out the window of the town car on Wednesday as Julian's driver, Reed, maneuvers along narrow streets where the wealthiest members of society play for the summer. High hedges and security gates prevent the outside world from peeking in, but it doesn't stop me from gawking at the sprawling estates that pop up every quarter-mile. The closer to the shore we get, the larger and more impressive the properties. This is some serious money.

When I don't think the houses can get any more extravagant, Reed pulls off the main road, stopping outside a secure gate. After punching in a code, the impressive steel gates open, allowing us entry. My heart thumps in my chest as he continues up a long, stone driveway.

I haven't seen Julian since Friday. Hell, I haven't even spoken to him since our conversation Saturday, apart from an email from his assistant telling me that his driver would pick me up today at ten in the morning. At first, his curt tone left a sour taste in my mouth. Maybe it's a good thing. I've already felt myself wanting to blur some of the lines I insisted we draw. How much longer will they remain if he continues to flirt with me?

As the house comes into view, my jaw grows slack. It's a sprawling three-story, shingle-style historic home that's obviously been updated and taken care of rather well over the years. The pristine exterior has a sweeping lawn out front, the grass greener than any I've seen recently. Then again, I've been living in New York for the past several years. The only grass I see is when I visit Central Park, which isn't often. It's amazing how much you take the little things, like grass, for granted until they're no longer part of your daily life.

Reed brings the car to a stop, then hurries to open the door for me. Immediately, a woman in her fifties or sixties rushes out of the front door, hustling along the stone walkway. She wears a dark suit dress, her hair pulled into a tight bun at her nape. Her kind blue eyes are filled with joy as she approaches me.

"You must be Guinevere." She holds her hand out toward mine, shaking it excitedly. "I'm Camille, the head of staff."

"Head of staff?" I repeat. "You mean there's more than one person?"

She laughs merrily at my question. "Of course, dear. At least during the summers. Someone must ensure the household runs smoothly, particularly during parties. But the rest of the year, it's just me keeping his Manhattan apartment in order. Reed will bring your things up to your suite while I give you the tour."

With wide eyes, I follow her up to the front door, unable to mask my complete awe and amazement when she pushes it open and we enter a grand foyer, the ceiling over thirty feet high with a stunning crystal chandelier. It's a circular room with a single round table holding a floral centerpiece of red roses, white lilacs, and blue orchids, tying in with the Fourth of July theme of the weekend. I step closer, the familiar aroma of powder-fresh flowers floating through my senses.

Camille leads me past a curving staircase and into an open living area. The cream-colored walls have wood and stone accents, the high-end furniture made of heavy wood. It's a stark contrast to the tiny room and pull-out couch I've been sleeping on, which seems ready to collapse if I breathe too hard.

"This is the living and informal dining area." She brings me to an expanse of floor-to-ceiling windows lining the eastern wall and I take in the panoramic views of the pool deck overlooking the ocean. I find it a bit of overkill to have both an ocean view and a pool, but what do I know?

"Wow." It's all I can manage.

I've seen places like this in the movies or online, but never in my wildest dreams would I have imagined being here myself. It's crazy to even consider that this will be my life for the next two months. I wonder if this is how Cinderella felt when Prince Charming whisked her away to his castle after he finally found her. Did she realize her life would be forever changed when she called her Fairy Godmother and went to the ball? Is my life about to be forever changed, too?

"It's pretty amazing, isn't it?" Camille comments.

"I don't think I've ever seen anything so…majestic."

She places a hand on my bicep, her smile warm as she meets my eyes. Her soft-spoken and caring demeanor reminds me of my grandmother. "Wait until tomorrow morning."

"What's tomorrow morning?"

"Sunrise. I checked the weather report. It's supposed to be a clear day, which means the sun coming up over that horizon…" She points out the window, "is sure to be fantastic. If you want to get up early to watch, I'll make sure to have coffee prepared. If you like coffee, that is. I'll need a list of any allergies and food preferences, as well as any other items you'll need on hand during your time here."

"And you'll get them for me?"

"Of course," she answers, as if it's no big deal.

"So if I say I like to snack on apples dipped in peanut butter, you'd get them?"

"What kind of apples? And do you have a preference for brand of peanut butter?" She withdraws a notepad from her suit jacket and proceeds to jot down notes.

I blink repeatedly at her proficiency. The closest I've ever been to this level of pampering was the one time I'd ordered room service. I thought having someone bring food to my hotel room was magical. That's nothing compared to this.

"I… It was just an example."

With a warm smile, she returns the small notepad to her pocket. "It's Mr. Gage's desire that you have everything to make your stay comfortable. So anything you need, please let myself or any of the other staff members know. Okay?"

"Okay." With every second that passes, I feel more and more like Julia Roberts in *Pretty Woman*. Well, if she weren't a prostitute. Still, there are similarities, like the way she gawks at his lavish lifestyle, not used to anyone waiting on her. The way she's confused about which fork to use. I can completely sympathize with her struggle there.

I continue to follow Camille as she shows me the formal dining room, library, theater room, game room, and even a gym. I want to ask for a floor plan of the house so I can find my way around. Or at least a bag of breadcrumbs.

Finally, we head up the staircase and down a long hallway lined with what I assume to be expensive artwork, coming to a stop outside a wooden door. When she opens it, revealing a large bedroom, I step onto the lush carpet. The aroma of fresh air mixed with the sea breeze flows in from an open window, and I walk to the far wall, the views of the ocean just as breathtaking up here.

"There's a balcony," Camille offers as she strides toward a pair of French doors, pushing them open. "Right out here."

I follow her out onto a large wrap-around balcony. A pair of chairs sits in front of the windows to my room, a small side table placed between them. Another pair is placed several hundred feet down, as well, in front of windows to what I assume to be another bedroom.

"That's Mr. Gage's suite," she explains, gesturing toward the end of the balcony to the north. Then she nods in the opposite direction. "And those are additional guest bedrooms, but will not be occupied during, well…during your little arrangement."

"Our…arrangement?" I repeat, making sure I heard her correctly.

"Yes, dear. Don't worry. I'm the only one aware of the truth, other than Reed, of course. It was my idea, after all, although my motivation may not have been completely innocent."

I square my shoulders as I face her. "What do you mean?"

"I've been on the household staff longer than you've been alive, dear." She smiles. "Even longer than Julian's been alive."

There's a familial affection in her tone as she caresses his name, like a mother would her child. It's the first time she's referred to him as Julian instead of Mr. Gage. I can't help wondering if their relationship is more than employer and employee.

"I see things. I hear things. Mr. Price's children are still around, and they like to make things difficult for him, unduly influencing people who can help him. It's been several years since Mr. Price's passing, but no thanks to his children, who like to perpetuate the rumor that Mr. Gage took advantage of an old man, people still view him as a billionaire playboy, a passing fad who will end up blowing his fortune. Regardless, being around so long, you hear things. Many people's biggest criticism is that he's thirty-eight and isn't married. So I suggested he finally date someone."

"Well, I guess he must really look up to you since he took your suggestion."

She bursts out laughing as she leads me back into the room. "He certainly did not. Much to my dismay, he shot me down right away at the mere mention of him dating anyone. So I suggested he *purport* to date someone instead. He was hesitant at first, but he eventually figured it was worth a shot. At the very least, it would get the social clingers off his back for a summer."

"Camille?" I ask as I follow her past the four-poster bed, the sheer material draped over the sides billowing with our movement. Everything about this room is peaceful and serene. I'm not going to want to leave at the end of the weekend.

"Yes?"

"What *is* this project he's working on that appears to be so important to him?" I lower my eyes. "Or at least important enough to ask a complete stranger to pretend to be his girlfriend?"

She avoids my eyes as she continues toward a door just past the sitting area. "Oh, he never discusses his business plans with me." Her response comes fast and shaky. "They'd go right over my head anyway. Dana, Mr. Gage's stylist, has already been by to organize all the clothing she's selected for you. It's all here in the closet." She doesn't even pause to take a breath as she changes the topic, opening another door along the far wall.

I want to push and find out what the big secret is, but I'm rendered speechless at what she referred to as a closet. I have to stop myself from laughing. If Chloe and Nora could see me now, they'd piss their pants. This "closet" is bigger than my old apartment. Instead of only a handful of items for me to choose from over the course of the next few months, the walls are lined with a wardrobe suitable for any occasion imaginable, along with several dozen cubbies filled with shoes.

"Mr. Gage provided Dana with a copy of your itinerary for the summer," Camille explains. "She's taken the guesswork out of everything." She heads toward a table in the center of the room and opens a binder.

"Each article of clothing is labeled with a number that corresponds to an event in here." She points to the first page in the binder. I see today's date, the event, followed by a list of numbers, indicating what I'm to wear. "Sometimes things come up, so in the back are a handful of outfits in case of an emergency." She closes the binder as she faces me, her stare harsh and direct. "Under no circumstances are you to wear the same outfit twice. Do you understand?"

I'm overwhelmed as I take in everything. The house. The staff. The clothes. When I'd agreed to be Julian Gage's fake girlfriend, never in a million years did I expect it to be like this. Rules about what to wear and when. But the planner in me appreciates it. There are no surprises. I find comfort in that fact.

"Perfectly."

"Wonderful." She clasps her hands together. "Well, I'll leave you to get situated. Can I bring you anything? I'm sure you're hungry after the long drive."

I place my hand over my stomach, which is in knots. "Actually, I had a big breakfast," I lie.

"Okay, dear. Just dial 2111 on the house phone if you change your mind. I'll be back to check on you a bit later." She begins to retreat.

"Camille?"

"Yes?"

I pinch my lips together, unsure what I even want to ask. Perhaps I'm feeling a little out of my element and want someone to tell me I didn't make a colossal mistake in agreeing to this.

"Never mind," I say quickly.

"Certainly." She continues toward the door. When she's about to close it behind her, she catches my eyes and speaks again.

"Don't worry. You'll do fine. Mr. Gage wouldn't have asked you to do this if he didn't think you could handle it. It may seem overwhelming right now, but once you get settled in, you'll forget what life was like before you came to the Hamptons." She gives me an encouraging smile, then closes the door, leaving me alone to absorb this strange life I've been thrust into.

"That's what I'm afraid of," I sigh.

This would be most women's dream come true. A gorgeous bedroom overlooking the Atlantic Ocean, complete with palatial walk-in closet, which is stocked with designer clothes and shoes. So why am I having such a hard time with this?

Restless and unnerved by the unusual silence, particularly compared to Manhattan, I head back into the elaborate closet, flipping the binder open. I scan the first page to find the pre-selected outfit for today's event — a pool party beginning at three o'clock. Turning my attention to the clothes, I locate the items Dana indicated and place them on a railing by a 180-degree mirror, scowling at the navy-and-white polka-dot two-piece bathing suit. At least she chose more of a vintage, pinup style with a high waist and full coverage for my girls.

"Well, I guess I should shave my legs," I say to myself, spinning around and going in search of the bathroom. Thankfully, it's right next to the closet.

Like the rest of the house, it's impressive and extravagant. Marble tile. Spacious shower with several showerheads. Tempered glass behind an enormous claw-foot tub overlooking the ocean. I can't remember the last time I've lived somewhere with a tub, so I opt for a bath.

I turn on the faucet, spying a canister of bath salts sitting on a shelf above the tub. After sprinkling some into the steaming water, the fragrant aroma of lavender fills the air. I twist my hair into a knot on top of my head, then rid myself of my clothes.

Once I step into the bath and lean against the porcelain, tension rolls off me as all my worries about what this afternoon may bring evaporate. So what if these people don't think I fit in? That's never bothered me before. It's just a few months. After that, I'll never have to see any of them again.

Basking in the serenity of my luxurious bath and surroundings, I all but lose track of time until I notice the water's gone tepid and my skin's begun to prune. I shave quickly and grudgingly step out of the tub. After toweling myself off, I set about readying myself for my first event of the summer. I'm surprised how well the bathing suit Dana selected fits. Then again, she was rather meticulous in measuring me. I expected nothing less.

After applying copious amounts of sunscreen to my fair skin, I accentuate my natural peachy hue with a hint of blush. Then, as per Dana's instructions, I smooth my signature red lipstick on my lips. It brings together the vintage look. I tie a band around my head, knotting it at my nape, allowing the excess material to fall in front of my chest. I complete the look by draping a sheer white, floor-length coverup dress over my body.

When I step in front of the mirror in the closet, I gawk at my reflection. I still look like myself, but I don't feel like myself. Normally, I loathe wearing bathing suits. That's the benefit of living in the city — there's no real reason to wear one. But Dana chose one that accents what I consider my best assets — my hips and chest — without revealing too much skin. If she was able to work her magic on selecting the perfect two-piece, I can only imagine the gown she chose for tomorrow night's gala.

Curious, I spin from the mirror and head to the binder, about to turn the page to see exactly what I'll be wearing, when there's a knock on the door. Assuming it's Camille to check on me, I simply call out, "Come on in."

As I round the corner into the bedroom to meet her, I stop in my tracks when Julian stands in front of me. All six-foot-four of pure Julian Gage. Sinewy muscles. Consuming stare. Perfect lips turned into a subtle hint of a smile. He wears a white, short-sleeved, button-down shirt paired with blue checkered swim trunks. Yet again, it's another new look for him. Is there anything this man can't wear and make absolutely delicious? I doubt it. His skin appears darker than a few days ago, the ends of his hair lighter, kissed by the sun.

"Remind me to give Dana a raise," he murmurs as he circles me.

If anyone else regarded me in such a way, I'd probably feel like a prize pig on display during the annual county fair. That's not the case with Julian. He makes me feel coveted, admired…beautiful, something I never thought I would by wearing a two-piece bathing suit.

"A very *large* raise." Instantly, his hand clutches my hip and he drags my body against his. I gasp, taken aback by the gesture, particularly after our phone call Saturday.

"We're back to playing nice, are we?"

"Playing nice? What do you mean?"

I lower my head, feeling more exposed than I already am. "Nothing."

His thumb and forefinger grip my chin, forcing my eyes back to his, his deep pools of blue piercing me. "I don't keep secrets and don't expect you to, either. It's important we're both honest with each other about this arrangement. It's the only way it will work."

"It's nothing," I say once more, pushing away from him. I fold my arms over my chest.

"Guinevere…" His voice is a warning.

"You were…different when you called on Saturday. I guess I wasn't sure which version of Julian Gage I'd see today." I shrug half-heartedly, not wanting him to think his demeanor was a big deal, and turn from him.

"Which Julian Gage? You don't mean…" He trails off. I glance over my shoulder as he closes his eyes, dragging his fingers through his hair. When he looks up, he catches my gaze, his expression apologetic. "You thought I was short with you because I'd gotten you to agree to my proposition and no longer had to pretend to like you?"

"The thought crossed my mind." I face him, placing my hands on my hips.

He approaches me and tilts my head back. There's a power and earnestness as he stares deeply into my eyes. Unwavering. Determined. Honest.

"Listen to me, Guinevere. Everything I told you Friday is true. I *am* profoundly attracted to you. I was the instant I laid eyes on you. And I've only become more so with each second I spend in your presence. I'm sorry if I made you feel like you're anything but the beautiful, charming, witty woman I'm thrilled to spend the next few months with." He holds my gaze for a moment longer before stepping back, releasing his hold on me. "I was working Saturday. We all have our faults, and one of mine is being unable to switch from business mode to…pleasure mode."

I laugh slightly as the stress about the situation rolls off me. "And what exactly is 'pleasure mode'?" I smirk, chewing on my bottom lip.

He leans toward me, his voice a low growl. "Keep sucking on that lip and you'll find out."

Bringing my hand to his chest, I gently push him away. "I thought you said kissing's for amateurs."

"Who said anything about kissing you?"

I open my mouth to argue, but snap it shut. He's certainly got me there.

"That's what I thought." He flashes a devious smile before straightening his posture, extending his hand. "So, are you ready to convince the world you're my girlfriend?"

I pass him a flirtatious look as I link my fingers with his, his skin rough against mine. "Let the games begin."

CHAPTER EIGHTEEN

"SO WHAT'S OUR story?" I turn to Julian as he drives along the streets of Southampton. It's the first time I've seen him behind the wheel. There's something incredibly sexy about it. The natural confidence he exudes as he shifts from third to fourth, his free hand resting leisurely on the wheel. For most people, driving is a necessity, a way to get from point A to point B in the shortest amount of time. Julian makes it appear like an art form.

And let's face it, his car is ridiculously hot, too. I practically had an orgasm when we entered his garage and I feasted my eyes on a fleet of luxury cars — Land Rover, Porsche, Mercedes, Tesla, Bentley, Jaguar. But when Julian clicked a key fob and the lights to a red Ferrari Portofino convertible blinked, I all but had to wipe the drool off my lower lip. When he asked if I wanted to take it for a spin sometime, I offered to give him a blow job in return. Jokingly, of course. But that's how amazing this car is in the hierarchy of hot cars. It truly is blow-job worthy. The hum of the engine as he revved it to life only solidified my original assessment.

"What do you mean?" His smile is bright against his tan skin.

"People are bound to ask how we met. I can't come out and tell them the truth."

"Why not?" He's so cavalier about it, composed and in control, acting as if we're not about to walk into a party where we'll try to convince the Hamptons' elite we're an item.

"For one, we met in a bar. I'm sure you'd rather we make up something, like we met at a Sotheby's auction or doing something else people with a ridiculous amount of money do." I squint at him, pinching my lips together. "What is it you people do for fun?"

He laughs, shaking his head as he shifts into fifth. "*We* people…" He playfully lifts a brow, "do the same kinds of things you do for fun."

"Except you probably smoke better weed and do keg stands on twenty-four karat gold kegs with diamond-encrusted taps."

"Actually, the taps are hard to come by this year, but twenty-four karat kegs are a dime a dozen up here." He winks, his response taking me by surprise. Whenever I'd make a joke like that to Trevor, he'd scold me for being absurd, that I should be more serious. It's refreshing to be with someone who can appreciate my sense of humor.

"Thank God, because there is no way I'm drinking Natty Ice out of anything other than a keg that's plated in gold. A broad's got her standards."

"Of course."

It's silent before I speak again. "But seriously… Shouldn't we make sure our stories line up?"

"What's there to line up? We met in a bar." He glances at me. "*Not* at a Sotheby's auction."

"Horseback riding?"

"Definitely not."

"Golfing?"

"Hate the sport."

"At the racquetball club?"

"It's for men only."

"Chauvinistic bastards."

"They certainly are. Only men would make a competition out of smacking balls against a wall."

I shift my eyes to his, fighting against my smile. "Did *the* Julian Gage just make yet another joke? I thought the first one was a fluke, but a second one in so many minutes?"

"Why do you sound surprised?"

I face forward, allowing the strong rays of the sun to warm my face. I wonder if Dana knew which car Julian would take to the party and that's why she instructed that I tie a wrap around my hair. It does go with the vintage style of the rest of my wardrobe, but it has also proved to be rather practical.

"I had this image in my mind of you being so serious, like you were born shitting caviar and pissing Champagne."

"That's not true."

"I know." I fidget with the line of my coverup, hesitating before blurting out, "I Googled you."

"I figured you would." His voice shifts, no longer playful. Now it's more serious, cautious. He clears his throat. "Find anything interesting?" He steals a glimpse at me before staring straight ahead, his Adam's apple bobbing up and down in a hard swallow.

"No," I respond thoughtfully. "It simply solidified my opinion of you."

"Do I want to hear what that is?"

"That you're a good person, despite what some tabloids would lead people to believe."

Out of the corner of my eye, I notice his grip on the steering wheel tighten. According to my research, Julian came into his fortune nearly ten years ago now. I can't believe he's still dealing with the quiet whispers and upturned noses, even after all this time.

"I like to believe that karma rewarded your generous spirit."

Upon hearing my words, he flicks his gaze toward me as he lifts his hand from the gear shift and grabs onto mine, squeezing.

"Thank you." The corners of his mouth turn up in a gentle, heartfelt smile. It's not the sensual, flirtatious one I'm accustomed to. It's real, genuine, pure, a peek into who Julian Gage truly is.

"Of course."

He keeps his fingers intertwined with mine for a while as he drives. As we approach an intersection, he withdraws his hand to downshift, causing my shoulders to fall. But once he turns down another street and is back up to speed, he returns it to my thigh.

I snap my eyes toward his as a fluttering erupts in my stomach. My breathing increases, the skin beneath his fingers tingling.

"Is this okay?" he inquires in a low, smooth tone.

"Yes," I whimper.

"Good." His pupils dilate as he steals a glimpse at my exposed leg. Then he looks forward, squaring his shoulders. "Because we'll need to touch each other quite a bit over the next few weeks. If we're to make people believe what we have is real, we need our interactions to appear natural."

"Right." I form my mouth into a tight line, suppressing the flicker of hope his gesture gave me. "So is there anything I should know about the people who will be there today?"

"This is more of a casual get-together at David Gittney's house."

"Old money or found money?"

He passes me a sly smile as he shifts into fifth, then returns his hand to my thigh. "Very good. You remember. David is old money."

I purse my lips, trying to understand the proverbial caste system that appears to be in place here in the Hamptons. "If he's old money and looks down upon people with found money, as you claim—"

"Which he does."

"Then why does he invite you to his parties?"

"They like to flaunt the fact that this has been their lives for as long as they can remember, that they're the equivalent of American royalty. Old money invite new money so there are warm bodies at their parties, at least more than the few dozen people who'd attend if they kept it strictly old money. Found money goes in the hopes to finally be accepted. It's a game that's been taking place for ages now. And I have a feeling it will continue even when I'm dead. The current found money will eventually become old money and a fresh batch of newly minted millionaires and billionaires will strive for acceptance."

"Well…" I settle into the black leather. "I suppose I'm in store for a rather eye-opening summer. Anything I should keep in mind? Should I act a certain way? Not swear? Stuff like that?"

He flashes me his debonair smile as he pulls his car up to an elaborate iron gate. "Just be your normal, charming self. Don't change who you are for these people. I chose you *because* of who you are. Don't blend into the crowd. Stand out."

"It's hard not to stand out with bright red hair," I joke.

"That's not what I mean. You'd stand out even if you had a black curtain tossed over you. I'd never ask you to change who you are to suit my needs."

I face forward, reminded of my breakup with Trevor.

"I like you as you, and that will never diminish. Anyone who takes for granted how incredible you are doesn't deserve you. Remember that."

"But aren't you trying to convince these people you're someone you're not?"

"I'm not trying to convince them I'm someone I'm not." He returns his eyes to the driveway, continuing up an even more extravagant and impressive paved path than the one leading up to his estate. I didn't think such a thing were possible. Again, I'm proven wrong.

"But you said it yourself. You're not cut out for the relationship thing."

He pulls to a stop in front of a sprawling home that rivals many of the mansions I'd seen in Newport during a trip I'd taken with Trevor. When a valet attendant approaches the car, opening my door, Julian leans toward me. "And I'm not. But that doesn't mean I sleep around, either. Because I don't. I don't lead women on. I am upfront and honest with everyone from the beginning, just like I was with you."

He steps out of the car and I do the same, allowing one of the attendants to help me to my feet. When Julian reaches me, I part my lips, wanting to press further, but the warning in his gaze reminds me we're on display for everyone. I glance past him to see other cars pulling up behind his, curious eyes observing us. Some indifferent, others tainted with animosity.

"Ready?"

I nod quickly, swallowing down my nerves. He rests his hand on my lower back, steering me up a grand staircase leading into a palatial home that screams money. Crystal chandeliers. Marble tiles. High ceilings. Pristine furniture. Rare art. It is the quintessential display of wealth.

After navigating our way through the house, we step out of a pair of French doors and onto the back patio, the pool party already in full force. There must be over two hundred people in attendance, not to mention a band set up on a stage in the corner, playing hits of the 80s and 90s.

You know those cliché scenes in coming-of-age movies when a girl moves to a new school and walks into the cafeteria that first day, knowing absolutely no one? That's how I feel now. Except I'm at a five-star cafeteria and naked. At least I *feel* naked. That could be the only thing to explain the dozens of eyes that instantly zero in on us, the whispers washing over my skin.

Able to sense my nerves, Julian turns toward me and grabs my chin, tilting my head back.

"Be yourself. These first few days will be the hardest. People will wonder who you are. And some women here today will most likely be catty. Don't let them get to you."

He brings a thumb to my lower lip, brushing against my flesh. One touch and I'm completely intoxicated by this man and the way my body responds to even the slightest graze of his skin against mine. I crane my head back, the distance between our mouths diminishing with each heartbeat. I'm no longer paying attention to the band rattling off Jenny's phone number or the people squeezing past us to get through. It's just Julian. Just this. Just us.

"Don't let anything they say or do make you think you're anything less than the amazingly beautiful and vibrant woman you are. In my opinion, you're the most beautiful woman here."

He runs a lithe finger down the curve of my neck, the warmth of him so close unhinging me. My eyes flutter into the back of my head, my skin flushing, my knees weakening.

"I think that's enough to get them talking. Let's go enjoy the party."

When I no longer feel the heat of his breath so close, I open my eyes, struggling to calm my racing heart and act as if Julian hadn't brought me to the edge of complete and utter bliss with his words alone. After taking several deep breaths to compose myself, I link my hand in his.

"If whatever project you're working on doesn't pan out, you'd make a damn good escort," I joke in a husky voice as he leads me past a crowd of curious onlookers.

"Is that right?" His tone is amused.

"That's right."

"And what makes you say that?" He leans toward me, whispering into my ear, "Do I turn you on?"

"You could probably make a lesbian want to have a go with you just to be sure she really is gay."

He's silent for a moment before he bursts out laughing, the sound carrying over the band. It's so natural and addictive. How can anyone not feel a pull toward this man?

"Thanks for your vote of confidence, but I doubt I could ever be an escort."

"You never know. You could give August Laurent a run for his money. He's got a great voice, too, but not like yours."

We approach a bar and he places our drink order — manhattan for me, scotch for him. Then he faces me. "You've spoken to him?"

"I have."

His eyes brighten in genuine enthusiasm. "How did you manage that?"

"I got lucky." I shrug. "Someone mentioned I was looking for him…a little birdie, as he put it. He tracked me down, called my office line, and *bam*. Now we're email pals."

"Email pals?" He brings his glass to his lips as he steers me away from the bar and toward a vacant table tucked out of the way. For someone who needs to conduct business, he seems to be paying a great deal of attention to me.

"Yes." The perfect gentleman, he helps me into a wood slat chair. "We've been exchanging emails the past few days."

"Getting good material for your story?"

I bring the chilled martini glass to my lips, savoring that first sip of my drink. "He's a bit…aloof. He doesn't like to share much. But I'm working on it. I just need to establish a rapport with him. Then he'll open up."

"Good."

"Good." I watch as he shifts his attention away from me, searching the partygoers.

An unnerving silence settles between us as he rests his hand on my thigh like he did in the car. And just like in the car, I know it's not real. There's no emotion behind his fingers as they delicately brush my skin. No yearning building deep inside as he steals a glance at me. No unyielding desire as he leans toward me and nuzzles the crook of my neck. It's all for show. That's become my mantra these past few minutes. I have a feeling that will become my mantra these next few months, too, a constant reminder there's absolutely no meaning behind anything he does or says, despite what my heart wants to believe.

"Julian!" a voice shouts, snapping me out of my thoughts.

I follow his line of sight to see a man approach. He has short, shaggy, copper hair, fair skin, and a slight five o'clock shadow, although it's not too noticeable due to the light hue. His nearly six-foot frame is dressed in a pair of swim trunks and an open, white button-down. That appears to be the unspoken uniform amongst the men, while the trend with women seems to be who can wear the smallest piece of fabric and still be able to call it a bathing suit. Despite all the females being dressed as if ready to go for a swim, not a single one of them is in the pool. In fact, *no one* is in the pool. I wonder if that's customary at these things. Have a pool party, wear a bathing suit, but don't think about getting into the water.

"Christopher! Good to see you." Julian stands from the table, appearing genuinely happy to see him. Then again, it could be an act, too. I never know what to think with him.

"So this is her? The girl you haven't been able to stop talking about?" He looks from Julian to me, then back again.

"Sure is. Christopher, this is Guinevere Fitzgerald. Guinevere, this is Christopher Albright."

"Nice to meet you." I stand up, holding out my hand.

He grasps it. "You, as well. I've heard a great deal about you, Guinevere. Please. Sit. Sit." He gestures to my chair as he occupies the free one across from me.

"You can call me Evie," I instruct as I return to my seat. "Everyone else does. Except this guy." I jab Julian playfully in the stomach once he lowers himself back to his chair.

"He's always been pretty formal, at least as long as I've known him, which is since freshman year of college."

"Is that right?"

"Sure is. I can tell you some incredibly embarrassing stories about the guy. Trust me. He used to be awkward. And scrawny."

"Please tell me you have pictures."

He smiles. "Of course."

"If you want to keep my company's 401k account," Julian interrupts, gritting a smile, "you'll keep those photos to yourself. And you were just as awkward."

At that moment, a stunning brunette wearing a yellow two-piece sidles up to the table, placing a kiss on Christopher's temple before turning her attention to me. Her eyes are the color of honey, her hair full with perfect beach waves falling to mid-back. Her smile is warm, which makes it difficult for me to hate the fact she has the physique most women would kill for — tall, slender, but still with a classic hourglass shape.

"Is this her?" she asks excitedly.

"Now I know why my ears have been ringing the past few days," I answer, holding my hand toward her. "Hi. I'm Evie."

"Sadie. And try weeks." She plops down on the last free chair, taking a sip of what appears to be a cosmo.

"Weeks?" I furrow my brow. "What do you mean weeks?"

"That's how long Julian's been talking about you. It's about time he found a good girl, instead of playing the perennial matchmaker."

"Matchmaker?" I look back at Julian. I never would have pegged him for a guy who'd go around setting people up on dates, considering he seems rather averse to being in a relationship himself.

"He introduced me to Christopher several years ago. Now we're about to celebrate our fifth wedding anniversary."

"Sadie is one of the first friends I made out here in the Hamptons," Julian explains.

"Is that right?" I smile nervously, looking between them. I can picture them as a couple. Both gorgeous with incredible bodies. They look more like a couple than Julian and I do. And Sadie and Christopher.

"Not like that," she interjects quickly, her eyes wide. "No, no, no. We never… Ya know. Our relationship's always been strictly platonic."

"Even if it hadn't, it's okay." I place my hand on Julian's thigh. It's the first time I've initiated contact between us. But it's what feels natural, what I would do if Trevor were here with me and we were having this conversation with one of his friends. I meet his eyes. "He's here with me now. That's all that matters. Not the past. Not the future. Just right now."

I keep my gaze locked with his, the outside world seeming to melt away. It's not until I hear Sadie that I look back at her.

"Aww…" She covers her heart, her eyes bright and smile wide. "That is the sweetest thing. Isn't it, babe?" She glances at Christopher.

"It's about time," he jokes in response. "Maybe now I won't have to field this asshole's phone calls about reinvesting portions of his portfolio at all hours of night or on weekends." He brings his beer to his lips, looking at me from over the bottle. "Promise me you'll keep him occupied outside regular office hours, okay?"

I lean into Julian, giving him a demure look. "I'm sure I can keep him *very* busy."

Christopher whistles as Sadie claps, but I don't look their way. I can't, the raw need covering Julian's expression catching me off-guard. If I didn't know any better, I'd think he were about to throw me over his shoulder and haul me into the house so we could find somewhere private. My thighs squeeze involuntarily at the notion.

Remembering where I am, I clear my throat, looking back at Sadie and Christopher. "So, how did Julian play matchmaker?" With a trembling hand, I bring my drink to my mouth, needing the alcohol to cool the flames building inside.

"At one of his parties," she answers.

"Sadie is what you'd call old money," Christopher adds.

"Well, used to be," she corrects.

I pull my brows together. "Used to be? How's that?"

She shrugs. "Marriage."

"What—"

"I'm old money, but married no money."

"Thanks for emasculating me, sweetie," Christopher quips as he drapes an arm across her shoulders, but the smile never leaves his face.

"Anytime." She lowers her voice. "You'll eventually figure it out, but there's a bit of a hierarchy out here."

"Julian's already given me the Cliff Notes." I glance at him, about to rest my hand on his thigh once more, but stop myself, his heated stare still trained on me. We're definitely playing with fire. I think he's finally realized that. "About old money and found money," I finish, facing Sadie once more.

"Well, I grew up in old money. Granddaddy was big in steel in the early 1900s. Made his fortune and was smart, so he didn't lose much during the Great Depression. Anyway, some of the more conservative families prefer their offspring to marry within their 'station'," she explains, using air quotes. "Like my parents."

"But you didn't."

"They may view love and marriage as a business relationship, one for profit, but I don't. When I first met Christopher, I couldn't help but feel a connection. He was smart, charming, funny, a breath of fresh air from all the stuffy people I've always known. My parents thought it was just a phase." Her expression drops as she toys with the ring on her left hand. It's stunning and a decent-sized rock, but not nearly as extravagant as some of the jewelry I've seen on other women here. "I think they sometimes think it's still a phase."

She smiles at Christopher, but it doesn't reach her eyes this time. I sense she still struggles with the tension that must exist between her parents and the man she loves. I couldn't imagine having to choose one or the other. I was lucky to have a boyfriend my parents adored.

"But that doesn't matter. They can drop my social standing a few pegs all they want. It won't change anything."

"Then why do you still come to these things?" I wave my free hand around. "I could be wrong, but it sounds like you're pretty fed up with the way things are and want no part of it."

She leans toward me. "That's true. But I love showing off the fact that I'm genuinely happy. Most of these people wouldn't know happiness if it slapped them in the face. And it ruffles their feathers to know I've found it. That no matter what they do, they can't take that away from me."

"Wow." I shake my head, absorbing Sadie's story. "It all seems a bit antiquated."

She raises her drink. "Welcome to the Hamptons, where the caste system is alive and well." After she takes a sip, she returns her glass to the table. "So, did you two really meet in a bar?"

I'm about to confirm this when Julian's voice cuts through. "We sure did."

I turn my head, meeting his eyes. There's still an intensity within, but it's not as pronounced as it was. He pulls me close, his fingers tracing a delicate circle on my bicep. I attempt to melt into his embrace, wanting it to appear as natural as possible.

"Her ex had just broken up with her and she decided to share her story with the entire bar."

Sadie's eyes widen. "You didn't!"

I blanche as Julian continues. "It was far more entertaining than any stand-up routine I've seen." Pride drips from his statement, his hold on me tightening. "Guinevere has a gift with words. So I suppose I should thank her ex for being a complete idiot. If it weren't for him, I wouldn't be sitting next to this incredible, amazing, captivating woman who seems to have weaseled her way into my heart practically overnight."

He speaks with such passion, such fervor, such affection, it's hard to imagine this is simply an act. But as Shakespeare so succinctly put it in *As You Like It*, "All the world's a stage, and all the men and women merely players." Now is my time to play the part of Julian's girlfriend. Come September, the curtain will close and I'll go on to the next act of my life.

CHAPTER NINETEEN

"AND THAT'S IMOGENE Joyce," Sadie says under her breath as we sit at the same table a while later. Julian and Christopher excused themselves earlier. I haven't seen them in over an hour. At least they left me in good hands. Sadie seems to know the dirt on everyone. And being the Hamptons, there's more dirt than usual. "She claims to be James Joyce's great-niece or some shit."

"Is she?"

Sadie shrugs. "Who knows? One can never be too sure of anything around here. People constantly say whatever they need in order to secure an invitation to the next big social event, or to make someone jealous, or to appear better than someone else. Hell, if you wanted, you could say you were a distant relative of F. Scott Fitzgerald and people would probably believe it. You'll soon learn that everything out here is a façade. Nothing is real. It's all for show. The smiles. The clothes. The houses. It's all a competition, a game we play every summer to see whose dick is the biggest."

"Then why do you come year after year?"

As she relaxes back in her chair, she crosses her legs. "It's too entertaining a show to miss. Not to mention it's good for Chris to network, considering he works in wealth management. Plus, Julian asked me to hang out this summer, as a favor to him."

"He did?" I furrow my brow.

"Yes." She smiles warmly. "He didn't want you to feel lonely. Thought you could use a little female camaraderie." She's silent for a moment. "He's a good guy. A *really* good guy. Loyal to a fault. Caring. If you have a problem, he'll do whatever he can to help you, regardless of what he has going on in his own life at the moment. He may look like he's this tough bad ass, and he's definitely perfected the mystery man persona he seems to exude, but to those of us who know the real Julian Gage..." She reaches across the table and clutches my hand in hers. "Well, you've hit the jackpot because there's no one better." She pulls back. "Well, except Christopher, but Julian comes in a very close second."

She winks as she sips on her drink. It warms my heart to hear someone talk about Julian with so much affection. It solidifies my original assessment of him. He truly is a good guy, not the playboy con artist some would have me believe.

"And I'm so glad he's finally met someone who makes him happy."

"That's all I want." I force a smile. "To make Julian happy."

It's not a complete lie. I *do* want to make Julian happy. If I didn't care about him, I wouldn't be giving up my weekends to be his proverbial arm candy, as ridiculous as the idea of me being anyone's arm candy sounds, especially when I'm surrounded by several women who actually *are* models and only here to be some rich guy's arm candy for the night.

"And this may be the alcohol talking," she continues, her voice slurring more and more with every word she speaks, "but I think you could be the one. Ever since I was a little girl, I had these…feelings about people. Like I could see a couple and know instantly if they were made to last. And you and Julian…" She slowly nods, waggling her brows. "You two are made to last. I saw the way he looked at you. That man could not take his eyes off you." Her playful expression grows serious. "Every woman deserves to find a man who looks at them the way he does you."

I chew on the inside of my cheek as I lower my head, a blush blooming on my face, wishing I could tell her it's all fake, but I can't.

"And every man deserves to find a woman who looks at him the way you do Julian," she finishes. "It seems I've been waiting for him to find a girl for years, at least someone who's more than a passing fling." She reaches for my hand and squeezes it again. "I'm so glad he found you."

"Me, too," I whisper, wishing I'd met her somewhere else. I could see us being real friends. I could see her joining Nora, Chloe, and me at our Thursday evening get-togethers. I could see her dropping whatever she has going on when one of us has an emergency. But that won't be possible, an unfortunate side effect of this arrangement I hadn't anticipated.

Needing to cut through the growing tension, I lift my eyes back to the growing crowd of people swarming around the pool, dancing as if the world is watching. In a way, I suppose the world *is* watching.

"So…who else do you have dirt on?"

"Everyone."

After draining her drink, she sets the glass back onto the table and scoots her chair even closer to mine, continuing to give me the rundown on the who's who in the Hamptons. Every so often, a few women approach, fabricated smiles on their faces as they hug Sadie, claiming it's good to see her. Then their disdainful stares settle on me. It doesn't take a genius to conclude that they know who I am. They probably came to talk to Sadie as a pretense to getting a closer look at Julian Gage's girlfriend.

"You should write a book," I joke after a while of soaking in the stories she's relayed. I used to watch soap operas during high school and college, thinking the plot lines were far-fetched. Or so I thought. These people have proved that soap operas aren't as ridiculous as I presumed. Secret babies. Amnesia. Arranged marriages. Mistaken identity. Faked deaths. It's all here, and then some.

"The thought's crossed my mind. I doubt anyone would actually believe any of the stuff is plausible. It all sounds crazy, don't you think?"

"Before today, I would have thought the same thing. Now I get the feeling the stories you've shared are only the tip of the iceberg."

"Oh, honey. You have *no* idea."

We both laugh and I finish the rest of my manhattan, standing up. "I'm going to get another drink. Want one?"

"Sure. Would you like me to come with you?"

"Nah. You stay here so we don't lose our table. We've secured a prime piece of real estate to people-watch." With a wink, I spin from her, squeezing through the throngs of people to make my way to the bar, ignoring the stares as I do.

Now that the party's in full force, the bar is much busier than when we first arrived. While I wait to place my order, I scan the pool area, amazed that this kind of party is an everyday occurrence here. Most people would plan all year to throw a celebration of this magnitude. Here, it's just Wednesday.

As I continue soaking in the atmosphere, I stiffen when I see a familiar face a few yards away. My heart drops to my stomach as he wraps his arm around a petite woman's waist before raising a scotch to his lips. Lips I once kissed. Lips that once told me how much he loved me. Lips I used to make smile daily. I'm no longer the reason they smile. The woman at his side is.

He leans down and kisses her forehead, bringing her even closer, as if he can't stand to be any farther from her than necessary. An ache builds in my throat, in my limbs, in my soul as I'm forced to witness their exchange. Sensing my stare, Trevor flicks his eyes in my direction. When he sees me, he flinches, his muscles growing taut.

I remain frozen in place, dumbstruck, unsure what I'm supposed to do. I should have anticipated running into them, considering Julian *did* mention Theresa is a friend of his neighbor. I just didn't expect to come face-to-face with them at my first party. Based on the confusion covering Trevor's brow, he didn't anticipate this, either.

Just then, an arm snakes around my waist and I snap my head up, meeting Julian's concerned gaze.

"Guinevere?"

I blink, wishing something as simple as a kiss didn't have this effect on me. But we were together twelve years. How can I just forget that? I'm on a see-saw. One minute, I want to write off Trevor. The next, I want him to tell me he's made a mistake.

"Are you okay?"

With a quick nod, I avert my eyes, hiding the emotions coming to the surface. But Julian won't let me, grabbing my chin and tilting my head back.

"He's a fool," he whispers, leaning toward me.

"He looks happy, doesn't he?"

"So what if he does?"

I pull my lips between my teeth to stop my chin from quivering, trying to avoid making a scene in front of all these people…and Trevor.

"Because *I'm* supposed to be the one who makes him happy. That's always been my job. How can he—"

"Like I said, he's a fool. You make me happy," he offers in consolation.

I lower my voice to barely above a whisper. "But it's not real."

"My happiness when I'm with you? It's more real than anything I've felt in a long time, even if the rest of this is only for show. And I want you to be happy, too. So tell me what it'll take to make you happy, and I'll do it."

I laugh as I blurt out the first thing that comes to mind. "A dartboard with Theresa's face on it."

"Consider it done," he responds in a lively voice. "Would you like another with Trevor's face? Or perhaps a punching bag?"

"I certainly wouldn't send it back." I wipe the few tears from my eyes. It's surprising how quickly Julian can make me smile, even when facing heartbreak.

"Good."

I peer into his eyes, his compassion seeming to mend the rips caused by Trevor. "Thank you."

When he brings his hand to my face, rubbing his thumb under my eye to erase one last tear, a shiver trickles through me, my sadness and despair turning into something else.

"I don't care what it takes. I want to show you that you deserve more than he gave you. No woman deserves to be with someone who doesn't appreciate them. And Trevor didn't appreciate you, not if he broke up with you because you no longer fit into his idea of perfection. You deserve someone who *will* appreciate you. Never settle for anything less. Okay?"

"It's not as easy as you make it sound, not after twelve years."

"I know. But with time, it will be."

I nod, unsure if I like the idea of getting over Trevor. Since I was eighteen, he's been a part of me. It's hard to picture life without him. Divorced couples must go through this, still sleeping on the same side of the bed, even though the other person's no longer there. Still sitting in the same chair at the dining room table, even though you now have your choice. Still using the same bathroom sink to brush your teeth, even though they're both now yours.

Feeling another crack in my armor, I look back at Julian. "I need to use the ladies' room. I'll be right back." I go to turn from him, but he grabs my arm, stopping me, forcing me to face him once more.

"Are you okay?"

"Yes," I insist. Sensing curious eyes watching us, I place my hand on his chest, then raise myself onto my toes, inching toward his neck. "Never better," I murmur. When my lips touch his cheek, he inhales a sharp breath.

All afternoon, we've shared more than a few sensual touches — a brush of his hand on my leg, a finger smoothing an unruly wave behind my ear, his hand intertwining with mine. But there's been nothing more. Until now. In fact, I've never had the pleasure of experiencing the warmth of his skin on my lips, the scruff from his unshaven jaw harsh and piercing, but invigorating at the same time. I didn't think I'd like it, considering Trevor always kept his jawline smooth. But something about Julian's two-day beard stirs me to life, replacing my despair with yearning, desire…hope.

When I pull back, Julian's eyes find mine, both of us powerless to look away. It was only a chaste kiss on the cheek, but in it I felt something I hadn't in a long time…a spark. Based on the bewilderment in his expression, I surmise he felt it, too.

"Bathroom," he says, finally finding his voice, snapping me out of my daydream.

"Right. Bathroom." I peer at him for a few more seconds, then spin from him, trying with everything to regain my composure.

As I'm about to duck into the house, I glance over my shoulder, a jolt of electricity coursing through me when I notice Julian's eyes glued to my body. In that moment, I don't even notice Trevor standing just a few feet away. Maybe this is why Julian walked into my life. Not to take Trevor's place, but to help mend my heart so I can move on. Maybe Chloe was onto something when she formulated her motto, "You live. You learn. You upgrade." Perhaps Julian is my chance to upgrade, even if for just a few months.

Feeling hopefully optimistic, I continue into the house, navigating the long corridors to the guest bathroom, which is just as spacious and luxurious as the rest of the house. To my surprise, there's no line. I step inside, allowing myself a minute to breathe for the first time all afternoon.

Once I'm refreshed and ready to face the party, I walk back through the stunning home. I didn't have a chance to truly admire its beauty when I first arrived, but now that I'm alone, I take a moment to soak up my surroundings. While Julian's house is impressive, this place makes it look like a shack. High, decorative ceilings. Crown molding. Furniture that looks like it's merely for show. Artwork. Sculptures. Fountains. I feel like I'm in a museum, not a person's home.

As I reach the ornate living room, my eyes focus on a painting hanging on the far wall. From the limited exposure I've had to art, it appears to be impressionist. Broad brushstrokes and muted colors. I step toward it to get a better look.

"Do you like art?" a voice inquires.

I whirl around to see a man I estimate to be in his forties approach. He has a touch of silver in his beard, making him look distinguished. He has a full head of dark hair and mesmerizing gray eyes I'd recognize anywhere.

"Holy crap," I say, covering my heart with my hand. "You're Ethan Ludlow."

"Guilty as charged." He winks, approaching me. "And you must be the lovely Guinevere I've been hearing about all afternoon."

"Trust me, I doubt anything you've heard is true."

"Not much you hear about in the Hamptons is." He leans against the wall, crossing his arms. "But it's not all bad. And it's not all lies. I can now confirm a few things with my own eyes."

"And what's that?" I smooth a strand of hair behind my ear, trying not to freak out over the idea that I'm standing here, having a casual conversation with Ethan Ludlow, child actor who rose to fame playing on one of the longest-running sitcoms in the 80s. He had a leading role in a few movies during his teens and twenties, then decided to try his hand directing and producing. The movies with his name attached are some of the most popular ones out there. And I'm standing next to him. I want to pinch myself to make sure this is real.

"You have some incredible…assets." He waggles his brows and a chill instantly envelopes me as he advances. The stench of alcohol wafts from his breath, and I back up as my heart drops to the pit of my stomach.

I grit out a smile, brushing him off as Sadie's warning about this kind of thing plays in my head. While there are some good guys here, a lot of them think their overflowing bank accounts allow them to have anything they want. They don't realize there are things in this world that *can't* be bought. And what they can't buy, they simply take.

"I suppose they could be saying much worse. If you'll excuse me, I should be getting back to the party."

"I heard you're a writer for a magazine," he says, preventing my retreat. "I'm always interested in meeting new writers to see what kind of ideas they have. Ever consider working in the film industry?" He leers at me.

I wish I had more than this flimsy coverup on. Every time Julian had stolen a glance, he gazed at me in a way that made me feel like the most beautiful woman around. This guy makes me feel like I'm a piece of meat. Is that how he looks at every woman?

"I'm happy at the magazine." I attempt to sidestep him, but he mirrors my movement, blocking me again.

"Come now. There's a vast difference between working for a women's magazine and working on a script for the next blockbuster. Who wouldn't want to be involved in something like that? People would kill to be in your shoes right now." He closes the distance, the heat of his breath like the blade of thousands of knives. "In more ways than one."

I swallow down the bile rising in my throat, unable to believe this is actually how Ethan Ludlow behaves. Growing up, he had the persona of being a wholesome kid from a great family. Hell, he's married to Sonia Moreno. They're *the* Hollywood power couple. Why would he be hitting on me when he has someone as stunning as Sonia at home?

"Like I said…" I attempt to mask the tremor in my voice, peering over his shoulder in the hopes of finding a familiar face. Unfortunately, no one here is familiar. "I'm happy at the magazine."

When he places his hand against the wall, I duck underneath it, walking as fast as my legs can carry me. I only make it a few feet before a pair of arms wrap tightly around me, pulling me against a hard body. Instinct kicks in and I struggle, thinking it's Ethan. But it's not, the arms holding me warm and familiar. When I look up, I stare into Julian's frantic and concerned eyes. He rakes his gaze over me, trying to figure out what has me so rattled. Then he glares over my shoulder, every muscle in his body tensing.

"Julian," Ethan says as he approaches. Julian's protective grip tightens around me. "Good to see you again. I was just getting to know your girlfriend here." He continues past us, smirking, holding his head high and acting as if he can do whatever he wants. "I'm looking forward to getting to know her even better over the next few months."

Julian doesn't utter a single word, staring him down until he disappears through the living room. Once he's out of view, Julian returns his attention to me, scanning my body for any hint of harm.

"Are you okay? He didn't hurt you, did he?" His voice sounds frenzied, desperate.

"I'm fine," I assure him. "He's just like every other asshole here who thinks they can treat women like property."

"Except for me."

I open my mouth to agree, but he *is* using me as a pawn in whatever game he's playing.

"Except for me," he repeats, this time firmer. "Right?"

"It doesn't matter." I push away from him, but he's in front of me before I can return to the party.

"It does, Guinevere. It matters to me. I don't…" He runs a hand through his hair, tugging at it.

"It's okay, Julian." I cup his cheek, offering him a comforting smile as I lower my voice so no one overhears. "I knew what I was getting into when I signed up for this. We're both using each other. We're both pawns in this game. Nothing more."

I drop my hold on him, exiting the house and immersing myself back into the party. The sun's begun to set, casting a glow on the pool deck. Without the hot rays beating down on me, the air is comfortable, especially with the gentle breeze coming off the ocean wrapping around my skin.

As I search for any sign of Sadie, a hand clutches my bicep, forcing me around to see Julian's determined stare.

"Don't ever think you're a pawn to me, Guinevere." His voice is harsh, powerful, yet sincere. As much as I want to think this is just another part of his game, something about it feels too convincing, too…real. "You're not." He takes a breath. When he speaks again, his words come out barely above a whisper.

"Yes, we may be putting on a show to get what we need, what we *both* deserve, but don't ever think for a second I view you as a piece of property. I respect you, more than you realize. Just because we have a bit of an unconventional relationship doesn't lessen that." He runs a soft finger along the contours of my face. I shiver, the reaction as surprising and unexpected as everything with Julian seems to be. "You are so much more than any of that. You are…"

"Yes?" I lick my lips as I tilt my head, losing myself in the depth of his eyes.

"You are…" He places a hand on the small of my back, pulling my body against his. My heart pounds against my ribcage. No longer out of fear or dread, but out of desire and anticipation. My chest rises and falls in a quicker pattern, every inch of me desperate for his next move. I shouldn't be this turned on by him. I shouldn't want his hands on me. Still, I can't help but wonder what *could* be.

"Yes?"

"You are…unexpected."

"Good unexpected or scary unexpected?"

He chuckles. "Good unexpected." His buoyant expression turns serious as he pulls his bottom lip between his teeth. I can see a war raging within. "*And* scary unexpected," he adds, releasing his hold on my lower back and bringing his hand to my face.

When he runs his thumb along my bottom lip, I plump it out. Electricity courses through my veins as the heat of his breath grows closer and closer. I brace myself for his kiss. I *welcome* his kiss. In twelve years, I've only known one man's kiss, one man's arms, one man's body. Perhaps it's time I experience something new, too. I may regret it tomorrow. Hell, I may regret it in a few minutes. But right now, I just want to be kissed again.

As I inch even closer, a body unexpectedly slams into me. Everything seems to play in slow motion as I struggle to regain my balance. Julian reaches out, scrambling to grab onto me, but gravity is not my friend, and with unceremonious grace, I fall into the pool.

When I resurface, I wipe at my eyes, seeing all the partygoers staring in my direction, and my cheeks flush in embarrassment. I normally don't care about making a complete fool of myself. But here, I'm self-conscious, especially when I notice everyone whispering amongst themselves as they gawk at the poor girl who got bumped into the pool.

Thankfully, Sadie soon emerges from the crowd, a cool confidence about her. "Well, it *is* a pool party, isn't it?"

She steps out of her sandals that I can only imagine cost a small fortune. Leaving her drink on a nearby table, she dives into the pool with the practiced expertise of a swimmer. When she pops her head above the water, she meets my eyes, winking.

I pass her a grateful smile, unsure how I'll ever repay her for doing this. I shrug out of my now soaked coverup and take my shoes off, tossing them onto the pool deck just as I notice Julian removing his shirt. I keep my eyes trained on him, unable to look away from his chiseled physique, everything about it near perfection, except for the scars on his abdomen. In my eyes, those scars are part of the fabric that makes up who he is, although I'd love to learn the story behind them.

With a smirk, he cannonballs into the pool, disappearing beneath the surface. Before I know it, dozens of people jump in, some of them wearing their street clothes, the alcohol encouraging them on.

As my eyes scan the sudden festive environment, I notice Theresa and Trevor standing off to the side. She pulls on his hand, attempting to get him to join in the revelry. He refuses, excusing himself and heading into the house. I shouldn't feel partly responsible for his sour mood, considering he broke up with me. But despite everything, I still care about him.

I'm about to find my way out of the pool to talk to him when an arm loops around my waist. Spinning around, I meet Julian's eyes, smiling. Like two puzzle pieces locking into place, I drape my arms over his shoulders, making anyone think we've done this dance dozens of times before. I do my best to ward off the electricity flooding through me as we remain chest to chest, our wet flesh pressed against each other.

"I thought you wanted people to take you seriously," I remark.

"I do."

"I'm not sure this accomplishes that."

"That's true, but I couldn't resist."

"Resist what?"

"Getting wet with you."

"Is that right?" I run my hand through his waterlogged hair, scratching at his scalp. He bites his bottom lip, groaning from the contact.

"I have a feeling I'm going to have trouble resisting a lot of things about you over the next few weeks."

I bring my mouth toward his, remaining just out of reach. "Only time will tell."

Chapter Twenty

"LET ME HELP you," Julian says once the valet attendant pulls up with his car. We approach the Ferrari and he reaches for my hand. The instant he touches my skin, he flings his eyes to mine. "Jesus! You're freezing!"

"That's what happens when the air cools down and you're wearing nothing but a wet two-piece."

"Why didn't you say anything?" His brows pull together in concern.

"It's not a big deal," I insist as I climb into the passenger seat. "I can take care of myself."

"I don't doubt that, but if you're uncomfortable, you need to tell me." He takes the key fob from the valet attendant and pops the trunk. After rummaging around in it for a minute, he closes it, then ducks into the driver's seat, handing me a sweatshirt.

I look at the big, bold letters printed on the front. "SUNY?"

He shrugs. "What did you expect?"

"I don't know. Harvard. Yale. Columbia." As I pull the enormous sweatshirt over my head, I inhale, instantly bathed in a scent that can only be described as Julian. It reminds me of waking up in his bed that first morning, panicked. I don't even recognize him as that person anymore. I don't recognize myself as that person, either.

He finds my hand and brings it onto the shifter, our fingers intertwined as he puts the car into first. "Nope. I enjoyed my higher education years out here in Stony Brook."

"Interesting," I muse, settling against the cool leather as he pulls around the elaborate driveway, navigating onto the quiet road, my hand glued beneath his as he shifts between the gears.

"Interesting? How so?"

"I had you pegged as more an Ivy League guy."

"I guess you had me pegged wrong." When he glances at me with a sparkle in his blue eyes, I can't reel in my smile.

"I guess I did."

"I'm surprised you didn't find out about this when you Googled me."

"I must have gotten distracted by other information that your college education didn't seem all that interesting in comparison."

"Like what?"

"Like Theodore Price."

When I say the name, he swallows hard, the mood shifting from playful to somber. He passed away over ten years ago now, but by Julian's unfocused stare, it's apparent he still grieves the loss of the man who, according to many reports, molded him into the person he is today.

"He sounds like a good man," I offer when he remains silent.

"He saved my life."

I want to ask more, my mind immediately going to the scars on his abdomen.

"Did he—"

"I want you to promise me something, Guinevere," he interrupts, his voice determined. His hardened expression is at complete odds with the way he clutches my hand, his thumb brushing against my skin haphazardly, as if it's second nature.

"What's that?"

"That you'll stay as far away from Ethan Ludlow as you can. That you'll come find me if he so much as breathes on you the wrong way. No matter what I'm doing, who I'm speaking with. I don't care if I'm in the middle of some negotiation."

I shiver as I recall my earlier exchange with Ethan. The excitement of standing next to this Hollywood legend. Then the sickness filling me when I realized what kind of person he truly was.

"I knew I'd need to warn you about him eventually, but thought I could put it off. Obviously not, because he's already interested. Word's gotten out you're a writer."

"I'm not really—"

"You are. Don't let anything Trevor said make you believe otherwise. You *are* a writer. That's probably why Ethan tracked you down. That, and you were there with me."

"Why? Is he one of the old money people who likes to constantly knock you down a few pegs?"

"You can say that. He's one of Theodore Price's children."

I can't hide the utter shock when I hear this. "What? I mean—"

"He uses his mother's maiden name in the industry. An homage to her legacy, I suppose. So yes, he has a tendency to make it difficult for me to get things done, considering he's a shareholder of the company, albeit a minority one. Outside of that, he's still a Hollywood slimeball. He'll offer you the moon and the stars, success, money, everything you've ever dreamt of. But trust me when I say it will come at a high price. Do you understand what I'm trying to tell you?"

I nod, swallowing down the bile rising in my throat at what could have happened if I hadn't taken the opportunity to get away from Ethan when I did. How did I not know he was one of Theodore Price's kids? I really need to read up on all my celebrity news.

"I don't want you to worry about me. You're trying to network at these events. You shouldn't have to stop what you're doing to make sure I'm okay."

"But I *will* worry about you." He laughs nervously, and I sense a chink in his armor, revealing a vulnerability I've yet to see. "It's a personality flaw. I worry. I always will. I just want you to be okay."

He briefly glances at me, his eyes pleading. His grip on my hand tightens, like he's scared something will happen if he lets go. I wonder if this protectiveness, this fear, is tied to those scars. I want nothing more than to ask about them, how they got there, if they're connected to Theodore Price and how he supposedly saved Julian. Instead, I simply murmur, "Okay."

"Okay," Julian breathes, as if my acquiescence allows a weight to lift from him. He brings my hand to his lips and places a soft kiss on the flesh, repeating, "Okay."

When he pulls his car into what he refers to as the carriage house a short while later, his property is devoid of all activity.

"Are these like your day-of-the-week underwear?" I ask as he helps me out of the Ferrari. They're the first words either one of us have spoken since our tension-filled conversation about Ethan.

"Day-of-the-week underwear?" He cocks a brow.

"Yeah." I gesture to the line of luxury cars. It's all I can do not to salivate over them. I've been living in New York so long I almost forgot what it's like to drive. It's one of those things I took for granted before moving to the city. Like grass. Now I yearn for that feeling of independence. "Monday is the Land Rover. Tuesday the Porsche. Wednesday is obviously the Ferrari."

"Obviously." He smirks, linking his fingers with mine as he leads me up to the main house.

"So what's the deal with all the cars? Most people I know only have one. Well, now that I live in New York, most people I know have zero."

"I like cars."

"I gathered as much."

"We all have our guilty pleasures." He narrows his gaze on me as he grins slyly. It's sinful to hear the words guilty and pleasure roll from Julian's tongue. I fight to silence the voice in my head telling me how nice it would be to be one of his guilty pleasures, if just for a day. "What's yours?"

"Sex," I answer, not even thinking.

He inhales a sharp breath, his eyes widening. I pull my hand from his, slapping both of them over my mouth, my face reddening to a shade that would probably rival my hair color.

"I mean—"

"Why would you consider sex a guilty pleasure? The term in and of itself infers it's not essential. If you ask me, sex is essential for the continuation of the human race."

"I didn't mean that," I flounder. "It just popped out. That happens sometimes. I don't have a brain-to-mouth filter."

He regards me in quiet contemplation as he opens the front door to the house, allowing me to enter before him. It's dark, apart from a few dim lights illuminating our path to the bedrooms.

"So you were thinking about sex?"

"What? No!" I exclaim. "I…" Trailing off, I exhale deeply, trying to calm my frazzled nerves. "I'd like to retract my original response. Books are my guilty pleasure, okay?"

"Books?"

"Yes." I face forward as we crest the top of the stairs. "Books. Final answer."

"Are you sure you don't want to phone a friend?"

Pinching my lips together, I smile coyly. "Did Julian Gage just make *another* joke?"

"What can I say? I think you're rubbing off on me."

As we come to a stop outside the door to my room, I'm about to reply with a flirtatious retort. Before I can do so, he faces me, zeroing in on my mouth. It reminds me of the tension sizzling between us when he dropped me off Friday night. But it's more pronounced, more intense this time. We've only spent a few hours together, but in those few hours, I have a better insight as to who Julian Gage truly is. Friday I was attracted to him. Now I *like* him. He's more than just a pretty face with an enormous bank account. And I want to know even more, despite the voice in my head warning me against it.

"So…" I chew on my lower lip as I fidget with the hem of the sweatshirt. Then I realize I'm still wearing *his* sweatshirt. "Crap. You probably want this back." I start to pull it off my body when he touches his hand to my arm, stopping me. I drop my hold on it, allowing it to fall back down.

"As fantastic as you looked in that bathing suit, I like you in my sweatshirt more." He advances toward me, the heat in his eyes forcing me to back up against the wall. He leans his forearm on it, curving toward me. "I had a wonderful time with you tonight, Guinevere."

"Me, too." I close my eyes as lust blinds me, the same craving that's teased me all day flickering through me, my skin, my core, my soul aching for this man's touch.

I hold my breath, bracing for his lips to meet mine. Instead, the warmth disappears and I flutter my eyes open. Julian steps back, readjusting his composure, clearing his throat.

"You have a spa appointment tomorrow at noon." It's like he's flipped the switch from fun, lighthearted, sensual Julian Gage to the practical and pragmatic businessman.

"A spa appointment? You didn't have to—"

"Yes, I did. It's part of the ritual, so to speak. If I want people to take our relationship seriously, you need to spend the afternoon at the spa with all the other wives and girlfriends. Sadie will be there. It's all part of the act we need to put on."

"Well then, who am I to complain?" I smile, but it's forced.

"Reed will be waiting for you out front at 11:30. Before then, make yourself at home."

"And where will you be?" I ask flirtatiously in an attempt to bring playful Julian back, but he's gone.

"I need to attend to business-related matters during the day. I'll be back in time to escort you to the gala." Without giving me a chance to ask any more questions, he turns, continuing down the hallway before disappearing into his bedroom.

"Good night," I murmur once I hear the click of his door.

I stare into space, trying to reconcile the two very different versions of Julian Gage. One minute, he tells me how much he worries about me. The next, he runs from me as if he can't stand the sight of me. What could cause these wide swings in demeanor in such a short time? I can't shake the feeling it's all related to the scars marring his perfect skin.

CHAPTER TWENTY-ONE

"OH, MISS GUINEVERE…," Camille breathes after she finishes zipping up my gown, clasping her hands together as she admires my reflection in the mirror. "You are absolutely exquisite."

The person staring back at me may as well be a stranger. My red locks are pulled out of my face and curled into loose beach waves. The cosmetologist at the spa gave me a natural look, only emphasizing my eyes with smoky shadowing, which if I were to try and recreate would end up making me look like a raccoon on a bender.

As amazing as my hair and makeup is, the real attention grabber is the sapphire blue dress. It's something I never would have taken a second look at, with the plunging neckline and slit that goes up to my mid-thigh, but it's a gorgeous gown. The fitted bodice is encrusted with jewels before ending at the waist and transitioning into a flowing tulle skirt. It's unlike any dress I've ever worn, and I doubt I'll ever wear anything this elegant again.

"Mr. Gage will be quite pleased."

I force a smile, pretending to be enthusiastic about the notion. It's a little bittersweet to know I currently feel more beautiful than I ever have, yet it's being wasted on someone who will never appreciate it. This is what I signed up for, though. There are worse ways to spend my Fourth of July than being pampered at a spa, then attending *the* social event of the summer on the arm of a dashingly handsome man. Who cares if he switches from hot to cold in the blink of an eye?

"Thank you, Camille."

"Of course, dear." She meets my eyes in the mirror as she smiles at me in adoration, like a mother would a child. Her excitement strikes me as odd. She knows the truth of what's going on. So why is she acting as if I'm about to leave for a ball to meet Prince Charming?

"Well…" She steps away, grabbing the shoes Dana selected to go with the gown, placing them in front of me. I slide them on, trying not to think about the fact that my entire ensemble probably costs more than my college education. "We shouldn't keep him waiting any longer. He's already on the brink of exploding in anticipation."

"He is?"

"Why wouldn't he be?" She hurries out of my room, striding down the hallway. I practically have to run to catch up. “You’re a beautiful, charming, enigmatic woman he appears to be quite taken with.”

“You and I both know appearances can be deceiving.” I give her a knowing look, silently reminding her this isn’t real. Reminding myself of that fact at the same time.

“They certainly can be. In more ways than you think. Sometimes we act a certain way because it’s all we know, because we believe it’s the only thing that can protect us.” She glances at me, her eyebrows raised.

I slow my steps, my mind racing with questions. It’s obvious she knows something.

“Camille!” I call out, running toward her. When I reach her, I ask, “How long have you known Ju— Mr. Gage?”

She stops walking, turning to face me. “Since he first met Mr. Price, God rest his soul.”

“You worked for him?”

“I did. Started as a housekeeper before he made me his head of household.”

I chew on my lower lip, then quickly release it, not wanting to smudge my lipstick, although I’m confident this stuff could survive the nuclear winter.

“And when did Julian enter the picture?”

She exhales and stares into the distance, searching her memory before looking back at me. “Oh, over twenty years ago now. Mr. Price became like a father to Mr. Gage. And he was the son Mr. Price’s own sons refused to be. At first, I was skeptical about Mr. Gage’s intentions. I guess a part of me thought he was just someone else who wanted to prey on a wealthy, lonely man. I’m normally not one to judge or assume, but when you see a boy of barely sixteen, who looks like he hasn’t had a decent meal in ages, befriend an older man, you assume the worst. But Julian proved me wrong, proved us all wrong.”

She smiles warmly before continuing down the hallway. My brain buzzes with even more questions. Julian Gage is a puzzle I’m eager to solve.

Bunching the fabric of my skirt in my hands, I walk quickly, following her down the stairs. Once we enter the living room, she faces me, doing one last check of my dress to make sure everything’s in place.

As she brushes away a thread, I whisper, “Where did he get the scars on his abdomen?”

She stiffens, inhaling a sharp breath. When she meets my pleading eyes, she slowly shakes her head, conflicted. “Do you believe in soul mates, Guinevere?”

“You can just call me Evie. And yes.” I nod. “I did at one point.”

“I do, as well, but not like most people. I like to think soul mates can include more than just a romantic relationship. I truly believe Mr. Price and Mr. Gage were soul mates. They were both in need of a certain kind of companionship, and they found it in each other." She clutches my hands in hers. "Julian hasn't had the easiest life. There's a darkness that continues to hang over him. Just… Be patient with him. He'll come around." She passes me a reassuring look before turning to walk out of the room.

"But I don't want him to come around." I spin to face her, then lower my voice. "This isn't real."

She glances over her shoulder, smiling. "Whatever you need to tell yourself, dear."

I open my mouth, about to argue my point further, when Julian rounds the corner, coming to a stop the instant he sees me standing in front of the large windows overlooking the ocean. The two-day scruff he's been sporting is gone, his face clean-shaven. His hair's wayward in a sexy sort of way, curling slightly over the collar of his jacket. And his tux… It should be a crime for a man to look this exquisite without being naked. The lines accent his chiseled physique in a way that almost makes me never want to see him with his shirt off again.

Almost.

I'm not that much of a sadist.

I didn't count on missing him as much as I did throughout the day. I shouldn't have longed for his touch, craved his scent, considering the brush-off he gave me last night. I tried to blame it on the fact that I spent the afternoon at the spa with Sadie where we talked with a few other women about my whirlwind romance with Julian. Some of the women, whom I expected to greet me with cold shoulders and upturned noses, ended up gushing over what they viewed to be a real-life Cinderella story, one I could sense they secretly wished for themselves.

"Guinevere…," Julian exhales, his gaze holding steady with mine, his pupils dilating. No one's ever admired me the way Julian does, even when I'm dressed more casually. No one's ever made me feel so beautiful.

Emboldened, I twirl, the layers of the skirt flaring around me as I show off for him.

"I stand corrected."

I stop spinning. "Regarding?" I arch a brow.

With determination, he strides toward me. In an instant, his hand palms my lower back, pressing my body to his. I wonder if this is what Cinderella felt like. If she struggled against hope, knowing once the clock struck midnight she'd have to go back to her ordinary life. Just like I'll be forced to return to the pieces of my life once the summer's over. But that didn't stop her from dancing, from dreaming, from living. Why can't I do the same thing?

Because life isn't a fairy tale. If you wake up missing a shoe, you're not a princess. You simply drank too much. There won't be a prince showing up on my doorstep, a glass slipper in hand, promising to make all my dreams come true. This is the real world, and in the real world, I have to chase my dreams myself.

"Dana."

"Dana?"

"She doesn't just deserve a raise. She deserves everything she could ever want."

He links his hand with mine and spins me around, his motions graceful as he soaks me in. I'm so swept up in this moment, I don't even have to concentrate on maintaining my balance or not tripping over my own feet, as I'm sometimes prone to do. Under Julian's watchful gaze, I feel like I'm flying.

"You look…" He stops twirling me, then brings my body back to his. One hand remains clasped with mine as the other returns to my back. He begins swaying to no music at all, except the song in our heads. And I hear it. It's low and struggling to break through the other noise, but it's there. "You are stunning, Guinevere." The hunger in his gaze softens as he lowers his voice. It's gentle, benevolent, earnest. "I won't be able to leave you alone for a second tonight, not with you looking like this." He leans in, his breath warming my neck. "I won't *want* to leave you alone for a second."

I do everything to keep my composure. Inside, I want to scream at how perfect Julian can be when he wants. He seems to always know exactly what to say so I'll never want to leave his side. I'm still supposed to be heartbroken over Trevor. But in the span of only a few days, Julian's completely endeared me to him. What will he do by the end of the summer?

Placing my hand on his chest, I push against him, needing to put a little distance between us for my own sanity.

"We should go. We don't want to be late, do we?"

He stares at me for a moment. I notice the subtlest hint of his shoulders dropping at the loss of contact. Or perhaps I simply imagine it, my desperation for him to feel this growing connection between us forcing me to see things that aren't real. Then he fixes his expression, that flirtatious smirk I remember from the first time I saw him crossing his mouth.

"I suppose that would be a bad thing." He holds his elbow out for me to place my arm through. "Come on, Princess. Time to get you to the ball."

CHAPTER TWENTY-TWO

DURING MY FIRST month at the magazine, Viv insisted I attend the opening of an art installation at an eclectic little gallery in SoHo. It was the most upscale event I'd ever attended. Waitstaff in tails and gloves. Men in beautiful suits. Women in gorgeous gowns. And Champagne flowing like it grew on trees, which I suppose one could argue it does, since grapes are grown on vines and Champagne comes from grapes.

Nevertheless, that gallery opening was mere child's play compared to the posh and glamour of the annual Red, White, and Blue Gala. Anyone who's anyone is here. And if you don't get an invitation, you're not someone worth knowing.

Which is why my already antsy nerves are even more so, considering the importance of tonight, especially for Julian. As the newcomer to this elite group, all eyes will be on me. Because of that, I need to do everything in my power not to embarrass him. As long as there's not a pool nearby, I think I'll be okay.

The gentle sounds of a jazz band fill the air as Julian leads me through the foyer of a magnificent home situated on the beach. I expected this to take place at a function hall, but I've once again been proven wrong. Why rent a hall when you can show off the grandeur of your home in front of several hundred of your closest friends? That's all life in the Hamptons seems to be. One giant competition. And this place is the crown jewel. It's like a mansion straight from the Gilded Age. Lush tapestries. Grand staircases. Painted ceilings. Now I really do feel like Cinderella.

We follow the flow of guests, smiling polite hellos every few feet before emerging into a large ball room. Waitstaff are in abundance, circling the room, carrying trays of Champagne and *hors d'oeuvres*. I tilt my head back, admiring the intricate detailing on the ceiling.

"It's like the Hall of Mirrors in Versailles."

"*La Gallérie des Glaces*," Julian says in the perfect French accent. "You've been?"

I look back to him, laughing slightly. "No. I've never been out of the country. But I've always dreamed of visiting Europe, particularly Paris."

"You've never traveled abroad?" He sounds genuinely surprised by this fact. I suppose in his circles, it's an odd occurrence.

"Can't say as I have."

"You were with Trevor for twelve years and he never took you?"

I open my mouth to defend him, but Julian interrupts me before I can utter a word.

"You can't tell me he didn't have the money, because I know what that firm pays their attorneys. He could have afforded it."

My eyes shift nervously around the room. Have I really been so blind as to overlook so many of Trevor's shortcomings? "We've both been so busy," I respond, but my words lack any conviction.

"You need to go to Paris. Everyone should experience the city once in their lives. There's nothing like it anywhere else in the world." The more he speaks, the more excited he becomes. There's a boyish gleam in his eyes as his obvious adoration for the City of Lights shines through. "When the summer is over, I'll take—"

I quickly hold up my hand. "Don't."

He scrunches his forehead, perplexed by my sudden change in demeanor. "But—"

"No." I lean toward him, my voice nothing more than a low whisper. "I can pretend to be your girlfriend all summer. I've agreed to that much. But I won't do the fantasy game with you. I won't have you making me promises you have no intention of fulfilling."

"Who said I have no intention of following through?"

"Me. That's who. You're so accustomed to being able to just hop on a chartered jet and fly off to Paris for lunch. That's not my reality. That will *never* be my reality. It's already difficult to remain grounded when I'm surrounded by all this." I wave my hand around. "I don't need you making this any harder than it has to be."

I pull my bottom lip between my teeth, fighting against the lump in my throat. I wish I hadn't revealed this vulnerability to him, but this is challenging enough. The more I remind myself that this is nothing more than a fantasy, the easier it will be when the dream ends.

"Guinevere, I…" He shakes his head, running a light finger down the curve of my face before cupping my cheeks in his hands. He rests his forehead against mine. It's such a tender moment, one I wish were real. "I'm sorry. I guess I got swept up in the moment. I didn't realize…"

"It's okay. But I feel like some lines have been crossed that I may not have originally anticipated. Don't get me wrong," I add quickly. "The past few days have been great. Better than great. And you've been…great." I laugh. "Better than great." My eyes turn back to his, serious again. "And that's why I don't want to blur the lines anymore. It will only set ourselves up for failure. At least me. Because, at the end of the summer, you'll walk away without a single look back, and I'll still be picking up the pieces of a life I don't even recognize right now. Years down the road, we'll both remember this summer and smile. You from your palace overlooking Central Park, and me from whatever apartment I can afford, which will probably be somewhere in New Rochelle. Hell, one day, maybe I'll be able to tell my kids about the summer I experienced a real-life fairy tale. But that's all this is. Just a fairy tale. Not real life."

He opens his mouth, his expression pensive as he gazes at me. I can almost sense him wanting to tell me I'm wrong, that the fairy tale *can* be real. That this *doesn't* have to end after the summer. Instead, he blows out a long breath, nodding.

"I can respect that. I know what it's like to be surrounded by constant disappointment. I won't lead you on. No more fantasies."

"No more fantasies," I repeat, a pang in my heart at the idea.

"No more fantasies," he says once more, then pulls back, smiling a small smile. We return our attention to the party, everyone oblivious to our emotional exchange. Resuming the roles we're here to play, he links his hand with mine. When a waiter carrying a tray of Champagne passes, Julian swipes two flutes, handing me one.

"For the record…" He lifts his glass and I do the same. "I know you'll soon meet someone who will give you the trip to Paris you deserve." He sips the effervescent liquid, his eyes unwavering as they remain glued to mine.

"I hope so," I murmur absent-mindedly.

"Evie!" an excited voice exclaims as I'm about to take a sip.

I search for its source, seeing Sadie and Christopher gliding toward us. That's exactly what it looks like. As if Sadie is walking on air, everything about her poised and put-together. She looks as stunning as I expected she would, wearing a pale white silk gown that hugs her slender frame. Her brown hair is pulled into a bun at her nape, a few strands framing her face. And around her neck is a dazzling diamond necklace that must have cost a small fortune.

"Oh, my goodness…" Grabbing my hand, she spins me around almost in the same fashion as Julian did earlier. "You look incredible. This dress…" She shifts her attention to Julian. "Dana?"

"Who else?" he answers with a laugh.

"Who else indeed. She truly is the best. You'd better keep your eyes on this one tonight, especially around Ethan." She laughs, indicating she's simply making a joke, but Julian knows it's not.

He shifts, wrapping an arm around my waist. For once, I'm certain it's not just for show but his innate need to protect me. The fear streaming from his eyes when he saw Ethan around me last night was far too real to simply be an act.

"He has a thing for the ladies. That's probably why Sonia left him."

This is news to me. I wonder if Chloe knows. "She did?"

A smirk forms on Sadie's lips as she leans closer, her eyes brimming with excitement. She would get along famously with Chloe, both of them bonding over a shared love of gossip. Maybe that's why I've formed such a strong bond with Sadie after only a few days. She reminds me so much of Chloe.

"It's quite the scandal," she whispers. "Last summer, after the Fourth of July, she was mysteriously absent from all festivities, forcing Ethan to attend alone. Then, earlier this year, she was rumored to have been staying with another man while on location for an upcoming movie that was shooting in Vancouver."

"That's not exactly a scandal, Sadie," Christopher interjects, rolling his eyes.

"That's not the scandalous part," she insists, her gaze floating to his before returning to mine. I'm with Christopher. Two celebrities ending their relationship isn't newsworthy these days. "It's rumored this man was a male escort."

My interest piques at this tidbit of information.

"Which sounds ridiculous. I mean, why would someone like Sonia Moreno need to hire an escort? Any man would love to be with her, so why should she pay someone to sleep with her?"

"Maybe it's not about sex," I argue, my own words surprising me. All eyes instantly zero in on me, so I explain, using information I'd gleaned from my brief conversations with August Laurent. "Men and women are programmed differently. As such, they typically hire escorts for different reasons. Yes, most men do so in order to have a quick romp in the sack. Women are different, and I would argue far superior to the male species." I wink as I bring my Champagne flute back to my lips, taking a sip.

"I won't argue with that," Christopher quips. "Not if I want to sleep in the same bed as Sadie tonight." He looks to Julian. "And I wouldn't argue if I were you, either, not if you want to share Evie's bed with her."

"Duly noted." Julian's eyes find mine, wistful and eager. A part of me wonders if he wishes he could share my bed, too.

"As the superior gender," I continue, tearing my gaze from Julian's, "our reasons for hiring an escort are much more complicated than simply wanting to get laid. We do so to feel a connection, to feel adored, to feel beautiful."

The instant I say the words, the air is sucked from my lungs. That is precisely what Julian's done for me. After only twenty-four hours with him, I'm no longer clinging to a life I may never have again. All because he made me feel beautiful. And if Julian, an amateur, can make me feel like this, I can only imagine what August Laurent could do for someone over the course of a month.

"If it's true, I understand why she did it. An escort is discreet."

"Especially this one," Sadie says. "Apparently, he's the most sought-after escort in the country."

My eyes practically bulge out of their sockets as I choke on my Champagne. "August Laurent?" I cough out.

She smiles deviously, waggling her brows. "You've heard of him."

"Evie's working on a story about him for her magazine," Julian explains, his tone boastful. "She hopes that giving the world the inside scoop on the elusive escort will land her a promotion to assistant editor."

"I'd pick up the magazine for that article alone."

I clear the last remnants of Champagne from my throat. "That's what I'm hoping for."

"How's the research going? From what I hear, the guy's an enigma."

"You seem to know a lot about him, Sadie," Christopher teases.

She playfully jabs him in the stomach. "I need to stay educated in case I ever need to use his services." She winks, then turns her gaze back to mine.

"Somehow, he caught wind that I'd been looking for him and reached out to me. I won't reveal too much of what he's told me because I want you to buy the magazine." Everyone laughs politely. "But based on the little information I've gathered so far, I can understand why someone like Sonia Moreno would hire him, especially if she were in the middle of a problematic separation. My boyfriend of twelve years just broke up with me. Ending a long relationship is difficult, even if you've fallen out of love. You think no one will ever love you again, that you're past the age where anyone will find you beautiful. That's what Julian's done for me."

I tilt my head, meeting his eyes. The past twenty-four hours have been a whirlwind, a constant battle of not wanting to get swept up in the fairy tale. Maybe I deserve the fairy tale, regardless of the fact that it's bound to end. That didn't stop Cinderella from going to the ball and dancing with her Prince Charming, even though she knew it was over at midnight. Maybe it's time I take a page out of her book. Stop planning for a future. Live in the moment. Not care about what awaits me a month, a week, a day from now. Right now, I've never felt so cherished, even if this man was a stranger mere days ago.

"He's made me feel beautiful," I continue. "Even if this is just a fleeting romance, I'll always have that."

Staring into his deep pools of blue, everything around us seems to disappear into the background as we share in this moment, this realization that, no matter what happens, I'll forever be grateful to Julian for the gift he's given me. His lips curve into a smile, our mouths inching toward each other.

"Ah, young love," Christopher sighs playfully.

Julian and I snap our heads forward, reminded that we're not alone. He wraps his arm around my waist, then kisses the top of my head. "That it is."

Chapter Twenty-Three

JULIAN AND I spend the next few hours dancing and mingling among the upper crust of the Hamptons. He's unmistakably surprised by the familiarity with which I speak to several of the women, ones who had their noses turned up at me yesterday because I was the new girl. But, just like in high school, people eventually come around.

"And here I was, worried about how you would get on without me," he jokes after dinner as we all file to the expansive exterior verandah to watch the fireworks display.

"I suppose knowing that I'll never see these people after this summer relaxed me a bit. Yes, some of them still don't like me, probably because they secretly wish they were sharing a bed with you instead of their overweight, balding husbands. But the others…" I shrug. "Once they heard our story, they couldn't get enough. I had them swooning and sighing in the salon. They're not much different than anyone else. They want the same things all women do."

"And what's that?" His blue eyes sparkle as he smiles down at me, everything about him relaxed.

"Love. Happiness. And the occasional mind-blowing orgasm."

Julian's throaty laugh fills the air, music to my ears. "Is that all?"

"It's not too much to ask, is it?"

We come to a stop at the stone ledge and I lean on it. "Of course not. We all deserve love and happiness."

"Don't forget mind-blowing orgasms. I'm pretty sure those will inevitably lead to love and happiness. Let's face it. If I found someone who could give me a mind-blowing orgasm, I'd fall in love with him. Which is probably why I've fallen in love with Mr. Winky."

Julian passes me a bemused look. "Mr. Winky?"

I love how easy conversation is with him. Now that I've stopped worrying about a future and am simply living in the moment, I'm no longer on edge. Yes, there are still intense moments between us, but I don't care whether it's real. It doesn't matter. All that does is that I'm happier than I've been in a long time, all because of Julian.

"Please don't tell me you nicknamed Trevor's dick, because I'll never be able to look at him the same way again."

My core clenches when I hear him say dick in his gruff voice. I can only imagine what he's like in the bedroom. Based on the way he acts around me while we merely pretend we're madly in love, I presume he's just as impassioned, if not more so. And I bet he's one hell of a dirty talker.

"No." I fight against the heat washing over my face at the idea of Julian's bedroom voice. "I didn't nickname his dick. And he certainly never gave me mind-blowing orgasms." I add the last part as an afterthought.

"So who's Mr. Winky?" he inquires, and I'm grateful he doesn't push the Trevor issue. In fact, until Julian brought him up, I haven't thought of Trevor all night, regardless that he's also here with Theresa. I'm simply too consumed with Julian and everything he is. The way he dotes on me and takes care of me doesn't leave any room to worry about Trevor.

"Only the best battery-operated boyfriend I've ever had."

He laughs loudly and slings his arm over my shoulders. "I love that you're not embarrassed to talk about this stuff."

I shrug. "It's my job to talk about sex. Literally. Nothing fazes me anymore. I've seen it all. Some things I wish I could unsee."

"I'm not sure I want to know."

"You definitely don't. All I'm saying is there's a fetish for everyone and everything. And I do mean *ev-ry-thing.*"

"Duly noted."

I turn my eyes back to the shore, able to make out the sound of the crashing waves and the fizzling of foam as the saltwater spreads across the sand. It's a cloudless night, the stars twinkling above us against the dark. There's a slight breeze, as there usually is along the coast, causing a chill to run through me, despite the moderately warm temperatures.

Noticing me shiver, Julian shrugs out of his tuxedo jacket, draping it over my shoulders. I glance behind me, offering him a smile of thanks. I expect him to return to my side. Instead, he wraps his arms around my body, pulling me against him, my back to his front. As if this were a dance we'd done dozens of times before, I melt into him, reveling in his embrace. Nothing about this feels stilted or awkward. It's so natural, so familiar, so effortless.

Bathing in his warmth, I smile at a few nearby guests as they assemble to watch the fireworks. Out of the corner of my eye, I spy Trevor standing with Theresa. I must admit, he's rather handsome in his tuxedo, his hair freshly trimmed. Twelve years together and this is the first time I've seen him in a tux. The thought should anger me more, but it doesn't. Maybe if I'd never met Julian I'd be sitting on Chloe's couch, lamenting about how Trevor could leave me for someone boring like Theresa, but it no longer bothers me. Julian's right. So is Chloe. Why should I want to be with someone who doesn't appreciate me for me?

As I observe their awkwardness, struggling to see any connection between the two, Trevor glances in my direction and our eyes meet. He swallows hard when he sees me safe and secure in Julian's arms. Julian must notice Trevor staring. His embrace tightening, he caresses my stomach with his left hand, the one closest to Trevor. The gentle contact sends a rush of exhilaration through me, each brush of his thumb moving higher and higher. I hold my breath as he nears the curve of my breast.

"Is this okay?" he murmurs into my ear, his breath hot on my neck. "I'll stop if you say so. No hard feelings."

"Don't stop," I exhale. There's no way I could tell him no. Not now. Not when I'm wound this tightly. I'm fully aware it's just for show, to make people think we're a real couple, but if that's the only reason Julian's putting on this display, so be it. Who cares if it's not real? All I *do* care about is savoring in this moment. And in this moment, I just want Julian's hands on my body.

"Goddamn," he hisses as he grazes the bottom of my breasts. When he pulls my body even tighter against his, he groans, grinding against me.

"Down boy," I joke. Feeling how turned on he is gives my confidence an added boost. Say what you will, but there's nothing as empowering for a woman as knowing she has the ability to turn on a man, to bring him to his knees, to make him desperate for just a taste, a feel, a touch.

"I can't help it. He has a mind of his own, especially when you're around."

Music fills the exterior speakers and, seconds later, a loud boom echoes. Everyone "oohs" and "aahs" as their attention shifts to the horizon, the brilliant colors of the fireworks bright against the dark canvas. But Julian's attention remains focused entirely on me.

When his hips circle a slow, sensual rhythm against my body, I moan, leaning my head against his chest. I try to concentrate on the fireworks in the sky, not the ones erupting in my core at the sensation of his seductive teasing. My nipples strain against my dress, my body's reaction at odds with the warning my brain sounds, telling me to retreat, that I'd drawn lines for a reason. I couldn't retreat now if I wanted to, a carnal need to experience more of Julian driving me forward, regardless of the possible consequences.

"Do you have any idea how many times I've thought of you these past few weeks?" His teeth skim against my neck, causing a jolt of electricity to rush through me, hot and needy. Surrounded by all these people, I fight to maintain my composure. With each word, each nip, each touch, it's becoming more and more impossible.

"How many?" I manage to squeak out as I keep my eyes glued to the gorgeous display in front of us commemorating our country's independence. I can't help but feel that this weekend marks the start of *my* independence, too. The start of a new chapter in my life.

"I lost count. At the office. In the shower… In my bed."

I bite my lower lip, fantasies clouding my brain. Barging in on Julian when he's at work and seducing him at his desk. Surprising him in the shower and having him slam me against the cool tile, the way he fucks me hungry and insatiable. Then crawling in beside him in the middle of the night. Without a word, he'd show me the tender lover I sense is hidden somewhere beneath the mask. I barely know this man, yet the fantasies in my head are so real, as if someone's able to show me a piece of him I'll never be able to have.

"Have you thought of me?"

"Y-yes," I stammer, squeezing my legs together as pressure slowly builds inside me, on the brink of bubbling over. I fear if it's not released, I'll explode into a vibrant show more brilliant than the fireworks in the sky.

He runs his hands along my stomach, my muscles clenching. With each journey north, he retreats with a path traveling farther south. He presses me into the ledge, shielding curious onlookers from noticing when he dips his hand into the slit of my dress.

"Have you thought of me during one of your dates with your so-called Mr. Winky?"

Normally I'd giggle at the sound of anyone else calling my battery-operated boyfriend by his name. But I'm too turned on to find humor in anything right now. Instead, all I can do is answer truthfully.

"Yes."

"When was the last time?"

"Last night."

"Fuck." His grip on me tightens. The warmth of his hand brushing against the waist of my panties causes my breathing to increase, my chest to heave at the promise of what's to come. "Is this okay?"

"Yes." I adjust my stance, parting my legs slightly, signaling him with my body how much I want this. Chloe and Nora have done the no-strings thing. I can do that, too. I hope. "God, yes."

When he slips his hand beneath the line of my panties, I grip the ledge harder, my jaw clenching as I do everything in my power not to draw attention to us.

"Is this okay?" he asks once more as his fingers leisurely make their way farther south.

"Yes." I'm no longer standing on the verandah of a ridiculously opulent mansion in the Hamptons overlooking the ocean as we watch an excessive fireworks display. I'm flying, the ground nothing but a speck of dust.

He groans again as he brushes his fingers against my skin. "He really did make you get waxed, didn't he?"

"He did."

When he grazes my center, I whimper, in another place, another time, another universe. "Is this okay?"

"Yes."

"I was hoping you'd say that."

His touch becomes firm as he explores me, this entire experience completely out of character for me. Or maybe it's simply because my ex never would have so much as entertained the idea of doing something like this in public. I think that's what makes it even more exciting. The notion that, at any moment, someone could look our way and realize what's going on. But they don't, everyone too immersed in the fireworks, the musical accompaniment being piped in through the sound system loud enough to drown out my pants and pleas for more.

"Guinevere," he growls as he explores me with more intensity, pushing one finger inside before adding another. "Did Trevor ever turn you on like this?"

"No." It's the truth. Never. Not once. There was no spontaneity with him. I thought I liked that. I knew when we'd be having sex. I knew what position we'd be in. I'm starting to think that certain things can't be planned.

"I love that I do this to you. Because you have no idea how fucking hard I am right now. How hard I get every time I think of you. You do it for me. And this isn't me saying it as part of our game. This is me saying it because it's true. I'm starved for you."

"Oh god." My eyes roll into the back of my head as the thunder of fireworks becomes more and more fevered. I was right. Julian is a damn good dirty talker. I'm pretty sure I could come from his words alone. Add in how expertly he massages me and brushes his thumb on my clit and I soon climax in time with the grand finale of the fireworks display, screaming out in utter bliss as applause and cheers fill the air.

Every inch of me trembling, I struggle to make sense out of what just happened, how I should feel about it when I desperately wanted to keep the lines from being blurred. Not only did I just blur them, I pretty much eviscerated them, all because I got swept up in the moment.

"Don't," he rumbles into my ear as he removes his hand, adjusting my dress to hide our indiscretions. I stare forward, my mind racing, chest heaving. "Don't think this is anything more than what it is — two consenting adults enjoying each other's company."

I nod subtly, swallowing hard. How does he know my thoughts are currently clouded with guilt and embarrassment over what we'd just done, how easily I'd allowed him to touch me like that when only one man has in over a decade? I haven't even been single a full month, yet am already spreading my legs for someone else, a relative stranger. Granted, Trevor doesn't seem to be bothered by the idea of being with someone new so soon, but it feels…wrong.

"You deserve to feel beautiful, to feel desired, to feel adored. That's all I wanted. Okay?"

I turn around, locking eyes with him, his expression a mixture of hunger and remorse, a near mirror image of the war currently battling inside my own heart. How can I tell him I want him, but with every second we spend together, the harder it will be to walk away from him at the end of the summer? That if he keeps touching me like that he'll ruin me for all the men who come after him? And there will be men who come after him. He made sure of that. We both did.

"The ball's in your court, Guinevere. If you want to explore this connection further, I'm more than willing. If you're not comfortable with having a strictly physical relationship, I understand that, as well. Just know that I am insanely attracted to you. And I will be no matter what you choose."

My breathing is still labored from the after-effects of the orgasm rolling through me as I peer into his eyes, desperately wanting to crush my lips to his, wrap my arms around him, and allow him to consume me in a way I believe only he can. But can I really do this? I feel like I'm standing in the door of a plane, torn between jumping out and experiencing the exhilaration of flying, or returning to the ground from the safety of my seat.

I'm about to share my fears when Sadie's familiar voice cuts through. "There you two are!"

I jump away from Julian, as if we'd just been caught doing something we shouldn't. I'm not Catholic, but I have a feeling this is what the Catholic guilt I've heard so much about must feel like. I search the area, my eyes settling on her approaching with Christopher and a man I estimate to be in his fifties.

"I've been looking everywhere for you. I wanted to introduce you to my uncle Clinton." She leans in, lowering her voice. "He's my cool uncle." She winks an exaggerated wink as he laughs politely.

"Trust me," Clinton says. "It's not a stiff competition. Most in the family are—"

"Uptight," Sadie offers.

"Pricks," Clinton interjects immediately. "I was going to say pricks." He beams down at Sadie, an affection between them I haven't seen much out here. It's obvious she has a great deal of respect for her uncle, and he has a great deal of admiration for his niece, regardless of any fallout from her marrying Christopher. "But I suppose uptight is more agreeable." He returns his attention back to us, extending his hand toward Julian. "Clinton Alderman."

I stare at it, horrified over the idea of Julian shaking his hand after what he just did, then realize he used his left one with me. If he was that talented with his left hand, I can only imagine what he could do with his predominate one. A blush heats my cheeks as they shake politely.

"Julian Gage."

"Nice to finally meet you, Julian."

"And you." He turns his attention toward me. "This is my girlfriend, Guinevere Fitzgerald."

Clinton looks toward me, his eyes finding mine. But unlike so many other men I've met here, he doesn't appraise me like a piece of meat. He looks at me like I'm a human being. It's refreshing.

"Lovely to meet you, Guinevere."

"Evie," I correct. "You can just call me Evie."

"Evie."

After we all exchange pleasantries, Clinton turns back to Julian. "Sadie mentioned you're in the process of expanding your charitable branch overseas and are trying to get the ball rolling to open up shelters for women in high-risk areas."

I snap my head toward Julian, surprised by this. I'm not sure what I thought this big project of his was. I simply thought it was to build some ridiculously luxurious hotel in Dubai, something that could increase his income substantially. But to find out it's a charitable project? Another piece of the Julian Gage puzzle snaps into place.

"I'm sure I didn't get all the details correct," Sadie adds. "Just what I picked up from Christopher."

"It's something I've been wanting to do for a long time." He turns his attention to Clinton, his demeanor becoming serious, flipping the switch from seductive Julian to businessman Julian. "When I inherited Theodore Price's fortune, the first thing I did was begin a charity here in the States. Our mission is to provide a safe haven for women in abusive relationships. At least here, we get some assistance from criminal justice agencies. Which got me thinking about what it must be like for women in countries and cultures where this kind of abuse isn't frowned upon. In fact, it's *encouraged* as part of their customs. I want to do something to help these women, but expanding overseas isn't as easy as I thought it would be. There's quite a bit of red tape I have to cut through to even consider the possibility."

"Well, I may just be able to help you. I'm not sure what Sadie's told you about me, but I'm in the oil industry."

"I know."

"And in the oil industry, red tape is our specialty." He winks, then jovially slaps Julian on the back. "Come with me. A few of us are digging into Graham Salazar's cigar stash. You should join us."

"I'd love to." Smoothing the lines of his shirt, he steps away from me, exuding all the confidence and poise I've come to expect from him.

"Chris, you should join us, as well."

Christopher's dark eyes widen. He drops his hold on Sadie, joining Julian and Clinton.

"Great to meet you, Guinevere," Clinton offers with a smile.

"Likewise." My gaze shifts from him to Julian. We haven't finished our conversation about the unexpected fireworks display earlier. Maybe it's for the best. Maybe it's one of those things we shouldn't discuss, that we should just forget happened. "You boys enjoy those cigars."

Clinton tips his imaginary hat, then turns, leading Julian and

Christopher away from the verandah.

When the men are out of sight, Sadie winks. "That never would have happened if you weren't here."

"What do you mean?"

"My uncle. He's great, don't get me wrong, but he's from a different generation. He recognizes things aren't how they once were, but he's still from old money. He hasn't fully embraced this new dynamic. It shouldn't matter if Julian *were* a bit of a playboy. But it does to these people. They don't want to be associated with someone like that. So seeing him with a woman…" She shrugs. "Some of them are coming around and accepting him as someone who *will* be around for the foreseeable future, someone they could benefit from doing business with. They're starting to see what I see."

"And what do you see?" I ask, although I'm unsure I want to know the answer.

"I see a man falling hard for a fun, down-to-earth woman."

My face reddening, I avert my gaze, looking back out over the ocean. A breeze picks up and I pull Julian's jacket tighter around my shoulders, basking in the warmth and earthy aroma from it.

"And I see a woman living the fairy tale we all secretly hope for. Enjoy it."

I meet her eyes, smiling a small smile. "I am."

We remain on the verandah for a little longer, making the rounds as Sadie introduces me to even more people. After a while, I politely excuse myself, wanting to take a moment to freshen up. I feel as if my earlier indiscretions with Julian are plastered on my face, in my eyes, on my complexion.

Once my makeup is refreshed and I ensure it doesn't appear as if I'd just had one of the best orgasms of my life, I make my way out of the bathroom and back toward the ballroom. As I skirt past dancing couples, I spy the bar and decide to make a detour before rejoining Sadie.

Approaching the counter, I catch the bartender's eyes and order a manhattan, draping Julian's jacket along the surface of the bar. When he places the drink in front of me, I thank him, opening my clutch to leave a tip. All I have are a few hundreds that Julian left me this morning to use for gratuity at the spa. With a shrug, I place one down. The bartender doesn't even flinch. I surmise he must get that a lot at these kinds of parties.

"You really love those things, don't you?" a voice comments as I take my first sip. I look over the top of my glass to see Trevor standing before me.

"It's a step up from the Boone's Farm we drank freshman year."

He laughs at the memory, a boyish glint in his eyes. It reminds me of the Trevor I first met all those years ago. The one who used to paint his face red for football games. Who used to drag me out to have snowball fights during the winter. Who stood on one of the tables in the dining hall and shouted to the world, or at least a small portion of the student body of the University of Nebraska, how much he loved me.

Then his expression hardens, leaving the man he's turned into. A serious, workaholic who bears no resemblance to the Trevor I fell in love with. Does he feel the same when he looks at me? Is that why he ended things? Did we really commit the awful crime of being too blind to realize we'd fallen out of love with each other?

"You look good, G."

"You clean up pretty nice yourself." Spying a piece of lint on the lapel of his tuxedo jacket, I reach for it and brush it off, an old habit. Once, it felt normal to do something like this. Now it's different. It's not my job anymore. I don't *want* it to be my job anymore.

I raise my glass to my lips, looking around the ballroom. A few weeks ago I would have done anything to have a chance to talk to Trevor like this. Now all I can think is that I hope Julian won't be upset I'm speaking to him, as ridiculous as that sounds.

"I mean it. You look... Wow. I barely even recognize you."

"I could say the same about you."

He furrows his brow. "What do you mean? I wore suits nearly every day the past few years. But you... You seem like a completely different person than I remember."

"That's the problem then, isn't it?" I place my drink on the bar, squaring my shoulders. "Because I'm the same exact girl I was when you broke up with me, Trevor. I haven't changed much in the past twelve years. Sure, I may have a few more pounds and bigger breasts, but everything about me is the same. The way I sleep. The way I talk..." I trail off, my voice wavering, more out of frustration than heartache. Frustration I didn't see the truth years ago. "The way I love. It just wasn't enough for you."

I'd kept my feelings locked up for years, even though I constantly advised my readers not to, that the hallmark of a solid relationship is being open and honest, that keeping your feelings hidden is simply a ticking time bomb. I did just that. I smiled and pretended to be someone I wasn't so Trevor would love me. Nothing about our relationship was ever real. This thing I have with Julian is more real than the love I thought I shared with Trevor.

I lean toward him, my eyes fierce, the veins in my neck strained as I finally tell him exactly how I feel.

"At least now I'm with someone who thinks I *am* enough, who thinks I *am* serious enough to be with. He appreciates me, quirky sense of humor and all." I grab Julian's coat off the bar and turn from Trevor. I only make it a few steps before I stop, whirling around to face him once more.

"You know what? Maybe I *have* changed. Maybe I was tired of having to be someone I wasn't just to make you happy. I'm done with that. Now is the time to make *myself* happy. And Julian makes me happier than you ever did." My chest heaves as emotions overwhelm me. Then I lower my voice. "I'm just sorry it took me twelve years to realize this. Goodbye, Trevor."

CHAPTER TWENTY-FOUR

"OKAY, TELL ME everything," Chloe orders as she flies into my cubicle a little before five on Monday.

She plops onto the free chair, interrupting me from sorting through more of my scribblings about August Laurent. We exchanged several emails over the weekend, in which he revealed more information about his background. Now I'm trying to organize everything into an outline to make it easier to determine which direction to go with his story.

"Nice to see you, too," I respond sarcastically. "Where have you been? And why are you just getting in when it's practically time to leave?"

She smooths her hair behind her ear, avoiding my eyes, which is the Chloe tell that she's purposefully being evasive. "This isn't about me. This is about you. How did it go?"

I study her, unable to shake the feeling she's keeping something from me, but I've been itching to see her since Julian dropped me off at her apartment yesterday afternoon. A nice surprise since I expected Reed to drive me again. When she wasn't home, I had no option but to obsess over every little thing that happened, which resulted in the conclusion that Julian is obviously bipolar. Or, better yet, suffering from multiple personality disorder. What other explanation is there?

"Come on, Evie! Dish!"

"I don't even know where to begin." It's true. It seems like a lifetime's passed since I stepped into that chauffeured town car and was whisked off to the Hamptons for a weekend of excess and privilege.

"Start with what happened when you got there."

I sit back in my chair as I stare into the distance, trying to collect my thoughts. "To be honest, I wasn't sure what to expect, how Julian would act around me, considering this is just supposed to be a business relationship. But when I saw him and he saw me…" A blush builds on my cheeks as I recall the adoration in his eyes when they fell on me wearing that two-piece.

"Yeah?"

"There was a spark."

"But…" She arches a brow, sensing there's more.

"But every single action, every word made me question his motivation. I constantly got swept up in the moment and believed it was all real, only to be reminded it wasn't the next minute. The entire weekend, I felt like we were on a see-saw or playing a constant game of tug-of-war. He'd have me so wrapped up in him I'd forget the reason I was there. Then he'd retreat, acting like I had some infectious disease. And at the gala…" I trail off.

"Yeah?"

"It's just…" I fidget with my hands, still struggling with how to process what happened on the verandah during the fireworks display. Once we left the party, we hadn't spoken of it. For the rest of the weekend, it was as if it had never happened. At first, I considered it to be a good thing. Now I'm not too sure.

"What is it, Evie?" She places her hand on my knee, her voice filled with compassion. "You know you can tell me anything."

I blow out a breath, lifting my eyes to meet hers. "Things got a little…heated." Butterflies flit in my stomach at the memory. "Actually, things got *very* heated."

"Heated?" This catches Chloe's attention. "Heated how?"

I chew on my lower lip, trying to find the right words.

"Come on, Evie!" she all but shrieks. "You're a sex and dating columnist for crying out loud. This shit is what you do for a living."

"He touched me," I blurt out.

She waggles her brows as a slow smile builds on her mouth. "Where? Your arm?"

"You know where," I scoff, rolling my eyes before swooning from the memory. "God, Chloe…" I squeeze my legs together. Just discussing this leaves my body desperate for more. "It was so wild, so crazy, so out of character for me." I lower my voice, inching closer to her. "We were on the verandah. It was a little chilly, so he draped his tux jacket over my shoulders. Then he wrapped his arms around me, keeping me warm. One thing led to another and before I could stop the train from derailing, he slipped his hand under the slit of my dress and took me to pleasure town."

She stares at me, processing my story.

"I wore this dress with a long, flowing skirt. There was so much fabric, it masked what was really going on."

She waves me off. "I know what you were wearing."

I blink at her. "You do?"

"Of course. Photos were all over the gossip websites as everyone tried to figure out who the mystery woman on Julian Gage's arm was. That's not what I'm questioning."

"It's not?" I ask, unsure what to think of my photo being plastered all over the Internet. I knew this would happen, but I'd been living in my fantasy world all weekend. This explains why my mother's been trying to get in touch with me. She probably saw my picture with someone other than Trevor. I make a mental note to call her and tell her we broke up, considering I no longer have any interest in getting back together with him.

"Pleasure town, Evie?" Chloe bursts into a giggling fit. "Really? That's what you're going with? Did you ride his rocket all the way there, too?"

"No! There was no rocket riding. There was no rocket fondling. Hell, I never even caught a glimpse of the launch pad, although I certainly felt it." I laugh along with Chloe. This is exactly what I needed, a few moments with one of my best friends to make sense out of the weekend.

"But he worked your…command center?"

"Did he ever. The fireworks in the sky were nothing compared to the explosions down below. He knows his way around…ground control."

"Okay, okay." Chloe waves her hands in front of her, tears forming in the corner of her eyes as she struggles to breathe. "You need to stop with all these spaceship references or I'll never be able to watch *Apollo 13* again, and you know how much I love Kevin Bacon."

It takes a few minutes, but our laughter gradually wanes. When it does, she comments, "So you broke the no kissing rule."

"What? No."

"But you let him—"

"Explore ground control," I interrupt with a smile.

"Find your pleasure center," she corrects, "yet you still refuse to kiss him?"

"It worked for Julia Roberts' character in *Pretty Woman*."

"Actually, it didn't. She still ended up falling for Edward."

"Because she kissed him. I haven't kissed Julian; ergo, I won't fall for him."

She assesses me with her analytical stare, then states, "Are you sure you haven't already?"

"I'm not sure of anything, Chloe," I admit after a pause. "All I do know is being with Julian made me realize I haven't been true to myself. I put on an act for Trevor so he'd love me. You were right. I shouldn't waste my time on someone who doesn't appreciate me for me. And Julian does. He makes me happy, makes me feel beautiful. Even if it's only for a few months, it'll be worth it."

Her eyes brimming with enthusiasm, she wraps her arms around me, planting a kiss on my temple. "I'm happy for you. Don't think about the future. Have fun. Live in the moment. Let Julian explore your command center until he has all its functions worked out properly. Hell, maybe you can even play on his launch pad."

I laugh, this entire conversation bordering on ridiculous, but in a way that makes me feel incredibly grounded in reality.

Pulling away, she holds me at arm's length, her eyes trained on mine. "You've always been a planner, and I love that about you. Your obsession with planning out every second of every day with stickers and notes is quirky and adorable and what makes Evie…Evie." She drops her hold on me, then continues. "I'll admit, I was skeptical of this arrangement at first, since I know how you are, but now… I don't know. You're...different. I *like* this side of Evie. You're confident and self-assured."

I give her a sanctimonious look. "I've always been confident and self-assured. Need I remind you I got up in front of an entire bar a few weeks ago and told them all about my embarrassing breakup?"

"That doesn't make you confident and self-assured. All that evidences is the fact you've been screaming for someone to notice you because Trevor never did. Now someone finally has. So who cares if nothing comes out of this? Stop making plans for the future. Enjoy the ride." She pulls me closer again.

"On his rocket ship," I add, then we both burst out laughing.

"Come on," Chloe says when she sees it's after five. "Izzy's off today. Let's all go surprise Nora at the yoga studio and hijack one of her classes."

I get up from my chair, grateful for one night of normalcy in a life I have trouble recognizing these days. "That sounds perfect."

I gather my things, and within a few minutes, we're in the elevator on our way to the lobby. As it descends, I steal a glance at Chloe and smile. She scrunches her brows, knowing I'm about to do something crazy. When I start singing Elton John's "Rocket Man", she stifles a laugh, covering her mouth with her hand. Everyone else in the elevator glances sideways at us. Then Chloe joins in, which causes me to sing louder. Much to my amusement, a few of our fellow passengers join in. By the time the elevator reaches the lobby, we're all singing the chorus. But we don't stop once we exit. We continue belting out the lyrics as we all make our way toward the doors.

I'm so wrapped up in the strange, impromptu moment that could only happen in a place like New York City, and in a building that houses a slew of magazine offices, I almost don't recognize the man leaning against a column in the lobby until Chloe grabs my arm, forcing me to stop.

My breath hitches when my eyes fall on Julian. He looks rather dashing in the charcoal gray suit he makes casual by foregoing the tie and leaving the top few buttons of his shirt undone. Sunglasses obscure those deep blue orbs that are permanently ingrained in my head, but I can still feel their heat. Everything about him is so effortless, so confident, so compelling. It's no wonder everyone passing him pauses to look. A few women even giggle, probably wishing they were lucky enough to spend time with him. But I'm the lucky one. I think…

He pushes off the column and walks toward me, lowering his sunglasses. "Guinevere…"

The way my name rolls off his tongue is incredibly erotic. Even more so now that I've been treated to a taste of his bedroom voice.

"Julian." I straighten my posture, doing everything to make it appear as if his presence doesn't have my stomach in knots.

"Do I want to know what caused that impromptu rendition of 'Rocket Man'?"

"Definitely not." I can only imagine his reaction if he were to find out Chloe and I reduced what happened on the verandah to aeronautical terminology.

"I didn't think so."

I attempt to slow my racing heart as we stare at each other. I hadn't expected to see him again until Friday morning when I'm to head back to the Hamptons to attend a charity art auction aboard some heavy hitter's ridiculously large yacht. At least I didn't think I was supposed to see him. Perhaps I overlooked something.

"Good to see you, Chloe," Julian says, finally acknowledging I'm not alone.

"You, as well, Julian. To what do we owe the…pleasure?" She discreetly pinches my side. I bat her away, struggling to maintain my composure.

"I came to collect Guinevere." He shifts his gaze back to mine, a mysterious aloofness about him.

"Did I forget about something?" Frantic, I reach into my commuter bag to retrieve my planner, where every event I'm set to attend has been written down and color-coded. "I could have sworn—"

A hand reaches out, forcing me to let go of my planner, my life. Glancing up, I'm met with Julian's smirk.

"Put the calendar away. You didn't forget anything."

I blink, swallowing hard at the intensity in his stare. "I didn't?"

His lips turn into a playful smile as he shakes his head, slow and flirtatious. "No."

"Then—"

"I stopped by to see if you wanted to do something."

"Chloe and I were planning on dropping by Nora's yoga studio—"

"But I was just telling Evie how exhausted I am from a crazy weekend," Chloe interrupts, faking a yawn before winking conspiratorially. Squeezing my arm, she passes me a sly grin, then leans toward me, her voice a low whisper. "Don't think. Enjoy the ride…on his rocket."

I snort out a laugh, then instantly cover my mouth.

"Bye, you crazy kids!" Chloe calls out, waving as she heads off.

Once we're alone, Julian returns his attention to me. "So it's settled. We'll do something."

"What about the itinerary?"

"The itinerary?"

"Yes. The itinerary." Passing him a coy smile, I bat my lashes. "That was part of our deal. You promised we'd only have to see each other during pre-approved times."

In an instant, his playfulness disappears, his expression turning impassioned and carnal as he closes the distance between us. When his hand palms my back, forcing me against him, I gasp. My legs weaken as every synapse in my body fires at the same time.

It's official. Julian Gage is the most potent drug known to man. He should be regulated and come with a warning to all females…and perhaps a few men.

Side effects include wet panties, labored breathing, and irregular heartbeat. May cause multiple orgasms upon even the slightest touch. Consult a doctor prior to repeated use.

He leans toward me, his voice a heady growl. "Fuck the itinerary."

CHAPTER TWENTY-FIVE

FUCK THE ITINERARY indeed.

Over the next several weeks, that's precisely what Julian and I did. I still accompanied him to the myriad of events that seemed be the hallmark of summer in the Hamptons, where he continued to try to convince many of the power players that his project was worth them investing their time and connections, but we also spent time together away from the Hamptons.

On more than one occasion, he made the trek back to the city to take me to dinner, or for a walk through Central Park, or to see *Hamilton*…after I'd mentioned I'd yet to see it and doubted I'd ever be able to score a ticket. He claimed he needed to come into the city for work anyway, but the fact that he seemed to spend many work hours with me made me believe otherwise.

When I wasn't with Julian, I worked tirelessly on getting more of a feel for who August Laurent truly is. Now I know why Viv was so eager to green light this story. He's incredibly tight-lipped. Yes, over the course of our phone conversations and email exchanges, he's given me some insight into what he does and why, all revolving around the theme of empowering women and making them feel beautiful during a difficult time. But the article is missing something. No matter how many times I've written and rewritten it, it's not the gripping exposé I'd originally envisioned. Not without more than he's given me.

I tried to press for details about his clients, even asking if I could talk to a few with a guarantee of complete anonymity, but he denied my request instantly. Without any other option, I asked if the rumors about him and Sonia Moreno were true. I thought perhaps that would encourage him to open up more. I may have overplayed my hand because an entire week has gone by without so much as a response to any of my emails.

Before Viv approached me regarding this promotion, I'd always enjoyed my work. Writing for the sex and dating columns has been one of the least stressful jobs I've ever had. Yes, there are deadlines and Viv can be particular with how the articles are worded and presented, but after a while, I learned what she liked and adjusted my style to match her preference. Now I can't help but feel like a complete failure, like I'm not cut out for this. Maybe my parents are right. Maybe I'm better suited to teach.

When Julian picks me up on the second Friday in August for my obligatory weekend in the Hamptons, I try not to let this roadblock affect my mood, but it's obvious something's bothering me. The instant I'm in the front seat of his Porsche Spyder…or as I've affectionately renamed her, Monday…Julian notices.

"You okay?" He steals a glance at me as he merges into traffic.

I float my eyes from the trendy buildings that make up the East Village, forcing a smile. "Of course."

"Are you sure? You seem…off." He shifts into third as he continues up First toward the interstate.

"I'm fine. Everything's fine."

"Fine?"

"Yes. Fine."

"Hmm."

"What?" I tilt my head.

"During his lifetime, Mr. Price offered a great deal of advice, most of it regarding operating and building a successful business. But he also gave me real-world advice." Licking his lips, he glances at me, our eyes locking before he returns his attention to the road. "One of the things he told me was if a woman ever says she's fine, I should run for cover."

I laugh softly as I gaze at him, a nostalgic twinkle in his eyes.

"You're not fine, Guinevere. Remember what I said at the beginning. No lies. It's the only way this will work. Tell me what's bothering you." His voice is soft and comforting as he grasps my hand in his.

"I thought we weren't going to do the whole sharing of our sob stories?"

"Is it a sob story?" he asks hesitantly.

"No. Just some trouble at work." I grit out a smile. I've tried to keep my troubles to myself, considering Julian has his own problems with getting his project up and running. "Nothing to concern yourself with. Don't worry. I'll be my usual charming self this weekend. I need to figure out my next step. That's all."

He abruptly pulls the car to the side of the road, putting on his hazards. In typical New York fashion, horns blare and drivers shout expletives as they pass, flipping him off. It doesn't deter him.

"What are you doing?"

Once he shifts into neutral and engages the parking brake, he faces me, his eyes hardened. "I never intended this arrangement to cause you problems at work. You don't have to come with me this weekend."

"It's not," I insist. "This is a me issue. It has nothing to do with our arrangement. I guess I didn't realize how difficult…" I trail off.

"How difficult what?"

"Don't worry about it."

He brings his hand to my cheek and I melt into him. He tenderly grazes his thumb over my bottom lip. It's a subtle, gentle touch, one most may not react to. But that's all it takes to ignite the spark, the unquenchable thirst building inside me. Now that I know exactly how it feels to have Julian's hands on the most intimate parts of my body, that thirst has only increased. There have been so many instances I've been on the brink of initiating something more.

Like when he took me to a pottery class. I thought it would be fun to recreate the scene from *Ghost*, complete with appropriate background music, which I sang myself. The way he stared at me, his eyes dancing with amusement as he tried not to laugh at the spectacle I made, only increased the connection I felt to him. Trevor would have tried to hide out of embarrassment. Not Julian.

Like when he surprised me with a trip to one of the most beautiful bookstores I'd ever seen. He barely took his eyes off me as I roamed the aisles in wonder of all the stories filling the gorgeous space. I'd asked Trevor to take me there dozens of times. I never even had to ask Julian. He did it because he knew I'd enjoy it.

Like when he realized I started waking up early to watch the sunrise over the ocean. He began getting up, too. Now, whenever I open the French doors and step onto the balcony of his exquisite home, he's waiting for me, holding a cup of coffee prepared the way I like it. Trevor never made coffee for me.

Regardless of how close we've become, the ball's remained firmly in my court. There have been countless opportunities for me to toss it back to him. But I haven't, scared it will ruin what we've built.

"I told you. I'll always worry about you. If you'd rather stay in the city to focus on work, I understand."

"Thank you." I sigh, finding comfort in his words. There are so many sides to Julian, I can't decide which I like best. One minute, he can be mysterious and aloof. The next, sweet and compassionate. And still the next, tortured and defeated. All parts that make up this man who's unwittingly found his way under my skin where he's burrowed so deeply I'm unsure whether I'll be able to let go. But, in less than a month, I have to do just that.

Swallowing hard, I pull back, forcing him to drop his hold on me. "Maybe a weekend away to clear my head is what I need. Sometimes the best medicine is a little sun and sand." I turn my lips into a small smile.

"Are you sure? I really don't mind—"

"It's fine," I interrupt, crossing my arms in front of my chest as I tap my foot, feigning annoyance. "And if you don't take me, I'll hop on a train and show up at your house, so you may as well enjoy my company for another two hours." I pass him a playful look, winking. "Plus, as if the hair weren't a dead giveaway, I'm Irish, and I have the stubbornness to prove it. You're not going to win this battle with me, Mr. Gage."

Pinching his lips together, he studies me for a moment, then pushes out a breath. "Fine. We'll compromise."

"Compromise?"

"Precisely." Disengaging the parking brake, he presses his foot on the clutch before shifting into first and pulling back into traffic without signaling. Horns honk all around us, but Julian ignores them.

New York drivers.

"And what would that be?" I lean against the seat, tilting my head to admire him. God, I love the confidence he exudes when he drives, the way he handles the car stirring too many fantasies to the surface of my subconscious.

"You can spend the weekend with me in the Hamptons, but just me." He lifts his brows.

"Just…you?" I swallow hard, my pulse increasing.

"Exactly. No parties. No dinners. No distractions. Just us and whatever we want to do. We'll be on our own schedule. No one else's."

"Just us?"

Approaching a traffic light, Julian presses on the brake, coming to a stop. As he licks his lips and curves toward me, I almost combust right there, the proximity of his mouth to mine making me want to erase the last bit of space between us and finally have a taste of what I've fantasized about since my first weekend in the Hamptons. Since he picked me up for our first dinner together. Since I first saw him from across the bar on what I thought was the worst night of my life.

"Just us," he confirms.

On a hard swallow, I slowly nod. "Okay. Just us."

"Perfect." He grins, pulling away from me. "Oh, and by the way..."

"Yes?"

"You have no idea what hearing you call me Mr. Gage does to me, Guinevere," he growls, the husky rumble hitting me deep in my core. I open my mouth, stunned, unsure how to respond to his brazen flirting. Thankfully, the light turns green and he puts the car back into gear, following the flow of traffic.

I blow out a long breath, smoothing a ringlet behind my ear as I squeeze my legs together, praying he doesn't pick up on how on edge I am. If he does, he doesn't say anything.

When we walk into Julian's house after an uneventful drive, it's unusually quiet. Normally the foyer is bathed with light, heavenly aromas of whatever Camille has prepared for me to eat upon my arrival meeting me. Now it appears like a ghost town.

"Where is everyone?"

"I gave them the weekend off," he explains as he heads toward the stairs.

"You did?"

"Yes."

"When did you do that?"

"When you dozed off on the drive."

"I'm sorry. I'm a horrible fake girlfriend. I've just been really tired lately, and—"

"Has anyone told you how adorable you are when you snore?" He continues up the stairs and down the corridor leading to the wing where our bedrooms are located.

"I do *not* snore."

"You do. Don't worry," he adds quickly. "It's not this big, gravelly snore that makes me worry you're about to keel over and die. It's this little snore, almost like a whistle."

"A whistle?"

"Yes. A whistle. Music to my ears, baby doll."

When we reach the door to what's become my room, he doesn't stop, continuing toward his, leaving me confused. Every other weekend, there's been an itinerary full of events for us to attend. Without that, I'm uncertain what to do, how to act, who to be.

"Julian?" I call out. He spins around, arching a brow. "What are we doing?"

"You wanted a bit of sun and sand. Go put on a swimsuit. I'm taking you out on my boat."

I chew on my lower lip. "I'm not sure I have one for this weekend. This wasn't on the itinerary, so I doubt Dana set one aside. There are a few outfits in case of emergency, but I didn't see an extra bathing suit."

"Just put on one you've already worn. If I can make a suggestion…" He grins a devious smile. "That two-piece you wore your first day here was…" His eyes harden as his pupils dilate, the vein in his neck throbbing.

"Yes?" I bat my lashes.

"Hot, Guinevere. It was fucking hot."

Chapter Twenty-Six

"HOLY CRAP," I moan as I revel in the flavors dancing on my tongue. Garlic. Butter. The spiciness from the bold cabernet Julian opened to complement our meal.

"Why do you sound so surprised?" he replies in a smooth voice, smirking as he raises his wine glass and takes a sip, swirling the liquid around his mouth. His eyes never leave me as I indulge in his exquisitely prepared dinner. I sense he likes watching me enjoy the fruits of his labor.

"I never pegged you for the type who could cook." I tear my gaze from his, looking at the darkened ocean from the small bistro table on the patio overlooking the pool where we currently dine. The breeze wraps around my skin that's sun-kissed after spending several hours relaxing and reading on the deck of Julian's boat. But any chill that would normally find me is chased away by the fire pit.

Everything about today has been perfect. For the first time since we began this charade, it felt authentic, like we were a real couple enjoying each other's company instead of putting on a show for everyone. He took me out on his boat, then let me drive one of his cars into the downtown area, where we indulged in ice cream. Seeing a farmer's market, we stopped and picked up the steaks we're currently savoring.

"Especially this well," I add as I slice into the filet mignon once more, the preparation rivaling that of any steak I've had in recent memory.

"I guess there's a lot about me you don't know."

"There certainly is, Mr. Gage. So why don't you tell me something else most people don't know about you."

After a moment of contemplation, he shakes his head. "You first."

I lift my brows. "Me first?"

"Precisely. You just learned I enjoy cooking. I want to know something interesting about you, Miss Fitzgerald."

"Okay." I adjust my posture, squaring my shoulders. "What would you like to know?"

He pinches his chin, studying me. "What would you like to tell me? What are your likes, dislikes, hobbies, stuff like that?"

"I enjoy saying 'You're welcome' loudly when someone doesn't say thank you."

Julian bursts out laughing. "I'd love to be around to see that. But how about something serious?"

"That is serious."

Not saying a word, he narrows his eyes.

"Fine." I push out a breath. "I speak four languages."

"Is that right? And here I was trying to impress you with my knowledge of French. Which do you speak?"

"English."

"Obviously."

"But I'm also fluent in profanity, sarcasm, and pirate."

He chuckles, but it quickly fades, his expression contemplative. "Why do you do that?"

"Do what?"

"Use humor as a mask."

I blink repeatedly, his words surprising me. "I don't use humor as a mask," I insist as I avert my gaze.

"You do. Over the summer, I've picked up on that. Anytime we broach a subject you're uncomfortable with, you make a joke. Granted, I think your sense of humor is incredibly sexy, but I often wonder what you're hiding, what skeletons lurk in your closet to cause this uncertainty or apprehension."

"There are no skeletons in my closet."

"Everyone has skeletons."

"Do you?"

Julian's jaw hardens, his stare becoming distant. I'm reminded of the scars on his abdomen, of Camille's warning that there's a darkness hanging over him. I've seen it firsthand. One minute, things will be great. Better than great. Then something happens to force him to withdraw into himself.

"I do," he finally says, surprising me. I expected him to avoid the question. "Like I said. Everyone has skeletons."

"Well, I don't." I stab one of my brussels sprouts with my fork, bringing it to my mouth. "I had the perfect life. My parents are still married and live in the same town. Dad was my high school principal and Mom's an Honors English teacher in the next town."

"Siblings?"

"An older brother."

"And what is it he does?"

"He's an English professor at the University of Nebraska."

"And you studied English, as well, didn't you?"

"Yes."

"But you're not a teacher. Excuse me for saying, but it appears as though that's the normal track, at least in your family."

"That's true, but—"

"But you didn't want to teach, did you?"

I shake my head as a small smile forms on my lips. "That was *their* dream for me, not mine."

"Then tell me…" He leans back in the chair, his eyes bemused. "What is Guinevere Fitzgerald's dream?"

"This conversation feels awfully one-sided."

"How so?"

"You're giving me the third degree, yet you don't have to answer my questions?"

"You can find anything you'd like to know about me on the Internet. The same doesn't go for you."

"Not everything…," I draw out, but he ignores my comment.

"So tell me your dreams, baby doll."

When he uses such an endearing term, I'm cast under his spell, opening like a flower, urged to spill my secrets, hopes, frustrations, things I never even shared with Trevor, mainly because I didn't want him to worry about my problems when he had his own worries with college, law school, and his career.

I've often told my readers that relationships aren't fifty-fifty. Sometimes you have to do a little more heavy lifting to help your partner through a difficult time, just like they'll have to do the same for you. It's more like a see-saw. There are ups and downs, but it eventually evens out.

It was never really even with Trevor. I was always the one using all my weight to lift him up, sacrificing my dreams so he could achieve his own. I deserve better than that. Now, thanks to Julian, I realize that. This makes me want to share things I've kept inside.

"Ever since I was a little girl, I've dreamt of being a writer," I say finally. "That's all I wanted. I remember sneaking into my parents' room and stealing one of my mother's romance novels when I was only twelve or thirteen. I'd hide away in my room and devour it in hours. That's when I fell in love with…love. And unrealistic expectations." Laughing at how naïve I was back then, I look at the ocean waves with an unfocused gaze. When I sense the heat of his stare on me, I return my attention to my dinner, taking a bite of my steak before I continue.

"Sure, I read the classics, like any person who loves the written word. But like my mother, sometimes you want the fantasy, too. Although I don't think I realized it was just a fantasy. So, being the planner I am, I made a list of who my dream man would be. I pictured it all in my head. I'd meet the love of my life in college when I was old enough to have some experience, but young enough that we'd both come into adulthood together. We wouldn't rush into getting married right after graduation, as I researched the statistics and the success rate of marriages increase as you near thirty. He'd be a professional of some sort. A doctor…"

Julian lifts a brow. "Or lawyer…"

"Yes. Or a lawyer. We'd spend our twenties finding out who we are individually and as a couple, as we'd both navigate our chosen career paths."

"And what would your chosen career path be? In this plan you made for your life, I mean."

"I always wanted to write for a magazine. Being a writer is often considered a lonely profession, and it is. I love the idea of being part of a team, so that's why I wanted to go the magazine route."

"Then why didn't you study journalism?"

"I did my research. Many of the columnists at the top magazines had non-journalism degrees — English, political science, art design. So I studied English, despite my parents insisting I study education with an emphasis in English, if only to have it as an option in case things didn't work out. For a while after graduation, I thought maybe I should have taken their advice. I moved out to New York. Yes, it was to be near Trevor, but also to be in New York, where so many magazine offices are located. I had so much hope and drive those first few months…until I realized how difficult it was to crack into the industry. They were all looking for someone with experience. I had none, apart from working on the university newspaper and magazine. It was by pure luck I even landed the job at *Blush*. When I saw the posting, Trevor told me I was crazy for applying since I lacked any of the qualifications. But that didn't stop me. I figured it was better to get rejected by the magazine than myself."

"If you weren't qualified, how did you get the job?"

I shrug. "By doing what it appears I do in all uncomfortable situations." I pinch my lips together, giving him a knowing look. "I made Viv laugh. I used humor in my cover letter. It caught her attention, so much so that she brought me in for a chat. She was trying to shake things up at the magazine, bring in fresh talent. So she told me to come back in a week with a piece she could run in the sex and dating column. That was when I concocted a tongue-in-cheek article about what all women should do for the first thirty days of any relationship in order to keep the guy interested. It starts out pretty innocent, but as you continue reading, you realize it's satire."

"I'm not sure I want to know what's in it."

I smirk. "You probably don't. But Viv loved it. Better yet, readers loved it. It was the most read article on the website the week it published. So Viv hired me, much to my parents' chagrin. Like Trevor, all they think I do is write about sex without any substance. So having a chance at this promotion and writing an article about something other than the best sex position for maximum pleasure is exactly what I've been searching for ever since I told my parents I didn't want to pursue teaching. But now…"

"Yes?" He places his elbows on the table, leaning toward me.

"The story's falling apart and there's nothing I can do to stop it."

"I'm sure it's not that bad."

"It's not to the level I need it to be if I want this promotion."

"This is the August Laurent piece?"

I nod. "All I have is his perspective, his side of things. It's too one-dimensional. There's no drama, no compelling reason people would want to know more about this guy. But I know there's a story there, that there's more to him than he's told me. But to figure that out, I need to talk to some of the women who've hired him. Unfortunately, he flat out refused to reveal any of their identities, even when I guaranteed their names would never be disclosed. I thought I'd try to encourage him and mentioned I'd heard the rumors of him and Sonia Moreno, asking if it were true. He never responded. It's been over a week.

"So not only is the piece complete crap, he's no longer cooperating. There's no way I can submit this story to Viv like it is and hope to be promoted. Hell, as it stands now, she won't even publish this piece as a column, let alone a feature story."

"You sure about that? There must be another way, a different angle you can take to make it compelling."

"I've tried." I push my now empty plate away. "Boy, have I tried. I've written and rewritten that article a couple dozen times. No matter what I've done, it still falls flat." I stare into space, trying to figure out a solution, but it remains out of reach. I shake off the thought, smiling at Julian, my voice brightening. "But I don't want to think about that right now. The idea that my parents were right about teaching being the best career path for me will only depress me. For the rest of the weekend, I want to pretend I'm not a complete failure."

"You're not a failure, Guinevere. You're an extremely talented writer. You just need—"

I shoot up my hand, silencing him. "Not now."

"Going to pull another Scarlett O'Hara?" He smiles slyly as the memory of the night we met fills me with warmth. We certainly have an unusual story, one most people would never believe, one you read in romance novels and fantasize about. Like I've said from the beginning…it's a real-life Cinderella story. Except this version won't end with Julian tracking me down after he finds my glass slipper. It will end when the clock strikes midnight, no matter what.

"Why, Mr. Gage…," I coo in my best Southern accent, burying the thought. Maybe he's right. Maybe I *do* use humor to mask my emotions. "That is absolutely what I plan to do. Because—"

"I know, I know. 'Tomorrow is another day.'"

When I hear Julian speak with a Southern drawl, I practically come in my chair. It's almost as beautiful as listening to him speak French. Truth is, the mere sound of his voice sets my heart aflame.

"Yes, it is."

He pushes back from the table and takes a few steps toward me, extending his hand. I eye him as my fingers link with his, standing up.

"So what would you like to do *tonight*?"

"We can always make a fashionably late appearance at whatever party's scheduled. That way, you're not sacrificing your entire weekend."

"Out of the question. This weekend is all about you. If you weren't here, what would you be doing? How did you spend most of your Friday nights before we met?"

"Usually watching a movie and being a complete couch potato."

"Then let's be couch potatoes."

I step back, brow furrowed. "Really?"

"Yes. What's so surprising about that?"

"You don't strike me as the couch potato type."

"Didn't that steak teach you?"

"Teach me what?"

Leaning toward me, his breath tickles my neck. "I'm just full of surprises."

With that, he pulls me away from the patio and into the house, despite my protests that we need to clean up. He assures me he'll take care of it later, then leads me to a part of the house I've yet to spend any meaningful time in…the theater room. It's impressive, an enormous projection screen across the far wall. About a dozen leather recliners fill the tiered setup, along with a lush sectional in the front, which is where he heads.

"What do you want to watch?" He settles into the corner of the couch, draping his arm over the back. "Name the movie and it's yours."

"Any movie at all?"

"Any movie at all," he confirms.

"Even a chick flick?" I walk toward him, sitting next to him on the couch, but leaving a few inches between us. "You'd seriously be happy watching some sappy romance?"

"Like I said, this is *your* night. If you want some sappy romance, sappy romance you shall have."

"And if I wanted to watch porn?"

His eyes grow intense as he narrows them on me. "*Do* you want to watch porn?"

"If I did?"

"Whatever Evie wants, Evie gets." The sensuality in his tone has me squirming in my seat. "What does Evie want?" He toys with a few tendrils of hair in my ponytail, the light touch sending a shiver down my spine. "What movie makes you happy?"

A slave to his touch, I say the first thing that pops into my mind. "*Breakfast at Tiffany's*."

His mouth gradually curves into a brilliant smile. "You got it." He grabs a remote and presses a few buttons. The screen sparks to life. After sorting through a few menus, he hits play and the familiar strains to the opening measures of "Moon River" fill the room.

"We don't have to watch this if you don't want to," I say quickly, crossing my arms. "I'm sure you'd much rather watch something with big explosions and lots of boobs."

Shaking his head, he wraps his arm around my shoulders, enclosing me in his embrace. "Absolutely not." He props his long legs onto the cushioned ottoman in front of us. "Actually, this is one of my favorite movies."

I tilt my head, meeting his eyes. "It is?"

"It is."

I peer into his deep blue pools. "Why is that?"

"I like the story. How even someone who didn't think she was worthy of being loved eventually found someone who did love her."

"Everyone deserves to be loved," I whisper as my gaze remains locked on his. He reaches out, brushing an errant curl behind my ear, his finger tracing the lines of my face. My heart rate increases as desire heightens deep in my core. I focus on his lips, what they must taste like. I've thought of little else the past few weeks, how much I want to kiss him, but I fear I won't be able to stop at just a kiss. I'd want more. I'd want everything he's adamantly insisted he could never offer me.

"Come on." He clears his throat, the moment breaking before it had a chance to begin. He gestures to the screen. "Watch the movie."

I peer at him for a moment longer, then shift my eyes to the movie, watching as Holly Golightly, wearing an oversized nightshirt, accessorized with an eye mask and earplugs, meets Paul Varjak. I laugh at the absurdity, reminded of my own initial meeting with Julian, how I was thrust into his life just as Holly and Paul were thrust into each other's.

I nuzzle into Julian's chest, inhaling a deep breath of his familiar scent. The first time I smelled this soothing aroma, I nearly had a heart attack, thinking I'd just had a one-night stand. Heat radiates through me as I reflect on how far we've come since the night I expelled the contents of my stomach all over my dress and his shoes.

He rests his hand on my hip, lightly tracing different patterns on the small slice of exposed skin between my tank top and maxi skirt. It relaxes me even more than Julian's mere presence does.

"I like this," I murmur, no longer worried about how he'll respond to my admission.

Leaning down, he places a soft kiss on the top of my head. "I like this, too."

That's the last thing I remember before dozing off, the gentle beating of his heart the perfect metronome to lull me to sleep.

Chapter Twenty-Seven

A SOFT SNORE rips through my slumber and I flutter my eyelids open, my surroundings unfamiliar at first. Then the day trickles back… Spending the afternoon with Julian. Having dinner with Julian. Falling asleep cocooned in Julian's warm embrace as we watched *Breakfast at Tiffany's*, where I remain. The movie still plays on the screen, but it's the final scene where Holly Golightly frantically searches for Cat in the alley, rain pouring down on her.

When she locks eyes with Paul, I lift my own to Julian, observing the gentle rise and fall of his chest as he sleeps peacefully. The sight brings a smile to my face. Despite practically living together these past several weeks, I've yet to see him sleep. I should feel like a creeper, watching him like I am, but there's something so tranquil about his expression, I can't look away. It's the most relaxed I've seen him. The darkness can't find him there, allowing his brain a moment's rest.

As the music in the movie swells, I float my eyes back to the screen as Audrey Hepburn slowly walks up to George Peppard, Cat stuffed safely in her trench coat. When they kiss, my heart expands with the emotion between them. I've seen this movie more times than I care to admit, can probably recite most of the lines from memory. But the kiss in the rain between Holly Golightly and Paul Varjak, once she finally realizes love isn't such a bad thing, is one of my favorite kisses of all time. So much passion. So much heartbreak. So much hope.

Looking back at Julian, I stare at his face, his eyes still closed, deep in slumber. His lips part with every exhale before his chest expands on a short inhale. My gaze remains transfixed on his lips, unable to look away. I've exhibited extreme restraint all summer by not kissing him, by keeping the ball firmly in my court. How much longer can I hold out?

Chloe's been pushing me to step out of my comfort zone and do something I didn't plan. Thanks to Julian, I've done just that. I haven't opened my planner once in the past two weeks, a tremendous feat for someone who usually spends several minutes of every day updating and meticulously planning out my life months in advance. Lately, I haven't given much thought to what awaits me down the road, mainly because I know what awaits me… Life without Julian. Do I really want to walk away without knowing how his lips taste? I know the answer to that. It's been evident from the beginning.

Shifting in his arms, I carefully adjust my position, my eyes unwavering as I admire him. I inch toward him and my pulse increases, my racing heart thundering in my ears. All I can do is pray my clumsiness doesn't decide to make its presence known and turn what I want to be a moment full of passion into one I'll never live down. There's no going back after this. I'm about to cross the line I insisted remain firmly drawn. But as I gaze upon Julian's breathtaking face, I realize the reason I'd kept the line firmly drawn is no longer applicable.

I've fallen for him. I've allowed him to burrow deep under my skin and into my heart. Kissing him won't change any of that, won't make it any less painful when the clock strikes midnight and I turn back into a commoner.

Resolved that this is the path we were always meant to take, I graze my lips against his. They're warm, soft, electrifying. It's the slightest hint of a touch, but it still sends a shiver through me, the dull ache that settled in me during our first meeting growing more intense and prominent. I've fantasized about this moment on more than one occasion, but nothing could have prepared me for the real thing, the fireworks in my core, the music filling my heart. If this is how I react to the mere whisper of his lips against mine, I can only imagine what would happen if we took this further.

Lost in the sensation, I almost don't realize when Julian's body tenses beneath mine, his breath hitching. I should pull back now that he's caught me stealing a kiss, but I'm physically unable to retreat. And he doesn't push me away, either. We remain in place, our lips barely touching, neither one of us moving. The meaning behind this isn't lost on either of us.

We're at a crossroads.

I can pull back, apologize, and pretend this never happened. Or I can take a risk on something new, something exhilarating that will inevitably end in heartbreak. I've spent all my adult life planning every second of every day. I allowed myself to be locked in a cage, feigning happiness in a life that made me miserable. It wasn't until Julian, until I took a leap and did something out of character, that I finally felt alive. I want more of that.

Threading my fingers through Julian's wayward locks, I press my mouth more firmly against his. With a groan, he wraps his arms around my waist, pulling me into his lap, forcing my legs on either side of him. His embrace is powerful, dominating, consuming, yet he allows me to remain in control, to decide how far to take this. There's no question that the ball's still in my court. I get the feeling that's exactly where it will stay.

I brush my tongue along his bottom lip, begging for entrance, which he's more than eager to grant me. A hand goes to the back of my head as he digs his fingers into my scalp, urging me on. Moaning, I deepen the exchange, my nerve endings stirring. He tastes of mint, wine, and something unique to Julian. A flavor I'll crave long after we say our final farewell. The way he kisses me, his tongue sweeping against mine, exploring me as if trying to imprint every tiny sensation to memory, only increases my need for more.

My fingers digging deeper into his hair, I press my body against his. But no matter how I try, I can't get as close to him as I want, as I need. Even a whisper of air between us is too much.

I circle my hips, desperate to satisfy the ache building inside, but I doubt anything can ever extinguish the fire within. Julian's kiss has sparked an inferno, one I fear will continue to burn for years to come.

I rip my lips from his, panting, pressing my hand against his chest as I struggle to catch my breath. Chests heaving in near unison, we stare at each other as if seeing one another for the first time. I try to tell myself it was just a kiss. People kiss all the time. But deep down, I know this isn't just a kiss. Not with him. Not with us.

"Does this mean I can finally kiss you now?" he asks when I don't say anything immediately.

I peer into his blue eyes, a brow raised in question. He doesn't close the distance between us, indicating this is my decision and mine alone. But it's not even a decision. Not anymore. Not after a taste.

"Yes," I breathe.

He brings a hand to my face, cupping my cheek. I fuse into the contact, closing my eyes. "Even though that's all this will ever be?"

His voice is soft and timid, almost as if he doesn't want that any more than I do. I wish I understood why he seems to deprive himself of love, of happiness. But now's not the time for that conversation.

"I don't care about that," I insist. "All I care about is this, right now." I bring my lips back to his, skimming them. I feel him harden against me. "You taught me that, Julian. You taught me it's okay to live in the moment, to stop planning for every minute of every day. And right now, in this moment, I just want to kiss you." I swallow hard, grateful he can't see the truth in my eyes. "Nothing more."

"Nothing more?"

"Nothing more," I confirm.

"Nothing more."

There's something in his voice as he repeats our promise to each other. Sadness. Remorse. A reminder. I can't quite pinpoint what it is. Before I can dissect it further, he loops his arm around my waist and flips me onto my back, hovering over me.

I'm breathless from the sudden shift, my heart rate spiking. As our eyes meet, I smile a small smile, a glow washing over me. He rests his elbow by my head, leaning toward me. Then he kisses me, fully, madly, completely, reminding me why I chose this path, why I want to live in the moment.

Because this moment is everything.

CHAPTER TWENTY-EIGHT

MONDAY MORNING, I walk into the office with a smile on my face, still in the clouds from my weekend of making out with Julian. After these past few days, I doubt anything can burst my bubble. It was one of the most enjoyable weekends I can remember in recent history. It allowed me a peek into yet another side of Julian Gage…the *real* Julian Gage.

We got up to watch the sunrise over the ocean. He made me breakfast. We walked along the beach, fingers intertwined. He even took me to some local bars most of the people in his circle would never be caught dead in. We ate fish sandwiches as he shared stories of going there with Christopher during his college days. Throughout the weekend, it felt like we were a real couple, especially when he'd steal a kiss as we cooked dinner together, or lounged by the pool, or sunbathed on his boat.

By the time he dropped me off at Chloe's apartment, leaving me with a sweet goodbye kiss, I didn't think anything could dampen the high I'd been on…until I sit down at my desk and open my latest draft of the August Laurent feature and am reminded of how lackluster this story is. Julian's kisses are magical and make me feel things I never thought possible. But they can't fix this. Only I can.

So that's what I attempt to do, spending hours toiling over my notes, looking for anything that could spice up a story that should sell itself, but it still falls flat. It's nothing more than a piece about how a man went from helping a friend at a wedding to being a highly sought-after escort, empowering women who are going through a difficult breakup or divorce, making them feel beautiful again. Why? Why would a woman believe she has no other option but to hire him? And why does he do this? Why does he sacrifice having a personal life of his own to help women, help strangers?

I'm about to throw in the towel and refocus my attention on writing articles for my column when I hear a ping from my computer, indicating an incoming message. I glance at the alert on my screen, my breath hitching when I see it's from August Laurent.

Navigating toward my email program, I find the message and click on it, bracing myself for him to back out of the article altogether.

To: Evie Fitzgerald
From: August Laurent
Subject: On Second Thought...

Dear Miss Fitzgerald,

I hope this message finds you well. I'd like to apologize for my somewhat rash behavior as of late. I was quick to shoot down your request to interview some of my past clients without giving it the careful consideration it deserves. I've spent the weekend doing just that, and after reading a rough draft of the article you sent with your latest email, I'm in agreement with you. It's missing something.

Attached is a list of times and locations for four interviews I've set up between you and a few of my former clients. I hope speaking with these four women in particular will give you a greater insight into why I do what I do, more so than I've been able to provide you.

I look forward to reading a revised draft of your story upon completion of the interviews.

All the best,

A

A renewed hope builds inside me as I click on the attached document. When it pops up, I scan the contents. It's a simple one-page file, but in that one page is everything I've been searching for. I get to work, alerting Viv to this new development so she can have the proper legal documentation drawn up. Before I know it, it's past two and I'm rushing out of the office to get to my first interview.

When the cab slows to a stop in front of a five-story brownstone in the Upper West Side a few minutes before three, I crane my head, my mind reeling. I have no idea who I'm about to meet, considering the document August sent only contained places and times, no names. Based on this house, whoever I'm here to see has money…and a lot of it.

After I pay the driver, I step out of the cab, double checking the address on the bronze plate beside the door with the one August provided. It matches.

Taking a deep breath, I ascend the steps, doing my best to settle my nerves at the idea of walking into a situation I doubt anyone can properly prepare for. I press the buzzer, then smooth the lines of my dress as I listen for footsteps. After a few seconds, the door opens, revealing an older woman I estimate to be in her sixties. Her hair is short and graying, her face devoid of any heavy makeup.

"Hi, I'm Evie—"

"Yes. Yes. I'm Margaret, the housekeeper. Come in. Come in." She ushers me inside, quickly closing the door behind me and leading me through the foyer. I barely have a chance to take in the ostentatious surroundings of the late nineteenth-century home as I'm led into a small cage elevator. I can just imagine the parties the walls of this house have probably seen during its time.

"I've never seen one of these," I comment, running my finger along the intricate latticework of the screen door. "It's beautiful."

"It's the original elevator. The motor and cables have been replaced over the years, but the owner insisted the house retain its original charm. Too many people buy these homes, gut them, then design them in a style in complete contradiction to the history within. If you want sleek lines and modern furnishings, buy an apartment in Central Park West. Don't buy one of these historic homes and destroy it."

I love the passion with which she speaks. I surmise this isn't the first house she's been in charge of. Hell, just a few months ago, I wouldn't have known how to act in the presence of a housekeeper or head of household staff. Now I do. I've had the pleasure of being waited on hand and foot all summer, thanks to Julian. Although those days are numbered.

"And who exactly is the owner of this home?"

"You'll see."

"So much secrecy."

"It's for good reason." Margaret narrows her gaze on me. It's a look of warning, telling me whatever I'm about to learn will make me rethink everything, open my eyes to what's truly going on.

The elevator slows to a gradual stop on the top floor and we exit into the hallway, which is bathed in natural light. I follow Margaret toward a sunroom, then step onto a rooftop terrace.

If it weren't for the woman sitting at an outdoor patio set, I would have taken a moment to soak in the stunning views of New York City, the Hudson to the west and Central Park to the east. But as I slowly walk toward the poised woman sipping her tea, I'm speechless.

I rewind to the information Sadie shared with me at the Red, White, and Blue Gala, thinking her story about Sonia Moreno was just sensationalized gossip. Now I know it's not.

Not when I'm staring at Sonia herself.

CHAPTER TWENTY-NINE

"SO YOU'RE GUINEVERE Fitzgerald." It's a statement, her tone showing her knowledge of me isn't tied to the article I'm writing about August Laurent, but because of my connection to the world in which she normally resides during the summer months.

"Sonia…," I breathe, momentarily dumbstruck. Her dark hair falls to her mid-back, barely a strand out of place. She wears a fitted, thigh-length black shift dress, her skin olive-toned and tanned. From what I know of her, she's around my age, but has a sophistication that makes her seem older, even if she doesn't look it. "I mean, Ms. Moreno." I reach my hand toward her and she takes it, her hold delicate. "It's wonderful to meet you."

"You, as well." A hint of her Spanish accent comes through. "Please…" She gestures to the chair across from her, indicating for me to sit down.

"Is there anything else you need, Ms. Moreno?" Margaret asks.

"We're okay for now."

"Very well. Call if anything comes up."

"Certainly." Sonia offers the woman a smile as she turns from us, then focuses her attention back on me. "Tea?" She raises the teapot.

"That would be lovely."

Lovely? I don't even sound like myself. I've never called something lovely, apart from a brief period during high school when I became obsessed with all things related to British literature. I refused to speak in anything but a British accent, which I'm sure sounded horrendous when coupled with my subtle Midwestern tone.

Sonia pours a bit of tea into a small cup, then places it on a china saucer with a floral design, handing it to me.

"I have to say," she begins as she leans back in her chair, bringing her tea to her lips, "I was quite surprised to learn August had agreed to an interview, considering how private he is."

"I've assured him I'll protect his anonymity, along with everyone else I speak with. This isn't a sensational story meant to reveal who the mysterious August Laurent is. It's simply a piece about the man, what makes him tick, why he does what he does…" I hesitate before adding, "Why women feel compelled to use his services."

"Well, now that I see you and realize who you are, it makes sense."

Her statement catches me off-guard. "Who *I* am?"

"Of course."

I shake my head, placing my cup back onto the table in front of me. "I'm not sure I follow."

"You *are* dating Julian Gage, aren't you?"

"Yes." Normally, I probably would have thought it odd that a complete stranger…a celebrity, no less…would be familiar with my personal life. But there's been nothing private about that this summer, not with all the photos of Julian and me that have graced the pages of the gossip websites.

She squints, studying me, as if attempting to put a puzzle together. Then her expression brightens. "Well, that must be why August agreed. He probably saw you with him and figured if anyone would understand, it would be someone who's been thrust into the lifestyle."

"And why is that important?" I lower my voice. "Are many of his clients from this…lifestyle?"

"You mean famous?"

"Yes."

"Some are. Some are ordinary housewives."

"And they can afford his fee?"

"What fee?"

"His fee…" My words lack the conviction I wish they had. I want to kick myself for never asking him about this. I assumed he charged. It never even crossed my mind he didn't. My curiosity only grows. Why would he do this if he wasn't getting paid?

"He doesn't ask for a single dime in return for his services."

My jaw becomes slack as I swallow hard. "He doesn't?"

"Not anymore. Yes, August Laurent was, at one time, a bona fide escort, but several years ago, it turned into something more. It's no longer about the money. It's about something bigger."

That's all it takes for me to become enthralled with this story, my mind spinning from this small piece of information, something I could have learned if I'd known to ask.

"Do you mind if I record this?" I swiftly remove my phone from my purse. "Your identity will never be revealed and the recordings never published. I just don't want to miss anything or get something wrong."

"August mentioned I'd get approval before publication?"

"Absolutely." I retrieve a document the legal team gave me and push it across the table toward her. "Everything's stated in there. Essentially, I'll never disclose anything to anyone without your approval. Anything published in the article will be done in a way to ensure no one can connect you to this story. And you'll get approval rights. If we publish anything you disagree with, you can sue the magazine for everything it's worth."

She scans the papers, her eyes glossing over the legalese before she returns her attention to me. "Okay. You can record this."

"Thank you." I open the voice recorder app on my phone and place it on the table. I pull out my notepad to take notes of our conversation, as well. I scratch the date on the top of a fresh piece of paper, then look up at Sonia. "How did you meet August Laurent?"

She smiles, contemplating. "I think a better question might be how I met my husband."

"Your husband?"

"Yes. Had I never met Ethan Price…or, as the world knows him, Ethan Ludlow…I never would have needed August Laurent."

"Okay." A chill trickles down my spine. "How did you meet your husband?"

"It's your typical Hollywood romance. I was an actress trying to catch my big break. And Ethan was a big shot producer who could make those dreams happen. We met at a cliché party in the Hollywood Hills. The guest list included a mixture of nobodies dying to be somebodies, and somebodies who wanted to take advantage of those nobodies. I just didn't realize that then."

"Is that what happened? Did Ethan take advantage of you?"

"Not at first, no." She looks into the distance, as if recalling happier times. "He was sweet, exactly as I thought he'd be from the characters he played on the sitcom when he was a young boy. Back then, he had a reputation in Hollywood as being down-to-earth and compassionate, someone who would bend over backwards to help those he cared about. And he cared about me, a girl who left a small town in Texas to chase her dreams in Hollywood. He made those dreams come true.

"Those first few years, I was so wrapped up in everything that I missed the little signs. I made excuses, saying he was just under stress, or I shouldn't have been so friendly to one of his associates, or I should've worn a less revealing dress. I was only twenty-one when we met. He was forty-five. I figured the tension could have just been due to the age difference. Regardless, with his name attached to mine, I started getting calls for auditions. And not just crap, two-bit parts like before. These were real roles, ones that eventually made me a household name."

Instead of smiling, as one would think when telling the story of how she finally achieved everything she could have imagined, her expression falls, her lips forming a tight line as her chin trembles.

"What happened?"

"About five years ago, I was in romantic comedy where I played opposite Matthew McConaughey. It was one of the biggest hits of the year. Made millions. Before then, I was known as Ethan Ludlow's girlfriend. After that, I was simply Sonia Moreno. Worse…" Her voice becomes strained through the obvious lump in her throat. "He became known as Sonia Moreno's boyfriend."

"I take it he didn't like the blow to his ego."

She laughs slightly, crossing her legs in a practiced way that makes it appear smooth and swanlike. "He certainly did not. How would you feel if you were a child star desperately trying to stay relevant as a producer and director and your newbie girlfriend was now more popular than you ever were?" She brings her tea back to her mouth, taking a sip. I do the same, allowing her a moment to collect her thoughts.

"He increasingly grew more and more controlling, possessive, angry. I couldn't even give an interview without him having a meltdown over something I said, regardless of how meaningless it was. He found something wrong in everything, something to make him think I was being unfaithful, that I was going to leave him. I insisted I'd never leave him, that I owed him everything, that I loved him. Because I honestly thought *I* was to blame for his insecurity, I did what I thought I had to in order to fix it and assure him he was the only man I wanted.

"So the next week, we boarded a plane to Bora Bora and got married in front of our other celebrity friends. It was so different from the wedding I imagined when I was a little girl."

"Why was that?"

Her eyes light up at my question. All women love talking of their childhood fantasies. It brings us back to that time in our lives when we believed the world was our oyster.

"I'd always envisioned marrying the man of my dreams in the church in Mexico where my parents said their vows, then have a reception at this gorgeous restored farm near my grandparents' house there. Instead, our guests were Hollywood types there just to say they were. I remember having second thoughts, thinking I could just fly away and start over again, but it seemed impossible. I was too recognizable. I couldn't disappear. It was the first time I felt trapped. And that only increased over the years.

"Don't get me wrong. Ethan and I had some wonderful times, times when I did love him. There were moments he was so full of life and excitement. But as I learned, for every up, there would eventually be an even bigger down. And when that happened, it was near impossible to reason with him. He'd find something lacking with me, something that made him lose his mind. In those moments of mania, I believed that to be the case, believed I was at fault."

I lick my lips as I prepare to ask my next question. "Did he hurt you?"

She lowers her eyes, nodding slightly.

"How often?"

Blowing out a long breath, she looks up. "I lost track over the years. After a while, I could predict when it would happen. It was a cycle. Things would be great. Then he'd grow increasingly irritable. It was only a matter of time before something set him off and he'd lose all control. The next day, he'd apologize, beg for my forgiveness, promise to get help, to never drink, to make it right, and he'd be the man I remember him to be when we first met.

"This went on for years. Each cycle got increasingly shorter and more volatile. In retrospect, I should have jumped ship ages ago, but when Ethan was in a good mood, he was sweet, charming, endearing." She laughs to herself, a shimmer in her eyes. "I used to joke he could charm the skin off a snake. He had this energy you wanted to be around. And when he looked at you in a way that made you think he saw no one else, well… There's nothing like that."

"I've heard a few rumors that he…"

"Cheated on me?" she finishes. "I blamed myself for that, too. *He* blamed me for it, told me if I was the type of wife he needed, he wouldn't have to seek comfort in another. I should have expected this, considering he was still married to his previous wife when we met. So I did what I could to be the perfect wife just to save some poor girl who was trying to make a name for herself in this industry from suffering the same fate I did."

My mouth grows dry at her words, a chill enveloping me. "What made you seek out August? There must have been some triggering event, something that made you say enough."

"The premier of my latest movie." With shaky hands, she places her cup back on the table. "Until then, I'd done mostly upbeat romantic comedies. But my latest film was more of a romantic drama. A very sexy romantic drama."

I nod. "I've seen it."

"Honestly, I was surprised when Ethan suggested I throw my name into the hat for the lead, but he claimed he was okay with the nudity and intimate scenes. It wouldn't be my first sex scene, but all my previous ones were lighter and more fun. When I got the part, he was thrilled for me. But after we got home from the premier, he was different…aloof, sinister. He accused me of enjoying those intimate moments too much, more than when *we* were intimate. I told him he was crazy, that I was merely acting. Things spiraled out of control, and before I could make sense of what was happening, he forced himself on me, demanding I tell him he's the best lover I'd ever had."

I cover my mouth with my hand, shaking my head. I can't even begin to comprehend what she's been through. I never would have imagined it was something like this. She's been dubbed America's Sweetheart, a gorgeous woman who came from nothing and made a name for herself in an industry that's notoriously exclusive. I may have complained about Trevor's lack of attention, especially later on in our relationship, but he always treated me well, always respected me. I couldn't imagine feeling so trapped, so degraded, so worthless.

"You'd think that would have been enough for me to leave."

"It wasn't?"

She shakes her head. "No. I stayed, mainly because I believed his threats that I'd never work again, that he'd use his sphere of influence to make sure no producer or director ever hired me again. Not only did he have a long history in the movie industry, his father was Theodore Price, owner of half the world, it seemed. It didn't matter that his father had been gone several years. Ethan was still connected to many of his powerful friends. It wasn't until the Red, White, and Blue Gala in the Hamptons last summer that something changed."

"The gala?"

"Often, the household staffs from the surrounding homes work the event, as well. During the fireworks display, I politely excused myself, the weight of the lies I'd been forced to tell all night suffocating me. Every time someone else congratulated me on my latest role, all I heard were Ethan's threats, all I felt was the burn of his body covering mine as he forced himself on me, destroying my soul."

"Why didn't you go to the police?"

"I didn't think they'd believe me. Ethan had me so brainwashed that I honestly thought they'd dismiss me. I was his wife. I'm supposed to want to have sex with my husband."

"But that wasn't sex. Regardless of any marriage vows, consent is still required."

"I know that now," she says. "I knew it at the time, too. I was worried what he'd do if I said anything. Acting was all I had. I couldn't lose that."

"What happened at the gala?"

She straightens her spine. "I went to the ladies' room. It was vacant, apart from one attendant."

"Who?" I press, my gut telling me this woman might be integral to the story, someone I could potentially speak to this coming weekend.

Pulling her bottom lip between her teeth, she considers what to tell me. "I'd rather not say. I don't want to put anyone else in Ethan's line of fire, so to speak. I'd never be able to live with myself."

My shoulders fall as I blow out a breath. "I can understand that."

"After I finished washing my hands and reapplying my makeup, she stopped me. Without saying a word, she carefully lifted the flutter sleeves of my gown, revealing the bruises on my biceps from where Ethan had restrained me the previous evening during one of his rage-filled moments. I could have said we were into the rough stuff, but there was no masking the fear in my eyes. Then she withdrew a business card from her back pocket. No name. No address. Nothing. All that was on it was a phone number. She said when I was done living in fear to call it. After that evening, I left the Hamptons and locked myself away, trying to figure out my next move. I didn't call until February twenty-seventh."

"Why did you wait so long?"

"I wish I had an answer," she exhales, shaking her head. "There are times I wish I could go back and shake myself, force myself to wake up, but it's not that easy. Ethan manipulated me to the point that I truly believed

I'd be nothing without him, despite the fact I now had a career of my own. I never saw myself as this successful celebrity. I still saw myself as the struggling actress who would do anything just to get an audition."

"What caused you to finally call?"

A blank look crosses her face as she stares straight ahead. "A photo of me from a movie I'd shot a few months earlier appeared on the front page of some tabloid with a headline about me leaving my husband for someone younger. Ethan saw it and flipped out. He wouldn't listen to reason, didn't care that the actor was gay or that it was a scene from the movie. He pulled out a knife, brought it up to my throat, and told me the only way he'd ever allow me to leave him was in a casket.

"The following day, after he'd apologized profusely and promised yet again to seek treatment for his anger issues, I kissed him goodbye, then called the number. In a matter of hours, I was on a plane to Vancouver where I spent the next two months with August Laurent.

"What did you tell Ethan? He had to notice you were gone? Did you tell him you'd had enough?"

She pinches her lips together, slowly shaking her head. "I told him I'd just gotten a project thrown into my lap and would be on location shooting for a few months. I offered to fly him out, knowing he'd never take me up on it. Once my star got bigger than his, he balked at the idea of joining me on set."

I sit back, trying to wrap my head around the story she just shared with me. Whenever I saw Sonia and Ethan together on TV, I assumed they were the perfect couple, the one everyone aspired to be, that their love was what we all hoped to find. As with everything, appearances can be deceiving. I got my first taste of that earlier this summer when he came onto me. I figured he was just drunk. I suppose Sonia made the same excuse I did when, in reality, there's no excuse for that behavior.

"And what was your time with August like?"

"Exhilarating." The tension seems to roll off her shoulders in waves as she reflects. "He was exactly what I needed. He took care of me and made me feel beautiful, something I hadn't experienced in years. I would talk about my time with Ethan, and he wouldn't judge me for staying with him. He had a level of understanding I never expected. He showed me what a real relationship should be like, what real love should look like."

"Do you love him?"

She scrunches her brows, chewing on her lower lip. "It's an interesting question, one I've never really thought about, but I suppose you can say I do. I love how his encouragement empowered me, how he helped me realize I *do* have worth, how he gave me the strength to walk away from it all.

"You see, hiring August Laurent isn't about a fleeting physical attraction. It's more than that. It's about sharing a connection, something

I hadn't had in years. He gave me that. He gave me the greatest gift anyone could. If it weren't for him, I shudder to think where I'd be right now. I wouldn't be on the brink of finally saying goodbye to my past. And it's all thanks to August Laurent's influence on me. Because now I know I have worth. Even if Ethan's threats are realized and he makes sure I never work in this industry again, he can't take away the most important thing, not anymore."

"And what's that?"

A brilliant smile forms. "My freedom."

CHAPTER THIRTY

A HEAVINESS SETTLES in my chest as I stare at my overnight bag, packing up the few essentials I'll need for my final weekend with Julian. I'd been dreading this for weeks, especially once we kissed. Thankfully, I haven't had time to think about it too much lately. Most of my free time has been filled with interviewing other women who'd been referred to August Laurent. Every single one of them helped me view him as who he truly is — a man who used his notoriety for good. He could have continued as a traditional escort, someone women called if they needed a date for a wedding to make their ex jealous or didn't want to sit through another Christmas with family members asking why they're not married or in a serious relationship just yet. At first, that's what he did, smiling, playing the role he'd been hired to play. But then something changed. I can't help but wonder what that was.

As I grab a few of my toiletries out of my vanity, I pause when my eyes fall on a strip of photos. On our way out to Southampton last weekend, Julian made a surprise stop at Coney Island. He couldn't believe I've lived in New York for nearly ten years and had yet to go. It was exactly as I'd imagined — cheesy, dirty, obnoxious…and magical. We played carnival games and ate food I'm sure will take the rest of my life to work off.

Neither one of us wanted to leave. So much so that we ended up being three hours late to the dinner we were scheduled to attend. That didn't seem to faze us. Nothing mattered much lately, except for being with each other. Now I'm on the brink of never seeing him again.

Despite the shift in our relationship, Julian's carried on as if it's business as usual, that he's still planning on walking away after this weekend. Two months ago, I looked forward to having my freedom back, as well as a beautiful new wardrobe. Now I'd trade all of that for just one more night, one more hour, one more minute with Julian.

Tears well in my eyes and I fall onto the bed, my throat closing up as I look to the ceiling, frustrated with myself. I'm not supposed to cry over him, not when one of the reasons he asked me to help was because I'd remain detached, because I wouldn't get emotionally invested. But I have. Regardless of what he wants me to believe, I know he has, too. How can he walk away now? How can anyone walk away after forming this kind of connection, this amazing bond? Isn't it human nature to want to pursue something like this and see where it leads?

As I consider the predicament I now find myself in, I'm reminded of August Laurent and how every single woman I've spoken to has admitted they love him. Surely after spending a month or two with these women, he must have formed feelings for them, yet he still walks away every single time. How does he keep his heart guarded? How can he leave them, knowing there's something there?

Grabbing my phone, I open my email. I may regret this, but I need words of encouragement. As much as I love Chloe and Nora, I can't talk to them about this, not when I've refused to admit I'm falling for the guy. Despite the change in me they've both picked up on, I insist there's nothing between us, that I'm still looking forward to the end of the summer. I need advice from someone who's been in my shoes. There's only one person who will understand.

To: August Laurent
From: Evie Fitzgerald
Subject: ???

How do you do it?

Short and to the point. I hit send, then continue packing up my things. Only a few seconds pass before my phone rings. I snap my eyes toward it, the familiar Blocked appearing on the caller ID.

"Evie Fitzgerald," I answer, although I know who it is. By now, it's become a routine with us.

"I thought we were past this, Miss Fitzgerald. Haven't you figured out by now I'm not taking advantage of vulnerable women?"

"It's not that," I respond quickly. "That's not what I'm talking about. I understand now."

"Then what is it?"

I draw in a shaky breath. "How do you do what you do and not feel like you lose a piece of yourself every few months?"

"A piece of myself?"

My chin trembles and I struggle to speak through the lump in my throat. "How do you find the strength to walk away from someone you've grown to care for?" I choke out in a strained voice, one that evidences my frustration and sadness.

There's a brief pause on the line before he speaks again. Everything about his words exude the compassion I surmise is why women are desperate for his companionship.

"Is this line of questioning coming from somewhere…personal?"

I exhale deeply as I swipe at my eyes, erasing my tears only for new ones to fall. "Let's just say I find myself in a somewhat similar situation. Apart from the whole escort thing." I laugh slightly and look down, surprised to see the strip of photos from Coney Island clutched in my hand. I can't even remember grabbing them. My chest tightens and I swallow hard. "I agreed to help out a friend for the summer…"

"And now that summer's ending, you're having trouble walking away."

My words caught in my throat, I nod. It doesn't matter he can't see me. He knows what I'm going through. This is why I reached out to him. I *need* his reassurance that I'll get through this.

"Listen, Evie…" His tone softens, taking on a friendly, more familiar quality. Until this point, we've been fairly professional in our correspondence and discussions. This is the first time he's called me Evie, despite my insistence he do so. It's always been Miss Fitzgerald. "I never said I didn't struggle with walking away."

"Then how do you do it? How do you form this amazing connection with another person, one that makes you truly believe you're soul mates, and still leave?"

"Because I remind myself I'm there to serve a purpose."

Now his own voice trembles. It's not as prominent, but it's obvious his words are laced with emotion, proving he's not this detached machine who has no trouble jumping between women. He truly does care about each one. The world needs more people like August Laurent.

"I'm there to give women the companionship they desperately need to put them on the track to what's next. Perhaps that's what you need to focus on. That whatever arrangement you had was just to get you to the next step in your life. It won't be easy. You'll find pieces of him in places you never expect, and it will knock the breath out of you. Like when a commercial you laughed over comes on the TV, especially all those pharmaceutical commercials where the side effects seem worse than the condition it's meant to treat."

I close my eyes, remembering doing the same thing with Julian just a few weeks ago. Now the tears that fall are no longer tears of sorrow but of joy, of comfort, my heart expanding.

"Or you hear a song on your playlist and remember dancing to it. Or you see a car that looks like his, only for your heart to deflate when it's not. But I assure you, the memories will eventually stop being painful, and you'll look back on this time with fondness instead of heartache. It won't happen right away. But it *will* happen."

"But—"

"My advice to you, since I'm assuming these are your last few days together?"

"Yes."

"Don't dwell on the future. Enjoy the present. Savor every last second you have together. Create more memories instead of lamenting on old ones. I promise these memories will carry you through the difficult road ahead, where you'll question everything. Everyone comes into our lives for a reason, Evie. This…friend. Maybe he didn't come into your life to be your soul mate. Or maybe he is your soul mate, but not in the way you think. Maybe he's like Virgil guiding Dante through Hell and Purgatory, showing you who you are so you can start living."

As I hang up and continue packing my things for the last time, I do everything to follow August's advice. I try not to dwell on the idea of the sun setting on this magical summer, focusing instead on enjoying the little time I have left with Julian. Maybe he came into my life to help me realize I deserved so much more than what Trevor gave me. That I deserve to be with someone who supports my dreams, regardless of how ambitious and out of reach they may seem. Julian gave that to me. For that, I'll forever be grateful. The notion keeps the tears at bay.

Until the buzzer sounds and I step out of the building to see Julian standing on the front stoop, the car I've nicknamed Thursday, the Jaguar, idling by the curb. He looks as beautiful and captivating as when I first saw him from across a bar during what I thought to be the worst night of my life. But now that I know his inner beauty matches that on the outside, he appears even more beautiful, more captivating. It forces the ache to return, tears sliding down my cheeks.

Julian's quick to pull me into his chest, holding me tightly as my tears soak his white linen shirt. His arms comfort me at the same time they remind me this will be the last time they'll be here to do so.

"It'll be okay," he murmurs, his own voice showing signs of strain. "This was always how it was going to end. Nothing will change that. You deserve more than I can give you, Guinevere."

I lift my head and peer into his eyes. "How do you know?"

He brings his thumbs up to my eyes, wiping at them. "It's the truth. I am not a good man. I won't bring you down with me. You deserve the sun and moon and stars." He brings his forehead to mine. "I can't give that to you."

I cup his face, relishing in the scruff of his unshaven jaw. "What if you already have?"

He swallows hard as his eyes lock with mine. I can see the internal struggle through those vibrant blue orbs, ones I've seen look at me in a way I never thought another man would. So much admiration. So much devotion. So much…love?

Before I can react, he swallows me in his embrace, crushing his lips to mine, his kiss ravenous, desperate, needy, as tears slide down my cheeks. I arch into him, returning his kiss with the same intensity, wanting to remember every groan, every circle of his hips, every swipe of his tongue before the candle is extinguished.

CHAPTER THIRTY-ONE

THEY SAY TIME seems to drag when you're excited about something. The opposite is true, as well, because my final weekend with Julian flies by, time rushing when I'd love nothing more than for it to slow down.

The myriad of events I attend on Julian's arm are marked with a celebratory atmosphere reminiscent of the last days of school. I hate lying to all these people as I make plans to get together with several of them in the city. But that won't happen, not once word of our breakup gets out. I'll be back to my normal life, and my summer with Julian will be nothing but a distant memory. In my heart, I know that will never be the case. Not for me. And not for Julian. He's struggling with this, too. I can see it in his eyes as he looks upon me with a hint of longing, feel it in his arms as he holds me a little tighter, taste it in his lips as he presses them against me with a bit more desperation.

As I stare at my reflection in the full-length mirror as Camille helps zip up the stunning charcoal-colored ballgown I'm to wear to the final gala, it's bittersweet. I've kept my emotions at bay all weekend in front of everyone, only allowing Julian to see them in the hopes he'd change his mind. Now that it's almost over, a tear escapes at the knowledge that this is it, my last night by his side. It's not about the glitz and glamor. What's killing me is never experiencing the same adoration, devotion, or affection I have this summer. Even if it's not real. In my heart, it is. It has been since the beginning.

"It'll be okay." Camille fetches a tissue and holds it out when she notices the tear sliding down my cheek. I offer her a smile as I bring it to my eyes, grateful I'd worn waterproof mascara. "He's struggling, too."

"Right," I scoff. All weekend, Julian's been his usual charming self. Yes, there's a hint of sadness surrounding him, but not enough to make a change.

"Trust me, sweetie. I've known Mr. Gage a long time. I've never seen him this...unsure."

"Then why doesn't he say something? Why does he insist he can't give me what I deserve? Who is he to make that determination?"

Camille clasps my hands in hers as she leads me toward the sitting area, both of us lowering ourselves onto the couch. "Did you know that Mr. Gage spent his younger years in the foster care system?"

Swallowing hard, I shake my head. After those first few days, I tried to steer clear of all articles about him, mainly because I was mentioned in a lot of them. The last thing I wanted was to read gossip about myself, something Julian had warned me against earlier in the summer.

"How did he end up there?" I lower my voice. "Does it have something to do with the scars?"

She pinches her lips in contemplation. "That's not my story to tell, but being in the foster system can change you. The system failed him, didn't get him the help he needed after what he went through… Didn't give him the *love* he needed. That boy spent his most impressionable years desperate for love, only to never have it bestowed on him. It's my belief he gave up and decided he's undeserving of love."

I stare straight ahead, absorbing her words. Julian never spoke of his childhood much. Whenever I asked, he closed up, saying it was unimportant. Now I understand why. The scars have never fully healed. Physically *and* emotionally.

"Maybe if you show him he's deserving of love, if you tell him how much you love him—"

Whipping my eyes toward hers, I inhale a sharp breath. "I never said I loved him."

She pats my hand affectionally. "You didn't have to. It's written all over you, dear. You love that man, probably more than you've loved any other person in your life."

"I—"

"And he loves you, but refuses to admit it…to himself or anyone else. Yes, he's a grown man, but at times, he's still that lost little boy desperate for even the slightest show of love, the one who cries himself to sleep because he doesn't think he deserves to be loved. Prove him wrong. Show him he is." She holds my gaze a moment longer, her eyes pleading with me to love Julian like he deserves. *Do* I love him? I don't want to admit the answer. It will only make tonight more difficult than it already is.

"Come on, Cinderella. Let's get you to the ball," she says, ripping me out of my thoughts.

"Except Prince Charming won't be hunting me down afterward to see if the glass slipper fits."

"Cinderella didn't think that would happen, either, but that didn't stop her from enjoying herself. Don't let the knowledge of what tomorrow brings stop you."

With a nod, I silently follow her out of my room, walking this path for the final time. Earlier in the summer, I'd given myself the same pep talk Camille just did. It was easier then, back when we still had time.

As I round the corner into the formal living room, my Christian Louboutin heels clicking on the wood flooring, a figure in a black tuxedo turns from peering out the windows, Julian's gaze settling on me. On a hard swallow, I blink back a new wave of tears. My throat constricts over the idea that this is the last time he'll ever look at me in amazement as he soaks in the dress Dana selected for the evening's festivities. Even when we were just scheduled to attend a casual barbecue or beach bonfire, he still had a way of admiring me as if I were bathed in priceless diamonds.

"Hey," I say with a smile, cutting through the silence.

"Guinevere..." His voice catches as he says my name. He clears his throat, taking slow steps toward me. Just like all those weeks ago, he grabs my hand in his, spinning me around to get a better view from every angle before tugging my body against his. He places his free hand on the small of my back, and I drape my arm over his shoulder, toying with a few tendrils of hair that hang over his jacket collar. We remain still for what feels like an eternity, but in reality is only a second. Our eyes lock, midnight blue to my emerald green. Neither one of us utters a single word. There's no need. In this silence, in this moment, in this space, we say everything we want to.

A low hum cuts through the quiet. It's a familiar song that will always remind me of the moment I finally succumbed to my desire and kissed him. He squeezes my hand, then leads me around the room. Unlike our first weekend together, when dancing with him felt stilted and awkward, we move with practiced grace.

Julian begins to sing the lyrics to "Moon River", husky and deep, and it takes every bit of willpower I possess not to burst into tears. I've never truly paid attention to the words before. It was just a song that reminded me of one of my favorite movies about two drifters who were wrong for each other, but so right at the same time. Just like Julian and me. But we weren't meant to see the world together. Our rainbows' end isn't the same, and I'm not sure anything can change that.

We slow our steps as the song comes to an untimely end and we stand in place, our hands still clasped together, our bodies a breath away. If this is our last private moment together, I want to savor it. The way he holds me, admires me, cares for me.

Too soon, he releases me from his hold. "Guinevere, I..."

"Yes?" I respond, hope building in my voice.

"I..."

"Yes?" I rest my hand on his cheek, his clean-shaven skin soft against mine. I wish I knew he planned to shave. I would have loved one last kiss with his scruff scraping against my lips, jarring and bruising, yet making me feel more alive than anything else in my life. Never again. The thought rips at my heartstrings.

"I, uh..." He licks his lips, blinking rapidly. "I got you something."

"You didn't have to get me anything." I drop my hold on him. "You already bought me a wardrobe that could probably pay for the first year's rent at the apartment of my choosing in the city," I joke.

"You're not going to sell it, are you?" he asks frantically. "Because if that's what it takes for you to afford your own place, I'll buy you an apartment. I—"

"It's a lovely gesture," I interrupt. "But not necessary. Now that I've had the opportunity to revamp my piece on August Laurent, at least I have a decent shot at that promotion. It'll be nice to have my own bathroom again."

"And a door."

"Yes. And a door," I laugh, grateful for the short reprieve of tension. "It's amazing how we take those little things for granted until we no longer have them. I'll never take doors for granted again."

He smiles, but it doesn't reach his eyes.

"So..."

"Right." He spins, heading toward the wet bar. After retrieving a square white box, he walks back to me with a smile on his lips. "This is for you."

"What is it?" Taking it from his outstretched hand, I feel the weight, knowing it must contain more than just a t-shirt, as the size of the box would normally indicate.

"Open it."

Eyeing him suspiciously, my heart thumps in my chest. With trembling fingers, I pull at the red ribbon. When I lift the cover, I gasp at what I see inside. It's another box, but that's not what surprises me. It's the Tiffany's blue shade that steals my breath.

"I was planning on getting you something from Cartier, but I figured Tiffany's would have more meaning."

"It could be an empty box and it would be infinitely better than even the most expensive piece you could get from Cartier," I gush.

"Phew," he exhales, swiping at his brow. "That's a relief, because it really is just an empty box."

Laughing, I shake my head and pull out the square blue box, placing the other one on a nearby table. "No, it's not."

"You're right." His expression turns serious, his eyes trained on me. "It's not," he admits in a soft voice. "Open it."

I hold his gaze for a moment, then shift it to the box. Butterflies flap their relentless wings in my stomach as I slowly raise the lid. When I set my eyes on what's contained within, all the wind is knocked from my lungs. An exact replica of the necklace Audrey Hepburn's character admires during the scene when she takes Paul to Tiffany's for the first time. The light reflects against the stunning yellow-colored diamond in the center, the intricate latticework of diamonds along the neckline like a vine surrounding a lone flower.

"Julian..." I cover my mouth with my hand, speechless.

This isn't the first piece of jewelry he's purchased for me. I have an entire jewelry box in the dressing room filled with pieces to accent the various outfits I've worn over the course of the summer. This one is different. It's something he's given to me because he wanted to, not as a complement to my wardrobe.

"Now I know why Camille insisted I not wear the necklace Dana had paired with this dress."

He grins a devious smile. "It's good to have her on my side." He winks, then extends his hand toward the box. "May I?"

I remain motionless as he takes it. He removes the stunning necklace, then stands behind me. I catch a glimpse of my reflection in a mirror hanging over the fireplace, watching as he brings it to my neck, securing it. When he's finished, his hands stay on my shoulders. I touch my fingers to the stones. I've never worn such a weighty piece of jewelry in my life.

"Wow," I murmur. "I'm not sure I want to know how much this cost, or how many carats I'm currently wearing around my neck."

"The large stone is a forty-carat yellow diamond. A rarity. Ten carats in white diamonds accent the neckline."

"So fifty carats worth of stones." My breathing becomes labored as I try to grasp onto the concept. "*Please* don't tell me what this cost you."

"It's not about the money. Not to me—"

"Because you have money."

"All the more reason for me to do this for you, to give you something to show how appreciative I am for everything you've done for me this summer. This is the least I could do."

I practically choke on my saliva. "I could understand giving me a Starbuck's gift card or something, but this?" I spin around to face him. "I don't feel right accepting."

"You will accept it." He grabs my hands in his, bringing them to his lips. He places a gentle kiss on each. "Please. Let me do this for you. Let me give you something to remember our time together."

"I'll never forget." I lock eyes with him, silently pleading for him to acknowledge that our time together doesn't have to end, that *we* don't have to end. Why should it have to? Why should we walk away from each other because the summer's over? Yes, that was the original plan — an end date so I could have my life back, so I could *plan* the rest of my life. Now I want nothing more than to deviate from the plan, to throw the planner out the window and see where this could take us.

"It doesn't have to end," I say, one last attempt as I touch my mouth to his. He kisses me softly, gently, but in his tenderness is more emotion than any of Trevor's kisses could even hope to contain.

"It does, Guinevere. You deserve to be happy." He pulls back, his fingers digging into the skin of my cheeks as he cups my face. "I can't give that to you. I can't give you more than this."

I've heard the same thing all weekend whenever my emotions got the better of me in his presence. I want to push it more, but not at the risk of marring our last few hours together. Instead, I simply nod, my lips finding his once more.

The sound of the ocean waves fills the room from the open windows and we melt into each other, our kiss passionate, yet restrained, two words that describe Julian Gage perfectly. Despite how much I can tell he wants me, he'll never admit it. To me, or himself.

When he pulls away, a hint of moisture dots his own eyes. "We'll always have Tiffany's."

I pull my lips between my teeth as I struggle to swallow through the pain in my throat. "We'll always have Tiffany's."

***

The Farewell Gala is exactly as I expect it to be — filled with glamour, pretension, and bravado, yet another display of extreme wealth amongst the country's upper crust. But tonight, as opposed to the previous few weeks, Julian doesn't leave my side to talk business with someone interested in investing in his project. Whenever anyone approaches, he requests they reach out to his assistant to set up a time for a meeting or a phone conference when he returns to the city on Tuesday.

The entire evening, he's the perfect date, doting on me, making sure I have everything I need. More than once, part of me considers the possibility he's acting like this because Ethan Ludlow seems to circle like a hawk, although to anyone else, he's no more harmful than a parrot. Not to me, not after the story Sonia shared. And not to Julian, either. Despite that, I truly believe he stays with me because he doesn't want to waste a second of the little time we have left.

Before I know it, Julian and I are dancing to the final song of the night, then saying our goodbyes to the friends I've made over the summer, some of them women who turned their noses up at me during that first pool party. It's amazing how much can change in just a few months.

After a silent limo ride back to Julian's house, we head through the dimly-lit living room and toward the staircase for the last time. His hand finds mine, our fingers interlocking as we walk those final steps toward my room. When we reach the door, he drops his hold, turning to face me. Our eyes meet, neither one of us saying a single word.

I've been dreading this for weeks. It's not just good night. This is goodbye. I'd insisted it be a term of our arrangement. As did Julian. A clean break.

There's nothing clean about this.

I open my mouth, about to make one final plea for him to reconsider his position, that he *can* give me what he believes I deserve, but before I have a chance, his lips are on mine, stealing my words. His touch is so light, it's akin to kissing a ghost. And tomorrow, that's precisely what Julian

Gage will be.

Desperation takes over and I wrap my arms around him, curving my body into his as I deepen the kiss. He's more than eager to match my intensity, pressing me against the wall. He kisses me as if he needs it to breathe, as if his lips were made just for mine, as if it's the last time he'll ever taste me. Because it is.

He releases his hold on my face, his hands traveling down my frame, exploring, needing, wanting. When he brushes against my breast, I moan as he hardens, grinding against me. There's so much longing, so much yearning, so much despair in this kiss, electrifying and satisfying me in a way I fear no one else will ever be able to do. Pulling him closer, I claw at his back, drawing everything out of him I possibly can. And I give him everything I have. My devotion. My respect. My love. I don't need to tell him exactly how I feel. I show it in the way I worship him, hold him, cherish him.

He moves his lips from mine, kissing a hot trail along my jawline, his hands teasing and torturing as he tries to imprint everything about me to his memory. I throw back my head, savoring in the warmth of his mouth on my skin as he nibbles on my neck. Our heavy breathing fills the hallway, my heart racing. Regardless of what tomorrow may bring, I know one thing… I need this man. His kisses. His touch. His soul.

My fingers thread into his thick hair, tugging as his mouth journeys along my collarbone, his hand squeezing my breast. With my body pressed against the wall, I hook a leg around his waist, gently thrusting against him, urging him to continue, telling him I'm ready for whatever he's willing to give.

Eventually, his lips find mine again. At first, the kiss is impassioned and animalistic, but transitions into something…different. It's full of pain and heartache as his tongue sweeps against mine, slow and measured.

When he pulls back, he stares at me with a haunted look, as if on the verge of telling me something but can't seem to form the words. It reminds me of the same tortured expression in his eyes my first night in this house.

And just like that night, instead of saying a single word, he drops his hold on me and retreats with quick steps, disappearing into his room before I have a chance to whisper "goodbye".

Chapter Thirty-Two

I STARE AT the bright moon over the ocean as I lay awake in bed, sleep evading me. Since my first night here, I've slept well, the room designed to emphasize maximum comfort and relaxation. Tonight, nothing can get my brain to shut off, not when I wonder if I blew it with Julian. What if I'd made one final plea for him to reconsider? Would it have changed anything?

I'll never know.

Feeling like the walls of this luxurious bedroom are suffocating me, I throw the covers off and my feet find the cool floor. I grab my silk kimono robe off the bed post and toss it over my tank top and sleep shorts, securing it around my waist. When I open the French doors and step onto the balcony, I inhale a long breath. The ocean breeze kisses my skin as I walk toward the ledge, leaning my arms on it. It's so tranquil and serene, the sound of the waves soothing the fire and indecision within.

As I smooth a few tendrils of hair behind my ear, I spy a figure standing at the end of the deck, staring at me. My breath hitches and my body shoots upright. His eyes, bloodshot and tired, find mine. It's clear Julian hasn't been able to sleep, either.

He pushes himself away from the ledge, walking toward me with slow steps, a heat in his gaze. Hungry. Ravenous. Desperate. I straighten my spine, facing him, the tension between us mounting with every inch he erases. When he's a breath away, he stops, his expression wrought with turmoil. It's reminiscent of the indecision covering his face earlier tonight when he left me in the hallway. I worry the same thing will happen, that he'll retreat instead of push forward. I can't let that happen.

Without saying a word, I reach for the sash of my robe, pulling at it, allowing the material to fall to my feet. A chill washes over me as the breeze wraps around my exposed skin, but the raw need covering Julian's expression chases it away, empowering me. Finding the hem of my tank, I pull it over my head, leaving me in just my shorts.

He sucks in a breath, his eyes breaking from mine as they rake over my chest. This is a bold and rash move, especially for me. I've never had to put it all on the line and risk rejection. But this is the eleventh hour. There's no tomorrow, not if I don't take a leap.

When he returns his gaze to mine, there's something unfamiliar in it.

It's more than lust or desire. He's not ready for me to walk out of his life any more than I am. But is that enough for him to ask me to stay? Or will the demons that still haunt him return, forcing him to withdraw back into himself?

I don't have a chance to think about it as he tugs my body to his, his mouth covering mine. His kiss is fevered, intense, wild. He seems to feed on me, needing me for sustenance. He breathes into me, causing a flutter in my chest. His hands shift to my ass and he squeezes, his raspy groan satisfying and electrifying. When he lifts and places me on the ledge, my legs wrap around his waist, his fingers digging into my skin. Desperate to feel every inch of him, I kiss him with more force, pulsing my hips against him. It feels like we've done this dance thousands of times before, our bodies in tune with each other so perfectly, so succinctly. A growl rips from his throat and his grip on me tightens. Before I can make sense of what's happening, we're moving, his lips never straying from mine as he carries me into my room.

Once he deposits me onto the bed, he leans back, peering at me, a question in his unwavering gaze. Not a single word has been spoken between us since we left the gala. We don't need them. After spending this amount of time together, we can read each other. We started out as strangers and became so much more than simply friends. I struggle to see a world without Julian in it.

I don't *want* to know a world without Julian in it.

As I nod in silent confirmation that this is what I want, I grab the back of his head, capturing his lips once more. When our tongues meet, he moans, and I hook my legs around him. Moisture pools between my thighs as I squeeze them, desperate for Julian to extinguish the flames he sparked months ago.

His mouth moves from mine, traveling along my jawline, nibbling on my earlobe before beginning the journey down the rest of my body. He takes his time to worship every inch of me, every curve, every dip, every valley, feasting on me as if I'm the finest delicacy known to man.

When his tongue swirls around my nipple, I fist the sheet in my hands, lightheaded. But that's nothing compared to the immense pleasure shooting through me when his teeth scrape against the sensitive flesh. My breathing increases, my pulse skyrocketing. Unmatched need fills me and I close my eyes, thrusting against him with increased urgency.

"Patience," he finally says. "I want this to last."

Taking several deep breaths, I try to slow my racing heart. But he's already struck the match. He did so the night I first saw him at the bar in Manhattan. All summer, he's fueled the flames to the point where I'm now ready to combust.

He returns his mouth to my nipple, sucking before continuing his exploration of my body. Every nip, every scrape, every lick pushes me higher and higher. When he reaches my hips, he hooks his fingers into the waistband of my shorts. A single brow arched, he peers up at me. I nod quickly, lifting my ass off the bed, desperate for him to hurry. With a sly grin, he leisurely lowers my shorts and underwear down my legs, tossing them to the floor, then settles between my thighs. Not a single self-conscious thought fills my mind as he seems to admire me from this vantage point, like a man who's been starved for too long.

He gradually breaks his gaze from mine and licks his lips. Every muscle in my body tightens as I hold my breath, waiting for the warmth of his mouth on my most sensitive spot. I've spent the summer in a perpetual state of heightened arousal. I fear all it will take is the slightest swipe of his tongue for me to shatter.

I close my eyes, gripping the sheets even tighter, my core clenching in anticipation. Finally, he presses his tongue against me, and I moan, relaxing my body as I lose myself in this sensation of bliss I've only fantasized about. I do everything to prolong it, but it's impossible. The past two months have been one big buildup to this moment. Now I regret what I've deprived myself of to keep my heart guarded, when Julian was able to burst through those walls without even a brush of his finger against my skin. In my heart, I know this was the path we were meant to take. We were meant to wait until this moment to experience this mind-blowing passion neither one of us believed possible…until now.

My breath quickens as that familiar sensation of warmth and ecstasy fills me, the peak in sight. As if able to read me like a book, Julian increases his motion, filling me with a finger, then another, pushing me to the brink until I succumb to his touch, convulsing around him. But that doesn't make him stop. He continues worshiping me until the last of my tremors cease.

As he crawls up my body, a smirk on his lips, I grab his face, crushing my mouth against his. The taste of me on his tongue reignites the flame and I'm instantly desperate for more of him, for all of him.

"I need you," I plead in a throaty voice, frantic and delirious.

He simply nods, pushing his shorts down his legs. As he's about to toss them to the floor, he reaches into one of the pockets, retrieving a foil packet.

"I was standing out there for over an hour before you walked onto the balcony," he answers the question written on my face.

"So this was your plan all along?" I ask coyly.

He releases a short laugh. "I don't think anything about this was ever planned, Guinevere." I smile at how true his words ring. Nothing about this summer went according to my original plan. Maybe that's the beauty of it. Because it was completely unexpected in the most satisfying of ways.

He touches his lips back to mine, treating me to a soft kiss. "I never planned this." His voice is contemplative.

"Me, either."

"Now I can't think of anything I want more."

"Me, either," I repeat, running my fingers through his hair and down his back, relishing in the feel of his skin. He briefly closes his eyes, melting into my touch, arching his back before returning to a kneeling position. He secures the condom, then positions himself between my thighs. I swallow hard, this moment bigger than I ever thought it would be.

Julian arches a brow, silently asking if this is what I truly want. I nod once more. He pushes into me, slowly, deeply, completely. My body fuses to the mattress as a sensation of absolute fulfillment washes over me. He leans down, cupping my face in his hands. His eyes sear mine as he moves so reverently inside me, taking me by surprise. I expected sex with Julian to be…different. Less emotional, less passionate, less…intimate. But this isn't sex. Not with him. Not with us. It would never be just sex.

I move with the steady rhythm he sets, relishing in every gentle thrust as he fills me to the brim, stretching me in a way no man ever has, then pulls back before continuing the same pattern. Neither one of us speaks a single word. There's no need, no requirement to fill the vacant space with declarations of lust or desire. The silence is more striking, the unspoken words more poignant than insignificant ramblings just to make it seem as if we're in the moment. Because we both know we're there, that we've finally made it to this place we fought against for too long. No more.

Julian rolls his hips into me, his motions measured and penetrating, delivering the utmost pleasure. As he nuzzles the crook of my neck, he finds my arms, pinning them on either side of my head.

"I don't know how much longer I can hold back." His voice is strained.

"It's okay." I wrap my legs tighter around his waist, circling him. "Let go," I whisper, taking his earlobe between my teeth, nibbling on it. That's all it takes for his muscles to tighten, his harsh grip on my wrists painful, yet satisfying. As his movements become increasingly more intense, I close my eyes, my core clenching as another wave of desire washes over me, much to my surprise.

"Don't fight it," he murmurs into my ear, his own breathing labored. "Just let go."

He drives into me with even more ferocity and I scream out, shattering around him as explosions of light obscure my vision. His mouth clamps onto my neck as he finds his own release, his body trembling and jerking. He thrusts one final time, then loosens his grip on my wrists, collapsing on top of me, spent and sated.

My fingers drift up and down his back, savoring the grooves of his tattoo, toying with his hair as I try to calm my breathing. I stare at the ceiling, everything seeming different now.

"Wow," Julian exhales, struggling to catch his breath just like me.

I laugh. "You can say that again."

He rolls off me and stands, removing the condom and tossing it into the trash bin next to the nightstand before crawling back into bed, draping the duvet over our bodies. His arms wrap around me and I blow out a contented sigh.

But I still don't know what this means for us, if this changes anything. I open my mouth, about to ask, when Julian places a soft kiss on my shoulder blade, tightening his hold on me.

"Shh," he soothes. "I'll be right here when you wake up. I'm not going anywhere."

All the tension immediately leaves my body as I melt into his embrace, his promise filling me with hope.

CHAPTER THIRTY-THREE

THE MELODY OF the lapping ocean waves and Julian's gentle breathing meet my ears as I slowly rouse from a restful sleep. The sun shines in the room as seagulls squawk, the sheer curtains blowing near the open French doors we never shut last night in the frenzy of finally experiencing each other. And experience each other we did. At least four times.

Sensing I'm awake, Julian traces a delicate circle around my hipbone. I moan, relaxing into his touch as he stirs my desire once more. I flip over to face him and place gentle kisses on his chest. He's so warm. So virile. So…perfect.

He grabs my chin, tilting my head back and leaning down to kiss me. I tear away, covering my mouth with my hand.

He cocks a brow. "What is it?"

"Morning breath," I say from behind my hand. "No one likes morning breath."

He chuckles, the rumble hitting me deep in my core. He wraps his arms around me, bringing me closer into his body, the heat coming off him electrifying.

"I like morning breath."

"Then you're weirder than I thought."

"Nah. I'm just weird for you." He grabs my chin once more. When he leans in for a kiss this time, I don't hide, his mouth touching mine. "Mmm," he moans, tongue tracing along my lower lip, coaxing me open. A slave to whatever he wants, I part my lips, our tongues meeting in a gentle dance.

I hook my leg over his waist, inching as close as I can. As our kiss becomes more heated, his hold on me tightens and he brings my body on top of his. Straddling him, my hips circle a slow rhythm against him. He groans as he hardens even more, craving me as much as I hunger for him.

"Do you feel what you do to me?" He grips the back of my neck, fierce, jarring, intoxicating.

"Yes." I close my eyes, continuing to tease him.

"Do you want me?" His hands find my waist, controlling my motions as he thrusts against me.

"God, yes."

That's all he needs to hear. He reaches for the nightstand, grabbing the last condom. He's about to open the packet when I rip it from his hands. Passing him a flirtatious grin, I tear it open, my eyes remaining locked on his as I carefully roll the condom on him. My touch on his length causes his nostrils to flare, his jaw to clench.

Once the condom is in place, I hover over him, my mouth a whisper from his. Our breath intermingling, I lower myself onto him, taking him as deep as I can before pulling back. He brings his lips toward mine, but I escape them. I'm no longer concerned about morning breath. I like this game, the playful desperation as Julian tries to capture my mouth with a kiss, to no avail.

My motions remain slow and sensual as I savor in him. Just like he did to me the night before, I grab his wrists, pinning them on either side of his head as I shade his face with my hair. He flexes his fists, and I can tell it's killing him not to be able to touch me. I know all too well. I was in his place last night.

Our eyes linger on each other as we remain in this moment. I give Julian everything he deserves as I take everything he's willing to give me until neither one of us can take anything else and I collapse on him, both of our bodies quivering and trembling.

In the aftermath, I remain locked in his embrace, my head nuzzled into his chest as I relish in the sound of his steady heart. He delicately traces circles on my shoulder blade, my arm slung over his waist. As we lay there in solitude, my attention is drawn to the scars on his abdomen.

"What's the story behind these?" I ask as I shift my hand to the three circular marks, brushing my fingers against them.

The instant I do, he grabs my wrist in a harrowing grip. I snap my eyes to his, wincing in pain. But he doesn't relent. Something inside him snaps and he's not himself, an old defense mechanism kicking in, forcing him to become someone else.

"Don't." It's not a plea. It's a demand. A warning. The atmosphere changes as he glares at me. Gone is my charming, endearing Julian. In front of me is a broken man. A haunted man. A shattered man. His entire body seems to tremble, his stare darkening as he squeezes my wrist so hard I yelp, tears forming in the corner of my eyes.

When he hears my piercing cry, he releases his hold, his eyes widening as he stares at me in confusion, as if snapping out of whatever trance he'd been in. Then he quickly pushes away from me and jumps out of the bed. I rub my wrist, flexing it, able to discern the place where each individual finger was wrapped around it. He focuses on my skin where a bruise is already forming, then looks back at me, turmoil covering his expression.

"Why don't you want to talk about your scars? What happened?" My brain tells me to retreat, to drop it, but I can't. I reach for him again, but he steps away, grabbing his shorts off the floor and yanking them on.

"I don't talk about them."

"But I want to know. I want to know this part of you. I want you to open up."

"Why?" His tone is harsh, one I've never heard him use with me, with anyone. "Why do you need to know about this? It doesn't matter."

"It *does* matter! It's a part of you. Based on your reaction, it's a big part of you. This is what people do when they care about each other. They share themselves. The good. The bad. And the gritty darkness."

He stares at me, his jaw tight, then lowers his head. "I can't do that." He avoids my eyes as he walks toward the door.

I scramble off the bed, rushing to pull on his oversized SUNY sweatshirt. When his hand touches the doorknob, I blurt out the first thing that comes to mind, the only truth I know that will make him see that whatever idea he's concocted in his head is ridiculous.

"I love you!"

He stills, his body stiffening as my declaration hangs in the air. The silence is so penetrating, you can probably hear a pin drop from a mile away. My heart thumps in my chest as he remains motionless, staring at the door.

"What did you say?" he asks in a soft voice, peering over his shoulder at me.

I advance toward him, my eyes unwavering. "I said I love you."

"No, you don't." He digs his fingers into his hair, yanking at it, pained at the mere notion. "You can't."

"I didn't want to believe it at first, either, but I can't avoid it anymore. I've fallen in love with you, Julian."

"No. You're just in love with the *idea* of me. None of this is real. That hasn't changed just because we slept together." He opens the door, storming away from me, but I follow him into the hallway.

"Aren't you tired of it all?" My words carry through the empty space. I can make out the typical morning sounds of the household staff cleaning and preparing breakfast, but I make no attempt to lower my voice. "Aren't you fucking exhausted of constantly running away from anything that *is* real? I know *I'm* exhausted *watching* you do everything you can to remain closed off to everyone who actually matters. Everyone who cares about you. Everyone who loves you."

He pauses, his lips curling, his fists clenched. A few weeks ago…hell, a few days ago, I would have dropped it, thinking it wasn't worth the argument. But I'm tired of this. Of him pushing me away the second I open up. I won't do it anymore.

I approach on timid steps, grateful when he doesn't try to escape. "Take it from me… It is *exhausting* pretending to be someone you're not just so you're accepted. I did it for twelve years of my life…until *you* showed me I was good enough as myself."

"This is who I am." He remains in place, but his voice lacks any conviction.

"No, it's not. I know it's not. I don't believe the Julian Gage who asked me to pretend to be his girlfriend for the summer is the real Julian Gage. I don't believe the only reason you needed me to pretend to be your girlfriend was to get your project up and running. I see how you are. You're resourceful. You already have hotels in several countries, so you know how to navigate all the bureaucratic bullshit."

He shakes his head. The more I speak, the more tension seems to mount inside of him.

"So that got me thinking. Why would you possibly want me on your arm? Then it struck me. You only did it because you thought it would help you be accepted into these people's inner circle. That's all. Not for some project, as noble a cause as it is. You just wanted them to accept you. Why? Why do you care? Why is this so important to you? Why, Julian?!"

"You wouldn't understand!" he shouts back. "You don't know what it's like being an outcast, of never being accepted!"

"So… What? You decide it's worth sacrificing happiness and who you are just so some asshole one-percenter will talk to you? That's not who you are. I know it. You're not that self-centered. I saw pieces of the real you through the cracks in your armor."

"No. No. No." He continues shaking his head, his body trembling with the force of his anger.

"That's the real Julian Gage!" I state over the lump in my throat, my voice becoming louder as relentless tears fall down my cheeks. I let them fall. At least I'm not hiding my feelings. At least I'm finally being true to myself. "Not this person standing in front of me lying through his teeth because he's too scared to admit he has feelings for someone. That, God forbid, he might just *love* someone!"

My words must have hit a sore spot because he punches his fist against the wall. The noise startles me and I jump, my heart ricocheting into my throat.

"You can't fix me, Evie!" he thunders, his eyes red as the vein in his neck strains against his skin. "No one can. So stop—"

"I don't *want* to fix you!" I scream, my chest heaving through my heavy sobs. The house has grown eerily quiet as my words seem to echo against the lifeless walls. Drawing in a deep breath, I lower my voice. "I just want to love you. Why is that so hard for you to accept?"

"Because love doesn't last," he chokes out. "The second you get a glimpse at who I really am, at all the shit I've done, you will run for the hills. So let's save each other the hassle now and cut our losses. You wanted a firm end date to our agreement. We've reached that point. It's come to an end."

"Is that truly what you want? To end it? To walk away and keep pretending to be someone else?" I look at Julian through my tears, desperate for him to admit he's never felt anything as real as he has with me.

He swallows hard, his Adam's apple bobbing up and down as the harshness in his expression softens. "This is all I know."

I hang my head low, emotionally and physically exhausted. I want to shake him out of this, to slap him and make him wake up. Will it work? Is it worth it? I don't know if I'm strong enough to pull him from the depths to which he's already fallen.

When I don't say anything else, he takes a step back. "Goodbye, Guinevere."

I float my eyes to his, not saying anything. I just stand there, studying the apprehension on Julian's face. He starts to turn from me, but hesitates, a flicker of indecision in his eyes. If this is what he wants, I'm not going to beg him to reconsider. Not anymore. I'm too drained to stay on his path of self-destruction, fighting against hurricane-force winds that will only pull me under and drown me. I won't do that to myself. I don't deserve it. Julian taught me that.

With a heavy sigh, he eventually turns from me and continues down the hallway. Just as he's about to disappear into his room where he can hide away from the world, I call out one last time.

"You were right."

He pauses, lifting his head, his eyes filled with sorrow.

"I do deserve better than you."

He nods, his shoulders falling.

"You deserve better than you, too."

I allow my words to linger for a moment, then step into my room, slamming the door behind me. Throwing myself onto my bed that still smells of Julian, I hold out hope that he'll change his mind and knock on my door.

He never does.

CHAPTER THIRTY-FOUR

"YOU SERIOUSLY DON'T want any of this stuff?" Izzy asks in disbelief as she sorts through hangers filled with the clothes I was treated to over the summer. "Why would you want to get rid of it?"

As much as I've wanted to share what happened between Julian and me, I couldn't bring myself to do so. Yes, my friends are aware we fooled around that first weekend, but I insisted that was the only time. I never even told them we'd kissed. And often.

When we all got together the Tuesday after Labor Day and they asked about my final weekend with Julian, I lied and said it was just like every other weekend, that I was thrilled to put the summer behind me and focus on my possible promotion. I must be a good actress because none of them questioned me, not even when my phone would ping with an incoming text and I'd jump to my feet in the hopes it was Julian apologizing for his behavior.

It never was.

Now, nearly two weeks later, I'm beginning to think I'll never hear from him again. Which is why I need to get all these clothes out of here. Not only do I have nowhere to store them in Chloe's tiny apartment, but I can't bear to look at them. Every time I do, the memories of my time with Julian come rushing back.

Like the way he looked at me the first time he saw me in that navy blue-and-white polka-dot two-piece. The way his mouth felt against mine the first time we kissed when I was wearing a beige maxi skirt and loose white tank. And the way we danced to him singing "Moon River" when I wore the stunning gray ballgown on our last night together.

"It's not my style," I say. "Take all the clothes you want. Or shoes." I gesture to another trunk filled with dozens of shoes I only wore once. "Jimmy Choo. Manolo Blahnik. Christian Louboutin."

Nora's eyes widen as she darts toward the trunk, throwing it open. "You have Christian Louboutins?" A peacefulness crosses her expression as she pulls out a pair and examines the signature red sole.

"Take them. We're the same size."

She grins dreamily. "I love you, Evie. If I swung that way, I'd totally whore myself out for you."

"I love you, too, Nora." I return her smile, although it's not as full as normal. How can it be when I'm surrounded by memories of Julian? And this is precisely why I need all this stuff out of here. I never wanted it to begin with. I purposely left them at Julian's place, but the day after I returned to Manhattan, a delivery man appeared on my doorstep. I'd hoped Julian had sent flowers to apologize for his behavior. Instead, he had the contents of my room packed up and delivered here. No note. No apology. Nothing.

"Are you sure you don't want anything?" I ask Chloe.

Standing, she gestures down her petite body. "If you haven't noticed, you're at least six inches taller than me. And have boobs. Whereas I, well… I'm lucky to fit in a B cup most days."

I nod toward a smaller trunk. "There's jewelry. And sunglasses. That stuff will fit. Check out some of that."

Chloe's hesitant at first, but her curiosity eventually gets the better of her. I lay back on my bed as I watch my friends pillage the spoils of my own war.

"You really don't want any of this stuff?" Chloe inquires yet again, a hint of skepticism in her tone.

"I really don't want any of that stuff," I confirm for what feels like the hundredth time.

"Even this?"

I glance up as she pops open the lid on the signature blue Tiffany's box, revealing the exorbitant necklace Julian gave me.

Everyone's eyes zero in on the brilliant stones encrusted in the intricate neckline, leading to an obscenely large yellow diamond.

"Holy fuck!" Nora gasps.

"Is that *real*?" Izzy asks.

Chloe lifts the necklace out of the box. Instantly, her gaze settles on a sheet of paper beneath it I hadn't noticed before.

"What is it?"

"Certificate of authenticity," she replies, reading it. "Fifty carats worth of diamonds. The stone is a forty-carat fancy vivid yellow diamond, with an additional ten carats of flawless diamonds in the neckline." She looks up, meeting my eyes. "Appraised value…one million."

I try to hide my utter shock at her words. I knew it was an expensive piece of jewelry, but I estimated maybe a hundred grand or something like that. Shows you how educated I am about the value of jewelry. But a million dollars? I can't even wrap my mind around that amount of money. Does it matter? Chloe routinely reminded me of Julian Gage's net worth during my time with him. A million dollars barely puts a dent in it. It's akin to most people buying flowers for their loved one. All Julian cared about was making an impression. He used me to do so.

"Take it. I don't want it."

My friends share a look before turning their inquisitive stares on me.

They simultaneously advance toward me, sitting on the edge of my bed in concert.

"Okay. What the hell is going on?" Nora starts.

"You haven't been yourself since Labor Day," Izzy adds.

"And now you want to give me a necklace from Tiffany's worth a million dollars?" Chloe continues. "Are you out of your fucking mind, Evie? How do you even *have* a necklace worth a million dollars? I mean, the rest of this stuff is nice, maybe worth a grand here and there, but a million dollars? What aren't you telling us?"

"That she has a magic pussy," Nora jokes.

"You guys know everything," I argue, my face heating as I try to convince them the lies I've told are true. "Our entire relationship was for show. Julian needed a companion to conduct business and make deals over the summer months. And like you mentioned, Chloe, this was a great way to clear my mind and help me forget about Trevor. We'd agreed it would only last through Labor Day. It's after Labor Day, so the agreement has ended. Plain and simple. Nothing more to tell."

Chloe squints, analyzing my demeanor. I've seen that look before. The look of disbelief mixed with annoyance, the one that means she's about to unleash an interrogation worse than I'd be subjected to if arrested for murder. Thankfully, the buzzer rips through the space and she exhales, pointing a finger in my face.

"This isn't over. You're not off the hook just yet."

She jumps up from the bed and leaves to answer the door. I watch her disappear into the living room, then blow out a long breath. When I shift my eyes to Nora and Izzy, forcing a smile, they harden their glares.

"That's right, Evie." Nora pinches her lips, trying to frown.

I stifle my laugh at the idea of her being some badass bitch. She doesn't even like it when I kill spiders, preferring to set them free instead. This woman doesn't have a bitchy bone in her body. She's all about peace and tranquility, the balance of mind, body, and spirit. She is the typical yoga instructor. So to see her trying to appear angry and annoyed only causes me to giggle.

"You're not off the hook yet."

"Oh, Nora. I almost forgot!" Scrambling to my feet, I head to one of the racks and flip through the hangers, grabbing an adorable shoulder dress in a subdued tropical print. "I'd set this aside for you earlier. I thought it would be great pre-wedding wear."

She protests at first, but stops when I say wedding, allowing me to pull her off my bed. Since her engagement, I've learned discussing her upcoming nuptials to Jeremy is a surefire way to distract her. Normally, I hate discussing her wedding. Now it's my saving grace.

"Don't you think?"

Holding the dress up to her body, I spin her so she's facing the full-length mirror propped against the far wall that's surprisingly not obstructed with the array of trunks and boxes filling the space. The fire department would have a field day if they ever saw what a fire hazard it is.

"You're right!" Her voice oozes excitement as she flips the switch from suspicious friend to glowing bride-to-be. "This would be great for the rehearsal dinner! Did I tell you?"

She whirls around to face me in full wedding planning mode. I widen my eyes, feigning enthusiasm. Izzy simply laughs, fully aware this was just a diversionary tactic.

"We're doing it at a luau. Figured everyone's making the trip just for us, we should make sure they all get a taste of the islands." She leans toward me. "And there are dancing Samoans blowing fire. Maybe you can nab yourself a hot local while you're there." She winks, then turns back to the mirror.

"The only hot local I'm interested in is Jason Momoa, but I think he's already spoken for." I smile, expecting Nora to swoon with me over his tattoos, which I know she's a complete sucker for. Instead, her body becomes taut, her breath catching as her eyes widen.

I look into the mirror, wondering what could account for her sudden change in demeanor. The instant I do, my heart drops at the reflection of Julian standing in the doorway.

CHAPTER THIRTY-FIVE

"GUINEVERE," JULIAN BEGINS in a shaky tone as I remain frozen in place, barely able to breathe. My mouth agape, a heaviness settles in my stomach. Ever since I walked away, I hoped for this moment. I didn't think it would actually happen. Things like this only happen in fairy tales.

When Nora squeezes my arm, I snap out of my shock, floating my gaze to her and Izzy, who both smile in encouragement. I suppose that's the thing about best friends. I don't have to tell them a single word. They'll still see the truth, despite my lies. Just like I see the truth in Julian's eyes right now…despite *his* lies.

Slowly, I turn around. The confident, self-assured man I spent my summer with is nowhere to be found. He looks like a different person, a shell, broken, defeated.

"You know what, Nora?" Chloe's voice cuts through the tension in the room. "I just realized I haven't seen any of the invitation samples you received."

"Me, either," Izzy offers.

"I thought you both didn't care which one I chose. That—"

"What kind of maid of honor would I be if I didn't give you my honest opinion on which type and style of paper will eventually end up in a landfill?"

"But I don't have them with me. I left them at my apartment. You said you wanted one day where I didn't mention the 'w' word."

"Nora…," Izzy says through clenched teeth, glancing between Julian and me, urging her to put two and two together.

It takes a few seconds, but realization finally washes over her. "Oh! I get it." She winks conspiratorially, following Izzy out of the room. As she walks past Julian, she pauses, lifts herself onto her tiptoes, and leans toward him. "Good luck."

"Thanks." He laughs slightly, then refocuses his unwavering stare on me. "I have a feeling I'll need it to fix the mess I've caused."

The girls glance back at me, giving me a hopeful look before making their way out of the apartment, leaving me alone with Julian. Neither one of us moves for several long moments. I want to ask why he's here, but I keep my mouth closed, simply staring at him with a blank expression. I've already said everything I wanted to. The ball's in his court.

Anxious from the awkward tension, he shoves his hands into his pockets, tearing his eyes from mine as he takes in the disaster that is my room. With a furrowed brow, he walks past me and toward all the trunks. My lungs expand as I inhale the aroma that is quintessentially Julian, memories flooding back.

"What are you doing with all your things?"

He stops in front of a box labeled GARBAGE and reaches in, retrieving the familiar polka-dot two-piece. I've always been self-conscious about my body…until I met Julian. I'd never felt as beautiful as I did when he first saw me in that bathing suit…except it wasn't real.

"They're not mine," I say dismissively. "I have no need for them, so I told Nora, Izzy, and Chloe to take anything they'd like before I donate what I can to a women's shelter. I figured you'd appreciate that."

He faces me, narrowing his gaze. Out of the corner of his eye, he spies the open Tiffany's box and flinches. "All of it?"

"All of it." I hold my head high, squaring my shoulders.

On a long sigh, he lowers himself onto my bed, his head hanging. I'm about to berate him for being so bold as to make himself at home when he interrupts me.

"I was in Paris this morning." He peers up at me through his long lashes, the confidence he typically wears like a shield absent. He still looks amazing in his dark suit, and smells even more sinful, but he's pale, dark circles under his eyes from an obvious lack of sleep.

"Did you come here to rub that in my face?" I press my lips in a tight line, my tone sharp. "If that's the case, mission accomplished. I've never had the luxury. I hope you enjoyed some macarons while you were there."

He shakes his head, briefly lowering his gaze. "I didn't mean it like that. You see what you do to me? You make me so…flustered."

He runs his hand through his sandy locks, tugging at them. My fingers twitch at the memory of what his hair feels like.

"I was there for work. This morning, as I went through my routine of reading the newspaper while having coffee, the TV was on as background noise, some classic movie channel. Do you know what was playing?"

I swallow hard, not saying a single word. My heart echoes in my ears as my eyes fixate on the despair and remorse hanging over him.

"*Breakfast at Tiffany's*," he says in a measured tone. "It was the final scene. You know the one when Paul finally calls out Holly Golightly for who she really is, for being scared of falling in love because she doesn't want anyone to put her in a cage?"

Tears form in my eyes as I recite one of the most poignant lines from the film. "'No matter where you run, you just end up running into yourself.'"

"Exactly." In an instant, he's on his feet, striding the short distance toward me. When he cups my cheeks in his hands, a current runs through me, my body waking after a nearly two-week slumber.

Drawing in a deep breath, he rests his forehead on mine. "I don't want to run into myself anymore. I am absolutely petrified of this, of you, of us. But I'm even more scared of not feeling this anymore."

I close my eyes, allowing his words to fill me with the hope and promise I'd been yearning for since it all came crumbling down. But is it enough? Does it change anything? How do I know it's real?

Shaking my head, I release myself from his hold. I need more than that, more than him being scared of losing me. I need…him. All the broken, damaged pieces that make up who he is.

"Thank you for finally admitting that. I can only imagine how difficult it is. But just because you're scared of losing me isn't enough reason for me to stay, not after…" I trail off.

"Guinevere…" He grabs my hands in his, pleading with me. "You have to believe me when I say I'm willing to try. For you. That's all I can give you right now. Please understand."

"I do understand." I pull away, glancing at all the clothes he spoiled me with, all of it as artificial as he is. All glamour, no substance. "But I need more than that. Just two weeks ago, you wanted me to believe you'd never change who you are for anyone."

"I lied." He rubs his temples, his jaw clenching. "Okay? You *know* I lied, too!" He returns his impassioned gaze to mine. "You saw the truth."

"You're right. I did." I sling my purse over my shoulder, retreating from him into the living room and toward the front door. When I reach the foyer, I pause, glancing back at him standing a few feet away, looking confused. "The truth is, I don't know what to believe. You can say you made a mistake today, but how do I know it's because you truly believe it, not because you have some ulterior motive?"

"Please, Guinevere." He closes the distance between us, his chest heaving in desperation. "I want this. I want *you.* I can't function without you in my life. Nothing is right in the world. And I'm sorry I was a fool and pushed you away. I promise. I won't push you away again. Just please… Give me a chance to prove it to you."

Pulling my lips between my teeth, I consider his plea. Then I place my hand on a hip. "Okay."

"Okay?" His eyes light up as he goes to close the last bit of space between us, but I step back, holding up my hand to stop him.

"Prove it. Now. Prove you won't push me away again."

He parts his lips, his brows pulling together. "How?"

"You say you want this, that you want something real with me."

"I do." He reaches for my hands, clutching them in his. "More than I've ever wanted anything."

"Real relationships aren't all romantic dinners and snuggling on the couch. They require a connection, sharing yourself. *All* parts of yourself, even the ugly ones. That's what makes it real. Looking past the ugly at all the beauty hidden beneath the surface."

Julian swallows hard, his fingers growing cold as understanding of what I'm asking rolls over him. He drops his hold on me and turns from me, staring blankly into space.

"I want your ugly, Julian. It's the only way this will work. The only way I'll know you're in it for real. So I'm going to ask you one question. Whether you respond will determine whether I walk into your arms or out that door." My voice trembles as I struggle to hide the emotion at the thought of walking away from him yet again. But I can't be with someone who only allows me part of the way in. I made that mistake with Trevor. I won't do it again. "How did you get your scars?"

Julian slowly glances over his shoulder, lifting his eyes to mine. Moisture pools in the corners as he pleads with me to ask him another question…*any* other question. But I can't. This was the question that started it all. And it may be the question that ends it all, too.

I'm unable to move, my heart caught in my throat as I wait for him to finally answer me. He doesn't. Instead, he faces forward, shaking his head.

My shoulders fall as my heart deflates. "I understand," I manage to squeak out. I turn from him, heading toward the front door. I only make it a few steps when his voice stops me.

"My step-father shot me." His words are low, devoid of emotion. He speaks so softly, I'm unsure I heard him correctly.

I whirl around. "What did you say?"

"The scars." Facing me, he pulls his shirt out of his pants, lifting it and revealing the marks on his abdomen. "From my step-father."

"Why?" I return to him as he tucks his shirt back in.

He rubs the back of his neck, drawing in a pained, shaky breath. "I was trying to protect my mother." He slumps onto the couch, the truth weighing him down.

"Your mother?" I sit beside him, unable to take my gaze off his remorse-filled expression.

"It wasn't enough. He killed her. She was trying to get us away from him so he couldn't hurt us again."

I lean into the cushion, briefly closing my eyes as I put the pieces together. No wonder he used a large portion of the inheritance he received from Mr. Price to open a women's shelter. He lost his mother to domestic violence.

"The instant she slumped to the floor, all I saw was red. I charged at him. He pointed the gun at me, warning me not to do anything stupid. But I didn't care. And he was drunk. So I grabbed a knife out of the butcher block and stabbed him, but not before he got off three shots. Thankfully, a neighbor, who was a paramedic, heard and burst into the house. If he hadn't, I probably wouldn't have made it."

"And that's what landed you in foster care." I tilt my head at him, studying him.

He shoots his eyes to mine, surprised at my statement. Then he pinches the bridge of his nose, exhaling. "Camille."

"You didn't have any other family you could live with?" I press. I come from a rather large extended family. The idea that there was no one else Julian could count on boggles my mind.

"Mom was young when she got pregnant. The result of an affair with a college professor. Her parents were well-respected, affluent members of their community. They saw her pregnancy as a blemish on their reputation. When she refused to get rid of the baby, they cut her off. She raised me on her own. We were all each other had. When she died, there was no one to claim custody of me, so I was put into foster care. Since the system's so overworked, none of the foster parents wanted to deal with an adolescent boy suffering from emotional trauma. Sure, I was in therapy, but I got moved around between therapists, too."

"Julian…" I shake my head, unsure what to even say. I'd learned about pieces of his past in the research I'd done on him. I could never have anticipated this was the real story.

"I push people away, Guinevere." His eyes intensify, the blue hue becoming darker. "It's what I've always done. Actually, I've never let anyone get remotely as close as you. No one's cracked the shell. Until you came into my life." His expression softens as he leans toward me, grabbing my hand in his. "You saw through me when no one else ever could. You were right about all of it. How I acted the way I did because I was scared. I knew it was true, and I hated you for calling me out on it. Worse, I hated myself because I thought it made me appear weak."

I bring my free hand up to his cheek, reveling in the scruff. "It doesn't make you weak. It makes you human."

He covers my hand with his, my heart swelling with the longing I feel in his touch. "I understand that now. I've spent my entire life running from anything real…including love. I'm just not sure I know *how* to love."

"Oh…" My heart deflates as I pull my hand from his cheek. I begin to slink away, my eyes watering, but he grabs my chin, forcing my gaze to his.

"But I want you to show me how."

I part my lips, my brows furrowed. "Show you how?"

"Yes, Guinevere. I need you more than I've needed anyone." He releases his grip on me, then stands and starts to pace. "But I'm messed up. *Really* fucking messed up. I wasn't lying when I said I'd hurt you. I probably will. Just please…" He stops, dropping to his knees in front of me, his hands clasped together. "Be patient with me. I have a lot of scars, ones that will take me a while to finally share with someone after keeping them all to myself for years. But I *want* you to know all these things about me. I *want* you to know my ugly."

"That's all I want. Just you." I bring my hand to his face, brushing my thumb along his cheek. "The real Julian Gage. No more lies. No more pretending. No matter how bad you think it is, lying is worse. So just be honest with me. And if I ask something you're not ready to talk about, don't push me away. Just say you're not ready. That's all I ask. Just be honest."

A flash of hesitation crosses his expression as he chews on his lower lip. I want to question it, but before I have a chance, he's on his feet, pulling me up with him. His arms swallow me as his lips find mine. Any doubt is instantly erased as his kiss consumes me, heart, body, and soul. For the first time, I feel like I'm actually kissing Julian, not the man he pretended to be all summer long.

"I like this better," I murmur against his lips, a tingle trickling down my back from the subtle contact.

"Like what?"

"Kissing you. Not the other person you were."

"And I like kissing you like this, too." He circles his hips, then yanks my body, hard and fast, against his. His erection pushes into my stomach, making me gasp. "And I'd like to do more than just kiss you. You have no idea how hard these past few weeks have been, especially now that I've gotten a taste."

I pass him a coy look. "Oh, I have a pretty good idea just how *hard* it's been." I palm his erection, which only causes the fire in his gaze to burn brighter.

Before I can protest, he lifts me up, forcing my legs around his waist. His mouth slams against mine, his kiss voracious, hungry, desperate as he carries me toward my makeshift bedroom.

When he reaches the doorway, he pauses, looking around. "Where the hell's the door?"

"I told you. This is just a den."

He glances at me, then out to the open living room before back at me again. "Oh, fuck it," he growls, practically tossing me onto my clothes-covered bed.

"Julian!" I squeal, laughing at the playful deviousness in his expression.

He hurriedly shrugs off his suit jacket while I rip my t-shirt over my head, both of us frantic to scramble out of our clothes. Finally, once his boxer briefs land on the top of our discarded things, he retrieves a condom from his wallet and climbs onto the bed, crawling up my body.

Impassioned lips find mine and I melt into him. He tastes as I remember…citrus, spice, and Julian.

"Guinevere…," he pants.

"Yes," I exhale.

"I'm buying you a fucking apartment with a door. And a better bed than this pullout sofa."

I laugh, the sound echoing through the room. "And why would you want to waste your money on that when I can just crash at your place?" I bat my lashes, passing him a demure look.

"So I can show up at your place anytime I want." Leaning back, he rips the packet open with his teeth, then rolls on the condom.

When he teases me with his length, I grab the back of his neck, every inch of me alive with anticipation. "And why would you want to do that?"

"So I can have you anytime I want." He exhales as he pushes into me, slow and restrained, filling me in a way only he can.

Our eyes meet as our bodies connect, but unlike before, it's not just the joining of our bodies. It's the joining of our hearts, our minds, our souls. I thought Trevor made love to me all those years we were together. He never did. But Julian… This moment, this feeling. This is exactly the love I've been searching for my entire life.

Maybe four isn't such a bad number, after all.

CHAPTER THIRTY-SIX

My fingers draw light circles around the grooves of Julian's scars as we lay in his bed, the motion now as innate as breathing. It's a far cry from the morning I woke up in this same bed and had a panic attack about where I was, *who* he was. Now, this is the only place I want to be. It has been for the past two months.

As summer made way for fall, our relationship truly blossomed. We've opened up to each other in a way I never did with Trevor. I want Julian to know everything about me. And I want to know everything about Julian. Thankfully, he wants me to know everything, regardless of how sad and horrible. He shares these things because he knows I won't judge him. I'll love him in spite of it.

I'll love him *because* of it.

It doesn't matter that he still hasn't uttered those three magic words to me. He will when he's ready. In the meantime, I shower him with my own love.

"How did you meet Mr. Price?" I ask in a lazy voice, spent and sated after our latest round of lovemaking. As much as I enjoy going out with him and being seen on his arm, my favorite place is still in his bed. He's an exciting and enthusiastic lover, one I can admit I'm incredibly addicted to.

"Mr. Price?" He peers down at me from where I rest in his embrace, relaxed from the steady rhythm of his beating heart.

"Yeah." I continue tracing circles around his scars. At first, it made him self-conscious. Now, I like to think it offers him the comfort he needs, that he deserves. "I know what Camille and you have shared, but I get the feeling there's more to it."

"What? You don't think I'm some criminal mastermind who took advantage of an old guy, like his children do?"

His words bring a smile to my face. Now that I know the real Julian Gage, thinking of him as a criminal mastermind is absurd.

"Absolutely not." I shake my head. "Plus, I did the math. When you met him, he was in his sixties, not this elderly, feeble man his kids made him out to be."

"That's for sure. He had more energy than I did some days. Thankfully, the judge realized his kids were greedy and pissed off their father didn't give them the bulk of his wealth."

"But I also think there's more to the story than you befriending a lonely man over a game of chess."

"I can't get anything past you, can I?" he comments on a long sigh.

"No, you can't."

His lips curve into a small smile, eyes sparkling as he stares into space. He pulls me closer into him as he sighs, relaxing. If I asked this same question a few months ago, he would have closed up. Now he talks about his past with no hesitation. It hasn't been easy. There have been moments he's struggled to share certain things, especially when I asked about the aftermath of his mother's death and he told me about the six months he spent in a juvenile detention facility before the judge ruled he acted in self-defense. Regardless, he's slowly learning how to open himself to me.

"No one really knew how to handle me in any of my foster homes. I never got the help I should have when I was first placed in the system. I went to therapy, but it didn't work…at least not for me. I kept blaming myself for what happened. When I got to be too much for my first family, they sent me on to the next home. The cycle repeated for years, so much so that I thought this was my penance for taking another man's life."

"Julian…" I tighten my arm around him, kissing his chest. "You don't honestly believe that, do you?"

"I did at the time. And I'll admit there are times I still do. I had no direction in life. When I first arrived at a new home, my foster parents would care for a little while, hoping to save some poor kid from becoming another statistic so they could brag to their friends about all the good they were doing. Until they realized how difficult it was. They'd quickly lose interest and wait for Child Services to come and take me to a new placement so they could try all over again with a new kid. By the time I was sixteen, I was so used to the cycle, I stopped caring, stopped trying. I'd been through so many foster homes, I'd lost count."

"It couldn't have been all bad. I'm sure you had friends at school."

"I was never in the same one long enough to make friends. Child Services did everything to keep me in the same district, but it wasn't always possible. I always had to start over again in new schools. After a while, I stopped trying to form friendships with anyone there, since I knew it would only be a matter of time before I was uprooted again. Plus, I hated being teased by everyone about the fact that I didn't have real parents. I acted out, allowed my anger to get the better of me. I was suspended from school a lot. And that's actually what brought Theodore Price into my life."

"How so?"

"I was living in a foster home with five other kids in Fort Lee, just across the Hudson from New York. My foster parents had their hands full, so they never realized when I wasn't there. Hell, when I brought home my notice of suspension, they signed it without even reading it. They were just going through the motions, knowing the clock on me was ticking. I was a few years from being eighteen and aging out of the system, with no hope for a future.

"When my mother died and Child Services came to take me away, they let me bring a few items with me. I'm not sure how, but my mother's old address book ended up in my things. I think I just wanted something with her handwriting on it and that was the first thing I could find. Well, as I grew older, I became more and more angry about the shitty hand I'd been dealt. I figured everything would be different if I had a real family, people who actually cared about me. So I looked in my mother's address book and paid her parents a visit at their multi-million dollar home in the Upper West Side."

"Did they know who you were?"

He exhales loudly. "Yes, but they turned me away. Said my mother's death was due to all the bad decisions she'd made. That she was dead to them years before her actual death. That I never existed in their eyes."

"My god." I cover my mouth, struggling to understand how anyone could say that, especially to their own blood. No wonder he has trouble accepting love.

"I had a lot of problems, Guinevere. A lot. I battled depression, anxiety, along with a slew of other things. After they said that to me, I started to think maybe it *would* be better if I didn't exist."

Tears well in my eyes at the pain I hear. I squeeze him tighter, reveling in his warmth, reminding myself he *is* alive. I can't imagine a world without Julian in it.

"I never went back to my foster home that night. I just walked and walked. Hours passed as I tried to think who would care if I weren't alive. I couldn't think of a single person..." He trails off, his voice wavering before he clears his throat and continues.

"As I crossed the George Washington, I came to a stop. I remember standing there, looking at the Hudson swirling below, wondering if I could actually do it, if I could really jump. I kept wondering if it would hurt, if dying would be painful. Regardless, I knew it would be nothing compared to the pain I lived with every day.

"I was about to hoist myself over the railing when I heard someone say, 'The bravest thing I've ever done is continue to live when I wanted to die.' It stopped me cold. I looked to my right. Mr. Price stood a few feet from me. And that's exactly where he remained for the next hour, talking to me about everything and nothing. By the time the sun rose, I was no longer interested in jumping. But that wasn't enough for him. He made a phone call and got me in to see his therapist, the man who helped him with his own depression after his youngest son had jumped from that same bridge years before."

"Oh, my god."

"That's why he was out there. It was the anniversary of his death, so when he saw me in the same place, he felt compelled to save me. And that's exactly what he did. He was the first person to take a genuine interest in me. Everyone else only did because they were getting paid to do so. But not Mr. Price. He had nothing to gain, yet he still cared. Not only did he get me the help I needed, he encouraged me to focus on school. He told me if I graduated, he'd pay for college. Before then, I never put any effort into my education. By the time college rolled around, I'd no longer be considered a ward of the state and would be on my own. Why bother studying when I couldn't afford college? But Mr. Price did something no one else had. He made me see I had potential outside my life circumstances."

"You went to SUNY, right?"

"Not the typical Ivy League school you hear most successful men attend, but that was an accomplishment for me in and of itself. Once Mr. Price offered to fund my college education, I buckled down and raised my grades. Having a great therapist helped.

"After I turned eighteen, Mr. Price helped me find an affordable apartment near campus. He even offered me an entry-level job at his company to earn money. He wanted me to learn how to take care of myself, how to budget and pay bills. With him, everything was a lesson. Yes, he had more money than I could even wrap my head around, so he wouldn't miss a measly $800 a month that was the rent on my studio apartment. It wasn't about the money. It was about teaching me to live on what I made."

"My parents did the same. When I got my license, they made me get a job so I could pay for car insurance. I had to give them $20 every week. They wanted me to understand that everything has a cost, that we have to work for things we want."

"And that's what Mr. Price taught me. The life lessons he shared with me were more valuable than anything I learned in school."

"So you remained close, even in college?"

"We did. Every Sunday, he invited me to his place in Manhattan…" He looks around. "Here, actually," he adds with a smile. His brows scrunch in contemplation. "It's funny, isn't it?"

"What is?"

"When he first passed and I inherited everything from him, I still called this his place. I thought I always would."

"I'm sure he'd want you to think of it as your place, don't you?"

He pulls his lips between his teeth. "I suppose."

"So… Sundays?"

"Right. Every Sunday, I came over here and Camille would cook us dinner. I often found myself hating to leave. He shared his story with me, how his success was due to simply being in the right place at the right time. He told me about his wife and children. His wife died from breast cancer ten years earlier, just a few months after he lost his son to depression. She was the glue that held the family together. Once she passed, his kids drifted away, leaving him mostly alone, except when they needed money."

"That's so sad."

"I guess you could say we both needed each other."

"He sounds like a really good man."

"I owe him everything." He shifts to his side, his hands cupping my cheeks as he stares intently at me. "Just like I now owe *you* everything."

I swallow hard. "Me?"

He slowly nods as he brings his lips to mine. "Yes, Guinevere. Mr. Price showed me I was deserving of love, but he never did what you did. He couldn't."

"And what's that?"

I feel his lips turn into a smile. "You taught me *how* to love. If you never did what you did, if you never had the balls to call me out on my shit, I doubt I'd be here, that *we'd* be here." He covers my mouth with his as he pushes me onto my back. "And I *really* like being here with you."

His deep kiss leaves me breathless, a panting bundle of hormones. When he moves to the crook of my neck, I moan, closing my eyes, relishing in the roughness of his day-old scruff against my skin. I bring my hands up to his back, digging my fingers into the flesh, my nerve endings firing as he travels down my body.

"Are you only using me for sex?" I breathe.

"Never," he croons. "Although I *really* like having sex. But it's not just sex with you." His lips circle around my nipple, his tongue torturous as he tastes me. "It never was. It never will be."

I throw my head back, my hand moving to his scalp. My fingers dig into his hair, guiding him as he worships me in a way only he can. "Never."

"Never." He flicks his eyes to mine. I grin deviously as I place my hands on his broad shoulders and push him down my body. "Can I help you with something, Miss Fitzgerald?" His voice is playful and coy. As much as I love learning about his past, I love this side of him more. The flirtatious man I found him to be during our time together.

"You know there is." Spreading my legs, I prop my feet on the bed.

"And what would that be?" He blows out a long breath as he settles between my thighs, the warmth driving me wild.

"Your mouth on me."

"Anything for you, baby doll."

I brace for his tongue to work the magic it always does when a loud ringing cuts through the room.

Julian stiffens, his eyes widening as he remains motionless for several seconds. This isn't the first time a phone's rung when we were about to go at it, but this ring… It's not coming from either of our phones. It's coming from down the hall.

"Ignore it," I whisper, running my hands through his hair. That's normally all the encouragement it would take. Not this time. He pulls his bottom lip between his teeth, visibly torn about what to do. Then he sighs.

"I have to get that." Rolling off me, he grabs his discarded boxer briefs from the floor and yanks them on as he darts out of the room.

My mouth agape, I sit up, staring at the door in disbelief. What could be so important that he left me when he's rarely answered a phone call in my presence, and certainly never during sex? He's been adamant in his insistence that when we're together, he wants to devote all his attention to me. What changed? And what phone was that? His cell is sitting on the nightstand.

My curiosity getting the better of me, I throw my legs over the side of the bed and grab my robe, pulling it over my body. I carefully tiptoe down the hallway, stopping shy of the open door to his study.

"Slow down. Slow down. Tell me what happened." His tone is calm and compassionate as he pauses. I can faintly make out the voice on the other end — a female voice. "Where are you right now? … Shh. Shh. It's okay. It'll all be okay. You're stronger than this. Don't let him get into your head."

My heart's caught in my throat as I listen to his conversation. A sickness forms in my stomach at the idea that he hasn't been faithful, but my rational side screams for me to slow down and look at the situation realistically. We've spent practically every night together the past few months. If Julian were sleeping with someone else, I would have known about it. I would have at least smelled the perfume on him. Since he confided in me about his past, the only perfume I've smelled on him is my own. But the secret cell phone doesn't ease my worries any.

Lost in my own thoughts, I almost don't hear him end the call. When the sound of footsteps meets my ears, I hurry back toward the bedroom on light feet, tossing my robe to the floor and jumping back into bed.

When he appears in the doorway, I smile, but it doesn't reach my eyes. "Everything okay?"

He parts his lips as he steps toward me, hesitant. Then his shoulders drop. "Actually…" He worries his bottom lip and my heart deflates. "I have to go."

"Go?" I prop myself onto my elbows, doing my best not to act dejected, but it's impossible, especially with the knowledge that he was speaking to a woman.

"Work thing. It's an emergency." He heads to the closet and retrieves a pair of jeans and a sweater, pulling them over his body. "You know I'd never put work ahead of you. You're more important than that, but this is a matter of life or death…" His voice trails off as he swallows hard. "So to speak. I don't know how late I'll be, but stay. You don't need to leave just because I'm not here."

Returning to the bed, he leans down, kissing my forehead, then steps back. In the silence, we hold each other's gaze. Something in my expression must tell him I'm not convinced this is a work thing. Regret creases his brow.

"I'm sorry, Guinevere," he says in a soft voice. He looks as if he's about to say something else. Then he shakes his head, turning from me and hurrying out of the room.

Chapter Thirty-Seven

I CAN'T SHAKE my melancholy mood as I shuffle from the elevator toward my cubicle. The atmosphere at the magazine office usually fills me with energy, especially this time of year when Christmas lights and decorations seem to hang from every available surface. But nothing lifts my spirits.

As I lay in Julian's bed last night, I tossed and turned, unable to shut off my mind. The smell of him on the sheets was anything but comforting as I came up with a thousand scenarios about where he was and what he was doing. They all seemed so outrageous, so out of character for him…except for the truth that he abandoned me to go see another woman.

I try not to dwell on that as I stare at my laptop screen, needing to focus on my work, but it's impossible. I'm so consumed with what's really going on, I almost don't register Viv's voice saying my name.

I glance up from my computer, doing my best to force a smile as she leans against the wall to my cubicle. "Good morning, Viv."

"I was hoping it would be; unfortunately, I just read the rough draft of the escort piece you sent over."

I swallow hard, my stomach rolling. To Viv, it was a rough draft. For me, it was the result of hours of writing, rewriting, revising, and editing. I wanted Viv to be so impressed by the initial draft that her suggestions were merely stylistic. Based on the displeasure on her face, that's not the case.

"And?" My voice is shaky, hesitant. I brace for her to rip it apart, as she's been known to do.

"It's good. But good doesn't sell magazines, Evie. The picture of this August Laurent character you've drawn is compelling, and the idea of a male escort empowering women is one that will intrigue readers. Many women will empathize with what his clients have experienced. He's helped all kinds of women, from the single woman left in a circle of friends to women whose spouses never appreciated them. You've painted him in a light that will make readers think twice about judging him as merely a male escort taking advantage of women. Hell, *I've* thought twice about judging him as a male escort who takes advantage of women."

"Thank you?" My voice lifts, waiting for the punchline.

"But it's one-dimensional. I want more August Laurent."

"The whole article's about August Laurent."

She smiles a thin-lipped smile. "No. It's about the women who've hired him."

"And through each of them, you learn something about him."

"I learn about the man he is when he's with each woman. That's not who he really is. I want the *real* August Laurent. I want to know what makes him do what he does, what makes him want to sacrifice friends, family, *love*."

"The article talks about that," I protest, although she's right. There's no big insight into who August Laurent truly is, which is why I pressed to talk to some of his clients. There's still a piece missing. The *why* is missing.

"Something must drive him to choose this path, to help the women he does. There's a story there. I want to know what that is. And so do your readers."

She holds my gaze for a moment longer, then turns, walking away. I open my mouth to argue, but it won't do any good. After all, this is her magazine. If I want this promotion, I need to give her the story she wants...and then some.

Mentally exhausted, I return my attention to my laptop, opening the file I'd amassed on August Laurent and the handful of women who agreed to let me interview them. My notepad in hand, I scour through everything once more, searching for something I may have overlooked or deemed unimportant. The more I review my email exchanges and phone conversations with August, the more it hits me. He seemed to evade all my questions about his younger years, often shifting the focus back on me. It almost reminds me of how Julian used to do the same thing until I convinced him to open up.

As I consider what I can do to persuade August to share what caused him to get into this line of work, Chloe flies into my cubicle, her eyes wide, expression grave. "Did you hear?"

"Hear what?" I peer at her, brows furrowed. This level of excitement could mean Diego in accounting finally asked out Rachel in design. Or it could be actual news.

"Sonia Moreno was murdered. She was a friend of Julian's, wasn't she? I thought I saw a photograph of them together at some fundraiser earlier in the year."

Blinking repeatedly, my heart drops to the pit of my stomach as a chill rushes over me.

"Yes," I answer in a small voice. But her connection to Julian isn't what has me out of sorts. It's the fact that she's a client of August Laurent's. And not just any client. A woman who claimed he saved her from an abusive marriage. During a few follow-up interviews, she mentioned she was getting her affairs in order before going public with her abuse and officially filing for divorce. I wonder if she finally did it.

"How was she killed?" My voice trembles, tears forming in my eyes. She seemed so confident, so happy, like a weight had been lifted off her shoulders at the thought of starting over, even if she never worked another day in Hollywood again.

"Details are still sketchy, but a few of my sources say she had stab wounds covering her chest and abdomen. Police are operating under the theory it was a burglary gone wrong. She'd just returned from being on location for the past month, so authorities think her place had been scouted for a break-in. She must have surprised them by being home."

I shake my head, my heart squeezing under the weight of everything I know. It could have been a robbery, but my gut tells me it's not. Not after everything Sonia shared with me.

Jumping to my feet, I grab my coat and my bag, needing to do something, *anything*. I can't remain silent about this.

"Where are you going?" Chloe calls after me.

I whirl around, meeting her questioning stare. She probably came into my cubicle to share the juicy gossip before it hit the airwaves. Never could she have predicted my response, or the fact I may hold the missing link to what happened. I refuse to believe Sonia went through everything she did, *survived* everything she had, just for some thugs to kill her. It's too much of a coincidence.

"I have to go." It's all I can tell her, at least for now.

I spin on my heels, about to race to the elevator when Viv approaches, her own expression frantic. She doesn't even have to utter a word. I know she's here because of the news about Sonia. Viv is the only other person who's aware of the identity of the women I interviewed, including everything they've been through.

"It's okay." Her voice is a low whisper. She squeezes my biceps, giving me a reassuring smile. "Go. Be her voice."

I nod, then hurry from the office, doing everything to keep my emotions under control. I barely knew the woman, but in the brief time we spent together, I felt a connection to her. I can only imagine how August feels, if he even knows.

I stop in my tracks, imagining him watching this story break on the news. I can't stomach that. No one deserves to learn about the death of a loved one that way. So I reach out to him the only way I can.

To: August Laurent
From: Evie Fitzgerald
Subject: Sonia Moreno

Dear August,

Please call me as soon as you receive this message. It's about Sonia. News just came over the wire. I'd rather tell you over the phone instead of through email.

I stare at my phone the entire ride toward Police Plaza, waiting for him to call.

He never does.

By the time the cab drops me off a block from police headquarters, news of Sonia's death must have already spread. Reporters are camped out front, setting up cameras and preparing to go live to break the news, all for better ratings. As I hurry up the stairs and into the lobby, the place is a madhouse. Everyone passing appears as if they know exactly where they're going. I'm lost and out of my element, unsure if I'm even in the right place or if they'll take me seriously.

"Can I help you?" a woman asks in a thick New York accent as I look around.

I turn, my stare falling on a young brunette sitting behind a pane of what I imagine is bulletproof glass. My heart breaks a little at how far our society's fallen that you can't even feel safe in a police station anymore.

Straightening my spine, I step toward her. "My name's Guinevere Fitzgerald. I work for *Blush* magazine."

Rolling her eyes in annoyance, she points to the front doors. "Reporters have to stay outside and wait for the press conference."

"No," I interject. "I'm not here to *get* information. I'm here to *give* information. I just recently interviewed Sonia Moreno. I may have evidence to help in finding her killer."

"The detectives already have someone in custody who was seen in the vicinity of her house."

"Have you questioned her husband?" I press.

"Her husband?" She arches a brow. "The director?"

"Yes." I retrieve my cell phone from my purse, unlocking the screen and scrolling through the audio files until I find the one I need. "She spoke of him. How she was getting ready to file for divorce, but was worried about what he might do." I hit play. Sonia's voice fills the room. Her subtle Spanish accent leaves no question that it's her.

"Turn that off," the desk sergeant orders, glancing at people lingering close by. She gets up from her seat and walks away. A few seconds later, the secure door opens and she holds it for me. "Are you coming or not?" she presses when I don't move.

"Right. Of course." I walk toward her and follow the sergeant down several long corridors. I stay as close to her as possible, worried I'll get lost or trampled by people rushing around if I stray. I barely breathe until we step into the elevator and the doors shut, allowing me a reprieve from the chaos. I love the busy atmosphere at the magazine, but it's never like this.

When the elevator stops, we exit onto the twelfth floor, the words "Homicide Unit" in bold letters hanging on the wall in front of us.

"This way."

We continue down several hallways, the sound of two-way radios and loud voices filling the maze-like space. Approaching a door labeled "Conference", she points to a line of chairs against the wall.

"Wait there. Detective Mulroney will be with you shortly."

"Thanks," I say, but she's already disappeared.

Taking a seat, I smile as a man in a dark suit with a buzz cut, a detective shield hanging from his neck, rushes past, carrying a bunch of papers. I pull my planner out of my bag, scratching down notes in one of the free pages. There's no doubt in my mind Ethan is involved, not with the threats he'd made. What I have to say may not be useful, but I must try. I'll never be able to live with myself if I don't and he continues to walk free. Julian would want me to do the same. He stood up to an injustice and protected his mother. I need to protect Sonia's legacy.

When the door to the conference room opens, I snap my head up, looking in its direction, my hands growing clammy. I'm innocent of committing a crime, but I'm just as nervous as I would be if that weren't the case.

"Thank you for coming in and sharing this with us, Mr… What do I even call you? Now that I know who August Laurent is…"

My pulse skyrockets when I hear that name.

"Call me whatever you'd like," a familiar voice interjects. But it's lacking the normal vitality I'm used to hearing during our conversations. It's somber, solemn, not to mention the subtle French accent seems to have disappeared, as well.

The door widens and two men step out. I freeze, unsure how to act, whether August would want me to acknowledge him. He knows what I look like. But I have no idea what he looks like. Every single woman I've interviewed has remained incredibly tight-lipped about his appearance, about his true identity.

But as the detective moves to the side and I meet the eyes of the man I've spent months obsessing over, my heart plummets. The room spins, my grip on my planner loosening. It falls to the floor, pages spreading in every direction as the world seems to give out from beneath me.

CHAPTER THIRTY-EIGHT

"JULIAN?" I SAY through the thickness in my throat, fighting to capture a breath as I stand. Chills rush through me, my limbs trembling as flashes of the past several months play before me. What I thought was a coincidence when I ran into him at the Steam Room. August calling me because a "little birdie" told him I was looking for him. His sudden change of heart after he'd adamantly refused my request to interview a few of his clients. His agreeable attitude wasn't because of any skillset I possessed. It was all because he wanted to sleep with me.

"Julian?" I squeak again when he only stares at me, his jaw slack. My expression pleads with him to finally say something. But he doesn't. He simply bows his head, shaking it, silently confirming the awful truth. My eyes burn with the betrayal filling me and I spin from him, running down the hall, searching desperately for the elevator.

"Guinevere! Wait!" he calls out, but I continue, wheezing as my sobs remain trapped in my throat.

With each step I take, the more it makes sense. I often mentally remarked about the parallels between the two men. But I never considered Julian *was* August Laurent. He would have told me. Wouldn't he? A voice in the back of my head reminds me he wouldn't if he were trying to hide the truth. And there's only one reason he would do that… Because on the nights he wasn't with me, he was keeping another woman company. The thought turns my stomach.

I somehow find the bank of elevators and send a prayer of thanks to the big man upstairs when there's already one waiting. Once inside, I repeatedly hit the button for the lobby. Julian's voice grows closer, calling my name, begging me to stop. I bang the button faster, willing the doors to close. They finally do just as he reaches the elevator, the echo of his fists slamming against the doors filling the car. I release a relieved breath and slink against the wall, needing the support to keep me upright.

When the elevator arrives on the main floor, I dash from it, keeping my head lowered, refusing to look over my shoulder in case Julian…or August…or whoever he is manages to catch up. I barrel past the front desk, ignoring the desk sergeant's questions about how it all went, and continue through the large glass doors.

The instant I step outside, a coldness hits me like a wall, and not just from the frigid temperatures on this December morning. There's a strange feeling in the air. The sky is a foreboding shade of gray, one I've grown accustomed to over the years.

I inhale a breath, tasting the impending snow in my mouth. Based on the weather report I caught earlier, that's exactly what's supposed to happen over the next few hours. The first snowfall of the season. Normally, I'd play hooky from work and enjoy the beauty of snow falling around New York City. But my mood's been drastically altered.

Tugging my jacket closer, I do my best not to slip on the slick brick as I hurry past the growing number of reporters, evading their shouts asking if I know anything about Sonia Moreno. I ignore everything, until *he* bellows my name, his voice carrying across the plaza, echoing against the tall skyscrapers.

"Guinevere!"

I glance behind me, watching as Julian frantically runs toward me, panic and desperation covering him. His stare is distressed, neck stiff, jaw tense.

"Leave me alone!" With quick steps, I continue toward the corner, raising my hand to hail a cab. When one pulls up to the curb, I open the door to get in, but come to an abrupt stop when an arm blocks me.

"Guinevere, please. Just hear me out."

I keep my eyes forward for a moment, my vision obscured with tears. This truth is worse than Trevor walking away after twelve years. He may have had his faults, but he never lied to me, never misled me, never used me.

"Hear you out?" I squeak, biting down at my bottom lip, hoping to transfer the pain from my heart to another part of my body. "Why? So you can make up an excuse about why you lied to me? I've heard them all before. I don't need to listen to you go on about how you wanted to tell me the truth but didn't know how. That's a bunch of bullshit. You just wanted a guaranteed piece of ass every goddamn night." A shiver rolls through me, acid burning my stomach. "Nothing more."

I go to duck under his arm and into the cab, pausing when I hear his voice again.

"I haven't taken on a client since the beginning of June."

I have no reason to believe him, but something in his tone makes me second-guess myself. I still, one foot in the cab, one foot on the ground. So what if he hasn't taken on a client since June? Does that change anything?

"Lady, are you in or out?" the cabbie asks in a thick Middle Eastern accent, glancing at me. I look at him, then back at Julian, torn.

"Don't run from me, Guinevere. Not without knowing the truth. Please."

I close my eyes, squeezing them tightly. Once again, I'm entangled in a battle between my brain and heart. My heart screams at me to stay, but my brain tells me to walk away and never look back.

"Please," he says once more, this time softer. "'No matter where you run, you just end up running into yourself.'"

The instant Julian utters that quote from *Breakfast at Tiffany's*, I exhale a protracted breath, shaking my head. I hate that he's using that movie against me. It's unfair, but it still makes me stop and think rationally for a moment. And a moment is all it takes for me to realize I'll never move on unless I have answers.

Blowing out an exasperated sigh, I step away from the cab and close the door, but don't turn around. If I peer into Julian's eyes, I fear I'll crack. "You wanted to explain. Here's your chance. Explain."

"Please, look at me."

"Explain," I repeat, this time harder.

At first, it's silent, then he exhales deeply. I picture him running his hands through his hair in resignation. "I never intended things to get this messed up."

"No? What was your intent then, Julian? Or is it August?" Spinning around, I throw my hands up in frustration, paying no attention to the snow beginning to fall around us. "I don't even know your real name."

"Julian Gage is my real name. I was born August 10, 1980, in Jersey City. I never lied to you about that."

"But you failed to mention you also go by August Laurent, the man I was doing a story on." With each word, my voice gets more and more agitated. "You called me repeatedly, pretending to be this other person, when all along it was *you*. Hell, you even used a fake French accent so I would be none the wiser. You had so many opportunities to come clean, yet you deliberately kept the truth from me. Why? Why would you do something like this?"

"I never meant to hurt you, Guinevere."

"*Bullshit*! Bullshit, Julian. You *did* mean to hurt me! The second you made a conscious decision to lie to me, to deceive me, you intended to hurt me. You know what they say about secrets, don't you?"

He remains silent.

"Two can only keep a secret if one of them is dead. At some point, the truth was bound to come out. Or were you going to wait until we were married to tell me you had to leave on occasion to go screw some other woman?"

He grabs my biceps, his eyes imploring. "I know I fucked up. I knew it the second I walked into the guest room of my beach house and saw you wearing that stunning two-piece. That entire weekend, there were so many times I considered telling you the truth. Because I had started falling for you. Even in those early days. For the first time in my life, I wanted somebody to know every part of me. The good. The bad. The ugly. You know my ugly. The reason I *am* August Laurent is because of that ugly."

"Tell me this, Julian…" My voice wavers as my next question remains on the tip of my tongue, my throat closing up at what his response will most likely be. "When you approached me with your proposition, did you only do so because you knew I was on the hunt for August Laurent?"

He briefly closes his eyes, hanging his head as he drops his hold on me. "I wasn't planning on calling you as August Laurent that Monday after our first dinner. I was just going to let it go. But I found myself forming feelings for you. And I liked the idea that I could help you get promoted. So I picked up the phone and did the one thing I swore I'd never do. I called a journalist who was hoping to do a story about me."

"Did you not even stop to think about what this would do to *my* career?" I shriek, pacing in front of him. "All along, I honestly thought I did something right to get the elusive August Laurent to agree to an interview when he's refused everyone else for years. I thought that maybe, just maybe, I could prove everyone wrong and show them I *am* good at what I do. But all along, the *only* reason August Laurent agreed was because Julian Gage wanted to get into my pants!"

"That's not true. That's not the only reason." He advances toward me, but I step away.

"Oh really? If I weren't the one sitting at that coffee shop trying to get a lead on August Laurent, if it were someone else, would you have reached out to them?" I lean into him, my nostrils flaring and fists clenched as I wait for his answer. "If I hadn't shared my frustrations over the direction of the story, would you have granted me access to some of your clients?"

He averts his eyes. His silence is the only confirmation I need.

I push past him once more and hail a cab, keeping my back turned. I can't stomach the sight of him, of the visible reminder I'm not enough, that I never would have gotten this far with this story, with this promotion, if he hadn't made it so.

When a cab pulls up, I go to pull the passenger door open.

"I love you, Guinevere!"

I stop in my tracks, choking out a sob at his admission. I've waited months for him to finally say those three beautiful words. I pictured him sweeping me into his arms, showering me with kisses as he declared his love for the first time. Instead, it tastes of desperation, one final act to make me stay.

"That's the truth. That hasn't changed. You taught me that. *You*. That has to count for something."

"Maybe. But you know what you taught me?" I look over my shoulder at him, but he doesn't answer. "That being spontaneous comes at a cost, one I'm no longer willing to pay." I hold his gaze for a moment, watching as the snow falls around him.

"I'm ready to give it all up for you. All of it." His voice is strained and wrought with emotion.

I bite my bottom lip to stop my chin from quivering. "I wish I could believe you. I just don't know what's real and what's not. Goodbye…whoever you are."

Chapter Thirty-Nine

"Are you certain this is the direction you want to take?" Viv looks at me from over her horn-rimmed glasses.

I rub my clammy hands along my pants, glancing out the window of her office. The city is dark, despite it only being three in the afternoon. A downpour soaks Manhattan, the weather matching my mood.

"Like I said, I've given this serious consideration over the past few weeks. I didn't get the story because of my talent or tenacity. I got it because…" I trail off as I attempt to compose myself. The last thing I need is for Viv to see how the truth of who Julian is has affected me. "Because I had a personal relationship with my…subject, although it was unbeknownst to me at the time. That still doesn't change anything." I straighten my spine, rebuilding the wall around my heart. "I would have never gotten remotely close to landing that story had he not had a personal interest in me. You should choose your new assistant editor based on their talent, not luck…or the fact that the subject hoped to get something out of our agreement."

Telling Viv I no longer want to be considered for assistant editor has been one of the most difficult things I've ever done, but it's necessary. I could never accept a promotion I didn't earn.

When she doesn't respond, I stand, heading toward the door.

"Do you honestly believe that?"

I turn around. "What do you mean?"

She removes her glasses, chewing on the end of the frames. "That you didn't get the interview with Mr. Laurent based on talent."

"Of course I do, Viv. I dated him without realizing it. He admitted he—"

"I understand that. But do you really think people agree to be the subject of a story based on the goodness of their heart?"

I step away from the door, sucking in my lower lip. "What are you saying?"

She stands from behind her desk and walks toward me, her mouth formed in a tight line. "I've been in this industry for more years than I care to admit. It's one of the toughest jobs out there, especially for a woman. No matter what you do, how much you try to present yourself as serious, there are times when you'll only get the interview if you turn on the charm, if you make them think there's a chance of something…more."

"I didn't just make him think there was a chance of something more. I gave him something more. And then some."

"No. You gave that to Julian, not August."

"I still didn't get the story based on my talent alone, regardless of whether the man I slept with was Julian or August. I didn't plan for it to happen this way."

"Evie…" She runs her hands down my arms. "Life sometimes doesn't go as planned. It's how we handle the unexpected that determines our strength. Do you go on to fight another day? Or do you give up because it's too hard?"

"I'm not giving up," I mumble.

"No?" She spreads her arms. "Then what do you call this? So you were lied to. It doesn't lessen your ability to do your job and do it well."

"But I'd know the truth." I point to myself, my jaw tensing. "If I continued on and, by some miracle, you gave me the promotion, every time I walked into that office and saw my name on the nameplate, assistant editor below it, I'd question whether I earned it. I *need* to know I earned it. I'd never…" I stop short. I can't tell her the other reason. That every time I walked into that office, I'd be reminded of Julian. Ever since I learned the truth over two weeks ago, I vowed to erase him from every aspect of my life. That includes my work life, too.

"I've always known you were stubborn," she says when I don't finish my thought. "I just didn't realize you were stupid, too." She spins and grabs a large envelope off her desk, shoving it at me.

"What's this?"

"An early proof of the February issue. It's not final yet, but it has the feature story and the layout you designed. Figured you'd want to see the fruits of all your hard work."

"Oh."

She crosses her arms. "Yeah. Oh."

After several long moments pass and she doesn't say anything further, I take it as my cue to leave.

"You're damn good at what you do, Evie," she offers as I reach the doorway. "You should be proud of everything you've accomplished, regardless of *how* you did so."

I glance over my shoulder and smile, wishing I could be as proud of myself as it appears Viv is. I walk out of her office, returning to my cubicle and the only thing that makes me feel grounded in a world that seems to have fallen to pieces around me. I pull my new planner out of my desk drawer and make new plans…better plans. *Happier* plans.

But it still doesn't heal the gaping hole in my heart. I wonder if anything will.

* * *

"Coming to Nora's to help her decide on centerpieces?"

When I hear Chloe's voice, I pull my attention away from my planner, which is now covered with decorative stickers and color-coded based on my itinerary for the day. I've even started making daily, weekly, and monthly goals for the next three months. It makes me feel like I'm slowly regaining control of my life, like I will move on from this little hiccup.

"The hotel…" She focuses on my desk, then snatches the planner off the surface. "What in the holy hell is this?"

"You know what it is." I tear it away from her, hugging it to my chest like a baby would a security blanket. "It's my planner. A new planner. For new plans."

"Oh, I know that. But what is it doing out here?"

"Nothing." I hold my head high. "I just like being organized. I dropped the ball the past few months and am now suffering the consequences. Life is better when it's planned. No surprises. So that's what I'm doing. Making a new plan for the new year."

"Does this new plan include finally growing a pair and talking to Julian? I'm not sure how many more bouquets of roses we can fit into the apartment before the city zoning committee tries to evict us for running a floral shop out of a residence. Or are you *planning* on ignoring him forever?"

"I'm not ignoring him," I answer calmly. "I just have absolutely nothing to say to him. Eventually, he'll move on. He'll go back to being August Laurent, screwing whatever rich socialite calls him that month, and forget I even exist."

She considers my words for a moment, then sits on the spare chair. "But will you?"

"Will I what?"

"Move on? Forget about him?"

"Yes. I have a plan."

She rolls her eyes. "Of course you do. And what does that entail?"

Flipping my new and improved planner open to the correct page, I push it toward her, keeping a protective stare on her the entire time to ensure she doesn't do something crazy.

"What is this?"

"New requirements for a potential partner."

"You're joking, right?"

"No. Goals are important. Of course, I set the bar a little lower than I did when I first did this in high school. I'm thirty. Most women are twenty-seven when they marry, and the men are twenty-nine. So I can't be as selective as I was twelve years ago. Ideally attractive, a decent job—"

"I can read," she shoots back. "It's all here on your list."

"And not a secret escort."

"Well…" She closes my planner and pushes it toward me. "I don't think you have to worry about that."

"I wouldn't be so sure. I didn't take that into consideration last time and look where it got me."

Chloe glares, her lips pinched together as she leans toward me. "Did you ever stop to put yourself in his shoes? Try to figure out *why* he did what he did?"

I open my mouth, shaking my head. "What are you—"

"Julian!" She slams her hands on the desk, her eyes fierce. "Have you considered what *he's* gone through during this pity party you've thrown for yourself these past few weeks?"

"I know why he did it. So he could have his cake and eat it, too." I look away from her heated stare, crossing my arms over my chest.

"You know that's not the case. You said yourself he claimed to have stopped taking clients the beginning of June. When you met. The *first* time. Before you ever agreed to be his fake girlfriend."

"Who knows how true that is?" I mutter under my breath.

She brushes off my comment. "If he told you who he was back then, would you have given him a shot?"

"No." I chew on my fingernails when I notice a word spelled wrong on my itinerary for January second. My hands itch to reach out and grab my planner to fix it, but I have a feeling Chloe would toss it into the incinerator if I did that.

"Then maybe that's why he did what he did. Because he knew lying to you was the only chance he had to get to know you. Trust me, as much as I was initially skeptical of the whole arrangement, that man has always had eyes for only you. I saw it that first weekend when the photos of Julian Gage's mystery woman started appearing online. The way he looked at you… Well, it's a way all women yearn to be admired, revered, worshiped. There's no question in my mind he worships the ground you walk on. That he would do anything for you." A smile lights up her face. "I've never seen you as happy as I have when you were with Julian. Trevor certainly never made you that happy."

"At least Trevor never lied to me. He didn't have a secret escort business he never told me about. Remember this…"

I open one of my desk drawers, shifting through the contents until I find the list I'd scratched out after Julian called to take me to dinner all those months ago. On one side are Trevor's pros and cons. On the other are Julian's. I haven't updated this list since that day. I could probably add many more cons to Trevor's side and dozens of pros in Julian's. But there's one con that outweighs everything else. The con he played on me.

I shove the list at Chloe. "Trevor's a much better choice than some man I'm not sure I ever knew."

"On paper, maybe, but I recently read this dating advice column where the author said that love is fickle and makes no sense. That just because someone has all the traits you deem important, it doesn't mean you love them. That only the heart decides that. Sound familiar?"

I lower my eyes, pulling my lips between my teeth. "Maybe."

"So tell me…" Chloe places her hand on my arm. I lift my head. "What does your heart say about Julian?"

"That none of it was real," I answer in a quiet voice, my throat pained.

"I think it was as real for him as it was for you."

I shake my head, refusing to believe it. "This entire thing taught me that life is better when you stick to your plan. Trevor was my plan. I should never have let a pair of beautiful blue eyes and a smooth-talking mouth stray me from that. Not only do I have to live with the knowledge I messed up, but I also destroyed any chance I had at making Trevor realize he made a mistake."

Chloe glares at me before sighing and standing. "He came to see me."

"Who? Trevor?"

"No. Julian." She pulls on her jacket, securing it with a belt. "When you refused to talk to him, he reached out to me. You know what he told me?"

I remain silent.

"That even if you never speak to him again, he doesn't regret what he did, not when you gave him the greatest gift imaginable."

"Guaranteed sex?" I quip back sarcastically, but it's missing my usual bite.

"No. He said you taught him how to love." She pauses, allowing her words to linger. "But I think he gave you an even greater gift."

"And what's that?" I ask hesitantly.

"He taught you how to *live*. If he had to lie to get you to stray from this picture-perfect life you imagined for yourself, from constantly making lists of pros and cons of every decision, from micromanaging everything, I'm grateful he did so. And I think if you looked hard enough, you'll realize you feel the same way."

CHAPTER FORTY

I LOUNGE ON the couch in Chloe's living room, glaring at the envelope Viv gave me earlier while *It's a Wonderful Life* plays on the television in the background. In retrospect, it probably wasn't the best movie choice, considering I'm currently going through my own internal crisis. I wish I had a guardian angel who could come down and show me what *my* life would look like had I never met Julian Gage. Would it help matters any?

Always a glutton for punishment, I grab the envelope off the coffee table and lift the flap. I'm most likely going to regret looking at this. Then again, I *did* just wish for a guardian angel. Maybe that's Viv. Unexpected and impractical, but so was Buster Poindexter as the Ghost of Christmas Past in *Scrooged*.

My stomach tenses as I pull out the magazine and flip it over. When I stare into a pair of familiar blue eyes, my throat tightens. I haven't seen Julian since Sonia's funeral, and even then, I kept my distance, disappearing before the end of the service so he couldn't approach me. At one point, whenever I peered into these eyes, I saw a man willing to take a risk and love me. Now all I see are his lies.

As Jimmy Stewart begs Clarence to take him back to the life he'd wanted to end, I thumb to the page Viv marked with a sticky note, landing on the featured article — *August Laurent: Unrobed.* The initial two-page spread is a combination of photos of him along with the text of the article I'd poured everything into the past several months.

I peel the note off and read it.

> *E,*
>
> *I made a few adjustments to the final draft you submitted. Mr. Laurent requested additional information be included to give the reader greater insight into why he does what he does. This piece will still run, regardless of what decision you make, but I hope I won't have to change the byline. The ball's in your court.*
>
> *- Viv*

I shift my eyes to the caption beneath the title, running my fingers over the glossy page.

By: Guinevere Fitzgerald, Assistant Editor
Contributor: Chloe Davenport, Columnist

It's strange to see my full name in print. I've always gone by Evie Fitzgerald. In a way, it's satisfying, like I'm turning over a new leaf, starting a new life. No longer writing about the best condoms for maximum pleasure, but about subjects of value.

Encouraged by George Bailey shouting about wanting to live again, I turn my attention to the opening paragraph of the story I pitched on a whim, thinking nothing would come of it. I can't help but smile at how wrong I was. In more ways than I care to admit.

> *When I first pitched the idea of getting the inside scoop on the man who, over the past decade, has become one of the country's most sought-after escorts, I selfishly did so because a story about a male escort would appeal to a large percentage of female readers. I envisioned the cover in my mind... A man dressed in a suit, tie draped around his neck, white shirt unbuttoned revealing chiseled abs, head cut off to keep the mystery alive.*
>
> *I suppose that's how I assumed this man's story would be. All eye candy. No substance.*
>
> *Well, dear reader, you're in for quite the ride, just as I was.*
>
> *August Laurent's tale is one you can't truly appreciate until you have the full picture. I confess, I didn't have that until now. I assumed he was a womanizer, a heartbreaker, a philanderer... Someone who had no qualms about taking advantage of women for monetary gain.*
>
> *I couldn't have been more wrong.*

My heart squeezes as I zero in on that one line. When I first wrote it, I believed it with every fiber of my being. Has any of that changed because I know *who* August Laurent is? Maybe I'm wrong about him again.

Bringing my eyes back to the article, I lose myself in the world I spent my summer living. But it's better now, the pieces Chloe contributed adding another dimension. Now, instead of being a story that seemed to focus on the women August helped, I'm left with a tale of a boy forced to become a man when most kids his age only cared about the latest video game. A boy who had to say goodbye to the only family he had when the rest of us were at an age we wished our parents would disappear. A boy who refused to get close to anyone because he didn't think he deserved to be loved.

But that didn't stop him from giving love when it was needed, despite his insistence that he didn't know how to love. He did. In giving that love, he helped so many women realize their true worth. Some of them just wanted to feel secure in their decision to focus on their career instead of getting married and having kids. Others needed to feel as if they were worthy of love after being with someone who took them for granted. And others needed him to save them, just as he was saved. Regardless of the fact that it was strictly a business arrangement, he still made them feel beautiful, made them feel worthy, made them feel loved.

He did the same thing for me, too, but as Julian.

Can I learn to look past his faults because of the way I felt when I was with him? The way I *still* feel when I hear his name, look into his eyes, recall the heat of his hands on my skin? I want to. God, I wish I could run into his arms and start over again, like he's begged me to do over the weeks that have passed. But this is a man who's made a living out of giving the women who've hired him the fantasy they need, learning how to read them and tell them what they need to hear. How do I know anything he's told me is real?

I'm so consumed with indecision, I barely register the sound of the buzzer, thinking it's the apartment next door. When I hear it again, I shoot my gaze toward the door, holding my breath as I stare. I've ignored that buzzer for weeks now, regardless of Julian's pleas from the front stoop to talk to him. A few hours ago, I was happy to continue to ignore him. Now, I wonder if I can give him the second chance my heart urges he deserves.

Placing the magazine on the coffee table, I stand, taking measured steps toward the entryway, my pulse increasing the closer I get. I place my hand on the knob, able to feel the electricity. When I open the door, I expect to stare into pleading blue eyes. Instead, the eyes looking back are hazel.

"Trevor..." I wrap my arms around my stomach, warming myself as I walk out onto the front step, remaining out of the rain. "What are you doing here?" I hug myself, Julian's SUNY sweatshirt providing me with warmth.

He shoves his hands into his pockets, nervously rocking on his heels. "I, uh... I was in the Village for a meeting with a client and thought I'd stop by to see how you're doing."

"How *I'm* doing?"

I haven't seen Trevor since my final weekend in the Hamptons at the Farewell Gala, which he attended on Theresa's arm. And I haven't spoken to him in even longer, both of us happy to ignore each other all summer. Truthfully, it wasn't a conscious effort on my part. Julian's presence consumed me to the point that I ignored everything else...including the ex-boyfriend often standing only a few feet away.

"No plans with Theresa tonight?"

"We broke up around Thanksgiving." He laughs slightly. "Mom and Dad came to visit, like they do every year."

"And how did that go?"

"Let's just say it made me realize how different Theresa and I are."

"Sorry to hear that."

He lifts his eyes to mine as he shakes his head. "No, you're not."

I part my lips, about to argue with him, but snap my jaw shut. "You're right. I'm not."

"I deserve that, especially after the way I handled things."

Neither one of us says anything for several long seconds, an awkward tension building. I used to feel comfortable around him. This is a man with whom I had no qualms, even sharing all the dirty details of my period…much to his chagrin. Now I don't know how to act.

"How's Julian?"

I hold my head high, doing my best to maintain my composure at his question. "We're not together anymore."

"I figured as much."

"You did?" I arch a brow.

"You were both at Sonia's funeral but didn't acknowledge each other. I wasn't aware you were friendly with her."

"I could say the same about you," I shoot back, not wanting to discuss the fact that my connection to Sonia is actually through Julian's alter ego, August Laurent.

"The firm represents her." He pauses, then corrects, "*Represented* her."

All I can do is nod, silence falling between us once more.

"Can I come in?" Trevor finally asks, his eyes imploring me as he hunches his shoulders, trying to shield himself from the rain. "Just for a minute. I just… I just really want to talk to you. If you don't like what I have to say, I'll leave and never bother you again. Okay?"

I study him in quiet contemplation. After the way he ended things, I don't owe him anything. But my curiosity gets the better of me.

"Fine."

Turning from him, I enter the apartment, the warmth thawing my cold fingers. After shaking the water off his coat, Trevor leaves it in the entryway, then follows me into the living room. I grab the proof copy of the magazine off the coffee table and shove it back into the envelope, keeping the identity of Julian's alter ego a secret for now.

"Do you know what today is?" Trevor asks.

I scrunch my brows together, wracking my brain, but nothing comes to mind. A few months ago, I would have been able to remember every anniversary we shared. Now those memories have faded.

"December fifteenth?"

"Exactly." He steps toward me, a heat I haven't seen in years crossing his expression. "Do you remember what happened on December fifteenth twelve years ago?"

I shrug. "I don't know."

"We were at a football game. But not just any football game. It was a momentous game, and not because of any Bowl placement for the Huskers. Something else happened at that game. Do you remember what that was?"

Closing my eyes, I chew on my bottom lip, the memory of the game he's referring to returning with striking clarity. I can almost hear the roar of the crowd in the stands. Smell the hot dogs and beer. Feel the frigid wind whip against my face.

"You told me you loved me, and not just as a friend."

When I open my eyes, there's a smile on Trevor's mouth. It reminds me of the carefree, spirited person I met my freshman year, not the Trevor he turned into. He's *my* Trevor again.

"And do you remember what happened after that?"

"The game went into double overtime. By the time we won, I was so cold. I joked I had hypothermia and the only way to make sure I didn't perish was by stripping so we were skin to skin."

"You sure did." As he continues closing the distance between us, our chests rise and fall in sync. Suddenly, everything about him becomes familiar, simple, easy, like riding a bike. Despite the passing of time, you don't forget how to hop back on, even after a nasty fall. It may take some time to build up the courage to ride full on again, but you eventually do.

"I didn't really have hypothermia," I say in a breathy voice.

"I know. But I would have been an idiot to turn away your offer for some skin-to-skin time." He adjusts his stance, his hand going to the small of my back and bringing my body flush with his. He lowers his mouth toward mine, the warmth of his breath dancing on my lips. "I was such an idiot to push you away, Evie. I knew it was a mistake, but refused to admit it. I hated seeing you with another man. It drove me crazy to think someone else was enjoying *my* laughs, *my* smiles…*my* lips."

Hypnotized by his heartfelt plea, I succumb to the pull Trevor has on me, all reason leaving me as his lips brush against mine for the first time in over six months.

"I don't care what I have to do to win back your heart, I'll do it. You'll never have to doubt me again, just please… Give me a chance."

He doesn't even allow me to respond as he presses his mouth even firmer against mine, kissing me like he did for so many years. When he first broke up with me in June, this was exactly what I wanted. But now, it feels lacking, foreign…wrong. It's missing something…something only Julian's kisses ever provided me. A feeling of love. I'm no longer thinking of kissing Trevor, but of Julian, recalling the magnitude of his blue eyes in the photos Viv selected for the article. I'd expected to see all shots with his head cut off, recalling the numerous times the man I thought to be August Laurent insisted his anonymity was all he had. Instead, every single photo was of him, August…

Trevor kisses me deeper, but his hand roaming my frame lacks the confidence Julian's touch had. I'm transported to the Steam Room the day I received that first phone call from August Laurent, his voice still strong in my memory.

"If I ever find someone worth giving this all up for, I'll gladly grant your magazine an exclusive photo shoot and you can plaster my face from here to kingdom come."

The realization hits me like a freight train. Breathless, I stumble away from Trevor, as if he holds some contagious disease. I stare into his eyes, but all I see are Julian's. The same deep pools of sorrow and pain staring back at me from the pages of the magazine. It's not August in those images. Not to me. It's Julian.

Bringing my hand to my lips where the ghost of Trevor's lackluster kiss lingers, I step back. The truth has been glaring at me all along, but I was too stubborn to open my eyes. Yes, I was angry at Julian for lying, but what really irritated me was the idea of him sharing himself with all those women. He never did that. They only got to know August Laurent…mysterious, enigmatic, aloof.

I got to know Julian Gage.

My broken, damaged, tortured Julian.

My lascivious, passionate, amorous Julian.

My beautiful, caring, kindhearted Julian.

"Evie?" Trevor's concerned voice cuts through. "Are you okay? I thought—"

"He's showing his face."

He tilts his head to the side and pinches his lips together. "What are you talking about?"

"He's showing his face," I repeat, this time louder. My heart pounding, I snap out of my stupor and grab my boots, tugging them over my leggings. "He said it himself." My voice grows increasingly excited and frantic with each word I speak, my heart ready to burst. "He would only reveal who he was when he found someone who made it worth giving up. He's willing to walk away just to have a chance with me. If that's not love, I don't know what is."

I whirl around, heading toward the front door. As I'm about to open it, I pause, facing Trevor once more. His brow furrows in confusion at my sudden change of demeanor. I don't know how to explain it, either.

Flinging my arms around him, I plant one last kiss on his cheek. It's fitting, in a way. Trevor is the reason I met Julian in the first place. Now he's the reason I finally opened my eyes to what's been staring at me all along.

"Thank you, Trevor!"

I spin from him, dashing out of the apartment. As I run into the rain, I feel a little like Jimmy Stewart in *It's a Wonderful Life* when he rushed through the streets of Bedford Falls, desperately trying to get home to the people he loved. And that's what I'm doing, too...trying to get home.

Julian is my home.

CHAPTER FORTY-ONE

ADRENALINE COURSES THROUGH me as I jump out of the cab in front of Julian's building. The entire drive from Chloe's, I tried to figure out what to say. I'm not sure any words will be adequate, but I suppose apologizing for my behavior, admitting I was wrong, is probably a good start. He claimed he'd give it all up for me, but I refused to listen, insisting I'd never be able to believe another word out of his mouth. So he did one better. He *showed* me. Now it's time I show him how much he means to me, how sorry I am for all this wasted time.

I'm a nervous wreck as I ride up the elevator to his penthouse apartment. I don't know what to expect when he opens the door. I *hope* he opens the door. I never even stopped to consider he might not be here or, worse, is here but refuses to speak to me. After all, I deserve it. I refused to speak to him.

When the elevator slows to a gradual stop and the doors open, an emptiness settles in my stomach, my mouth growing dry. This is it. My grand gesture. I like to think Julian wouldn't want those photos to be published in an article revealing August Laurent's identity if he'd given up on me. Then again, I could be wrong. It could all be a ploy by Viv to get me to agree to the assistant editor position. I have no way of knowing anything for sure, not until I see Julian again. And for the first time in weeks, I *do* want to see him.

Heading toward his door, I square my shoulders, summoning every ounce of courage I possess to swallow my pride and admit I made a colossal mistake. I was the one who had the balls to admit my feelings to Julian in the first place. Now I have to be the bigger person and admit I was wrong about him, about both August and Julian.

I bring my hand up to the door, but before I have a chance to knock, it swings open. I still, momentarily taken by surprise before a familiar smile greets me warmly.

"Guinevere," Camille sighs, holding out her arms and taking me in them, hugging me. "It is so good to see you." She pulls back, not a hint of disapproval in her gaze as I'd expected to see. I'm more than aware of how close she is to Julian. I have no doubt he told her what happened. "Although I suspect you're not here to see me."

I laugh. "While I have missed you and your cooking, no. I've come to talk to Julian."

"He'll be so happy to learn you're here. He's been an absolute bore these past few weeks." She smiles, then her expression falls flat. "But he's not home."

"He isn't?"

"No. He left about an hour ago. He's at a charity auction for the foundation Sonia's sister started in her name."

"Of course." I chew on my lower lip, contemplating my next move. Now that I've had my big epiphany, I hate having to wait another second.

"It's just over at the Four Seasons."

I glance down at my clothes before lifting my eyes back to hers. "I don't think I'm dressed for that kind of event."

"So? That didn't stop Cinderella from going to the ball."

"She had a Fairy Godmother. And a bunch of talking mice as friends. I don't exactly have any of that."

Camille's eyes dance, her expression turning conniving. "I don't think I can help you with talking mice, but I have something better than a Fairy Godmother."

"Oh yeah? What's that?"

"Come see for yourself." With a wink, she turns from me and walks back into Julian's home. I hesitate at first, then step inside.

The instant I do, his warmth and energy fill me. For the past few months, this place was like a home. I felt more comfortable here than I ever did in the apartment I shared with Trevor. Julian never reminded me he was the main bread earner in our arrangement, as Trevor so often did. The difference is just another reminder of the person Julian is. He never flaunted his money, except to spoil me. Our relationship was never a competition. It was a true partnership.

Camille stops outside one of the guest rooms, then pauses before pushing open the door. Curious as to what's going on, I walk inside, my gaze instantly falling on a stunning sapphire blue ballgown hanging outside the closet. The fitted bodice has a sweetheart neckline and off-the-shoulder sleeves. Jewels overlay the satin material down to the waist, then the dress juts out into a flowing skirt Julian seems to like, considering most of the formal gowns I'd worn all summer were of a similar style.

"Like I said," she sings as she approaches me from behind. "I may not have a magic wand or mice that can sew, but I do have a dress."

My mouth agape, I spin around, my mind reeling with various thoughts, the most pressing being why there's a dress waiting for me when I haven't spoken to Julian in several weeks.

"He had Dana set something aside," she explains, answering the question written on my face. "He'd hoped you'd have a change of heart by tonight."

I can't fight against the smile pulling on my lips. I want to be angry at him for being so arrogant and assuming, but I can't. It's further proof that I never left his mind, that he wasn't lying when he insisted I was the only woman he thought of since he met me.

"He's a bit cocky, isn't he?" I mutter in a playful tone.

"He certainly is. I've known Julian Gage over twenty years now. The one thing I've learned is when he sets his eyes on something, he doesn't stop until he has it."

"And he wants me." I look back at the dress.

"Yes, sweetheart. He does. He has since the night you met." She places her hands on my shoulders, forcing me to face her. "He may have lied to you, things may not have gone as planned, but I don't think your story could have been written any other way. Do you?" She cocks a brow.

There's only one answer that seems fitting. "No, I don't."

"Good." She beams. "Now, let's get you ready for the ball, Cinderella. This time, there's no turning into a pumpkin at midnight."

CHAPTER FORTY-TWO

I LOOK DOWN at my dress, a hint of the same inadequacy I experienced my first weekend in the Hamptons with Julian washing over me. Curious eyes float in my direction the instant I enter the elaborate ballroom at the Four Seasons. I summon every ounce of courage I possess, aware most of the people present have learned of our breakup and are probably wondering why I'm here. Men don crisp tuxedos. Women wear stunning gowns, glittering jewels covering their necks and ears. Impressive crystal chandeliers hang overhead, the ambient lighting not too bright as couples dance to a jazz band playing an old Ella Fitzgerald tune.

As I continue farther inside, my eyes zero in on the bar. My nerves are at an all-time high and I need something to help settle the butterflies in my stomach. With each step I take, I feel the whispers of the other guests against my skin. All summer, I never felt as out of place as I do now. I had Julian at my side back then. This is just another reminder of everything he did for me, how he made me feel empowered amongst those who view it their duty to judge others.

Once I have a manhattan in my hand and take a sip, I return my attention to the enormous ballroom, searching for Julian. But it's hard to find him in a sea of what I estimate to be over five hundred people.

After Sonia's passing, I'd received word of this event to raise funds for the foundation her sister had started in her name with the purpose of providing help and resources to other women in similar situations as Sonia found herself in.

Thankfully, the police brought Ethan in for questioning based on the information I, as well as Julian, provided. When the robbery gone wrong angle didn't pan out, they took a closer look at Ethan and ended up arresting him after his alibi fell through. Once I learned that, I felt a bit of vindication for Sonia, knowing Ethan wouldn't get away with what he'd done. But there are times I turn on the TV and listen to newscasters discuss recent developments in her case that I can't help but feel I could have done something to prevent this from happening in the first place. I can only imagine what Julian must be going through, the guilt that must consume him over the fact he tried to help, but it wasn't enough. Just like with his mother. I should have stood by his side and comforted him during this difficult time that must have reopened old wounds. I hope it's not too late to do that.

As I search for Julian, or at least a friendly face who could point me in the right direction, a voice comes over the speakers and everyone turns their attention to the stage in the center of the room. Cameras flash, reporters lifting audio recorders to get a few snippets. That's how it usually is at these functions. The media is invited to ensure the event makes headlines, padding egos. But here, it's not about that. It's about sharing Sonia's story and encouraging more people to help those in similar situations.

"Hello, friends," the woman says in a slight Spanish accent. Her olive-toned skin and dark hair make it apparent she's Sonia's sister, their appearance nearly identical. "My name is Isabella Moreno. I wanted to take a minute to thank all of you for coming out tonight to support this foundation." She smiles, but it doesn't reach her eyes. "Sonia would have wanted to know her death wasn't in vain, that something good could come out of it, that perhaps she could have a hand in preventing the same tragedy from happening to someone else. It's because of your generosity that can become a reality."

There's polite applause from the crowd before she continues. "I had no idea what was going on in her personal life. When the cameras were on, she was all smiles, telling everyone how happy she was in her marriage. We all believed it was the perfect love story. It wasn't until this past year that I learned the truth. It all started when she told me she'd hired an escort named August Laurent. Or, as many of you know him, Julian Gage."

She steps away, revealing a man in a perfectly tailored tuxedo, like many of the other men here. But he's not like any of the others, not to me.

Low murmurs and a few gasps ring out as he steps up to the podium, many of the attendees just as surprised about this revelation as I was when I first learned the truth.

"Good evening." Placing his hands on the podium, he pauses in contemplation, briefly closing his eyes before looking at the assembled guests. "Since Sonia's death, I've debated what to do, what to tell all of you. I've kept this secret for years. My work depended on me being able to maintain my anonymity, and it worked. But losing Sonia made me reconsider things. It made me realize the importance of telling those you care about how you feel. You may not get another chance."

He momentarily averts his gaze, drawing in a deep breath. "Sonia was surrounded by people she thought were her friends and was in a marriage that, on its face, was the picture of perfection. But she'd never felt so alone. That's why she sought me out. And over the weeks we spent together, she confided in me. I think she just wanted someone to talk to, someone who would listen and not judge her for staying in an abusive relationship. Because of our time together, she finally found the strength to file for divorce."

He grips the podium tighter, his expression fraught with emotion. When he looks at the audience again, tears are visible in his eyes and his voice wavers.

"Unfortunately, despite the courage she demonstrated, her husband carried out his threat. She called me that night, panicked. I tried to get to her. But I was too late."

My heart drops to the pit of my stomach as I recall the night he left me for what I thought to be another woman. He claimed it was a matter of life and death. I can't believe how true that was.

He clears his throat, his voice becoming strong once more. "And that's why this work is so important. Sonia had her freedom ripped from her, but our hope is that other women won't have to suffer the same tragedy.

"Sonia isn't the first victim of domestic violence, and she certainly won't be the last. But we can try to combat this epidemic, this idea of patriarchy and male dominance that seems to permeate society. Yes, men can be victims of domestic violence, too. It's the idea of exerting power and authority over another person that needs to stop. It happens far too often and to people we never expect because of how happy they appear on the outside. Hell, Sonia always smiled, no matter what. I should have known something was off, considering my mother did the same thing…until she was murdered by her husband, my step-father, when I was twelve."

An eerie silence falls over the room as people absorb his confession, his truth. This is a man who's spent the past decade in these social circles, pretending to be someone he wasn't so they'd accept him. It warms my heart to witness him finally discuss his past so freely. I hope it will encourage more to do the same.

"I haven't spoken about my mother in years, not until a few months ago when I had the pleasure of meeting a woman who made me rethink everything." He laughs slightly, a sparkle in his eyes, as if recalling happy memories. "She had this strange habit of being herself all the time, which completely captivated me, considering we all have a tendency of pretending to be someone we aren't. Not this woman. And by being herself, she helped me see that it's okay to talk about my past, about the skeletons in my own closet. All the past trauma, torment, hurt… She called it my 'ugly'. And she embraced the ugly. It's what makes us who we are. We can't erase it. Do we wish we could? You bet your ass. Instead of doing everything to bury it, we should embrace all the pieces that make us uniquely us.

"So tonight, in honor of Sonia, I'd like to announce the groundbreaking of a project I've been working on. For those who may not be aware, when I inherited Theodore Price's fortune, I used a great deal of that money to open women's shelters here in the Tri-state Area. A few years ago, I wanted to do something bigger, so I expanded my charitable foundation reach into every state in the country. But it still wasn't enough. I wanted to do more. Now, thanks to all your generosity, I'm able to do that. Working with Isabella, we'll be going overseas, helping women born in cultures where abuse is so pervasive, it's considered normal. It's not. And it's my mission to help even more women realize this. Thank you."

Thunderous applause erupts as he steps away from the podium, pausing for a few photos before making his way from the stage. Reporters descend on him, all of them shouting questions about his identity as August Laurent. Instead of humoring them, he responds that they'll have to wait until the February issue of *Blush* magazine hits the newsstands to get the answers they're looking for. My heart expands, thinking how those magazines will now fly off shelves even more so than they would have.

I'm so lost in the gift he's given me I almost don't realize he's leaving. Snapping out of my stupor, I rush toward him, but after his revelation, it seems everyone wants to know more, people swarming him as he makes his escape. He must have predicted this would happen because two bodyguards flank him, ushering him out of the room as other security personnel escort the media from the event now that the speech portion is over.

I call Julian's name, but he can't hear me over everyone else. All I can do is watch as he's whisked away, without a single glance in my direction. As the excitement comes to an end, the sound of saxophones and piano playing a jazz standard fills the space. Out of nowhere, I hear my name.

I whip my head up to see Sadie rushing toward me. I don't have a second to brace myself before she barrels into me, hugging me enthusiastically. Thankfully, I'm quick enough to save the remnants of my drink from spilling.

"I've missed you!"

I still at first, surprised by her sudden attack. Then I melt into her embrace. "I've missed you, too, Sadie."

She pulls back, her eyes frenzied. "Did you know?"

"Know what?"

"About Julian being August Laurent? My god!" She loops her arm through mine, not taking a breath. "You were together while you were doing a story on August Laurent!" She gasps as she puts two and two together, facing me once more. "That's why you broke up, isn't it?"

"It is."

Her brows furrow as she surveys me. "But if you broke up, why are you here?"

I take a long sip of my manhattan, draining it. "I realized I made a mistake and came here to tell him." I shrug in defeat. "But I missed my chance."

She gives me an encouraging smile, squeezing my bicep. "It's okay. It'll all work out. Trust me." She winks.

"Thanks, Sadie." I sigh as I place my glass on a nearby hightop table.

"But now that Prince Charming has left the ball, there's no reason for Cinderella to hang around. It was great seeing you again." I start to turn from her.

"Wait!" she yells, forcing me to stop. I look over my shoulder at her, an eyebrow raised. Her frantic expression softens. "Since you're already here, how about a drink? I'm buying," she jokes, considering it's an open bar.

"Honestly, I'm not sure I'll be the best company right now. I should just—"

"Come on, Evie. One drink while I update you on all the gossip, and there is some *juicy* gossip. For old time's sake."

On a long exhale, I reluctantly nod. "Okay. One drink. Then I'm going home and curling up on the couch with a plate of Christmas cookies."

"One drink. That's all I need."

I follow Sadie to the bar. She orders two manhattans, then we find a hightop table in the corner. The out-of-the-way location reminds me of the day we first met when we sat at a table hidden away, which allowed her to give me the dirt on the who's who of the Hamptons. She does the same now, updating me on affairs, unplanned pregnancies, and even a few paternity tests. It's like being brought up to speed on my favorite soap opera.

As she's telling me about one of the guest's affairs with the nanny, the music changes and the opening notes to an all-too-familiar song in three-quarter time fills the room. I stiffen, my breath hitching as memories of dancing to this song with Julian return.

The lighting in the room lowers, apart from a spotlight on the dance floor. When I look in its direction, my heart catches in my throat at the man I see standing there, a small smile forming on his mouth. His eyes locked on mine, he extends his hand toward me.

Sadie swipes the drink out of my hand and pushes me away from her. After passing her a look of appreciation, I slowly walk across the ballroom, the sea of people parting for me. With each step, my heart beats a little faster, my lungs struggle to capture a breath, my skin tingles with the memory of Julian's touch.

Approaching him, I float my gaze to his outstretched hand, briefly hesitating. His expression falls, panic overcoming him at the idea of me walking away.

"Got ya," I tease as I link my fingers with his.

Relief rolls off him in waves and, like so many times during our summer, he twirls me around to get a better look at the dress before yanking my body against his. He places his hand on my lower back and I drape my free arm over his shoulder. Then he leads me around the dance floor to the band leader singing "Moon River", neither one of us saying a word. There's no need. We share a connection, one that allows us to say everything we need with a simple look.

Months ago, it would have bothered me to share such a personal moment in the company of others. Now it doesn't. All I see is Julian. He's all that matters. This moment is all that matters. Not his past. Not my past. Just us. Just now. He taught me to embrace the moment, to stop living life according to a predetermined itinerary. Life doesn't always go according to plan. Julian's living proof of that. *I'm* living proof of that.

"You came back," I finally say once our song ends and we stop moving.

"I'll always come back for you, Guinevere. Always."

I run my hands through his sandy hair, relishing in the sensation I'd deprived myself of these past few weeks. "And I'll always come back for you, Julian." I bring my lips to his. "Always."

He cups my cheeks, his grip firm and demanding. Then he covers my mouth with his, his kiss soft, sweet, and delicious in all the ways I remember it to be. But he doesn't stop at a simple exchange, despite our audience. He sweeps his tongue against my bottom lip, begging for entrance, which I can't deny him. His hold on me tightens as he pulls me closer, exploring my mouth in a way that makes it feel like it's the first time. And that's what this is. I'm finally kissing every side of Julian Gage. And I'm willing to accept every piece of him.

Pulling back, he rests his forehead on mine. "A symphony," he murmurs.

"What's that?" I ask in a breathy voice.

"That's what I hear when I kiss you. Have since the very first time. And I have a feeling I will until our very last kiss, which I hope is when we're both old and gray."

"Is that right?" I flirt.

He nods slowly, his eyes locked on mine, the fire sending a chill down my spine. "That's a promise. No more lies. No more games. Only the truth. Only you. You're all I want. All I need. And I hope I can be that for you, too."

It takes every ounce of resolve I have not to melt into a puddle on the floor. The only reason I don't is because he's supporting me, just like he always has, both as August and Julian. Truth be told, I love both men. They've molded the man in front of me into the person he is. For that, I'll always be grateful.

"You're more than that." I beam, then chew on my bottom lip, my expression falling. "There's just one thing."

"Anything. Whatever you want, it's yours," he promises in desperation.

"Can we still play a few games?" I waggle my brows, giving him a coy smile. "Because I'd really like to try some roleplay with you."

His jaw clenches as his eyes widen. Then he brings his lips back to mine, his kiss ravenous and insatiable. "What am I going to do with you?"

"I have a few ideas."

Before I have a chance to register what's happening, he hoists me over his shoulder in a fireman's hold. The entire place erupts in cheers and applause. When I hear a familiar whistle, I crane my neck up, meeting Sadie's infectious smile. I beam at her, grateful she encouraged me to stay. The moment fills me with so much joy, I don't even care about the scene we're making as he carries me out of the gala, through the hotel lobby, and down the busy Manhattan sidewalk, tourists staring. It's not until we're a few blocks away that he finally puts me down.

Always the gentleman, he shrugs out of his tuxedo jacket and places it over my shoulders. When I glance at the storefront to see where we are, I fall in love with him a little more.

Tiffany's.

For someone who said he wasn't cut out to be in a relationship, he sure knows how to make a woman happy.

Brushing my hair behind my ears, he brings his hands up to my face, admiring me as the tension between us shifts from one of playfulness to one of devotion. "I love you, Guinevere Fitzgerald."

"And I love you, Julian Gage. And August Laurent. And any other personalities hiding in there. I love them all."

He chuckles, the sound exactly what's been missing. There's nothing like hearing him laugh. I used to be desperate to make everyone around me laugh to mask the fact I wasn't happy with the life I'd planned. Now I only care about making Julian laugh.

"That's good to know, but from this moment forward, there's no one else. Now that I finally have you, I don't need to be anyone other than myself."

He brushes his lips against mine and kisses me in front of the display window of Tiffany's. I couldn't think of a more perfect spot to begin our story of forever. It just goes to show you. The greatest things in life can't be planned.

Love can't be planned.

CHAPTER FORTY-THREE

I STARE AT THE pink hue of the sky as the sun setting in the west casts a beautiful glow over the ocean outside the windows of Julian's home in the Hamptons. A smile curves my mouth as I consider how far we've come since the first time I stepped foot in this house. Back then, I never would have imagined I'd be kicking off another summer with someone who was only supposed to be a fun distraction, or my key to revenge. Now I can't imagine my life without him.

The sound of my phone ringing tears my attention away from the stunning view. I pull it out of my clutch, grinning when I see Chloe pop up.

"You made it!" I say as I answer her FaceTime call. "How are the islands treating you?"

She lifts the oversized sunglasses off her eyes as she brings a tropical concoction to her lips. She flew to Hawaii early this morning, but if I didn't know any better, I'd think she'd been there for days.

"I may never leave."

I smile. "I don't blame you. I'm counting down the hours until we hop on a plane tomorrow."

"Yeah," she scoffs, rolling her eyes. "Because you have it so rough, having to hold off on coming to Hawaii so you can go to some high-class party in the Hamptons. Let me get out my violin, Evie."

Shaking my head, I can't stop the grin from crawling across my lips. She's right. I do have it pretty good. Not only do I have an incredibly supportive man in my life, but I also have a job I only dreamed about. Thankfully, Viv knew I wasn't thinking clearly and refused to offer the assistant editor position to anyone until the beginning of the year. By then, I'd come to my senses.

My new position isn't without its challenges. I wouldn't trade it for anything, though, especially whenever I pass a newsstand and see the new edition of a magazine bearing my name as the assistant editor. You can Google me now, and the search will return information unrelated to my relationship with Julian Gage. I wouldn't have been able to say the same if I gave up and went home to become an English teacher, as I considered when everything fell apart.

"Have you seen Nora yet?" I ask.

"Yes." She rolls her eyes. "She's in full bridezilla mode, but in the best way possible. I think you've rubbed off on her."

"How so?"

She grimaces. "She has lists."

"Lists?"

"Lists," she repeats with a nod. "And itineraries. She has one for you when you get here. I've already warned Izzy."

"Do I want to know what's on these lists or itineraries?"

"I can't say for certain what's on yours, but based on mine, I'm convinced she's lost her damn mind. You need to come and run an intervention. Stat."

I grin. "Why's that?"

"I thought I'd enjoy a week of relaxation before the wedding. That girl has shit scheduled every day. Sightseeing shit."

I stifle my laugh at the look of absolute displeasure crossing her face. I've often wondered how Chloe and Nora were such good friends. While Nora's idea of a fun vacation is packing as much sightseeing and adventure into as short a time as possible, Chloe would much prefer to sit on a beach and have attractive men bring her fruity drinks as she works on her tan.

"At least you're in Hawaii. It could be a lot worse."

"The fact that I'm in Hawaii is what makes it unbearable. I should be shacking up with some hot islander who will breathe fire in my pussy. Instead, do you want to know what I'm tasked with doing during what should be a sex-filled vacation?"

"What's that?"

"Making sure Jeremy's best man keeps his dick in his pants. Apparently, he flirts with anything with a pulse. And since Nora knows I have a low tolerance for bullshit and charm, I've been given this exciting task."

I laugh once more as Chloe brings her drink back to her lips. "I'm going to need this shit in an IV."

"Remember. It's all for Nora."

"Yeah, well, Nora owes me after this. Anyway, I don't want to take up much more of your time. I know you have a big thing tonight. I just wanted to call and wish you a happy birthday." She lifts her glass once more, toasting me. "Here's to thirty-one. May this birthday be more memorable than the last."

"Actually…," I begin after a moment of contemplation, "my last birthday was pretty amazing. It just took me a while to realize it."

"At least you finally did." She holds my gaze for a moment longer, then seems to look past me. I glance over my shoulder to see Julian descending the staircase. I return my eyes to my phone. "Looks like Prince Charming's here to take you to the ball. Have a good night, Evie. And happy birthday."

"Thanks, Chloe. Love you."

"Love you, too."

I end the FaceTime call, then drop my phone into my clutch, whirling around as Julian approaches, his impassioned gaze raking over my body. It doesn't matter we've known each other a year and are past the so-called honeymoon phase. He looks at me with the same desperation and desire every time. I get the feeling he always will.

His hand finds mine and he twirls me around, wanting the full effect of the cocktail dress Dana suggested I wear to tonight's gathering. It's more of a low-key event to celebrate the opening of Julian's first overseas women's shelter in the Middle East, something that wouldn't have been possible without all the networking he did last summer.

He tugs my body into his as his free hand wraps around mine. Just like so many other times, I drape my arm over his shoulder, toying with the curls that fall over his jacket collar. Our bodies sway as he hums "Moon River", which has become our song. There are times I hear it even when he's fast asleep beside me. It's the song of our love, one I hope will continue until we're long gone.

He leans his forehead on mine, barely a breath between our bodies as we share this moment. We've done this same dance so many times over the course of our relationship. It's never gotten old. I still feel the same spark, the same fluttering in my heart, the same craving to be in his universe. In fact, I feel it even deeper now that I finally know all sides of Julian Gage. And every day, I continue to fall more in love with every part of him.

When he stops humming, he lifts his head from mine and looks at me with a focused gaze. "You look beautiful, Guinevere."

I bring my hands to the lapels of his suit jacket, smoothing them. "You clean up pretty good yourself." I wink.

"I got something for you."

"I told you…" I narrow my eyes on him. "No presents. You spoil me enough as it is. All I wanted for my birthday was to spend it with you."

"What if I told you it's not a birthday present?"

"I still don't want it."

"How about we test it out? I bought it to go with your outfit. Dana said it would really accentuate the jewels on the straps of your shoes. If you don't like it, I'll return it, okay?"

I playfully roll my eyes, feigning irritation. As much as I hate the thought of him spending money on me, I love that he spoils me. I love that he thinks of me so much.

"Okay."

"Okay." He smiles, but it's not as confident as usual. Reaching into the pocket of his pants, he pulls out a small box in that familiar blue hue unique to Tiffany's. "I was planning on getting you something from Cartier instead, but figured Tiffany's would have more meaning."

My breath hitches as he repeats the same words he uttered on what was supposed to be our last night together. There's only one possible way for me to respond to that. Tears fill my eyes as I stare at the leather box, knowing all too well what's inside.

"It could be an empty box and it would be infinitely better than even the most expensive piece you could get from Cartier."

"Phew." He laughs nervously. "That's a relief, because it really is just an empty box."

"No, it's not," I whisper through the lump in my throat.

"You're right. It's not."

He drops to one knee and pops open the ring box, then grabs my left hand in his. I exhale at the stunning diamond that greets me. It's a princess-cut stone that's easily three carats, the band thin and inlaid with even more diamonds.

"Guinevere Shea Fitzgerald, I couldn't have planned for you to walk into my life even if I tried. I'll never forget sitting in the corner of a bar after meeting with a client, wondering if it's all worth it, hearing you tell the entire place how you were dumped. All I could remember thinking is that I needed to know you. I'd spent most of my life running from love. And then there was you.

"Our relationship may not have been conventional by any stretch of the imagination, but that's what I love about us. We broke the rules. We weren't supposed to find each other, but we did." He brings the ring up to my finger, unshed tears forming behind his eyelids. "We weren't supposed to fall in love with each other, but we did. And I fall in love with you all over again every day. I want to continue to fall in love with you every day for the rest of my life. Do me the honor of being my wife, of taking a risk on me, of loving all the pieces of me."

His words are everything I could have dreamed for a proposal, and more. I never expected Julian to drop to one knee after only a year. I thought he'd need more time to get used to being in a real relationship. But that's what makes this so exciting, so exhilarating. I never saw it coming. It was never planned.

"I'm not quite sure getting engaged was on the itinerary," I joke, remembering our early days when I insisted on a firm schedule of events. "At least, I didn't see it there." I grin, playfully batting my eyelashes.

He's on his feet in an instant, yanking my body hard and fast against his, stealing my breath. He doesn't even wait for me to say yes as he slides the ring onto my finger, where I plan to leave it for the rest of my days.

"Fuck the itinerary," he growls as he kisses me for the first time as my fiancé.

Fuck the itinerary indeed.

THE END

PLAYLIST

Memories Are Made of This - Dean Martin
Live Learn - The California Honeydrops
Little Black Dress - Sara Bareilles
S.O.B. - Nathaniel Rateliff & The Night Sweats
Showboat - Josh Ritter
Anybody Else - Jon McLaughlin
A Little Fire - Parker Millsap
Falling Slowly - Glen Hansard
Classic - MKTO
Fool In the Rain - Led Zeppelin
Fight Song - Rachel Platten
Run - Matt Nathanson
Without You - Parachute
Reaching - Jason Reeves
Moon River - Henry Mancini
Summer is Over - Jon McLaughlin
Always Midnight - Pat Monahan
Put Me Back Together - Grace Grundy
What About Us - P!nk
3 Hours - Canyon City
Scarecrow - Alex & Sierra
The Shape of Us - Ian Britt
This Will Be Our Home - John Lucas
Never Got Away - Colbie Caillat
Capital Letters - Halloran & Kate
Dammit - Jana Kramer
Dear John - Julian Sheer
Extraordinary Magic - Ben Rector
Guiding Light - Mumford & Sons
I Hear a Symphony - Cody Fry
Have It All - Jason Mraz
First Try - Johnnyswim
Say You Do - Graham Colton
You - A Great Big World

DATING GAMES

Wicked Games

USA TODAY BESTSELLING AUTHOR

T.K. LEIGH

CHAPTER ONE

I'VE OFTEN WONDERED what hell would be like.

Not really out of fear. More like curiosity.

Is it full of fire and brimstone, as I heard them speak of the handful of times my parents dragged me to church as a child?

Or maybe everyone's hell is personal. Maybe Hitler's hell is filled with all the people he thought were inferior to him. Jack the Ripper is probably surrounded by prostitutes who emasculate him, cutting *his* throat and abdomen. And Ted Bundy is most likely alone, not a single person there to impress or feel self-important around.

Just like my hell would be a nightclub fifty stories above the Vegas strip, drunk people grinding up against each other. And the sentence Lucifer would give me when I arrive at the fiery gates? To serve eternal damnation at a bachelorette party that never ends.

Yup. I have arrived at my own personal hell.

"Blowjobs! That's what we need right now!"

I close my eyes, summoning the strength to feign excitement over the idea of drinking a disgustingly sweet mixture of Bailey's, Kahlúa, and half-and-half, all topped with whipped cream. If my cousin, Hannah, and I weren't like sisters when we were kids, I wouldn't be wearing a a necklace of penises and a tight black tank top, "Bride's Bitch" bedazzled on the front, enduring this bachelorette party that's filled with one cliché after another.

I sure hope this city's marketing slogan is correct. This entire experience needs to stay in Vegas.

"Yes!" Hannah slurs, agreeing with Bernadette, her older sister and maid of honor, who planned this excursion to the tenth circle of hell. She struggles to get up from the couch where she's sitting, tripping over several pairs of legs as she attempts to flag down our cocktail waitress. "Blow jobs all around!"

Whistles and cheers erupt as two guys with far too much hair product jump at the opportunity to join us. "I'll buy you those if you return the favor with the real thing," the tall, slender blond says, his suggestive gaze scanning our group in a way that reminds me of someone selecting produce at a farmer's market, looking for the ripest tomato, the juiciest peach.

I glance to my left, giving Izzy a knowing look. Hannah, Izzy, and I were inseparable growing up. For the longest time, I couldn't imagine my life without them at my side. We went through all of life's big changes together. Puberty. First boyfriends. First kisses. Then my parents divorced and my mom took me from Connecticut to New Jersey, where she unsuccessfully attempted to piece her life back together.

"I'm not sure you could handle the real thing," a petite brunette named Carmen says, suggestively licking her lips.

Desperate for a break from what's become a sex-charged day in the city of sin, I extract myself from our group.

"Bathroom?" Izzy asks. "Or did you change your mind on the scavenger hunt and decide to…" She picks up a printed piece of card stock and reads, "build a penis with objects found at the bar?" She rolls her eyes at the absurdity of it all.

"Tempting…" I give her a tight smile, "but I think I'll pass. I'm going to the bar to get a drink."

"But they ordered blow job shots," she retorts sarcastically, taking a sip of her vodka tonic.

"I refuse to do any shot made in such a way to make it appear I have cum on my face when I drink it."

Izzy coughs, liquid spraying out of her nose and mouth.

"Who the hell invented that shot? Probably someone who didn't give or receive blowjobs that often. If you do it right, you won't end up with cum on your face. Unless that's what you want. If that's the case, more power to you. To each their own."

She coughs a few more times, then clears her throat. "God, I've missed you, Chloe."

"Missed you, too. Want anything?"

She holds up her glass. "I'm good."

"Okay. I'm off to brave the elements." I spin on my heels.

"Good luck," she calls out.

At least now that night has fallen and we're in a darkened space, the stereotypical tank top that's been my bachelorette party uniform isn't as noticeable. Bernadette thought each of us wearing a shirt with "Bride's Bitch" on it was hysterical, and hers saying "Bitch of Honor" even more so. I bit my tongue so hard it almost bled in order to prevent myself from telling her how juvenile I think this entire weekend truly is. That it's not the kind of bachelorette party Hannah envisioned. She's too nice to say anything. She's always been that way.

Strobe lights pulse as I maneuver my way through crowds of people congregated around small tables and lush leather couches. The smell of perfume, combined with beer and fruity alcohol mixtures, fills the air.

Scantily dressed waitresses pass by carrying trays overflowing with drinks while the vibration of the driving club music seems to make the floor shake.

Despite the temperatures being on the chilly side, considering night's fallen, the sheer number of people present increases the heat level, causing perspiration to form on my brow. All walks of life are represented here, everyone pretending to be someone they're not for one weekend of sin.

I don't need a weekend of sin. I sin on a regular basis.

I squeeze my way up to the bar and catch the bartender's attention immediately, my gray and lilac-colored ombre hair standing out in a sea of blondes and brunettes.

"What can I get you?"

"Martini. Dirty."

"You got it." He turns and grabs the vodka bottle, pouring a heaping amount into the cocktail shaker. "Having a good time?"

"Absolutely." I grit out a smile.

"Liar," he responds with a wink.

"That obvious?"

"Maybe I'm just observant. You don't seem to fit in with your friends over there." He nods toward the bachelorette party.

I look at him incredulously, wondering how he'd notice me when pouring drinks all night. Then I glance back at the girls, raising my five-foot, two-inch frame onto my tiptoes to peer over the ocean of people, grimacing when I see Bernadette's shoved a brightly colored shooter between her boobs and one of our new "friends" is taking the shot from her without the use of his hands. We're definitely hard to miss. Bernadette made sure of that.

"What makes you say that?" I muse when I return my attention to him.

"You don't exactly scream 'desperate housewife'." He grabs a long metal spoon and stirs my martini. If nothing else, he understands a great martini should be stirred, not shaken, as Mr. Bond would have you believe.

"At least I'm doing something right."

"You certainly are." He pours the liquid through the strainer and into a chilled glass, then pushes it toward me. "Enjoy."

With a smile, I place a bill on the counter and turn from him. If I were anywhere else, I might have given him my number with instructions to call when his shift was over. I'd rather not leave any piece of myself in this town.

As I emerge from the mosh of people, I look in the direction of the girls, only to find most of them grinding with complete strangers. Except for Hannah and Izzy. They're off to the side, distancing themselves from the debauchery currently underway amongst the rest of the women. All I can do is pray this kind of behavior doesn't rub off on Hannah. Then again, she's twenty-eight. She had her fun during her younger years, unlike her sister, Bernadette, who got married when she was twenty — a shotgun wedding because she was pregnant.

"How much?" I hear a voice say as I start toward them. It's so random and out of context I don't react at first. Then a hand grips my bicep, preventing me from taking another step.

I whirl around, my fierce eyes settling on a man of average height and build. His black shirt is tucked into a pair of dark jeans, a gray blazer finishing the ensemble. "Excuse me?"

"I said..." He loosens his grasp on my arm, licking his lips as he leers at me, wavering slightly. I can smell the alcohol on his breath. Great. Another guy emboldened with the help of Jim Beam, Jack Daniels, or Jose Cuervo. Possibly a combination of all three. "How much?"

"For what?"

He chuckles in feigned amusement. Then his expression falls, his eyes heating as they rake over me.

"I get it. You're discreet. I can be discreet, too." Winking, he reaches into his pocket and retrieves his wallet, flashing what I estimate to be several thousand in hundreds. He either got lucky shooting craps or hit up a few ATMs earlier. I'm guessing the latter. "Like I said, how much?"

I shake my head, backing away from him. "I am *not* a prostitute." My tone is firm, leaving no room for argument.

He blows out a laugh. "Sure. You're not a prostitute, just like I'm the fucking Easter Bunny. I can pretend to be someone I'm not, too, sweetheart. Trust me. I have an eye for these things, and any woman who comes into a club wearing a ridiculously tight tank top, a skirt that rides up her ass, and has hair colored like yours just screams whore."

Fire flames on my face and I ball my free hand into a fist. Before I can reel back and land a blow, he grips my hip, yanking my body against his, causing my martini to splash between us.

"We can do this the easy way or the hard way, but every second you play hard to get, the amount I pay you will decrease. If I were you, I'd give careful consideration to the next words that come out of your mouth. Ya got me?"

My jaw clenches as my distaste for him grows with each heartbeat. "Like I said..." I place a hand on his chest, glowering, "I am *not* a prostitute. So I'd suggest taking your disgusting paws off me before I kick my apparent hooker heel into your balls and press so hard they'll hear them pop all the way in Los Angeles. Ya got me?" I finish, throwing his words back at him.

His composure cracks momentarily, but he's either too drunk or too dumb to get the hint. "You're a feisty one, aren't you? I dig it." He loops his arm around my waist, pulling me even harder against him. "Come on. Tell me your price."

My heart rate spikes and bile rises in my throat when his erection pushes against my stomach. What the hell is it about men these days who think they can treat women like property? Who think it's their God-given right to exert dominance over the opposite sex?

"Like I told you. I'm not—"

"Oh, there you are!" a deep voice bellows, cutting through.

I whip my eyes in its direction, disoriented when an arm wraps around me, prying me out of the creep's grasp. I'm startled at first, taken aback by the strong embrace currently holding me. But unlike before, I don't feel the overwhelming sense of dread and disgust.

"I can't leave you alone for a second, can I?"

When he pulls back, I meet brilliant green eyes that seem to penetrate deeper than they should, considering they belong to a stranger. Then again, there's something oddly familiar about him, making me think I should know him. But I'd remember someone like him. Wouldn't I?

He towers over me, making me estimate he's six-three or six-four, since I only come up to his pecs. He has a proud face, chiseled cheekbones, square jaw, masculine nose. His dark hair is a little messy, but in a sexy kind of way. Although he sports a beard and mustache, it's impeccably groomed. In fact, everything about him is impeccably groomed.

Granted, we're at a club in Vegas with a rather strict dress code, at least for men. But something about the way he carries himself with a cool confidence makes him stand out amongst a sea of men just looking for a quick piece of ass. The dark jeans and tweed jacket make me think he'd be more comfortable at a cigar bar, sipping scotch, jazz standards playing in the background.

"Can I?" he repeats, giving me a knowing look, encouraging me to play along. So that's what I do.

"I guess not." I face the creep, a smug smile on my face as I burrow deeper into my mystery man's embrace. "Like I said. This…" I gesture down my body, "isn't for sale. Even if it were, you would never be able to afford it, baby. Not with that wallet you flashed me."

He opens his mouth to argue, but all my mystery man has to do is puff out his chest and he snaps his jaw shut, turning from me.

"And for future reference," my mystery man calls out, keeping his arm wrapped around me, despite the threat waning.

The creep looks back at him.

"When a lady says she's not interested, it's not an invitation to press the issue. If I find you've caused any more problems or offer any other woman money to sleep with you, there are two rather large gentlemen manning the front door who will have no problem helping you learn this lesson differently." He smiles a fake smile. "Ya got me?"

"Yeah. Sure. Whatever." He shuffles away.

"What a tool," my mystery man remarks as he drops his hold, turning to face me, his eyes filled with concern. "Are you all right? He didn't hurt you, did he?"

"I'm fine," I snap. "I can handle myself. But thank you for intervening on my behalf. It wasn't necessary."

I begin to retreat from him. If I didn't hate Vegas before, I do now. With it being the stereotypical destination for a hormonally charged bachelor or bachelorette party, it's open season to hit on anything with a pulse. I wish people had to take a test before entering the proverbial Vegas wildlife, like hunters have to in order to obtain their license to hunt prey. That's what this place is like. A jungle. During mating season.

"Got a name?" he calls out before I can take more than a few steps.

"Yup," I shout over my shoulder with a smirk. "Thanks for checking."

"You're not going to tell me?" he yells when I continue to squeeze my way through the hordes of people. "What am I supposed to call you? Dick Girl?"

His words seem to carry over the beat of the music and I stop in my tracks, sensing curious eyes watching our interaction. I spin around, stalking toward him.

"Dick Girl? Why? Because I'm wearing a short skirt and my hair's a little different so I must really enjoy dick? I'm pretty sure there are lesbians out there who wear short skirts and color their hair differently, too. That doesn't mean they like the dick, does it? Or is it just because we're in Vegas?"

He's about to respond, but I cut him off before he has a chance to utter a single syllable. My presence in my least favorite city for a ritual I find cliché, trivial, and ordinary, all things I try to avoid being, causes the thin filter between my brain and mouth to evaporate.

"I get it. Some guy who probably considers himself a marketing genius concocted a brilliant ad campaign all those years ago when he came up with this city's tagline. Can you imagine being in the room when the creative team discussed that gem as an option? It's almost like their mission was to come up with the slogan most likely to result in surprise pregnancies, STDs, and infidelity, all of which do *not* stay in Vegas."

He tries to speak again, but I hold up my finger, silencing him.

"So, as tempting as the idea of living out my wildest fantasies is…and truthfully, you're not so bad to look at, and I do have quite an active imagination…I do not hook up with random strangers, not in this town anyway. But fear not." I give him a trite smile. "This city is full of bachelorette party attendees who would love to have a piece of you. Hell, you could probably even score a threesome or foursome. Maybe even a fivesome, like a sorority porno gone incredibly wrong. A simple online search will lead you to any number of sex clubs within a short Uber ride from here. But that shit won't be happening with me." I gesture to my crotch area. "This pussy is on a much-deserved break."

I remain in place as my words seem to ring out between us. I expect him to be stunned and unsure how to respond, maybe offer an apology for his assumption about me. Instead, he reaches out. I attempt to step back, but before I can, he toys with the chain dangling from my neck.

Smirking, he says, "I was referring to your necklace. Dick. Girl."

A tingle sweeps across my cheeks as my shoulders drop. Thankfully, it's too dark for him or anyone else to see my complexion turn red. "Oh."

"Yeah. Oh." He chuckles as his full lips curve in the corners. He flashes his white teeth, his smile exuding a confidence I'm not used to seeing. Something about it intrigues me. It's such a simple thing. The flexing of muscles to turn up your lips, demonstrating happiness, amusement, or any other number of positive emotions. But with that one smile, I feel something I've avoided for years now…

Vulnerability.

"Have a nice night… Dick Girl."

He turns from me, the crowd seeming to part to allow him passage. Then he stops, facing me once more.

"And, for the record, I didn't ask your name as a preface to sleep with you. I did so because my mother taught me manners, to treat everyone with respect." He keeps his dark eyes locked with mine, allowing his statement to sink in. "Stay safe tonight. It's a jungle out there." He treats me to one last smile, then disappears into the crowd, leaving me bewildered.

Has being single in New York so long jaded me to the point that I assume every straight man only approaches me because they want to get into my pants?

At one point, I dreamed of having the love story I read about in fairy tales…until I realized all fairy tales eventually end. Soon, the Prince will question Snow White's devotion to him whenever she runs off to the forest to spend time with the dwarfs. Prince Phillip will accuse Aurora of always just lying there, practically asleep, during sex. And poor Aladdin and Jasmine… He'll never stop feeling emasculated every time they have an argument and she so kindly reminds him that if it weren't for her, he'd still be a street rat.

If that's a fairy tale, I want nothing to do with it.

CHAPTER TWO

THE SPICY, ROBUST flavor of red wine dances on my tongue as I relax into my barstool, savoring these last few moments to myself before embarking on another night of bachelorette party fun. About to flag down the bartender for the check, I stop when my phone pings with an incoming text.

Nora: *On a scale of one to murder, how's the bachelorette party?*

I laugh at how well Nora knows me. After all, she was my college roommate. Even though I ended up leaving before the end of my second year, we've managed to remain friends.

Me: *Let's put it this way... Most would consider Ted Bundy a compassionate serial killer compared to my brutality. However, any murder I commit would probably be excused as justifiable. Or, at least, I could plead not guilty by reason of insanity. I believe the courts recognize the bachelorette party defense in homicide cases.*

Her response comes almost instantly.

Nora: *I'm not so sure that's a thing.*

Me: *It should be. And in case I haven't told you, I'm so glad you don't want any of this stuff for your wedding. It makes my job as your maid of honor much easier and won't require me to resort to murder.*

Nora: *Blech. The last thing I want is to make my friends suffer through a night of penis jokes and scavenger hunts that border on sexual harassment. Try to have a little fun while you're there, although I know how much you despise Vegas. New York misses you. See you in a few days.*

I sigh as I lean back in my chair, typing out one last text.

Me: *And I sure miss New York. See you soon.*

I close out of our message and open my email, scanning my inbox. As a celebrity news columnist for one of the top women's magazines, I'm required to keep a constant pulse on what's going on in the world of the rich and famous. But this weekend has been quiet. No big breakups. No pregnant celebrities giving birth. No arrogant has-been who thinks he's above the law getting arrested for drinking and driving.

"For you, miss."

I snap my head up just as the bartender places a martini in front of me. "I didn't order this." I start to push it across the bar, but he smiles, leaving a cocktail napkin beside the glass. Scribbling in blue ink catches my attention, the pen stroke masculine, but still legible.

Thought I'd make up for the martini you didn't get to enjoy last night.

There's only one person who could have sent this. On a sharp inhale, I scan the lounge. It's on the darker side, the lighting dim, votive candles placed sporadically on the bar and each table to add to the romantic ambience, despite being mere feet from a roulette wheel.

As I search for familiar green eyes, I sense a warmth approach from behind. The hairs on my nape stand on end, and I freeze.

"I wasn't sure what kind of vodka you preferred, so I had to guess based on what little I know about you. But something makes me think you're a Belvedere girl. Smooth. Layered. Sophisticated."

I take a moment to compose myself before facing him. The instant my gaze floats to his, an involuntary shiver rolls through me. "A rather astute assessment. I prefer Polish vodkas."

"Smart woman."

His eyes dance as he gestures to the free chair beside me, silently asking permission to sit. I nod, then turn forward once more, smoothing the lines of my gray silk tank, adjusting my navy blue blazer. I'll most likely get shit from Bernadette for not wearing my "Bride's Bitch" shirt tonight, but I need to draw the line somewhere. One night was fine. There's no way I'm going to wear that sweat-stained, smoke-infested thing again.

As he assumes the chair beside me, his scent filters through my nose, addictive and mouthwatering. It's a woodsy and manly scent, reminiscent of rain on a hot summer day. He flags down the bartender and orders a few fingers of a top-shelf scotch. My assessment of him last night wasn't that far off after all. He would have fit in better at a quiet bar sipping scotch instead of a dance club where everyone was just one tequila shot away from alcohol poisoning.

Truth be told, it wasn't my scene, either. I'm not sure *what* my scene is.

Once he takes a sip and exhales in satisfaction, he returns his gaze to me. I tap my nails against the counter, the silence painfully loud. I've never felt so on edge in the presence of a man, so out of sorts. But I felt it last night. And I feel it now.

This man is different.

Despite him being a stranger.

Despite him barely uttering more than a few sentences to me.

Despite my not knowing anything about him.

When the heat of his stare becomes too much, the connection too palpable, I turn my eyes from his, taking a sip of my martini, the combination of dry vermouth, vodka, and just a hint of olive juice perfect.

"How did you know I liked my martini dirty?" I ask in a smooth voice, trying to calm the butterflies swimming in my stomach by bringing the glass back to my mouth.

He licks his lips, leaning toward me. "I had a feeling you liked things…dirty."

I choke on my drink, coughing as I struggle to breathe. He hands me a napkin and I cover my mouth. If anyone else used that line on me, I'd roll my eyes and send them on their way. But this guy isn't saying it to get into my pants. At least, I don't think he is. It's all part of his personality — cool, confident, yet lighthearted.

"Wouldn't you like to find out?" I quip once I clear my throat.

"You have no idea." His voice is guttural and wanton as he inches closer. I zero in on his lips, drawn to them like a moth to a flame.

Then he pulls back, bringing his drink to his mouth, acting as if his statement didn't leave me squirming. When he speaks again, he sounds different, his tone lighter and more conversational, a complete one-eighty.

"More bachelorette festivities planned for the evening? Or is that all over?"

I draw in a deep breath to compose myself. "Don't I wish. I stopped by here to ensure I'm in the right…frame of mind for what awaits me."

"And what is it that awaits you?"

"I'm not sure you want to know," I respond with a roll of my eyes.

"Is it as bad as doing blowjob shots while wearing a string of penises around your neck?"

Squinting, I cock my head, his statement catching me off guard. There's no way he'd know about those shots unless he were watching me earlier in the evening. I remind myself it could just be a coincidence. I *was* at a bachelorette party. It's not a big stretch to assume we'd do blowjob shots. They tend to go hand-in-hand.

"That was child's play compared to tonight's festivities." I flash him a coy smile over the top of my glass as I tilt it back, then return it to the bar.

"Do tell. You can't leave me hanging with a statement like that." His eyes sparkle with amusement and intrigue.

"What would you say if I told you I'd be learning how to strip and pole dance?" My voice comes out breathy, laden with desire, as I inch toward him.

His expression widens momentarily, muscles clenching, before he recovers, that unaffected attitude returning. "I'd say I'd love to see that."

I lean even closer, barely a breath between us. "I bet you would." I scrape my lips ever so slightly against his. The touch is no more than a whisper, yet it ignites a spark deep within. "Maybe later, I can give you a private show of what I learned."

"But I thought you didn't hook up in this town?" I can feel his mouth turn into a wry smile. "I thought you said your pussy was on a break."

Moisture pools between my thighs, the combination of his proximity and words making me want to blow off tonight and do my own private striptease with my mystery man.

"An exception can be made."

A slight growl escapes his throat, his lips about to press firmly against mine when a loud, shrill voice cuts through.

"There you are!"

I quickly tear away, snapping my eyes to my right as Bernadette rushes toward me, her blonde curls bouncing with each long stride, a woman on a mission. As expected, she's still wearing her "Bitch of Honor" tank top. I wonder if she slept in it.

"I've been texting and calling you the past five minutes. The party bus is out front. Izzy said you were coming here for a drink and a quick bite…"

She trails off, halting in her tracks the instant she notices the man beside me. The way his body is positioned makes it apparent we're not simply strangers sitting next to each other at a bar. Her eyes rake over his crisp suit, unshaven jaw, and wayward dark locks. A smirk forms on her lips as she all but salivates over him.

"I guess you *did* come for a quick bite." She flirtatiously waggles her brows.

He opens his mouth to say something, but she advances, closing in on his personal space like a lioness in heat. He scoots back in his chair to put distance between them, but she doesn't get the hint. I wonder if her husband knows how she's behaved all weekend, that she's shamelessly flirted with anything with a pulse, male *and* female.

"Want to come with us? We're about to go to a striptease and pole dancing class." She sticks out her chest, squeezing her arms against her body to make her cleavage pop. "I'd love someone to perform for."

Rolling my eyes so hard I'm confident I see my ass, I scoot off my stool, stepping between them. I hope I didn't come across as desperate as Bernadette when I propositioned the same thing. I don't think *anyone* could come across as desperate as Bernadette.

"I'm ready," I announce, pulling my wallet out of my purse. "I just need to pay for my dinner first."

I'm about to ask for the check when he places his hand on my forearm. The instant I feel his skin on mine, my pulse skyrockets, breath quickening. I look at him, questioning. I expect him to withdraw his hand. Instead, he lingers, his fingers tracing light circles.

"It's taken care of," he states with authority.

"But—"

"It's taken care of." This time, his voice is harsher, leaving no room for argument.

I part my lips, my words stuck in my throat. How can I make him understand why I don't like the idea of anyone paying for my meal or my drinks? That it makes it easier to walk away after a night, a week, a month, whatever it may be? That it's helped keep my heart guarded? It helps keep their heart guarded, too, safe from the inevitable destruction my life will unfold on them.

That it brings up too many memories of a past I want to forget.

"Say okay." His tone is a cross between a plea and demand.

Hypnotized, oblivious to everything other than giving him what he wants, I respond, "Okay." My voice doesn't even sound like my own. I'm a puppet and he my master pulling the strings.

He brings his fingers to my chin, tilting my head back. "Say thank you."

My pulse skyrockets. It's so simple, so innocent, yet has me wondering what it would be like to hear him tell me what to do in the bedroom. And based on what I've observed, he'd do just that.

"Thank you," I whimper.

His lips inch toward mine, every synapse in my body firing. "You're welcome."

I close my eyes, bracing for his kiss, but it never comes. Instead, he drops his hold on me, the warmth of his breath disappearing. I flutter my eyes open, disoriented. Then I spy Bernadette standing off to the side, smirking like an older sister would when catching the younger one kissing a boy. It's not that far off. At one time, Bernadette *was* like an older sister.

Trying to settle my raging hormones, I hop off my barstool, pretending I'm a composed, professional twenty-eight-year-old woman. Bernadette's smirk only grows wider. I keep my head lowered as I loop my arm through hers, dragging her away.

"Who *was* that?" she whispers once we're outside the restaurant, glancing over her shoulder.

The realization hits and I blink repeatedly. "I don't know." I stop walking and look back to where I was just sitting. He's no longer there, as if he vanished. If Bernadette hadn't seen him, I'd think I imagined the entire thing. "I never got his name."

"Pity," she replies with a dismissive shrug of her shoulders. "He was quite the looker. But fear not. There will be more than enough eye candy for us tonight."

She grabs my hand and pulls me toward another night of bachelorette torture.

Chapter Three

RELIEF ROLLS OFF my shoulders as I make my way through the quiet corridors of the hotel and toward a bank of elevators, pulling my roll-a-board behind me. I don't think I've ever been so happy about a vacation ending as I am about getting on that plane in a few hours. As much as I love Hannah, I'd rather be stuck in my cubicle at the office than in this city for another second.

Once I'm in the elevator on my way to the lobby to meet Izzy, I pull my phone out of my purse and type out a quick text to my friend and coworker, Evie.

> **Me:** *Headed to the airport. I should be back in town around 7.*
>
> **Evie:** *I can't wait to hear all about it. You should do a piece about bachelorette parties for the magazine, but in a way only your cynicism can truly deliver.*

I respond, arguing I'm not *that* cynical, when the elevator slows to a stop on another floor and the doors open. Keeping my eyes glued to my phone as I finish my text, I step back to make room for anyone about to get on. That's when a familiar scent hits me, earthy and raw. I snap my head up, my body stiffening when I see *him*.

I thought the first time we ran into each other was simply a chance encounter. The second a coincidence. But a third time?

At first, he remains frozen in place, gaze glued to mine. Then a mischievous smile gradually replaces his stunned expression and he enters, standing unnervingly close as he leans toward me to press the lobby button that's already illuminated.

The elevator doors close, leaving us alone in this tiny space that's abuzz with electricity. Conscious of every sound, every heartbeat, every breath, I stare straight ahead. With each drawn-out second, my pulse increases, mouth growing dry. I shift from foot to foot, ready to burst from the tension.

When the silence becomes unbearable, I float my eyes to his, only to notice he's unabashedly staring at me. Unlike our previous encounters, he's dressed casually in a white linen shirt with the sleeves rolled up to just below his elbows, revealing his muscular forearms. Khaki shorts hang from his hips, a pair of tan flip-flops on his feet.

"Taking a day off from ruling the world?" My voice breaks through.

"Ruling the world?"

"Exactly. You always act so in charge. So…in control."

His lips curve up into one of the most sensual grins I've ever seen. Screw Matt Damon's sexy smirk, or Brad Pitt's flirtatious smile. They have nothing on this guy.

"I do like being in control."

I attempt to fight against the blush building on my cheeks, averting my gaze. All I hear is his voice from the other night.

Say okay. Say thank you.

And I did. It was so simple, so innocent, yet it lit me up in a way that left me craving him all weekend. His words. His presence. His…dominance.

"I didn't mean it like that." I chew on my bottom lip, fidgeting with the hem of my jacket. "I meant you look and act like you have some high-powered job. Master of the universe and all that."

"Master of the universe?" He arches a single brow.

"Yes." I return my eyes to his, shrugging. "You know, like He-man."

"Well…" Licking his lips, he closes the distance, the heat of his breath on my neck making me tremble. "Appearances can be deceiving. Wouldn't you agree?" He pulls back, meeting my gaze.

"They can be," I reply thoughtfully, masking my shaky voice. "But something tells me they're not. Not when it comes to you."

"Even the master of the universe deserves a day off to enjoy life's…pleasures."

My nerve endings tingle as that one word hangs in the air, making me hyper-aware of my heartbeat, which I'm confident they can hear in the casino. Hell, they can probably even hear it all the way at the Hoover Dam.

I swallow hard, my gaze fixated on his lips, thinking how much pleasure they could give me. Suddenly, the elevator comes to a stop and the doors open, the clanging bells of slot machines breaking our moment.

I snap out of my daze, squaring my shoulders as I scramble out of the enclosed space and into the casino, able to breathe again. Normally, I hate the loud noise that meets me every time I step off this elevator, feeling much like the Grinch when he complains about all the "noise, noise, noise" down in Whoville. But right now, I find it comforting, at least compared to the anxiety that consumes me whenever I'm in this man's presence.

"Headed home?" When I hear his voice, I look to my right to see him catching up to me.

"Thankfully, yes. One night in Vegas is too long. I've been here four." I slow my steps as I near the front doors, scanning the enormous lobby for any sign of Izzy. She's probably still in a ridiculously long line for coffee.

God, I hate this city.

"Aren't you headed out?" he asks when I don't follow him outside.

"I'm waiting for a friend. We're on the same flight."

"Oh." His expression momentarily falls, but he recovers quickly, smiling, although it doesn't make his eyes sparkle as it usually does. "Well, it was nice seeing you again."

"You, too."

He hesitates briefly, and I can almost see the words on the tip of his tongue. Then he turns from me, walking out the revolving glass doors. I can't help but admire his long strides, muscular legs, broad shoulders, and what I can only imagine is a firm ass. I almost don't want to look away. But when a ping sounds from my phone, I do just that.

Unlocking the screen, I read a text from Evie saying she's spending the night at Julian's and not to worry if she's not at my place when I get home. I reply, telling her she should just officially move in with him.

When her boyfriend of twelve years broke up with her, I offered her a place to stay, considering how difficult it is to find an affordable apartment in the city. But now that she has a new man in her life, she hasn't spent much time at my apartment. I'm pretty sure she's also stopped looking for a place of her own.

As I finish my text, a slight movement out of the corner of my eye catches my attention. It shouldn't, considering it's Vegas. This entire place is a constant wave of motion. But something draws my gaze toward the doors.

When I see my mystery man standing there, his impassioned stare trained on me, I'm stunned, frozen in place, in time, in this moment. The intensity in his stormy green eyes sends a rush of exhilaration through me, leaving me breathless. No man's ever looked at me this way. Or maybe they have, but I ignored it. But I can't ignore him.

He starts toward me and everything else seems to disappear. It's…quiet. Gone are the obnoxious sounds of slot machines, the tourists rushing by, and the ridiculously loud club music filling the space, even at eleven in the morning. Reaching me, his hand palms the small of my back and he pulls me against him. A spark shoots through me, low and deep, igniting a flame I didn't think would ever be lit again.

He brings his other hand to my hair, wrapping his fingers around it, forcing my head back. I stare into his eyes, unable to escape. And I don't want to, don't want to flee this bubble.

"I can't leave," he begins, his voice husky, low, sensual.

"Sure you can," I murmur. "All you have to do is put one foot in front of the other and walk through those doors."

He slowly shakes his head. "No. What I meant to say is I can't leave without…" His mouth inches even closer.

"Without what?" My lips tingle in anticipation.

"Without kissing you."

My nerves stir as my stomach fills with the wings of a thousand butterflies, all of them screaming at him to finally get on with it.

"Then what are you waiting for?"

His grip on me tightens and he yanks my body harder against his, his eyes flaring with unyielding desire. He gradually decreases the distance, this torturous dance of seduction making me even more on edge. I'm desperate to feel his lips, to know how they taste. All weekend, I've fantasized about his kiss. Most people would probably wonder what he was like in bed, how he screwed. Not me. There's nothing personal about that. Kissing is much more intimate.

Based on what little I know of him, I imagined he kissed with all the confidence he seemed to do everything else. At first, it would be controlled and reserved, but still addictive. He wouldn't be able to hold back for long. It would explode into a passionate exchange, leaving me thoughtless, breathless, soulless, ruining me for all men who would come after him.

When his breath dances on my flesh, I close my eyes, bracing to feel his full lips on me. Instead, boisterous voices infiltrate our bubble, a body slamming into me, causing me to teeter on my heels.

Forced out of my trance, I glare at a bunch of drunk guys in their twenties, all of them carrying those huge plastic cups containing sugary, frozen drinks. It's not even noon, yet they already look like they've been overserved.

"Are you okay?" my mystery man asks, and I return my eyes to his.

"Of course." I straighten my jacket, even more happy to be going home than I was before. I'm about to ask where we were when an alert interrupts. He reaches into his pocket, withdrawing his cell.

"My Uber's here." He offers me an apologetic smile. Then he leans in, his mouth a whisper from my neck. "Safe travels." He kisses my cheek, his lips lingering on my skin for several long moments. When he pulls away, he holds my gaze before retreating, leaving me feeling like a hormonally imbalanced high school freshman who was nearly kissed by the hot senior quarterback before the prom queen pulled him away.

I exhale a breath, taking a moment to collect myself. But I don't have a moment. Izzy hurries toward me, eyes wide in curiosity.

"Who was *that*?" The tone of her voice indicates she must have seen him kiss my cheek, at the very least.

All I can do is shake my head as I shift my attention to the front doors and watch my mystery man slide into the back seat of a dark sedan.

"Just some guy."

CHAPTER FOUR

"SO YOU MEAN to tell me that, of the three times you've seen him—"

"Four, if you count him coming back to try to kiss me."

"Whatever…" Izzy waves me off. "That's not the point. The point is that you never thought to ask him his name?" Her voice is filled with disbelief at the story I just relayed to her about my run-ins with Mr. Mysterious over the course of the weekend.

"I *did* think of it." I relax into my plush lounge chair, bringing my espresso to my lips as we sit in a quiet corner of the airline club. The hectic atmosphere of the airport is nowhere to be found. No screaming children being ignored by their parents who are exhausted after a long day of traveling. No annoying businessmen who feel the need to shout on their cellphones in the hopes that someone thinks they're important. No assholes bitching out the poor airline employee who had nothing to do with the delay of the flight going to Denver, where there's probably snow. In here, I'm able to have a moment of peace.

"A name is usually the *first* thing I ask," she interjects before I can say anything else. "You'd think with all the time you spent 'bumping' into each other this weekend, you would have gotten that much."

"It's just… Every time I saw him…" I shake my head, struggling to come up with the words to describe how his mere presence consumed me. Normally, *I'm* the confident one. *I'm* the one calling the shots. *I'm* the one saying whatever's on my mind without a care for what anyone thinks about me. But not around him. "It was quiet," I finish thoughtfully.

"Quiet?" Izzy gives me a sideways glance. "What do you mean?"

I place my espresso on the table separating us and lean closer, lowering my voice. "All the noise of my life. It was…gone."

Understanding immediately washes over her, and her expression relaxes.

Izzy's one of the few people who truly knows me, all my secrets, all my scars. Yes, Nora's been a great friend since we were college roommates, and once Evie was assigned the cubicle next to mine at the magazine, we formed a quick bond, considering she lacks any brain-to-mouth filter, much like myself. But Izzy knew me *before*. She knew me when my parents were still together. She knew me when it all fell apart, when I had to lie to my father about being sick so I could miss my weekend with him to take care of my mother during another one of her drinking binges. Something no teenage girl should have to do. But what choice did I have? She was the only family I had left after my father upgraded to a new one.

"Sometimes you just need someone to quiet it for a minute," she remarks.

"Because of that, I didn't think a name was necessary." We share a look before I curl my lips into a wicked grin, lightening the mood. "You *do* have to admit the entire scenario is kind of hot. Not knowing his name, anything about him…"

"*Kind of* hot?" She fans herself, giggling. "Try off the charts! I noticed the chemistry between you two right away, even if all he did was kiss your cheek. It was incredibly…sexy. I can't imagine how it made *you* feel."

"Like I could let go," I reply without hesitating. "For once, I didn't worry about the fact that we're polar opposites. That he's presumably this guy who has his shit together, whereas I'm lucky if I don't lock myself out of my apartment on a daily basis. But each time I saw him, I didn't think about any of that, didn't try to distance myself because of how it would play out. It's almost like we were in our own little bubble."

"Bubbles can be good." Then her eyes turn conniving. "Especially a bubble that sexy."

We both break into laughter. I lean back into my chair, at ease with the familiarity of joking with one of my oldest friends. If nothing else, at least I got to spend a little more time with Izzy this weekend than I usually do. While we both live in New York, her job as a nurse in the pediatric oncology unit at one of the local hospitals doesn't give her much time off. Izzy's one of those friends who you can go months without seeing, then pick back up as if you just saw them yesterday.

"So, what do you think the girls are up to today?" I ask after a few minutes.

"Knowing Bernadette, something cliché and inappropriate."

I roll my eyes. "Promise me if I ever get that lonely and desperate for attention, you'll smack some sense into me and tell me I don't need to stay in a loveless marriage. That there's better out there for me."

"You know I will."

A chiming cuts through and I float my eyes to the coffee table to see a text from my mother wishing me safe travels. I grab my cell and fire off a quick response, not wanting her to worry.

"She doing okay?" Izzy asks, obviously having seen who the text was from.

"Yeah." I take another drink of my espresso, finishing it. "She's been dating this guy who works in the same building." I stare into the distance, smiling. "It's actually a sweet story. Somehow, they kept riding up to their floors in the same elevator. After about a week, he mentioned it to her. Said he couldn't ignore it anymore, that it was a sign."

"Hmm… A sign?" She smirks knowingly.

"That's not the same thing," I argue, fully aware what she's referring to. "Mom works in the same building as Aaron. There's a decent likelihood of running into him again. This thing with me and…whoever he is, well…it's different. I have a better chance of winning the lottery than seeing him again."

Izzy shrugs. "You're probably right, but what if you do?"

"It'll never happen," I say incredulously. "I'm about to get on a flight back to New York. He was headed…" I wave my hand around, "wherever. So yeah. Not going to happen."

"But if it does?"

"It won't," I insist.

"But if it does?" she presses again.

"It won't."

"Yeah, but if it does?"

I groan, remembering how persistent and annoying Izzy can be. This could go on for hours, even days. "Fine. If by some miracle I *do* see him again, maybe I'll admit there might be a reason for it all."

She nods, leaning back in her chair, happy with herself.

"But it won't happen."

She glares at me, feigning annoyance. "Always have to have the last word, don't you?"

I grin. "Always."

My phone dings again and I reach for it, assuming it's a reply from my mother. Unlocking the screen, I see an alert from the airline.

"Shit," I mutter as Izzy's phone begins to beep.

"What is it?" She scrambles for her cell, presumably reading the same message I received. "Dammit."

"Yup. Flight to JFK is canceled."

She groans, closing her eyes in frustration. "Just how I want to spend my day. Stuck in the airport."

"And not any airport," I remind her, pointing at the busy terminal that resides just outside the lounge, the subtle sound of slot machines inching their way into our peaceful recluse. "McCarran Airport in *fabulous* Las Vegas." My voice is laden with sarcasm. "If the Strip is the tenth circle of hell, this place is purgatory."

"Glad to see all those literature classes paid off."

"What flight did they rebook you on?" I ask, opening the airline's app on my phone to get my new flight information.

"Red-eye. Eleven PM. And here's the kicker. No seat assignment available." She holds out her phone so I can see her new itinerary.

"Me, too." I mirror her movement.

"It looks like they're cramming everyone onto that flight. What are the chances of us actually getting on?"

"I'd like to say they wouldn't rebook us just to tell us no in ten hours."

"My mother used to work for an airline. They absolutely *would* do such a thing." She pinches her lips together, deep in thought, then jumps up. "I'll be right back." A woman on a mission, she starts toward the front desk of the lounge.

While Izzy speaks to an agent for what I presume to be a solution, I return my attention to my phone, opening the web browser to see if there are any other options. Despite it being a Tuesday and a light travel day, most of the flights to JFK are sold out or, if there are seats available, are way out of my price range. Not to mention, it's after one in the afternoon. The next flight into New York doesn't leave until later tonight, even on a different airline.

"Hey," Izzy says breathlessly. I look up from my phone, eyes brimming with hope. "I can get us guaranteed seats on the noon flight tomorrow. The red-eye is oversold and they'll most likely be forced to rebook again if they can't get enough people with confirmed seats to give them up. You in? Guaranteed seats or take a risk on the red-eye."

I push out an aggravated breath, pinching the bridge of my nose. As much as I hate the idea of staying in Vegas another night and having to waste even more vacation time, it doesn't seem like there's an option.

"Guaranteed seats."

"Give me your boarding pass and I'll get you rebooked."

I grab my phone and find my boarding pass, then hand it to her.

"Thanks. Be right back."

I watch as she scurries back to the front desk. She's come a long way from the little girl who was too scared to approach Hannah and me when her family first moved into the neighborhood. Now, Izzy's a typical New Yorker. Confident. Assured. And always gets her way.

After a few minutes, she returns and hands me my phone along with a new airline printout. "Here you go. You're all set."

"Thanks," I say, surprised at her efficiency. If she weren't here, I would have sucked it up and hung around the airport in the hopes of getting on the red-eye. But now that we're flying out tomorrow, there's another problem.

"Umm… Izzy, we can't go back to the same hotel, not unless we want to get roped into day 317 of the never-ending bachelorette party."

A sly smile builds on her lips. "Don't worry. I've got that covered, too."

CHAPTER FIVE

"WHERE THE HELL are we?" I ask as our Uber driver slows to a stop in front of a gated driveway on the outskirts of Vegas. "David Copperfield's house?"

"No." Izzy rolls her eyes. "But my sources say he lives around here somewhere."

"Sources? What sources? *I'm* your source for all things celebrity."

"Maybe there are some things about me you *don't* know." She passes me a devious grin before opening the door, stepping onto the street. A little bewildered, I take a minute to collect my things. When she said she had a friend who was more than happy to let us stay the night, I didn't expect to pull up in front of a piece of property that looks like it belongs in Bel Air.

A knock on the window rips my attention away from the impressive entrance and I snap my eyes to Izzy as she opens my door.

"Are you coming? Or do you want to call Bernadette and see if you can crash with her tonight? Maybe stay up and do a makeover, then go to some Pure Romance party."

"I wouldn't mind going to a Pure Romance party." I scoot out of the car. "I'm all for women exploring their sexuality. But I'd pass on the Bernadette makeover," I say as I head toward where our driver stands, holding the handle of my suitcase for me. "With the amount of makeup she'd cake on my face and the revealing outfit she'd stuff me in, I'd come out of there looking like a blowup doll." Smiling, I take my bag from the driver as he eyes me up and down, discreetly adjusting the waist of his pants.

The Vegas sun beating down on us, I follow Izzy toward the front gate, watching as she enters a code into a box. I can't help but feel like she hasn't been forthcoming about who we're staying with. Granted, I'm not as close to her as I once was, but she would have mentioned knowing someone who owned a palace in Vegas, wouldn't she?

"Are you coming?" she asks when the gate opens and she continues up the elaborate drive.

"I suppose…," I respond in a drawn-out voice, taking slow steps toward her as I absorb my surroundings. The driveway is made of pavers, the brick matching that of the flowerbeds lining it, which are filled with succulents.

Palm trees shade the path, as well as offer privacy to the occupants.

As we round the corner, the house finally coming into view, my jaw drops. I knew we were in a wealthy neighborhood, but I didn't expect this. The sprawling two-story house looks like a snapshot from a home design magazine, a rare peek into how the rich and famous of Las Vegas live and play.

I glance at Izzy, my curiosity increasing with every step. She knew the exact house we were going to, told the driver to stop when he was about to pass it. That means she's been here before.

"Iz?" I say as we approach the short flight of steps leading to the front door.

She stops, flashing her eyes to mine, a single brow raised.

"Who lives here?"

"Just an old friend from my undergrad days." She avoids my inquisitive stare, smoothing a lock of nearly jet-black hair behind her ear, her olive-toned skin becoming flushed.

"A...friend? Does this 'friend' happen to be of the male persuasion?"

"Yes." She holds her head high, but still doesn't look directly at me.

"Call me crazy—"

"You certainly are."

"But I get the feeling there's more to the story than this guy..." I wave my hand around at our surroundings, everything pristine and glamorous, "being just a 'friend'."

Her eyes finally meets mine, a flash of indecision filling them. I can physically feel her turmoil, like she wants to tell someone whatever this is, but is scared of the potential backlash. Izzy has a habit of taking everyone's feelings into account with every decision.

I rest my hand on her arm. "What is it? You can tell me anything."

"I know that. But this..." She shakes her head, conflicted, pulling her lip between her teeth. When she looks at me again, a hint of shame covers her expression. Her shoulders fall. "It's Asher York."

I remain motionless as the name rings out between us. "Asher York as in Jessie York's older brother?"

She blows out a nervous laugh. "It's not exactly a common name, is it?"

"Asher York, the handsome, struggling musician?"

"Yup."

"The Asher York with a singing voice that makes you forget your name?"

"That's the one."

"The Asher York who looks like a fucking Adonis with a guitar strapped to him?"

"Yes, Chloe. *That* Asher York," she admits, her voice growing louder, her face blushing even more as the tension momentarily lightens.

"The Asher York who would have been your brother-in-law if you hadn't smartened up and called off your engagement to Jessie?"

Her expression falls and she slowly nods. "Exactly."

I stare at her, unsure how to react to this. She still didn't admit anything's going on between them, but she doesn't have to. I can see it in her eyes as she silently pleads with me not to make a big deal out of this. And I won't.

I never liked Jessie to begin with. He was arrogant, pompous, and conceited. They dated in college. Got engaged young. I pretended to be happy for her. She's my friend, after all. Deep down, I questioned whether it would last, considering they were both so young…*too* young to decide to get married. Thankfully, she realized that before it was too late, thanks to Jessie not being able to keep his dick in his pants.

"Well…" I take in my surroundings, my voice brightening. "It looks like Asher's not a struggling musician anymore, is he?"

"Oh, this isn't *his* place. He's just kind of…staying here."

"Like, house sitting?"

"Not exactly. He, uh…"

Before she can finish her sentence, the door swings open and we both snap our heads to the entryway. I almost can't believe my eyes when they fall on Asher York leaning against the doorjamb, arms crossed in front of his chest, his biceps stretching the fabric of his shirt, a wicked smile on his full lips as he admires Izzy.

This is not the same Asher York I remember from all those years ago. He's more mature, more muscular, more…experienced. There are hints of the man I saw a handful of times during some of Izzy's pre-wedding festivities, but his short, dark hair is now longer, the strong jawline sporting a sexy five o'clock shadow. It's only been six or seven years, but he seems like a different person. Then again, he could probably say the same about me.

"When I told you it was okay for you both to crash here, I meant *inside* the house. Not on the front stoop," he jokes, his eyes never leaving Izzy.

"Hey, Ash." A blush blooms on her cheeks, her lips kicking up into a brilliant smile. Then she looks away, nervously pushing her hair behind her ear. "Thanks for this."

"It's nothing, Iz. You know that." His words are laden with a sincerity I feel deep in my core. "I was thrilled to hear your voice, considering I thought you'd be 35,000 feet in the air by now."

"I guess the universe had different plans."

"I guess so."

Izzy peers up at him through thick lashes, her chest rising and falling in a quicker pattern. Something about the way Asher holds her gaze makes me think he doesn't want to look away. Then he glances in my direction, clearing his throat.

"Chloe. Good to see you again. I like the hair. It suits you."

I pass him a wry smile. "Thanks for letting us stay here."

"Anytime. I'd never turn away a friend in need." He steps back, gesturing for us to enter the house.

I lean into Izzy. "Hear that? He'll never turn away a *friend* in need, Iz." I waggle my eyebrows at her as we walk into the magnificent foyer complete with high ceilings and modern chandelier hanging overhead.

"Oh, hush. It's not like that."

I grin. "You want it to be like that, though, right?"

Chewing on her lower lip, she shrugs. "Maybe."

* * *

"All right, Asher," I say when Izzy and I step into the kitchen after getting a brief tour of the luxurious house and changing into our bathing suits. "Whose house is this?" I turn around slowly, craning my head back, my voice seeming to echo against the tile in the cavernous space. "Izzy said you're not house sitting, so what *are* you doing in a place like this?"

"Don't think I can afford it myself?" He looks up from forming a mixture of ground beef and onions into patties.

"Last I heard, you were playing bars in LA, trying to make it big."

"Maybe I've made it big."

"Have you?" I place my hands on the large island, leaning toward him, my lips pressed into a tight line. If he'd made it big, I would have heard.

He considers my question for a moment, then shrugs. "Not yet, but I'm one step closer."

"What do you mean?" I look from him to Izzy, an amused expression on her face. I notice her eyes shift ever so slightly and I follow her line of sight, my gaze falling on a glass case in the living room.

I walk toward it, my brow furrowing when I see six Grammy awards enclosed within. Squinting, I read the gold plate, then whirl around, my expression wide.

"You're in Fallen Grace?" I can't hide the disbelief in my voice.

Fallen Grace is this decade's most popular boy band, five twenty-something-year-old guys from London who girls scream and fawn over everywhere they go. I would have noticed Asher York standing amongst their numbers. I notice *everything* about *everyone*.

He shakes his head, laughing. "Certainly not. They're not really my style."

"Then what—"

"They hired me to work on their new album with them, and to help with their engagement here in Vegas."

"If they're not your style, why are you working with them?"

"They're going for a more mature sound…less pop, more rock."

I absorb what he's saying, my mouth agape as I shake my head. "How the hell did you even land this job?"

"Dumb luck," he laughs. "About six months ago, I had a gig with my band in Hollywood when one of the guys came by. He grabbed one of our download codes, listened to the tracks, then played it for the rest of the band. After doing a bit of research, they found out I wrote all the songs. Their manager called to see if I was interested in helping on their next album."

"So you're… What? Writing their songs for them?"

"More or less. Some of them write their own stuff, too, but I'm helping fill in the gaps and produce the record." He smiles, a hint of nostalgia in his eyes as he stares into space, his expression thoughtful. "Before I got their call, I was months behind on my rent and facing eviction. I was ready to throw in the towel, tell my parents they were right and I should never have left my teaching job. It goes to show that sometimes good things happen when we least expect it."

He looks from me to Izzy, admiring all five feet, seven inches of her slender physique, which is now on display in just a black bikini and sheer coverup. She pulled her dark locks into a messy bun, a pair of oversized sunglasses pushed up onto her forehead.

His Adam's apple bobs up and down in a hard swallow before he returns his attention to the burgers, his hands shaking slightly. It's adorable how nervous she makes him. That's all any woman wants. To know she affects a man in such a way as to completely fluster him.

"So…" He clears his throat. "What can I get you to drink? Beer? Wine? Cocktail? You name it, and it's yours, unless you ask for something strange. I may not have all the ingredients. But considering the parties the guys throw here, I'm pretty well-stocked."

I lean toward Izzy, whispering into her ear. "He certainly is, isn't he?"

She slaps me away, hushing me. "I'm happy with a beer." She looks toward the rear wall that consists of floor-to-ceiling windows overlooking the pool area. "It's a beer kind of day."

"A woman after my own heart," he comments with a wink, causing the blush on her cheeks to build even more. Then he lifts his eyes to mine. "Chloe?"

"Beer's fine with me, too."

With a nod, he turns toward the refrigerator and opens it, taking out two Coronas, popping the top off them. "Lime?"

"Yes," we answer simultaneously.

He retrieves a couple lime slices from a bowl on the island, sticks them into the neck of the bottle, then slides the beers toward us. We get to work pushing the lime past the neck, plugging the bottle with our thumbs, and flipping it so the lime sinks toward the bottom.

"Here's to making the most out of a canceled flight." Izzy raises her beer.

I mirror her movements. "I'd much rather be here than stuck at the airport."

"I'll drink to that," Asher agrees, bringing his beer toward ours. We clink bottles, then tilt them back, taking a sip.

"Is there anything we can help with?" Izzy asks.

"I have it all under control. You ladies are guests here. Just relax and enjoy yourselves. Come on."

He grabs the plate of burgers and starts toward the open French doors. We follow him, emerging onto the back patio area, the aroma of burning charcoal filling the air.

"Lincoln!" Asher calls out as he strides toward the grill off to the left, leaving the plate on a table beside it. "Get off your phone and be social."

I scan the pool area, following Asher's line of sight. A tall man with dark hair holds up a finger, not looking in our direction as he walks toward a fence beyond the pool, leaning his arms against it as he admires the view of the Vegas skyline from this vantage point on the outskirts of the city. It is quite impressive. I can only imagine how incredible the view must be at night. As much as I hate Vegas, I can certainly appreciate the beauty of it, especially from afar.

"He'll be done soon, I hope."

"Who's *he*?" I don't actively follow Fallen Grace, but I don't recall any of them being named Lincoln.

"Lincoln Moore," Asher answers, placing the burgers onto the grill. It instantly sizzles. "We went to college together. In fact, he was a workaholic back then, too, constantly studying. He was one of those guys who lived according to the motto 'work hard, play hard'."

"I like to think that now it's 'work hard, play even harder'."

When I hear that deep rumble, every muscle in my body tenses, my breath leaving me. It couldn't be, could it?

I slowly turn around, momentarily disoriented as I stare into those green eyes once more. Izzy pinches my side, just as surprised as me.

"Chloe, Izzy...," Asher begins, oblivious to the tension. "This is my friend, Lincoln."

I stare, seeing him differently now that I know his name. It suits him. Strong, yet flirty.

"Lincoln, this is Izzy and—"

"Dick Girl."

"Dick Girl?" Asher looks between us, confused. "Do you two know each other?"

Lincoln subtly nods. "We've had the…pleasure." The way that word leaves his tongue has my nerve endings stirring. "Or perhaps I should say *I've* had the pleasure of experiencing her sharp tongue."

"Yes." I offer him a flirtatious smile, extending my hand toward him. "It's nice to see you again, to *formally* meet you, Lincoln."

He takes my hand in his, raising it to his lips, his pupils dilating as he feathers his mouth against my skin. The touch is subtle, yet it has my stomach doing backflips.

"Likewise, Chloe." He passes me a devilish grin, then lowers my hand. "I didn't think we'd see each other again."

"Either did I."

"Funny how that keeps happening, isn't it? How we keep…bumping into each other. If I didn't know any better, I'd think someone, some*thing* wants us to keep seeing each other."

I lift my beer to my mouth. "I'm beginning to think I should buy a lottery ticket."

CHAPTER SIX

"CAREFUL. CAREFUL," I caution, biting my lower lip, my breathing ragged, wracked with nerves. "No, not there." My voice is frantic as I meet Lincoln's fervid eyes, his concentration so intense I fear it may be our undoing.

"This isn't my first rodeo," he reminds me.

"I figured as much, but you have to watch what you're doing or it won't end well." My words come out husky, my body taut with anticipation. "One wrong move and it'll all come tumbling down."

"I've got this," he insists through clenched jaws, his nostrils flaring.

Licking his lips, he pauses, the pressure so thick I could almost burst. My chest heaves, the seconds seeming to stretch as I watch his every move. He inches closer and closer and I brace myself, my hands forming into fists, the past several hours, hell…days, culminating in this moment.

Then he pushes a finger in, his motions measured and practiced. I exhale, the tension rolling off me.

"See, Chloe." He meets my eyes, waggling his brows. "I told you I knew what I was doing."

He waves the Jenga block in my face, jutting out his chest. With his head held high, he barely pays attention as he places the block on top of the tower we've spent the past hour building. It instantly falls, the pieces scattering across the table and the ground, the sound echoing throughout the patio.

Groans emanate from everyone as we watch our hard work topple over.

"See! That's what you get for being so cocky," I taunt.

"Don't you know it, baby," he says with a wink before turning his attention to the mess, picking up the blocks.

I can't remember the last time I've played this game. It was probably in college. Back then, of course, it was more of a drinking game. When I stumbled on a collection of board games in the living room, I figured it would be a better way to spend our time than sitting around and drinking.

"What's next on the agenda for game night?" Izzy asks once all the Jenga blocks are back in their box.

"Game night?" I repeat.

"Yeah." She gives me a knowing look. "Game night."

"Oh, no." My response comes quick. "This isn't game night. That's something bored, married couples do to mask the fact that they have nothing in common with each other. The arrogant husband acts as if he's a know-it-all anytime his wife answers a question wrong in Trivial Pursuit. And she realizes exactly how little her husband listens to her during a rousing game of Taboo. No thanks. Not interested."

A sly smile crosses Izzy's mouth, her eyes alight with excitement. "Not all games are boring."

I've seen this look before, the most recent being when she dragged me to what she thought was an intimate Cher concert at a club in the Village. It sounded too good to be true. And it was. The "Cher concert" was a drag show. Regardless, we had one hell of a time.

"What did you have in mind?"

Her grin widens. "You'll see." She stands and heads back into the house, a bounce in her step.

"I'm not sure if I should be scared or intrigued," Asher says, keeping his eyes trained on her.

"The one thing I've learned about Izzy is that she's rather unpredictable."

He blows out a laugh, nodding. "Truer words have never been spoken."

Izzy reappears in the doorway seconds later and walks toward us, a box in her hand. She places it on the wicker coffee table between us, her expression smug.

"I told you, Chloe. Game night doesn't always have to be boring. What do you guys think? Want to take things up a notch?" She grins mischievously. "Or are you too chicken?"

That's all it takes for the guys to puff out their chests, raw masculinity oozing from them. I almost expect them to bang their fists against their pecs and roar like cavemen.

"Never Have I Ever?" I say, reading the words on the box. I didn't realize they'd made a board game out of it.

She shrugs. "Why not? I thought you were an open book, that you had no shame."

"I don't."

"Then what's stopping you?" She smirks, briefly shifting her eyes to Lincoln before returning to mine.

"Fine," I relent with a sigh. "But if we're going to play this, I'll need another beer." I begin to stand from the couch when Lincoln places his hand on my arm, gently pushing me back down.

"I got it." He meets my gaze, which seems to linger on my lips. Then he drops his hold on me, looking at Asher. "I'll grab another round for everyone. I have a feeling we all may need it." He focuses on me once more before disappearing into the house.

"I might as well take advantage of this break and go change." I stand, stretching my arms over my head after sitting for the past hour.

We spent all afternoon lounging by the pool, drinking beers, eating burgers, and playing board games. But now that the sun has disappeared beyond the horizon, the temperature has fallen, making it a bit too cold to be out here in just a bathing suit and a flimsy coverup.

"Are you sure you're not planning to take advantage of something else?" Izzy calls after me as I start toward the house.

I roll my eyes, ignoring her comment, and continue into the kitchen, glancing back at them to see Asher stealing my spot next to Izzy. I'm definitely intrigued by their obvious connection, wondering how long this has been going on. At least I have a five hour flight tomorrow in which to get some answers.

Distracted by concocting a plan to pry this information out of Izzy, I don't pay much attention to my surroundings… Until a movement catches my eyes. I attempt to halt in my tracks, but velocity from my quick strides prevents me from stopping and I crash straight into Lincoln, the beers in his hands jostling and splashing.

"Oh, my god." My face reddens as I stare at his linen shirt, which is now soaked with beer. "I'm so sorry." I rush to take the fizzing bottles out of his hands and place them on the island. Grabbing a kitchen towel, I bring it to his shirt, dabbing at it.

"Don't worry about it." A smile illuminates his face as he looks down at me. "It's just beer."

"I know, but I—"

He wraps his hand around my arm, preventing me from fussing over him any longer.

"Chloe…"

I straighten, swallowing hard. "Yes?"

While we've spent all afternoon together, this is the first time we're alone. The atmosphere is just as charged as it has been the previous times we've seen each other. I have to remind myself to breathe.

"I said it's okay. Nothing a blow dryer can't fix." He pauses, pulling his lips between his teeth. "You wouldn't happen to have a blow dryer, would you? All my stuff is back at the hotel."

I pinch my lips together. "A girl never leaves home without her favorite blow dryer. Come with me."

I leave the towel on the island and lead him up the stairs, doing everything to settle my overwrought nerves. When we reach my room, I walk to my suitcase sitting on an ottoman by the window.

"Please don't tell me that's how you pack," he comments as I rummage through my haphazardly arranged things.

"What's wrong with it?"

He shakes his head. "It's so…unorganized."

"Perhaps to some people…" I grab the dryer, a satisfied look on my face as I wave it in front of him. "But I thrive on the chaos. If you think that's bad…" I spin around and head into the bathroom, "you should see my desk at the office."

He follows, leaning against the doorjamb, observing me as I plug in the dryer.

"And what is it you do?"

"I work at a magazine."

He raises his brow, obviously surprised. "Doing what?"

"I'm a celebrity news columnist." I offer a forced smile.

He studies me for a moment, gaze narrowed. "Why do I get the feeling you wish you were doing something different?"

My posture stiffening, I peer at him. This guy barely knows me, yet he's picked up on something my close friends haven't. That Evie never picked up on, even though she works at the same magazine.

I shrug. "It's a good job. It pays the bills. That's the important part. And I don't hate it. People would kill to have the job I do."

I'm not ungrateful for the opportunity I have at the magazine, but I didn't exactly get it on my own merits. My father's the only reason I'm lucky enough to have that job.

After I was forced to drop out of college to support my mother, who'd been fired because of her alcohol problem, I begged him to help me out with money. Instead, he called in a favor.

I thought I'd eventually go back and finish my degree, be able to get a job at a different magazine because of my own qualifications. Maybe *Rolling Stone*, or even *Time*. But life always seemed to get in the way.

Correction.

My *mother* always seemed to get in the way. I'm just waiting for the bottom to fall again. That's why I'm only taking a few classes at a time, inching toward my degree. I figure even if the bottom *does* fall, it won't be impossible to juggle my job, a couple of classes, and my mother.

"Chloe? You okay?"

I snap out of my thoughts, meeting Lincoln's concerned eyes.

"Sorry. Just thinking about…work." I clear my throat, then turn on the blow dryer. "Come here," I order, and he walks toward me. I point the air stream at the beer stain on his shirt.

He instantly flinches. "Damn. That burns."

"Well, what do you expect? The only way to dry something is with hot air." I return the dryer to the spot, and he cringes again. Men. No wonder women are the ones who get pregnant. They probably wouldn't survive period cramps, let alone pushing a watermelon through a straw.

"Enough." He steps away and I turn off the blow dryer. "New idea."

He unbuttons his shirt, allowing it to fall open, which has the unfortunate side effect of my mouth growing dry. I'd be lying if I said I hadn't fantasized about what he'd look like without a shirt. The reality certainly lives up to the fantasy. Broad shoulders. Sculpted biceps. Firm abs. And a little trail of hair disappearing into his shorts.

"Fuck me," I murmur, entranced with the thought of what he has farther south.

He lifts his eyes to mine, his lips curving into a flirtatious smile.

"I mean…" I look away, flustered, trying to come up with an excuse for my verbal vomit.

His grin widens as he steps toward me, his gaze narrowed. Warmth spreads through me, my heart drumming a feverish rhythm. It's so intense, I expect it to leap out of my chest at any moment. I remain locked in place, unable to move, fearing my knees would buckle if I tried to walk. He curves toward me and I swallow hard, barely able to breathe.

When his mouth is a whisper from mine, my eyelids flutter closed and I crane my head. My body aches in anticipation of his kiss, desperate to finally know how his lips taste.

"Allow me," he murmurs in a seductive voice that makes me even more light-headed. Then he removes the blow dryer from my hand. I fling my eyes open as he pulls back, a smirk on his lips.

In an attempt to steady myself, I place my hand on the vanity counter, drawing in several deep breaths as I try to make sense out of what just happened. What *did* just happen?

"You're familiar with the story of the tortoise and the hare, correct?" He glances at me before returning his attention to his shirt. Flicking on the blow dryer, he aims the air at the material.

"Yes…," I answer in a drawn-out voice, confused about this line of questioning.

"My litigation professor in law school often spoke of it in relation to a trial."

"So you're a lawyer." I place a hand on my hip.

I'm not sure what I thought Lincoln did, but I didn't expect him to say he's a lawyer. I grew up around lawyers. My father's chief general counsel for the biggest newspaper in the country, if not the world. None of the lawyers on his staff ever looked like Lincoln. If they did, I might visit him more often, attend more of his work functions.

"Not master of the universe. Master of the courtroom."

"In a manner of speaking, yes. But that's beside the point."

I saunter toward him. "Then what *is* the point?"

He shuts off the blow dryer, running his hand over the fabric to check for any dampness. Content, he shrugs his shirt back on, much to my disappointment. A shirtless Lincoln Moore truly is a sight to behold. In the shirtless Olympics, he'd wow the judges with a near perfect score.

"Do you know what the hare's mistake was?"

"Yes." I smirk. "He was cocky. Thought he'd get what he wanted no matter what."

He laughs, the sound causing my demeanor to momentarily crack. "That's true. But his problem was sloppy execution."

"Sloppy? How so?"

"He went out of the gate at full speed. There was no warm-up..." Fire builds in his gaze. "No buildup. And when he saw he was in the lead, he took a break."

"You don't think it's okay to take a break?"

"I think it's lazy. Certain aspects of life require a bit more finesse, a bit more planning, a bit more...effort. And let's not forget the most important part."

"And what's that?"

"That the tortoise is the one who crossed the finish line first." He leans toward me, so close I can taste the sweetness of the beers he's consumed. "And I am *very* interested in crossing that finish line."

A shiver rolls down my spine, the double meaning in his words driving me wild with need.

Then he straightens, buttoning his shirt the rest of the way. "But not until I've fully run the race."

"Well... I guess it's time for me to fire the starter pistol."

I start to walk past him, but he grasps my arm and yanks my body against his. It feels like all the air's been sucked from my lungs as I stare into his striking green eyes.

"Haven't you figured it out by now?" His lips skim against mine.

"What's that?"

"I already fired that pistol Saturday night, Chloe. We've just been running laps around each other since then."

"But even when you run laps, you need to stop for a drink of water. You need to quench your thirst."

"Is that what we're doing now? Quenching our thirst?"

"Why don't you tell me?"

His grip on me tightens as a groan falls from his throat, heady and sexy, forcing a stirring deep in my core. He licks his lips, yearning covering his expression as he closes the distance. I brace myself for his kiss, mouth tingling, synapses firing, when every light in the room suddenly snaps off, shrouding us in darkness.

We both stiffen, remaining still, waiting for the lights to come back on. When they don't, he pulls away, releasing me. I look around, but the bathroom is pitch black. Of course, we'd be stuck in the one room with no windows.

"I'll go see what's going on," he states with authority. "The door's around here somewhere."

I put my hands out in front of me, reaching for something to tell me exactly where we are in this ridiculously opulent bathroom that's probably bigger than my entire apartment.

"Why did you close it to begin with?"

"In case we needed a bit of privacy."

I follow Lincoln's scent, confident we must be near the door. "And why would we need a bit of pri—"

My leg hits something, the velocity of my strides catapulting me forward. Without being able to see, I wave my arms around, grasping onto the first thing my hand finds, which also happens to be Lincoln, and we land on the floor with a loud thump. At least my fall was cushioned by his body. He, unfortunately, didn't fare as well and grunts.

"You okay?"

"Great," he answers in a high-pitched falsetto.

"Did I…" I trail off, noticing my knee's putting pressure on something. "Shit. I'm sorry." I adjust my position and hear his exhaled breath.

"I had a feeling you were a ball buster," he groans. "I didn't think you'd literally bust my balls."

"Want me to massage them to make them feel better?" I joke.

He's silent for a moment, then breaks into a throaty laugh. It echoes against the tile, filling the space. "Thanks for the offer, but right now, I'm pretty sure my dick is shriveled up. It'll need some coaxing to come out and play again."

I run my hands up his firm chest, the sensation of being this close sparking a need for even more. To feel more of him. Bringing my mouth toward his, I murmur, "Challenge accepted." He instantly hardens beneath me, and I crook my mouth into a smile, feeling powerful that I have this kind of effect on him.

Cautiously raising myself back to my feet, I step around the room, extending my arms in front of me. When my hand brushes against a metal object, I stop, wrapping my fingers around it. I turn the knob and open the door, the light of the moon illuminating the bedroom through the windows.

"There you are!" Izzy says breathlessly as she rounds the corner into the room. Asher follows, carrying a flashlight. When Lincoln steps into the bedroom, she halts. "Both of you," she adds, her tone not quite a statement. Not exactly a question, either.

"Did we blow a fuse?" I ask in an attempt to steer the conversation away from the curiosity in her gaze.

"I don't know," she responds slyly. "Did you?"

"I don't think it was a fuse," Lincoln interrupts.

I look in his direction to see him staring out the back window that displayed a beautiful view of the Strip earlier. Now the only lights visible are those of cars snaking up Las Vegas Boulevard. No green glow from the MGM Grand. No Eiffel Tower at the Paris Hotel beckoning people to have their photo taken. No gigantic Ferris wheel spinning a slow circle. It's all dark, the sky black, apart from the moon and stars.

"Like I said," Lincoln continues when we all remain silent, congregating around him and staring into the darkness. "I don't think it was a fuse."

CHAPTER SEVEN

"WAIT A MINUTE. Wait a minute," I say, struggling to capture a breath, my stomach aching from laughing so much over the past hour as we played a toned-down version of Never Have I Ever on the back patio under the light of the moon.

After realizing there was nothing to do but wait for the electricity to come back on, we decided to continue on with our game night. What else could we do? It took our minds off what could have happened to cause all of Las Vegas to lose power.

"You were cursed by a…cat?"

"Fluffy was not a normal cat." Lincoln sips on his beer, but keeps his eyes focused on me.

"The cat's name was Fluffy?"

"Should have been Satan," he mumbled.

"What did the cat do to make you so terrified of it?"

"Existed."

"One of his girlfriends adopted the dang thing from the shelter," Asher pipes in, sharing the story of Fluffy, the devil cat.

"She was nuts," Lincoln adds. "Certifiable."

"Are we talking about Fluffy or the girlfriend?" I ask.

"The girlfriend," he answers, then pauses. "Well, both. I'm pretty sure Mia's psychosis rubbed off on Fluffy."

"What could a cat do that's so bad to make you think it cursed you? I love cats," I offer. "They're the perfect pet. They shit in a box and clean up after themselves."

"They're nature's little serial killers. You cannot trust a cat. Or a cat person."

"Well then…" I settle into the couch. "I guess you can't trust me. Because I'm a cat person."

"Were any of your cats cockblockers?" he presses.

"Umm…no. But I never bring guys to my place to begin with."

This piques Lincoln's interest and he tilts his head. "Ever?"

"It's one of her rules," Izzy states. "Don't shit where you eat or something."

His brow furrows. "Doesn't that phrase refer to sleeping with a coworker?"

"To some, but I expand it to mean not wanting to ruin anything that's important to me."

"And not bringing a date home is important."

"It complicates things. And I like…uncomplicated. The rest of my life is difficult enough. So rule number one is never let them into my home."

"After all…," Lincoln begins, "home is where the heart is."

I peer at him, my mouth falling open. People I've known most of my life don't fully understand why I refuse to invite a guy to my apartment. But Lincoln gets it. Maybe we're not as different as I originally believed.

"This isn't about me," I say quickly. "This is about Fluffy."

"Right. Fluffy. Like Asher pointed out, my ex adopted him. Referred to him as our 'baby'. When I ended things, she went a little crazy."

"How crazy? On a scale of one to *Single White Female.*"

"She would have been more than happy to pin some murders on me," he replies, understanding my movie reference. "At least she never attempted to adopt my appearance. Suffice it to say, she didn't deal with the breakup well. One day, I got home from work to find she left the cat on my front stoop with a note saying she couldn't handle being a single parent and I needed to step up my game."

I choke on my beer at the ridiculousness of it all. I've done some crazy things in my life, but nothing like this.

"Sounds like you found yourself a clinger."

"I think she was just lonely and looking for attention," he responds thoughtfully. "Because once she started dating someone new, she forgot about me…and Fluffy."

I can certainly understand that. My mother's the same way.

"At first, I couldn't believe she'd leave the cat outside for what could have been hours in the middle of winter in Manhattan."

"Wait a minute." I shoot my eyes to his. "You live in New York?"

There's a sparkle in his gaze as he nods, brushing the pad of his thumb against his bottom lip. "Chelsea."

"I'm in the Village."

"Hmm… What are the odds?"

I sip on my beer, hiding my smile. "I'm thinking I *really* need to play the lottery now."

He smirks before continuing his story. "So I took the cat in. As much as I'm more of a dog person, I wouldn't abandon an animal. He was a pretty easy-going cat. Like you said, he shit in a box and took care of himself. But that first night…" He trails off.

"Yes?"

"I woke up in the middle of the night to use the bathroom. That's when I noticed him sitting on the opposite side of the bed, staring at me."

"He was probably curious," Izzy offers.

He slowly shakes his head. "No, because he would have eventually gotten bored. But he just sat there, watching my every move. And it happened night after night after night. Then, about a month later, I started seeing this new girl. Things were going pretty good, so I brought her back to my place."

I ignore the pang of jealousy at the idea of Lincoln bringing a girl home. I have no stake over him. Hell, we haven't even kissed. There's no reason for me to be jealous of any women in his life, past or present.

"Things started heating up and we were about to…"

"Cross the finish line," I say, completing his thought, giving him a knowing look.

"Precisely. And that's when they waved the red flag."

"On what grounds?"

"Due to the cat staring at us. It was creepy, and I couldn't…"

"What?" Asher laughs. "You couldn't get it up?"

"It's not that I couldn't get it up, but knowing that cat was looking at us with his beady eyes… Nothing helped. It's almost like Mia knew that would happen. Like the cat had some mystical powers and she purposefully left him to live at my place so I'd never have sex again."

We all burst out laughing, and I swipe the tears forming in my eyes.

"Well, I hope you found a way to get rid of the curse." I look at Lincoln beside me on the couch.

"I sure did. About three months later, my boss was going through a tough time because the family cat was hit by a car and his kids were distraught over it. I said I had a cat I could part with if he thought it would help. He refused at first, but I insisted. So now I'm free to… Ya know."

"See the checkered flag."

"Precisely."

"But what about your boss and his wife?" Izzy asks. "Don't they—"

"That's the thing!" Lincoln interrupts excitedly. "I asked him about it."

"You *asked* him? How does that even come up in conversation? I'm not quite sure a cockblocking cat is a normal topic."

He waves me off. "He invited me over for a dinner party. We both had a bit to drink, so I asked. He was convinced I was messing with him. Which leads me to the only possible conclusion. My ex tried to curse me with her cat."

We all roar with laughter once more, and it's a remarkable sound, particularly against the emptiness. It's strange how silent everything becomes when there's no power or cell service. No constant pings or vibrations from phone alerts. No hum of electricity. We've been forced back to simpler times when we actually have to communicate face-to-face, our only source of light and heat the fire pit we're sitting around.

"Okay. Who's next?" Izzy returns her attention to the coffee table, then frowns. "We're out of cards."

I chew on my bottom lip. "Maybe it's time we go off script. We stopped with the board game part of this a while back." I gesture to the game board where all the pieces were abandoned long ago in favor of just going through the stack of cards containing different scenarios. "Maybe it's time to make things more interesting and ask different kinds of questions."

"What kinds of questions did you have in mind?" Izzy waggles her brows, grinning mischievously.

"I don't know. Something deeper. A little more…personal."

"Therapist personal or *sexy* personal?"

"Therapist personal," I answer confidently. Then I catch Lincoln's gaze. "And sexy personal."

There's an instant shift in the atmosphere. Until now, we've all been relaxed, just a bunch of people getting to know each other, or catching up with old friends. But with those two words, we're about to change the rules.

"I'm okay with that." Asher takes a swig of his beer, his demeanor giving off the impression that he has nothing to hide. "We're all adults. Not much makes me uncomfortable."

"We *are* all adults, aren't we?" Izzy comments, her mouth a tight line as she taps a fingernail against her upper lip.

"What's going through that brain of yours?" I ask guardedly.

Instead of sharing, she jumps up, grabbing one of the flashlights off the table, then proceeds into the house.

"What is she doing?" Asher floats his gaze to me.

"Your guess is as good as mine."

We sit in silence, apart from the music coming from Asher's phone, all of us curious as to what Izzy's up to. Finally, she reappears, a wide smile on her face.

"What's going on?" I ask as she approaches.

"Like Asher said…," she begins with authority, "we're all adults, correct?"

"Yes…," we mumble, more or less at the same time.

"I'm declaring a circle of trust…a bubble, so to speak." She waves her arms in a circle through the air around us, enclosing us in an invisible dome. "I submit for your consideration a new take on Never Have I Ever."

"I'm not sure I want to know what this new take is," Asher jokes.

"You probably don't, considering it's how I met your brother, but…" She holds out her arms, wavering slightly, physical proof of how much she's had to drink. "Circle of trust." She pauses, waiting for us to agree, which we all do with a quick nod.

"We'll go around in a circle, saying something we've never done. If someone says they've never done something and you have, you drink. The changed rules apply to the person speaking. For example, if I say 'Never have I ever shot Abraham Lincoln', obviously, no one here will drink. In that case, we go to the penalty round."

She opens her palm, revealing a pair of dice I recognize from the goody bags we received this weekend. But they're not your traditional dice. Instead of little dots indicating a number, they have words. One is an action, the other a body part.

"How do we know whose…" Squinting, I read off the first words I spy on the dice, "thigh we have to bite?"

She grabs her nearly empty beer and drains it before waving it in front of us. "That's what this is for. Whoever the bottle lands on is the lucky winner… Or perhaps *unlucky*."

"I am *not* biting Asher's thigh," Lincoln says in a voice that sounds even deeper than his usual one.

"And I am not…" Asher grabs the dice, watching as they roll across the surface of the table, "sucking his finger."

Izzy sighs an exaggerated sigh, flopping back onto the couch beside Asher. "Men. This game is much more fun with only girls. They don't care about this shit. We have no problem licking each other's tongues."

Both guys instantly snap their eyes to her. It's so adorable that just the idea of two women making out gets their hormones running wild.

"But fine," she continues, ignoring the way Asher adjusts his shorts. "How about this? Everyone gets one free pass. Of course, just say something you know at least one other person sitting here has already done and you won't have to worry about spinning the bottle. Unless you *want* to…" She scoops up the dice and rolls, "blow on someone's neck." She looks around, lifting her bottle. "Are you all in?"

Lincoln flashes his eyes to me, a devilish glint in them. It is a bit juvenile and reminiscent of drinking games we played in college. But we're in the city of sin. What fun is being here during a blackout if you can't sin a little?

"Blackout Club," I say.

"What?" She scrunches her brows.

"The first rule of Blackout Club…"

"You don't talk about Blackout Club," Asher and Lincoln finish in unison. Every man in their twenties and thirties knows a *Fight Club* reference when they hear one.

"Exactly." I raise my beer, meeting Izzy's eyes. "Like you said, this is a bubble. We're all consenting adults… *Single* consenting adults. I'm in."

"Me, too," Asher says, lifting his own bottle.

We all shift our attention to Lincoln. He raises his beer and we all clink bottles, sealing the deal. "Let the games begin."

CHAPTER EIGHT

AN HOUR AND two beers later, Asher confidently says, "Never have I ever gotten so drunk I had to be carried out of a bar."

I glance around our little party, our circle of trust. Neither Lincoln nor I raise our beer to our mouths. I've carried more than my fair share of drunk people out of a bar, but I've never been carried out myself.

When I look at Izzy, she smirks, slowly bringing her bottle to her lips. Something about the smug expression on Asher's face leads me to believe he was aware of this incident.

"Okay." I place my lukewarm beer on the coffee table and lean across it to where she sits next to Asher. "There's obviously a story here. I need to hear it."

"Fine." She takes another sip of her beer, then faces me. "It was Christmas break my junior year of college. I was spending it in Connecticut with my family. Jessie was in Massachusetts. I had planned to visit him, but decided to surprise him and go early."

"Jessie? Your brother?" Lincoln asks, looking to Asher.

"Yes. They were, well... They were—"

"Engaged," Izzy finishes. "Until that night." A flicker of heartache passes across her expression before she recovers. "Their parents are snowbirds who flee the cold north for the south every winter. The guys usually went down to Florida for Christmas. Well, Jessie was getting back into town that day. Asher was already back, since he was a music teacher and school had resumed. Anyway, I told Asher my plan to surprise Jessie when he got home that day. I had this entire scenario in my head.

"At first, it all *did* go according to plan. Asher left me a key to Jessie's place so I'd have enough time to freshen up after the two-hour drive. I even made him the lasagna he loved, thinking he was probably going to be hungry after traveling all day. When I heard the car pull into the driveway, I went into the dining room, taking a page from Julia Roberts in *Pretty Woman.* You know, when she surprised Edward wearing a tie...and that's it. Sexy, right?" Her expression falls. "Until Jessie walked into the house and I could hear moans and giggles."

"Oh, Iz," I exhale, my hand covering my heart. I may not have the healthiest approach to relationships, but I've never cheated. I've never been anything but honest about what they were getting into with me — laidback, no strings, uncomplicated fun. Nothing more. Still, a pang squeezes my chest, thinking how Izzy must have felt at that moment.

"He tried to apologize, promise it was just a one-time thing, but in my heart, I knew that wasn't the case, that it had probably been going on a lot longer, especially considering *she* was the one he ran to the second he landed in Boston, not me. So I stormed out of there. After getting dressed, of course," she says, her voice lightening.

"I was a mess and not thinking clearly. I was so convinced he was the perfect man for me, although hindsight's always twenty-twenty. As I tried to figure out what to do, I passed a bar."

"Which just so happened to be where my band was performing that night," Asher continues. "Around the time we finished our first set, I looked up to see her sitting at the bar, some punk putting his hands all over her. But she was too drunk to realize what was going on."

"Not one of my finer moments."

"I knew some kind of shit had to go down for her to be there when she was supposed to be with Jessie. So I hauled her out of there before something untoward happened. Canceled the rest of our gig that night, much to the displeasure of the bar's owner, and took her to my place to sober up."

"The next morning, as he helped me nurse one of the worst hangovers of all time, I told him what happened. To which he said—"

"You deserve to be with someone who looks at you every day as if they won the lottery." He meets her gaze, a tender moment passing between them before Izzy quickly averts her eyes, clearing her throat.

"So that's how I was carried out of a bar. Who's next?" Her voice brightens, an obvious attempt to get the focus off her and Asher. "It's your turn, isn't it, Chloe?"

I stare at her, dozens of questions on the tip of my tongue. I want to know why she never told me about this, why she never mentioned Asher at all. Did they hook up that weekend, but she hid it because of how Jessie would react? Despite the heartache and pain he'd caused her, she'd still care about him. She probably still does. That's the type of person she is.

Izzy narrows her gaze on me, wordlessly telling me not to press the topic. So I don't. Not now. I don't want to ruin the fun we've been having. And I do admit I've had a lot of fun. I suddenly have a new appreciation for game night.

"Okay then." I adjust my posture. "Never have I ever given or received a lap dance."

"Try again," Izzy sings. "Already asked."

"Crap. That's right."

I pull my lips between my teeth, trying to come up with something that hasn't already been said *and* at least one person has done. This has proven to be the difficult part of the game, considering Izzy's the only person I know well and I'm running out of risqué things I'm confident she's done. Factor in the rule that you must say something before time is up, added after Asher took several minutes during one of his turns, and it's a bit more stressful, yet exciting.

"Ten seconds, Chloe," Lincoln taunts, waving his phone in front of me, displaying the countdown.

"Okay, okay." I bounce on the seat, adrenaline filling me as I wrack my brain. Then I look back at Lincoln, the timer only showing two seconds, and say the first thing I think of. "Never have I ever gotten freaky in an elevator."

My voice rings out as I bring my own beer bottle to my lips, taking a small sip. I expect someone to drink with me, indicating they've done it, but no one does.

"Remember, we're in a bubble. Circle of trust. Blackout Club and all that. It's okay if you have." I shift my eyes around, everyone shaking their heads.

"Looks like you earned a penalty round." Izzy pushes the bottle and dice my way, her lips kicking up into a sly grin.

So far, everyone else has done this at least once. The first time, Izzy had to touch Lincoln's finger. We all laughed when they did a little E.T. finger touch with each other, Izzy fanning herself afterward, pretending to be all hot and bothered from the contact.

A few minutes later, Lincoln had to roll after he couldn't come up with something in enough time. Lucky him. He had to blow on Asher's chest. Things started to heat up a little when Asher had to bite Izzy's ear. The instant his teeth clamped onto her lobe, her face flushed and lips parted as her eyes fluttered closed. She can insist they're just friends all she wants. There's more going on.

Doing my best to push down the nervous flutter in my stomach, I reach for the dice and toss them onto the coffee table. They teeter on their edges before falling over, landing on SUCK and TONGUE.

A chorus of "whoa" and a few whistles fill the night sky as I swallow hard.

"Looks like things are about to get *very* interesting," Izzy comments.

"I suppose they are." I grab the bottle and give it a spin. Now I know how contestants on *The Price is Right* must feel when they spin the wheel, trying to get as close to a dollar as they can without going over. The anticipation and tightening in their body as it nears that magical number, then the despair when it lands on a nickel. I wonder if Lincoln is *my* dollar, or if he's simply a nickel and I should spin again.

The seconds seem to stretch as the bottle takes a few more turns around the circle, each journey getting slower and slower until it gradually bypasses Asher, then stops close to Lincoln, which causes Izzy to whistle.

With all the confidence I've found sexy since the beginning, he leans back, draping an arm along the back of the couch.

"You can use your pass if you want," he says flirtatiously, raking his gaze over my body before zeroing in on my lips. "I'll understand."

"Rules are rules," I reply in a throaty voice, batting my lashes. "Plus, I'd rather save my pass for when I have to suck on Izzy's chest."

Both men groan. I can't help but laugh. What is it about two girls together that always seems to force men to revert to hormone-crazed teenagers?

"Please don't," Asher begs. "Use your pass if you have to touch her ear, but not that. *Anything* but that."

"We'll cross that bridge *if* we get to it. But for now…" Smiling a coy smile, I turn to Lincoln, crawling across the couch and into his lap, my legs straddling him. He stiffens beneath me, jaw clenching, eyes darkening as they remain focused on me. Inching my mouth toward his, I murmur, "I believe the dice have spoken."

"I believe they have."

"And that red flag that was being waved earlier?"

"It's green, baby." He brings his hand to my head, digging his fingers into my scalp. "Conditions are *very* favorable."

"I can feel that."

Slowly, I erase the last bit of distance between us, pressing my mouth to his. The kiss is soft and reverent at first, neither one of us pushing forward. I can't, not yet, breathless from the sensation of this first touching of our lips, my body buzzing to life. If this is how I react from an innocent kiss, I shudder to think what will happen when he deepens it.

As if able to read my thoughts, a groan rips from Lincoln's throat, his hold on me tightening as he yanks me harder into him. I gasp at the feel of him, how excited he is. He takes advantage of my open mouth and swipes his tongue against mine. Instant fireworks erupt in my stomach, the raw need making me kiss him with more urgency, more desperation, more unsatisfied hunger.

I grasp at him, subtly circling my hips to relieve some of the pressure building inside me. But I fear nothing will extinguish the match he lit at our first meeting, the spark he's flamed with each subsequent encounter, so much so that the fire won't be put out easily. Not anymore.

He brings his hands to my face, our fevered kiss turning into something sweeter, more ardent, more personal, offering me a different side of him. An unexpected side. He exhales, breathing into me. It's such a strange thing, feeling another person's air expand in your lungs, giving you life. I don't even know this man, but that's what he's doing — making me feel alive.

He sensually caresses my tongue with his, heat curling down my spine as I try to remember the last time a kiss made me feel *this*. I don't even know what *this* is. And for once, I don't care. I'm just enjoying the moment before our bubble bursts.

Our motions slowing, I gradually pull back, still resting my lips on his. I don't want to stop feeling them, tasting them, savoring them. Not yet. His kisses are the sweetest drug and I an addict, wanting to squeeze every last drop I can.

"Say you want more," he whispers, his grip on my head keeping me from escaping his demand. I wouldn't try to escape him even if I could.

"I want more."

A smile slowly curves his mouth. "I want more, too. I want so much more."

CHAPTER NINE

"MMM…," I MOAN, squirming in my seat. My breathing is labored as I run my hand down my chest and along my stomach. "That's it. I've always wanted someone to blow on my finger."

I stop moving, opening my eyes to Lincoln's and Asher's disappointed pouts, Izzy's giggles echoing around us.

As the night wore on, it's become increasingly difficult to come up with something original before time's up, which has resulted in more throwing of the dice and spinning of the bottle. When Izzy spun and it landed on me, Asher's and Lincoln's eyes lit up like a kid running downstairs on Christmas morning. But when they looked to the dice and saw all she had to do was blow on my finger, both wore a similar expression, this time of a little kid who was told they're about to go to Disneyland and end up at the dentist instead.

"What? Were you hoping for something hotter?" I smirk as Izzy returns to the couch, Asher draping his arm along her shoulders.

As things got more personal and heated, the sexual tension within our little bubble has become palpable. Where Izzy and Asher once kept some space between them, they're now practically on top of each other. And Lincoln and I… Well, I'm desperate for another lap around the track. I get the feeling he is, too, considering last time I excused myself to use the bathroom, he waited for me in the hallway, where he proceeded to slam me against the wall, stealing another kiss. But when I attempted to drag him up to my room, he resisted, said we weren't there yet. If nothing else, the man has incredible restraint. I imagine when we finally *do* make it to the bedroom, that restraint will make things even more mind-blowing.

"Honestly, yes," Asher responds, tearing me out of my hormone-filled thoughts. "We've been waiting for one of you to spin the other and it hasn't happened. When it finally does, all you have to do is blow on her finger? I feel short-changed."

"Rules are rules," Izzy sings. "We can't just make out because you want us to, hornball." She playfully jabs him in the stomach. "If you want to see girls make out, go watch a porno."

He waggles his brows, giving her a mischievous smirk. "Want to join me?"

"Maybe later," she murmurs seductively, inching even closer to his mouth. The raw need I see coming off Asher has me wanting them to kiss, too. I can only imagine the sparks that will fly when they finally do. "Too bad there's no power. It's your turn."

She abruptly pulls back, leaving Asher momentarily bewildered, and grabs Lincoln's cell from the table. Opening the timer, she hits START. "Go."

Asher takes a beat to compose himself, then says, "Never have I ever taken a sexy selfie."

"Nope!" Izzy responds, then imitates an annoying buzzer. "Already asked. Try again."

Asher leans his head against the back of the couch. "Never have I ever slept with someone whose name I couldn't remember the next morning."

"Try again!" Izzy shouts once more. For being as buzzed as she is, she has an incredible ability to recall everything that's been said. Then again, she's always been ridiculously smart.

"Shit," Asher mutters as he licks his lips, squeezing his eyes shut.

"Tick-tock," Izzy teases.

"Never have I ever…" He runs his hand through his hair as he struggles to come up with something.

"Five seconds," Lincoln taunts.

"Never have I ever…," Asher says again, but still nothing.

"Four. Three."

"Never have I ever…," he repeats once more.

We all join in with Lincoln's countdown, shouting, "Two. One!"

Izzy grabs the bottle and thrusts it into his hand. "Spin it, baby!"

He groans in playful irritation as he places the bottle back onto the table. Taking the dice, he rolls as we all lean closer to see under the dim lighting of a few flickering candles and the firepit. When they land on KISS and LIPS, Izzy and I erupt into cheers and whistles.

"I'm so looking forward to watching you two make out," I joke, jabbing Lincoln playfully in his side.

He wraps his arm around my shoulders. The heat of his breath against my neck makes my heart skip a beat. "I'd much rather make out with you again," he murmurs in a barely audible growl that has me involuntarily squeezing my thighs together. "I'd much rather do a lot *more* than make out."

"Like what?"

He leans closer. "Be a good girl and you'll find out."

I float my eyes to his, closing the gap between us, our breath intermingling. "Maybe I like being bad."

"Is that so?"

I slowly nod, my lips hovering near his. "Oh, baby. You have no idea how bad I can really be."

He shifts in his seat, a low groan escaping his throat, just as Izzy says, "Time to spin, Asher."

Reminded we're not alone, we tear away from each other, returning our attention to the game. At first, it thrilled me, the promise of what could happen. Now all I want is to go to my room and have a different kind of game night with Lincoln.

Asher grabs the bottle and gives it a spin. Every time it closes in on Lincoln, Izzy's eyes brim with hope.

As it slows and inches toward me, Lincoln's hold on me tightens. His reaction to the mere thought of me having to kiss Asher is endearing. Then again, I doubt it will be a problem. He'd use his pass, just like Izzy used hers when she was supposed to suck on Lincoln's earlobe. I wouldn't have minded. But we don't exactly have the same history Izzy and Asher apparently have.

Finally, the bottle rolls past me and lands on Izzy. She gives him a flirtatious smile. They've had to do a few risqué things over the course of the evening, like sucking on an ear or biting a neck, but nothing more than that.

"Well then…," he begins smoothly, a smirk tugging on the corners of his lips as he looks her up and down. "I suppose it's time we finally kiss."

His statement momentarily surprises me. I'm not sure what I thought. I guess I assumed they already had.

"Unless—"

Before he can say another word, she clutches his cheeks. "I suppose it is." She lowers her back onto the couch, bringing him on top of her.

"I suppose it is," he repeats, brushing his mouth against hers, nipping on her lower lip.

"The dice says kiss my lips, not *bite* them."

"I know, but I've imagined this for years now. I need to take advantage of it while I can, while we're still in the bubble."

Izzy tenses below him. "*Years*?"

Asher nods, rubbing his nose against hers. "Yes, Iz. Years."

All the tension seems to roll off her as she hooks a leg around his waist, yanking him even tighter against her.

"What are you waiting for?"

Their kiss starts out simple and innocent, just a light meeting of mouths. But it doesn't take long for it to become more intense, more heated, more…greedy.

A finger trails down my neck as I watch them, feeling like a voyeur, but I can't look away. When Lincoln brushes my hair behind my shoulder, exposing my skin, I crane my head, silently giving him permission to keep touching me. His soft lips feathering against me causes a shiver to roll through me.

"I don't recall you rolling the dice," I whisper.

I feel his mouth curve into a smile. "It'll be our little secret." He brings his hand to my leg, brushing up and down my thigh.

"Our little secret," I repeat.

Glancing across the table to see Asher and Izzy still going at it, oblivious to the world around them, I part my legs, an open invitation for Lincoln to continue.

His teeth clamp onto my neck and I struggle not to yelp. His hand inches higher and higher, my chest rising and falling in a quicker rhythm. When his fingers ghost against my center, sparks shoot through me. I really wish I hadn't changed into jeans. If I still had on my bathing suit, this would be even more erotic, if that's possible.

"I want you," he says gruffly.

I swallow hard, biting back my moan.

"Do you want me?"

"Yes...," I whimper.

He steals a glimpse to make sure Izzy and Asher are still occupied, which they are. "Here's what I want you to do. When the two lovebirds break away, you're going to excuse yourself. Say you're tired. I'm sure they'll want to have some privacy themselves. Once they head up, I'll come to you. Okay?"

I stare straight ahead as Izzy and Asher's passionate exchange wanes, their kiss slowly coming to an end.

Lincoln squeezes my thigh."Okay?" he asks again, more forceful.

"Okay," I answer in a breathy voice.

"Okay," he repeats, removing his hand from me, increasing the distance between us.

A giggle bursts through, and I glance up to see Asher helping a rather flushed Izzy back into a sitting position.

"Well, that was unexpected."

"Hopefully in a good way." He wraps his arm around her, pulling her close.

"In an amazing way." She beams, fanning herself. "Now, I believe it's Lincoln's turn. Or is it Chloe's?"

"Actually..." I stand up. "I hate to be the one to put an end to game night, but I'm beat. It's been a long day. And tomorrow will be another long one with heading home, provided the power comes back on."

Izzy pouts playfully. "Always the responsible one, aren't you?"

"Always."

Her expression brightens. "It's okay. I'll probably be going to bed soon myself."

"Alone?" I lift a brow.

She bites her lower lip, flicking a mischievous grin to Asher as she squeezes his thigh. "Only time will tell."

After saying my goodbyes to Asher, thanking him once more for allowing us to crash here, I start to head inside.

"Let me walk you," Lincoln offers, surprising me. This certainly was not part of the plan.

"I'll be fine," I insist.

"I'm sure you will, but I'd feel better if I walked with you." The tone of his voice makes it clear that this isn't up for debate. I actually like the idea of him walking me to my room. I've never been with someone who so much as walked me to my Uber or the subway station after a date. Hell, a lot of them couldn't even be asked to get out of bed to walk me to the door of their apartment.

"Okay," I say.

"Okay." He places his hand on the small of my back, shining the flashlight of his cell in front of us, illuminating our path.

Once we reach my room, I turn to him, about to thank him, when he advances toward me, pressing me against the wall, his mouth covering mine. Momentarily caught breathless by his sudden invasion, I still. But the shock eventually wanes and I melt into him, grasping his face, needing more of him.

Lincoln tears his lips from mine, growling like an animal starved for too long. "You're incredible, Chloe."

Throwing my head back, I revel in his unshaven jaw scratching against the flesh of my neck. I scrape my nails down his back, wrapping a leg around him, pulsing against him as he nips at my shoulder. Our heavy and labored breaths fill the silence, every synapse in my body firing.

His hand roams my frame, his touch needy and reckless. As he reaches my waistband, I inhale a sharp breath, my core clenching when he unbuttons my jeans.

He kisses a hot trail along my collarbone, inching his way back up my neck. His fingers swipe a line along my stomach, teasing me. Finally, he lowers the zipper and brushes the top of my panties. My muscles tighten in anticipation. He bites my earlobe, tugging at it. A bolt of need shoots through me as I struggle to maintain my composure.

"Keep going," I murmur, a slave to his touch. "Don't stop."

Growling, his teeth bite down harder as he sweeps a finger under the line of my panties.

"Do you feel what you do to me?" He subtly thrusts against me.

"Yes," I moan, my eyes rolling into the back of my head. "Yes."

He inches his hand farther south, my muscles tightening as he nears the spot I need him to touch. When he finds my center, I sigh. "And I can certainly feel what I do to you."

I bring his lips back to mine, my tongue plunging in his mouth, fireworks erupting in my core. Finally, he pushes a finger inside and I relax, bliss filling me.

"You're so wet. So tight. So fucking sweet."

"Just wait till you get a taste. You'll never want another pussy again."

"Is that right?" He arches a brow, his expression playful as he continues stretching me.

"That's right," I exhale as I move with his motions. "God, that's so right." I grab his head again, bringing his mouth to within a whisper of mine, my breathing becoming more erratic with each push, each thrust, each drive. My teeth chatter, my entire body trembling, close to unraveling.

Instantly, he pulls his hand away, releasing his hold on me. I fling my eyes open, staring at him incredulously, a panting bundle of hormones.

"What are you—"

"Suck," he demands, interrupting me, touching a finger to my lips.

My eyes remaining glued to his, I slowly open my mouth, swiping my tongue against the tip of his finger. The contact is subtle, barely there. But the way his pupils dilate tells me he's on edge, that he needs more, that he's been fantasizing about this as much as I have.

With a a moan, I wrap my lips around his finger, sucking every last drop of me off his flesh, giving each of his fingers the same treatment.

"Tell me how you taste."

Flirtatiously batting my lashes, I pass him a demure look. "Why don't you find out for yourself?" I force his lips against mine. The second our tongues touch, he groans. He tastes of need, of want, of unmatched desperation.

Too soon, he tears away, chest heaving, eyes dark. "Go. Get in your room. I'll be with you shortly."

Before I can do or say anything else, he spins around, heading toward the stairs with determined strides, leaving me a quivering mess.

"Oh, and Chloe?"

I meet his heated stare. "Yes?"

"You'd better not even think about getting yourself off while you wait for me. Tonight, I own you." His voice becomes deeper, more demanding. The hairs on my nape rise. "And that includes all your orgasms. Do you understand?"

I swallow hard. No man has ever spoken to me this way, so brazen, so confident, so…hot. There's only one way to answer him.

"Yes, Lincoln," I respond in a sultry voice as I walk the few feet toward where he stands at the top of the staircase. "I completely understand." When I reach him, I stand on my tiptoes, skimming my lips along his neck. "Hurry back."

I remain motionless for several protracted moments, my breath warming his skin. His chest rises and falls quicker, and I notice him clench and unclench his fists. I can't help but grin at how much he wants me. Then I lower my heels to the floor and turn, walking into my darkened room and closing the door behind me without a single look back.

Game night really is a lot of fun.

Chapter Ten

I'VE OFFICIALLY WORN a path in the lush carpet.

I thought Lincoln would only be a few minutes, especially once I heard Izzy come upstairs. I took a lukewarm shower, needing the tepid water to dull the flames building inside me. I figured he wouldn't be much longer once I got out, considering how needy he seemed.

But as I pace in front of the window overlooking the patio, I can still make out the gentle sound of Asher and Lincoln each strumming a guitar. As if Lincoln weren't delicious enough, he has to play the guitar, too. My ovaries all but exploded when I peered down into the yard and saw how effortless he made it look. Yet another piece of the Lincoln Moore puzzle.

Finally, the music stops, as does my pacing, my libido perking up. Any other time, I'd be upset over that, but not tonight. Not when that means Lincoln's that much closer to knocking on my door. If he's even planning on doing that. I wouldn't be surprised if he simply barges in.

I walk up to the window, doing my best to remain out of view so neither one of them realize I've been snooping. I strain to listen for the telltale sound of the French doors closing. When they do, I light up, turning to look around the room.

Should I lay on the bed in a provocative pose, beckoning Lincoln to come in if he knocks? Should I put on something sexier than my t-shirt and yoga pants? Should I be wearing anything at all?

As turned on as I am about the prospect of answering the door naked, I don't want to miss out on Lincoln undressing me. We only have one night together. I need to experience everything he has to offer.

When I hear footsteps growing closer, my heart ricochets into my throat and my eyes zero in on the door. Then the knock I've been waiting for echoes.

I rush over, pausing to inhale a calming breath. But the instant I open the door and see Lincoln holding a bottle of wine and two glasses, I can't stop my stomach from doing backflips.

"May I come in?" he asks politely, yet seductive at the same time.

"Of course." I step back and allow him to enter. Using the flashlight on his phone to light the way, he walks toward the desk by the window, placing the bottle and glasses on it. He yanks out the cork and pours a deep red liquid into each glass, handing me one.

"To blackouts," he offers as he raises his wine.

"To blackouts." I clink my glass against his, then take a sip.

"I hope you like it. I wasn't sure what kind of wine you prefer, but remember you drinking a red when I saw you Sunday night."

I allow the robust flavor to dance on my tongue, a nice change after the beer. "This is more than acceptable," I say with a smile, unable to mask the tremble in my voice. "Shiraz?" I arch a brow.

He smiles over his glass, lowering it, licking the wine off his lips. "How could you tell from just the taste? Apart from a professional sommelier, I don't know many people who could do that."

I shrug nonchalantly. "I know my wine."

"Really?"

I hold his gaze, trying to act serious. Then I laugh as I nod at the bottle, the light from the moon casting a glow over the label. While most people would have to get a better look, I'd recognize the familiar script of that logo anywhere.

"Penfolds," I say. "If there's one thing Australian winemakers are known for, it's a fantastic shiraz."

"They certainly are." He brings his glass back to his lips, but his gaze never leaves mine. I've never felt so exposed, as if Lincoln's doing more than mentally undressing me. Maybe that's what makes him so different. He *looks* into my eyes, instead of everywhere but, as I'm accustomed to.

I take another sip of my wine as I attempt to calm my racing heart. This isn't the first time I've slept with a guy I just met. But I've never been this jittery, this desperate.

When I lower my glass, he reaches for it, not saying a single word. I allow him to take it and he places them on the desk, then faces me. My chest expands with my increasingly irregular breathing, my body aching to feel him. Finally, he palms my lower back and tugs me against him. He leans down and I crane my head, inching my lips toward his. But instead of feeling his mouth cover mine, he changes course at the last second, bringing his lips to my neck, clamping down his teeth.

I yelp, struggling to make sense of the sensations filling me, the pleasure, the pain, everything in between. I now know where that saying "it hurts so good" comes from, because Lincoln… He definitely hurts so good. I don't even care that the harshness of his bite will most likely leave a rather prominent mark. I want him to mark me. I want to walk around, have people stare and know what I did, what I let this stranger do to me. The idea makes me burn even hotter.

When his lips finally make their journey to mine, his kiss is jarring, intense, lust-filled. He tastes of mint, spice, wine, and a flavor I surmise is uniquely Lincoln. One I fear I'll crave for weeks to come.

He clutches my face, keeping me in place, his grip powerful, demanding, confident. Everything I believe this man is. Then his eyes lift to mine, the fire in his gaze replaced with a hint of amusement.

"What?" I ask, pinching my lips together.

His smile only grows as he reaches into the pocket of his shorts and pulls out something. He opens his palm, revealing Izzy's dice. "She let me have them. Said she already has some of these back home."

"Is that right?" I pass him a flirtatious grin.

He nods. "That's right."

"Well then…" I lift myself onto my toes and brush my lips against his. "Let the games begin."

I abruptly spin from him, sauntering toward the bed. When I feel the heat of his stare on me, I glance over my shoulder, a shiver rolling through me from the lust in his eyes.

"Coming?"

"I hope to." With determined strides, he walks toward me, only needing four steps to close the distance.

I lower myself to the mattress, scooting up toward the headboard, the only light coming from the moon. Lincoln's hooded eyes lock on mine as he crawls onto the bed, advancing toward me like a lion stalking its prey.

Apart from our breathing, not a single sound can be heard in the room, the lack of any power leaving everything silent. You don't realize how many noises a house makes — air conditioning, refrigerator, whirring hum of computers — until you no longer have electricity. Every little thing seems more noticeable, more intense, more amplified. Like the way Lincoln stares at me in a way I can't recall a single person ever admiring me. Like the way our chests seem to rise and fall in perfect rhythm with each other. Like the way his tongue swipes along his lips, causing them to glisten, leaving me desperate for another taste.

Clutching his cheeks in my hands, I pull him closer and press my mouth to his, exhaling into the kiss. It's gentle, yet bubbling with a passion that's been missing from my life for too long now. He threads his fingers through my hair as I wrap my legs around his waist, needing to feel all of him. When I circle my hips against him, he groans, his tongue brushing mine with more need, more ferocity, more desperation.

"I don't remember you rolling the dice," he murmurs, throwing my own words from earlier back at me.

"Those dice don't have what I want to do on them."

"Is that so?" He lifts a single brow. "And what's that?"

I run my fingers up and down his back, my nails digging into his skin. He arches into my touch, biting his lower lip as he closes his eyes, a look of bliss washing over him. The rippling of his muscles against my hands makes me want to explore every single inch of his warm, firm body.

Curving toward him, I nibble on his earlobe. "I want to taste you."

He stares down at me, his expression playful. "You can taste me if you roll LICK and FINGER." He winks.

I slowly shake my head, my gaze unwavering. "That's not what I want to taste."

He takes my bottom lip between his teeth. I grow lightheaded, wanting him to keep doing that, but harder, and to other parts of my body.

"Tell me what you want to taste, Chloe," he demands.

"You."

He loosens his bite, shifting position. "Oh, come now. I didn't take you for being shy, Pixie."

"Pixie?" I lift my brows in question.

"Exactly. You're so tiny, like a fairy, or an angel." The mood changes as he touches his lips to mine, treating me to a delicious kiss, so different from the way he just had his teeth clamped on me. "*My* angel."

"I'm not shy," I insist, pressing my hand to his chest, forcing him onto his back. Straddling him, I circle him, my motions greedy, insatiable, wanton. "And I am certainly no angel. Especially not in the bedroom."

He cups my face in his strong hands. I can't help but marvel at how big they are. Everything about us seems to be polar opposite.

He's larger than life with an intimidating physique. I'm tiny with a stature that makes me often feel overlooked.

He's a professional, intelligent man who seems to have his life together. I'm a bit of a drifter who's still trying to figure out who she is.

He looks like the quintessential all-American boy who probably played football in high school and could have his pick of any woman. I was the troublemaker, the promiscuous girl with piercings in her eyebrows, nose, and tongue.

He probably has a family who loves him, who's always supported his decisions. I often feel like my mother blames me for the divorce, a heavy burden to bear as a teenager. And it's only grown heavier now that I'm an adult.

"Is that right?"

I nod. "That's right."

"Prove it. Tell me what you want, what you want to taste."

I open my mouth to respond when he cuts me off.

"And don't just say 'you'. I want to know *exactly* what you want to do."

I briefly press my mouth to his, then meet his gaze. "I want to suck your dick."

He stares at me for several seconds, his jaw hardened, eyes on fire. Then he slams his mouth against mine, his tongue pushing through my lips, his kiss ravenous and greedy.

When he pulls away, he grabs my hips, lifting me off him and onto the mattress beside him. Standing, he extends his hand toward me, and I allow him to help me off the bed.

"Lift your arms."

Not saying a single word, I simply follow his demand. I'd normally protest, insist on remaining in control. But we're in the bubble. Maybe the bubble's my own personal Wonderland, a place where I can lose all control and live out the fantasies I've been too scared of in the real world.

He grabs the hem of my t-shirt and pulls it over my head before tossing it to the floor. His Adam's apple bobs up and down as his eyes zero in on my bra. "Turn around."

Excited nerves simmer in my veins as I obey, facing away from him. When his lips feather that place where my neck meets my shoulders, I moan.

"That's the spot, isn't it?" he murmurs, his fingers traveling toward my bra, unhooking it with practiced expertise. His hands go to my shoulders and he pushes the material down my arms. "Does that turn you on?" He returns his mouth to me.

"Yes." I subconsciously squeeze my legs together as his hands find their way to my stomach, the pressure building to a level I didn't think possible.

He takes his time caressing my flesh. Whenever he nears the swell of my breasts, I hold my breath, only for him to change direction and return to my stomach. I squeeze my thighs together tighter, biting down on my lower lip. I'm on the brink of telling him to bend me over the desk and fuck me already, seduction be damned. But he won't do that. He's the tortoise, not the hare. This is a marathon, not a sprint. And I have a feeling he wants this race to last all night long.

"Spread your legs," he orders when I continue to squirm. I don't immediately comply, needing something to dull the ache. He tugs my body against his, pushing a knee between my thighs, parting them. "I need you as desperate for me as I am for you." He brings his hands to my breasts, tugging at my nipples. "Because I've spent the past weekend desperate for a taste of you, Chloe."

He removes his hands from my chest, his motion quick as he spins me around. Stepping back, he crosses his arms and stares at me with a menacing gaze. "Take off your pants, but leave on your panties."

I peer at him through my lashes. "Any reason for that?"

"A magician never reveals his secrets." He winks, a hint of playfulness amidst the sexual tension.

More curious than anything, I lower my yoga pants down my legs and step out of them, waiting for Lincoln's next directive. But it doesn't immediately come. He simply stares at me in wonder, his expression softening. There's something incredibly tender about this moment as we admire each other, the moon casting a serene glow in the room, illuminating pieces of us.

"You are so beautiful." He reaches for my face, brushing a tendril of hair behind my ear. The gentleness of his statement and touch has my knees growing weak. I search my memory for someone else who looked at me the way Lincoln does, for someone else who called me beautiful. Nothing comes to mind. Sure, I've been called hot, cute, even charming, but never beautiful.

Needing to break the intensity of the moment before I allow his compassion to burst through my walls, I dig my fingers into his chest, leaning into him. "Now it's your turn."

"Yes, ma'am." He unbuttons his shirt and shrugs out of it before pushing his shorts down his strong legs.

"And Lincoln?" I arch a brow.

"Yes?"

"No need to keep on your boxers. Not for what I have planned."

"Yes, ma'am." With haste, he rids himself of his boxer briefs, and they join the rest of our discarded clothes.

Approaching him, my eyes don't waver, the atmosphere shifting from playful to sensual. His taut skin is warm as I run my fingers along his chest, savoring the little tufts of hair that dot it. Soft lips skate against mine, but I pull back, depriving him of a full kiss.

"Do you want me?" I murmur, feeling unusually powerful as I scrape my hand down his torso, wrapping my fingers around his erection.

"Fuck," he hisses, his eyes squeezing shut. I study his expression, ecstasy and need filling the lines of his face, his muscles tensing.

I raise myself onto my toes. "Say you want me." I feather my lips against his neck, my touch barely there.

"You know the answer to that."

"Oh, I know," I respond coyly. "I can feel the answer to that. But I want to hear you say it." Bringing my mouth back to his ear, I nibble on it. "Two can play your little game, ya know."

When I pull away, he opens his eyes, his stare intense and bold.

"Is that what you think this is? Just a game?"

Unwrapping my hand from his arousal, I bring both of them to his chest. "Isn't that all life is? Just a game?" I drag my tongue along his lips, retreating when he parts them for a taste. "Tell me you want me."

He jerks my body against his, grinding his hips. "I want you, Chloe. So fucking much."

The look of pure torture on his face is almost more than I can stand. Almost. But he deserves a taste of what I had to endure.

"How do you want me? What do you want me to do?"

"What do *you* want to do?"

"I already told you what I want to do. But I don't want to presume you're agreeable."

"Presume away, baby."

The intensity monetarily cracks, and I laugh. I love how he's seductive, sensual, and carnal one minute, then lightens the mood the next. I never thought it would be possible to have both. Then again, I've never met anyone like Lincoln.

Recovering, I pass him a heated stare. "Tell…me…what…you…want."

"Your mouth."

I'm about to ask him where, when he interrupts.

"On my cock. Now."

His hands land on my shoulders, putting pressure on them. Happy to oblige, I rake my fingers along his chest, allowing him to push me to my knees. When I dig my nails into his skin, he releases a growl, his nostrils flaring. Not out of anger. Out of unbridled need.

Keeping my eyes locked on his, I kneel before him, taking his erection in my hand once more. He holds his breath, every muscle in his body becoming even more rigid. And I do mean *every* muscle.

I run my tongue over my lips, my heart hammering in my chest as I pause. I may be on my knees, but I've never felt so powerful. When I slide my tongue along his length before taking him into my mouth, tension rolls off him.

"Damn, Pixie…" He digs his fingers into my scalp as he begins pumping into me, his rhythm slow at first. "You have some mouth on you, don't you? I knew that about you the instant you went off on me at the bar, but this…" His grip on my hair tightens as he wraps his hand around it, pulling it. So hungry. So desperate. So determined. "This is something I only fantasized about."

His hold becomes more forceful, guiding my head. I swirl my tongue around his tip, savoring the taste of pre-cum before relaxing my throat, taking him even deeper.

"Fuck," he groans, on the brink of unravelling. He drives harder into me, then releases my hair, suddenly stepping back.

"Wha—" I begin, but I'm soon interrupted.

"Get on the bed."

I arch a single brow, confused why he pushed away when he was seconds from his release.

"Now, Chloe," he demands.

I scramble to my feet and hurry toward the bed, scooting up to the headboard. I stare at him, expecting him to join me, but he doesn't. Not right away. He simply admires me. I grab the duvet to cover myself, but he shakes his head.

"Don't. Let me look at you."

I swallow hard, feeling exposed, but I follow his command, keeping my arms to my sides, allowing him to examine every inch of me. His admiration gives me an added boost of confidence and I prop my legs up, spreading them, an invitation to see even more of me.

His green eyes darkening, he stalks toward the bed, his steps deliberate, drawn-out, measured. When he lowers himself onto the mattress, he rests his elbows by my head and finds my lips, his kiss sweet and addicting, at complete odds with the way he just fucked my mouth. I fear this strange dichotomy will be my undoing. As much as I love being spontaneous, I prefer being able to read people, determine their next move. With Lincoln, I never know what he has planned, what his intentions are.

He moves along my jawline, down my collarbone, hovering over my alert nipple. I squirm, bracing for his touch. *Desperate* for his touch.

"Something you need, Pixie?" His voice is deep and soft.

"Yes."

"And what's that?"

I lock eyes with him. "For you to taste me."

"With pleasure." When he covers my breast with his mouth, I throw my head back, my body fusing to the mattress. "With immense pleasure."

His teeth tug on my nipple, his tongue circling it, driving me wild. I'm not sure how much more of this teasing, this buildup, this foreplay I can take before I explode. I'm on edge as it is. I've *been* on edge all day. Hell, all weekend. Now isn't the time for teasing. I'm already at my breaking point.

As if able to read my thoughts, he traces soft, tantalizing lines along the curve of my breasts, down my stomach, circling my belly button before settling between my thighs. He hooks his fingers into my panties, and I lift my hips to allow him to lower them down my legs. Instead, he grabs my ass, propping me up. I furrow my brow, unsure what he's doing. But before I can utter a single syllable, his mouth covers my panties, the warmth of him against me driving me crazy. My underwear could be a pane of bulletproof glass instead of just a flimsy piece of fabric, for all I care. It's still a very unwelcome barrier.

"Please," I moan as he continues licking and sucking on me through my panties.

"Something I can help you with?"

"Yes." I narrow my eyes. "I need your mouth on me."

"It is on you."

"No. On my skin. No panties."

He studies me for a moment, then shakes his head. "I told you before that all your orgasms belong to me tonight, did I not?"

"You did," I exhale, desperate for release, to have him consume every inch of me.

"That means I get to decide exactly *how* you come. And I want you to come like this." He brings his mouth back to me, sucking and nibbling, and I melt into it, moving with the rhythm he sets. I have to admit, there's something incredibly erotic about this.

It doesn't take long for that familiar sensation to bubble in my core. My muscles tense as I pulse against him with more urgency. He moans, the vibration pushing me higher and higher. Then he scrapes his teeth on my clit, sucking, and I scream, waves of ecstasy washing over me as I come undone, riding out one of the most intense orgasms for what feels like hours, but is probably only a minute or two.

When I finally start to return to earth, he meets my eyes and smirks, hooking his fingers into my panties and sliding them down my legs. Then he returns to me, burying his mouth between my thighs. I exhale in utter bliss, savoring in how expertly he tastes me, his tongue drawing out my orgasm even longer.

"Fuck, you're wet."

"It's what you do to me." I lower my hand, toying with my clit, spreading my juices around. Bringing my finger to my mouth, I suck on it, recalling how much it turned him on before. And that's all it takes to turn him on again. He grabs my hips, his movements quick as he flips me onto my stomach. His arm snakes under my waist and he props me onto my knees.

He leans over me, his chest hair tickling my back. "Is this okay? Having you from behind?"

"Y-yes," I stammer.

While I prefer being on top so I can be the one in control, I'll take Lincoln however he wants. This position is probably better anyway. I won't have to look him in the eyes. I'll be able to stay detached. I'll be able to walk away and carry on with my life when the blackout is over.

"Good." He straightens himself and steps off the mattress. I watch as he grabs his shorts, pulling a condom from his wallet.

Not saying a word, he returns to the bed and grasps my head, forcing my eyes forward once more. I don't argue. Don't protest. Don't return my gaze to his. I stare at the headboard, every noise putting me more on edge.

Finally, the bed dips and I feel his erection against me, teasing me. I close my eyes, rocking back into him.

"You're greedy, aren't you?"

"Yes." I bury my head into the pillow.

"Tell me what you want." He inches himself inside. I sigh, bracing for him to push the rest of the way. But he doesn't. Instead, he pulls out, waiting for my response.

"I want you to fuck me," I pant, aching for him.

My desperate plea ringing in the air, he slams into me. Both of us still as he fills me to the hilt, savoring this sensation of fullness that's so new, so unexpected, yet so satisfying. He exhales, as if also surprised at how incredible it feels.

Then he covers my body with his, his hands gliding up my arms, his fingers linking with mine. When he moves, gently at first, I sigh, matching his rhythm. He kisses my shoulder blade, skating his teeth against my skin.

"And for the record, I'm not fucking you, Chloe."

"Then what do you call this?"

"Possession, plain and simple."

I moan at his gravelly voice, losing myself in this erotic moment.

"Possessing your mind, your soul..." He clamps his teeth onto my neck, pain pulsing through me momentarily before being replaced by the unmatched pleasure building from his measured movements. "Your body."

"Oh god..." I ball my hands into tighter fists, my grip on his fingers intertwined with mine growing stronger. I bury my head into the pillow, biting down on it.

I can honestly say I've never been with a man like Lincoln, a man so practiced in the art of seduction. Sex is supposed to be an act that tantalizes your senses, hypnotizes your mind, captures your heart, breathes life into your soul. But not for me. I've made sure of that. Until now.

He moves with greater urgency, his own breathing erratic and uneven. With each thrust, he drives deeper and deeper, forcing my body to climb higher and higher until I scream, falling apart, my mind becoming hazy, unable to form a coherent thought.

"That feels incredible," Lincoln exhales, his voice strained as he pumps faster, drawing my orgasm out. When I'm not sure whether I can take any more, he grunts, thrusting deep into me, holding my hips in place as he jerks through his own release.

We remain motionless for several long moments, both of us struggling to get our breathing under control. As his body covers mine, I feel his heart beating violently in his chest. Satisfaction fills me at the idea that I did this to him, that I worked him up to this point of exertion.

"Goddamn," he says, slowly withdrawing and peeling off me.

His touch is gentle as he supports my stomach, helping to lower me onto the mattress. My legs have never shaken or quivered as much as they are right now. I've never been this sated after sex. A woman could get used to this.

Once he's certain I'm okay, he pushes off the bed, grabbing the duvet and covering my body with it. He rids himself of the condom, tossing it into the nearby trashcan before returning to me. Without saying a word, he crawls in beside me, pulling me into his arms, my back to his front. I need to clean up, but I'm content in this moment, my brain quiet for a change.

“I don’t remember inviting you to stay the night,” I tease in a lazy voice.

“You didn’t.” He plants soft kisses along my neck and shoulder, causing that fluttering to erupt in my stomach once more.

“Then what makes you think I want you to stay?”

“Because I know something you don’t.”

“And what’s that?”

“That I’m a huge fan of morning sex. If you thought that was incredible…” He circles his hips. Moisture pools between my thighs and I’m instantly ready for round two, or three. I’ve lost count at this point. “That was just a warm-up for tomorrow.”

I turn around to face him. “You think so, do you?”

“I don’t think…” He brings his lips toward mine. “I know.”

When he leans in to kiss me, I press my hand against his chest, pushing him away. Taking advantage of his momentary surprise, I force him onto his back and crawl on top of him.

“Well, *I* know something you don’t, too.” I bring my mouth to his.

“And what’s that?”

I bite his lower lip and tug at it before releasing it. “That I’m not done with you yet.”

“God, I love blackouts."

CHAPTER ELEVEN

AN OBNOXIOUS PINGING wakes me from one of the best night's sleep I've had in a long time. Then again, Lincoln worked me to the point of utter exhaustion. I've never been with someone as enthusiastic and salacious. And let's not even talk about his stamina. With him, it certainly is a marathon. Slow and steady won the race. Again. And again. And again.

It takes me a few moments to register what I'm hearing, the sound strange against the silence. Then it hits me — my cell phone.

I bolt up, grabbing it off the nightstand, surprised to learn I have service again and am being bombarded with texts from my concerned friends.

> **Nora:** *Ohmigod. I just saw the news. A blackout in Vegas? What happened? You'd better text and tell me you're okay. You guys better be okay. Please text. Like now.*
>
> **Evie:** *Hey. I heard about the blackout in Vegas. I know you and Izzy are still stuck in that shithole. Just let me know you're okay. The news says cell towers have been affected so I don't expect an immediate response, but I promised Nora I'd text. You know how she can be about stuff like this. There's no reasoning with her. Love you. Stay safe.*

Flopping back onto the bed, I check my flight status to see it's not canceled, then type out a quick text to both of them to let them know I'm okay and that I'll be getting into New York later today. Curious as to what happened to cause the loss of power for a little over twelve hours, I open the web browser and run a quick search. Unfortunately, there's not much information, apart from the fact that Vegas lost power for a period lasting a little over twelve hours, but that all power and cell service is now restored.

I'm about to check my email, cringing at the idea of all the unanswered messages waiting for me, when an arm snakes around my waist. If it were anyone else, I'd shrug them off, make up some excuse, like needing to get to the airport to catch my flight, which I do, but I crave one last taste of Lincoln before our bubble bursts.

Moaning, I melt into him, craning my neck to give him better access. He feathers light kisses against my skin, his touch different from the commanding, dominant lover he was last night. Now he's gentle, tender, affectionate. Truth be told, I like this side of him just as much. Maybe even a little more.

His hand roams from my stomach, creeping its way up to my chest. As his fingers ghost over one of my nipples, I whimper, my body coming alive. He pushes me onto my back, then crawls between my legs. His vibrant green eyes are lazy in the light of day, his exhaustion from our night of sin evident. But that doesn't stop him from wanting me again.

Lowering his mouth to my breast, he delicately scrapes his teeth along the sensitized flesh of my nipple, and I lose myself to his touch yet again. Synapses firing, I wrap my legs around his waist, thrusting against him, my body a slave to sensation.

"Say you want me." His voice is raspy from broken sleep.

I smile, running my hands through his hair. Every time he woke me up in the middle of the night, he demanded the same thing. Now, whenever I hear those words, I'll only think of Lincoln, of his desperation to have my desire.

"I want you."

"Say you need me." This time, his plea is filled with more urgency.

"I need you."

Groaning, he pulls away. I loosen my grip around his waist, allowing him to lean back and roll on a condom.

"And I need you. More than I've needed anything." He covers my mouth as he pushes into me, filling me to my breaking point before retreating, continuing the same torturous, yet satisfying rhythm. Over. And over. And over.

Unlike last night, there are no carnal words, no harsh, punishing motions. It's sweet and affectionate, making me feel more fulfilled than any previous sexual encounter. My body quivers, my heart quickening as I struggle to think of something else, *anything* other than the amazing way Lincoln seems to strum me, like a practiced musician would his instrument.

He lowers his mouth to my neck, licking and biting before he murmurs, "Let go, baby. Let me have it."

My breathing grows ragged when his motions increase. Before I can fight against it, I unravel, a kaleidoscope of lights blinding me. He moans my name, finding his own release before collapsing on top of me, nuzzling his head against my chest.

I run my fingers through his wayward hair, swiping at the sweat on his brow. My eyes shift to the window, sunlight beaming into the room. Everything seems so different in the light of day. I'm not sure if it's a good different or bad different.

"Come to dinner with me." Lincoln's voice cuts through the tranquility.

I smirk. "Did you forget I'm headed home today? My flight's still showing as being on time."

"Not here. Back in New York. I want to take you out."

My heart catches in my throat, my body becoming rigid, my brain unable to tell my lungs to breathe, to perform that simple task of drawing in air, then exhaling.

Noticing my reaction, Lincoln pulls back, meeting my eyes, his brow wrinkled in confusion. "What is it?"

I shake my head, my lips parting. Most normal people would agree, would want to see if these feelings were real, if they'd survive outside the bubble. But I'm not most people. I don't have the luxury of being able to pursue a fantasy.

Pushing against him, I free myself from his hold and roll off the bed, scrambling around the room for my discarded clothes.

"Chloe, what is it?" He stands, stepping toward me. "I thought you—"

"Trust me," I interrupt, finding my yoga pants and tugging them on after the search for my panties ends up being fruitless. "You don't want that. We're not exactly compatible, are we?"

I stumble across my t-shirt and yank it on, feeling much more comfortable having this conversation now that I'm dressed. Lincoln doesn't seem to mind his lack of clothes, though. He's still as confident as he was last night. As he was yesterday when he gave me that lame tortoise and the hare analogy. As he was that first night I saw him.

"We're as opposite as they come," I continue, my tone frantic. "Not just in physical appearance, but in personality. There's no way this…" I gesture between our two bodies, "would ever work out. We don't even know each other."

This was never an issue with any of the other guys in my past. But they were aware of the score going in. They were *happy* with the score going in. I broke one of my rules. I failed to have that important conversation with Lincoln. I didn't think I had to. We all agreed last night. What happens in the bubble stays in the bubble.

"And once you get to know the real me, you'll—"

"Do you always try to control everyone else's decisions?" he interrupts, his voice calm.

"I don't try to control everyone else's decisions."

"You're doing it right now. You're standing here, claiming I'd never want to be with you, the real you, but you won't even give me a chance to get to *know* the real you. That's all I want. A chance."

I wrap my arms around my torso, shrinking into my tiny frame. "Once you get to know the real me, you'll understand how much of a mistake it is. Last night was great. Better than great. But we were in the blackout bubble."

"What about this morning? The blackout bubble is gone, yet I still want to know you. I still feel the same thing I did last night. That hasn't changed just because the power's back on. I still feel this connection. And I know you do, too."

"That wasn't a connection. That was just the result of too much alcohol, being stuck in this house, and a pair of dice."

"You're wrong. I felt it the instant I touched you Saturday night. The entire time you were going off about how much you loathed Vegas, all I could think was that I wanted to know you, but that I'd never get the chance. And then I did. We kept running into each other. Over. And over. And I knew it wasn't a coincidence. That it wasn't just a chance meeting. I didn't even know your name, yet what I felt for you was stronger than anything I've felt for anyone in a really long time. It makes no sense, and I can't even attempt to explain it without sounding like I'm fucking crazy, but there it is… I just…" He licks his lips, his chest heaving as he collects his thoughts.

It takes every ounce of resolve I possess not to avert my eyes to steal a glimpse below his waist. But that's not a solution. Not here, not now.

"I'm not asking you to move in," he says, his voice softer. "Hell, I'm not even asking you to be my girlfriend. I'm just asking you to take a chance on getting to know me, on allowing me to get to know you. To see if this has the potential I feel in my heart it does."

On a long inhale, I close my eyes. Maybe if my life weren't so complicated, I'd be able to say yes. Just like it takes a certain type of person to date a woman who already has children of her own, it also takes a certain type of person to date a woman who has an alcoholic mother. When she falls, I'm the only one who cares enough to catch her. And when I do, Lincoln will just let me fall, too.

I open my mouth, wanting to tell him all of this so he'll understand. Instead, all I can muster is, "I'm sorry." I hold his gaze for a moment, then dash into the bathroom, closing the door behind me.

Seconds stretch as I lean against the wall, hyper-aware of every sound. Every heartbeat. Every breath. Every frustrated sigh. Finally, after what feels like an eternity, I hear his footsteps retreat, the door to my room closing. I exhale deeply in what should feel like relief, but it isn't. It's something else.

Regardless, I shake off the exchange, convinced I made the right decision. As great as last night was, it wasn't real. We were in a fantasy world where nothing else existed outside the bubble. Fantasy and reality don't mix. Lincoln and I in the real world won't mix.

Not wanting to get stuck in Vegas yet another night because I missed my flight, I turn on the water and take one of the quickest showers of my life. As I rush around the room, throwing my few belongings back into my suitcase, I spy a piece of paper placed on the desk next to the full wine glasses from last night.

I stop in my tracks, my heart thumping as I walk toward it, admiring Lincoln's neat, yet masculine scrawl.

Dear Chloe,

I meant what I said. I do believe we have a connection. This connection won't go away simply because the blackout is over. I felt it before. And I still feel it now. There's a reason we kept running into each other. The universe has a plan for us. You just need to finally realize that.

Until then, I'll be yours...

Lincoln

P.S. - I took your panties. If you want them back, meet me at The Living Room in the Park Hyatt. Thursday night. 9 o'clock.

The sound of a door slamming reverberates through the house, and I snap my eyes away from the paper, dropping it on the desk. I listen as heavy footsteps storm from Izzy's room, past mine, continuing down the hall. I get the feeling things didn't end well between Izzy and Asher, either.

My phone dings, alerting me to a text message and I rush to it, finding a message.

Izzy: *Requested an Uber. Will be here in ten. Meet me by the front gate.*

I type out a quick reply.

Me: *Okay. Just packing up.*

I hit send, then finish throwing all my things into my suitcase. Once I'm confident I have everything I came here with, well…*almost* everything, I open the door to head out to catch our ride to the airport. Glancing behind me one last time, I spy Lincoln's note, taunting me.

"Oh, fuck it," I exhale, rushing to the desk and stuffing the paper into my bag.

The house is silent as I make my way down the steps, everything about this place different from the day before. It lacks life, vitality…hope. All the more reason I need to get out of this town as quickly as possible.

I step out the front door and walk down the long drive toward where Izzy's already standing, looking down the street for our ride.

"Hey, Iz."

"Hey, Chloe."

Neither one of us says anything else for several long moments. Despite the silence, our thoughts are deafening. I glance at her, catching her eyes. We both shrug at the same time, then say, "Vegas."

Our laughter fills the air as we wrap our arms around each other, offering the comfort we know we both need.

When our laughter dies down, Izzy comments, "So you're not going to see him again." It's not a question. She knows me, is fully aware of my reasons for not getting involved.

I pull out of her embrace. "What choice do I have?"

She pinches her lips together, nodding. Thankfully, she doesn't press the issue.

"You're not going to see him again?" I ask.

She meets my eyes. "What choice do *I* have?"

CHAPTER TWELVE

"NOTHING INTERESTING HAPPENED in Vegas? At all?"

I smile at Nora's doe-eyed expression, grateful to be back in New York and doing something I do every week — Thursday happy hour with two of my best friends.

"It was just an uneventful weekend in the tenth ring of hell," I say dismissively, taking a sip of my martini.

"Apart from the blackout," Nora says. "Do you have any idea how worried we were?"

"I read the texts," I respond, rolling my eyes. "All 187 of them, Nora."

"I did *not* send 187," she scoffs, indignant, smoothing her strawberry-blonde hair. Then she gives me a devious smile. "It was more like 186."

The sound of our laughter carries through the trendy bar. This is exactly what I needed after my weekend. A night with my girls. As I take in my surroundings, it's almost like I never left New York. The city's still the same. Nora still gets distracted anytime I ask her a question about her own wedding plans. Evie is still madly in love with her boyfriend, Julian. And I'm the perpetual single girl. Same as it was last week, and the week before that, and the week before that. My experience in Vegas didn't change any of that.

At least that's what I tell myself.

"So, tell me…" Evie squares her shoulders. "How *was* the bachelorette party? Did you have to wear something ridiculous, like a crown of penises?"

"No crown of penises, but I did have to wear a necklace of phalluses." I furrow my brow, deep in thought. "Phalli? Phalluses?"

I look between my two friends as we all murmur amongst ourselves, as if trying to answer a riddle.

"Actually, it can be either," Aiden, our bartender, interjects with a wink.

I turn my attention to him and tip my glass toward him before taking a sip. "Thanks, Aiden. What would we do without you?"

"Pay a lot more for your drinks than you do."

"I'll drink to that." Evie salutes him with her manhattan before sipping it.

"Please tell me there are pictures of you wearing a line of phalluses around your neck." Nora's eyes all but plead with me to admit there are.

"Probably. But that's not even the worst part."

"There's something worse than wearing penises around your neck?" Evie asks in disbelief.

"Oh yes. We all had tank tops. *Bedazzled* tank tops."

"Oh god," she laughs, a devilish glint in her eyes. "What was on it?"

"Mine said 'Bride's Bitch'. And the maid of honor wore one that said 'Bitch of Honor'."

They look equally horrified at the thought.

"I can promise we won't be doing anything that cheesy for my wedding."

"And this, my darling Nora, is why I love you." I raise my martini glass, toasting her.

"You'd love me even if I made you wear a crown of penises."

"You're right. I would." I pass her a sincere look, then bring my drink to my lips, sipping on it. When a song I recognize from Fallen Grace comes over the speakers, I choke on it, liquid shooting out of my mouth.

Before Vegas, I never paid much attention to the band. In the past twenty-four hours since I landed back at JFK, I feel like I see and hear them everywhere, a constant reminder of what I did in their Vegas house while they were back in London.

Almost like the universe refuses to let me forget it.

"What is it?" Evie asks in concern.

"Nothing. Drink went down the wrong pipe. That's all."

At that moment, a bar back rushes behind the counter, his arms filled with bottles. "Here's the Belvedere you needed," he says, handing them over to Aiden, who gets to work on restocking the shelves. All I can do is stare at the sleek bottle, trying to convince myself it's just a coincidence. It has to be. I'd purposely ordered a different kind of vodka for my martini to avoid the memory of Lincoln. Yet someone, some*thing* doesn't want me to forget.

"Chloe?" Nora says.

I whip my eyes to hers, my expression panicked, confused, and everything in between. "I—"

A flicker from the large screen television hanging over the bar catches my attention. I lift my eyes, scrunching my nose at the low-budget commercial for a used car dealership. Normally I wouldn't give it a second glance, but I can't stop staring at the actors dressed as George Washington, Benjamin Franklin, and you guessed it…Abraham Lincoln.

I could deal with hearing Fallen Grace. The radio stations play them at least once an hour. But the Belvedere vodka and a commercial with Abraham Lincoln? It's too much. Maybe Lincoln was right. Maybe the universe *does* have a plan for us.

Pushing out of my barstool, I grab a few bills to cover my drink and throw them onto the bar. I check my phone to see it's just a few minutes after nine. If I hurry, I can still make it.

"Where are you going?" Evie asks as I shrug into my jacket, then pull on my gloves and wrap my scarf around my neck.

I meet their curious expressions, parting my lips as I struggle for a way to explain this. There's so much I *should* tell them, but time is not on my side. Instead, I give them the short answer.

"I need to go see a man about a pair of panties."

Then I turn from their confused faces, running as fast as I can in my rather impractical boots away from the bar and toward the Park Hyatt, pushing through the crowded sidewalks, tourists and locals not moving as quickly as I want them to. At least Lincoln chose somewhere close to our usual Thursday evening spot. I would've been screwed otherwise.

The air is frigid, the wind whipping my face, but I've never felt so warm, so sure, so happy. When I reach the hotel, I momentarily pause, staring up at the tall building. Everything's about to shift. I'm taking a risk if I walk inside. And I'm taking a risk if I don't. But now I know which risk I *want* to take. I can no longer deny there's a reason our paths crossed. The universe made that loud and clear tonight.

Resolved, I step into the foyer, then take the elevator to the lobby. The ride seems to last an excruciatingly long time instead of the few seconds it actually does. When the doors open, I exit and am instantly swallowed up into the frenzied atmosphere of the lobby in the Manhattan luxury hotel.

Spying The Living Room past the check-in desk, I move toward it, my heels seeming to echo in the cavernous space as I cross the threshold into the swanky lounge. Couches and chairs fill the area, giving it the feel of being an actual living room instead of a bar.

My eyes float between the tables, looking for a familiar face. But I don't see one. I grab my phone out of my purse to check the time. 9:30. Maybe I'm too late. Maybe he's already left, thinking I wouldn't show up.

My shoulders dropping, I turn around, hoping the universe will ensure our paths cross again. At this point, it's all I can do. Or Facebook stalk him. Thank god for social media.

Just as I'm about to head out, my gaze settles on a pair of familiar green eyes at a table in a secluded corner, and my mouth ticks up into a smile, a tiny exhale of air escaping. He's dressed similarly to the way he was during our first few encounters — tailored jacket, crisp shirt, designer shoes. It's been less than forty-eight hours since I last saw him, but it feels like it's been an eternity.

His stare unwavering, he slowly stands, buttoning his suit jacket as he makes his way toward me. You know those scenes in movies when everything else falls away, leaving just the two main characters? That's what happens here. The world around us instantly disappears. We're no longer in a popular lounge in Midtown Manhattan. I'm no longer thinking about all the stress in my life. It's just Lincoln. Just us. Just this bubble. An incredibly sexy and addictive bubble.

As he approaches, his scent grows stronger, wrapping me in comfort. I thought it would be strange to see him anywhere other than Vegas, but it's not. It feels…right.

"You're late." His deep voice sends heat curling down my spine.

"I'm rarely on time."

Several silent heartbeats pass as he peers at me, almost convinced I'm not real. "These panties must be pretty special if you came all the way here just to get them back."

I slowly shake my head. "You can keep them."

"Then why are you here?" He arches a single brow.

I stand on my toes, my mouth feathering against his. "For you."

He brings me into his warm body, enclosing me in his perfect embrace. "God, I was hoping you'd say that."

He's about to kiss me when I press my hand on his chest, stopping him. "But this doesn't mean I'm going to move in with you," I say, repeating the same words from his own plea. "This doesn't mean I'm going to be your girlfriend… Not right away. All this means is that I'm willing to get to know you. That I'm willing to let you know me. That's all this is. Just a chance."

"That's all I ever wanted with you, Pixie. A chance."

CHAPTER THIRTEEN

I'VE OFTEN WONDERED what heaven would be like.

Not really as motivation to live a virtuous life. More like…curiosity.

Is it like floating on clouds with beautiful music playing in the background, St. Peter welcoming you with open arms, as is depicted in popular folklore?

Or maybe everyone's heaven is personal. Maybe Mother Theresa's heaven is filled with all the people she strove to help, no more signs of hunger or abuse. Robin Williams is probably free from depression, cracking jokes about anything and everything. And Steve Jobs' heaven is probably a replica of that garage in Los Altos where he built the first Apple computer.

Just like my heaven is wrapped in the arms of a man who was a mystery mere days ago, one I never planned to see again. But I couldn't stay away.

Yup. I have found my own personal slice of heaven here on earth. And his name is Lincoln Moore.

An arm snakes around my midsection, pulling me against a large, firm body. Chest hair tickles my back as I relax into him. Nuzzling his nose into the crook of my neck, he inhales, then moans. The deep, guttural sound sparks my libido to life, although it doesn't need much help. Not after our night of some of the most amazing sex I've experienced. Of acting like two long-time lovers who haven't seen each other in months, maybe years.

In reality, we're practically strangers. All I know about Lincoln Moore is he's a lawyer I kept running into while I was in Vegas for the bachelorette party from hell.

Oh, and that he's incredible in bed.

And against a wall.

And on the kitchen island.

I'm looking forward to finding out how amazing he is in even more places and positions.

"How are you feeling?" he rasps out as his tongue traces a circle on that spot where my neck meets my shoulder, causing a shiver to trickle down my spine.

It's amazing how he's learned to read my body in such a short amount of time. What I like, what turns me on. A trained musician playing an instrument, familiar with the exact spot that makes me hum, makes me vibrate, makes me sing.

"Horny."

It's silent for a beat. Then his throaty laugh echoes against the walls of his bedroom. "What am I going to do with you?"

I shift in the bed, peering into his lazy eyes, the green still dazzling first thing in the morning. Hooking a leg around his waist, I subtly circle my hips, his need for me already prominent.

"I have a few ideas."

In one swift move, he rolls onto his back, pulling me on top of him. My legs fall on either side of him and I lean down, allowing my hair to form a curtain around us. I feather my lips against his, then retreat. He cranes his head, chasing my kiss, but I remain just out of reach.

"Do you like being a tease?"

Readjusting my position so I'm sitting upright, I bite on my lower lip, smiling coyly as I move against him. "I think *you* like it when I'm a tease." My voice is demure as I bat my lashes.

With a growl, he grabs the back of my head, his fingers digging into my scalp as he brings my mouth within an inch of his. My breathing becomes ragged, raw hunger flowing through me.

No man has ever turned me on to the level Lincoln has. No man has ever brought me to the brink of the kind of pleasure I didn't think possible, then pushed me over the edge to the point of oblivion. No man has ever brought me to my knees, made me want more.

But I do.

I want so much more from him.

I lick my lips, then plump them out, encouraging him to dive in for a taste. Instead, his teeth clamp onto my lower lip. The ache hits me in my core, making me burn even hotter for him. He wraps his arm around me and flips me onto my back, covering my body with his. Brushing my hair away from my face, his eyes lock with mine, vibrant green to my lackluster gray. I wonder if he can read my thoughts, if he knows I'm mentally comparing him to every man in my past, every mistake, every reminder of why I've always done things my way.

"Don't." A single word is all I need to confirm my suspicions.

I part my lips, but he captures my protest with a mind-erasing kiss.

In my lifetime, I've been treated to thousands of kisses. Not one of them has touched me like Lincoln's do. Have made me feel like they were invading my soul. Like I needed them to breathe. Like I'd perish without them.

"I don't want you to think about anything else when you're with me," he whispers against my mouth, the roughness of his unshaven jawline invigorating as he leisurely makes his way down my body. "Like we said last night." He floats his eyes to mine as he settles between my legs. "I'm just asking for a chance. We'll take things slow."

When his tongue lands on that spot that brings me extraordinary pleasure, I sigh, succumbing to him. I doubt this qualifies as taking things slow.

But it feels too good to tell him to stop now.

* * *

"Shit. Shit. Shit." I check my watch to see it's almost eight in the morning, then drop to my hands and knees and search under Lincoln's bed for my panties. It's a mystery how they always seem to disappear around this man. Then it hits me.

Jumping to my feet, I grab my boots and head down the hallway of his apartment in the heart of Chelsea's art center. The exposed brick, combined with steel accents and reclaimed wood furniture, give it a masculine vibe. It's not a huge place, but given the real estate prices in this part of the city, it's probably valued at a couple million. Yes, he's a lawyer, but he's still young. At least he seems young. I'm not sure how old he is. I'm not sure I *want* to know how old he is.

I round the corner into the living room and skitter to a halt, the scene that greets me leaving me breathless.

From the instant I met Lincoln, I found him attractive. Dark hair. Mesmerizing green eyes. Muscular build. A perpetual five o'clock shadow that had me fantasizing about what it would feel like scraping on my thighs.

When I was treated to the vision of him playing guitar, I didn't think anything could top that in terms of sexiness.

I was wrong.

So fucking wrong.

Because I've discovered something even sexier than Lincoln Moore, all six-foot-three of pure masculinity, playing guitar.

And that's him sitting at the round bistro table in his breakfast nook, an impressive view of the Manhattan skyline visible in the wide expanse of windows behind him, reading the *New York Times*, a pair of dark-framed glasses on his face.

"Fuck me," I murmur, then slap a hand over my mouth.

He looks up, a brow cocked. With a smirk, he folds the paper and pushes back from the table, standing. I don't think I'll ever tire of seeing him dressed this way. Something about the dark jeans and tweed blazer makes him look like a sexy college professor. Maybe if my professors were as attractive as Lincoln, I would have been more excited about learning. Hell, I may have even taken them up on their offers of extra help.

"I think I did." He leans toward me, his lips brushing against my cheek.

It's an innocent gesture, but it still leaves me lightheaded. "Quite a few times, if I'm not mistaken."

He pulls back and winks. I briefly consider dragging him back into the bedroom for one more quickie.

With the glasses on.

Increasing the distance before I make us both late for work, I cross my arms over my chest, pinching my lips into a tight line.

"On that note, you wouldn't know where my panties are, would you?"

"Why? Have they gone missing?" he asks in faux surprise.

"Indeed." My hands rest of the lapels of his jacket, able to make out the defined muscles even through the few layers of clothes.

"Hmm. It's quite the mystery, isn't it? We should open an investigation into the matter."

I shake my head, inching my lips closer to his. It doesn't matter how many kisses he showered me with over the past twelve hours. I still need one more.

I have a feeling I'll *always* need one more.

"That's unnecessary. I already have a suspect in mind."

He playfully arches a single brow. "Is that right?"

"That's right."

He palms my lower back, yanking me hard and fast into his body. "And who is this panty thief?"

"You," I breathe.

"Prove it."

"I can't. Not yet. But it fits your M.O. You *do* have a track record of stealing my panties and using them as a bargaining chip."

His lips feather against mine. "You know what they say, don't you?"

"What's that?" My husky voice is unrecognizable. I suppose that's the Lincoln Moore effect. He has me acting like a completely different woman.

Or maybe being with him allows me to be myself for a change.

"Desperate times call for desperate measures." His lips move from mine, trailing hot kisses along my jawline, settling in that spot where my neck meets my shoulders. He nibbles as I throw my head back, allowing him to push me against the floor-to-ceiling windows. The chill of the January air on the other side of the pane tempers the heat coiling in my veins.

"And what had you desperate enough to steal my panties?"

"It worked last time, didn't it?" His gaze locks with mine, his smile revealing the devil hiding beneath the tweed jacket. "I had to make sure you came…" He smirks, then finishes, "back."

I thread my fingers through his hair, pulling him to me. "I knew I could get you to admit you took them."

A beat passes before he groans, grinding his body against mine. "Naughty girl. You play a wicked game, don't you?"

"It's how we got here, isn't it?" I say breathlessly. "By playing wicked games?"

"There's no one else I'd want to play these games with, Pixie." The sincerity in his voice almost has me running for the hills. Instead, I lean in, savoring in the heat of his mouth pressed firmly against mine.

When he retreats, I avert my eyes, out of my comfort zone. I've never stayed the night with a guy before. Well, I suppose I did Tuesday night when I let Lincoln sleep in my bed during the blackout. But there was no awkward goodbye. I ran off and locked myself in the bathroom before we could get to that point.

But now, I'm at that point. What do I do? What's the proper protocol? Do we make plans to see each other again? How soon is too soon? I wish I'd asked Nora or Evie. But that would mean telling them about Lincoln. I'm not sure I'm ready to share him with anyone yet. I'm not sure we're at that stage in…whatever this is.

"Well…" I clear my throat, pushing against him. "I should get going, so…" I arch a brow, expectant.

"So?" he says when I don't finish my thought.

"My underwear?" I hold out my hand.

"What about them?"

"Aren't you going to give them back?"

"I wasn't planning on it." There's an arrogance about him as he retreats from me, bringing his now empty coffee mug into the open kitchen area. I look around his clean apartment, marveling at the simple act of him washing out his coffee mug. I tend to allow mine to collect for days before I finally throw them all into the dishwasher.

"Why?" I follow on his heels. "Concerned the only thing of value you can offer me is my own underwear?"

He ponders my question for a moment, then advances toward me as I stand near the island, a hand on my hip. "I'm more than confident I can offer you something else of value."

"And what's that?"

He shrugs, the heat that was present in his eyes turning into something…more. "Me."

"I—" I stammer, words escaping me. I've never met anyone so transparent, someone who laid it all out there for the world to see. In a way, I envy that about him, wish I could be more like that. But I can't. Not with my past. Or my present.

Able to sense my unease, he covers my mouth with his. "Whenever you're ready. No pressure. Like I said—"

"I know," I breathe. "Just a chance."

"Exactly. Just a chance." His reassurance lingers as he places a hand on my lower back and leads me toward the foyer. "But I'm still keeping your panties."

Huffing, I playfully roll my eyes. "I'm going to run out of panties soon. Then what are you going to do to lure me back to your lair of sex?"

"I'll figure something out." When we reach the door, I face him, and he curves into me, our lips meeting. "I can be pretty resourceful."

"I've heard that about you."

CHAPTER FOURTEEN

THE FAMILIAR DRONE of a frenzied newsroom meets me the second I round the corner behind the reception desk of *Blush* magazine. Nails click at keyboards. Phones ring incessantly. Low music plays from some cubicles…except those belonging to the fashion department. Their little area is often akin to a rave.

Glancing at my watch to see it's five minutes before ten, I hurry to my desk and drop my bag before continuing through the open space, a woman on a mission.

I duck into the breakroom to find it empty, considering most of the editors are probably already in the conference room waiting for the weekly meeting. I'll need to pull some sort of story out of my ass to pitch today. It won't be the first time.

I make a beeline to the Nespresso machine, pop a pod into the brewer, and place a cup beneath the spout. The instant the nutty aroma fills my senses, my shoulders relax. After my night of little sleep, I need this magical concoction. Espresso is the perfect pick-me-up when you want something stronger than coffee but weaker than cocaine.

"You needed to see a man about a pair of panties?" a familiar voice cuts through my moment of peace.

I curse under my breath, then whirl around, meeting Evie's hardened expression as she leans against the doorjamb, arms crossed over her chest, an inquisitiveness in her green eyes.

How was I going to explain my sudden retreat from the bar last night? And the panties? I hadn't given it much thought this morning, thanks to the spell Lincoln cast over me.

With my head held high to make my five-foot-two frame appear bigger than it is, I grab my espresso and walk toward her. "One of my hook-ups kept a pair of my underwear. I wanted them back."

I avoid her stare as I skirt past her, heading toward the conference room. I've never looked forward to our Friday staff meeting as much as I do right now, if for no other reason than to give me a few minutes to figure out what to tell my friends.

I should be able to gush about this new guy in my life. But that's never been my thing. In fact, there's never been a guy in my life *to* gush about.

Isn't there a waiting period required by law before doing that or something? Lincoln and I aren't even an item. At least, I don't think we are. I'm not sure *what* we are. All I know is he's got me all out of sorts.

And he likes stealing my panties.

"I wasn't born yesterday, Chloe." Evie's right on my heels. Relentless, as always. "We've known each other over five years now. Hell, we practically worked on top of each other until last week when I moved into the assistant editor office. If you think you can say you went to get a pair of panties back from one of your 'hook-ups' without me calling bullshit…" She steps in front of me before I can disappear into the conference room. "You'd better think again."

I take a sip of my espresso, doing my best to remain confident.

"There's no way this was just a hook-up," she continues. "Not with that shit-eating grin that was plastered across your face last night. I know that look. It was the look of someone *excited* about something. You had a glow about you. Come to think of it…" Squinting, she scans my body.

I wonder if this is how criminals feel when they've finally been apprehended and try to convince the officer the bag of drugs in their coat isn't theirs. Except I wasn't caught with drugs, although Lincoln's more addicting than even the most potent narcotic.

"You *still* have a glow about you." Her eyes brighten. "You had sex last night!"

"Evie," I hiss, trying to hush her.

While I've never been one to keep my sex life to myself, this is different. I *care* about Lincoln. I don't want to broadcast our fantastic sexcapades for all to hear. I don't want to share him with anyone. Not yet. I want to keep him all to myself for a little longer. I fear the second I talk about him, it'll make it real. I'm not ready for that yet.

"I have sex a lot… Well, not *a lot*, but enough that going to see some guy isn't a big deal." I straighten my spine. "It's not the first time I left you and Nora at the bar to hook up with somebody."

"No, it's not." She wraps a strand of her striking red hair around a finger, toying with it as she continues assessing my demeanor. "But I don't think last night was just a hook-up. I think you *like* someone."

I open my mouth to protest when the conference room door swings open, Maggie, the editor-in-chief's assistant, standing there, an air of superiority about her. "Are you two coming? Viv's waiting on you." She spins around. "As usual," she adds under her breath.

My expression brightens as I smile cheerily. "Come on, Evie. We don't want to be late," I chirp as I head inside.

She leans toward me. "This conversation isn't over," she murmurs, her voice low.

"I didn't think it was."

* * *

Thankfully, after the pitch meeting, Evie's too busy with assignments to continue to press me about the new man in my life, which gives me time to figure out how to address the elephant in the room.

Or at least the very large cock in my life.

As I attempt to catch up on all the work I missed while I was out of the office, as well as come up with a way to spill the beans about Lincoln to my friends, my phone dings with an incoming text. At first, I ignore it, assuming it's a tip about a breaking story in the world of the rich and famous. I can't be bothered with that stuff, not with a deadline looming on articles that go to print in just a few days.

But when it beeps again, I float my eyes to the screen, smiling when I see it's not from a source, but from my very own panty thief.

And that smile only grows wider when I open the text, which reveals a photo of a familiar pair of panties.

> **Lincoln:** *Missing you like you wouldn't believe. But at least I have a souvenir. And the scent is intoxicating.*
>
> **Me:** *You really do have a fetish, don't you? Is it 'bring some random girl's panties to work' day? I didn't receive the memo.*

I hit send, relaxing into my chair as I focus all my attention on my phone. One text, yet I've forgotten everything I'm supposed to be working on. Hell, if Lincoln asked, I'd probably sneak out of work to meet him for a quickie, although I'm not sure Lincoln's capable of a quickie. His bedroom skills are those of an expert, a man who's made sex an art form. He's a masterpiece I doubt I'll ever tire of experiencing.

> **Lincoln:** *You're not just some random girl, Chloe. You never have been.*

My heart warms as I read his words. Then the text bubble appears, indicating he's typing more.

> **Lincoln:** *And to answer your question, I do have a bit of an underwear fetish. At least when it comes to your underwear.*
>
> **Me:** *Well then, I hate to disappoint you. I haven't had time to do my laundry since returning from Vegas, so I had to go commando today.*
>
> **Lincoln:** *Fuck...*

A part of me wishes I were with Lincoln so I could see his expression. Pupils dilating. Green eyes darkening with unbridled lust and need. Jaw clenching. Muscles tightening. God, I love that look on him, knowing I make him react that way.

Lincoln: *You really know how to torture a man, don't you, Pixie?*

Me: *Only you.*

Lincoln: *I like the sound of that.*

I want to say I like the sound of that, too, but I don't, responding with something safer instead.

Me: *Think of me today.*

Lincoln: *I haven't been able to stop since the moment I saw you.*

Me: *Me, either.*

I hope that's enough to make him believe I'm willing to try, even if my words aren't overly amorous. I'm just a work in progress.

When no additional texts arrive, I return my attention to my computer, concentrating on my work once more, hours passing. I'm so focused, I don't tear my eyes away from my screen until I hear a slight knock on the exterior wall of my cubicle, the receptionist holding a large white box with a pink bow wrapped around it.

"A courier just dropped this off for you." She places it on my desk.

I eye the box much like one would glare at a device with a timer and wires attached. "What is it?"

"I'm sure if you open it, you'll find out," she snips, then whirls around.

I've always wondered how some of our receptionists got their job, since they all seem to have a stick shoved up their asses, unless a handsome man walks through those doors. I can't really complain. I started at that desk myself. I'd like to think I wasn't so bitchy, but I probably was.

As I look back at the box, a suspicion it's from Lincoln forms in my gut. Who else would send me something at work? How does he know *where* I work? I don't think I told him, apart from the fact that I work at a magazine. But there are hundreds of magazine offices in New York City.

After loosening the ribbon, I lift the lid and pull back pink tissue paper, laughing when I see what lies beneath it. I reach for the envelope placed in the center and slide out the small card, Lincoln's familiar scrawl greeting me.

My dearest Chloe,

I've worked out a solution to our little...dilemma. And your lack of undergarments for the day.

I glance at the contents, my cheeks flushing at the dozen or so pairs of panties before reading the rest of the note.

They're all laundered and ready for you to wear. It was torture sitting here, thinking about you not wearing any panties. No one's allowed to steal a glimpse of what's mine. And rest assured, Chloe, you will be mine.

I'm already yours…

Lincoln

P.S. - In addition to the panties, there's a little extra something for you. I'd love to see you in it. Whenever you're ready.

I place the card on my desk and rummage through the box, pushing the panties aside. My pulse increases when I find a sexy black lace negligee with a matching thong. The thought of Lincoln's reaction to seeing me in this has my blood pumping, electricity coursing through my veins.

Phone in hand, I type off a quick text.

Me: *What makes you think I'm interested in seeing you again? A little cocky, don't you think?*

Lincoln: *Not a little cocky. At least I think it's impressive. It gets the job done.*

I burst out laughing as my fingers fly over the screen.

Me: *It certainly does.*

I'm about to type out another reply when my cell rings, Lincoln's name appearing on the screen. My heart catches in my throat, face heating as I bring my phone up to my ear.

"Hello," I answer as seductively as I can get away with at work.

"Say thank you."

His deep voice murmuring those words brings me back to that bar in Vegas when he picked up my tab.

Say okay. Say thank you.

It hypnotized me, and I succumbed to his request without a moment's hesitation. That spell is still cast over me.

"Thank you."

"Good girl."

A shiver rolls down my spine, renewed desire igniting deep within. This feels so surreal. How far will I take this? Will I always do what he demands? The idea doesn't scare me. It excites me. I *want* him to tell me what to do. I like not having to think about all the potential ramifications of every single one of my actions. It's refreshing to turn it off for a minute. To quiet all the noise and drama that usually clouds my mind.

"Now, tell me… *Do* you want to see me again?" he asks, his voice as calm and collected as ever.

I picture him in a large office sitting behind an impressive wooden desk, one wall lined with AmJurs and the CJS, much like in my father's own office, despite no one using hard copies of legal encyclopedias these days. Everything is probably impeccable. It's not stacked high with boxes containing evidence or notes or other case material. There's a place for everything, and everything's in its place. A far cry from my cubicle, which on a good day looks like a bomb went off.

"Or are you having second thoughts about giving me a chance?"

"Never," I admit breathlessly.

"Good answer. Then I look forward to seeing you…soon."

"You're not going to ask me when?" I blurt out after a beat.

"No, I'm not. I understand this is new territory for you, so I won't push. When you're ready, so am I." His tone lightens. "Although I hope you don't wait too long, because now that I've had a taste, I'm not sure how long I'll be able to go without you in my arms."

A flutter erupts in my belly and I feel like I'm floating, the force of the butterflies' rapid wings lifting me up.

"Have a good day, Pixie."

"You, too." I linger on the line a moment longer, about to hang up when I call his name. "Lincoln?"

"Yes?"

I chew on the inside of my cheek. "How did you know where to send my…gift?"

It's quiet for a beat before he answers, "What would you say if I Googled you?" I can hear the smile in his voice.

"You…Googled me?"

"I wanted to surprise you. I don't know much about you, other than your name, what you do for a living, and that you make the most adorable sound when you're about to come."

"Yeah. It's called a moan."

"No. It's not that. It's more like a…mewl." His voice grows heated, wanton, lustful. "This excited mewl I can't get enough of. So please, don't make me wait too long to hear that again."

"I won't," I respond before I can stop myself. "Promise."

I imagine him smiling at my response. Hell, *I'm* smiling at my response.

"Goodbye, Pixie."

"Goodbye, Lincoln."

I stay on the phone a moment longer, then end the call. With a sigh, I try to return my focus to what I was working on, but all I can think of is Lincoln.

There's this mysteriousness about him, which makes me want to learn even more. Was he born in New York? Where did he go to law school? Does he have brothers? Sisters? What's his family like?

These are all things I've never cared enough to learn about any other man. Now I'm desperate to have a fuller picture of Lincoln Moore.

Navigating to my Internet browser, I type his name into the search bar. I hit enter just as a voice startles me.

"What is this?"

I quickly close out of my browser before I have a chance to look at the results, snapping my eyes up to see Evie hovering in my cubicle, staring at my gift.

"I was low on underwear and didn't feel like doing laundry," I lie nonchalantly.

"Bullshit." When she reaches for the card, I don't fight her. It was only a matter of time before she found out anyway. We spend over forty hours a week together.

She takes a few seconds to read. Then her wide eyes dart to mine. "Who's Lincoln? How does he know you're not wearing any underwear? Is he the one you went to go see about your panties last night? And why is he…yours?"

"He's…a guy."

"I gathered, but—"

I hold up my hand, cutting her off. I take a deep breath, summoning the strength for the conversation that's about to follow. "He's a guy I like. And yes, he's the panties guy." My lips quirk into a smile. "A panty thief."

Evie stares at me, her mouth agape, her response similar to one she'd have if she just learned I'd been leading a double life as a sex abstinence advocate. Then she squeals, her words coming out a mile a minute.

"Who is he? Where did you meet? What's he like? What does he do? What does he look like? Where's he from?" Her questions come like rapid gunfire.

"Evie… Evie… Evie!" I say in between each question, having to shout the last one to get her attention.

She snaps her mouth shut. "You're right. This calls for reinforcements."

"Reinforcements?"

"Exactly."

CHAPTER FIFTEEN

"OH MY GOODNESS!" Nora squeals, placing her hand over her heart as we sit in a row of spin machines, sweat dripping from our bodies. Upbeat music blares, overpowering the sound of wheezing breaths and the whirring of the wheels on the stationary bikes. "It's better than any movie! It was meant to be!"

I roll my eyes at her reaction to the story I'd just told, slightly breathless, about meeting Lincoln in Vegas.

"It's a total fairy tale."

"Fairy tales all end with 'And they lived happily ever after'," I taunt, using air quotes, imitating her light, dream-like voice. "That's not us."

Nora scowls, an adorable pout on her face, as if she'd just learned a car had hit her childhood dog. "What makes you think that?"

"It's too soon to be planning a future with him." I pedal harder, pretending to focus on my workout when, in reality, I want to flip off the instructor, who seems to get off on people's anguished expressions. If I hear her say "Pain is weakness leaving the body" one more time, I'll show her some real pain. "We agreed to take things slow."

Evie snorts a laugh. "Yeah. Him practically telling you he owns your pussy is *really* taking things slow."

"He didn't say he owns my pussy," I protest, somewhat loudly.

A few people glance in our direction, the women scrunching their nose in disgust at my use of the word "pussy". It makes me want to shout it repeatedly at the top of my lungs.

"He'd stolen yet another pair of my panties, and I haven't been home long enough to drop off my clothes at the laundromat, so I had to go commando."

When an attractive man in his thirties looks our way, I flash him a smile, then notice the wedding band on his hand as he not so subtly adjusts his shorts. Facing my friends, I lower my voice to avoid any more stares.

"Once I told him that… Well, you can fill in the blanks. He didn't want anyone to catch a glimpse of what *could* be his. But don't worry. It's not his yet. I still own this pussy."

"And his cock, by the sounds of it," Nora chimes in.

"I don't own his cock."

Evie and Nora share a look before fixing their gazes back on me. "You do," they say simultaneously.

"Impossible. We haven't even known each other a week. Not to mention, I didn't know his name until Tuesday. That's only three days ago! Hell, the only thing I know about him is that he's a lawyer. I don't even know what kind of law he practices…" I trail off as I shift my eyes to the large mirrored walls, the reflection of dozens of people's legs cycling on their spin machines dizzying. "But there's one way to find out." I grab my phone off the bike and navigate to the browser.

"What are you doing?" Evie asks, a brow quirked up, slowing her pedaling.

"Googling him."

Her eyes widen as she shares a look with Nora yet again. In a heartbeat, she snatches the phone out of my hands. "No. Don't."

"Wha—"

"I get that you're a curious person by nature, that you love digging for dirt on every celebrity out there. And you're damn good at it." She waves my phone in front of me. "But don't do that here."

The instructor increases the resistance on the bikes and we all pedal even harder, the ache in my legs a temporary distraction.

"When I agreed to that first non-date with Julian," Evie continues, panting, "I had no idea who he was. And it's probably a good thing. I'm not sure I would have gone. I probably would have second-guessed the entire scenario. Hell, I did that anyway, but having no clue who he was allowed me to relax and get to know him. I never looked him up, apart from that one time you showed me his Wikipedia page. I got to learn about Julian from him, not the Internet."

She exhales a breath, her face reddening. "And who the fuck decided spin classes were a good idea?" Her eyes dart to Nora. "It was you, wasn't it? Sadist. Why can't we have girls' time with ice cream instead?"

"That's a different situation, E," I argue when Nora simply shrugs in response to Evie's accusation. "Julian Gage is well known. Lincoln Moore isn't."

"How do you know?" Nora asks, then does a double take, brows furrowed. "Wait a minute. His name is Lincoln Moore?"

"Yes…," I answer in a drawn-out voice.

She stares at me, mouth agape. I brace myself to find out he's now officially off-limits due to the girl code. Before she settled down with Jeremy, her fiancé, she was a date-aholic. We often compared "war stories" about what it's like finding someone you feel a connection with in the New York City wildlife. I never cared about the connection, not like Nora, although she claims she didn't, either. That she was simply enjoying her twenties. Secretly, I could tell she was looking for more than a fleeting romp in the sack.

Maybe I was, too, but I didn't realize it.

"Damn, that's a great name. Lincoln Moore." She fans herself, continuing to pedal, making it appear effortless when everyone else in the class is ready to stick the instructor's head on a spike in revolt. I suppose running a yoga and meditation studio has its benefits. "Does he have you begging for *more*?" She grins mischievously.

"No." I pause before breaking into a smile. "More like screaming."

"That's my girl." Nora reaches toward me and we bump fists. Some may find our conversation inappropriate, but we've never shied away from topics some consider taboo. That's probably why I've remained friends with Nora and Evie…and even Izzy…for as long as I have. They're as comfortable with discussing sex as I am.

"Scream for more all you want," Evie interjects. "Just promise you won't Google him."

"He Googled me first."

"I bet he did," she says under her breath.

"To send you underwear," Nora reminds me. "Not to figure out who you are. I know how you work. You'll find something random and convince yourself not to pursue him. Don't. Get to know him. Don't assume he has some weird fetish because you misread something while stalking his social media profiles."

"Well, he *does* have a weird fetish."

They perk up.

"For my panties."

We all erupt in laughter, eliciting a few glares, but we ignore them.

"I'm happy for you, Chloe," Nora says in all sincerity.

"Me, too," Evie adds. "And, for the love of a magical penis, will you take some of your own advice?"

"My own advice?"

"Exactly. When I wasn't sure what to make of Julian going from hot to cold in three point five seconds, do you remember what you told me?"

I don't immediately respond.

"You told me to enjoy the ride."

"On his rocket," I add to cut through the tension.

She smiles for a second before fixing her expression once more.

"Yes. And I'll give you the same advice here. Chloe, I've known you five years."

"And I've known you ten," Nora pipes up. "I've never seen you this excited about a guy."

"I don't think I've *ever* seen you excited about a guy, period," Evie offers, then adds quickly, "Don't get me wrong. It's not a bad thing. I just… I want you to be happy. If that means pursuing something serious with

Lincoln Moore, great. If you want to keep things casual, that's great, too. Don't think too much. Let life lead you down the path you're meant to travel."

I take a swig of my water, giving her a smug grin. "Strange words coming from a woman who, six months ago, used to plan every minute of every day down to the nanosecond."

Evie playfully punches my bicep. "I did not. At least not down to the nanosecond." She winks. "But you know what I mean. I understand how it is when you find yourself in uncharted territory. You over-analyze everything. I know *I* do. And as much as you'd like to think we're opposites, we're more alike than you think. So have fun with Lincoln Moore—"

"You can just call him Lincoln."

She pauses, her eyes scrunched together in contemplation, before she quickly shakes her head. "Nope. Can't do it. His name rolls off the tongue too perfectly."

"She's right," Nora agrees. "It does."

"It really is the perfect last name for a sex god." Evie giggles.

"I never said he was a sex god."

"You didn't have to," Nora states. "It goes with the territory."

"What territory?"

Nora and Evie share yet another look. It makes me wonder if they have a secret code when it comes to me. I've never exactly given them a reason to focus on me.

For the past five years, our friendship has focused on Nora's seemingly never-ending search for Mr. Right while insisting all she cared about was a decent lay, although we all knew she wanted more. To our surprise, she met someone on Tinder who felt the same.

Then there was Evie's breakup with her long-time boyfriend and her whirlwind fake relationship with one of Manhattan's most eligible bachelors, which ended up being a lot more real than either intended. Compared to them, my life is boring, mainly because I tend to keep the details to myself.

Evie pinches her lips together before answering. "You have high standards."

"Says the girl who once berated me for sleeping with anything with a pulse."

"To which you replied you were sampling the buffet before you went back for seconds."

"Precisely."

"My point exactly, Chloe. You *rarely* go back for seconds."

"I've seen a few guys more than once," I argue.

"True," Nora says, finally piping up. "But I think this time's different."

I roll my eyes. "All I promised him was a chance to get to know me. He left the ball in my court, so to speak."

"Well, if I were you," Evie begins, "I wouldn't wait to throw that ball. I'd toss it now. Hell, I'd spike it to show him you're not stringing him along."

"He knows I'm not."

"Trust me," Nora interjects. "A single, attractive man who's interested in more than a quick fling is a rarity, especially in New York. Most men you'll meet are either married to their career, married to their bachelorhood, or married to their wives. Yes, you say all he's asking for is a chance to get to know you, but he's giving *you* a chance, too. Don't fuck it up."

"Gee, thanks for the words of encouragement." My tone oozes sarcasm.

She shrugs. "What are friends for?"

* * *

Nora's and Evie's warnings seem to play on repeat in my mind for the rest of the afternoon and evening, festering, making it impossible for me to concentrate on anything other than Lincoln and what he's doing. Is he out with friends? At work? Having dinner with another woman he's also sent panties to?

The idea of him stealing another woman's panties is all the motivation I need to get off the couch, shower, and make my way to his apartment. He surprised me with a present at work today. What better way to spike the ball back onto his side of the court than by showing up at his apartment wrapped in a present for him?

Bringing my hand up to the door, I knock softly, my insides vibrating with anticipation of how Lincoln will react. I strain to listen for any sound coming from within. At first, there's nothing but silence. Then I hear a faint rustling. Shoeless footsteps gradually grow closer. There's a pause, and I assume Lincoln's checking to see who could be here at ten on a Friday night.

When the door opens, he peers at me with a furrowed brow. He parts his lips, presumably to ask me what I'm doing here, but I place a finger over them, silencing him.

Without saying a word, I loosen the belt on my coat and slowly unfasten each of the buttons, allowing my jacket to fall open, exposing my body clad in the negligee he'd sent me earlier.

"Fuck," he hisses, his jaw clenched, nostrils flaring, a bull in heat. His gaze rakes over me, calculating, agonizing, as if imprinting every inch of me to memory.

Approaching him, I stand on my toes, my lips ghosting against his. "That's the plan, Mr. Moore."

A growl rips from his throat as he tugs my body hard against his, his mouth covering mine, devouring, possessing, consuming. I curve into him, signaling with my acquiescence to his touch that I'm his for the night.

Maybe longer.

Chapter Sixteen

MY HEELS SKID on the tile in the lobby of the journalism building on campus as I rush to the elevator, checking my watch. Ten minutes past three on Thursday afternoon. Meaning I'm ten minutes late for my first day of class. I shouldn't be surprised. I'm notorious for being late, especially when sexting with Lincoln Moore.

Lincoln. Just Lincoln.

Ever since I appeared at his door last Friday, scantily clad, we've seen each other every day. And every day, I grow more and more addicted to his touch, his essence, his everything.

Once the elevator doors close, I pull out my phone and read through our most recent exchange, unable to stop the smile from tugging on my lips.

> **Lincoln:** *Have I mentioned today how much I love your legs?*
>
> **Me:** *My memory's not what it used to be. I am closing in on thirty. Why don't you refresh my memory?*
>
> **Lincoln:** *You're still a baby. And I love your legs. Actually, I'm not so sure love is the correct word. I think about them nearly every waking moment.*
>
> **Me:** *Nearly?*
>
> **Lincoln:** *Yes. Nearly. Except when I'm buried deep inside you. Then I can only think about how amazing your pussy feels when it clenches around me.*

Desire, thick and intense, coils in my core as I attempt to come up with a response, having left him hanging once I realized I was running late. The elevator doors open and I scurry down the hallway toward my classroom, typing out a quick reply.

> **Me:** *Sorry to leave you with your dick in your hands. Lost track of time. Have class. Maybe I can come over after and you can feel my pussy clench around you. You know, so you can take a break from thinking of my legs.*

Once I hit send, I shove my phone into my bag, slowing when I reach the classroom. Fixing my frantic expression, I open the door and do my best to slip in unnoticed without interrupting class, smiling at a few familiar faces who don't seem surprised to see I'm late on the first day.

I make my way toward one of the vacant seats in the middle of the room, trying to be as quiet as possible. It's obvious by the stiff posture and annoyed breathing of the professor he's not exactly pleased with my disruption.

When I'm about to slide into my chair, he finally turns around from where he's written out the text of the First Amendment, and our eyes meet.

Ever have one of those dreams where everything seems perfect? Maybe your boss called you into his or her office and gave you that promotion you've been hoping for. Maybe Publishers Clearing House, if that's even still a thing, showed up at your door with one of those oversized checks. Or maybe you ran into one of the hottest guys you've ever seen while grabbing your morning coffee. All great things, right?

Until you look down and realize you're naked.

That's what this moment feels like.

Correction.

This is worse.

Because this isn't some dream.

This is real.

Lincoln Moore is my college professor.

I've been sleeping with my college professor.

Without knowing it.

Fuck…

A throat clearing cuts through the heavy silence. Unsure what else to do, I slink into my chair, doing my best to hide behind the girl sitting in front of me. Even so, the slight tremble in Lincoln's hand as he writes on the board doesn't escape my attention, evidence he's as surprised about this turn of events as me.

Had I walked into this room and one of the other men I'd slept with had been lecturing the class, I wouldn't have been so dumbfounded. But this is different.

Lincoln is different.

I try to convince myself this is for the best, that this never would have worked out. Listening to his lecture solidifies this assessment. He needs someone who can be his intellectual equal. Someone he can debate about what should be classified as obscene and not deserving of First Amendment protections. I'd barely be able to get out a few words without stumbling over them.

Conversation breaks out in the room and I glance up from the blank page of my notebook to see the other students packing up their things. When I glance at my watch, I'm surprised to see it's fifteen minutes to six. I'd just sat through almost an entire three-hour class without hearing a word, too consumed with this strange, new reality.

Snapping out of my daze, I scramble to shove my belongings into my bag and leave without having to confront Lincoln and endure an awkward conversation where we pretend we don't know each other. I'm not sure what I'm supposed to do, but I'll figure something out. Try to drop the class. Do an independent study. Something…*anything* so I don't have to come back to this classroom.

My eyes averted, I attempt to escape unnoticed when a familiar deep voice foils my plan.

"Miss Davenport."

I stop in my tracks, my shoulders tensing as I exhale a frustrated breath. I hate that he used such a formal tone. It's one he's used with me in the bedroom, but it was part of our game. This isn't a game.

In an effort to appear unaffected by this turn of events, I fix my expression and slowly face him, staring into green eyes that mere hours ago looked upon my naked body with an unmatched hunger. "Yes, Professor Moore?"

When I address him this way, he flinches. "I'd like a word."

"I have somewhere I need to be."

"I insist." He widens his stance, his gaze darkening. It's not quite a glare, but it's not a compassionate look, either. It's a new expression, one that tells me not to test him, that this isn't something we can avoid discussing. "Just a few moments of your time, then you can go on with your life."

His statement hits me hard. By the way his Adam's apple bobs up and down in a thick swallow, I get the feeling it was just as difficult for him to say as it was for me to hear.

On a deep inhale, I nod, trailing a few steps behind him as he leads me toward the faculty corridor. This entire scenario makes me feel like an errant teenager who acted out in class and is being handed off to my guidance counselor, who will press me to talk about my parents' divorce and how I'm "coping".

Except I'm an adult.

Who just found out she's been screwing the professor of the one class she needs to finally graduate this spring.

So much for proving to my father I'm not a complete fuck-up.

Once the door to the office closes behind us, allowing us to talk in private, he heads to the window, peering at the city surrounding us. I simply stare at him, unsure what to say. Then he glances over his shoulder.

"Did you know?" There's a hint of pain in his tone.

Aghast, my eyes widen. "What?"

"When you saw me in Vegas…" He fully faces me. "Did you know who I was and not say anything in the hopes of getting me in bed?"

"Of course not! Why would you think that?"

"How could I *not* think that, Chloe?" He runs his fingers through his hair, tugging at it. "This seems to be *too* much of a coincidence."

I cross my arms over my chest. "Yeah. Because I'd go through the trouble of starting to fall for a guy, only to have to walk away when I learn he's my goddamn professor!"

"I don't know. I—" He stops short, inhaling sharply. "What did you say?"

"That you're my professor…," I answer in a drawn-out voice.

"No." He shakes his head, licking his lips. "Before that." His tone becomes tranquil, expression softening.

I replay the words and stiffen at the truth that poured so freely from my mouth. His eyes plead with me, and I can't deny him this.

"That I wouldn't fall for a guy if I knew there was zero chance of survival."

"You were falling for me?" He steps toward me, his gaze raking over me, as if searching for something. What, I'm not sure.

"It doesn't matter anymore." I tear my eyes from his.

A part of me wants him to tell me we'll make it work. That the connection between us is too strong to throw away over something as trivial as this. But he doesn't, the compassionate Lincoln transforming back to the man he was the past three hours as he lectured the class.

"You're right. It doesn't matter anymore. It *can't* matter anymore."

He walks to his desk and pulls out a thin book, Policies and Procedures written on the front in bold letters. He flips to the table of contents before turning to the appropriate page, scanning it.

"Right." His tone is firm when he looks up. "According to the conduct code, as long as the previous relationship is disclosed, it's not a big deal."

I hug my jacket tighter around my body, my stomach queasy as I listen to Lincoln talk about me as if I'm just a problem in need of fixing, not a person he once cared for.

"I'll go to the dean and let him know, assuring him we ceased all contact once we learned the truth. I'll request a third party grade all your papers and exams, and I'll forego having class participation be a part of the final grade this semester in order to appear neutral."

I nod, still having difficulty coming to terms with this new reality. My eyes scan his desk, everything about it as neat and orderly as I imagined it would be. As I continue looking around, I spy a copy of the syllabus he probably handed out before I'd arrived. I pick it up, my throat tightening even more.

"And you're only going to disclose this to the dean, right? No one else?"

"Of course not," he insists, then corrects himself. "Well, there are ethical concerns, so to err on the side of caution, I'll be informing my boss at the newspaper where I work."

"You're an associate attorney at the *Times*," I state, reading his credentials listed at the top of the paper.

"Yes," he answers, ignoring the forlorn expression on my face. "My boss *is* friends with the dean and is actually the one who recommended me for the adjunct position here, so…"

Our eyes lock. "I can't let you do that. Can't let you tell either of them."

"I don't have a choice," he whisper-shouts, placing his hands on the desk and leaning toward me. "This is my career."

"That may be true, but your boss at the newspaper? David Jensen?"

Lincoln's expression blanches, seeming to sense I'm about to drop yet another bomb on him. Which I am.

"He's my father."

Chapter Seventeen

THE SURPRISE THAT covered Lincoln's expression when he turned around and realized I was one of his students is nothing compared to the utter and morose shock now plastered on his face. His jaw drops open, his eyes scanning me, probably for any hint of resemblance to the man who hired him…and could fire him.

"But your last name is Davenport." He shakes his head, brow furrowed, as if hoping the fact I don't share his last name will negate the DNA running through me.

"After he divorced my mother, I took her last name. I didn't want a reminder of that man attached to me for the rest of my life."

He exhales, pinching the bridge of his nose. "Chloe, I—"

I step toward him, folding my fingers together as I beg for him to keep this quiet. "Please, Lincoln. Maybe if it were just the dean, it wouldn't be so bad. There'd still be a chance he'd mention it to my father, since they're friends, but this… With my father being your boss? There's no way the dean *won't* tell him. And my father can*not* find out."

"It's not up to me! I *have* to report this. It's right here in black and white." He points to the book in front of him. "I'm obligated to report any prior relationship with a student to the dean."

"Who will tell my father since you work for him," I hiss back. "Please. I am *begging* you." Tears dot my eyes, my throat closing up.

"Why don't you want him to know?"

I wrap my arms around my stomach, warming myself against a sudden chill enveloping me. Do I feed him some line in the hopes he'll grant my request? Or do I tell him the truth, revealing another fragmented piece of myself?

"Help me understand." His voice softens, reminding me of the way he'd whisper sweet words in my ear as I drifted off to sleep in his arms. I want to curse the world for being so cruel. For giving me a taste of something I never thought possible, never thought I wanted, only to rip it away, dangling it in front of me like a memento of something I can never have again.

"You never could. You probably had the perfect life. The perfect fucking family who supported you through everything."

He parts his lips, but I hold up my hand.

"Well, I didn't. As you've figured out, my father's a bit of a hard-ass."

He snorts out a laugh, the tension momentarily cracking. "You can say that again."

"And he's always been that way." I draw in a deep breath, attempting to compose myself, swiping at the few tears that had managed to escape. "All my life, I've been nothing but a disappointment to him and his impossibly high standards. I get that all parents want their children to succeed. But nothing I did was ever good enough. Nothing I *do* is ever good enough."

I pull my lips between my teeth. "For once, I'm close to finishing something on my own." I lower my voice. "I'm close to finally being able to prove to my father I'm not just a massive disappointment."

"Chloe, I—"

"I know it makes no sense," I interrupt before he can utter a single word of sympathy for my fucked-up childhood and adolescence. "Why should I care what he thinks? I ask myself that same question constantly. A part of me doesn't care. But as you've learned, my father is extremely stubborn. And that stubbornness is genetic. So instead of writing him off like I should have years ago, I keep trying. Just to say I proved him wrong."

I meet Lincoln's eyes that are awash with compassion. Something about the way he gazes upon me makes me think he's dying to wrap me in his arms and comfort me. But he can't do that. Never again.

"If you report this and he learns I had a prior relationship with my professor, with one of his employees, he'll never let it go. He'll always think I only passed because I screwed my way to a passing grade. Just like he thinks the only reason I was promoted from receptionist to columnist at the magazine is because I was the only one willing to trade my body for tips on celebrity comings and goings. While there may be *some* truth to his opinion, it's not the only thing that's gotten me to where I am. If he finds out about this…" I shake my head, swallowing. "If you report this, he'll always see me as the naïve twenty-two-year-old girl who made a terrible decision and got herself in a bad situation just to prove she could do more than answer a phone."

He stares at me for what feels like an eternity, dozens of questions on the tip of his tongue after this admission, something I didn't think I'd ever share with him, or anybody. Finally, he blows out a long breath, his shoulders falling.

"I can't believe I'm about to do this, but okay." He brings his eyes back to mine. "We'll keep this between us."

All the tension rolls off my body, gratitude filling me. "Thank you."

His expression hardens, his jaw tightening, nostrils flaring. "But if I hear the faintest hint of whispers about us, it will leave me no choice. So do *not* speak a word about this to anyone. Do not say anything during class that would lead anyone to believe there has ever been anything between us."

The compassionate Lincoln is gone, serious and stern Lincoln taking his place. "For all intents and purposes, the relationship happened before you were my student anyway, and once we were aware of the situation, we ceased all contact. Neither one of us is taking advantage of the other, so if we keep it quiet, no one will ever know about it, considering I have no intention of continuing this relationship."

"Such a lawyer," I comment, his words stinging more than I thought they would. "Trying to get off on a technicality."

"Do you see any other option?" He pinches his lips together. "Need I remind you, I'm the one whose ass is on the line here. I'm doing this as a favor to you. I can go down the hall and report this right now. I *should* go down the hall and report this."

"No," I respond urgently, advancing toward him, desperate. "It's okay. You're right." I swallow hard as I straighten my spine. "There *is* no other option."

We stare at each other in silence for several moments. Then he nods. "So we're in agreement. We'll continue on with our lives as if this never happened. We'll forget about everything." His tone rises in pitch at the end, his words neither a question nor a statement.

I bite on my lower lip to prevent Lincoln from seeing how difficult this is.

"It's already forgotten."

CHAPTER EIGHTEEN

I BARREL INTO our normal happy hour meeting spot and make a beeline for the bar, plopping into the empty barstool to the right of Evie, Nora and Izzy sitting on the other side of her. While I'm thrilled Izzy was able to find time in her schedule to come out with us, seeing her only reminds me of Lincoln, considering she was present during the blackout that started it all.

Fuck Vegas.

And fuck whoever's responsible for that damn blackout.

Why couldn't Vegas have lost power and cell service one day later? Better yet, why couldn't our flight not have been canceled? Why did Lincoln have to steal my panties? And why did I have to go get them back?

I should know better. Hell, did I not learn anything from the story of Orpheus and Eurydice? He lost everything that was important to him because he looked back, a lesson to all to only look forward. Not only did I look back, but I made several return trips to the all-you-can-eat buffet. Now the hostess is telling me I've overstayed my welcome.

"Is everything okay?" Evie's brow wrinkles as her analytic eyes survey me.

"Fucking marvelous." I wave down Aiden, our handsome, yet very gay bartender. He begins pouring my usual martini. "Get me a shot of Jameson, too."

He peers at me quizzically, as do my three friends, particularly Izzy, who's more than aware of my reasons for not drinking much. I need it today, though.

"What's going on?" Izzy asks once I slam back the shot.

"Did something happen at class?" Nora chimes in.

"Did you get kicked out for being late?" Evie presses.

I draw in a deep breath, placing my palms against the cool wood of the bar. "No, I didn't get kicked out for being late. This is undergrad, Evie. Not the fucking Marines." I playfully roll my eyes, which elicits a laugh from Nora and Izzy. "But something *did* happen at school."

"What is it?" She leans toward me.

"I—"

She holds up her hand. "Wait. Are we talking 'need to take the edge off' kind of something? Or is it more like 'line 'em up and let's get wasted'?"

"It's more along the lines of 'I don't think there's enough bourbon in all of Kentucky to handle this'."

The girls look at each other, eyes widening, before zeroing in on me, sitting on the edge of their seats.

"Okay. Spill." Evie fishes the Maraschino cherry out of her manhattan and tugs it off the stem with her teeth.

I bring my own drink to my mouth, taking a sip of the smooth vodka. And of course, being a martini, it only serves as another reminder of Lincoln. I've known this man less than two weeks, yet I find pieces of him in every part of my life. Is that how it will always be? God, I hope not.

Exhaling, I place my glass back on the bar, squaring my shoulders to address my friends, their expressions akin to children meeting Santa for the first time.

"When I got to campus today, I was only about ten minutes late. No biggie. At least for me," I add when I see the absolute horror on Evie's face at my admission. "So I snuck into the classroom and grabbed a seat in the middle of the lecture hall." I bring my drink back to my mouth with a trembling hand, forcing a smile. But even a fake smile can't mask the hurt in my voice. "And that's when the professor turned around and I found out *who* would be teaching my First Amendment class."

"Oh god," Nora exhales. "It's your father, isn't it? Did you not check the schedule to see who it would be?"

I wave her off. "It wasn't my father. Thank fuck for that."

"Then who?" Izzy asks.

On a hard swallow, I allow his name to roll off my tongue. "None other than Lincoln Moore."

"Holy shit." Nora takes a big gulp of her drink, as if she were the one who'd walked into class and learned the guy she'd been sleeping with was her professor.

"Oh, my god," Evie exhales.

"Hold on a second," Izzy says, her mouth agape as she stares at me, knowing I wouldn't have told Evie and Nora about Lincoln if there weren't still something there. "You've been seeing Lincoln Moore and never said anything?"

"His name is just Lincoln," I respond, not wanting her to pick up on Nora's and Evie's habit of referring to Lincoln by his full name. "And you'd know about it if you stopped working long enough to meet me for coffee. I haven't seen or talked to you since Vegas, so I didn't exactly have a chance to tell you."

She waves me off. "Whatever. That's not important right now. What *is* important is what's been going on with you and Lincoln."

"Nothing now."

"Well, before."

I shrug. "We…reconnected."

"Reconnected how?"

I chew on my lower lip. "He kind of took my panties. And I kind of went to get them back."

"And what? You kind of slipped and fell on his dick?"

"It *is* an impressive dick."

It's silent for a moment. Then the girls' laughter carries through the bar, overpowering the chatter and music.

"Guys," I whine. "It's not funny. This is serious!"

"I know, I know," Nora says, tears forming in the corner of her eyes. "We're not laughing at the situation."

"Then—"

"You tripped and fell on his dick?" Evie giggles.

"Kind of. I mean, that guy has some serious game."

"What are you going to do?" Nora asks the question on everyone's mind.

I shrug. "Hope my advisor agrees to let me fulfill these credits with an independent study instead. This is the last class I need to graduate, but I don't want to sit in that room every Thursday for fifteen weeks or however long the semester is."

"I'm sure she'll agree," Evie assures me. "After you disclose your relationship to Lincoln, there's no way they'll let you stay."

"Right." I avert my eyes, taking another large gulp of my drink.

"What is it?" Izzy tilts her head.

I glance at her sideways, then blow out a breath. "We kind of agreed to keep it quiet."

"You *what*?" Evie shrieks, aghast.

"That's crazy," Nora adds.

"Not to mention a horrible idea," Izzy offers. "No matter what you may think, these kinds of things never stay quiet forever."

Briefly closing my eyes, I clench my fists. "I understand that, but there's no other option."

"Yes, there is," Nora pushes. "My replacement roommate after you dropped out made the mistake of hooking up with her TA. It went on her record. On *both* their records. And it affected him for years, all because they got drunk one night, messed around, and someone eventually found out about it."

"It's not optimal, but…" I release a heavy sigh. "It's not just the fact he's my professor. I knew he was a lawyer, but I assumed he worked at some high-power law firm."

"Is he some ambulance chaser instead?" Evie presses.

I bury my face in my hands, shaking my head. "No. Worse." When I finally lift my eyes and stare at my friends, the truth is plastered in my expression, at least enough for Izzy to put the pieces together. Who better to teach First Amendment Law than someone who practices it on a daily basis?

"He works for your father, doesn't he." It's more a statement than a question.

I slowly nod.

"And you're worried if Lincoln reports this it'll get back to your father."

"It's not a question of if. It *will* happen. My father and the dean golf together. Plus, Lincoln teaches at the university *because* of his experience as a lawyer for the newspaper. *Because* my father recommended him for the job. He was adamant about telling his boss...until he found out my relationship to his boss."

"And your father cannot know," Izzy says in understanding.

"Precisely."

"I don't follow." Evie scrunches her nose. Out of the three of them, she's known me the least amount of time, coming in at a point in my life when I'd already distanced myself from my father.

"We have a...difficult relationship."

"Difficult? How? He's your father."

I can understand how she'd be confused. She comes from the stereotypical family. Two loving parents. An older brother who adores her and most likely put the fear of God into all the boys she'd dated in her past. Hell, they probably even have a cookie-cutter house with a picket fence, à la *Leave it to Beaver*.

"He may be my father, but that always came second. Maybe even third or fourth on his list of priorities. His job always came first. Always. It still does."

While he did remarry soon after divorcing my mother, it's a strange marriage. I don't feel any love between him and Tiffany. No passion. No intense need to be with each other. I think my father simply wanted to have a woman on his arm during important functions. And Tiffany was more than happy to have a career as a housewife. It's not like it was with my mother, a woman who had strong aspirations of her own.

"He's always had impossibly high standards."

"So did my parents," Evie offers, still trying to understand this.

"Nothing I did was good enough. If I won the class spelling bee, he'd point out I failed to win the school-wide competition. If I won a fencing match, he'd comment how my opponents weren't well-trained. If I were cast as the lead in the school play, he'd mention all the flaws in my performance. All of this in the hopes of encouraging me to work harder."

"Did it?" Evie's voice is hesitant.

"At first, yes. I worked my tail off trying to make him happy. Then I discovered boys. And I mean *really* discovered boys. Do you know what I discovered about them?"

Evie and Nora shake their heads, transfixed. Izzy listens with polite attention, fully aware of this part of my life.

"That they were nothing like my father. That they didn't put me down after we kissed by telling me my technique could use some work. And I liked that feeling. Of course, my father hated the fact I became more focused on boys than school. Why should I care, though? No matter what I did, it wouldn't be good enough, so why try?" I take a sip of my drink, needing the liquid encouragement to share this piece of myself with my two friends. "Despite it all, there's still this part of me that wants to make him proud, to prove to him that I *am* good enough."

"And if he learns you slept with your professor…," Evie begins, putting the pieces together.

"He'll never think you earned this degree," Nora finishes.

"I know it sounds stupid, that it shouldn't matter."

"We all want to make our parents happy." With a smile, Evie places her hand over mine, squeezing. "Or we want to prove them wrong."

"And I'd love to prove my father wrong, make him see I'm not a failure."

"So if you're keeping it a secret," Nora begins after a brief pause, "will your advisor agree to an independent study?"

"All I can do is hope she does."

"If she doesn't? Do you think you'll be able to handle him teaching the class?" she asks in all seriousness. "I mean without picturing him naked every time he talks about briefs, or penal violations, or getting a client off."

I lift my eyes, staring at her for a protracted moment, then burst out laughing, grateful for the break in the tension. It's a relief, especially after the day I've had.

I fidget with the stem of my martini glass, a pang squeezing my heart as I watch a couple walk into the bar holding hands, an obvious affection between them.

"Actually, I *don't* think I'll be able to deal with it, so I'll just pray my advisor is on my side and allows me to do an independent study." I swallow thickly. "Then I can forget about Lincoln Moore."

CHAPTER NINETEEN

MY STOMACH ROILS as I look up at the journalism building on campus, the structure feeling more like an unwelcome fortress than a place of higher learning. A chill washes over me, having nothing to do with the frigid January temperature and everything to do with what awaits me inside those doors. The last thing I want to do is walk into this building and sit through class with Lincoln — *Professor Moore.* But I no longer have an option. Not if I want to graduate this semester.

Because I'd taken this class twice before with less than stellar results, thanks to problems with my mother, my advisor refused to sign off on an independent study. I'd considered withdrawing from the class altogether, but like Izzy reminded me, it's my last one. There's no guarantee someone different will teach it next semester, either, so I may as well get it over with.

Spine straight, I summon the determination to walk into the lobby, my steps quickening when I see the elevator doors begin to shut. Thankfully, someone notices me and places their hand on the door.

"Thank you," I say breathlessly as I sneak inside, keeping my head lowered.

"You're welcome."

As the doors close, my breath catches, every muscle becoming rigid. I fling my eyes to my left to see Lincoln standing there, all poised and confident.

It's official. The universe is out to get me. I wrack my brain to think of what I could have done to piss it off this much. I consider finding the nearest Catholic church, despite not being religious, just to go to confession. Then again, I doubt any priest would be prepared to listen to the number of sins I've committed. He'll probably say a plethora of Our Fathers and Hail Marys to cleanse my soul, too.

"Professor Moore." I stare ahead, pretending this isn't anything more than a teacher and student sharing an elevator. It's not the first time I've shared one with a professor of mine. But they weren't Lincoln.

"Chloe." When he says my name, it's soft, compassionate, endearing.

"Don't," I snap, refusing to so much as glance at him.

In the silence, I can sense his turmoil. Sense he wants to say something but doesn't know what. I doubt they teach this kind of thing in whatever law school he attended. Probably Harvard, just like my father. Another reason this is for the best. Lincoln would turn out just like him — in love with his career and nothing else. Better to cut my losses now.

"For the record," he states as the elevator slows to a stop on our floor, "I'm sorry things had to end this way."

The sincerity in his voice forces my eyes to his, and I look at him. Actually look at him. I'm not sure what I expected to see. Maybe the same demeanor I've come to expect from him — self-assured, bold, a hint of arrogance. But that's not what I see at all.

The way his sad eyes trace over my face with longing is all the proof I need that this has been as difficult for him as it has for me. The green is lackluster, the circles under his eyes evidencing lack of sleep. It could be due to having to pull extra hours at work, but the wistful expression as he focuses on my lips makes me think he's been tossing and turning at night, cursing fate, just like me.

The doors open, breaking our moment, and he scurries off. I watch his long strides as he continues down the hall, turning into the faculty wing just as I whisper, "Me, too."

Pulling myself together, I shake off the interaction and head toward the classroom. It's relatively empty when I arrive, a handful of ambitious students discussing the assigned reading.

I assume the same seat in the middle of the lecture hall and pull out the few notes I jotted down as I attempted to absorb this week's material. It turned out to be a lost cause. Whenever I tried, all I could think of was Lincoln. I fear I'll be faced with the same problem every time I open the textbook. I play Lincoln won't be cruel enough to call on me to discuss the reading. I can only hope he'll avoid bringing attention to me these first few weeks while we attempt to find a new normal in this strange dynamic.

"Is all this legal talk as much a foreign language to you as it is to me?" a smooth voice asks after several minutes.

I glance to my right as a man I estimate to be in his thirties sits down in the empty chair beside me. I thought I was one of the oldest students in the department, considering most everyone else isn't even able to legally drink yet. How did I not notice him last week? Oh, yeah. Because I was dealing with the fact that I'd been fucking my college professor. Another day in the life of Chloe Davenport.

I meet my fellow classmate's eyes. They're a dull combination of brown and green, completely uninspiring. "You have no idea."

"That's a relief." He pretends to swipe sweat from his brow, his smile comforting. "After the last class, I thought I was the only one who felt lost."

"I barely retained anything." It's not a complete lie. I couldn't tell him a single thing that was discussed last week.

"Right? I get that all this First Amendment stuff is important as a journalist, but can't they teach it to us in simpler terms?"

I smile politely. While I find it difficult to concentrate on the material because of *who* is teaching it, it is fascinating. I can understand why my father chose the path he did. Spending your time ensuring people's First Amendment rights aren't infringed unnecessarily is certainly admirable. Why couldn't he exhibit that kind of enthusiasm toward his family?

"I'm Owen," he says, extending his hand toward me.

I eye it before placing mine in it. "Chloe."

"Nice to meet you, Chloe." He keeps his grip firm on my hand, holding it a little longer than socially appropriate. When he finally lets go, my skin tingles with his phantom touch.

Part of me wants to feel something — desire, craving, lust. Owen *is* an attractive guy. Sandy hair with hints of copper. Deep-set eyes. Full lips. Clean-shaven jawline. I estimate he's about six feet tall, and based on the muscled forearms I see, the sleeves of his white shirt rolled up, I assume he has a nice physique.

Regardless, my body has no reaction to him. Almost like my ten days with Lincoln have now ruined me for any man who's to come after him.

"You, too," I say, although it's more of a polite formality than a truthful statement.

"So, what's your story?" he asks as I turn my attention back to my notes.

"What do you mean?"

"The usual. What do you do for a living? Why are you studying journalism? What's your favorite sexual position?"

I dart my wide eyes to his, unsure how to respond to this inquiry.

"You know. Those usual ice-breaker questions people don't give two shits about but ask each other in an attempt to make inane conversation." He winks, his smile growing wide.

I don't know what it is, but something about his cavalier attitude is refreshing. He *does* have a point.

"Well, since you're not going to pay attention anyway," I begin with a grin, "I work at a magazine as a celebrity news columnist. Started as a receptionist just trying to make a living wage and worked my way into the newsroom. So I guess that's why I'm studying it. I've got a foot in the door of an industry that's notoriously exclusive. I figure having a degree will only help me move on to something bigger and better."

"You mean you *don't* enjoy reporting on what celebrities had for lunch or whether they're good tippers?" He looks at me aghast, a playfulness about him.

I chuckle, tension rolling off me. Maybe having a friend in this class is exactly what I need. If nothing else, Owen makes me laugh, something I haven't done in days.

"Shocking, I know. So, how about you?"

"Oh, I'm not too complicated. I tend to follow my partner's lead."

I furrow my brow.

"Favorite sexual position," he clarifies, his tone light. "Whatever my girl wants, my girl gets."

I stare at him, assessing. If some random guy at a bar said that to me within seconds of learning my name, I'd write him off. But something about Owen's good-natured demeanor makes it more than clear he's using humor to break the ice. So, instead of being turned off by his statement and doing everything to avoid him in the future, I laugh, the sound carrying through the room, echoing against the walls. I don't even care that I'm drawing attention to myself.

Until a loud, booming voice cuts through.

"Miss Davenport!"

I fling my gaze to the front, seeing Lincoln standing there, his arms crossed, stance wide, expression severe.

"If you don't mind, I've called class to order. Or is your conversation more important than the First Amendment?"

I blink, my heart caught in my throat. I consider arguing that I was exercising my own First Amendment right, but decide against it. "Of course not. I apologize."

Several protracted moments pass as he stares at me, making me feel small and insignificant. Then he flits his glare to Owen, his jaw clenching as he does so. To anyone else, his actions wouldn't be seen as anything other than a silent warning to him, as well. But I know Lincoln. There's jealousy in those green eyes.

Finally, he breaks his attention from us and turns toward the whiteboard.

Owen leans close, whispering, "I'm sorry."

I nod, but remain silent, not wanting to draw any more attention to myself.

"And for what it's worth...," Owen adds. I glance at him as he passes me an encouraging look. "You have a beautiful laugh."

I smile. It doesn't reach my eyes, but it's something. "Thanks."

"You bet." He winks, and I feel the tiniest flutter in my chest.

If nothing else, Owen could serve as a very welcome distraction. Maybe this class won't be so bad after all.

CHAPTER TWENTY

"GOD, I HATE the suburbs," I exhale as the Uber driver comes to a stop in front of a well-maintained three-story house in an upper middle-class neighborhood in Greenwich. A thick layer of snow covers the front lawn, making the property look even more picturesque. Even more perfect. Even more idealistic. The quintessential place to raise a family.

I should know. It was once my home.

Until my father realized he didn't get it quite right the first time around and started over again from scratch. New wife. New kids. Kept the house. At least he got *that* right.

Prick.

You'd think Tiffany, my father's new wife, would have wanted to move, start their lives in a new house where they could make memories of their own. That didn't seem to matter to her. I wouldn't be surprised to learn she'd insisted he keep the house just to be able to gloat that she took my mother's place.

"You're doing this for Midge," Izzy reminds me.

I float my eyes to her and nod.

Midge, my half-sister, is the youngest of the four children Tiffany pushed out after marrying my father fifteen years ago. The first one appeared less than nine months after my parents separated, so it didn't take a genius to solve that little mystery. But one kid wasn't enough. So they kept having them. I thought they were trying to form their own basketball team. It seemed like every time I saw them, Tiffany was pregnant. In the end, she simply wanted a girl.

It must drive her crazy that the girl she so desperately wanted looks up to me. It's a mystery how the little pipsqueak formed an attachment to me, but when I show up for holidays and parties, she shoves everyone aside, clinging to me as if *I* pushed her out of my hoo-ha. It's probably the only reason I was invited today. Probably the only reason I'm ever invited.

"But if it'll help, we can make a pit stop at my parents' house and sneak some of the liquor bottles my mother stole from the airline." She waggles her brows.

"Iz, didn't she quit the airline, like, ten years ago?"

"Fifteen, but last I checked, she still has those mini bottles."

A horrified expression crosses my face at the idea of drinking anything that's been sitting in a plastic bottle that long. "Gross." I try not to gag. "That stuff wasn't good when it was fresh. Can you imagine how disgusting it would taste now? Not to mention…" I gesture toward the house. "My father has a *very* well-stocked bar." I slide out of the back seat of the Uber and step onto the street, meeting Izzy as we walk up the driveway together, the March air crisp on my cheeks. "Sharing his DNA has its benefits, like being able to steal some of the thirty-year-old scotch he keeps hidden away for special occasions."

"And you just so happen to know his hiding spot?"

I pass her a mischievous look as we approach the front porch, the sounds of children laughing and screaming filtering out, as I suspected it would. "His youngest daughter's sixth birthday should be a reason to celebrate. Don't you think?"

"I suppose you're right." About to open the door, she pauses, looking to me, silently asking if I'm ready.

I nod, steeling myself. At least Izzy agreed to come with me, since she knows how uneasy being in this house makes me. She was there when I learned my parents were separating. When I packed up my room. When I got into my mother's car and left this neighborhood behind. Regardless of the months that would sometimes pass without speaking to each other, our connection has remained strong. She'll always put her life on hold to help me out, especially when it involves my father.

We walk into the house, my eyes immediately going to a series of framed photos on the entryway table showcasing my father and his new family. I can't remember ever seeing a photo of my parents and me. Sure, there are photos of my mother and me, as well as some of my father and me. But I don't think there's anything in existence of the three of us, like we never were a family.

"Chloe!" an excited voice calls out, followed by two small arms flinging around my mid-section, squeezing me tightly. "I was worried you weren't going to make it!"

I briefly close my eyes, relishing in Midge's unbiased love. Regardless of her mother's feelings toward me, it hasn't rubbed off on her. I wish she could stay this innocent the rest of her life. It's only a matter of time until she picks up on her mother's animosity. After all, we're not born programmed to hate. We're taught that. And I know her mother will eventually teach her to despise me, even if she doesn't do it deliberately. All I can do is savor the fact that Midge hasn't learned to hate me yet.

"I wouldn't miss this party for anything. It's not every day my favorite sister turns six." I tousle her perfect blonde curls as she releases her hold, looking up at me.

"I'm your *only* sister."

"But you'd still be my favorite," I sing.

"Midge, sweetie," a high-pitched voice calls out, the sound of heels clicking against the hardwood growing closer. "Where did you—"

Tiffany stops in her tracks when she sees Izzy and me in the foyer. Her dyed blonde hair doesn't have a single strand out of place. I imagine she went to the salon early this morning to have it styled and her makeup applied so she'd look impeccable in the presence of all the other house vultures she invited.

"Oh... Chloe. You made it."

She leans in, pretending to kiss both my cheeks before pulling back. It must kill her to have to be nice to me because of Midge.

"Unfortunately, you missed all the cake and presents. Perhaps we should start telling you to be here an hour earlier so you'll show up on time."

For Midge's sake, I bite my tongue at her passive-aggressive statement. "I'd figure it out, then show up two hours after you said it started." I look down at Midge, handing her the gift bag. "Happy birthday, pipsqueak."

Tiffany huffs, crossing her arms in front of her chest. She's made it more than clear she doesn't believe in pet names for her children. But I do.

"Is this for me?"

"Of course it is, silly."

"Can I open it?"

"Absolutely."

With pure joy in her eyes, Midge plops onto the floor and tears at all the tissue packed inside the bag. She shrieks as she pulls out her gift. I steal a glimpse at Tiffany, who feigns enthusiasm. I saw the wish list she put together for Midge's birthday. Books about important figures in history. Educational toys. Computer programs to help her learn a foreign language. Nothing any young girl would be remotely excited about.

At Christmas, Midge had asked me if her parents were actually Santa, since he seemed to get her the same kinds of toys they did, while other kids at school received fun things to play with. So, I asked what she really wanted, then knew exactly what I'd be getting her for her birthday.

"You got me an American Girl doll?" She jumps to her feet and squeezes her arms around me as I crouch down to her level.

"You deserve it, pipsqueak. One of these days, I'll take you into the city so you can go to the American Girl store yourself. You can bring your doll, pick out some clothes for her. We can even take her to lunch there."

She squeals even more, hugging me again. This makes it all worth it, being able to give her something she really wants. Giving her one moment of happiness.

"Yes, well, we'll have to see about that," Tiffany snips, head held high. "Chloe does have a very busy schedule."

"But I'm never too busy for you," I tell Midge directly. "Okay?"

"Okay." She beams, looking from me to her doll. I sense she's itching to show off her new toy to her friends.

"Go play."

"There are a bunch of accessories and other things to use with your doll in here," Izzy offers, handing Midge a second gift bag.

Midge's gray eyes light up again and she wraps her arms around Izzy. "Thanks, Auntie Izzy."

"You bet. Now go."

Grinning, she spins, hurrying into the living room, excited shrieks coming from all the girls.

Able to feel the heat of Tiffany's glare on me, I shift my eyes to hers. "I thought we were clear that only gifts on the pre-approved list were to be purchased for Midge."

"Oh, you were clear. But as I'm sure you've learned, I don't exactly like rules." I return Tiffany's condescending smile, then spin from her.

The instant I enter the living room, all conversation ceases among the house vultures, as I've affectionately referred to them for years. I've never quite understood this group of women. They're all in their forties. All happy not to have a career, to be completely dependent on their husbands to provide for them. Granted, each is married to someone who does well for himself, all of them having married a man in their fifties or sixties, but I'd never want to be known as "Adam's wife" or "Joe's wife" or "Nathan's wife". No identity. So handmaid-ish.

Perhaps that was why my father wasn't happy with my mother. She was ambitious. Didn't want to sit at home and raise children. She wanted to show me that women could be just as successful as men. And she did, as much as she could when forced to sacrifice her own career to take care of me as a child.

"Chloe," one of the house vultures says, smiling and pretending they hadn't spent the past several minutes talking about me.

If I remember correctly, her name's Stephani-with-an-i, as she introduced herself to me when we met a few years ago. Not sure why it mattered, but apparently, that unique spelling was important enough that she was no longer Stephani, but Stephani-with-an-i.

"So glad you could finally make it. We were beginning to worry."

I meet her fake smile and raise her a fabricated grin. "The trains out of the city were behind schedule."

Izzy and I move toward a few vacant chairs, and I take a minute to absorb my surroundings, the place barely recognizable as the home I remember from my youth. The furniture and window treatments are so over-the-top, probably meant to be a display of wealth but missed the mark and are downright gaudy.

"I don't know how you can stand living there," another one of the women offers, dressed almost identical to Tiffany and Stephani-with-an-i.

I wonder if there's an unspoken rule that every housewife in Greenwich must adhere to the same uniform. Hair just past their shoulders, preferably blonde, with perfect beach waves. Skin bronzed year-round, despite the fact it's only March and not yet beach weather. Pastel-colored sheath dresses showing off the figures they pay personal trainers thousands of dollars to help them achieve. I must stand out with my skinny jeans, oversized cardigan, and knee-high boots, not to mention my gray and lilac ombre hair.

"I know," Denise, another one of the house vultures, adds. "It's so big. And noisy. And chaotic. Not a place I'd ever be proud to live in."

"Well, I could never live in the suburbs," Izzy states in my defense, as she's prone to do whenever I leave Manhattan and come out to this place that often feels like a foreign country after living in the city so long. The fresh air, chirping birds, and large expanses of open space make me uneasy. I much prefer concrete, tall buildings, and a barrage of honking horns.

Denise looks at her with a wavering smile, then shrugs, sipping on her Champagne, oblivious to the children running around the house.

Izzy leans toward me. "Drink?"

"The stronger, the better." I'm usually not one to drink during the day, but there are exceptions to that rule. And today is an exception.

"You got it." She squeezes my side, then heads toward the kitchen.

"So, Chloe," Stephani-with-an-i says. I look in her direction. "The barista at the Starbucks by the elementary school recently colored her hair similar to yours. What's her name?" She scrunches her brows, glancing at a few of the other women.

"Lottie," one offers.

"No. I think it's something like Lauren."

"No," another woman says. "It's something strange. Like a stripper name. Lola maybe?"

"Possibly." Stephani-with-an-i still doesn't look convinced. "Or is it…" She pulls her bottom lip between her teeth. "Not Lola. Poppy!" She tilts her head and looks at me as all the women nod in agreement. "Do you know her?"

"I don't live here," I remind her. "So I haven't had the pleasure of having suburban Starbucks."

"Oh, I know you don't live here. I figured since your hair…"

I blink repeatedly, trying to mask my utter shock at the stupidity spewing from Stephani-with-an-i's mouth. This conversation further proves we need to put more money into our educational system and encourage women to have a career, instead of aspiring to be a trophy wife.

"So, since our hair is similar, you figure we…know each other?"

She peers at me like it's not a ridiculous idea. "You don't?"

I have to bite back my laughter, desperate for Izzy to return with that drink. "Simply because we have similar attributes doesn't mean we're BFFs. I doubt you're BFFs with every woman who's had a shitty blonde dye job." I pause, smiling as I glance around the room at the sea of blonde. "Actually, I stand corrected. It appears you are."

Her expression falls, her nose turning up in disgust. "Well, you don't have to be nasty about it. I was only trying to make conversation. Apparently, your mother never taught you manners."

"She was too busy teaching me common sense."

"Here you are," Izzy says breathlessly as she flies into the room, handing me a glass. She meets my eyes, her expression a look of warning to play nice for Midge's sake.

With a smile, I take it from her. "Saved by the martini," I mumble under my breath.

If nothing else, being here does have a certain entertainment value. Whenever I attend one of Tiffany's parties, I often feel like a prostitute who just walked into church.

And not one of those "we accept everyone regardless of your sexual orientation, past failings, and current drug habits" kind of churches. More like those judgmental, holier than thou churches that quote the Bible when it suits them but refuse to practice any kind of forgiveness, humility, or charity.

Hypocrites.

"As always," Izzy sings.

"Is Hannah coming?" Stephani-with-an-i inquires in an attempt to recover from her earlier blunder.

"I believe she's still on her honeymoon," Tiffany pipes up. "And her parents are decompressing in Fiji now that the wedding's over. A gift from Hannah and her husband."

All the women *ooh* and *aah* over their generosity.

"It was a beautiful wedding," Denise comments.

"Just perfect," Theresa adds. "And her husband will be able to provide such a wonderful life for her. She's so lucky to have found a man so successful. She'll be able to quit her job and focus on raising their children."

I snort-laugh as I bring my drink back to my mouth, taking a long sip to cover my reaction.

"Something funny?" Tiffany asks in a pleasant voice, a smile plastered on her face as she exudes all the manners she was taught during the years of etiquette lessons her upper-class family insisted she attend.

"The idea of Hannah staying home and raising children."

While she *did* marry a very successful man and the wedding a few weeks ago *was* gorgeous, Hannah's not the kind of woman who would be happy adhering to such a societal role. Whenever she comes to one of Tiffany's parties, mostly as moral support for me, she rolls her eyes at the ridiculousness of these women. How they have no drive to have a life of their own. To have an identity of their own. Plus, for as long as I can remember, Hannah has wanted to be a teacher. I don't see her giving up that career anytime soon. Or ever.

"Who else will raise her children when she has them?" Carrie asks.

"She gets summers off."

"Yes. But what about the rest of the year?"

"Gosh, that *is* a problem, isn't it?" I scrunch up my brow, pretending to be deep in thought, as if this predicament is one no one has considered before. Then my expression brightens. "Actually, I read about this new concept that's been around for…oh, probably only forty or fifty years. What is it called?"

I glance at the ceiling, pinching my lips together. Izzy stifles a laugh, the only one amused, since I can feel the daggers the rest of the women are shooting at me. "That's right." I snap my fingers and return my gaze to them. "Daycare. Hannah can put her spawn in daycare. That's assuming she even *wants* to have children."

"Why would you get married if you didn't want to have children?" Stephani-with-an-i asks.

"I don't know. Maybe because you're in love and want to commit your life to each other." I take a sip of my drink, many of them still looking at me like I'm crazy, so I go in for the kill. "Plus, Hannah mentioned wanting to adopt. She works with a lot of kids in the foster care system. Some of them get moved around so much that their education suffers. It's a noble thing."

"That is true," Tiffany says, always trying to be diplomatic. "But aren't a lot of kids in foster care…" She trails off, wanting us to fill in the blank so she doesn't have to say it. But I'm not going to let her off so easily. She's always been prejudiced against anyone who isn't white and what she considers perfect.

"What?" I press.

"They're… You know."

"I don't think I do." I smirk. "Perhaps you should embellish so there's no misunderstanding."

"Just say it," Izzy interjects harshly, her dark eyes growing even darker.

She has very strong opinions on this subject. After all, she *is* Hispanic. And adopted. But it seems they all forget that because, as Tiffany puts it, she doesn't "act" Hispanic, whatever that means.

"They're something other than white," Izzy states firmly when she remains silent.

Tiffany's eyelids flutter as she holds her head high, placing her hands in her lap. She steals a glance at the children. I wonder if any of these sheltered kids have ever seen a person of color.

"Well, yes. Wouldn't she want her child to look like her? What will people think when they see their mismatched family?"

I've always found it odd that as staunch of a defender of the First Amendment as my father is, often filing suits against our own government when they try to suppress the media, he married someone as closed-minded as Tiffany. Then again, I'm not sure my father's ever loved her. I'm not sure he's capable of loving anything other than his career. And I doubt Tiffany's capable of loving anything except a large bank account.

"Oh, I don't know," Izzy mocks. "Maybe that Hannah has a heart of gold. So much so that she'd jump through hoops to take in a child who isn't her own and love him or her like they were. Do you have any idea how difficult it is to adopt?"

All the women stare at her in silence.

"It's damn near impossible. Most people give up after so many years because they can't take the constant roller-coaster ride anymore. I would never prejudge a family because they don't fit into some mold. It's the twenty-first century, for crying out loud. I see all walks of life come through the doors of the pediatric oncology wing at the hospital. And yes, some of those kids are adopted. It's heartbreaking to watch those parents struggle to find their child's birth parents to have any hope for a bone marrow transplant. But you know the one thing that's universal. The only thing that matters in any family?"

The room becomes eerily still, her voice seeming to reverberate against the walls. Izzy darts her eyes to the kids who've stopped playing and are focused on her. She briefly pulls her lips between her teeth as she regains her composure.

"Love. Regardless of whether you're related by blood, *love* is all that matters. *Love* makes a family."

I reach for Izzy's hand, squeezing it, offering her a comforting smile.

"Like how I love Chloe, even if she's only my *half*-sister," Midge's voice breaks through the awkward silence.

"Exactly." Izzy smiles at her. "And you don't only love her because you're related, right?"

"No. I love her because she wears cool clothes, has awesome shoes…" She grins, lowering her voice to a dramatic whisper. "And she swears a lot."

A few women snicker, but quickly cover their mouths when Tiffany shoots a glare their way. In my defense, I've made a conscious effort to curtail it when I'm around Midge. I've yet to drop an F-bomb. I think.

"Just like Daddy," she finishes. "So they probably *are* related. Where else would Chloe have learned to swear if she didn't learn it from Daddy?

That's where *I* learned."

I glance at Tiffany over my martini glass to gauge her reaction, an odd sense of satisfaction filling me at the sight of her squirming. After the number of kids she's had, she should know you can't say anything in front of them. At least nothing you want kept private.

"The apple certainly doesn't fall far from the tree," she says in a saccharine voice, neither confirming nor denying Midge's statement. "Speaking of which, how's school going?" She smirks at me, probably expecting to hear I've withdrawn from yet another class because outside obligations interfered with my coursework.

"It's been an…interesting semester." I glance at Izzy and we share a knowing look. "But I'm happy to report it will be my last. I filed my graduation paperwork a few days ago."

I leave out the part about nearly dropping the class earlier in the semester. But as I'd hoped, Owen has made my situation increasingly tolerable. There's still a bit of awkwardness anytime my eyes meet Lincoln's, but it's not as thick as it was in the beginning.

"Is that right?" a deep, booming voice cuts through.

I whip my head toward the foyer to see my father standing there, much to my surprise, considering I'd assumed he was working today, as he always is.

But his presence here isn't what has my heart ricocheting to my throat, all the air sucked from my lungs.

It's *who* stands beside him that makes me feel like the walls are closing in, suffocating me.

Izzy nudges me, silently reminding me to pretend like it's a normal occurrence for Lincoln Moore to be in my childhood home. Based on the familiar greetings from many of the house vultures, it might be. Many of them fawn over him, batting their lashes, sticking their chests out a little. But he doesn't notice them.

Just like that night at the club in Vegas, just like when he sent that martini over, just like when he nearly kissed me in the lobby of the casino, he looks at me as if I'm the only person who matters. Or maybe he's just as surprised to see me here as I am to see him.

"Let me get you another drink," Izzy murmurs, forcing my attention back to her.

I nod, swallowing the rest of my martini in one gulp before handing her the glass. I meet my father's expectant stare beckoning me toward him, probably so he can demean me in front of his employee in a show of superiority.

On a long exhale, I raise myself from the chair and walk across the living room, skirting discarded shards of wrapping paper and boxes filled with clothes.

"Hey, Dad." I float my eyes from his, looking at Lincoln. "Professor Moore."

"Miss Davenport."

"So I take it you're giving your First Amendment class yet another try?" My father lifts a single brow. He's always had a distinguished look to him. Tall and lean. Salt-and-pepper hair. Clean-shaven, apart from the times he's working on a big case and foregoes normal grooming to pull all-nighters. Smartly dressed, even when he keeps it casual with a blazer and jeans, like today.

"I *do* need it to graduate." I fold my arms in front of my chest, casually leaning against the wall, trying to appear unaffected when, in reality, my heart thunders against the walls of my chest, threatening to burst through.

"I won't pop the Champagne bottle just yet. It's your fourth time taking this class, isn't it?"

"Third." I grit a smile. "There were extenuating circumstances preventing me from completing the course the previous two times."

"There are *always* extenuating circumstances with you. It's your *tenth* year, isn't it? In my experience, people who've been going to college as long as you would be graduating with their doctorate, not merely a bachelors." He laughs jovially, as if his humor rivals that of a comedian.

That's how it's always been. He makes snide comments about everything I've done that fails to live up to his expectations, shrouding them in humor. But he means every biting comment, even if made in a light tone. If making passive-aggressive remarks were an Olympic sport, he'd be more decorated than Michael Phelps.

I clench my teeth, my jaw tensing. Yet I still smile. It's my last line of defense to act as if I don't care what my father thinks. That his statements have no effect on me.

"What can I say? I've never been one to stick to the rules."

"Rules are there for a reason, which I'm sure you're learning from Lincoln… Professor Moore here," he corrects quickly.

I look at Lincoln, a hint of sympathy in his gaze as he witnesses this strange dynamic, observing the exact reason I begged him to keep our past a secret.

"He's only thirty-five, yet he's accomplished so much. Graduated at the top of his class at Tufts, then went onto Yale Law. Worked for an advocacy group in the city before I stole him away. He's one of the top constitutional scholars in the country, a remarkable feat for someone so young. And you know why he's already achieved everything he has?"

"Because he's a white man?" I quip, partly joking, partly serious.

He rolls his eyes. It's something my protest-happy, political strategist mother would say.

"Because he knows about dedication. About having a strong work ethic.

About putting in the time and effort to achieve goals, even if the path might be hard."

I inhale a deep breath through my nose, my lips pinching together as I do everything to maintain my composure and not completely lose it.

"Actually, Chloe is a wonderful student. The faculty speaks very highly of her, particularly her advisor, Lara Stone."

I whip my eyes to Lincoln.

"Lara Stone isn't exactly a pioneer of hard-hitting journalism," my father scoffs. "But I suppose I can understand why she'd say that, considering she ended her career at a daytime talk show. That kind of thing is right up Chloe's alley, not real journalism. Simply reporting on celebrity gossip. No wonder they get along so well."

"We all have to start somewhere." Lincoln's tone is polite, despite my father's clear displeasure over the idea of anyone standing up for me. "At least she's working in the industry and learning how a magazine runs."

He gives me a reassuring smile before looking back at my father. A part of me wants to stop this, to tell Lincoln I don't need him to stand up for me. I stopped standing up for myself in this man's presence ages ago. But that's at odds with this small part that wants him to keep going. To hear the kindness and compassion in his tone.

"Not everyone is fortunate enough to land a desk at the *Times* right out of undergrad," he continues, referring to my father's dumb luck. "But Chloe's been in my class for six weeks now. In those six weeks, she's demonstrated an incredible understanding of the First Amendment that would rival that of any law student. In fact…" He glimpses at me. "She'd make one hell of a lawyer."

My father peers at him with curiosity. Can he sense there's a history between us? Don't fathers have this kind of sixth sense about men who've been intimate with their daughters?

"Chloe in law school?" He bursts out laughing, the gritting sound making the hair on my nape stand on end. "That's rich. It took her ten years to finish her bachelors. Could you imagine how long it would take her to graduate law school?" He wipes at his eyes. "Come on. Let's get to work."

Jovially slapping Lincoln on the back, he forces him away from me. He probably thinks the longer he stays in my presence, the greater the chance of my inferiority rubbing off on the man who's obviously his star attorney. I remain frozen in place, summoning all my strength to pretend my father's comments have no bearing on me.

As they're about to disappear into my father's office, Lincoln glances over his shoulder, his eyes locking with mine. Then he mouths, *I'm sorry*.

That could have so many meanings. Is he sorry for what my father said? For not standing up for me more? Or is he sorry for us?

CHAPTER TWENTY-ONE

I MAKE A BEELINE for Izzy, ignoring the curious eyes from the house vultures, and snatch the martini from her. Shakily raising it to my lips, I gulp down a large swallow, the liquor burning my throat.

"Come on." She loops her arm through mine, pulling me out of the room. "Let's see what kind of food's left over. I saw a few of my mother's famous tamales." Her voice is bright, a stark contrast to the warring emotions filling me at not only seeing Lincoln unexpectedly but hearing him stand up for me.

Izzy doesn't release her hold on me until we're out of earshot and in the large eat-in kitchen. At least she didn't lie about her mother's tamales. As expected, they were barely touched, most likely because it's "ethnic food", as I'm sure Tiffany referred to it. At this point, Izzy's mother probably sends it to piss her off, considering my father loves her tamales.

I grab a plate and pile on one pork and one chicken tamale, peeling back the corn husk before slicing into it. Once I've taken a bite, I look at Izzy, my muscles relaxing. We stare at each other for a few seconds before simultaneously breaking out in laughter at the ridiculousness of the situation.

"The only thing that would make this even more awkward is if Asher shows up." I shove another heaping forkful of "ethnic food" into my mouth, moaning at how delicious it is.

"Considering I haven't spoken to him since we left Vegas, there's a greater chance of this house being struck by lightning." She grabs a plate, assessing the options, settling on a few tamales, as well. "What are the chances Lincoln would be here?"

"He *does* work for my father. I guarantee Dad tried to go into the office today, but Tiffany undoubtedly threw a fit of epic proportion. So work coming to him was probably the compromise."

"What did your father say?" She leans closer, her voice barely audible. "Did he pick up on anything?"

"No. As usual, our conversation revolved around the fact I'm a complete failure who doesn't follow through on anything. All jokingly of course."

She rolls her eyes. "God, I hate that. I don't know why you put up with it. If it were anyone else, you'd give them a piece of your mind, then knee them in the junk to make them think twice about speaking that way to anyone else again."

Shrugging dismissively, I glance at the refrigerator, the surface devoid of anything personal. No birth announcements. None of Midge's artwork. Not even her latest spelling test because it wasn't good enough, even though she'd received a high mark.

"I've learned to pick and choose my battles. It's like he *wants* to piss me off. *Wants* me to lose my temper with him. Why give him the satisfaction? It's best to suck it up for the ten minutes a year we actually *do* speak to each other, then go back to my normal life he no longer has any say over."

It's silent for a moment as she assesses my statement. "And what did Lincoln have to say?"

My cheeks warm as his deep voice complimenting me echoes in my mind. I smooth a strand of hair behind my ear. "He told my father I was one of the smartest students he's ever had. That my understanding of the material would rival that of a law student. Of course, my father nearly dropped dead from a heart attack at the suggestion of me going to law school."

"So Lincoln stood up for you."

"I suppose," I answer nonchalantly.

"That's sweet."

I shoot my eyes to hers. "What? No, it's not. It's demeaning and chauvinistic. I don't need Lincoln to protect me from my asshole father. I've done just fine handling him for the past almost twenty-nine years of my life. And I'll do just fine the next twenty-nine years." I shove more tamale into my mouth, barely chewing before swallowing and inhaling deeply, using the food as a distraction from the conversation.

"He could have simply said you were doing well in class. He didn't have to go the extra mile and say you're exceptional, yet he did." She narrows her eyes, pinching her lips together. "I think he's struggling with this as much as you are."

"What?" I practically choke on my food. "I'm not struggling with this."

Izzy bursts out laughing. "Nice try, Chloe. You wouldn't be eating your emotions right now if you didn't still have feelings for him."

I pause with my mouth wide open, about to shovel in even more food. "I'm not eating my emotions." I put down the fork, pushing the plate away. "I'm just hungry."

"Whatever you say."

"Like I said, we've agreed to pretend that Vegas never happened, or the few days that followed. It's for the best."

"Do you really believe that?"

"Of course I do!" I retort loudly before lowering my voice. "Even if I didn't, it doesn't matter," I remind her.

"I get that. I just…" She trails off, blowing out a long breath.

"Do you remember what you said while we waited for our flight out of Vegas before it was canceled? When I told you about the man I kept running into whose name I didn't even know?"

She subtly nods. "That maybe there was a reason you kept running into each other."

"The same can be said here. Maybe this is the universe's way of telling me it would have never worked out anyway. That we really *are* too different to be compatible. You should see the man's apartment! There wasn't a speck of dust anywhere. And his closet?"

Izzy smirks, crossing her arms in front of her chest, clearly amused. "Yes?"

"The clothes were actually hung up. On hangers."

"What?" she shoots back in faux shock, bringing her hands to her cheeks. "You mean they weren't thrown all over the bed and floor? This isn't right. It must be some sort of witchcraft."

"You know what I mean," I whine.

Her joking expression lightens, and she looks upon me affectionately, placing a hand on my bicep. "I don't know Lincoln all that well, but there's something to be said about playing Never Have I Ever with complete strangers. You learn things. I don't think you two are as opposite as you believe."

Footsteps sound from the hallway, and I snap my head up, expecting Tiffany to come in and berate me for being antisocial by hiding away in the kitchen and stuffing my face with food.

Instead, Lincoln rounds the corner, coming to an abrupt stop when he sees Izzy and me. He hesitates, forehead wrinkling as he seems to weigh his options.

"Lincoln," Izzy greets, breaking through the silence. "What a surprise to see you, and here, of all places."

I pinch her side, an unspoken warning.

He pulls his lips between his teeth, and I sense him mulling over his words. Then he recovers his composure, posture straight, eyes distant.

"David said there's coffee?"

Pushing away from the counter, she passes him a sly smile. "Chloe can show you while I use the little girl's room."

I dart my wide gaze toward her. But even with the death stare I give her, she doesn't change course, floating out of the kitchen without a single look back as she sings, "Good to see you again, Lincoln."

He remains silent, not acknowledging her. Once we're alone, he brings his eyes back to mine. But I can't bear to look into their depths, spinning from him, my purposeful strides taking me toward the coffee bar in the corner of the kitchen.

"I can do it."

"It's fine," I practically bark out, grabbing a pod and placing it into the one-cup brewer. I groan, realizing someone turned it off so now it needs to warm up and heat the water, drawing out Lincoln's presence even longer. I press the power button, staring at the machine as it hums to life.

"I'm sorry about what your father said before," he offers after several moments of strained silence.

"Don't." I whirl around, my hardened stare cautioning.

"I just—" He steps toward me, but I hold up my hand, preventing him from coming any closer.

"I don't need your help," I seethe, my nostrils flaring. "I've been dealing with that man fine my entire life. Got it?"

He stares at me for several intense moments, then nods, his shoulders falling. "Got it."

"Good." I spin around, staring at the screen on the brewer, willing it to stop preheating.

"Has he always been that way?" he asks after a pregnant pause.

I shrug.

"You mentioned he's why you didn't want…" He trails off. "I guess a part of me thought you were over-exaggerating. I didn't realize how…"

"What?" I face him once more. "How much of an asshole your boss is?"

He shoves his hands into his pockets. "I knew he was a hard-ass. He has a reputation for being one, but that's what makes him a great lawyer. He doesn't stop pushing, even when facing adversity. But…"

"You assumed he'd leave the job at the office?"

He brings his bottom lip between his teeth. I look away, the memory of how those lips felt against mine only making this more difficult. It's one thing to have to watch him during class, but at least there's distance between us. Now that distance seems to evaporate with every beat of my heart.

"Yes, I did." He takes another step toward me. My brain tries to tell my body to retreat, but I'm still drawn to him, the magnetism I felt that first meeting ever present. "That's why you're here, isn't it?"

"You think I come here so he can use me as a verbal punching bag? Hell, I'm only here because I assumed he'd be working. Like he always is. If I had known he'd be here, I never would have made the trek out of the city."

He peers at me thoughtfully, peeling away layer after layer. "I don't think that's true. You do this for her."

"Who?"

He floats his eyes to my wrist where the beaded bracelet Midge made me sits. She put so much effort into it, telling me how she learned to spell "sisters" so she could make it. It's the most thoughtful gift I've ever received. But it allows Lincoln a peek into who I am, even more so than he's already had.

"Your sister."

I quickly cover the bracelet with my free hand, shifting my feet.

"Midge, right?"

I nod, the movement borderline imperceptible.

"You come here for her, don't you?"

"It *is* her birthday party." My tone is sarcastic as I try to shrug off his insinuations. "*Everyone* is here for Midge."

Slowly shaking his head, his eyes rake over my face. "That's not what I'm talking about. You leave the city and come to suburbia, which probably stands for everything you despise, just so Midge feels loved. You'll do whatever you can to make her realize she's perfect, that everything she does is perfect." He smiles, laughing slightly. "Even if she misspelled sisters and mixed up two of the colors in the bead pattern, you'd never point it out to her. You probably told her how much you loved it, how you'd always treasure it, more so than some ridiculously expensive piece of jewelry from Cartier or Tiffany's some guy bought you just to have a shot with you. Isn't that right?"

Bewildered, I stare at him, his words so accurate it's frightening. "Maybe."

He forms his mouth into a tight line, squinting, as he continues to analyze me, the space between us decreasing. "You're quite the conundrum, Chloe Davenport."

"What makes you say that?" My voice is low, wanton, husky, his nearness casting a spell over me.

"That morning in Vegas, you made it sound like you were incapable of being loved. That you were incapable of loving anyone. You may not have come right out and said it, but I've been practicing law long enough to know how to read between the lines, to make educated assumptions."

"And what assumptions did you make?"

"That you wanted to take a risk but were scared of the potential ramifications. Worse, that you were scared people would think you aren't as strong as you want them to believe because of your feelings. But you can love someone and still be strong."

"I don't see how," I manage to croak out. "Love makes you weak."

"No. It makes you human." His breathing increases as his lips hover even closer, barely a whisper away. "Don't you want to feel human again? Don't you want to *feel* again?"

I close my eyes, convinced this is a dream. There's no other explanation for this conversation, for this moment. Not after he insisted we keep our distance, that we forget each other, that we pretend we don't know each other. But if it *were* a dream, I wouldn't feel the heat of his breath ghosting against my lips. I wouldn't feel the tingle of what's to come overtaking me. I wouldn't feel my knees growing weak in anticipation.

I lift my chin, my heart drumming violently in my chest as we flirt with the devil. The fact that touching Lincoln is forbidden only makes me want him more. Makes me want him in ways I've never craved another man.

"I do want to feel," I whimper, the past several weeks of not tasting his lips pushing me past my breaking point.

"Then feel me." His voice is a low growl as he erases the final distance between us. Suddenly, footsteps echo, growing closer, cutting through our trance.

My eyes widen, breath catching, at the same time Lincoln jumps back, the tenderness mixed with yearning that covered his expression replaced with fear…and regret.

"There you are," my father's familiar voice bellows. He comes to a stop when he sees me. "Oh, I apologize. Was Chloe bothering you? She should know better than to try to butter you up just because she's realized you work for me."

I turn around, taking a moment to settle my flushed complexion as I finish preparing the coffee. "I wasn't buttering him up. I offered to make him a coffee since he's a guest in this house." I whirl around, gritting a smile. "Then again, I suppose I am now, too. Here you go." I hold the mug out toward Lincoln. "I prepared it how—"

His sharp intake of breath, coupled with his frantic expression, cuts my statement short. I snap my mouth shut, horrified at what I was about to say. The last thing I need to mention is that I know how Lincoln likes his coffee. That's not exactly something a professor includes on the class syllabus.

"How I like it," I finish, recovering. "I hope only a hint of sweetener is okay."

"That's fine." His lips curve up in the corners. I wonder if he's recalling the few times I brought him coffee in bed. Along with another kind of morning "pick me up".

"Tell her if it's not," my father insists. "You shouldn't have to drink something you're not happy with because Chloe wasn't paying attention. I taught her better than that."

"Actually, it appears I take my coffee like she does." His eyes remain locked on mine. "Even if I didn't, I'd never depreciate someone's kindness and generosity that way," he adds, but my father glosses over his comment.

"Right. I just got off the phone with the legal department of a small newspaper down in Texas where that school shooting happened."

Lincoln nods. Normally, I tune out once my father discusses anything work-related, since it acts as a reminder of how he'd never love anyone as much as he does that job. But something about watching the wheels spin in Lincoln's head turns me on, has me glued to him. The same way I find myself mesmerized in class when he plays devil's advocate with the other students, sometimes to the point of almost being an asshole. The passion he exudes for the subject is unmatched by anything I've ever witnessed.

"The court sealed the criminal record of the accused's father, from whom he stole the gun he used in the massacre. They've asked us to help prepare an emergency motion unsealing it. I don't have to tell you the importance of this information, so let's get back to work."

He spins on his heel, walking out of the kitchen, past the living room, not acknowledging Midge. I wonder if he even wished her a happy birthday. Based on my experience, he most likely didn't.

Lincoln hesitates, his gaze locking with mine, and I can sense a part of him wants to stay to clear the air we've now muddied.

"Are you coming?" my father calls from down the hallway once he realizes Lincoln didn't immediately follow him.

My eyes beg him to tell my father no, to ask me to go somewhere with him, regardless of how wrong it is. This once, I want a man to choose me, to want me, to *fight for* me. But he doesn't. Instead, he shakes his head, turning from me without a single glance back.

Chapter Twenty-Two

"EARTH TO CHLOE," Owen sings. I lift my eyes to his, wondering what we were talking about, having zoned out. "Welcome back, sunshine."

"Sorry." I offer an apologetic look. "I'm a bit preoccupied." I shift my attention to the front of the room where Lincoln will deliver his lecture. It'll be the first time I've seen him since our near kiss this past weekend, and I'm not sure how to act.

I've spent the past several days convincing myself that everything having to do with Lincoln Moore has been one big mistake. From sleeping with him in the first place, to agreeing to give him a chance, to nearly kissing him during Midge's birthday party.

With a few sweet words, I allowed him to see behind the mask, to peer into my soul. Never again. From now on, I'll treat Lincoln exactly how he'd asked when we started this charade back in January. I'll act as if I have nothing more than cold indifference toward him.

"Everything okay?" Owen asks.

"Yeah. I've had a lot on my mind. The last thing I want to do today is sit through this class."

"Well, you might get lucky." He gestures to the clock right above the doorway. "It's ten minutes after. Five more minutes and we get to leave."

"That's odd. Li— Professor Moore is usually punctual."

"True. Unless he got distracted with Professor Gordon." He playfully nudges me in the side. "If you know what I mean."

Heat washes over my face, my heart plummeting. "Actually, I don't."

"*Everyone* knows about Professor Gordon and Professor Moore." He looks at me as if I just asked what color the sky was, as if it's a fact that just is. No explanation necessary.

"Professor Gordon and Professor Moore are an item?" My voice comes out more like a squeak.

"I figure you knew. Like I said—"

"Yeah, yeah. *Everyone* knows." I chew on my lower lip, doing my best to pretend this news has zero effect on me. It shouldn't, but I can't stop the myriad of questions that pop into my mind. Was he dating her when we met? When he begged me for a chance? When I gave him that chance?

The relationship makes sense. He's ridiculously handsome. Intelligent. Successful. And Professor Gordon is what many of the guys in the department refer to as a solid eleven on a scale of ten. Like Lincoln, she's young and incredibly ambitious. In fact, she's the driving force behind a website, the sole purpose of which is to give unbiased news in an age when corporations and big money buy newspapers and television stations in order to skew the message.

"I guess I just kind of tune out all the gossip here at school," I add, my voice lacking any emotion. Owen doesn't seem to pick up on my sudden change in demeanor, though.

"I can understand that, considering you must get your fair share at work."

"Yeah."

When the door opens, all eyes shift in its direction, watching as Lincoln walks into the room. His hair is a bit disheveled, his tie not as tight and straight as it normally is. I do my best not to glare, but fail miserably.

"Well, I guess he was able to pull himself away, after all," Owen mutters.

Jealousy, raw and ugly, rears its head. There could be a perfectly reasonable explanation for his harried appearance and tardiness. Maybe an emergency filing at the paper. But a sinking feeling forms in my stomach that it has nothing to do with work.

"I apologize for the delay. I had something to take care of. Now, who wants to tell the class about the infamous 'cake' case?"

Owen leans toward me. "I bet he did." He waggles his brows.

"Mr. Campbell."

"Dammit," Owen utters under his breath, barely audible.

"Why don't you tell us the background of this case."

Owen straightens in his chair, looking through his notebook. When he speaks, his voice evidences his nerves. It doesn't matter how often he gets called on in class. It's more than apparent he hates public speaking.

"A couple went to a popular local bakery to discuss a design for their wedding cake, but the owner refused to serve them because they were gay."

"Did the owner refuse to *serve* them?" Lincoln shoots back. "Or was it something else?"

"Well, he refused to make the cake for them."

"Better, Mr. Campbell. It may not seem it, but there is a difference. Technicalities are extremely important in the law. Now, what did the couple do?"

He hesitates, flipping through his notes, searching for the answer. I shift my notepad so he can see, subtly pointing to my own scribblings on the case.

Owen offers me a grateful smile as he glances at my notes, which are surprisingly much more organized than his. "Filed a complaint with the local anti-discrimination commission."

"And why does that matter?"

Owen looks at his pages again, but it won't be in there. He can talk about social injustice and current events with an understanding and expertise I doubt I'll ever possess, but when it comes to the law, he has trouble wrapping his head around procedure and how it all fits together.

I tap loudly on my notebook, getting his attention once more, and he steals a glance.

"Oh," he says after reading, lifting his eyes to address Lincoln. "Because the state had enacted an anti-discrimination statute, preventing any business from discriminating on the basis of race, gender, or sexual orientation, among other things."

"Correct. So it sounds like this is an anti-discrimination suit. Then why are we studying it in a First Amendment class?"

Owen stares, uncertain, pulling his bottom lip between his teeth as he attempts to formulate a response. "I—"

"I'll wait while Miss Davenport gives you the answer." His tone is biting, and I hate that he seems to pick on Owen disproportionately to the other students in class simply because we've formed a friendship over the past several weeks. Well, I'm done playing this game. Done letting Lincoln use Owen as his own verbal punching bag.

"The owner of the bakery argued the anti-discrimination law violated his First Amendment rights," I say without raising my hand.

Lincoln shoots his eyes to mine, as does everyone else, considering I've yet to speak in class.

"More specifically, the Free Exercise Clause. He claimed the state overreached in commanding him to make a cake for a wedding he objected to on religious grounds."

"Thank you, Miss Davenport. Should I assume you're Mr. Campbell's mouthpiece now?"

"I suppose that's better than the other way around." I pinch my lips into a tight line, crossing my legs.

Lincoln scowls, an unspoken warning in his eyes, before he shifts his attention back to Owen. "Now, Mr. Campbell, what did the court decide?"

I don't even give Owen a chance to respond before answering. "They sided with the asshole baker. But not on the bigger issue of the intersection of using the First Amendment as a defense to an anti-discrimination statute, but because they believed the commission exhibited hostility toward the baker's religious beliefs in its decision."

"Thank you for that rather astute analysis, *Mr. Campbell*," he barks out in a condescending tone. "As you so succinctly put it in a voice that's much more feminine than your normal one, the court never decided the issue of the intersection of anti-discrimination statutes and the Free Exercise Clause. So why would I require you to read this?"

"To demonstrate the lack of balls the court exhibited," I quip sarcastically.

"Lack of…balls?" Lincoln repeats. Several of the other girls in class giggle at his statement.

"Exactly."

He folds his arms in front of his chest, widening his stance, turning his attention fully to me. My pulse increases as I focus on his biceps, the flexing muscles stretching the material of his suit jacket. I push down the memory of having those arms wrapped around me, how it felt to be enclosed within them.

"And if *you* were on the court, what would you have decided, Miss Davenport?"

All eyes in the room shift toward me. Most every other student would probably say something well-thought-out and educated, based purely on legal precedent. But that's not me. I've always been much more emotionally driven.

"That the baker shouldn't be permitted to not serve a customer just because of his bigoted view, which he shrouded in religion. I'm not an expert, but I'm pretty sure Jesus would be pissed. Or God. Or whomever makes the rules."

The corners of his lips curve up. "So you wouldn't afford him his constitutional right to the free exercise of religion?"

"Where would it end?" I counter, everyone's attention shooting back to me. "Should we allow restaurant owners the ability to refuse service to gay couples, too?"

Lincoln grins. I thought he'd be upset by my persistence. Maybe he was at first. But now I can't help but feel he's getting some kind of satisfaction out of me arguing with him like this.

"Then let's take the anti-discrimination law out of it. Let's just look at this from a First Amendment standpoint. Should a state be able to force a citizen to create art for someone else? Regardless of whether they're straight, gay, black, white, woman, man. Take away all the complications here. Shouldn't people who create have the right to decide which commissions to take?"

I smirk. "So baking a cake is a protected form of speech now?"

"Art is considered speech. Just a different form."

"But where does it end?" I say once more. "Going back to my example from before. A chef could consider plating his entrees art. Does he get to deny people service?"

"That's not the same thing. Those entrees, although pleasing to the eye, aren't created for their aesthetic qualities."

"And a cake is?" I arch a brow.

He shrugs. "While I've never been married myself, I have plenty of friends who have. Choosing the wedding cake is one of the most important items on their to-do list. They go over designs for what seems like days. Hell, some of these people aren't even called bakers or pastry chefs, but cake artists. These cakes can take days to finish. If we were discussing a simple sheet cake with a layer of plain frosting, like one you'd buy at a local grocery store, I'd be inclined to agree with you. But that's not a wedding cake. At least no woman I know would ever stand for something so ordinary and trivial. You may not like it, but these distinctions are important. These lines are important."

"Of course," I shoot back, my voice growing louder and increasingly annoyed. "I understand how important it is to have *clearly drawn lines*."

My words come out biting, causing Lincoln's eyes to darken and narrow on me in a look of warning. I should stop right now. Get back on track and apologize for my outburst, make up some story about having a gay friend who should be able to have the wedding cake of his dreams. But I don't. All the heartache at having to sit in Lincoln's presence for weeks and not be able to touch him, feel him, kiss him has come to a head. Add in the knowledge that he's been seeing someone else, and I've lost the ability to give a shit about keeping my mouth shut.

"I'm sure your anal-retentive nature needs the ability to put everything into boxes. Boss. Employee. Male. Female. Rich. Poor. Teacher. Student." I pause briefly, noticing Lincoln shift uncomfortably, the cords in his neck straining, his fists clenching. When I continue, my voice becomes increasingly agitated with each word. "No gray area. No crossover. No risk. But lines sometimes get blurred. Sometimes those blurred lines are okay because you finally feel something so perfect and beautiful and you just want to tell society to fuck off and let us be together."

My voice rings out as shocked gasps fill the space. Lincoln's posture stiffens as he gives me a death glare. It's not until I see his reaction I realize exactly what I've said in front of a class of several dozen journalism students who love nothing more than a juicy story.

"Them," I correct softly, my tone wavering. "Let them be together."

His jaw twitches as his lips curl almost into a snarl, his stare cold and vindictive.

"Class is dismissed. Miss Davenport, my office. *Now*."

Without another word, he collects his things and storms out of the room, leaving everyone in stunned silence. Including me.

Chapter Twenty-Three

THE WALK FROM the classroom to the faculty corridor seems to be miles instead of the dozen or so yards it is. I can't help but feel like a condemned prisoner heading to the gallows. Hell, I can practically hear the warden yelling "Dead man walking" in the recesses of my mind.

I almost turn around countless times, deciding it isn't worth it, that I should withdraw. But my father's biting comments and my drive to prove him wrong push me forward.

With my head held high, I steel my resolve, about to knock on Lincoln's door when it swings wide, my executioner standing before me, his anger having only increased in the past several minutes.

Oh shit.

He yanks me inside, closing the door behind me. I barely have a minute to catch my breath before he leans toward me.

"What the fuck was that?" he seethes, the vein in his neck engorged. "Are you out of your goddamn mind?"

He paces, tugging at his dark hair, more frazzled than I've seen him before. A part of me wanted this reaction, wanted to see this passion, this intensity, this humanity, instead of the unfeeling, unaffected human who's been standing in front of the class for weeks, doing everything to ignore me, to pretend he never met me.

"What were you thinking?" He stops, turning toward me, his voice choked. "I promised I'd keep whatever we had a secret. *For you.*"

I blow out a laugh. "Right. For me. Not because you didn't want a certain someone to find out about us." I roll my eyes, allowing my heavy bag to fall to the floor with a loud thump.

He advances on me, his expression flashing with rage, jaw tense, lips achingly close. "What's that supposed to mean?"

"Exactly what I said." I step back, increasing the distance between us, my mouth formed into a tight line. "Did you not think I'd find out?"

"Find out what?"

I place my hands on my hips. "About you and Professor Gordon," I hiss. "Why did you beg me to give you a chance when you were already getting a piece of ass? Or is this part of your game?" With every word, my voice becomes more strained, the hurt that he was never serious about me causing my fists to clench, my body to quake with anger. "See how many women you can get to fawn over you as some boost to your fragile male ego?"

I fight back the tears threatening to fall, hating that this man has brought out these kinds of emotions in me. I've often prided myself on not allowing anyone to get to me. But Lincoln has. It makes me despise him even more.

"What are you talking about?"

"Oh please… Don't play dumb now. It doesn't suit you, *Professor*."

"I'm not playing dumb. I… You think I'm dating Tess? I mean, Professor Gordon?"

"Not just me. The entire student body of the journalism department claims you guys are an item. Apparently, it's common knowledge."

"And what makes them say that? Because I agreed to talk to her students about defamation one day?"

I shrug, not answering. The truth is, I'm not sure of the details, didn't stop to verify any information, not like I normally would, the shock of it rendering me momentarily incapable of doing so. Stealing a glimpse at his face, I study his features, searching for any sign he's playing me. But all I see is genuine confusion.

"Or maybe because I've been seen having dinner with her on occasion, considering she often reaches out to the *Times* for help with FOI filings when they affect matters of national importance."

Lowering my head, I pull my lips between my teeth, my confidence waning with every reasonable explanation he gives.

"Or maybe it's because I genuinely like her as a person and can trust her, so when we're seen having lunch together before class, it must be a precursor to something more. Because certainly men and women can't be friends. One must be interested in the other. Is that right?"

I shake off my indecision, turning my resolute gaze back to him. He can come up with different explanations all he wants. After all, he *is* a lawyer. That's probably one of the first things you learn in law school. How to bullshit. But he can't fool me.

"You haven't denied it."

When he steps toward me, his green eyes darken as he studies my face, taking his time to appreciate the curve of my cheeks, the heart-like shape of my lips, the fire in my stare. The heat radiating from him is reminiscent of our first night together. When he came into my room and looked upon me with so much hunger, wanting the night to last an eternity for fear that what we had would vanish the instant the lights came back on.

"Chloe…"

The way my name rolls off his tongue makes it sound like a prayer. A benediction. A supplication. I've missed the intonation when he says my name. My *real* name. I'm so tired of having to be Miss Davenport around him. Of him having to be Professor Moore. There have never been two lines I wanted to blur more than those.

"How can I date someone when I'm still hung up on the last woman in my life?"

I release a tiny exhale of air, blinking repeatedly, taken aback by his admission. "And who's that?" I barely manage to squeak out.

"This incredible woman I've been unable to stop thinking about since the moment I laid eyes on her when she was stuck at a bachelorette party in Vegas, where she was obviously miserable."

"Sounds like a smart woman," I retort, my tone lightening. In the blink of an eye, Lincoln's able to shift my outrage into something else, something much more electrifying. "Bachelorette parties are akin to torture."

"Then you'd probably like this woman. I know I did from the instant she finally spoke and told me off because she thought I was trying to hit on her."

"But you weren't?"

"No," he answers smoothly, then quickly corrects himself. "Well, I mean, in a way, I suppose. I don't know. But something drew me to help this stunning woman when some drunk guy, who thought she was a prostitute, wouldn't leave her alone. Regardless of whether I was lucky enough to find out her name, I needed to go to her, to remind her there are decent people in the world." He leans toward me and cups my cheeks in his hands. "That there are people who think the world of her, regardless of what others have led her to believe."

As I relish in the heat of his rough skin on mine, I whimper, not wanting this moment to come to an end before it has a chance to begin.

"That *I* think the world of her, regardless of what my behavior has led her to believe."

All sense of where we are, *who* we are, flees from my mind at his captivating words, and I grab the back of his neck, forcing him to erase that final bit of space between us. The instant his lips press against mine, sparks shoot through me. Every inch of me floods with warmth, with desire, with need, our bodies molding together as we greedily reignite this connection we've done everything to pretend never existed.

I swipe my tongue along the seam of his mouth, begging to taste what I've been deprived of for too long. With a growl, Lincoln deepens the kiss, enclosing me in his firm body.

His hands move to my hips and he lifts me with ease, forcing my legs around his waist. Losing myself in him, I remain oblivious to how wrong this is. In this beautiful moment, nothing else matters. That he's my professor. That I'm his student. That we've just eviscerated any line we had drawn. But the truth remains. There is no line. Not when it comes to Lincoln. Not when nothing else has ever felt so fucking right.

A man obsessed, he deposits me on the desk, sending neatly stacked files and papers to the floor. Tearing his lips from mine with a heady groan, he trails a hot path along my jawline, sucking and biting on my neck. The scruff of his trim beard is jarring and bruising, yet so wanted, making me feel more alive than I have in weeks.

"I could never forget you," he assures me, his voice laden with desire. "You're all I've been able to think about, Chloe. Every time I walk into class and see how incredible you look, all I can focus on is getting you alone again. Of feeling you again."

"Then feel me."

Pulsing against him, I reach for his pants, unbuckling his belt, desperate for him. As I'm about to lower his zipper, he grabs my wrist, stopping me. My eyes dart up, meeting his. I brace myself for him to tell me this is a mistake, that he lost his head. But he doesn't. Instead, he brings his lips to mine, feathering soft kisses.

"I don't have a condom." He chuckles, the deep rumble electrifying. "I don't exactly make a habit out of bringing girls back to my office for this sort of thing."

"I don't care," I breathe. "Let me feel you."

His mouth slams against mine once more as he squeezes my thigh, the pressure leaving no question there will be a mark. And just like our first night together, I'm confident that's exactly what he wants. That every time I look at my body and see the bruises on my thighs and bite marks on my neck, I'll be reminded of who put them there, who marked me, who branded me as his.

"I'm yours," I exhale, giving him the confirmation I know he needs.

"Mine," he snarls, an animal in heat.

"Yours. Always."

"Mine," he says again, this time softer, more heartfelt.

His hand moves up my leg, disappearing under my dress. When he pushes the skirt up around my waist, I meet his eyes. A devilish glint appears within as he hooks his fingers into the band of my panties…ones he bought for me. With quick movements, he lowers them down my legs before shoving them into his pocket.

"And those are mine, too." He kisses me, starved and greedy.

"Yes. Yours."

His teeth clamp onto my bottom lip, the pain dueling with the pleasure of what's to come. Then he leans back, his eyes locking on mine. He runs his hand along my collarbone, traveling between the valley of my breasts, down my stomach, coming to a stop just shy of that place I'm desperate to have him touch, explore, command.

I should feel cheap and dirty, considering he has me on his desk, legs spread, leaving me exposed to his fully clothed body, but I don't. I just want Lincoln. Any way I can get him.

He brings himself out of his pants, raising his arousal to me. My pulse skyrockets and I hold my breath, bracing to experience him with no barrier. He looks at me, an unspoken question in his tender gaze. I nod.

His pupils dilate, about to drive inside, when a knocking rips through the space. "Linc? It's Tess."

Every muscle in his body grows taut, all the color draining from his face. "Shit."

Eyes that overflowed with primal heat mere seconds ago widen, filling with remorse and disgust. In a heartbeat, the Lincoln I met in Vegas is gone, transforming into the Lincoln I saw the first time I stepped foot in his classroom. Into Professor Moore.

"Just a minute," he calls out, his voice trembling with anxiety as he hurriedly shoves himself back into his pants, readjusting his suit.

"I heard you ended class early." There's a pause before she speaks again, her voice lower. "That you got into it with Chloe Davenport. I wanted to make sure everything's okay."

"I'm in the middle of a phone call," he replies as he practically throws me off the desk, pushing my skirt down to hide any hint of impropriety. When I remain in place, shocked from the sudden shift in demeanor, he grabs my bag and thrusts it at me.

I blink repeatedly, feeling like an errant child who was caught with her hand in the cookie jar when she knows it's off-limits.

Like I know Lincoln's supposed to be off-limits.

That doesn't make this any easier.

"It was a misunderstanding. We've straightened it out. I can assure you it will *never* happen again." His eyes narrow on me, his expression severe. It doesn't take a genius to hear the true meaning behind his words.

"Okay," Professor Gordon's sweet voice carries through. "I'm around if you want to grab a drink."

"Sounds good. I'll be with you once I put out this fire."

I listen as her footsteps retreat. Heat covers my face, making me momentarily oblivious of the consequences, and I reel back, landing a hard slap against his cheek, the sound seeming to reverberate in the small space.

At first, he's stunned, his body frozen. I gave Lincoln a chance because I thought he was different. Thought nothing would turn him into an asshole. Thought he wouldn't become like every other guy who made me feel cheap, useless.

But he's just like them. Willing to get a piece until they're reminded they have a wife, a girlfriend, a life they don't want to lose. Maybe my father's been right all along. Maybe I'm *not* good enough. Maybe I'll *never* be good enough.

Lincoln's expression softens as he licks his lips. "Chloe, I—"

I quickly shoot up my hand, cutting him off. I want to tell him I'm going to the dean with the details of our relationship to spite him, but he'll know it's an empty threat. *I* was the one who didn't want him to tell anyone.

"You're right." I square my shoulders, my words straining past the lump in my throat. "It was a misunderstanding, one that will absolutely never happen again. No matter what." I storm toward the door, about to open it when he calls out to me.

"Chloe..." The timbre of his voice is tender, a complete contradiction to the way he just spoke to me.

As much as I know I shouldn't, I look over my shoulder. Turmoil covers his expression and he moves toward me, his eyes pleading. I fully face him, hope building inside me that he's about to apologize, say he made a mistake. Then he slowly reaches into his pocket, pulling out my panties.

"These are yours." He holds them out toward me, swallowing hard, a hint of reluctance on his face.

Remember in elementary school when your teacher tried to shape your behavior toward others and promote kindness by saying that actions speak louder than words?

Well, this moment proves that's true. Because this one action obliterates my heart more than any words ever could.

CHAPTER TWENTY-FOUR

"WAIT A SECOND," Nora says the following Wednesday as she zips up the back of one of the bridesmaid gowns she's considering for me.

Pulling the material to make it tighter, she glances at my reflection as I stand on a pedestal in front of a three-way mirror in the middle of a posh bridal boutique in Midtown. It's a silver dress that hugs my body through my hips to where it falls a few inches above my knees. Thankfully Nora's not sticking us all in the same color and style. We'll all be wearing different tones and cuts, based on our body type and coloring. Better than Hannah's wedding, when Izzy and I were forced to wear identical pink chiffon gowns that looked like a bottle of Pepto-Bismol got freaky with a cotton candy machine.

"You had sex in his office?"

Her voice carries through the space and I glare at her, but she doesn't seem to care. I doubt any of the ladies who work here will flock to social media to dish about whatever hot gossip they overhear. They've probably heard much juicier stories than one of the bridesmaids almost sleeping with her college professor.

"We didn't have sex," I correct. "We *almost* had sex."

"How close are we talking here?" Evie pipes up from her position on one of the uncomfortable looking chairs that would be more fitting in a Victorian tea room than a dressing room at a bridal boutique. "Are we talking 'about to rip open a condom' close? Or 'a little tip action before the first thrust' close?"

"There was definitely some tip. Although I'm not sure I'd call it just some." My cheeks heat. "Lincoln is rather…gifted."

We all giggle as I fan myself dramatically. As angry as I was initially, discussing everything with my friends is exactly what I need. They're better than any therapist. They make me believe I'll get through this little rough patch.

"What are you going to do?" Evie asks once our laughter dies down.

"What *can* I do? I should have stayed quiet. This never would have happened if I kept my mouth shut in class and pretended we have no history, just like he's done."

"And what? Risk an even bigger blow-up down the road?" Izzy quips before glancing at Nora. "By the way, that's a good style choice for Chloe. Simple, straight lines work best since she has… What?" She looks back at me. "Size A boobs and no waist?"

I stick out my chest a little, but she's not far off. "For your information, I'm a B-cup."

"So you *have* graduated from the training bra."

"Ha. Ha. Ha. Sorry I don't have triple D boobs like all of you."

"I'm only a C," she argues back. "Now, getting back to Lincoln Moore—"

"Just Lincoln," I correct.

"Whatever. This was bound to happen. Especially after the way he looked at you during Midge's birthday party."

"What?" Nora and Evie simultaneously fling their eyes toward me.

"He was at Midge's party?" Nora spins me around to face her. "When were you going to share this with us?"

"Eventually… Maybe."

"Why was he there?" Evie presses.

"Because instead of taking the day off to celebrate, my father had work come to him. Just like he did when I was growing up." I grit a smile.

"Did you talk to him?" Nora asks, her voice lower.

"It was impossible *not* to. He was right there."

"What happened?"

"What usually happens whenever I'm around my father. He made his usual cracks, how most people who go to college for ten years are doctors. And, of course, after learning I'll graduate this May, he said he'd wait to pop the Champagne. He's great for an ego boost, isn't he?"

"How did Lincoln react to all this?" Evie asks.

A smile lights up my face. "Actually, he defended me. Said I was one of the most promising students he's had the pleasure of teaching."

The girls look at each other and sigh.

"Aww…" Nora places her hand over her heart. "So sweet. Your knight in shining armor coming to your rescue."

I place a hand on my hip, fixing my expression. "I don't need a knight in shining armor to come to my rescue. And I told him as much when he came into the kitchen later on."

"I never asked what you guys 'talked' about." Izzy waggles her brows, grinning deviously.

I stare into space, recalling with striking clarity the conversation I had with Lincoln. We talked about a lot of things, but one stands out.

"Love," I murmur.

Three pairs of eyes instantly widen.

"What?" Evie gasps.

"In what context?" Izzy inquires, always the pragmatic one.

"Did he tell you he loved you?" Nora bounces on her feet.

"No, no, no." Since it appears we've settled on this dress for me, I head back into the fitting room. "Not like that."

"Then how?" Evie asks.

I pull on my jeans, then yank my top over my head before tugging my boots up my legs. Satisfied with my appearance, I walk into the sitting area, plopping down on a chair. "It was more in the context of my relationship with Midge and how he thought I was a conundrum."

"Which he's spot-on about," Nora comments.

"I'm not that difficult to figure out."

"Oh, come on." She exaggeratedly rolls her eyes. "You're hot, then cold. I can understand how Lincoln would be confused. You give off the impression you're this tough bitch who doesn't let anything get to her. And that's probably exactly what Lincoln thought because he didn't have a chance to get to know the real Chloe. Not like we do. So I can only imagine his surprise when he walked into your father's house to see you at a birthday party for the spawn of the man you loathe and his replacement wife, as you've always called her."

"It's not Midge's fault she has a father who will never be happy with anything she does."

My words linger in the air for a moment before Izzy speaks once more. "What happened next?"

I shake my head, trying to piece it all together. "I told him love makes people weak, to which he argued it makes you human. And then…"

"And then?" They all lean toward me, sitting on the edge of their seats. Literally.

Staring into the distance, a shiver rolls through me as I recall that exact moment. "He asked if I wanted to feel human. If I wanted to *feel.* He was so close. The closest he'd been to me in months. And then…"

"Yes?" Nora encourages as they all inch even closer, desperate for my story.

"We almost kissed."

"Almost?" Izzy asks.

"My father came in talking about some emergency filing they needed to get done. So Lincoln went back to work."

It's silent for a moment. I don't expect anyone to come up with a solution. This isn't a problem that can be fixed. It's just something I need to learn to live with for the next seven weeks. Then I'll never have to see Lincoln again. At least I get a break this week with it being spring break.

"That's it!" Evie slams her hand on the side table, startling us.

"What?"

"That's what this is all about."

"What is?" I scrunch my brows together, tilting my head.

"This whole thing with Lincoln. You're worried he'll choose his job over you."

"He *has* chosen his job over me. But it wasn't like he had a choice. It's right there in the code of conduct."

"Exactly." She shoots up, tapping a finger against her lower lip. I can see the wheels spinning in her head. Never a good thing. "*You* were the one who insisted he not tell anyone about your relationship. *He* wanted to report it. Then after the semester, if there was still something there, you'd be free to pursue it. But you made sure there was no chance, under the guise of your father not finding out for fear he'd think you didn't earn your degree."

"And if he knew, that's precisely what he'd think."

"I don't think that was the reason at all. Sure, that may be what you told Lincoln, but—"

"It was a preemptive strike," Nora breathes, turning her wide eyes to me, as if a puzzle piece just snapped into place.

"A preemptive strike?" I counter dismissively, averting my gaze. "You two are crazy. You've been reading too many romance novels. Or watching too much daytime TV. I did *not* tell Lincoln to keep this a secret as a preemptive strike against..." I wave my hand around. "Whatever you've concocted in those twisted brains of yours."

"Maybe not at the time," Izzy interjects thoughtfully. I shoot my eyes to hers, glaring at my traitorous friend. She's not supposed to take their side. She's supposed to support *me*, have *my* back. "Maybe at first, you genuinely *were* concerned about your father. But I also think, deep down, you were hoping Lincoln would fight for you."

"What? I didn't—"

She stands from her chair, walking toward me, squeezing my biceps. "I know you, Chloe. Probably better than anyone else. For you to take a chance on Lincoln, you must have seen something in him that made you believe he was different."

"Well, thank you, Dr. Nolan. Should I book my next session with you or your receptionist out front?" I joke, trying to lighten the mood, but Izzy doesn't let up. She never does.

"Your father was a crappy male role model. He still is. Which is why, when Lincoln didn't even try to fight for you, it broke something inside you."

I push out of her hold and cross my arms in front of my chest. "He didn't break me," I insist, but I can't look her in the eye.

"I think he did. I think he showed you what was possible. I think you felt hope that not all men are like your father or any of the other assholes you used to sleep with. So when he didn't fight for you, it reminded you too much of how your father chose his job over you and your mom. But I think if Lincoln knew how much you still want to be with him, things might be different. I think he *would* fight for you."

"I'm pretty sure lying on his desk with my legs spread sends that message loud and clear."

"That just shows you were willing to *sleep* with him. Maybe he needs to know you're willing to take a risk, like he'll have to. I doubt you've ever given him any indication you were serious about him."

"Since it appears you haven't been following along, I'll say it again. I never had the opportunity. I found out he was my professor before we could take things to that level."

"Or are you using that as an excuse?"

I open my mouth, trying to come up with some argument in my defense. I want to deny her words hold even the faintest hint of merit, that Lincoln wrote me off the instant he learned who I was, but I can't. His pained expression as he handed back my panties is still ingrained in my mind. A person who feels nothing but indifference doesn't look at you that way.

A loud ringing rips through and I blow out a breath, saved from having to respond. I rummage through my bag, pulling out my phone, a number I don't recognize appearing on the screen. Inwardly grateful for the reprieve, I offer the girls an apologetic smile, then bring my cell up to my ear.

"Chloe Davenport," I answer with all the professionalism I can muster, assuming it's a lead on a story.

"Chloe, it's Louise."

"Louise?" I wrinkle my nose, trying to place the name. I usually pride myself on my memory, but I'm drawing a blank here.

"Yes." She lowers her voice to almost a whisper. "Your mother's sponsor at AA."

I inhale sharply. In all the years I've played lifeguard to my mother's alcoholism, her sponsor has never called me, even when things got a little hairy. We took it in stride, simply trying to keep any temptations or triggers as far away as possible.

"I'm sorry. Of course." I give Izzy a knowing look, then stand and slip out of the sitting room, making sure I'm out of earshot before continuing our conversation. "Is everything okay?"

"Yes. It's just… Your mother hasn't attended her normal meetings the past two weeks. And she *never* misses a meeting without letting me know. I've tried calling, but she hasn't answered. I thought of phoning her work to see if anyone there knows anything, but I'm not sure what her co-workers know of her recovery. I didn't want to overstep, so that's why I called you. Have you spoken with her recently?"

I pinch the bridge of my nose, releasing a long sigh. "No, I haven't."

Guilt forms a knot in my throat at how I've dropped the ball these past few months. Apart from a few texts and phone calls, I've barely spoken to her since I got back from Vegas. It sounded like things were going great with Aaron, her boyfriend. I didn't think I needed to keep a close eye on her.

"I've had some personal stuff going on myself and I guess I kind of fell down on the job, so to speak."

"It's not your job to take care of her," she reminds me. "I'm sure it's nothing. I can be a bit of a worrier."

While I may not know Louise well, I can tell her concern goes above being a worrier. She's a recovering alcoholic herself. She knows how quickly someone can regress.

"You're right. She's probably fine, but I'll make some calls anyway."

"And you'll let me know?"

"Of course."

I hang up and draw in a long breath, fighting against the headache I feel coming on. Like Louise said, it's probably nothing. But I've been in this place before. It's never nothing, not where my mother is concerned. So I return my attention to my cell and call my mother's work number. On the first ring, a bright voice answers.

"Carsdale Associates. How may I direct your call?"

"Hi. It's Chloe Davenport."

"Hello, Chloe. How can I help you?"

"Is my mother around?"

"I'm sorry," the receptionist says with fake sympathy. "She's not. Actually, your mother hasn't been to work in about ten days or so. Said she needed some time away from the office to recenter herself after the last big PR nightmare she had to deal with."

"Of course she did," I mumble under my breath. "Do you know how long she'll be out of the office?"

"She didn't say," the receptionist answers, and my suspicions only grow.

It's not like my mother to take extended periods of time off, not now that she's working in crisis management and doing something she enjoys again. A part of me hoped that would be enough to keep her happy, to keep her from regressing. But I've also learned that, regardless of how put together someone may appear on the outside, they might be battling demons no one else can see.

"I'll call her cell instead."

"Okay," the receptionist chirps, unaware of any troubles. "Have a great day, Chloe!"

"You, too."

I hang up just as light footsteps sound from behind me. Whirling around, I meet Izzy's concerned eyes. I don't even have to say anything for her to know what's going on.

"Oh, Chloe…"

I shrug, doing my best to hold it together. Like I always have. "What can I say? When it rains, it fucking pours."

CHAPTER TWENTY-FIVE

I CLIMB OUT of the cab and glance up at the shotgun-style house in the East Flatbush neighborhood of Brooklyn where my mother lives. It's a quaint house in a quiet neighborhood. Well, as quiet as you can find within a short commute to Manhattan.

Ten years ago, I didn't think my mother would ever be able to hold down a job for long, let alone afford a house in this neighborhood. But once she started taking her twelve-step program seriously, things turned around for her. I just pray she hasn't fallen that far again.

Hesitantly, I climb up the stairs and pull back the screen door, the hinges groaning. I consider knocking. There could be a perfectly reasonable explanation my mother missed her meetings and didn't answer her cell when I called. Experience tells me otherwise.

Pulling my keys out of my bag, I find the one I'm searching for and insert it into the lock. The instant I step inside, my suspicions are confirmed. The scene is the perfect example of what it's like to have a high-functioning alcoholic in your life. The house is decorated with expensive furnishings, artwork hanging on the walls, high-end appliances in the kitchen. A demonstration of success.

But the wine bottles littering the island, kitchen counter, and living room coffee table tell a different story.

I curse under my breath. I should have known something like this was bound to happen. I've been so consumed with work, school, and all the drama going on with Lincoln, not to mention helping Nora with the final stages of planning her wedding. Most nights, I'm barely able to sleep more than a few hours. I thought my mom was doing good. She *had* been doing good. Better than good. So good that I made the mistake of moving her down my list of priorities. Now I'll have to suffer the consequences of that.

"Mom?" I call out timidly, stepping farther into the house. I walk to one of the windows and crack it open, allowing some fresh air to fill the place.

A crash sounds from the basement, the sound ominous against the quiet. I whirl around, darting down the stairs. When I round the corner, I expect to see her lying on the floor, having fallen in a drunken stupor.

Instead, I come face-to-face with a do-it-yourself nightmare. The walls have been repainted from the previous drab eggshell color to a deep gray, droplets splashed on the laminate wood flooring, since my mother didn't think to lay down any plastic first. Bubbles and streaks abound on the walls from the shoddy paint job. Various fabrics and cuts of wood are strewn all over the place, along with power tools I wouldn't trust this woman with sober, let alone in her current state.

My mother's personality when she drinks can range from happy to angry and everything in between. Over the years, I've learned to prepare myself for a wide variety of personalities, thanks to the alcohol. If she was drinking because she had a good day at work, she'd shower me with love and praise. But if something happened in her personal life, she'd curse and demean me in a way that made my father seem like an amateur.

But I'd take an irate drunk over a home-renovating drunk any day. I can handle her mood swings. I can't handle her with power tools.

"Mom?"

She spins around, her mouth falling open, eyes widening. She blinks, remaining still, trying to figure out her next move. Her gaze briefly floats to a corner of the room where several cans of paint sit. Beside them is a glass of red wine, the bottle next to it nearly empty. At three o'clock on a Wednesday. I'm not saying I'm perfect and never occasionally have a few drinks during lunch. But I'm also not a recovering alcoholic who shouldn't be drinking at all.

At. Fucking. All.

My glare narrows, lips forming a tight line, nostrils flaring. I don't even know what to say. As always, I want to blame myself. How much longer can I do that?

I'm about to ask her what she thinks she's doing, but when she sees the outrage in my expression, she attempts to distract me.

"Chloe!" Her movements are overly dramatic as she takes the cigarette out of her mouth, opening her arms to me, a lazy smile on her face. Her silver hair is pulled back, paint dotting her tanned complexion as well as the jeans and t-shirt she wears. "There's my baby girl!" She steps toward me, wrapping her arms around me. I can smell the liquor coming off her.

"What are you doing?" I push out of her hug before she burns me.

Taking the cigarette from her, I extinguish it in a nearby ashtray. I've never been a fan of her smoking. She picked it up when she finally got serious about getting sober, trading one vice for another, but I'd rather have her smoke than be drunk.

"What does it look like I'm doing?" She waves her hand around.

"Making a mess out of the basement?" I shoot back.

She jabs me playfully. "Oh, stop. No. I'm surprising Aaron with a man cave."

"A man cave?" I lower my voice. "Has he moved in with you?"

"Not yet, but he does spend a lot of time here, so I thought I'd do something to surprise him when he gets back from his business trip later today."

She looks around the space, scrunching her nose at the utter chaos surrounding us. The basement looked infinitely better when it still had its dreary wall color that lacked personality.

"I'm not sure it'll be done in time, though." She blows out a breath, then straightens, her voice brightening. "I'll tell you something. All those home improvement shows that make this kind of thing seem easy are full of it. This shit is hard. But look..."

She grabs my wrist, pulling me toward the far wall where it appears she attempted to install a custom entertainment center. I shudder at the idea of my mother using a circular saw and nail gun. She's lucky she didn't lose a finger. I steal a glimpse at her hands to make sure, counting ten.

"Isn't it incredible? I did that myself! Who would have thought?"

"It certainly is incredible." Feeling like I've stepped into an alternate universe, I wonder if my mother thought to use a level in her infinite wisdom. By the looks of the lopsided shelves lining the place where a TV would eventually sit, I assume the answer is no.

"Well, I'm glad you're here. I can use an extra set of hands if I'm to finish this before Aaron's flight lands in..." When she brings her watch to her face, her eyes bulge. "Shit. Is that the time already? His flight's supposed to land in a few hours and I haven't had a chance to start the coffee table. Come on." She clutches my arm again, dragging me toward several pallets, all in various stages of disrepair.

"Do I even want to know what this is supposed to be?"

"This is what we're going to make the coffee table out of," she answers proudly.

"Pallets?"

"Apparently, it's a trend. I printed out some instructions." She glances around, wavering slightly from the sudden movement. "They're around here somewhere." She begins moving piles of wooden slats, paint cans, and brushes.

"Mom..."

"Not now, Chloe," she barks, probably sensing what I'm about to say. "I don't have time."

"And like I had time to come here today?"

"Then leave," she snips, growing defensive.

"Mom, please," I implore, my voice strained as I try to take the wheel when the world spins out of control around me. "Just tell me what the hell is going on!"

"I told you. I'm renovating." The vein in her forehead pulses as she shuffles things around with increased annoyance. "Doing something nice for Aaron. Something you wouldn't know about since you can't exactly keep a man for longer than a few weeks, can you?"

My jaw tightens and I take a deep breath, counting to ten in an effort to stop myself from going off on her. I'd like to say this is the first time she's spoken to me like that, but it's not.

I wish I could say it'll be the last, but I know it won't, although I wish it were.

"This isn't about me." I keep my tone calm and even, despite the frustration bubbling inside me. She wants me to engage. Wants to shift the focus off the fact her house is littered with empty alcohol bottles. "It's about you."

"I'm doing just fine. So if you're not going to help me build this coffee table, you can help by finding your way out the door."

"Mom," I warn.

"What? It's not hard. You found your way in, didn't you?"

"Mom," I say again, this time louder.

"Chloe," she taunts, mimicking my tone.

"You are *not* doing fine."

"Why?" She whirls around. "Because I'm happy? You just can't *stand* the fact I'm doing well, can you? You're just like your father. You're not happy unless I'm miserable."

Hearing her compare me to my father sends me past my breaking point. As it always does. I can handle a lot of verbal abuse, but I refuse to be compared to a man I've spent the past twenty-odd years of my life ensuring I'm *nothing* like.

Heat flashes across my face and I ball my hands into fists, my body tensing. "Mom! Look at you!" I shriek before I have a chance to keep my temper in check. "When I walked into this house, it was worse than a fucking distillery. There are empty wine bottles everywhere." I spin in a circle, quickly counting four bottles tossed aside. "What happened? You were doing so good! I honestly thought this wouldn't happen again. That you cared enough about yourself and the people in your life who *love* you that you weren't going to drink anymore!"

"Don't speak to me like I'm a child!" she shouts back, indignant. "You seem to have forgotten that *I* gave birth to *you*. *I* raised *you*. *I* nurtured *you*."

"Yeah, you did. Until getting drunk became more important. I was the one who covered for you so Dad didn't know how bad it was. If it weren't for my constant lies to him, do you honestly think he would have allowed you to keep custody of me? Then what would you have done without his child support payments financing your addiction?

"Maybe that's where I fucked up. Maybe I *shouldn't* have kept this a secret. Maybe you would have gotten the help you needed earlier and we wouldn't be going through this cycle that doesn't seem to ever fucking end! But no matter the price everyone who loves you has to pay, you don't seem to care!" I bellow, tears streaming down my face.

"I *care*!" she snips. "I care so much that I'm renovating this entire basement for Aaron! So if you don't mind, I need to finish!" She storms toward the pile of pallets.

I briefly close my eyes to calm myself and inhale a deep breath. On a long exhale, I approach her.

"Mom." I soften my tone, hoping she'll relax enough so we can have a rational conversation.

"What, Chloe?" She spins around, her motions quick. Too quick.

Everything seems to happen in slow motion as the sound of an air compressor firing a nail echoes, followed by a sharp pain in my thigh just above my knee.

Darting my eyes up, I see the nail gun in her hand and collapse to the floor, clutching my leg as blood blooms on my jeans.

The sight is all it takes to push my mother over the edge. She loosens her grip on the nail gun and it falls with a clatter just as she passes out, her body slumping to the floor.

"Of course," I grit out through the pain. "It's not like she could have driven me to the hospital anyway."

Pulling my phone out of my back pocket, I unlock the screen and call the only person I can in this situation.

"Izzy, I need your help."

CHAPTER TWENTY-SIX

"HOW'S SHE DOING?" I ask several hours later when Izzy reappears around the privacy curtain in the emergency room where I'm lying on a bed, my leg propped up.

"She's fine. Had to get a few stitches over her eyebrow and suffered a mild concussion from the fall, but she'll survive. How are *you* doing?" She heads toward me, pulling off the thin blanket, revealing my heavily bandaged knee and thigh. "Is the local wearing off?"

"Yup. But they gave me some painkillers." I shoot up in bed. "You didn't let them prescribe any for my mom, did you?"

"No. I apprised the attending of her history, but it was in her chart already. Her injury is minor anyway. She'll just have to suck it up with regular ol' ibuprofen."

"Good." I relax back into the mattress, checking the time to see it's after seven. "I can't believe I wasted my entire fucking day on this. And for what? For my mother to shoot my knee with a nail gun?"

Izzy assumes the chair beside the bed. "Not *quite* your knee. She's lucky her aim was off. A few centimeters down and you could have faced some major reconstructive surgery. At least it didn't nick any bones and the doctor was able to yank the sucker out." She grins a devilish smile. "Did the doc let you keep it?"

"Why would I want to keep a bloody nail?"

"As a souvenir," she says, as if it's obvious.

I playfully roll my eyes. "I'd rather not have a reminder."

She shrugs. "To each their own. How long will you be off your feet?"

"Doctor Warren said I should be back to my old self in a week or so, but to take it easy and listen to my body, since the stitches need to stay in for about two weeks. Speaking of the handsome doc, is it a requirement for every doctor here to be ridiculously good looking?" I narrow my eyes at her. "Please tell me you've taken advantage of working here."

"I'm on the pediatric oncology floor."

"So? They have doctors there, too, don't they?"

"They do, and I'm sorry to disappoint you, but most of the hot doctors also have hot wives at home."

I sigh dramatically, leaning back against the pillows. "Yeah. Doctor

Warren told me he was happily married during my attempts to flirt with him after I was given anesthesia."

Izzy straightens her spine, her brows furrowing. "Chloe, they only gave you a local to numb the area."

"So?" A mischievous smirk skates across my lips.

She stares at me for a moment, remaining silent. Then she bursts out laughing. It's a strange sound in a hospital, as out of place as a nun in a strip club, but maybe we all need to laugh more. After this afternoon, *I* need to laugh more.

"You really have no shame, do you?" she asks, wiping at her eyes.

"I figure he probably sees enough depressing shit working here, so I may as well do something to make him laugh. Consider it my civic duty."

"Civic duty," she repeats, shaking her head, giggling even more.

"Excuse me, Chloe."

At the sound of a serious voice, I whip my eyes from Izzy, my own laughter ceasing when I see my mother's boyfriend, Aaron, standing in the opening of the privacy curtain. His graying hair is slightly disheveled, worry and guilt etched in the lines of his face. He's on the tall side, around six feet, and in great shape, considering he's in his sixties. But the energy and liveliness he usually exudes is lacking, his tie loosened, his suit wrinkled. Based on the suitcase beside him, I gather he took a cab straight here from the airport.

"Aaron." I sit up in the bed. "My mom is—"

"Actually," he interrupts, "I'd hoped to talk to you first." He shifts his attention, noticing Izzy at my side. "Thanks for taking care of my girls, Iz."

"You bet." She stands from the chair and walks to him. They hug briefly and he kisses her cheek. "I'll give you two a few minutes." She looks back at me. "You should have your discharge papers soon, but if you need anything in the meantime, shoot me a text."

"I will." I watch as she leaves, grateful to have a friend like Izzy, who immediately left Nora and Evie to get me to the hospital. Then I turn my attention to Aaron, apprehensive about his reason for wanting to talk to me.

"This is all my fault." He slumps into the chair, burying his head in his hands.

I exhale, knowing all too well what he's going through. I've done this same thing myself more times than I can count. Hell, I did this same thing earlier today when I walked into Mom's house and was met with the smell of alcohol.

"No, it's not," I say with all the compassion I can. "I promise you, nothing you could have done—"

"No." He darts his eyes to mine, his gaze intense and remorseful. "It *is*. I could have stopped it. I could have prevented it from starting in the first place."

I open my mouth, about to reassure him once more, when he says, "I gave it to her."

I shake my head. "I don't—"

"Alcohol. I gave her the alcohol."

His admission is a punch to the gut, the air knocked out of my lungs. "You…*gave* her alcohol?" I'm barely able to get the words out.

With a deep sigh, he closes his eyes, his shoulders drooping.

"How long has this been going on?"

He runs a hand over his face. "For a little while now."

"How. Long?" I demand again through clenched teeth.

Hesitant, he licks his lips. Then his unwavering gaze meets mine. "About three or four months."

His admission hits me hard, my jaw dropping, the world feeling like it's giving out from beneath me. My mother's been drinking for three or four *months*? I'd hoped maybe he'd brought over a bottle of wine a few weeks ago. But three or four months? So much could happen in that timeframe. So much could go wrong in that timeframe.

"I didn't expect it to get this out of control," he offers in a misguided attempt to not seem like the villain in all of this. But even if he'd only given her a sip, it would be one sip too many.

"Oh, you didn't? What *did* you expect when you gave alcohol *to…an…alcoholic*?" I hiss, trying to keep my voice low.

A part of me feels bad about speaking to him this way. It's one thing to have a shouting match with my mother when she's in one of her stupors. Sometimes it's the only way to get through to her. But Aaron is basically a stranger to me.

"It's not like I showed up at her door one day and force-fed her a bottle of vodka. It started out relatively innocent. A sip out of a glass of wine I'd order at dinner."

"That's the same thing as force-feeding her! And what were you thinking ordering wine when you were with her? You've been to meetings with her, haven't you?"

He nods, his eyes glassy from unshed tears.

"Then you know being around other people drinking could trigger a relapse."

"I didn't think it would be that bad. She's around worse stuff with some of the clients she works with, helping them cover up their own alcohol or drug abuse issues. I thought she could handle it." He blows out a long breath. "I guess I was wrong."

"Ya think?" I glare at him, a tightness in my chest. "Do you have any idea the damage this has caused?" I manage to say through the frustration building in my throat.

"But I read that most alcoholics who suffer a relapse come out stronger afterward."

"That would be true if her *boyfriend* hadn't been giving her the goddamn alcohol!"

"I wanted to tell you a few months ago, especially when the occasional sip turned to drinking half my glass, then a full glass, but I didn't want you to hate me. I care about your mother. You need to believe I'd—"

"You have a funny way of showing that."

He pinches the bridge of his nose, his jaw tightening. "I know I fucked up. And I don't expect you to forgive me. That's not what I'm asking for." His eyes float to mine, imploring. "I love your mother. Tell me what I can do to make it right. To help her get back on track."

I stare at him, sick to my stomach. "You want to know how you can make it right?"

"Yes." He clasps his hands in front of him. "Anything. Tell me and it's done."

"Leave her alone."

My words cause him to instantly straighten. "Wha—"

"*You* are her trigger." I lean as close as I can in the hospital bed, my gaze unwavering. "If you really do care about her, you'll keep your distance. She needs to get sober, something that won't be easy if the person who constantly fed her alcohol is around."

"I…," he stammers, chewing on his bottom lip. "Do you think that's best? Won't that upset her? Make it even worse?" He blinks repeatedly, grasping at the last straw he can pull. "Getting her sober again will put enough stress on her. Shouldn't she—"

"Not have a daily reminder of the man who gave her alcohol? Absolutely. She may love you, but now you're just one giant alcohol vending machine. And that's all you'll ever be to her. That's all she'll ever see when she looks at you. A man who will cave and feed her addiction when the people who truly love her would never have even imagined giving her so much as a sniff of their wine. So if you truly do love her, you'll walk away and let her heal."

Jaw tight, I glower at him, my chest heaving. I'm sure this conversation isn't good for my blood pressure. This entire scenario is shit for my blood pressure. Briefly closing my eyes, I suck in a steadying breath before looking back at him.

"I can't make you do anything you don't want to," I continue, my voice softer, more controlled. "I can beg for you to walk away, but you're two adults. It all comes down to how much you love her. Are you selfish enough to stay with her, knowing you're a crutch? Or are you self*less* enough to allow her the opportunity to recover, something she'll never have otherwise?"

He stares at me for what seems like an eternity, indecision flickering in his gaze. My heart thrums in my chest, my breathing echoing in my ears, my lips pinched tight.

Finally, he lowers his head, nodding in resignation. “Okay.” His agreement comes out as a strained whisper.

I offer him a compassionate smile. It doesn’t go unnoticed how difficult this must have been for him. I hate that I even had to force him to make this decision. But he forced me to put him in this position.

I just pray my mother understands why this was the only option.

Chapter Twenty-Seven

I STRETCH MY leg out in front of me as I work on the couch Saturday evening. It's been an interesting couple of days since the incident in my mother's basement. Upon being discharged, she apologized profusely, even went so far as insisting I stay at her house that night. I took her up on the offer. Partly because I was recovering. Partly so I could keep an eye on her.

To my surprise, the instant we got back to her place, she cleaned up all the empty bottles, then proceeded to pour every last drop of alcohol down the drain, all without me asking her to. The following morning, she was up bright and early, getting ready for work. She even attended an AA meeting on her lunch break. It gave me hope that this little relapse may not be as bad as all the others, which was why I felt comfortable enough to stay at my apartment tonight, since the weekends tend to be busy in my line of work.

If my mother weren't coping as well as she is, I would have been at her place. But she went to her normal Saturday Book Club meeting with some of her other AA friends, then texted afterward to say she was crawling into bed and relaxing for the rest of the evening. She even sent a photo as proof. I hate that she thinks she has to provide photographic evidence to back up her statements, but there's a certain level of trust that's broken whenever she has a relapse. She's used to it as much as I am.

Just as I'm about to stand and hobble into the kitchen to make a coffee, my phone rings, a number I don't recognize appearing on the screen.

"No rest for the weary," I murmur to myself before answering. "Chloe Davenport."

I'm instantly met by loud music, coupled with raised voices. "Is this Chloe Davenport?" a man practically bellows.

"Yes," I respond hesitantly.

"I need you to get to Spring Lounge in SoHo. There's a woman here. Very intoxicated, argumentative. I was about to call the cops when she begged me to call you instead. I'm assuming this is your mother since you have the same last name. Short. Silver hair. Mouth like a trucker."

With a heavy sigh, I pinch the bridge of my nose, fighting against the frustration filling me. Like the other day, I start to blame myself for this, but I can't keep doing that. I can't keep putting my life on hold to babysit her. When will it end?

"Yes. That's my mother."

I briefly entertain the idea of not bailing her out this time. Maybe a night in jail and criminal charges are exactly what she needs. But what will that do to her career? In her line of work as a crisis management specialist, they deal with enough scandals from their clients. The last thing they'd want is a scandal from one of their employees, as well. And I refuse to go back to the way things were years ago when I had no choice but to find more creative ways to earn money to help her pay the mortgage. It takes everything I have to afford my own rent.

"I'll be there as soon as I can."

"Don't take all night. There's only so long I'm willing to babysit her."

"All right. All right." I jump to my feet, wincing from the pain. "I'm on my way."

Yanking on a pair of sneakers, I limp out of my apartment without grabbing a jacket, despite the snow beginning to fall, and hail a cab. The drive takes a little longer than normal, thanks to the weather, but after fifteen minutes, the cab pulls up in front of the neighborhood dive bar.

When I step inside, I'm grateful to see my mother sitting at the end of the bar, a full glass of water in front of her, seemingly calm. I limp toward her, doing my best to forget about the pain shooting through my leg.

"Mom?"

Her movements are slow as she lifts her lazy eyes toward me. Then a wicked smile curls her mouth. "There she is. The prodigal daughter. This is her, everyone!" she shouts.

Several people look in my direction, more out of curiosity than interest. And maybe a little pity.

"My lovely daughter who asked my boyfriend to break up with me!"

"Mom," I hiss, grabbing her arm in an attempt to yank her to her feet. But my injury prevents me from being as strong as I usually am. I wish I'd taken this into consideration and called someone for help. But who? This has always been my burden, and mine alone.

"You just can't let me be happy, can you?"

"Come on. Let's get you out of here." I ignore her statement, attempting to pull her off the barstool, to no avail. "The bartender was nice enough to call me instead of the cops. The second we're outside, you can tell me all about how I'm a horrible daughter for asking the man who provided alcohol to an alcoholic to keep his distance if he really cared about you and your recovery."

"Well, your little plan backfired," she sneers.

"You've got to get her out of here," the bartender warns as his eyes float to patrons who start fleeing in droves. "I'm losing customers because of her."

"I'm sorry." I wrap my arm under her shoulder blades, but she's dead weight. There's no way I'll be able to get her out on my own. "Can you help me get her outside? Please. She has a problem—"

"No, I don't," my mother interrupts. "*You're* the one with the problem." She shoves a sharp finger into my chest. "You can't stand anyone being happy."

I clench my jaw, drawing in a deep breath before I do or say something I'll regret and make an even bigger scene, resulting in both of us getting arrested.

Looking back to the bartender, I implore one final time. "Please. I'm begging you." My voice trembles, a lump forming in my throat. I've been in this situation with my mother more times than I can count. I've had to drag her out of numerous bars before they called the cops. But I've never felt as helpless as I do right now.

The bartender blows out a long sigh, throwing the dishtowel hanging over his shoulder onto the bar. "Fine."

Gratitude fills me, the bald man akin to a guardian angel at this moment. "Thank you."

He simply nods, then comes out from behind the bar and hoists my mom to her feet with ease. Thankfully, she doesn't fight it. Once we're outside, I gesture to an empty bench at a nearby bus stop, and he brings her over, depositing her onto it.

"Thanks," I say again.

"You bet." He begins back inside before pausing, looking over his shoulder. "You did the right thing by asking that guy to stay away from her. I would have done the same."

I smile, savoring his words. It may not seem like much, especially considering he's telling me something I already know to be true, but living with an alcoholic, *loving* an alcoholic is a constant battle of doubt, second-guessing yourself, and wondering if you handled a situation correctly.

When he retreats into the bar, I dust some of the snow off the bench, then plop onto it, ignoring my mother's venomous stare. Opting to order an Uber instead of trying to hail a cab, I pull my phone out of my purse. Maybe if I offer a big tip, the driver won't mind helping a severely inebriated woman into the car.

"You must feel proud of yourself," she taunts. "Huh? You're responsible for Aaron leaving me, then decided to come here to gloat."

I shake my head, looking at my Uber app to see the estimated arrival time of the car, as well as the model and license plate. Thankfully, it's only a minute away.

"You're the one who called me," I remind her through gritted teeth. "If I didn't come, that bartender was going to call the cops."

"I should have let him." She wavers on the bench as she tries to sit up straight. Placing my hand lightly on her shoulder, I push her back. She barely notices. "I would have been better off spending the night in the drunk tank instead of having to sit next to someone who only wants to ruin everything good in my life because she can't hold down a relationship for anything."

I pinch my lips together, briefly closing my eyes, just wanting to get her home so I can put this night behind me. Like so many similar nights that came before it. Thankfully, the Uber I'd ordered turns the corner, and I wave the driver over.

"Okay, Mom. I need you to cooperate for a minute and get into the car."

"You want me to cooperate?" she retorts, barely able to even enunciate the word. "Like you wanted Aaron to cooperate with your plan to destroy my life?"

My hands ball into fists as I remind myself not to apologize for any steps I take to remove a trigger from my mother's life. Instead, I try to focus on the immediate task at hand. There's no rationalizing with her when she's like this.

"I understand your frustration. And I'm happy for you to make a long list of all the ways I'm a shitty daughter—"

"And you are."

"But when we're home," I plea in a strained voice, feeling like I'm trying to bargain with a three-year-old who doesn't want to take a nap. "Okay?"

"Hey, lady," the driver calls out. I lift my eyes to his. He points to my mother. "Is she drunk?"

"She's just a little under the weather." I return my attention to my mother, ignoring the curious stares from passersby on the street of the popular restaurant and bar area in SoHo.

I wrap my arm around her body and use every ounce of strength I possess to pull her up, gritting through the ache in my leg. When I realize I'm successful, I exhale, holding onto her as tightly as I can to prevent her from falling.

But the massive quantity of alcohol she consumed, coupled with my unsteady balance from my injury and the snow-slickened sidewalks, makes this a difficult task. She wavers on her feet before crashing to the ground, taking me with her.

When I land with a hard thump, I cry out in pain, which only causes my mother to laugh hysterically.

"This ain't worth it," the driver says. "Find another ride."

I don't even look up to watch him drive off. I can't. I fear I'll lose what little hope I've miraculously held onto through everything.

I've dealt with my mother in this condition for what feels like most of my life. I never thought twice. It was just always something I had to do. I honestly believed if I did everything right, if I focused on keeping the stress out of her life, regardless of the personal cost to myself and my own dignity, she'd eventually get back on her feet, eventually stop drinking.

But now I'm exhausted. Broken. Defeated. And for the first time since I realized my mother had a problem, I allow my tears to fall, allow the emotions I've kept locked inside to flow out.

"What did I ever do to deserve this?"

Despite the pain, I clutch my legs to my chest, wanting to hide from the world, to press that imaginary reset button on my life. Sirens wail, horns honk, happy voices converse as people pass, not one soul stopping to help the poor, injured twenty-something struggling with a drunk. I shouldn't be surprised. I learned long ago the only person I can count on is myself.

"Karma really is a bitch, isn't it?" my mother slurs. "This is what you get for ruining my life. For *always* ruining my life."

I shift my eyes to hers, tears obscuring my vision. I should just leave her here, should let her fend for herself, but I can't. No matter what she's done, no matter the vitriol she spews, I've always put up with it, refusing to abandon her like my father did.

"I would have been better off if you were never born. Then your father never would have left me. We were happy until you showed up."

"I know." I nod, swiping at my cheeks, my throat closing up. I don't have the strength to fight her anymore. Life has sucked everything out of me. I don't even have the energy to return to the bench, my limbs too heavy to move.

Instead, I stay on the sidewalk, my teeth chattering, my fingers growing numb from my lack of any winter attire. Another reminder of how I can't do anything right.

I pull my legs tighter against me, feeling like it's the only thing keeping me glued together. I try to cover my hands with the sleeves of my thin shirt, but my clothes are wet from the snow, my body shaking from the combination of my sobs and frigid temperatures. I'm not sure tonight could get any worse.

"Chloe?" a deep voice cuts through.

I stiffen, unable to breathe, to move, to think, wanting to wake up from this nightmare that keeps getting worse with every passing heartbeat.

I thought I'd hit the lowest of the low, sitting on a dirty New York sidewalk, too weak to drag my drunk mother into a cab, snow falling around me, my body shivering because I didn't have the wherewithal to protect myself from the elements. But no. Fate or karma or whoever had to make sure the one man I didn't want to see me like this bore witness to my breakdown.

"Chloe," he repeats when I don't react, keeping my head buried in my legs. This time, his tone is less confused, more sympathetic.

"Please go," I manage to get out through my wheezing breaths, my tears falling even more relentlessly.

His hand touches my shoulder. I snap my head up, shrugging him off. I have no idea what I did to deserve being saddled with an alcoholic mother for the past fifteen years of my life. But I took it all in stride. I didn't break down when my mother failed to show up for my high school graduation. I didn't break down when I had to quit college to work so she didn't lose the house. I didn't break down when I saw that first property tax bill and knew I no longer had a choice but to sacrifice the last shred of dignity I had in order to pay it. But this right here, having Lincoln look at me this way, his eyes glassy with emotion… It fucking destroys me.

He licks his lips, shaking his head, speechless.

"Please. Go," I say again, this time louder, my words drawing the attention of several passersby. "The last thing I need right now is you gloating about what a fuck-up I am," I sob, my entire body quivering, but no longer from the cold. From the raw emotions filling me. "I know I am. I'm trying so fucking hard. I just… Please. Leave me alone."

When he doesn't make any move to retreat, I bury my head back in my legs. "You're the last person I want to see right now."

"Chloe," he says again, just as Professor Gordon's familiar voice calls out to him.

"Linc, the car's here."

Without looking at him, I can sense his hesitation. I bring my legs closer to me, sending a silent prayer to the big man upstairs to grant me this one favor and make Lincoln leave. Seconds pass, seeming like hours. Finally, he exhales deeply. When I hear the crunch of his footsteps retreating in the snow, I steal a glance and watch him walk away. It's what I wanted, but it makes me cry even harder. Makes me feel even more alone.

Burying my face once more, my tears continue to fall, releasing everything I've kept hidden for years. It doesn't seem to faze my mother. She keeps her head on my shoulder, berating me. I tune it out. I can't listen to it anymore.

Officially out of options, I'm about to reach into my purse to call Izzy when I feel a warmth wrap around me. A weight lifts off me and I dart my eyes to my left, disoriented, watching as Lincoln hoists my mother off me and carries her down the block toward a yellow cab idling in front of an upscale French restaurant.

Once she's secure in the back seat, he returns to me. I want to scold him for not listening when I told him to leave me alone, but the comfort of his wool coat surrounding me is too inviting.

Fishing a handkerchief out of the inside pocket of his suit jacket, he hands it to me. I dab at my eyes and cheeks as he wraps his arms around me, helping me to my feet.

When I limp, he glances down at my leg, but doesn't ask what happened, as if he can tell I don't want to talk about it. It only makes him hold me even tighter as we make our way to the cab and he helps me inside before sliding in next to me.

"Where to?"

"My place." The last thing I want is to sit in a cab all the way out to Brooklyn when my apartment is mere minutes away.

"Which is?" Lincoln arches a brow.

I blink, caught off-guard that he doesn't even know where I live. I guess we never got to that point.

Turning my attention to the driver, I rattle off my address in the West Village. With a nod, he merges into traffic.

I relax into the seat, closing my eyes as a shiver rolls through me. Lincoln pulls me against him, rubbing my arm, and I rest my head against his chest, the metronome of his heartbeat offering a brief escape from my reality.

"I've been where you are," he says after a beat.

I raise my eyes to his, my brow wrinkled.

"Exactly where you are," he emphasizes, then looks forward, keeping me in his warm embrace.

CHAPTER TWENTY-EIGHT

"I GOT HER," Lincoln assures me, adjusting his grip on my mother's inebriated body as I lead him toward my building. "Go unlock the door, but try not to kill yourself while you do it."

"Are you her boyfriend?" my mom slurs, her eyes mere slits. The alcohol coming off her breath is pungent. It's a miracle she didn't throw up in the cab. Then again, she passed out the second the driver pulled into traffic, not waking until Lincoln started to get her out.

"No, I'm not." His tone isn't exactly friendly, but it's not icy either. Just…indifferent.

"Figured as much. Did he get tired of you like the rest of them?"

"Mom," I grit out in warning as I climb the front steps, searching my purse for my keys, grateful when my frozen fingers land on them. "We've never dated." I insert the key into the lock, pushing the door open and stepping inside, Lincoln close behind. I head into the living room, kicking off my shoes.

"Now that I *do* believe. All these years, you've claimed you weren't interested in settling down. But I finally figured it out. It wasn't *you* who wasn't interested in settling down. It was everyone else."

I draw in a slow, steady breath, keeping my eyes forward, biting my lower lip to prevent myself from flying into a seething rage.

"They saw you for what you really were," she continues, relentless as always. "Someone who would spread her legs for a story, or a great pair of shoes, or the latest designer purse."

"That's enough," Lincoln barks, his voice echoing. I spin around to see his expression tight, his lips pinched together as he glares at her, not allowing her to escape his words. "Your daughter is the *only* reason you're not sleeping on the street or sitting in a jail cell right now. She didn't have to help you tonight. Or any other time you found yourself in a similar situation."

"It's okay. I'm used to it." I give him a small smile, then limp from the living room and into the den to make up the pull-out couch.

"That's right. She's used to being nothing but a disappointment. All she does is ruin things. You're smart you didn't get involved with her. She would have found a way to ruin your life, too."

I peek at Lincoln, the vein in his neck throbbing, his nostrils flaring. The temperature in the apartment seems to rise several degrees. With determination in his stride, he brings my mother over to the reading chair, depositing her harshly onto it. Then he glowers, pointing a finger in her face.

"Don't. Move."

A chill runs down my spine. It has nothing to do with my damp clothes, but everything to do with the power and dominance in his voice. I swallow hard, my own heart thumping in my chest, observing my mother snap her mouth shut, nodding quickly.

My mother's always been tenacious, tough as nails. You don't get to be a political strategist, then work in crisis management unless you have thick skin. Seeing her obey Lincoln's command is somewhat surprising.

Although it shouldn't be.

I couldn't resist obeying him, either.

I watch as Lincoln stalks toward me, every muscle in his body taut. I return my attention to the task at hand, grabbing a cushion off the couch and tossing it into the corner. As I'm about to add another one to the pile, he stops me, grabbing my hands in his.

"This is *not* okay, Chloe," he says in a choked voice. "Nothing about this is okay." He drops his hold on me, ripping the remaining cushions off the couch before yanking out the mattress, taking out his aggression on it. Pausing for a beat, he runs his hands through his hair before facing me. "Nothing about the way she spoke to you is right. Don't you realize that?"

I'm about to argue once more that it's not a big deal, when he cuts me off.

"I know. She's your mother. If you don't take care of her, who will?"

I shrug. It's the truth.

His jaw twitches and he shakes his head, his distressed expression hitting me hard. Why does he seem so invested, so hurt by the things she said?

"Go change into some warm clothes. I'll get her comfortable. You've done more than you needed to."

"*You've* already done more than you needed to. I can handle this. This isn't my first rodeo." I start to turn from Lincoln when his fingers wrap around my arm. I lift my eyes to his, so much hurt and understanding within.

"I *haven't* done enough. And for that, I apologize. Let me do this for you." His Adam's apple bobs up and down in a hard swallow. "Please."

I part my lips, struggling to form a response. I should stand my ground, insist I'll be fine on my own, that it's not the first time I've been here. But the idea of having someone to lean on, even if for just a minute, lifts a weight off my shoulders.

"Okay," I murmur.

"Okay." He smiles a small smile, but doesn't release me, lightly dragging a finger down the length of my arm. My gaze remains transfixed on his, the feel of his touch sending a bolt straight to my core. When he reaches my hand, he squeezes, his thumb brushing across my knuckles.

"Okay," I say again, hypnotized.

"Okay," he whispers, curving toward me, his lips lingering just above my forehead, grazing my skin. I don't move. Hell, I don't even want to breathe, blink, anything. "Okay," he repeats, almost like an affirmation to himself. Then he releases me, heading to where he'd left my mother on a chair in the living room.

At first, I remain still, the tingle of his small kiss still trickling through me.

"I told you." He glances over his shoulder as he's about to hoist up my mother, who's passed out once more. "I've got this. You need to warm up."

Snapping out of my stupor, I limp toward my bedroom, hyper-aware of the heat coming off Lincoln's eyes as I pass him. Once I'm alone, I blow out a long breath.

I'm still not sure what to make of tonight's dramatic events, of Lincoln being in my apartment, but I'm not going to think about it. Right now, I just want to slip into something warm and allow someone else to shoulder the burden for a change.

CHAPTER TWENTY-NINE

Bottles clanging against each other rouses me from sleep. I bolt up, my eyes flinging wide. Disoriented at first, I hurriedly scan the living room, trying to remember how I'd fallen asleep on the couch. Then the events of the night trickle back. Working. Getting a phone call. Having to drag my mother out of a bar yet again…

Shit.

I jump to my feet, wincing as I hobble into the kitchen, expecting to see her raiding all the booze I was too tired to get rid of just yet. But when I round the corner, I'm surprised to see Lincoln pouring bottles of alcohol down the drain, the sleeves of his crisp button-down shirt rolled up, his suit jacket lying neatly across the counter.

Sensing my presence, he glances over his shoulder, offering me a sweet smile as he continues to drain the contents. When he's finished, he wipes down the sink, then fully faces me.

"I'm sorry. I hope you don't mind. If I were in your shoes, this is what I'd want."

"I was planning on doing it. I just needed a minute to decompress. I guess I dozed off. Did my mother give you a hard time?"

He shrugs. "She's fine. Tomorrow will be a completely different story."

I playfully roll my eyes. "You've got that right." The last thing I want to think about is the state she'll be in when she wakes in the morning.

"I didn't wake you, did I?"

"It's okay. I need to get some work done anyway. My voicemails and inbox are probably overflowing with messages."

"Ah, yes…" He leans against the counter, crossing his arms in front of his chest. I avoid staring at his biceps as I limp past him toward the one-cup brewer, trying to ignore the heat coming off him. It's impossible to escape it in such close quarters, my kitchen no bigger than the galley of a boat. "The gossip mills must be running full force, correct?"

"Celebrities seem to enjoy getting into trouble on the weekends." I grab a mug and place it underneath the spout, popping a pod into the brewer. I glimpse at Lincoln. "Want one?"

He worries his bottom lip, seeming to weigh the pros and cons of staying for a coffee, before finally answering. "Sure."

I refocus my attention on the coffee maker, neither of us saying anything while I prepare two cups. When I'm finished, Lincoln grabs them and heads into the living room, making himself comfortable on the couch.

Once I lower myself onto the opposite end, he hands me my mug and I take a sip, the nutty flavor relaxing me. Shifting my body, I stretch my legs along the length of the couch, placing a pillow under my injured one to keep it elevated, per my discharge instructions.

"So… What happened?" He keeps his voice low so as to not disturb my mother sleeping in the den.

"Are you asking about tonight with my mother or my leg?"

"As curious as I am to know everything, I'm more interested in your leg at the moment." He inhales a sharp breath, his eyes widening, expression flushing. "I mean… I didn't mean it like that. I just meant—"

"It's okay." I smile, then take another sip of my coffee. "On Wednesday, I was trying on bridesmaid dresses for Nora's wedding when I got a phone call. My mother's sponsor. Said my mother hadn't been to a meeting in a few weeks, which is unlike her. I called her work, only to learn she'd taken some time off. I had a bad feeling in the pit of my stomach, so I went to her house in Brooklyn…where she was drunk before three in the afternoon, working on remodeling her basement into a man cave for her boyfriend, Aaron."

I lift the leg of my yoga pants, revealing my heavily bandaged knee and thigh. "We got into an argument. When she tried to continue on her project of making a coffee table out of a bunch of pallets, she accidentally fired the nail gun. This is the result."

Lincoln's eyes widen. "Holy shit. Are you okay? I mean, I see you are, but—"

"I'm fine. I'll *be* fine." I lower my pant leg. "She missed hitting any bones, so they were able to remove the nail without surgery. I should be as good as new in a few days. Apart from the nice new scar I'll now have the rest of my life."

"Battle wounds. We all have them. Some you see. Some you can't." His voice is tender and understanding. I lift my eyes to his, a dozen thoughts on the tip of my tongue. He quickly looks away, breaking the moment. "And tonight?"

"I can't be certain, but based on the slurs my mother slung my way, I imagine she found out I'd asked her boyfriend to stay away from her, considering he'd been giving her alcohol the past few months, even though he knew she was a recovering alcoholic."

He leans forward and rests his forearms on his thighs, contemplating. Then he looks back at me. "How long has this been going on?"

"Since the divorce." My response surprises me. I've always kept this private. But Lincoln's already seen me at my lowest. I have nothing left to lose by sharing this piece of me. "She drank before, but I never thought anything of it until it was just us."

"And when was that?" He peers at me.

"Fourteen."

Nodding, he looks forward again, filing this information away in whatever category it belongs. "Did your father know?"

"I don't think he cared, but I never came right out and told him." I glance at him, hesitant as I open up even more. "He still doesn't know. The only person in my life who knows is Izzy. And now you."

"Why haven't you told him?" His brows furrow, that same pained expression from before returning. "Especially when you were so young?"

"I didn't want him to know. Didn't want him to have anything he could use against her to get custody of me."

"In your mind, an alcoholic mother was the lesser of two evils." It's not a question. More a statement of understanding.

"You know how my father can be. My mother might be an angry drunk, but my father's an angry *person*. At least my mother's harsh words are limited to when she drinks."

He's quiet for a beat, then admits, "My mother started drinking when I was in high school, too. After she found herself alone."

"Your parents are divorced?" I'm not sure why I find this more surprising than his mother being an alcoholic. I always pictured Lincoln having a flawless life and upbringing. From the beginning, everything about him was perfect. I guess no one's perfect. Everyone has scars. Some just know how to hide them better.

"No." He smiles briefly before faltering. "My father… He was killed on assignment."

"Assignment?"

"He was a bureau chief for the *Times* and living in Southeast Asia. He was kidnapped by some extremists and held for ransom."

I gasp, my hand covering my mouth. "My god. I'm sorry. I didn't know." These days, it seems we've become desensitized to these things, since they happen so often. It doesn't make them any less tragic.

"This was maybe six months after 9/11 and the U.S. government had taken a hard stance against negotiating with terrorists, given the current state of affairs."

As I listen, his story sounds achingly familiar. It was one of the first gruesome acts I'd read about in this post-9/11 world. Yes, the attacks themselves were horrific, especially for someone who's lived in the New York area most of her life. But I remember walking into the kitchen at my house one morning to see my father beside himself with an emotion I wasn't used to seeing from him. He actually hugged me. And there were tears. Later, I learned it was because he'd just received word that one of his colleagues, who'd been reported missing, had been found decapitated, his body evidencing signs of extreme torture.

"You're Elijah Moore's son," I breathe, the puzzle pieces locking into place.

He nods, his shoulders slumped slightly. "He died a few months before I graduated high school. My mom's drinking probably started much like yours did. A glass of whatever here and there. So innocuous and common you barely notice. But within a few months, one glass turned into two. Which turned into an entire bottle. Which turned into two. Like most other alcoholics, she still held down a job, made it appear to everyone she was doing fine, or as fine as could be expected when you lost a piece of yourself in such an inhumane way.

"I guess a part of me felt compelled to fulfill my father's legacy. I was originally a political science major, but added a double major in journalism. Graduated at the top of my class. Excelled in the field. Submitted articles to various papers and magazines during college. Got a job as a contributor for the *Post*, then attended Yale Law."

"That's why you're this crazy workaholic, isn't it?" I shift my eyes to him, seeing him in a different light now that I know the truth. For the longest time, I questioned what someone as put together as Lincoln could see in me. But he's as broken inside as I am. "It's the one thing you *can* control."

Children of alcoholics tend to gravitate toward one thing they're good at and put all their effort into that, since it gives us a sense of control we don't have with our parents. Of course, I didn't focus on school. Instead, my "relationships" with various men gave me that sense of control. I said when. I said how. I said where. Until Lincoln, it was the only thing I felt I had control over in my life. And I needed that control.

"You think I'm obsessed with my work?" There's a twinge of hurt in his voice.

"Trust me," I scoff playfully, trying to lighten the growing tension. "You are. I grew up with a man who always put his work before anything else. Still does." I shrug dismissively, not wanting to dwell. "Which is probably why I'll never measure up to his impossible standards."

Lincoln arches a single brow. "Yet it doesn't stop you from trying, does it?"

I blow out a breath, surprised at how forthcoming I am. Exhaustion can do that to a girl.

"Just once, I want to feel like I'm good enough."

"Chloe…" His tone is filled with compassion. He reaches across the couch, grabbing my hand in his, his thumb brushing my knuckles. "You're more than enough." Such a simple statement, but it's exactly what I need to hear. What I've needed to hear my entire life.

"You're more than enough, too," I barely manage to squeak out.

He squeezes my hand, the touch innocent, but the way he swipes his thumb along my skin has my cheeks heating. I lock my eyes with his, unable to look away. There's something new in his deep pools. Wonder. Amazement. Respect. And need. He can deny it all he wants, but people who are just supposed to be acquaintances don't look at each other the way Lincoln's currently admiring me.

The way I'm currently craving him.

Wanting to feel something good and pure, even if for a moment, I inch toward him. Hypnotized, he leans into me, his eyes focused on my lips as I part them. I promised I'd never put myself in this position again, especially after last week. Right now, I just need to wrap myself in something other than feelings of inadequacy and failure.

But am I ready for the feelings of inadequacy and failure that will follow when Lincoln realizes this is a mistake? When he looks at me with the same disgust as he did a few days ago?

Can I really put myself through that again?

I know the answer to that.

I've known the answer to that all along.

When Lincoln's a whisper away and I can almost taste his addictive kiss, I snap out of the spell, practically jumping from the couch. "You should go. I have work to do." I snatch his coffee cup and bring it into the kitchen.

Spying his suit jacket on the counter, I grab it, ignoring his bewildered expression as I shove it at him. He doesn't say anything at first. Just looks at me in a way that makes me want to wrap my arms around him and lose myself in everything he is. But that's not who we are.

His gaze trained on me, he stands, taking his jacket from me and shrugging it on. "If that's what you think is best." He arches a brow in question.

A flicker of hesitation passes. How do I answer that? Is this what I want? No. But is this for the best? It must be.

"I do," I answer with reluctance, a sinking sensation forming that this is our final goodbye. That this is our last chance.

"Understood." His shoulders fall as he retreats from me.

I cross an arm over my stomach, chewing on my lower lip. Am I ready for this man to walk away when I know in my heart we turned a corner tonight?

"Lincoln!" I call out as he's about to disappear out my door.

He pauses, glancing back at me, eyes brimming with hope.

I part my lips, struggling to form a single word.

"Your coat," I say quickly, then rush into my bedroom, grabbing his heavy wool coat off the floor. When I return, I hand it to him. His fingers delicately brush against mine as he takes it from me. A part of me thinks he did that on purpose, a reminder of the spark, the connection, the flame that hasn't dulled despite the obstacles facing us.

"Well, goodnight then?" His tone lifts toward the end, turning his statement into more of a question.

It takes every ounce of resolve I possess not to clutch his face in my hands and kiss him. But tonight's events haven't changed the fact that he's my professor and I'm his student. I need to remain firm. I need to keep that line drawn.

"Goodnight, Professor Moore," I say in as determined a voice as I can muster at the moment.

He briefly closes his eyes, exhaling a long breath. "Goodbye, Chloe."

CHAPTER THIRTY

As a little girl, I went through a phase when I was obsessed with all things supernatural. After learning about the folklore theory of the witching hour being a time increased supernatural activity could be present, I'd always hide under my blankets if I somehow woke up between the hours of three and four.

Tonight, as I toss and turn at three in the morning, the only increased activity is in my brain. No matter what I've tried, I can't seem to quiet my mind.

I can't seem to stop thinking about Lincoln.

I haven't been able to since we met.

I've tried closing the chapter on us, tried starting a new one, but it's hard to turn that page when the person you want won't be there anymore.

On a long exhale, I throw my arm over my head, staring at the ceiling, wondering if Lincoln is as restless as me.

If he's thinking of me.

If he wishes we could turn back the clock and take a different path.

A gentle rapping cuts through my thoughts. I still, unsure whether it's real or if I'm simply hearing things due to exhaustion. A few seconds pass, my apartment falling silent once more. Then the knocking sounds again, this time firmer.

More curious than anything, I get out of bed and limp toward the front door. Lifting myself onto my toes, I peek through the peephole, my heart catching when I see Lincoln pacing on my stoop, snow still falling around him, hair disheveled, demeanor frantic. From the looks of it, he's had as much trouble sleeping as me.

I steal a glimpse of my reflection in the entryway mirror, smoothing my hair before opening the door. The instant I do, he halts in his tracks, his wild eyes shooting to mine.

"Lincoln, wha—"

Before I can finish, he advances toward me and grips my face. All the air leaves me, the combination of his sudden movement and rough flesh on mine making me breathless. His fingers dig into my skin, a fevered energy about him as his lips inch closer, the heat of him causing my pulse to skyrocket.

"Invite me inside," he growls.

"I don't—"

"Please, Chloe." He releases me, wearing a path on my stoop again. "I've done everything in my power to stay away from you, to forget about what we shared. It was only… What? Ten days? There's no way two people can form that strong a connection in such a short period of time, right?"

"Right…," I say in a drawn-out voice, leaning against the doorjamb.

"Right." He stops pacing, peering at me through pained eyes. "So why can't I forget you?"

I stand straight. "I—"

"Why don't I *want* to forget you?"

I keep quiet, letting him get out whatever he came here to say.

"Because I don't, Chloe. Believe me…" He laughs to himself. "I've tried. I've tried dating other women. Thought it would make it easy. That it wouldn't hurt so much. But you have to know how *excruciating* it is to sit in class and watch you with Owen."

"We're not—"

He holds up his hand, and I snap my mouth shut. "It has destroyed me, Chloe, regardless of whether there's anything between you two. The idea that you can have an open conversation with him, even a platonic one, kills me."

The veins in his neck tighten as his hand squeezes into a fist, pure anguish oozing from every pore. His face reddens. His teeth clench. His body shakes.

"Because I. Can't. Do. That. I can't enjoy the luxury of making you laugh. Of taking you out and treating you like the amazing woman you are. Of kissing you in the middle of Times Square with the world watching. Not without jeopardizing everything I've worked so hard for. Without destroying my father's legacy. But I'm willing to do that. For you." Eyes focused and chest heaving, he steps toward me. "I just need to know you're all in. I need to know you're willing to take a risk. To take a chance."

"I told you I was," I reply softly.

He closes the final bit of space. "That was before. Things have changed. I need to know you're willing to do this. Right here. Right now. With who we are to each other. I need to know you're willing to lower your guard and let me past the wall you've built up throughout a lifetime of being made to feel inadequate. So please…" He lifts a hand to my nape, not blinking as he stares intently into my eyes. "Invite. Me. Inside."

I part my lips, searching his expression. It's a reasonable request, one most women would agree to without a second thought, especially with a man as handsome and addictive as Lincoln Moore standing in front of them.

But I'm not most women. Lincoln knows this.

Worse, he knows how sacred maintaining my own space is. I've never invited a man into my apartment. That meant giving them a piece of myself. It meant permitting them into my heart, something I've always avoided.

Until now.

Bringing my hands to his face, I savor the scruff of his unshaven jaw, ghosting my mouth against his. "Okay."

He vehemently shakes his head. "No, Chloe. Not just okay. Not yes. Not a nod. I need the words," he pleads with me like a man begging for his life.

Licking my lips, I focus my gaze on his. "Lincoln… Will you please come inside?"

His muscles relax, a tiny exhale of air escaping. Then he threads his fingers through my hair and crushes his lips to mine, his tongue exploring my mouth like it's the first time he's ever kissed me…sweeping, penetrating, needy.

I've been treated to my fair share of Lincoln's kisses since we met. Every single one left me addicted for more. But not one felt this electrifying. Not one had the power to hit me so deep, to fulfill me in a way I didn't think possible, to make me think we've finally found ourselves in each other.

When he tears away, he leaves me gasping for air. Peering up at him, I see his jaw clenched, eyes untamed. I remain locked in place, not moving, worried he changed his mind, came to his senses. Then a brilliant smile crosses his lips.

I cup his cheek and he melts into my touch, covering my hand with his. I pause to admire this man. The man who felt the need to rescue me from some drunk guy who wouldn't keep his hands off me. The man who smoothly sent a martini my way just so he could come talk to me. The man who begged for a chance.

His smile turning wicked, he swoops me into his arms and carries me toward my bedroom.

"Lincoln," I whisper-shout, "what are you doing?"

"Helping you follow doctor's orders by keeping you off your feet."

Once he kicks the door closed, he helps me find my footing, the playful atmosphere shifting. We stare at each other in the relative darkness, the only light coming from a streetlamp casting a slight glow into the room.

He brushes a strand of hair behind my ear, allowing him to see me unobstructed. His fingers linger on my face. I close my eyes, savoring the warmth of his skin on mine.

"You are so beautiful."

I bask in his ardent declaration, my heart expanding. Then he brings his other hand to my face, his grip becoming harsher.

"Say you want me."

"I want you," I whisper.

His lips touch mine, our kiss a tease. "Say you need me."

I grip the back of his neck, digging my fingers into his skin. "I need you, Lincoln." I move my mouth along his unshaven jawline, taking his earlobe between my teeth, his taste addicting. "I've always needed you."

With a growl, he forces my lips back to his, his tongue sweeping against the seam. His motions are the perfect combination of desperate and sweet. Greedy and reverent. Chaotic and controlled. His ravenous kiss leaves no question in my mind of how much *he* needs *me*.

His rough grip loosens, his urgent kiss becoming tender. He exhales into me, his arms wrapping around me, keeping me safe in his embrace. As much as I want more of him, *all* of him, I want this, too. These quiet moments between us. These reminders that he hasn't given up on us.

Our mouths never break from each other as I fall onto the mattress, bringing him on top of me. I can't stop kissing him even if I want to. He is the elixir for my suffering. The cure to my torment. The remedy to all the tragedy.

My perfect addiction.

As he peppers starved kisses along my jawline, I crane my head, a shudder rolling through me when his two-day scruff scrapes against my throat. I hook a leg around his waist, slowly circling my hips, my pulse increasing.

"Do you have any idea how much I've thought about this? How much I've fantasized about this?"

"Yes," I moan as his fingers lift the hem of my t-shirt, my body aching for him.

"Tell me you've thought about me."

"Every day," I answer without a moment's hesitation.

"Tell me you've fantasized about me." His voice becomes more demanding.

"Every night," I pant.

"God, Chloe. Why can't I stay away from you?"

My fingers rake through his dark locks and he arches his back, relishing in my touch. "Maybe because we're not meant to be apart."

Before I can utter another word, his lips are on mine, his hands running along my body, exploring, remembering. We only tear away from each other long enough for him to lift my top over my head. He cups my breasts, his fingers rolling my nipples, eliciting a moan from me. I claw at his own t-shirt, yanking it off.

The instant it joins mine on the floor, he wraps an arm around my waist, raising me to a sitting position, pressing my body to his. Skin to skin. Flesh to flesh. Heart to heart. We take a minute to calm our ragged breathing and temper our racing hearts.

Toying with a few tufts of chest hair, I rest my head against him, this moment more intimate than any other time I've been with a man. Because I'd never truly been intimate with anyone else. Not like this. I gave them my body, nothing more. But Lincoln captured my heart, captivated my mind, invaded my soul.

"Your heart's racing," I murmur, covering it with my hand, the pounding rhythm comforting.

"I can't help it." His deep voice is tranquil as he runs his fingers up and down my back, causing a shiver to roll through me. "It always beats faster when you're around." He touches my chin and tilts my face, bringing my eyes to his. "It's always burned for you." He brings his lips to mine, his kiss achingly perfect as he lowers me to the mattress once more.

Taking his time, he tastes me, feasts on me, experiences me, his journey down my body torturously slow. My nails scratch his scalp as I pulse against him, my muscles tightening. A low rumble vibrates from him, and I smile. Such a simple, innocent touch, but the sensation of my fingers clawing at his skin has always unhinged him.

I hope it always will.

When he reaches my breasts, he floats his gaze to mine, a hint of mischief within. Then he returns his attention to me, taking a nipple into his mouth.

I close my eyes, my body fusing into the mattress, sparks shooting through me. When his teeth gently scrape against the sensitized flesh, I yelp, then moan, my muscles clenching as I attempt to calm the myriad of sensations filling me.

His hands roam my frame, getting reacquainted with every dip. Every valley. Every curve. Each time he looms close to the waistband of my shorts, I grow hopeful, only for him to retreat.

"Please, Lincoln," I beg, my body a slave to his touch.

"Something I can help you with, Miss Davenport?" Lifting his eyes, his lips kick up in the corners.

"I need you," I pant, my chest rising and falling in a quicker rhythm, the ache in my core only burning hotter with each passing second. "I need to feel you."

"You *are* feeling me." He circles one of my nipples with his tongue, eliciting another moan, before tracing a line in the valley between my breasts, the sensation unhinging me.

"You know what I mean."

He cocks his head. "I *think* I do. But maybe you should tell me so I'm certain we're on the same page."

It takes all my resolve not to break into a huge smile at the memory of the games we played our first night together. Both outside and inside the bedroom.

His cheeks clutched in my hands, I look at him with a heated stare. "Lincoln, I need you to fuck me."

He keeps his gaze locked on mine for several seconds as my words linger in the air. Blowing out a long breath, he shakes his head.

"I'm not going to fuck you tonight, Chloe."

My heart falls as I blink repeatedly. "But—"

He presses a finger to my lips, silencing my protest. "This isn't just sex for me."

I swallow hard at his sincerity. "It's not just sex for me, either." My words surprise me. Despite trying to convince myself otherwise, it's never been just sex with Lincoln. It's always been something more.

"That's why I'm not going to fuck you. Not now that we've finally made it to this place. Tonight, I'm going to seduce you." He lowers his mouth to my neck, beginning his agonizing journey down my body once more. "Your mind." He briefly sucks on my nipple before heading farther south. "Your body." He dips his tongue into my belly button, drawing a line along my waist before meeting my eyes. "Most importantly, your heart." He holds my face in his hands, our connection strong. "Your heart is what I want more than anything."

"It's yours," I assure him, my voice a whisper as I struggle to speak through the lump in my throat. "It's always been yours."

He treats me to a sweet kiss before pulling back and lowering my shorts, leaving me in my panties.

"These look familiar." He smiles slyly, smoothing a finger along the silky material.

"They should." Not caring about the pain from my stitches, I manage to prop my legs up, spreading them. He takes the hint and brings his thumb to my center. "They're yours after all." Arching toward him, I scrape my lips against his. "Yours are the only panties I've worn since you got them for me. I never stopped being yours, even if you stopped being mine."

He presses his mouth more firmly against mine. "I never stopped being yours, Chloe. Never." He narrows his gaze on me, allowing his statement to sink in. Then his fingers hook into the waist of my panties, about to pull them off.

"Don't." I grasp his forearm, then grin deviously. "Leave them on. Like our first night together."

"You liked that?"

Biting my lower lip, I nod, my eyes heated. "You know I did."

"Well then…" He grabs my thighs, spreading them wider, positioning himself. "Who am I to disappoint?"

As he inches toward me, my pulse skyrockets, the seconds seeming to stretch, time standing still when I need it to hurry. Finally, he presses his mouth against me and I moan, my eyes fluttering into the back of my head.

The first time he did this, the unwelcome barrier of my panties only frustrated me. But this is what I need right now. A reminder of how far we've come since that night, but at the same time how we're still the same people. That nothing's changed. At least the important thing hasn't. This connection hasn't.

"Lincoln," I moan, scraping my fingernails against his scalp.

"Yeah, baby."

The vibration of his voice pushes me higher and higher, and I move against him with greater urgency. I never thought it possible to get off without him actually touching me. He proved me wrong back then. Just like he's continued to prove me wrong.

That familiar quivering sensation fills me, my toes curling, spine tingling, and I hold my breath, my brain unable to focus on anything other than the immense pleasure this man brings me. When I don't think anything could feel more incredible, Lincoln pulls back the fabric of my panties, his tongue tracing along my center. He pushes a finger into me, then another, stretching and twisting. Lights blind my vision and I shatter, screaming his name as I convulse on my bed, not wanting this euphoric sensation to end. And Lincoln won't let it, drawing out my orgasm as long as possible until he can no longer control himself.

"I need to be inside you," he states in a gruff voice, a man obsessed.

With haste, he yanks my panties down my legs, then lowers his own jeans and briefs. I don't take my eyes off him, admiring his beautiful physique. I want to pinch myself to make sure this is really happening, that I'm not dreaming. It all seems surreal, considering a little more than a week ago, he looked at me with absolute disgust as he kicked me out of his office.

He returns to me, crawling up my body. His motions are tender as he brushes the hair away from my eyes.

"Are you okay?"

"Newsflash." I smirk. "This isn't the first time I've done this. This isn't the first time *we've* done this."

"True. But there's no looking back after this. There's a lot more at stake now."

I gaze at him thoughtfully, trying to find a way to assure him I'm ready for everything that follows. "Are you familiar with the story of Orpheus?"

He cocks a brow, releasing a small laugh. "This may be the first time someone's brought up Greek Mythology during foreplay. At least, it doesn't seem to be a common topic in my circles."

I give him a sardonic look before my expression turns serious once more. "When his wife, Eurydice, died, he went to hell to bring her back from the underworld, risking everything. Hades and Persephone were so entranced by his musical ability that they permitted him to go into hell and bring her back with him, on the condition she walk behind him and he not look back."

"I know the story."

Grabbing the back of his neck, I bring his lips within a breath of mine. "He lost the love of his life because he made the mistake of looking back." I shake my head, emotion choking my words. "I won't make that mistake here. Not now that I know what living without you feels like. You're the only one who's ever quieted the chaos, who's made me feel I have worth. I'm never looking back again."

Overwhelmed, he covers my mouth with his, his hold on me tightening in a way that makes me think he'll never let go. "I'm never looking back, either."

"Promise?" I ask, allowing him a glimpse at my vulnerable side.

"Promise." He touches his lips to mine, then steps off the bed, fishing his wallet out of his pants' pocket. A condom in hand, he starts to tear the wrapper open.

"Wait."

He stops mid-rip, giving me a questioning look.

"I want to feel all of you. Like we were about to…" I trail off, averting my eyes.

"Hey." He drops the condom to the floor before returning to me, cupping my face in his hands. "I am *so* sorry about how I treated you that day. I never should have…" He pauses, collecting his thoughts. "I guess I was just scared."

"I get it. You're risking a lot by being with me."

"That's not what scares me."

"Then—"

"I was scared of what I felt for you. What I *still* feel for you. I needed to know you were all in, that you wanted this…whatever this is. That you wanted more than you've ever wanted before."

With a grin, I pull him on top of me. "I can unequivocally say I want more. Lincoln Moore."

"Because I've never heard *that* one before," he jokes.

"Hey!" I playfully slap him. "You're not supposed to allude to past girlfriends when you're about to have sex with the new woman in your life. Didn't anyone ever teach you that?"

"Possibly." He smiles a devilish smile. "But I'm happy to have you teach me that lesson." Lifting his arousal to me, he spreads my wetness around, then pushes into me. Slowly. Deliberately. Perfectly. "Over. And over. And over."

"God, I like the sound of that." I bring him closer to me, meeting his rhythm.

I expect him to pick up the pace, but he doesn't, drawing out his motions in an agonizingly slow rhythm. He was right. This isn't sex. This *is* a seduction. Of my mind. My body. My heart.

He buries his head into the crook of my neck as I wrap my legs around him, needing him closer. But no matter how tightly I squeeze, how deep he drives, it's still not enough, still can't extinguish the flame building inside, the fire that's been burning for him since the first time our eyes locked.

I scrape my nails down his back, which elicits a groan, causing him to increase his pace. I meet him thrust for thrust, our bodies a tangled mess of legs and arms as we share this beautiful moment, propelling each other higher and higher until we both shatter in an explosion of ecstasy and bliss.

Spent, Lincoln collapses on top of me, breathing labored. I wrap him in my embrace, kissing his sweat-stained brow.

"Thank you." He brushes his lips against mine.

"For what? Not making you use a condom?"

He chuckles. "No. I mean, it's certainly much more enjoyable without one, but thank you for letting me in. For choosing me."

"It was never a choice with you."

CHAPTER THIRTY-ONE

LIGHT FILTERS INTO my bedroom as I stir from a restful sleep, my mind quiet for once. My muscles sore, I stretch, yawning, then steal a glance at the clock on the wall, expecting it to be maybe six or seven in the morning. When I realize it's after noon, I shoot up, scrambling for my phone. I never sleep in like this, especially on a weekend. Hell, most weekends I *don't* sleep. I shudder to think of all the stories I missed last night.

Last night…

I dart my eyes to the opposite side of the bed, finding it distressingly empty, despite the evidence of a body having slept there. Maybe it *was* too good to be true. Maybe in the light of day, the reality of the risk he'd have to take finally hit Lincoln and he left.

I can't blame him. He's seen the mess that is my life. Alcoholic mother. Disappointed father. I just thought things would be different this time. Thought we'd connected in a way we never had. In a way *I* never had. I actually fell asleep feeling something I hadn't in so long… Hope.

I bury the notion, needing to focus on the more pressing issue of my mother's current condition. I step out of bed, yanking a t-shirt over my head before pulling on a pair of yoga pants. When I spy my panties lying on the floor, I stop, a pang squeezing my heart.

On a hard swallow, I pick them up, staring at them. Every other time we've spent the night together, we didn't part ways without him stealing my panties, claiming them as his. This solidifies my original suspicion.

"You'd better not be thinking about keeping those."

I whirl around, my breath catching when I see Lincoln standing in the doorway, hair mussed, a lazy smile on his face.

His green eyes narrowed, he strides toward me. "They *are* mine, after all." With a wink, he reaches for the panties, taking them out of my hand and shoving them into his pocket. When I don't react with a snarky comment as I normally would, all the playfulness disappears from his expression. "Are you—"

"I thought you left," I admit, my voice small. "That you realized this was a mistake."

"Oh, Pixie…" He wraps his arms around me, pulling me against him. I inhale his comforting scent, savoring in his use of my nickname again. "Nothing about you has ever been a mistake. Well, except the way *I* treated *you*." Gripping my chin, he forces my gaze to his. "And I won't do it again. I will never make you feel like you're a mistake. Like you're not worth the risk. Like you're not enough."

I swallow hard at the sincerity in his promise, doing my best to stop the tears from forming in the corners of my eyes. I should hate that I'm letting him see my vulnerable side, but it's cathartic. Around Lincoln, I don't have to pretend to be someone I'm not. I don't have to be this resilient person who's unaffected by anything. I can lower my walls and let him in. I can finally be me.

"I meant what I said last night. You're more than enough, Chloe." He kisses away the tear sliding down my cheek before bringing his lips to mine. "You're…more."

"You're more, too."

He skims his mouth against mine, the touch light, making me want it deeper. But responsibility dictates otherwise. With a sigh, I break away. "I should go check on my mom."

"She's fine," he says nonchalantly, as if it's perfectly normal for him to be here during one of her relapses. "Well, as fine as she can be." He lowers his voice. "I hope you don't mind, but I called my mother."

I furrow my brow. "Your mother?"

"She's a nurse. Used to work in OB, but once she went into recovery, she changed paths and now works in a rehab clinic. I figured it would be good to have some sort of medical professional around."

"Medical professional?"

He blows out a long breath, running his hand through his hair. "On my mother's advice, I found your mom's keys and went through her place this morning." He brings his hands to my biceps, his expression grave. "Chloe, I think your mother's been drinking a lot longer than you've been led to believe. Definitely much longer than just a few months. Possibly years."

"How? I—"

"I think she just got good at hiding it. Probably figured if she did everything she was supposed to — went to work, attended meetings, stuff like that — no one would think anything was amiss."

"But I already went through her house." I place my hand on my dresser to steady myself. "The night we were discharged from the hospital. When she was sleeping, I made sure she'd gotten rid of everything."

He arches a brow. "Hidden bottles?"

"What do you mean?"

"Even though it was *her* house, she had liquor stashed in places you never would have thought. A flask between the mattress and box spring. Some mini bottles hidden in the top of the toilet. She even cut out pages in a few of her hardcover books to fit a bottle. All places my mother also hid alcohol."

"But she promised..." I clench my fists. "After I had to quit school because she lost her job due to her drinking. After I..." I trail off, bile rising in my throat at the memory of everything I endured to keep a roof over her head. "She *promised.* Said she finally realized how it was affecting those around her."

"And she probably did...until the withdrawal got to be too severe and she started sneaking a sip here and there. Then a glass. Then an entire bottle. My mother did the same thing. The only thing that finally helped her beat her addiction was a full detox, not simply going to meetings and seeing a therapist. I won't lie to you. It's going to suck, especially with the length of time your mother's been self-medicating."

I shake my head, still trying to process the betrayal and lies, my limbs growing heavy under the truth.

He grabs my hand, running his thumb along my knuckles. "You don't have to go through this alone. I know you don't like the idea of depending on anyone, that you want to prove to the world you can handle anything and everything life throws at you, but it's okay to let someone else carry the burden for a while. That's all I want. To help you carry that burden. Tell me what you need."

"What I need...," I begin.

"Anything. Within reason, of course." He winks.

"What I need..." I meet his eyes, searching them.

"Yes?"

With a smile, I say, "What I really need is a strong cup of coffee."

He pushes out a laugh, his shoulders relaxing. Bringing me back into his embrace, he places a soft kiss on my head. I breathe him in, wishing I could stay here all day, maybe forever.

"I can do that. I already figured out how to use your espresso machine...thanks to Google." He winks.

"Good. Because you'll need to get used to making me espresso if you want to earn your keep around here." I lift myself onto my toes, brushing my lips against his.

"And I certainly plan on doing just that."

CHAPTER THIRTY-TWO

I WON'T LIE and say the next few weeks are a walk in the park, because they certainly aren't. In fact, I can't remember a more stressful time, a more agonizing experience. Watching my mother's body shiver and shake as it fights to rid itself of all the toxins has opened my eyes and made me come to terms with the idea that I failed her. That I should have done more than insist she go to meetings and see a therapist. That I should have demanded more than just her word that she'd quit drinking.

I still have trouble reconciling the fact that she hid it so well from me for so many years. Thankfully, Lincoln's mother, Wendy, has helped me understand better than any high-priced therapist ever has. Seeing how well she's doing has given me hope my mother will also make a full recovery. Finally.

I think it's given my mother hope, too.

"Have you left this place at all this week?" a deep voice says as I stand in my mother's kitchen, heating some soup Wendy brought over.

I look up from the stove, smiling when I see Lincoln standing in the doorway. He's been more than understanding of my need to stay with my mother these past few weeks. It's been a long process, one we've dragged out even longer by not having my mother quit cold turkey. At first, I didn't like the idea of continuing to let her drink a single drop, but Wendy eventually convinced me that stepping down her alcohol consumption over a period of a few weeks would be best. After reading up on the severity of alcohol withdrawal side effects, I have to admit, she was right, especially considering my mother's been able to detox in the comfort of her home instead of a clinic.

"I have," I insist, stirring the soup before putting the cover on it, allowing it to simmer.

He arches a brow, tilting his head. "For more than a few minutes to answer a phone call on the back deck?"

I open my mouth, then snap it shut. He's got me there.

"Chloe…" He exhales as he strides toward me, running his hands down my arms in a soothing manner. "You need to give yourself a break."

"I am."

"Really? You've been holed up here for nearly three weeks now. You've put your entire life on hold."

"I'm still working," I remind him. "My boss said it was okay for me to work out of the office." Granted, I didn't give her the exact details. Just said there was a family emergency.

When Evie heard, she'd called, wondering if everything was okay. I told her not to worry, using my mother's concussion from the nail gun incident as an excuse. I've kept her problem a secret for so long, I'm not sure *how* to tell my friends without them feeling betrayed.

"Yes, but you're sacrificing everything else." He licks his lips, hesitating before lowering his voice. "You haven't been to class in three weeks."

"Lincoln..." With a warning tone, I push away from him. I'd hoped we could leave the professor-student relationship in the classroom, where it belongs. To his credit, this is the first time he's broached the subject, although I have a feeling he's been wanting to bring it up since the first day I didn't show up.

"I'm worried about you."

"Well, don't," I snap, defensive, my face heating. I spin from him, stirring the soup with more force than necessary, the liquid splashing onto the stovetop. "Once my mom gets through these next few days, I'll go down to campus and officially withdraw from class. Your mom said the first few days without alcohol are the worst. It's Friday. We stopped permitting her any alcohol Wednesday, so I—"

"Withdraw?" he interrupts, his voice soft. He touches my shoulder, forcing me to face him. "What do you mean?"

"It's for the best."

"How?"

"If there's ever a question about us, you don't have to worry about any code of conduct." I'm unable to look into his eyes as I rattle off the response I'd prepared. "If asked, I'll say I'd already decided to withdraw. That you had nothing to do with that decision. That a family emergency prevented me from filling out the necessary forms. With me not having been in class since we slept together, it'll make any appearance of impropriety diminish."

"Why would you withdraw when you're so close to graduating?"

"Like my father loves to remind me, it's already taken me ten years to get my bachelors." Although the idea of him gloating about being right eats away at me. "What's one more? My mother needs me—"

"Are you sure that's the case? Or is it the other way around?"

"*I'm* the one who's dropped the ball on this for years now." My voice rises in pitch, my gaze fiery. "The least I can do is make sure I'm here for my mother so she knows she doesn't have to go through this alone. Like I should have been when I..." I trail off, collecting my thoughts, but Lincoln interrupts me anyway.

"And how do you think she'll feel when she learns her daughter, who's mere weeks away from graduating, withdraws to take care of her yet again?" he shoots back in an annoyingly calm tone. Which only irritates me even more.

I take several steps back as my eyes dart around the room, his analytical stare trained on me. He squints, a puzzle piece falling into place.

"Unless she doesn't know she's the reason you quit school in the first place." Advancing, he grips my chin, forcing my eyes to his. "Please tell me she knows."

"I didn't think it was important at the time." Pushing out of his grasp, I rummage through my mother's cabinets for a bowl. This is why I've avoided serious relationships as long as I have. People don't understand. Living with an alcoholic is a constant balancing act — balancing her already fragile emotional state against my needs. *All* my needs.

"Didn't think it was important?" he says incredulously, keeping his voice low. "Chloe, that is *extremely* important. Have you *ever* been honest with her?"

"What's that supposed to mean? If you're trying to tell me this is all my fault, I know it is. I should have seen the signs earlier. I should have known something was wrong the first time she supposedly quit drinking, yet didn't exhibit any of the normal traits of alcohol detox. I was barely a fucking adult, so I messed up! I get that! But now I can finally do it right! And I don't need you reminding me I ruined her life!"

Desperate for some fresh air, I storm past him, but he's in front of me before I can escape. It's hard enough dealing with the truth of how I've constantly failed my mother. How I was selfish enough to just take her word for everything, not wanting to return to the way things were when she was at her lowest because of what that would mean for me. I can't handle Lincoln's disappointment on top of this, too.

"Hey..." He wraps his arms around me, bringing me into his chest. As much as I want to be alone, I can't help melting into his embrace. "You did *not* ruin her life." He tilts my head back, our eyes locking. "I blamed myself, too. Thought if I paid more attention to my mother, maybe I would have prevented it. But the truth is, nothing either of us could have done would have stopped any of this from happening."

"But I've known she's struggled with alcohol most of my life. Hell, I lost count of the number of times I lied to my father when it was my weekend with him, telling him I was sick so I could stay and take care of my mother."

He pauses before asking his next question. "I know you've hidden this from your father and pretty much everyone else, but have you spoken to someone about everything you've been through?"

With a sigh, I push out of his embrace, heading back to the kitchen. "Izzy knows," I answer as I grab a ladle, scooping the soup into a bowl. "I talk to her about it."

"Anyone else? Maybe a professional?"

"I used to go to Al-Anon meetings, but it's been a while." I steal a glance as he lingers in the kitchen, a formidable presence. "I guess I wanted to think everything we'd been through was in the past. That it was just something I could lock away and forget happened."

"It *did* happen. You can't pretend this isn't real. You're surrounded by friends who love you, friends who would love nothing more than to help you through this. You don't have to do this alone."

I swallow hard. "I don't know how *not* to be alone," I admit. It's one of the most honest statements I've made in a long time. For as long as I can remember, it's just been me and my mom. I've kept her secret for years. Isolated myself for fear it was the only way to protect her, to keep her safe.

Lincoln approaches, enclosing me in his arms. "You are a remarkable, strong, resilient woman, albeit stubborn. But it's okay to let others hold you up once in a while." He slowly lowers his mouth to mine, his soft kiss leaving me wanting more. "It's okay to live your life."

"I don't even know how to do that anymore," I breathe.

"Then let me show you how." His lips press more firmly against mine as his hands go to my hips, their grip resolute and needy. He swipes his tongue along my bottom lip, and I open for him, reaching up and threading my fingers through his hair as I melt into the kiss, all the noise in my head alarmingly quiet.

When he pulls away, his expression is light and carefree. "You can start by finally coming back to class."

I huff. "Why do you care so much?"

"This may sound like a foreign concept to you, but I care about *you*. I want you to succeed." A salacious smile crosses his mouth as he steps back and leans against the counter, his brows waggling. "And I'd be lying if I said the past three weeks of not having you in class have been excruciating." His heated tone forces a shiver to roll down my spine. Foreign, yet so welcome.

"Is that so?" I ask in a husky voice, approaching him, running my fingers up his crisp shirt.

He slowly nods, his eyes darkening to a hunter green shade. "That's so."

"And why's that?" My hand wraps around his tie and I pull him toward me. He tries to lean in for a kiss, but I remain just out of reach.

"Even though you weren't there, I was still able to smell your perfume. Like it's permanently engrained in my senses." Looping an arm around my waist, he drags me to him, grinding his hips against me. "And I can't tell you how hard just the smell of you makes me."

"I don't think you have to." Releasing his tie, I stand on my toes and nuzzle the crook of his neck, flicking my tongue along the skin. "I can *feel* how hard it makes you."

Muscles tensing, he grips my face, fingers digging into my skin, about to press his mouth to mine when the sound of footsteps breaks through.

I jump away, snapping my gaze to the stairway at the exact moment Lincoln's mother appears. She comes to a stop, looking between us, smiling slyly. Now I know where Lincoln gets his smile from. Actually, I see a lot of him in her. While his six-foot-three frame has a solid ten inches over her, she has the same green eyes, dark hair, and compassionate personality.

"Mrs. Moore." I lower my head, shifting uncomfortably on my feet. Lincoln, however, appears just as calm and collected as ever, amused by my reaction. "How's my mother doing?"

"I told you. Call me Wendy."

"Right. Wendy."

Turning from her to hide my embarrassment, I head toward the refrigerator and hoist myself onto my tiptoes, reaching for the breakfast tray on the top, but my height works against me. Seeing my struggle, Lincoln approaches, standing unnervingly close. I attempt to get out of his way, but he places his hand on my hip, keeping me in place as he reaches past me and takes down the tray.

I expect him to let go of me once he sets it on the counter, but he doesn't, snaking an arm around me and pulling me close. Wendy's smile only grows in response.

"Your mother's doing as well as can be expected. She's had a few bouts of heart palpitations, but they've seemed to settle."

"Will we be able to keep her here?"

"She's not exhibiting any extreme symptoms that would require constant medical supervision. I'll continue to monitor her, but because we didn't detox cold turkey, I don't foresee the effects to be as severe as they otherwise would have been."

I blow out a breath, grateful I had a few voices of reason to help me make decisions about my mother's treatment plan.

"She asked to see you," she says after a few moments of silence.

"Oh. Right." I step out of Lincoln's grasp, hesitant. While I feel compelled to be here during this process, I've tried to keep my distance, not wanting to sit through another verbal battering. At least the outbursts and angry shouts have decreased the past few days. "I'll bring her soup up."

I place the bowl onto the tray, along with a bottle of water and a baguette.

"And, Chloe?" Wendy calls out just as I'm about to head up the stairs.

I glance over my shoulder. "Yes?"

"There's no need to jump away from my son whenever I enter the room. You're more than welcome to kiss him anytime you'd like. In fact, you're welcome to do *more* than just kiss him." She gives me a conniving look.

My eyes widen, my cheeks burning, and I face forward, continuing up the stairs as Lincoln's deep chuckles fill the house with warmth. Fill *me* with warmth.

Chapter Thirty-Three

"CHLOE? IS THAT you?" my mother calls out as I timidly approach her room.

I push open the door, peeking inside. I swallow hard at what appears to be a shell of the woman who raised me. The strong, tenacious woman who didn't take shit from anyone. Who would fight tooth and nail for a cause she believed in. Who, on more than one occasion, had gotten arrested during a protest. It's difficult to see her so weak that she can barely support her head, her hands shaking every time she attempts to bring a sippy cup to her mouth. All from drinking too much for more than a decade.

"Hey, Mom," I greet weakly. "I brought you more of Wendy's soup."

"Thanks, sweetie." She waves me over, the motion seeming to take all the energy out of her.

I set the tray onto the table beside her and prop her into a sitting position, placing a few extra pillows behind her to keep her head upright. "Can I get you anything else?" I step back.

"Actually, yes." She pats the mattress, smiling. It reminds me of my younger days when she'd beam, bestowing praise on me for accomplishing something ordinary and unexceptional, like help her decorate a cake, or set the table, or sing a song. She never berated me for not living up to my true potential, as my father would. "Sit down, baby."

With a nod, I lower myself onto the edge of the bed. She grabs my hand in hers. I have to swallow through the lump forming in my throat when I feel how cold they are, how violently they shake. I do my best to steady them, covering her hand with my own and holding her tightly, wishing I could fast forward through this part.

"Chloe, sweetie," she begins with a sigh, peering into my gray eyes. "You remind me so much of your father."

"What?" I stiffen, heat washing over my face. "I'm not anything like that man."

"Maybe not the man he is today, but back when we first met…" Staring into the distance, a nostalgic gleam fills her eyes. "I see a lot of him in you. You'll fight for something you strongly believe in. You'll bend over backwards to help a friend in need." Her smile fades and she pulls her hands from mine, leaning back against the pillows, her gaze slowly lifting to mine. "You'll sacrifice your happiness and well-being for those you love, often without them knowing."

Unsure where this is going, I remain silent.

"I overheard your conversation with Lincoln."

I glance at her sideways, hesitant. "What part?"

"Enough to realize how selfish I've been." Her gaze searches mine before she asks, "Did you really drop out of school to take care of me? I thought you left because you got a job in the field."

"I couldn't let you end up on the streets." I lower my voice. "You're my mother."

She closes her eyes, a few tears trickling down her cheeks. "And I've been a horrible one at that." She returns her determined gaze to me. "I want you to know that you bear no blame in any of this."

"But—"

"No. I won't have you blaming yourself. *I'm* the one who decided being numb would solve all my problems. I knew it wasn't the answer. I should have focused on my daughter, not ignore her for the bottle. Definitely not make her take care of me instead of the other way around."

"It's not your fault, Mom."

"It is. And don't you dare try to convince me otherwise. I will not let you walk out of this room thinking this isn't my fault. That you bear even a speck of blame here. You don't. So don't you even try to argue with me, Chloe Lynn, because I'll win." She winks. Then her light expression falls and she reaches for my hand once more. This time, it's a little more steady, but not much. "Promise me something."

"What's that?"

"I want you to finish this semester and finally graduate."

On a long exhale, I pull away. "It's not that easy. Things are…complicated."

"Why?" She crosses her arms in front of her chest. The way her body trembles makes it appear she's trying to warm herself, not suffering from the lack of alcohol in her bloodstream. "Because Lincoln's your professor?"

My heart drops to the pit of my stomach, eyes widening. If she knows, who else does? And *how* does she know to begin with? Yes, Lincoln's dropped by on occasion over the past few weeks, but we'd kept our conversations focused on my mother's recovery. Today was the first time he brought up class.

"When you have kids of your own, you'll understand how mothers develop this kind of…sixth sense about things. Plus, I've spent a lot of time talking to Wendy." She looks at me thoughtfully, her smile returning. "We actually met once many years ago now. At the company Christmas party a few months before…" She trails off.

She doesn't need to elaborate. I know she's referring to the death of

Lincoln's father.

"I remember talking to her about how she felt about her husband's new assignment as the Southeast Asia bureau chief, especially considering this was mere months after 9/11. She didn't seem too fazed by it, said the hardest part was being away from him. But it was a mutual decision they made so their son could finish his senior year of high school here in the States. Once he was off to college, she planned on settling in Mumbai with him."

"But she never got a chance, did she?"

"No, but that's not relevant here. The fact is I know who Lincoln is, Chloe. Wendy mentioned he worked for the *Times* and also taught at a local college. The same local college my own daughter currently attends. From there, we both kind of put the pieces together."

"Then you understand why I have to do this. Why I have to withdraw."

"No, you don't. I am more than aware that your father and I have done a horrible job at making you feel like you're deserving of this risk Lincoln seems willing to take, but you are. You are worth so much more than the hand you've been dealt. So promise me. Go back to school. Finish this semester. Graduate. Finally prove that smug father of yours wrong. Don't give him the satisfaction of being right. Okay?"

I chew on my lower lip, torn. Yesterday, this seemed like the right decision. I assumed Lincoln would eventually realize it was best for both of us, considering how much we've muddied the waters. Then again, we muddied those waters the instant I begged him not to report our relationship to the dean and he agreed. There's only four more weeks left in the semester. What can possibly go wrong?

"Okay."

CHAPTER THIRTY-FOUR

MY OFFICE LINE ringing sounds Thursday as I catch up on all the articles I'd pitched and need to deliver in the next few days. Despite my initial reluctance, Lincoln was right, as was my mother. I needed to live my life. And that life included returning to work.

Shuffling papers around my desk, I follow the noise of my phone, finally finding it under a folder full of photos of the latest royal baby. Quickly grabbing the receiver, I answer breathlessly.

"Chloe Davenport."

"Ah, Miss Davenport." A deep, gravelly voice comes on the line, the timbre making my body buzz to life. "It's Professor Moore. I do hope it's not too forward of me to call you at work." There's a flirtatious quality to his tone that has me playing along with his little game. And if I know anything about Lincoln, it's that he loves games.

"Not at all, *Professor*," I reply softly, facing the corner of my cubicle to have a bit more privacy.

"I was calling to see if you'd be available for a bit of a chat today before class. Regarding your…past performance."

"Past performance?"

"Precisely. Fifty-two West Thirteenth Street. Near Fifth. Meet me there in thirty minutes. Go to the front desk and give them your name."

"Not your office?" I ask in a demure voice, swiveling in my chair. "Isn't that against school policy?"

"It *is* frowned upon."

"Then I—"

"Don't play coy with me, Miss Davenport." His tone is gruff, demanding, a complete change from the flirtatious quality mere seconds ago. I snap my mouth closed, involuntarily clenching my thighs together in an attempt to dull the ache. "I see how you look at me every week."

"And how's that?"

"Like you want to part those legs of yours and let me have my way with you."

"Professor," I gasp, feigning indignation when, in reality, everything about this game turns me on in a way nothing has before. I've always craved Lincoln, am always desperate for more of him. But this… This takes carnal desire to a level I hadn't expected.

"Don't even try to deny it, Miss Davenport. Because I've been fantasizing about you all semester. How can I not when you come in and flirt with those boring classmates of yours, all to make me jealous?"

"I don't—"

"You do," he barks before softening his voice. "But I know something your male classmates don't."

"What's that?" I glance over my shoulder to make sure I'm alone. It would be just my luck that an audience of coworkers would be assembled, eavesdropping in on bits of our juicy conversation. Thankfully, that's not the case.

"That they can fawn over you all they want, then go home and jerk off as they imagine how you feel and taste. But the truth remains."

"And that is?"

"Every single one of them… They're just boys. You need a man. Someone who can satisfy even your most hidden desires." His voice becomes breathy, carnal, wanton.

"And you think that's you?"

"I don't think. I know. And you do, too." He pauses before adding, "Don't be late, Miss Davenport. You know how I feel about tardiness." He allows his words to linger for a moment before the line goes dead.

I remain motionless, staring at the wall of my cubicle, my heart racing. Then I jump to my feet, return my phone to the cradle, and hastily collect my things.

I don't want to be late for Professor Moore.

Or maybe I do.

* * *

I check my watch as I hurry down the street, the address Lincoln… Professor Moore requested I meet him at coming into view. I thought I'd be practical and take a cab instead of the subway or bus. I was wrong. I'm convinced the cab driver intentionally took the route he knew would be most congested to pad his fare. The drive, which should have only taken twenty-five minutes, took close to forty.

Frantically pulling open the door to the boutique, Georgian-style hotel, I burst down the short flight of stairs to the lobby. I scan the area for any sign of Lincoln, then remember his instruction that I give my name at the front desk.

I run my hands over my dress to calm my frazzled appearance, my heels clicking on the tile as I continue toward the registration desk. If I weren't in such a hurry, I'd take a minute to appreciate the beauty surrounding me. Brick walls. Wood accents throughout. Crown molding. Flecks of gold.

All elements I never would have thought to marry together, but it works here. The charming, yet sophisticated space fits in with the style of Greenwich Village.

"How can I help you, miss?" a blonde with a congenial smile asks.

"My name is Chloe Davenport. I—"

"Yes, Miss Davenport." She retrieves a keycard from the desk area and hands it to me. "Elevators are around the corner and to the left." She gestures in the general vicinity. "Enjoy your stay."

I offer her my thanks, then head in the direction she pointed, skirting past a family of tourists as they step off the elevator. I sneak on, glance at the room number, then hit the button for the sixteenth floor. Once the doors close and I'm alone, I rock on my heels, jittery, unsure what awaits me. But if the buildup is any indication, I have a feeling it will be better than any fantasy.

Once the elevator stops, I step off, padding down the short, quiet hallway to the correct room. I insert the key into the slot and turn the knob, stepping hesitantly onto the hardwood of the foyer, praying the woman at the front desk gave me the correct key and I'm not about to walk into some crazy swingers' party.

But if there *were* a party going on, there wouldn't be this striking silence, the only noise that of the air conditioning unit and the faint, ambient city sounds I barely notice now that I've lived in Manhattan this long.

I round the corner from the foyer and my feet meet plush carpet, the bedroom coming into view. I halt in my tracks at the sight of Lincoln sitting in a wingback chair, a view of Greenwich Village and beyond visible behind him. A leg rests on a thigh, today's edition of the *Times* spread in front of him.

My heart skips a beat as my eyes feast on him. So casual. So smooth. So sophisticated. The way he looks in a crisp, three-piece suit, coupled with his dark-framed glasses and designer tie, has my libido going into overdrive. I'm pretty sure the ol' girl is stretching in preparation for what she hopes to be a killer workout.

Finally, Lincoln's eyes lift to mine. Slow. Deliberate. Calculated. The heat in his stare sends a delicious shiver through me, ending between my legs, my core clenching.

"Miss Davenport." His voice is even, unaffected, as he folds the newspaper, placing it on the small table beside him.

"Professor Moore."

He raises his arm, using a single finger to beckon me to him, the severe expression he wears not allowing any room for argument. My eyes remain locked on his, ash gray to vibrant green. The closer I get, the more I'm attuned to the raw masculinity and sexuality coming off him.

I stop when I'm mere inches away. Closer than would be considered socially acceptable, but still far enough away that I'm not right in front of him. Not yet anyway. He places both feet on the floor, resting a hand on either thigh, but makes no move to get up, a king holding court over his subject. And I am more than willing to be his subject.

"You're late. You're aware I have a very strict policy when it comes to tardiness."

"My cab driver gave me a nice tour of Fifth Avenue, instead of taking a less congested route. Otherwise, I would have been on time." My voice is little more than a squeak, a complete shift from my normally assured tone.

"You also know how I feel about excuses, do you not?" He glares at me through condescending eyes.

"I do."

He grips my hips, yanking me between his legs in one swift move, his hands going to my ass, squeezing. I gasp, my pulse skyrocketing, as if this is new. I guess it is in a way.

Leaning toward me, his nose grazes against my waist before he dips lower, inhaling when he reaches the apex of my thighs. He squeezes tighter, a visible shiver rolling over him before he pulls away, his eyes on fire. It sears a hole straight through me. Or at least through my panties.

He releases his grasp on me, sliding a hand along my hipbone, my muscles clenching. I have to remind myself to breathe as his touch leisurely travels down my thigh, pushing back the slit of my skirt.

"Perhaps I should teach you a lesson so you won't let it happen again." He shifts his eyes to mine, his voice becoming gruff, unable to hide his own need for me. The heat of his finger looms torturously close to my center, but still too far. He may as well be in Jersey City. "Would you like that?"

"God, yes," I exhale.

"I had a feeling you would." Abruptly pulling away, he stands, his sudden shift forcing me to step back.

With purposeful strides, he moves past me, turning to face me once he reaches the bed. Eyes narrowed, he beckons me with that same finger. I could find a better use for that finger, but damn if this entire scenario doesn't have me running hotter than any previous sexual encounter...including all the other times I've been with Lincoln.

I keep my expression even as I walk toward him, my chest rising and falling in a quicker rhythm. When I'm within reach, he spins me around, yanking my body hard and fast against his, my back to his front. He runs a desperate hand along my stomach, over my breasts, up to my mouth, never staying in one spot too long.

"Tell me, Miss Davenport. What do you think an appropriate punishment is for your tardiness?" He finds my nipple through the fabric of my dress. When he pinches, I moan, my body pulsing with need. My libido has checked the laces on her sneakers and is officially ready for that starting pistol. But I know Lincoln. He has no intention of firing it anytime soon. His self-control is excruciating.

"Whatever you think is best…" I swallow hard. "Sir."

With a hungered growl, he grips my hair, forcing my head to the side, exposing my flesh for his pleasure. He clamps his teeth down on that spot where my neck meets my shoulder, and my legs turn into jelly.

An arm wraps around my waist and tugs me even harder against him, supporting me. He knows how much his mouth on this spot drives me insane. And today is no different, but something about this game we're playing has my body more alert, more needy, more desperate for him.

Too soon, he releases his hold on me, forcing me around to face him. "Strip," he orders.

I feign shock and a hint of innocence. "But, Professor Moore, I—"

"Don't play the virtuous card with me. You've been fantasizing about this as much as I have." He curves toward me, his delicious scent consuming me. "You can't stand here and tell me you haven't. I know the truth."

His hand goes to my chin, tilting my head up, his mouth a whisper from mine. All it would take is the slightest movement and I'd taste his lips. And I want to. God, I want to. But just like the night we first connected, I want this even more. The chase. The hunt. Then the kill.

"And what's that?"

His finger draws a line down my throat, through the valley of my breasts, then circles my belly button before disappearing into the slit of my skirt. "That you can't stop thinking about me every time you touch this delicious pussy of yours." His thumb brushes against me, teasing.

"You are so wet for me, aren't you?"

"Yes…," I pant, my eyes rolling into the back of my head.

"Yes what?"

I swallow hard, licking my lips, my chest heaving. "Yes, sir."

"Good girl."

He removes his hand from me, and I snap my eyes open, watching as he steps back. His demeanor is nothing short of collected and assured, as always. This is simply a game, an opportunity to pretend to be two different people for a minute, but I doubt I could remain as composed as he. I'm already on the verge of losing what little control I have left.

"Strip."

"Yes, sir." I reach behind myself and lower the zipper of my navy blue sheath dress, the sleeves off the shoulders. I take my time as I shrug it off, addicted to the heat building in Lincoln's eyes as he watches my every move.

"No bra?"

"Benefit of having nearly non-existent boobs," I answer shyly. "You can get away without a bra instead of having to wear a strapless that digs into your skin."

Lincoln's demeanor changes as he closes the distance between us, pressing my body to his. His mouth finds mine and I sigh into his tender kiss, a break in character. He cups my breast, his touch reverent, yet still filled with so much passion.

"You're perfect, Chloe," he whispers against my mouth. "Everything about you is perfect. Don't let anyone ever tell you otherwise."

Before I have a chance to respond, he steps back. With the flip of an internal switch, he turns into Professor Moore, stance wide, expression severe. He nods slightly, and I continue pushing my dress down my body, over my hips, allowing it to pool at my feet. I step out of it, about to kick off my heels when his voice rings out.

"No. The shoes stay on."

My libido gives me a high five. Apparently, she was hoping he'd say that. So was I.

"Yes, sir."

"But your panties do not."

"Yes, sir." Smirking, I hook my fingers in the waist of my panties, ridding myself of my last article of clothing while Lincoln remains fully dressed. I'm about to toss them on top of my discarded dress when he extends his hand toward me.

"I'll take those."

"Why am I not surprised?" I murmur in a sly voice, placing them into his palm.

He clutches my bicep, spinning me around, binding my body against his. "You're already in trouble, Miss Davenport. Shall I increase your penalty?" He slides a leisurely hand down my stomach, which only serves to heighten the pressure building inside me, growing more excruciating with the passing of each second.

When his finger slides beyond my hipbone, I discreetly part my legs. "And what penalty is that?"

"Maybe I won't let you come," he warns, his teeth skimming against my neck, a dull ache from where he'd marked me. "That should serve as sufficient motivation to follow my rules."

"No," I beg, desperate. "Not that. *Anything* but that."

"Anything?" he repeats, amused.

"Anything." The idea of being left in this state for the next several hours is enough to drive me mad. I need to get off. And soon.

He turns me around, his grin mischievous. "I do have something else in mind. Something *I've* been thinking about for quite some time now."

"And what's that?"

"You'll see." He brings my panties up to his nose and makes a show of inhaling, shivering dramatically before shoving them into the pocket of his pants. "Have you ever used a safe word?"

"I have."

"And have you ever been spanked?"

"I have."

He nods, seemingly unaffected by my response, as if I'd just told him I've been to Florida, not that I've been tied up, spanked, or blindfolded.

"I won't be too harsh. Not today anyway. We'll start slow, since we've never really explored much of this together. If you're not ready, that's okay, too," he adds quickly, cupping my face, my sweet, compassionate Lincoln returning. "I would never force you into doing something you're not ready for. It won't make me want to be with you any less. Okay?"

I simply stare at him, my expression even, not giving anything away. Then I rid myself of his hold, stepping past him.

"Chloe, I—"

When I glance over my shoulder with a sly smile and wink, he snaps his mouth shut, his eyes filling with wanton lust as he watches me crawl onto the mattress, my ass exposed to him.

As I wait in anticipation, the room becomes eerily silent, apart from my labored breathing, and I stare at the black-and-white print of the Brooklyn Bridge hanging over the headboard.

When I feel Lincoln's finger draw a line down my spine, I peek back at him standing to the side of the bed, his jacket and vest discarded.

"You're sure?"

I nod subtly.

"I need you to say it, Chloe. I need more than a nod."

"I'm sure. I want this."

His mouth quirks into a smile as he pulls away, loosening his tie. But just as soon as it appeared, the light expression vanishes.

"Face forward."

Like a trained pet, I oblige, jerking my eyes forward, the snap of his tie ripping from his neck as formidable as the crack of leather against skin. He brings the silk-like material up to me, using it to shroud my world in darkness. Without the sense of sight, everything else is heightened. Smell. Sound. Touch. Feel.

The shiver from his finger tracing a line from my nape down my spine nearly unhinges me. Such an innocent touch, barely there. But the depth of it hits places on my body I never knew existed.

The bed dips and my breathing increases, my heavy pants echoing in my ears. The heat of him prickles my skin as he leans over me, his teeth lightly pulling on my earlobe.

"If it's too much, say…panties."

"Panties?"

"Fitting, don't you think?"

I smile, a break in the charged atmosphere. "I couldn't think of a more appropriate word."

He turns my head toward his, covering my mouth, treating me to a taste of him, before he pulls away, resuming the role he's here to play.

The sound of a belt buckle loosening finds its way to my ears, followed by his zipper. I hold my breath, bracing myself for whatever's to come. But nothing does, the room still.

One second. Then another. And another. When I'm about to remove the blindfold, a hard slap lands across my ass, the shock of it causing me to scream and bury my head in the pillow. Not out of pain, but in unbridled ecstasy, my body craving more of his brutal touch, his stinging hand, his punishing caress.

I don't even notice how much I'm shaking until Lincoln grips my hips, steadying me. He covers my frame with his, his hands gliding down my arms, his fingers linking with mine.

"Are you okay?" His breathing is hard, labored.

"Yes."

"Good girl." He leaves a jarring kiss on my neck before pushing himself up, his touch gone.

I take several deep breaths, moaning when he lands another blow to my other cheek, harder this time. But it makes me burn for him even more. He brings his hand back to me, massaging my ass, then sliding a few fingers between my legs, pushing inside, stretching and massaging.

"Does spanking turn you on?"

"Yes." I move against his fingers, on the brink of shattering. I'm unprepared for him to withdraw and slap my ass once more.

"Yes what?" he growls.

"Yes, sir," I yell, gripping the sheets, my muscles tight.

"Better." He slides a finger back inside me and I move against him, my mind a haze.

"Don't come," he whispers in a gruff voice. "Not yet. I want to feel your pussy clench around my cock, not my hand."

"Then you'd better hurry because I'm ready to fall apart."

His chest hair tickles my back, his breath hot against my flesh. "Condom or no condom?"

"No condom."

"Good girl," he says again, removing his fingers.

He lifts his arousal up to me and runs his tip around my slickness, but doesn't slide inside, torturing me even more.

"Lincoln…," I moan.

He fists my hair, yanking my head back. "What did you call me?"

"I mean… Professor Moore," I stammer.

"Better. I shouldn't let you come from that little slip-up," he muses, pulling his erection away.

"No!"

He bites my neck. "Then beg for me," he orders, his mouth never leaving my skin, jarring and bruising.

I squeeze my eyes shut, my entire body stiffening as I breathe through the ache. "Please, Li… Professor Moore."

"Please what?" His bite becomes even more harsh, but still makes me hunger for him. I fear the second he pushes into me, I'll implode into a thousand tiny pieces. "Tell me what you want."

"Please fuck me." My voice is even, but still laced with desperation.

"Good girl." He loosens his grip, his tongue tracing gentle circles where his teeth just dug into my skin. "Or perhaps I should say bad girl."

"You know what they say, don't you?"

"What's that?" he asks, amused.

"Good girls go to heaven. But bad girls—"

"Bad girls make you *feel* like you're in heaven," he finishes as he thrusts into me. "And this is most certainly heaven." He kisses my shoulder blade, not moving as he fills me to the hilt. "You are my heaven."

He slowly retreats before pushing back into me, going even deeper. This torturous rhythm continues as he plunges into me in a punishing drive, stills for several agonizing moments before withdrawing, almost like he knows I'm close to losing my mind and is prolonging my pleasure.

His hand massages my ass, making me moan. Then he lands a hard blow at the same time as he pushes into me. The combination of the agony and ecstasy has my heart racing. If there weren't a blindfold obscuring my vision, I'd be blind from sensation.

The pattern continues, bringing me to the edge, only to slow down, waiting until I've recovered before thrusting and slapping again. Each thrust, each slap is more punishing, more enthralling, more addicting, making me cry out louder, my legs to shake more violently.

"Harder," I beg, so close to unraveling.

"Like this?" His breathing labored, he reels back, the force of his blow and drive pushing me forward.

"Harder!" I bite the pillow to muffle my cries.

He stills, preparing for his next assault, which is more brutal, yet erotic.

"Harder!" I scream once more, unsure how much more I can take, but I'm willing to find out, to test my limits.

Like a beast unleashed, he drives into me, pressing his hand to my back, keeping me locked in place so my pleasure is completely at his mercy. But the buildup to this moment was so intense, so drawn-out, it doesn't take long for me to fall over the edge, crying out his name as forceful waves of ecstasy wash over me, my legs trembling as I come undone.

"Fuck, Chloe." His words come out almost like a strangled plea. He increases his rhythm even more before he stills, clutching my hips as he finds his own release.

We remain motionless as we attempt to get our breathing under control, my body still shivering through the aftereffects of what is probably the most body-numbing orgasm I've ever had. Being with Lincoln has always been an adventure. He's able to satisfy me in a way I never thought possible. But this… This may be the hottest experience to date.

Looping an arm around my waist, he slowly pulls out, then helps me roll onto my back. When he unfastens my blindfold, I'm met with blazing green eyes.

"Hey," he says sweetly.

"Hey." I reach up, running my fingers through his hair, my arm quivering from muscle fatigue. Grabbing my hand to help steady it, he closes his eyes, arching into the touch before returning his gaze to mine.

"How was that?"

"Hot. Insanely hot."

"Are you sore?"

"A little." I curve toward him, brushing my lips with his. "But just think. Every time you see me squirming in class because of how uncomfortable those hard chairs are, you'll know it's because of you."

"I would offer to bring my office chair in for you, but I fear more students might expect the same treatment."

"There are quite a few girls who I'm sure would love for you to tie them up and spank them," I jest, although my statement's not a complete lie.

He wraps his arms around me, and I kick off my heels, allowing them to fall to the floor with a load thump. "I was talking about bringing a chair in. You're the only one I want to tie up and spank."

"Good," I say drowsily, closing my eyes, and he covers our bodies with the duvet.

"Good." His soft kiss on my temple is a stark contrast from his earlier dominance. I love that this man can give me both. He can be fire and ice. Harsh and endearing. Wicked and honorable.

And he's all mine.

"Can I ask you something?" I press after a few moments of silence.

"Anything. Except where Jimmy Hoffa's buried. I'm sworn to secrecy on that one."

I turn around, playfully pinching him in the side as I snuggle into his chest. "Why did you want to do this?"

"Have sex with you?" He touches my chin, forcing my eyes to meet his. "In case I haven't made myself clear, I am absolutely addicted to you."

"Not that. I meant the whole role-playing thing. Well, technically, it's not exactly role-play with us."

"True," he responds thoughtfully. "It's not. I guess I didn't want this to become an elephant in the room between us. Is our situation ideal? Far from it. When we're together like this, I want to be able to be us and not worry about life outside these walls." He returns his mouth to mine and pushes me onto my back, hovering over me, resting his weight on his forearms. "And I've been fantasizing about some role-play with you ever since I met you."

"Is that right?"

He leisurely licks his lips, his gaze darkening once more. "That's right."

"And what kinds of things did you have in mind?"

"Oh, you know…" The corners of his mouth twitch up in a flirtatious grin as he lowers himself, dragging his tongue along my collarbone, traveling farther south before tugging on my nipple. "The usual."

"And what's that?"

"Doctor-patient. Boss-secretary. The virgin college freshman." He moves to my other breast, giving it the same treatment. I close my eyes, hooking my leg around his waist, feeling his erection slowly return to life. "But I am certainly partial to professor-student, especially after today." He covers my mouth with his, trailing a hand down my torso before sinking a finger inside, my body reigniting.

"Oh, Professor."

CHAPTER THIRTY-FIVE

"CHLOE," A TENDER voice says, rousing me from one of the most erotic dreams I've had in quite some time.

I slowly blink my eyes open, taking in my unfamiliar surroundings. The instant my gaze locks on Lincoln, I realize it wasn't a dream. This afternoon was real. Lincoln lured me into a hotel room for the sole purpose of having hot, naughty sex.

"Here." He extends his hand, revealing two ibuprofen. "This will help with, well…any discomfort."

I scoot up, wincing, my ass sore. But I'd gladly suffer through this pain again, the pleasure I experienced still making me feel like I'm on a high.

"What time is it?" I place the pills on my tongue, then grab the bottle of water he holds out, taking a sip.

"After two thirty. We need to get to class."

"Uh-oh." Passing him a coquettish look, I reach for his tie that served as a blindfold mere hours ago. "It appears I'm going to be late again." I yank him toward me, my words coming out breathy. "Perhaps I need a reminder of your rather strict tardiness rules."

"Perhaps you do." He crushes his lips against mine, his tongue plunging into my mouth as sparks shoot through me. I rake my fingers along his back, about to push his jacket off his shoulders when he abruptly pulls away, adjusting his belt. "But at a later date."

"Oh, really?" I roll onto my side, propping my head in my hand as I narrow my eyes on his crotch. "From where I'm standing, you're hungry for more."

"I'll always want more of you." He brings his hand to my cheek, lovingly brushing his thumb along the skin. "My sweetest addiction. But we still need to go."

"Ugh…" I throw my legs over the side of the bed. "So serious."

He flashes a beautiful smile my way, then his expression falls as I turn to grab the dress he placed neatly over a chair, his attention focusing on my ass.

"Chloe, I—"

I press my mouth to his before he can utter another word. "Don't. I liked it. Actually, I *really* liked it. I don't want you to feel bad because then you won't want to do it again. And I really want you to do that again." With a bounce in my step, I head toward the bathroom. "But next time, you be the doctor. I'll be the patient, and you can give me a very thorough exam."

I close the door behind me, grinning to myself when I hear him curse under his breath.

Aware of what a stickler Lincoln is for being on time, I hurriedly run a washcloth over my body and freshen my appearance so I don't look like I've just been fucked, especially on my first day back to class after missing three weeks. A bruise has already formed on my neck, teeth marks visible, so I smooth my hair over my shoulder, covering it as best I can.

When I emerge into the bedroom, Lincoln's re-adjusting his tie. He appears just as put together as he did when I first walked into this hotel room, apart from his hair, which has a mussed-up, just-fucked look.

Sauntering up to him, I bring my hands to his neck, helping to straighten his tie. "Every time I look at you and see this tie, I won't be able to stop thinking about the things you did to me when you used it as a blindfold."

"That's the point." He waggles his brows.

I touch my mouth to his, then allow him to help me into my jacket. After a quick check to make sure I have everything, apart from my panties, he walks me to the door. "Thanks for this afternoon."

With a smile, I lift myself onto my toes, kissing him. "Thank you."

He pulls back the door, holding it open for me. I step into the hallway, turning around when he doesn't immediately follow. "Aren't you coming?"

Hesitation flickers in his expression. "I don't think it's a smart idea for us to walk out of a hotel together. We *are* only a few blocks away from campus."

"Oh…" My heart deflates.

"It's just…" With a sigh, he pinches the bridge of his nose before returning his eyes to mine. "We need to be careful. I want to be with you, but I'll lose my job. Probably *both* jobs, so…"

"Of course." I force a smile, the high I was on crashing to the floor now that reality has set in.

Will we ever be able to be seen together? Or is this all we'll ever have? A few clandestine meetings. Some really hot sex. Then being sent away before anyone realizes the truth. It reminds me a little too much of all the men who came before him.

"Well…" I hold my head high, re-securing my mask. "I'll be on my way."

He steps toward me. "Chloe…"

I hold up my hand, stopping him. "It's no big deal." My tone turns icy. "Thanks for the private session… *Professor.*"

* * *

By the time I step off the elevator and make my way through the familiar corridors of the journalism building, my blood is boiling. No matter the questionable things I'd done in my past, I've never felt as cheap as I just did with Lincoln. Why did I expect things would be different? It was stupid of me to think we'd ever have a normal relationship.

When I barrel into the classroom several minutes after three, all eyes go to me in expectation, then disappointment when they see I'm not Lincoln. A few of the girls rake their disapproving gazes over me. I wonder if I have a blinking sign on my forehead, advertising the fact that I'd just fucked our professor. This must be how Hester Prynne felt. Except she knew she wore a giant sign announcing her sins to the world. My sins are still invisible. How much longer will they remain that way?

I take a few seconds to compose myself, feeling unnaturally exposed without the panties I can only assume are still stuffed in Lincoln's pocket, and meet Owen's confused stare, which doesn't leave me the entire time I walk in his direction and sit down, shrugging out of my coat.

I pull a notebook from my bag, flipping to a free page, squirming in my chair. I smooth my hair over my shoulder, ensuring it adequately covers the mark Lincoln left. I should have sat on the other side of Owen so he wouldn't have as many opportunities to see it. Better yet, I should have kept my coat on.

"Where have you been?" he asks once I'm situated. "I figured Professor Prick kicked you out. And since you haven't responded to any of my texts—"

"He didn't kick me out. I had some…personal stuff come up." I fidget with my dress, tugging the skirt to cover a few bruises on my thighs. But as discreet as I try to be, it doesn't escape Owen's attention.

"Is something going on?"

"What?" I shoot my eyes to his. I notice his gaze flicker to my neck, so I quickly hide the mark with my hair once more. "No. I just…" I stammer, needing to come up with something to tell him, to bring his attention away from the questionable bruises that cover my body. "My mom's sick." It's not a complete lie. "That's why I haven't been in class. I had to take care of her."

"Oh god," Owen responds with all the compassion I've come to expect from him, his shoulders dropping. "I'm so sorry. I had no idea." He shakes his head. "Do you need anything?"

"Thanks, but she's doing much better now. We both are."

"That's good to hear, but next time, answer your damn texts. I was worried about you." He reaches for my hand, covering it with his before I have a chance to pull away. "Worried the Big Bad Wolf ran away with Little Purple Riding Hood."

"Mr. Campbell!" A booming voice fills the room.

Owen and I jump in our seats and I yank my hand from his, hiding it in my lap. I expect Owen to shift his attention to Lincoln, but he doesn't, his analytical eyes studying me. I straighten my spine, feigning confidence, praying he doesn't put the pieces together. He wouldn't, would he? Then again, the last time I was in this very room, class ended early due to some unexpected fireworks.

"Do you mind? Or is your conversation with Miss Davenport more important than, say, a journalist's privilege to keep their source anonymous?"

"No, sir. I apologize, sir."

Lincoln glares for several uncomfortable seconds before turning around, scribbling on the whiteboard. I keep my eyes glued to the blank page of my notebook, ignoring the way Owen steals a glimpse of the bruise on my leg, then shifts his attention back to Lincoln, as if on the brink of putting a puzzle together.

"Now, Mr. Campbell," Lincoln begins when he turns around, a cocky smirk on his face. "What can you tell the class about the Branzburg cases?"

I blow out a breath. As much as I hate when he intentionally picks on Owen because of our friendship, I'm grateful for it today, since it forces Owen to focus more on Lincoln's line of questioning and less on me.

All throughout the three-hour class, I do my best to focus on the material and compartmentalize this Lincoln from the Lincoln who called me his sweetest addiction, from the confusing Lincoln who recoiled the instant I suggested we leave the hotel together.

The more I stew over his behavior, the more my irritation grows. He can't order me to a hotel room, treat me like he's only interested in getting between my legs, then get mad if Owen, a *friend*, appears genuinely concerned about my mysterious absence. He wants to have boundaries about where we're seen together. Well, I need boundaries, too.

When the class finally ends, Owen turns to me, raking his hand through his sandy hair. "I didn't think I was going to survive that."

Thankfully, any earlier suspicion has disappeared, probably because Lincoln called on me, much to everyone's surprise. But I suppose it's best to remove any appearance of impropriety.

"You did great. You're smarter than you give yourself credit for." I playfully nudge him in the side as we walk toward the door. I pay no attention to Lincoln, pretending to be more interested in whatever Owen's telling me. If he wants to treat me like I'm disposable, two can play his game.

I know it's juvenile and a bit rash, but after this afternoon, he deserves a taste of his own medicine.

As I'm about to leave with Owen, Lincoln's voice sounds from behind me. "Miss Davenport, I'd like a word, please."

I turn to face him. "Oh, I wouldn't want to inconvenience you."

"I insist," he grits out, his jaw clenched. "We need to discuss your absences and devise a plan going forward."

"You can email me. I need to get to an appointment," I lie, although I *am* supposed to meet the girls for happy hour.

"You've already missed enough classes for me to fail you, Miss Davenport. A few minutes of your time to discuss this is the least you can do. Rest assured, despite any…connection I may have to your father, I have every right to fail you."

I clench my jaw, my hands balling into fists. The room is still, dozens of curious stares watching our conversation. The last thing I need is to draw any more attention to us. That's the last thing Lincoln needs, too. So why is he doing this?

Fixing my expression, I give him a saccharine smile. "I apologize, Professor. You're right. There are things we should discuss regarding expectations going forward."

Nodding curtly, he adjusts that damn tie, then grabs his messenger bag. "Follow me, Miss Davenport."

"With pleasure, *Professor*."

CHAPTER THIRTY-SIX

"WHAT THE FUCK was that?" I strain in an irate whisper the instant the door to Lincoln's office clicks closed. "You think you can order me around in class? Threaten to fail me just to get me alone? Like this is some fucking game?"

"I know it's not a game." His voice is soft, a complete juxtaposition to mine, which only aggravates me more.

"You don't get to treat me like that," I choke out. "You don't get to fuck me, toss me onto the street, then act all jealous when I talk to a classmate, a *friend.*"

He grabs my hips, his earnest gaze attempting to put out the fire within. "I know. And I'm sorry." His lips part as he struggles to find words, a rarity for a man who always seems to know what to say. "We're skating on very dangerous ice here. One slip and we can both sink. I just…" He releases me, pacing the office, tugging at his hair.

"We don't have the luxury of being able to go out to dinner wherever we want, or going to see a show, or going away with friends for a weekend. Hell, even if you weren't my student, I still wouldn't be able to tell any of my colleagues at the paper about you because you're the goddamn boss' daughter! Did I overreact when I saw Owen squeezing your hand? Joking with you?"

I open my mouth to say something, but he interrupts me.

"Absolutely. But I can't help it around you. I can't reel in this insane jealousy that rips me apart, Chloe."

The vein in his neck throbs with the passion and intensity with which he speaks, and I remain still, speechless, my earlier anger dissipating with every word.

"I can't even hold your hand in public without worrying about who could be lurking around the corner. About someone snapping a selfie that has us in the background, then posts it on Instagram for the world to see. For the *wrong person* to see."

He clutches my hands, his expression frantic, a man on the edge. "I want to be able to take you out. I want to be able to show you off and shout to the world how fucking amazing you are."

His face falls and he drops his hold on me, heading to the window. "But

I can't." He peers at the city surrounding us, his shoulders drooping as his realization this will never work rings out between us.

I stare at him, swallowing hard through the lump in my throat, my heart sinking to my stomach. It was nice while we were in our own fantasy world earlier, but the fantasy never lasts. It'll fade and all we'll be left with is the sad truth of who we are. Two people who can never be together. We were fooling ourselves to think otherwise.

"I understand." With timid steps, I turn around, heading toward the door, using every ounce of resolve not to look back. Now I know why Orpheus did. Because it is so fucking hard not to.

"But that doesn't mean I can let you go."

His emotion-filled statement reviving my hope, I pause with my hand on the doorknob.

"That night I found you and your mother struggling in the snow…" Lincoln approaches, his hands sliding down my arms. "I told you I was willing to risk it all for you, as long as you were willing to let me in." He spins me around, his eyes searching mine. "*Are* you still willing to let me in? Even knowing things aren't going to be perfect. That it's going to be hard. That we're going to fight."

I reach up, pushing back a lock of his hair. "If you ask me, perfection is grossly overrated. And let's not forget the most important thing."

"What's that?"

"That make-up sex can be really hot."

His mouth kicks up into a smile as he cups my face, a flicker of desire in his eyes. "That's all I needed to hear."

Without a moment's delay, he crashes his lips against mine, desperation and devotion and everything in between consuming him. I part my lips, treating myself to a taste of him. But like that first kiss, I won't be satisfied with just one taste. I need more.

Wrapping my arms around his neck, I arch into him, running my hands through his hair. I dig my nails into his scalp, and he emits a hungered groan, pushing me across the room.

When we reach the desk, I slide onto the edge, parting my legs as I hook them around his waist, tugging him even closer. His lips never leaving mine, he places his hand on my back and carefully lowers me onto the surface.

"Say you want me."

I grin. Some things never change. And this is one I don't want to change. I never want to go a day without Lincoln begging for my reassurance.

"I want you."

"Say you need me."

"I need you."

Tremors follow the line his hand draws up my leg, my pulse increasing as it disappears into the slit of my dress, his hold on my thigh possessive, sending sparks throughout my body.

"Do you have any idea how difficult it was to focus during class knowing you were a few feet away and weren't wearing any panties. How, if I turned your way at just the right moment when you uncrossed your legs, I may be lucky enough to catch a glimpse of what's mine."

I close my eyes as his tongue traces a line from my mouth, down my throat, then across my neck. When he reaches the tender spot where he marked me, he's surprisingly gentle, peppering the most delicate kisses on my bruised skin.

"And you *are* mine, Chloe." His hand continues traveling north along my thigh. When he hits my center, I moan, succumbing to his touch once more. "Say it." His voice isn't demanding. Not like it was earlier today. It's more pleading, as if he can't go another moment without my declaration.

"I'm yours. All of me."

His lips find mine, and he breathes into me. "And I'm yours, Chloe. Have been since I first saw you. I knew back then that there was something different about you. That I had to have you. And not just your body." He slides a hand up my torso, tweaking my nipple before he affectionately rests his palm my chest. "But your heart, as well."

I grab onto his wrist, keeping it there as his other hand continues exploring me, pushing a finger in, then withdrawing before stretching me even more.

Unable to endure another second without feeling him, I sit up and reach for his waist. With my gaze locked on his, I loosen his belt and lower his zipper, wrapping my fingers around his erection and pulling it out. I stroke him as he continues fucking me with his fingers.

His nostrils flare, his jaw twitching, his eyes dark as they look upon me with pure lust.

"Enough," he hisses, clutching my wrist, stopping me from jerking him off. Blind to all reason, he pushes me back and enters me in one quick thrust, filling me to the hilt.

Closing my eyes, I release a low moan, forgetting where we are.

"Shh…" He brings his hand to my mouth covering it. "Quiet."

I nod. He takes his hand away, his pace slow and languid so as to not make too much noise.

"Put it back."

He pauses, furrowing his brow.

"Your hand. Put it back over my mouth."

His pupils dilating, he does as I command. "Like this?" he asks in a husky voice.

I nod again, the temperature in my body rising, my core clenching at how dark this man can be. He continues pushing into me, filling me completely, just as a knock echoes between our labored pants.

"Lincoln, are you in there?" a deep voice calls out from the other side of the door.

We freeze, neither one of us so much as breathing. His wide eyes dart to the door, the seconds stretching. My heart is in my throat, adrenaline coursing through me.

"It's John Morrison."

"Shit," Lincoln utters under his breath.

"Do you have a minute?"

He blinks, his gaze shifting between the door and me. "I—" he stammers. "I'm on the phone."

We both wait in anticipation, praying he walks away. But when no response comes, Lincoln hangs his head and reluctantly pulls out of me, offering a silent apology.

"Give me a minute to wrap things up."

"Certainly."

"On the phone? Is that the only excuse you can come up with?" I whisper as Lincoln helps me to my feet, remembering his use of the same excuse mere weeks ago when Professor Gordon interrupted us.

"Would you rather I tell the dean I was in the middle of screwing one of my students and I'd be with him when I made sure she came?"

Despite the gravity of the situation, I can't help but laugh quietly. "I'd give anything to see the look on his face when you told him that."

"You may get your wish if I can't figure a way out of this."

"Relax…," I soothe, standing on my toes and kissing his cheek. "You're lucky you chose to screw the shortest student in class. And probably the most flexible."

"Why's that?"

"I can fit in some remarkably tight spaces." I waggle my brows, grab my coat and bag, then head behind his large cherrywood desk, crawling into the alcove between the drawers on either side.

"Chloe…" His Adam's apple bobs up and down in a hard swallow. "You don't—"

"It's okay. There's no other option right now. So go see what he wants before he gets suspicious."

He readjusts his composure, straightening the lines of his suit before walking to the door and opening it. I do my best to remain still, despite my uncomfortable position. I pray it's a quick conversation. My legs are still sore from this afternoon's calisthenics, not to mention the pain already screaming from my ass. I won't be able to stay here for too long.

"Dean Morrison," Lincoln greets, his voice deep and professional.

"I hope I'm not disrupting you."

"Not at all. Just had to answer a few questions on a filing we're making at the office." His steps draw closer and I see his shoes appear a few inches from me. I glance up at his intimidating physique, oddly turned on at how commanding he looks behind this desk with me at his feet. "Won't you have a seat?"

"Thank you."

There's a slight stirring as Dean Morrison assumes one of the chairs in front of the desk. Lincoln catches my gaze as he sits, but his eyes don't linger.

"What can I do for you this evening?"

"I heard through the grapevine that Chloe Davenport is back in class."

He shifts, discreetly adjusting his belt. "She is."

"That's good. At least she'll be better prepared for next semester."

He cocks his brow. "What do you mean?"

"The school only allows students to miss ten percent of class hours. For most courses that meet for an hour three times a week, that amounts to four missed classes. But since yours is three hours once a week, anything after two is grounds for an automatic failure. Well, technically, anything after the first hour of the second missed class is, but I'm being generous. If my calculations are correct, Miss Davenport has now missed three classes."

"I understand the school policy, but I've decided to excuse the absences due to extenuating circumstances."

"I see." There's a pause before Dean Morrison speaks again. "Professor Gordon mentioned you both saw Miss Davenport outside a bar in SoHo several weeks ago."

The tension in the room thickens, his line of questioning sounding more like an interrogation than a conversation between colleagues.

"Yes."

"She also mentioned you shared a cab with Miss Davenport."

I hold my breath, the seconds stretching uncomfortably. I crane my head, stealing a glimpse of Lincoln, his expression unaffected. I suppose that's the upside of being a lawyer. He has a damn good poker face.

"I did. Again, there were extenuating circumstances."

"I see."

I hear the chair push back, followed by footsteps. I send a silent prayer that the dean isn't about to walk behind the desk. I'd never forgive myself if Lincoln lost his job, lost everything because of me. But isn't that the game we're playing?

"The same extenuating circumstances you're using as grounds to excuse Miss Davenport from missing too many classes?"

Lincoln stands, straightening his tie. "As a matter of fact, yes. Since it's a confidential matter, I'm not at liberty to discuss the exact nature of the problem without Miss Davenport's permission, but it is sufficient enough to warrant excusing her. Last I checked, the school policy allowed professors the discretion to determine whether or not to excuse absences, and I've used that discretion here. These were the first classes she's missed—"

"This semester," Dean Morrison interrupts pointedly. "She doesn't have the best track record."

"Compared to her classmates who are fortunate enough to have their parents support them financially and emotionally, you're correct. But when you factor in that she works a full-time job, I'd say she's doing pretty well. In my opinion, she's a brilliant student. One of the most promising I've had in my class."

"I don't doubt that. Her father's a brilliant man. But Professor Gordon has voiced her concerns regarding your relationship with Miss Davenport. I must admit, I find it disconcerting you would share a cab with a student, even if she *is* the daughter of your boss. You're aware this school has a policy regarding personal relationships between faculty and students."

Lincoln places his palms to his desk, leaning toward the dean, his eyes narrowed. "What are you insinuating?"

"That your behavior is raising eyebrows."

"Well, it shouldn't." Straightening, he widens his stance. "You've been in higher education long enough to know this place is often worse than a soap opera. Miss Davenport needed help. I decided to act like a decent human being instead of ignoring her simply because my actions may, as you put it, raise a few eyebrows. If I saw one of my male students in the same predicament, I'd help him, too."

"That may be true, but I'd still like to take a look at all the coursework Miss Davenport has submitted so far this year. Make sure it's on par with the level you claim."

I study Lincoln's demeanor, arms defensively crossed in front of his chest, eyes unwavering, everything about him giving the impression that he has nothing to hide.

An impressive performance, considering he's hiding me underneath his desk.

I notice Lincoln's jaw twitch slightly, then he sits, careful to give me space, and opens a drawer. Tossing a file onto the desk, he leans back into the chair. "There it is."

I hear the subtle rustling of pages as Dean Morrison presumably flips through the few papers I'd handed in throughout the semester. Seconds turn into minutes as my heart thunders in my chest. I pray the dean can't hear it in the strained silence. And that he doesn't find my high marks suspicious.

"It appears she does have a knack for the law," Dean Morrison finally says. "Much like her father."

"She certainly does."

It's silent for a moment before the dean speaks once more. "Very well. I'll let you get back to…whatever it is you were working on. I apologize for jumping to conclusions. This school takes these kinds of things seriously."

"Completely understandable, sir. I should have informed you of the incident previously. In the future, I'll be sure to report any encounters with my students outside class or office hours."

"You do that."

Footsteps echo, followed by the welcome sound of the door opening. I don't think my heart has ever pumped as fast as it has these past few minutes.

"And I'd strongly advise you to stay as far away from Miss Davenport as possible. No more requesting she come to your office to discuss her work, as I've heard has happened. Even if it's innocent, you don't need anything else to add fuel to the fire, so to speak."

"You have my word."

"Good."

When the door finally clicks closed, I blow out a breath, never having been so relieved in my life.

"Hey…" Lincoln crouches down to my level, extending his hand toward me. "It's okay. I locked the door."

Nodding, I put my hand in his, allowing him to help me to my feet. "I am so sorry." Rattled, I adjust my clothes, then collect my things. "I didn't mean for something like this to happen. You could have lost everything because of how careless I was. You should have—"

"Hey…" He grabs my biceps, forcing me to stop. "You have nothing to apologize for."

"But you're risking so much to be with me. *Too* much. It was fun role-playing earlier, but this…" I step out of his touch and gesture between our bodies. "This isn't a game, Lincoln. It's not just a fantasy, although I wish it were. You *are* my professor. If you stay with me, I will ruin your life. There's no way around it. No possible way this will have a happy ending, no matter the risk you're willing to take."

He stares at me for several long moments, and I expect him to agree and send me on my way. Instead, he smiles.

"Do you know how my parents met?"

"No." I shake my head. "I've read about your father because of what happened to him, but other than that…"

"He was the teaching assistant in one of Mom's English electives. Granted, it's not the same as our situation, but they still weren't permitted to be together. They had to wait. They weren't allowed to date while he was the TA assigned to her class."

"So he waited for her?"

He lowers his mouth toward mine, his breath kissing my lips, sending a shiver through me. "He did. Said he knew she'd be worth the wait. But that's where I'm different from my dad."

"How's that?" I murmur, craning my neck back.

"I've already had a taste. And I'm greedy for more. So I'm not going to stand by and wait for you, Chloe. I need to have you now, even if that means we have to be careful while we figure this out." He traces my jawline with a single finger. "I already lost you once. Already pushed you away when I should have begged you to stay. It's going to take a lot more than the risk to my career for me to push you away again."

Comforted by his sweet words, I fling my arms around him, kissing him with everything I have. I've never been with a man who was willing to risk everything to be with me. I still don't know how I deserve this, but I won't question it. Not now.

"There's just one problem," I murmur against his mouth.

"What's that?"

I glance at the door. "How do you suggest we get out of here without raising any suspicion?"

A contemplative look crosses his face as he scans his office, weighing his options. "Right." He shifts his eyes back to mine. "I'll leave first. It's probably safer. When the coast is clear, I'll text you. I can't guarantee you'll have much time, so when you get my message, make it quick."

"But what about locking your office?"

"I'll double back and lock it once you're in the clear. Okay?"

"Okay."

He collects a few papers, meticulously separating them into their appropriate folders before sliding them into his messenger bag. He heads toward the door, pausing when his hand touches the knob. A thoughtful expression crosses his brow as he looks back at me.

"What are you doing tomorrow night?"

I give him a sideways glance, seeing the wheels spinning in his head. "Why?"

"I want to see you."

"What did you have in mind?" I saunter toward him.

His lips brush mine. "You'll have to wait and find out. I'll have a car pick you up at seven. Wear a dress." His eyes skate over my body before returning to mine. "And heels. Definitely wear heels."

"Any reason why?" I bat my lashes.

"Because I love the way they dig into my skin when I make you come."

I whimper, rendered speechless by his wanton and lust-filled statement, the way he says it with no hesitation. It makes me want him right now, code of conduct be damned.

Smirking, he twists the knob, pausing before opening it. "For the record, I don't regret a thing. We'll figure this out, Chloe. Promise."

My lips curve into a smile, my heart warming. "Okay."

He holds my gaze a moment longer, then says, "Seven o'clock."

"It's a date."

He beams, his eyes sparkling. "I like the sound of that." Then he disappears, closing the door behind him.

"I like the sound of that, too," I whisper into the darkness, feeling unusually content, despite our close call. He's right. Our situation isn't ideal, but it's better than the alternative of not being together at all. I don't want to go back to that. Not now that I have him again.

When my phone buzzes mere seconds later, I yank it out of my purse and read Lincoln's text telling me the coast is clear.

Drawing a deep breath, I crack open the door, peeking into the hallway. Once I confirm no one's lingering nearby, I sneak out of the office. Adrenaline pumps through me, making me hyper-aware of every sound, every cough, every sniffle. The corridors through the faculty area feel like they're miles long instead of just a couple dozen feet.

When I finally step into the main corridor, my muscles relax and I can breathe again. I pause briefly to collect myself, then continue to the elevators, grinning deviously when I see Lincoln heading toward me.

"Miss Davenport," he says as he passes, mischief in his gaze.

"Professor Moore."

"Have a great evening."

I glance over my shoulder, lasciviously licking my lips. "I already have."

CHAPTER THIRTY-SEVEN

ONE OF MY strongest childhood memories is sitting in my mother's room, watching as she got ready for some important function, usually a political rally or fundraiser. She'd always dress in smart pantsuits. Told me they made her feel more powerful, insisted skirts and dresses were tools the patriarchy used to keep women where they wanted them.

While I may not have acquired her flair for feminism, since I actually feel incredibly powerful in a skirt or dress, I did inherit a few of her other habits, like always spraying a bit of perfume behind my ears.

As I do that same thing now, peering at my reflection in the mirror, I pause. For the first time in years, I see my mother in me.

Correction.

For the first time in years, I *don't mind* seeing my mother in me.

The mass quantities of makeup I'd typically wear on a "date" is absent. Minimal contouring and eyeliner take its place, along with a bit of gloss on my lips to make them shine. But that's not the biggest change.

I wrap a lock of hair around my finger, the blonde hue mixed with darker highlights giving me a more mature look. Gone is the gray and lilac color that's become my signature style, something I've kept simply for the attention it garnered. I liked that guys came up to compliment my bold choice in hair color, then slyly invite me back to their place. I don't want that kind of attention anymore. Lincoln is the only person I want to notice me. And I want him to know who I really am. Want to show him I'm ready to let him in, to let him see the real me. The me few people have seen over the years.

The me I haven't seen much of these past few years, either.

The knee-length dress I chose for tonight has a halter neckline that accents my back and shoulders. It's not as tight-fitting as I'm used to, but the belted waist adds a sensuality, as does the slit going to my mid-thigh. I never would have been able to pull off the emerald green shade before, since I hated how that color contrasted with my hair, but now that I'm a blonde again, I can get away with it. It actually suits me, bringing out a few green specks in my eyes I hadn't noticed before.

When I hear the buzzer, I tear my eyes away from my reflection, my heart ricocheting into my throat. With shaky hands, I grab my clutch and shrug my belted coat over my dress, then walk toward the door, smiling a greeting at the chauffeur standing on the doorstep.

"Good evening, Miss Davenport. I'm Charles, your driver." He helps me down the steps and opens the back door of the idling dark sedan.

"Thank you."

Once I'm secure inside, he shuts the door before running around the car to get behind the wheel. Pulling into traffic, he glances at me in the rearview mirror. "We should be there in about fifteen minutes."

"Where are you taking me?"

"Mr. Moore requested I not give any information away."

I can't help but grin, the unknown of what awaits causing my insides to vibrate. It's been years since I've been on anything remotely resembling a date.

Actually, I don't think I've ever truly had a "first date". Not in the adult sense anyway. My only other serious boyfriend was Parker, but we met in college. I'm doubtful a stolen kiss at the local pizza place where the entire university hung out qualifies as a date. Or going to the dining hall together. Or holding hands as we walked across campus, since we both had the same class.

As Charles maneuvers through the streets of Manhattan, I stare at the buildings as they become increasingly taller the farther away from the Village we get. Each time we pass a hotel, I perk up, thinking this is all another buildup to whatever fun role-playing game Lincoln has in store for tonight.

So when the car pulls up alongside a French restaurant in Midtown, I'm convinced I'm in the wrong place. Less than twenty-four hours ago, Lincoln and I discussed how we had to be more careful, discreet. Now he's taking me to a restaurant mere blocks from Central Park? There's no way we won't be seen. The risk is too great.

Charles opens my door, helping me out of the car and walking me toward the restaurant. I steal a peek at the windows in an attempt to peer inside, but they're all made of mirrored glass, ensuring the patrons' privacy.

"*Mademoiselle* Davenport?" a voice says in a thick French accent.

I snap my eyes to see a man dressed in a dark suit standing inside the double doors, holding one open for me.

"*Monsieur* Moore is expecting you."

Aware of the domino effect I fear tonight will cause, I look from the man back to Charles, who gives me an encouraging nod. I don't exactly have the best of luck. Hell, Murphy's Law should be renamed Chloe's Law. If something in my life can go wrong, it will.

"Enjoy your evening," Charles says before retreating with a smile.

"*Mademoiselle* Davenport?" the *maître d'* repeats, his brows raised in expectation, extending his arm into the foyer.

I chew on my lower lip, torn. Isn't this what I wanted, though? Didn't I want Lincoln to treat me like he would a normal girlfriend, not kick me out of a hotel room after having sex? But at what cost? Lincoln's always been a very rational and pragmatic person. He wouldn't bring me to a popular restaurant without some sort of safeguard, would he?

On a deep inhale, I walk through the doors, allowing the *maître d'* to take my jacket.

Once the exterior door closes behind us, I'm met with serenity. There's no ambient chatter, no clinking of glasses, no scraping of forks against plates. The only sound is that of soft music coming from a piano.

When I turn the corner, following the *maître d'* into the dining room, I know why. The entire restaurant is empty…apart from Lincoln sitting at a table in the center.

The instant he sees me, he stands, buttoning his suit jacket. It's not unusual for me to see him in a suit. But tonight, he looks…different. His hair appears damp from a shower, his beard and mustache neatly trimmed to resemble just a bit more than a five o'clock shadow. Exactly how I like him.

"Chloe…" His Adam's apple bobs up and down in a hard swallow as he rakes his gaze over my changed appearance.

I was so wrought with nerves over the idea of being exposed that I didn't have time to obsess about whether Lincoln would like the new me. But it appears I had nothing to worry about, not with the way he currently admires me with nothing short of unabashed reverence.

"You look…"

Emboldened, I do a quick spin, allowing him to get a full view of the dress I bought just for him. For tonight. For this new me.

"You like?" I pass him a demure look.

His gaze unwavering, he takes several long strides toward me, drawing me into his embrace. "You're stunning."

I wrap my arms around his neck, toying with the few tendrils of hair that curl over his collar. "You're not so bad yourself."

He runs a finger down the curvature of my face, then grabs a lock of hair, twisting it around his digit. "You got rid of the purple."

"I figured it was time for a change. Time to be me." I pause, bringing my lips toward him. "Time to let you see the *real* me."

His mouth finds mine, the kiss ardent, yet still respectful as he communicates how much this gesture means to him. When he pulls away, he cups my face. "Thank you for letting me see who you truly are." He kisses my nose, then places his hand on my lower back and leads me toward the table. He holds out the chair, helping me into it before sitting catty-corner to me.

"Do I want to know what's going on here?" I glance around the space, still a little confused why one of the premier French restaurants in the city would be empty on a Friday night.

"What do you mean?" Lincoln responds nonchalantly.

I lean closer, lowering my voice. "This place. Being here. The lack of other diners." My brow furrows. "What's going on?"

He reaches for my hand, grabbing it in his. As he runs his thumb over my knuckles, his eyes remain focused on my skin. "I never thought I'd be able to do this in public," he remarks contemplatively, almost in awe.

"What?"

He lifts his gaze to mine. "Hold your hand. It's…everything I imagined it would be."

I'm pretty sure another piece of my heart floats across the table at his words, wrapping around him.

"I don't want to deprive you of the normalcy that goes along with a real relationship because of who we are to each other. You deserve better than that. All last night, I couldn't stop thinking about what we discussed yesterday. How we'll never be able to do normal things. Go out for a romantic dinner, hold hands, steal a kiss for no reason at all. Right now, there are definitely some complications."

I blow out a laugh. "Ya think?"

"But that doesn't mean I won't take you out. That all we'll ever be able to do is hide away in one of our apartments or a rented hotel room. Granted, yesterday, my plan for tonight *was* another hotel room. But you deserve romantic dinners. Starlit walks through Central Park. Surprise flowers at work. I promise you…" His grip tightens, his voice firm. "In time, I *will* give you everything you've ever dreamed of, and more. There will come a day I'll be able to shout to the world how fucking happy I am because of you." He moistens his lips, pausing as he collects himself, his tone softening. "But right now, I hope this is acceptable." A hint of a smile curves his mouth. "We *are* in public, even if there are no other diners present." He winks.

"You lawyers. Always trying to get off on a technicality," I jest.

"Only with you. I only want to get off with you." He waggles his brows.

"Good. And tonight is more than acceptable. Although I'm not sure I want to know who you had to sweet-talk in order to buy out this place for the night."

"No one." With a casual shrug, he leans back, releasing his hold on my hand. "I'm friends with the executive chef, so I called in a favor. He's been closed the past two weeks preparing for a menu revamp, so it worked out quite well."

"I'd say," I muse as a waiter approaches with a bottle of wine Lincoln must have ordered before I arrived. After he presents it to him, the waiter opens it, pouring a small amount into a wine glass, allowing Lincoln to taste it. When he nods in approval, the waiter fills both glasses.

Once we're alone, Lincoln raises his wine and I follow suit. "To a first date I hope you'll never forget."

"I doubt I will." I smile, then bring the wine to my lips, taking a sip of the robust red. "Although yesterday's role-playing was pretty unforgettable, too."

"I can't count that as a date. You deserve better than that."

"That may be true, but we can still play once in a while. You won't hear any complaints from me."

He grins mischievously, which makes me want to skip dinner and go straight to dessert. "I'll be sure to keep that in mind for future dates."

"A bit presumptuous, isn't it? To assume I'll agree to see you again? This first date could be a complete disaster and I may have to cut my losses."

He takes another sip of wine, his motion slow, deliberate, meticulous as he swirls the liquid around his mouth. It's strangely erotic to watch. Such a simple thing adults of drinking age do on a fairly regular basis. But the way Lincoln takes his time to savor the liquid that winemakers spent countless hours perfecting makes my heart beat a little faster, my breathing to become a little more labored, my skin to flush under his sensual stare.

Forget Pornhub. I could watch Lincoln swirl his wine all day long and probably get off numerous times.

"It may be presumptuous," he finally says when I'm on the verge of combusting. "But something about you makes me think you like a man who's bold, who's confident, who has no problem telling you exactly what he wants. Am I right?" He arches a single brow.

"Perhaps," I flirt, pretending to be completely unaffected by his charms.

"Then trust me when I say that, if I do my job right, I'm *confident* you will be so swept off your feet after tonight that I'll ruin you for any first dates that come after me…although I hope there won't be any." He reaches under the table, his hand settling on my knee. When he grips it somewhat harshly, I jump, yelping, before regaining my composure, nervously glancing around.

"And I'm also confident that after I get you in my bed tonight, the only name you'll scream again will be Lincoln Moore." Eyes flaming with need, he brushes his fingers up my leg before pulling back, acting as unaffected as ever. But I know the truth. That he's the tortoise, and this is part of his seduction, his first lap around the track.

I curve toward him, salaciously licking my lips. "It already is, Lincoln…" I pause, then moan out, "Moore."

The grip on his wine glass tightens and I'm surprised it doesn't shatter in his hand. Now *that* would be a first date I'd never forget.

The next hour seems to fly by as we talk about anything and everything that pops into mind. I search my memory for an instance we've done this, coming up empty. We've never really talked to each other, apart from playing Never Have I Ever during that fated blackout. But that was just part of a game. Here, we're finally learning about each other. More importantly, we're no longer hiding from each other, no longer trying to keep our past inside to prevent reopening wounds that probably never healed completely.

Throughout the course of our dinner, he tells me story after story about his father. It's clear from the excitement and hint of longing in his voice that he still misses him, even though it's been nearly twenty years. I suppose time can't erase all wounds. I'm living proof of that, too.

"It's not as romantic as meeting at a club in Vegas," he says after telling me how his parents met at a blood drive on campus at the start of the semester. She was a nursing student who was helping with the blood collection. The second he laid eyes on her, he was attracted to her.

Apparently, confidence and cockiness are traits among the Moore males. Instead of taking his time after giving blood, allowing the lightheadedness to wear off, Elijah insisted he was fine and attempted to stand. Of course, dizziness instantly took over and he fell, cutting his head, which required a couple stitches. Wendy found out where his dorm was and went to check on him. And the rest, I suppose, is history. Until she walked into class a few days later and learned he was her TA.

"I guess we all can't be so lucky." I roll my eyes.

He grabs my hand in his. I've lost count of the number of times he's done that tonight. It's something so many other couples take for granted. I doubt I ever will again.

"I actually like our story. I like that we kept running into each other, as if the universe was trying to force us together."

"Bet you never expected to learn I was one of your students, though."

"That certainly threw me for a loop." He gazes at me thoughtfully. "But I wouldn't change that, either."

"Really?"

"I like to think everything happens for a reason. And I like to think there's a reason you ended up in my classroom."

"And what's that?" I lean toward him, my eyes glued to his.

"I think we both needed to fight for this. If there weren't these huge obstacles facing us, I think we would have taken each other for granted. Taken our feelings for granted. Maybe it would have eventually turned into something more, something meaningful, but I think we needed this. Because I know something I didn't back in January. Hell, something I didn't even know a few weeks ago."

"What's that?" I ask again, my voice softer.

He brings my hand up to his mouth, placing soft kisses against my knuckles. "That I'll always fight for you, no matter the battle, no matter the cost."

And that's all it takes for the remainder of the wall protecting my heart to crash down, allowing Lincoln Moore to possess it.

CHAPTER THIRTY-EIGHT

I SLAM MY hand onto the kitchen island where I've been chopping tomatoes and cucumbers for a salad. "Oh, my god! I just thought of something."

Lincoln glances over his shoulder. "Should I be worried?"

"Fluffy!"

"Fluffy?" Facing me, he crosses his arms in front of his chest, and it takes every ounce of resolve I possess not to drag him back into the bedroom, especially when I see his muscles flex with the motion. There is nothing sexier than a man cooking in the kitchen. Except a man cooking without a shirt. And that's my current view.

Over the past several weeks, I've spent a great deal of time in Lincoln's apartment. It now feels more like home than my own place. We've gone out on occasion, usually to a late movie at a theater so far out of the way that the chance of seeing anyone we know is slim, but we tend to play it safe and have a "date night in", as he calls them. Cooking dinner together. Watching movies. Always adding a personal touch to make it more than just staying at home.

"Yes. Fluffy, your cat. The one you told us about in Vegas that you're convinced cursed you."

"I remember Fluffy." He returns to the stove to check on the steaks searing on the burner, coating them with some melted butter from the pan.

I do my best not to gawk. Yes, I love a muscular chest and chiseled abs, but there's something incredibly sexy about Lincoln's broad shoulders and sculpted back that tapers into a defined waist. And those dimples right above his shorts beg to be licked. But I don't. That might be a little creepy. I know I'd be creeped out if I were cooking and he came up and licked my lower back. Then again…

"And it's a good thing we just had sex because bringing Fluffy up in conversation would probably curse me," Lincoln adds as he turns around, his voice and sudden motion forcing my eyes up to his. A sly smirk tugs on his mouth when he realizes he caught me ogling his physique. He stalks toward me, using his body to press me against the island. "But I have a feeling you'd be able to lift any curse." He grinds against me, making his erection known.

"Down boy. Do you need a cold shower?" I push him away. "What I meant was it just occurred to me that Midge's cat, Pigpen, is Fluffy. You said you gave the cat to your boss after they'd lost theirs."

"I did." He walks back to the stove. "And yes. Fluffy's name is now Pigpen."

"Don't you find that incredible?"

"What do you mean?"

"Think about it. If you'd mentioned the name he has now, I would have pushed to find out who your boss was. Let's face it. Pigpen isn't exactly a common name for a cat."

"It is if you're a *Peanuts* fan." He transfers the steaks to a baking sheet before placing them into the hot oven, setting a timer for six minutes.

"True, but it would have provoked a follow-up." I squint, considering all the pieces that had to fall into place for us to end up together. "And if I'd learned you worked as an attorney for the *Times*, I never would have so much as entertained the idea of sleeping with you, let alone kissing you."

"So you would have friend zoned me?" Cocking a brow, he approaches me, pushing the cutting board to the side. With incredible ease, he grabs my ass and lifts me onto the surface of the island, settling between my legs.

"No. You would have been in the no-zone."

"Not even the friend zone? At least there I could have attempted to use my amazing powers of persuasion." He curves into me, his mouth landing on my neck, the way he sucks and licks the perfect mixture of carnal and reverent.

"That would have been futile," I respond breathily. "I draw a hard line in certain matters."

"Is that right?" He slowly circles his hips, the friction jumpstarting my libido, as if the ol' girl needs an excuse.

"God yes." I throw my head back as he continues moving against me, his unshaven jaw bruising my skin. "That is so right."

He abruptly pulls away, his eyes dancing with amusement. "*Now* who needs a cold shower?" With playful arrogance, he retreats from me, heading toward the counter to take the baked potatoes out of the foil.

Refusing to let him beat me at this little game, I slide off the island, nonchalantly sauntering up to the sink. I make it look like I'm about to rinse the berries I set aside to top the cheesecake I'd brought over.

"Cold shower, huh?"

"That's right."

In one quick move, I yank the hose from the faucet, spraying him with the water.

He stiffens, spinning around to face me, but he makes no attempt to get out of the line of fire. His lips curl with a sinister smile as he advances, his steps slow, deliberate, unforgiving. When he grabs the bowl of heavy cream I'd whipped to go with our dessert, a devilish glint flashes in his eyes.

I take the pressure off the water, but that doesn't stop him from scooping whipped cream out of the bowl and smearing it down my face.

I stand completely still for a moment, the shock leaving me frozen. Then I wipe some of the cream off my face, making a show of seductively licking my fingers, even though I shudder to think what I look like. With a devious grin, I grab a handful of blackberries from the carton on the counter. His gaze remains glued to mine, watching me with interest as I smash them into his chest, rubbing the juices all over his body.

He tries to remain serious, but I notice the faintest hint of his mouth lifting in a smile. "You're in trouble now, Pixie," he warns as he goes to hook an arm around my waist.

Squealing, I attempt to escape him, but slip on the wet floor, taking him down with me. We land with a hard thump, the room momentarily silent. Then we break out in laughter, the sound echoing against the high ceilings.

"I've always wanted to add food into the mix," I joke. "But I figured we'd start with whipped cream on my nipples. Maybe a little chocolate syrup. Not sure how erotic the face can be."

"Oh, baby, I guarantee I can make it hot for you." Grinning, he drags his tongue along my jawline, tasting the sweet treat, and I moan, succumbing to him.

When the timer buzzes, neither one of us are interested in those steaks anymore.

***

The sensation of warm lips brushing against my temple slowly stirs me from sleep. Normally I hate to be woken, treasuring every second of sleep I can get. But these days, my reality seems better than my dreams. And who wouldn't want to be awoken by such a beautiful kiss? It worked for Snow White and Sleeping Beauty. They didn't groan and roll over, pushing their Prince away, begging in a raspy voice for five more minutes of slumber. And neither do I.

"Morning," I say, melting into Lincoln's lingering kiss.

"Morning."

My eyes flutter open, but the room is still dark, day not having broken just yet, although the glow coming from the windows tells me it will soon.

"What time is it?"

"Six."

I shift, turning my eyes to his. "An emergency at work?"

A slight smile curves his lips. "No. It's my day at the university. I wanted to go early and finish grading papers so I can turn in my final grades."

"Final grades?" I arch a single brow.

Slowly nodding, he erases the distance between us. "And we'll be one step closer to finally being free. To finally being us."

A fluttering erupts in my stomach when his mouth skims mine, his kiss hesitant and soft. As much as I love his hunger-filled kisses that brim with so much desperation and passion, these are my favorite. These gentle exchanges in our stolen moments before dawn.

"I think this calls for a celebration."

I feel his lips curve up. "I agree." The scruff of his beard scrapes me as he trails kisses from my mouth and along my neckline.

"What did you have in mind?" I crane my head, allowing him better access. His hand roams the contours of my frame, and I part my legs, moaning when he grazes against me.

"I can think of a few things," he answers coyly, nipping at my skin, driving me even more wild. "One in particular that I've been fantasizing about for months now."

"What's that?" I pant.

He pauses, and I can almost see the smile crawling across his mouth. Then he pulls back. "Meet me at The Living Room in the Park Hyatt tonight."

My eyes fly open as I prop myself up onto my elbows, searching his gaze. "Are you sure?"

"Why wouldn't I be?" he says nonchalantly, straightening himself, buttoning his suit jacket. "It's fitting, if you ask me. Starting this new chapter where it all began. Where you finally gave me a chance." Then he gently touches his lips to mine, erasing any trepidation. "Even more so considering today marks four months since the blackout that changed my life."

I sigh into him, unable to believe it's been that long. In some respects, it feels like it has been longer than four months, considering everything we've been through. In other ways, it seems like it was just yesterday that I walked into that classroom and learned the man I'd been having incredible sex with was my First Amendment Law professor.

"The happiest, most excruciating, amazing, heart-wrenching four months of my life. But I'd do it all over again if it meant I'd still be here with you." When he cups my cheek, I close my eyes, savoring the feel of his rough hands against my smooth skin. His mouth brushes mine and I melt into his soft kiss. "So, eight o'clock?"

I simply nod, ignoring my internal voice of reason that tells me we should still be careful, that we won't be in the clear just because he submitted my final grade. But when have I ever listened to reason? If I had, I never would have run out of the bar all those weeks ago, telling Nora and Evie I had to go see a man about a pair of panties. Then I wouldn't be here. Sometimes, it pays to take a risk.

"I can't wait."

"Either can I." Lincoln treats me to one last kiss, then leaves me alone in his large bed.

Chapter Thirty-Nine

TAPPING MY FINGERNAILS against the bar, I check the time to see it's nearly 8:20, growing antsy with each passing minute that Lincoln doesn't show up. Did someone put the pieces together? Was my father nearby when one of my texts flashed on Lincoln's phone? Did someone see us during one of our supposed clandestine meetings and report him to the dean? Or, worse, my father?

A ding rips through the background noise of the bar and I flick my eyes to my cell, blowing out a breath when Lincoln's name pops up on the screen.

Lincoln: *Play along. No questions.*

Confused, I'm about to text back when I notice movement to my left and shift my eyes in its direction.

"Is this seat taken?"

"Fuck me," I murmur, swallowing hard as I stare at the man in front of me.

He's in a different suit than the one he wore this morning. His hair glistens, evidencing a recent shower, his beard neatly groomed. But that's not what has me squirming in my seat. It's the British accent with which he speaks. It sounds remarkably authentic. And sexy. Holy shit, is it sexy. I didn't think I could be any more attracted to this man. Didn't think it were humanly possible.

I was so wrong.

"Miss?" he says with a smirk, knowing all too well what has my panties about to combust.

Trying to play it cool, I take a moment to compose myself, then smile slyly. "It is now."

With a wicked shine in his eyes, he assumes the seat, flagging down the bartender. I simply watch him, trying to figure out exactly *what* game we're playing. No matter what, I have a feeling it's going to be a lot of fun.

"You here alone?" he asks after he swallows a sip of his scotch, his lips wet from the remnants of the liquid.

"It appears I am." I smooth the lines of my skirt.

"Is that so?"

"I was supposed to meet someone." I sigh in mock disappointment. "But it looks like he stood me up."

A salacious smile builds on his mouth. "His loss is my gain." He eyes my nearly empty martini. "Can I buy you another?"

I lean back in my chair. "I should probably just go home and forget about tonight, considering it appears my *date* has." I pinch my lips together, interested to see how Lincoln plays this.

"You're right. You definitely *should* go home." His gaze darkens, a warning. "But don't you think you'd have more fun with me than going back to your place with nothing to distract you from thinking about some prick who apparently has horrible taste."

"What makes you say that?"

"Isn't it obvious?"

I shrug. "Humor me."

"He stood you up." He rakes his gaze down my body, and desire flickers in his deep pools. I uncross and re-cross my legs, allowing the slit of my dress to reveal the skin of my thigh. Jaw tightening, nostrils flaring, he reluctantly lifts his eyes to mine. "No man in his right mind would stand up a woman as stunningly beautiful as you."

He inches toward me, his lips close. I'd give anything to erase that last bit of space between us and taste him, but I don't, remembering the game we're playing. And I certainly love these games.

"Give me one drink to prove it to you. If you're not convinced, you can go on your way."

"And if I am convinced?" I exhale.

"Then you come up to my room and I make you forget all about this man who isn't worth your time."

"And how do you hope to do that?" I bat my lashes.

"Use your imagination." His mouth skims against mine, causing a shiver to roll through me. Then he pulls back, the epitome of restraint.

"I do have a *very* active imagination."

He lifts his scotch to his lips. "That's what I'm banking on." My gaze lingers on him as he swirls the liquid, then swallows. Returning his glass to the bar, he focuses his attention on me. "So, what do you say? One drink with me, then maybe one night where you can have all your needs met? Or go home all alone?"

I pause, enjoying the anticipation in his expression before nodding. "One drink."

"Good girl." He leers at me for a moment, then waves down the bartender.

Once he turns his attention away from me, I exhale a long breath. I've shared a bed with this man numerous times, but the rush of exhilaration filling me makes me feel like we're two strangers, my heart pounding a thunderous rhythm.

When the bartender sets my drink in front of me, I offer him a smile.

"I took a guess at what kind of vodka you'd prefer," Lincoln states, reminding me of a similar conversation back in Vegas. "But something made me think you were a Belvedere girl." He leans toward me, running a finger down my arm. "Smooth. Layered. Sophisticated."

I take a sip of my drink before setting the glass back on the bar. "How did you know I liked my martini dirty?" I pass him a sly grin, more than aware of what line's about to follow.

He hovers closer still, the nearness of his lips unhinging me. "I had a feeling you liked things…dirty."

"Wouldn't you like to find out?"

His lips ghost against mine, teasing me, making me desperate for more, regardless of the fact we're in public and anyone can see. Lincoln may have turned in his final grades, but we're still on rocky ground. We will be for a while. Seeing us together like this when I'm still technically a student will certainly raise eyebrows. Hell, seeing us together like this even a few months from now will raise eyebrows.

"You have no idea," he growls, jaw tensing, pupils dilating. I brace myself for the kiss I sense is coming. But it never does. He retreats, the foot or so between us feeling like miles.

"So, I assume you're not from around here." Brushing a lock of hair behind my ear, I bring my glass to my mouth, trying to steady my trembling hand.

"What gave it away?" he jokes slyly.

"All non-New Yorkers have a sign on their foreheads. Only true New Yorkers can see it."

"Is that right?"

"Sure is."

"I see." He looks forward, pretending to pay attention to the Yankees game on TV, but I know the only interest he has in the game is the Yankees losing. Like his father, Lincoln has two favorite baseball teams. The Mets, and anyone playing the Yankees.

"So, where are you from?" I ask after a brief silence, trying to spark conversation.

"Does it matter?" His tone isn't curt. More sensual and amused.

"Excuse me?"

"Does it matter?" he repeats. "I'm not from here. I fly back home tomorrow, so after tonight, you'll never see me again."

"I was just trying to make small talk."

"Is that what you like? *Small* talk?"

After considering his question, I blow out a breath. "I find it dull and ordinary, but it appears most people opt for these kinds of mundane questions."

"And why do you think that is?"

"Because they're too scared to ask what's really on their mind. Scared to voice their deepest desires."

His mouth lifts into a grin, his eyes dancing with amusement. "Take all the rules off the table. Forget about propriety and custom. What would you ask me?"

I curve toward him, bringing my hand to his thigh. His pupils dilate as I inch farther up his leg. "If I were to agree to accompany you upstairs, what did you have in mind?"

"A magician never reveals all his secrets." He winks. "Need to give you a reason to come…if only for curiosity's sake."

"That may be true, but I never buy anything sight unseen. Or at least without a description of what I can expect."

"A description?" He cocks a brow.

"Yes. A description." I lean back, removing my hand from him in the hopes the lack of touch pushes him to his breaking point, just as it does me. But he's still as composed as ever.

"Very well." He faces forward, brushing the pad of his thumb along his bottom lip. "I'll finish my scotch, thanking you for the enlightening conversation, and slide my keycard your way, leaving the ball in your court, as the saying goes. You'll be unsure at first, wondering if you can do this, if you can really take that key and go up to a stranger's room. But your desperate need to forget your inhibitions for one night will get the better of you." His tone is even and measured, as if discussing an important business deal instead of his plans of seduction.

"You think so?"

"I do. So you'll take that key and use it. You'll walk inside my room, and neither one of us will say a single word. We won't need them. We'll communicate our need with our bodies. You'll be so overcome with an urge to feel me, you'll try to strip off all my clothes, but I won't let you."

"You won't?"

"No." He slowly shakes his head. "Not yet. That's the problem with all these other men you've dated."

"And what's that exactly?" I shoot back, playfully rolling my eyes.

He leans toward me. "They didn't take their time to seduce you. Because they're just boys."

"I've dated older men," I say very matter-of-factly.

"Doesn't matter. They're still boys. A woman should be savored, like a fine wine, like the delicacy she is. Boys screw. I don't."

"So… What? You'll 'make love' to me," I taunt.

"No. What I plan to do to you is so much more than that."

I swallow hard. "More?"

"Yes." The heat of his breath on my neck causes my lips to part, making me shift as I clench my thighs together to dull the ache. "I will consume you. Hold your desires captive. Possess your every thought from this moment forward. I'll bring you to the brink of utter bliss, only to pull back, drawing out your pleasure as long as possible. You'll beg me to let you come, to make you experience the mind-altering orgasm you'll now be convinced only I can provide for you. But I'll make you wait a little longer. Because you wouldn't have reached your breaking point. Not yet."

His breathing grows heavier, the muscles in his face tightening as the distance between us becomes nearly nonexistent. "I'll feast on your body, memorizing every dip and valley, taking my time to give every inch of you the attention it deserves. When you don't think you can take any more, I'll bring you to the bed. You'll be blindfolded and restrained, completely at my mercy. Your *orgasm* completely at my mercy. Your legs will be spread wide so you can't find any relief that way. You'll *need* me."

"I already need you," I pant, my voice not sounding like my own.

I don't even have to look at his lips to see his smile. "I was hoping you'd say that." He abruptly pulls back and drains his scotch. Then he coolly slides a keycard my way, winking before turning from me, leaving me a bundle of sensations.

I watch as he disappears out of the lounge, exhaling to calm my overwrought nerves. My legs shaky, I'm careful as I step down from the barstool.

Lost in my thoughts of how Lincoln can affect me like this, considering we spend almost every night together, I jump when a hand grips my arm, my heart ricocheting to my throat. I snap my head to my right, gasping at Lincoln's heated stare. Before I can utter a syllable, he yanks my body against his and kisses me as if it's a regular occurrence for him to do this. It's been so long since he's kissed me in public. Most people wouldn't think it a big deal. Before Lincoln, I never gave it much thought myself. But now I do. And I want nothing more than to keep kissing him.

There's a hint of reluctance as he pulls away, and I search his eyes, unsure if this man kissing me is Lincoln or my mysterious stranger. The sparkle in his gaze as he smiles tells me it's Lincoln.

He runs a soft finger along the contours of my face. "You are fucking incredible, Chloe." He opens his mouth, then stops, as if struggling to find the words. He grips my cheeks, his expression filled with admiration, respect, and something else… Something I've seen for a while now but have been too scared to label. "I…"

"Yes?" I urge when he trails off.

A look of peace washes over him. "I love you."

I blink repeatedly, my mouth falling open, my pulse increasing even more. A fluttering sensation builds in my stomach, making me feel lightheaded, but in the best way possible.

"I know it's not the way most people declare their love," he continues when I don't say anything in response. "The one thing my father's death taught me is to never wait to tell someone how you feel. There may never be a perfect time to say it, especially with us." He cracks a small smile before his expression turns serious once more. "But I love you. You don't have to say it back. I understand this is difficult for you. I just…" He licks his lips. "I just thought you should know."

My head makes a slight motion, like a nod, but I'm not sure what that means. A gesture of acceptance? This is new territory for me. No one's ever told me they loved me. Not like this. Sure, my one boyfriend in college said it, but I didn't hear the meaning behind those words. Not like I do with Lincoln. When he says he loves me, I believe it with every fiber of my being.

"Just give me a few minutes to get ready for you." He places a soft kiss on my nose, then turns from me. I can't take my eyes off him as he walks through the crowded lounge and toward the bank of elevators, my heart fuller than I thought possible from his surprise declaration.

Months ago, I would have run far away if someone told me they loved me. But Lincoln's love doesn't scare me. *Love* doesn't scare me, not like it once did.

Recovering my composure, I grab my purse and offer a nod of thanks to the bartender. Keycard in hand, I turn to make my way up to Lincoln's room when I come to an abrupt stop at the intimidating figure hovering nearby.

You know those scenes in a movie where the main character's worst fears are realized and the camera focuses on them while the background zooms out? That's what this moment feels like. Like my world is giving out from beneath me.

"Hi, Dad."

CHAPTER FORTY

"WHAT THE HELL are you thinking, Chloe?" Dad hisses, eyes wild, expression frantic. He grabs my arm and yanks me into a quiet corner of the lounge, offering us privacy.

Disoriented, I stare at him with my mouth agape, paralyzed, unable to form a coherent thought. What *do* I say? What does he know? What did he see?

"Are you *trying* to ruin his career?" he continues when I don't respond. "His life? What is it?" He throws up his hands in exasperation. "You couldn't pass the class on your own so you're trying to figure out another way to get a good grade?"

I should be floored my father would even suggest that the only way I'd get a passing grade is by offering my body in exchange, but I'm not. He's never understood me. It's always been easier for him to write me off.

"It's not like that," I argue, my voice trembling.

"No? Then tell me what it's like, because from where I'm standing, I can't think of another reason he'd be here with you, other than that you offered him something he couldn't turn down."

"I care about him. A lot." I should keep my mouth shut, but I'm tired of my father thinking so little of me that I'd stoop to that level. I've put those days behind me. "I want to be with him. And he wants to be with me."

My father looks at me as if I just told him zombies had overtaken the streets or aliens had invaded the country. Then he paces, running his hands through his salt-and-pepper hair. When he stops, he shoves a finger in my face. I stiffen, backing up.

"You can*not* do this. That man has worked his tail off, has made a name for himself in this field. I will not let him throw it all away for someone who will never appreciate it. For someone who will toss him aside when something better, someone with a bigger bank account comes along. His father's legacy deserves better than this. *Lincoln* deserves better than this."

"I won't toss him aside," I argue, but he won't hear it. He has this idea in his head of who I am and nothing I say or do will convince him otherwise. Which is why I don't remind him that it takes two to tango. That we both accepted this risk together.

Even if Lincoln were here trying to accept full responsibility, my father would still find me at fault, insist I've been around my mother too long and learned everything I needed in order to persuade someone to make a decision they normally wouldn't. She was once a powerhouse in politics, after all. She's mastered the art of persuasion. As have I…according to him.

"You go through life thinking people are disposable, just like your mother. You use people, get what you want, then walk away, leaving them to clean up the mess."

I shake my head, my teeth biting into my lower lip, doing everything to reel in my temper, every word he spews like another knife against my flesh. I don't want him to see how much his words hurt. But I've spent too many years pretending his indifference toward me doesn't affect me.

"You flash a smile, bat your lashes just enough to get them into bed. And that's all they are to you, isn't it? Just a bit of fun. That's how it's always been with you. And that's how it will always be. Hell, that's what got you your promotion. Now it can help you get your degree. Is that right?"

With each word, my rage increases until it bubbles over. Fists clenched, blood pressure rising, I bellow, "I love him!" My chest heaves as my voice rings out, everything going still.

His jaw snaps shut, his body paralyzed by my admission. "What did you say?"

Exhaling, I lower my voice, my expression relaxing as a small smile builds on my mouth. "I love him."

"You—"

"I know what you're thinking. I never thought I'd be the type of person to fall in love, either, but I love him. I love how excited he gets when talking about some hard-fought victory at the paper. I love the look that comes over his expression when he's deep in thought, about to figure something out. And I love how he makes me feel more loved than anyone else in my life ever has. I have no way of knowing whether this will work, whether we'll survive. But I want the chance to find out."

Dad rakes a hand over his face, his shoulders falling as he realizes this is more than a passing fling. "You really love him?" He lifts his eyes to mine, searching for any hint of deception. But there isn't any. This is my truth. Lincoln is my truth.

"More than anything."

In a flash, the compassion disappears, the stern, controlling man returning. "Then you'll walk away." He steps back, adjusting his tie.

"Wha—"

"Dean Morrison is in there." He points in the direction of the restaurant just past the lounge. "I'm having dinner with him and a few other colleagues. It's lucky *I* was the one who noticed you two, considering they're all professors at the university."

Nausea bubbles in the pit of my stomach, my pulse increasing at the idea that we very well could have been exposed by someone other than my father, who I hope will keep this to himself.

"Do you want to be the reason Lincoln loses everything he's worked so hard for? The reason he tarnishes his father's legacy?"

I want to say that Lincoln doesn't see it that way, tell him all the times he's reminded me I'm worth the risk. But this brings to the forefront all the internal debates I've had over the past several weeks...hell, months. Can I really ask him to sacrifice nearly twenty years of hard work for me? Will I be able to live with the guilt that will inevitably consume me when I'm forced to watch Lincoln try to find something else he's passionate about? And Lincoln loves his job, loves his career. Am I worth it? Are *we* worth it?

"Listen, Chloe..." Dad licks his lips, lowering his voice. There's a hint of sympathy and compassion about him. "I'll keep this quiet. For now. But it *will* get out. Hell, a few months ago, John Morrison brought up the two of you during a dinner meeting. Asked if I was aware of any other kind of relationship between you. I denied it, said it was ridiculous. At the time, I *thought* it was ridiculous. But it goes to show you that people *are* watching.

"The semester may be ending soon, you may be a few days away from graduating, but that won't matter. You will still be considered his student. And in a profession such as ours where we need to adhere to the highest standard of ethics, this can destroy any chance he has at teaching. Maybe even practicing law. Just..." He blows out a breath, shaking his head. "Think about whether it's worth it." He holds my gaze for another moment, then turns.

I watch as he retreats toward the restaurant. He doesn't need to come right out and say what he really means — whether *I'm* worth it.

This is a man who's always chosen his work over everything else. Over my mother. Over me. Hell, even over his new family. Work has always been his life. His *career* has always been his life, his one true love. When I was little, I often snuck down the hallway toward his office and would listen to him argue certain issues with whomever he was speaking to on the phone. I'd never seen such passion, such fervor, such intensity.

Until I walked into that classroom and observed Lincoln.

He had that same wild, untamed look in his eyes as my father did.

I instantly know the answer, although I fear I've known it all along but didn't want to admit it.

I take a minute to pull myself together, trying to find comfort in the fact my father didn't threaten to out us to the dean. Maybe it would have been better if he had. Then I wouldn't have to be the bad guy. But I knew from the beginning this was how it would end.

Fairy tales *aren't* real.

I've been fooling myself to think I could have my handsome prince and not suffer the dragon's wrath.

On timid steps, I walk through the lounge, the chairs where I'd sat with Lincoln now occupied by another couple who are free to share intimate moments. A brush of a hand. A stolen kiss. A heated stare. But not us. That would never have been us. And I can't ask Lincoln to give up his passion so I can have that.

Instead, I give up *my* passion in order for him to hold onto his. It's not the first time I've had to sacrifice what I want for someone else. And it won't be the last.

CHAPTER FORTY-ONE

By THE TIME I round the corner onto my street, my feet scream for relief. But I welcome the pain, need it to dull how much it hurt to walk away from Lincoln.

I spent the past several hours roaming the streets of Manhattan, wondering if I did the right thing, if I made the right decision. I couldn't even bring myself to read any of his texts or answer any of his calls, worried I'd crack and allow his assurances to convince me that we *can* have a future.

When my building comes into view, I quicken my steps, wanting to curl up in bed and tune out the world for a minute. But the instant my gaze falls on my front stoop, my heart plummets to my stomach. Lincoln sits on the top step, shoulders slumped, hair disheveled, forearms resting dejectedly on his thighs. It's nearly three in the morning. How long has he been here? I thought by now, it would be safe to come home. I guess I was wrong. What else have I been wrong about tonight?

I consider retreating on the off chance he hasn't noticed me. Then he lifts his weary, tired eyes, as if he has some sixth sense where I'm concerned. I've never seen him so distraught, so uncertain, so…lost.

My lips part. I want nothing more than to apologize, offer him the comfort he deserves. Maybe if I hadn't been so greedy, been more understanding of our predicament, he wouldn't have felt the need to take me out somewhere we could be spotted.

"Lincoln, I—"

"Was it too soon?" he interrupts.

I furrow my brow. "What do you—"

"It was too soon, wasn't it?" He bites his lower lip, a pained expression on his face as he pinches the bridge of his nose. "I knew it was. That's why I didn't tell you weeks ago. I wanted to tell you the night I found you struggling with your mother. Because I knew back then how I felt. Probably before. I just… There never seemed to be a good time, so I figured fuck it. I'll just tell her. But, apparently, you weren't ready to hear those words."

I blink repeatedly, trying to piece everything together. He thinks I ran out on him because he told me he loved me?

Of course… He has no idea my father saw us.

All night, I'd toiled over what to say to convince him this is the way it needs to be. If he learned my father knew about us, that the dean was suspicious, he'd quit tomorrow. He said himself it'll take a lot more than the risk to his career for him to walk away.

I suppose that's what I need to give him.

Holding my head high, I cross my arms in front of my chest, rebuilding the wall around my heart, brick by brick. "This was never supposed to turn into…this." I gesture between our bodies.

His eyes narrow into slits, anger seeping into his expression. "What are you saying, Chloe?"

I shrug nonchalantly, acting as if my heart isn't bleeding on this very sidewalk, each word I speak another set of feet stomping all over it. "I'm not really a 'fall-in-love' kind of girl." I sidestep him, walking up the stairs so he can't see the truth in my eyes.

"Says who?" He jumps to his feet, his fingers wrapping around my bicep, forcing me to face him. "Your father? Your mother?" The hurt in his words is all-consuming, but I can't let that get to me.

"Me! That's who!" I answer with ice in my voice, giving the performance of a lifetime. "You're a smart guy. You should have figured out by now that I'm incapable of loving anyone."

All I want to do is wrap my arms around him and tell him I don't mean any of this, that I do love him. But love is never enough. I've had a lifetime reminder of that. Love wasn't enough to keep my dad at home. Love wasn't enough to prevent my mom from drinking. And love wasn't enough to keep her clean.

"No, you're not. I see you're not." His voice turns pleading as he loosens his harsh grip on me. "You're just scared. I get that. I'm scared of these feelings I have for you, too. But I'm not enough of a coward to lie about them, to say I don't feel this way about you."

"I'm not a coward." I push out of his hold. "And I'm *not* lying. I feel nothing for you."

"So you say, but your actions these past few months indicate otherwise."

I shrug. "I've just mastered the art of figuring out what men want and giving them that so I can get what I need in return."

His Adam's apple bobs up and down in a hard swallow, his lip twitching. "And what did you need from me?" he asks, although I can sense his reluctance.

"What do you think?" I retort, passing him a demure look. "Do you know how many classes I've had to withdraw from because of my mother? I figured I could use a little insurance that, even if I missed too many classes, I'd still pass. That's all you were. An insurance policy."

"You…" He shakes his head, struggling to form any words.

"And now that you've turned in my final grade, I don't need you anymore." I jut out my chin, shoulders back, neck exposed, doing my best not to show a single hint of weakness, of vulnerability, of the lump growing in my throat, the words difficult to say. But this is the only way. I need him to hate me. Need him to forget about me.

Maybe if I didn't have the past I've had, I'd let him fight for me. But growing up with an alcoholic changes you. Just like growing up with a parent who is constantly disappointed in you. You go through life convinced you'll keep disappointing people, that you're not worth their time or effort. Life becomes a constant decision of "fish or cut bait". And you always cut bait. It's all you know.

It's all *I* know.

"And before?" he asks, his body shaking, lips pinched tight, stare cold and detached, yet filled with so much hurt and betrayal it makes me want to tell him the truth.

"What do you mean?"

"Before you learned I was your professor, what did you hope to get out of me?"

I place my hands on my hips. "I knew who you were in Vegas. I thought you looked familiar, then it hit me. Lincoln Moore, associate attorney for the *Times*. The same Lincoln Moore who would be my First Amendment professor, the last class I needed in order to graduate."

His head continues to shake, every muscle in his body taut.

"So, if you'll excuse me, it's Friday and the gossip mills are turning."

I try to spin from him, but his hand grips my wrist, forcing me back to him. I wince, but he doesn't let go. I watch as his nostrils flare like an untamed bull. I can tell it takes every ounce of self-control not to take his rage out on me further, not to hurt me like I'm destroying him.

"Why don't I believe you?" he growls.

"Well, you should."

"But I don't." He tightens his hold on me, the intensity of his quivering muscles causing my arm to tremble, the pain excruciating. But it's a welcome distraction from the ache in my heart.

With an anguished cry, he releases me, his entire body seeming to deflate. He stares into the distance, searching for an answer he'll never find. Then he floats his eyes back to me, the venom gone, replaced with a compassion I don't deserve.

"What we shared—"

"Was. Not. Real," I hiss through clenched teeth, refusing to soften my resolve. "So leave."

He studies me for what feels like an eternity, meticulously weighing my words against my actions. I wait as I stand judgment in front of him, praying he believes me. Finally, he blows out a breath and retreats down the stairs, defeated. Relief filling me, I turn back around, about to unlock my door when his voice stops me.

"It *was* real, Chloe. I know it was. In here."

I can't bear to turn around, to see the agony covering him as he points to his heart. I don't have to look at him to know that's what he's doing. I know him better than I've ever known anybody else. Which is why this is the only way. He promised he'd fight for me, regardless of the battle. But this is a war we'll never win.

"I don't know what happened to make you feel like you have to push me away—"

I whirl around. "I'm not—"

He holds up his hand, cutting me off. "But I'll go, even though that's not really what you want."

This time, I don't try to convince him otherwise.

"On the outside, you're this strong, enigmatic woman who doesn't take shit from anyone. But on the inside, you're still the same broken girl who convinced herself she doesn't deserve to be loved. Until you convince yourself you do, it won't matter how many times I try to tell you I love you. It won't matter how many times I tell you I'd risk it all for you. You'll never think you deserve it. I can't fight for someone who's not ready to fight for herself." His voice catches as he struggles to finish. "I can't keep loving someone who doesn't love herself."

I swallow hard, wanting to tell him we're at risk of being exposed. That we're no longer protected by that bubble we've survived in. But that would give him hope. And hope is a dangerous thing. These past few months have been proof of that.

"I know how to love myself. It's you I never loved. Now leave, before I report you to the dean." I storm into my apartment, slamming the door behind me.

CHAPTER FORTY-TWO

SCATTERED PAPERS AND half-full coffee mugs surround me as I work in the early hours of the morning, firing off story after story of the latest celebrity gossip. Like I've done every other weekend the past several years. I'm actually grateful for the busy news weekend. It helps keep my mind off Lincoln and how difficult the past week has been. How it feels like a huge part of me is missing.

As I put the finishing touches on a column about whether the heiress to a hotel brand is pregnant, based on photos where she's wearing something other than the usual skin-tight dresses, my buzzer sounds. I tear my eyes to my door, a flicker of hope building inside me that Lincoln's here to berate me for being so stubborn. But I know he won't be. I made sure of that.

Lifting myself off the couch, I stretch my legs, then move toward the door, squinting through the peephole to see Izzy, dressed in scrubs, standing on the front stoop. It doesn't surprise me. If my buzzer rings after midnight, it's usually Izzy. She's the only one who works stranger hours than me.

When I open the door, she enters without so much as an invitation. "So you *are* alive." She makes herself at home, plopping onto my couch.

"Umm… Yeah. What would make you think otherwise?" I follow her, sitting beside her, tucking a leg underneath me.

"Oh, I don't know. Evie mentioned you've been distant at work, and Nora said you haven't gone to a single yoga class to taunt her in over a week." She narrows her eyes. "That doesn't sound like the Chloe we all love."

"It's nothing," I lie with a shrug. "Between finishing up this semester, Nora's wedding in just a few weeks, and work, not to mention keeping an eye on my mom, I've been busy."

She tilts her head, lips pursed, eyebrows raised. "And nothing else? There's no other reason you're out of it?"

I meet her eyes, staying strong. "Nope."

She squints, her analytical gaze sweeping over me. I've known this woman since we were little. She's the one who first asked if my mom had a drinking problem before I really understood what alcohol was. She's always had an uncanny ability to pick up on things no one else could.

Leaning toward me, her voice becomes a low whisper, despite the fact no one is around to hear. "Did something happen between you and Lincoln?"

"What?" I exclaim, back straight, eyes wide. "I told you months ago. We cut all ties. Once I learned he was my professor—"

"Yeah, yeah, yeah. You kept things strictly professional," she mocks playfully. "Apart from the time you almost fucked on the desk in his office. I haven't forgotten about that. Evie and Nora may not be able to see through you, but *I* can. You've been secretly seeing him."

Her gaze traces over my face, then to the rest of my body, as if I'm wearing a giant scoreboard with a tally of the number of times we kissed, fucked, and did…other stuff.

"I think you've been seeing him for a while now, despite your insistence that there was nothing going on. But something happened…" She stares into the distance, chewing on her fingernails as she bounces her legs. Then she looks back to me, her tone a mixture of agitation and excitement. "It was around the time you learned your mom never stopped drinking, wasn't it? It makes sense. Traumatic events always seem to bring people back together, make people snap out of…whatever."

"Izzy, life isn't a fucking fairy tale. I am not a damsel in distress. And Lincoln is certainly no Prince Charming." Unless Prince Charming were into kinky role-play and spanking.

"That may be true, but you've never been the Prince Charming type, either. You're more interested in the bad boy who will break a few rules. You can sit here and claim nothing's been going on, but you've been…happy."

"I'm always happy."

"Not like this. Hell, look at your hair! You changed it back to your natural color. Almost like you finally felt you could be yourself and not put on a front."

"I don't know who else to be if I'm not myself."

"You haven't been yourself since you were fourteen," she quips without a moment's hesitation, her words surprising me. And she's right. I haven't been.

That was around the first time I walked into my mother's bathroom and found her passed out, head on the toilet, a mixture of vomit and spilled wine staining the tile. I forget how many times I slipped in it as I attempted to clean the room, then move her to her bed. My mother's no bigger than I am, but that night, she felt like she weighed a ton. It took hours, but I was finally able to get her into bed. The only thing that pushed me forward when I was ready to give up was my fear that my father would learn the truth and petition for custody of me.

"But lately, I've seen a more...carefree Chloe," she continues. She rests a hand on my bicep, and I shift my gaze toward hers, doing my best to keep it together when I've spent the past week on the brink of a complete breakdown. "I can't help but think Lincoln had something to do with that. Am I right?"

I look to the ceiling, chin quivering, eyes welling with tears. I've been through a lot of shit in my life and never cried, never showed emotion. But Izzy's sympathy pushes me over the edge. After what I did, I don't feel like I deserve it.

"Maybe." It's all I can manage to say before the dam bursts.

"Oh, Chloe..." Her arms are around me in an instant, all the tears I've kept at bay rushing forward.

"But Dad saw us," I choke out, soaking her shirt that's covered with SpongeBob SquarePants. "He said I would destroy Lincoln's career if I stayed with him." I pull back, swiping at my cheeks. "And he's right. If people found out about us, it *would* end his career. Any relationship, present or future, would forever be tainted by our past."

She holds me at arm's length, her dark eyes brimming with hope. "I may not know Lincoln that well, or have a full picture of what was going on, but he must have known the risk going in. And he must have been willing to take that risk."

"He was." I swallow hard, shaking my head. "But I couldn't let him do that."

"I'm not sure you have any say in the matter. If he wants to take his chances, isn't that his decision?"

"Not if I made sure he wouldn't make that decision."

Izzy leans back, giving me a sideways glance, almost not wanting to ask. "What did you do?"

"What I had to." I push down the bile rising in my throat at the memory of that night. The happiness, then the betrayal. The hope, then the despair. The absolute joy of having him declare his love, then the vice squeezing my heart when I used that love against him. "I made him think I was using him all along. That I knew in Vegas he was my professor and the only reason I slept with him was to make sure I passed."

She exhales, closing her eyes, shaking her head. "You didn't."

"I did," I squeak.

"Chloe..."

"It was the only way. Lincoln said himself that he would fight for me. He'd never give up, which would only continue to put his career at risk. Unless I made him hate me."

It's silent for a moment as she processes everything. "And he believed you? That doesn't sound like the Lincoln I know."

"Because I eviscerated that Lincoln. He said he wasn't going to fight for someone who refused to fight for herself." I look back to Izzy. "That he couldn't love a woman who didn't know how to love herself." I grab the box of tissues off the side table and blow my nose, the harsh sound echoing through my tiny apartment. But it doesn't faze Izzy. We've seen each other at our highest of highs and lowest of lows. Nothing is off-limits between us.

"Have you tried to talk to him?"

I snort a laugh at the ridiculousness of her question. "I'm the last person he wants to talk to. The things I said… There's no way he'll ever trust me again. I made him believe I only slept with him so he'd pass me." I shake my head. "There's no fixing this. Our ship has most definitely sailed."

Izzy peers at me thoughtfully. "Maybe Lincoln's right."

I whip my eyes to hers, confused. "What do you mean?"

"Maybe you need to fix yourself first. Then worry about fixing everything else."

My lips part as I consider her words. "I don't even know how to do that."

"Sometimes you need to go back to the beginning before you can get to the end."

"Will you stop talking in code and metaphors, Master Yoda? You've been spending too much time at Nora's meditation studio," I blurt out, exasperated. "We screwed during a blackout in Vegas. That's our beginning."

"No." She shakes her head. "Not your beginning with Lincoln. *Your* beginning as Chloe, as the woman you are. The woman who was born the instant you saw your mother take that first sip of alcohol. You need to come to terms with all of that. Until you do, I don't see you having a future with anyone."

"I've come to terms with it," I try to argue.

"Then why have you still not told Evie and Nora? I've kept my mouth shut because it's not my story to tell. But until you're honest with yourself, I don't see how you can possibly grow and move past this."

She holds my gaze for a moment, then places a kiss on my forehead. "I love you, Chloe." Her steely eyes lock with mine once more. "Think about what keeping this secret has done to you." She offers me an encouraging smile as she makes her way out of my apartment, leaving me alone to consider her statement. I hate to admit it, but there's a hint of truth to her words. But this is all I've known.

I've spent my life covering for my mother, hiding the truth. And where has it gotten me? Maybe I do need to go back to the beginning. Maybe I need to make peace with the girl I was all those years ago. Then I'll have a chance at finally moving forward. Finally realizing I deserve more than I've afforded myself.

With a fresh cup of coffee in hand, I open a blank document on my laptop and do the only thing that's brought me peace most of my life. The only thing that's helped me make sense of everything.

I write.

* * *

You come from the perfect family and live an idealistic life in an upper middle-class suburb a quick train ride from Manhattan. Both your parents are successful.

Both your parents are happy.

Or so you thought.

Then your father starts spending more time at the office, sometimes not coming home at all on the weekends. You're not sure of the reason. Mom says it's because he just got a huge promotion. You can hear the bitterness in her tone at the idea that his career is blossoming while hers withered up and died after she had you.

Soon, you notice your mother has a glass of wine with dinner when she normally drank club soda. One glass turns into two. Which soon turns into an entire bottle, then two. You wonder if that's normal. You want to ask your dad, but you're worried how he'll react. Because when your mother drinks that wine, she praises you, tells you how proud she is of you. Something your father never says.

So you stay quiet.

And the drinking continues.

Your father works more and more.

You wonder if he ever really wanted to have kids. Or maybe it's you. No matter what you do, no matter how good your grades, no matter how many sports you excel at, it's not enough for him to notice you.

It's not enough for him to take a day off work.

Most nights, you lay awake listening to your parents fight.

Then, seemingly overnight, boobs appear. And boys start to notice you.

You welcome it, considering the people who are supposed to love you don't have the time for you anymore.

The fights at home get worse.

You know the attention from boys at school isn't the type you want, but it's better than the lack of attention you get at home. So when you're only thirteen, you agree to play Seven Minutes in Heaven with a bunch of high school boys.

The fights at home get even worse.

You wear makeup and revealing clothing to make yourself appear older than you are.

The arguments continue.

You lie about your age just for those few seconds of being noticed.

You can't remember what a quiet house feels like.

You lose your virginity before you even understand what a condom is.

Suddenly, the fights stop. You think things are getting better, that you'll finally have a family. Then you walk into the house for dinner, surprised to see both your mom and dad at the table, something you haven't seen in years, their expressions filled with sorrow. They don't even have to say the words. You know.

They're getting a divorce.

You say goodbye to the only friends and family you've ever known and move to a new town with your mother. You're actually looking forward to it. A fresh start. A clean slate.

Then one day, you help your mother take out the garbage and notice one bag is filled with glass bottles. A dozen. Two dozen. Three dozen. All consumed since the last garbage pickup a week earlier. You hoped this habit wouldn't follow her here. But it has, and it's worse, since she doesn't have to hide it from your father.

Sometimes she's too drunk to drive you to your dad's on your scheduled weekends with him. He could come get you, but then he'd learn your mother's been drinking. You're worried the court will order you to live with your father, something you can't even stomach the thought of because of how inadequate he's always made you feel.

So you lie.

You cover it up.

You tell your dad you're sick.

You need to study.

You have a group project.

Anything to keep your mother's secret.

Thankfully, he's too consumed by his replacement wife, his replacement baby, his replacement family to even question it. He actually sounds relieved when you can't come, which only solidifies your original thought that you've never been anything but a burden.

Somehow you make it through high school. All those hours you lay awake studying to make sure your mother didn't choke on her own vomit means your grades are good enough to get a scholarship to a decent four-year school. You're thrilled to have that fresh start you thought you were getting years ago.

The morning you're scheduled to move into your dorm, you bound into your mother's room, only to see she's still drunk from the night before.

So you have to spend some of the money you saved for books to pay for a last-minute train ticket upstate. But it's worth it. Because you'll finally be able to close this chapter in your life. Finally have a place you feel like you belong.

Until you arrive at freshmen move-in and are surrounded by parents bidding tearful farewells to their children, telling them how proud they are of everything they've accomplished.

Your mother most likely hasn't even noticed you're gone yet. And your father probably has no idea you're even enrolled in college.

You meet your new roommate. At least you were lucky enough to be paired with the jackpot of all roommates. Caring. Compassionate. Sensitive to the fact that there are clearly skeletons in your closet you're not ready to share.

For a while, things seem to get better.

You can focus on excelling and proving to everyone you can be successful.

You can leave behind your somewhat promiscuous adolescence and become who you were always meant to be.

You can fall in love.

Until you learn your mother lost her job because of her drinking. There's no one else she can turn to, so you do the only thing you can in order to save her from losing the house, the only anchor you feel you have in your life.

You ask your father for help.

Except you don't tell him the exact reason. Just that you've decided to leave college.

Of course, he accuses you of never finishing anything you start.

He has a point, but you don't dwell.

You thank him when he says he'll call in a favor to see if he can get you a decent job. Or at least one that will pay a little more than the local Starbucks.

So you go to work as a receptionist at a women's magazine.

You're starstruck the first time a famous actor walks in.

Even more so when he shamelessly flirts with you.

With all the drama at home, you welcome the attention. It helps take your mind off the fact that you're not able to get your mother the help she needs. She promises she's trying to get clean. You have no choice but to take her at her word, the pile of bills preventing you from babysitting her. Your low-paying job isn't enough to afford rehab. You can barely pay the mortgage, but you refuse to let her lose her house. That may only make her drink more.

So you find a second job as a cocktail waitress, as ironic as that is.

The tips are good.

But the stack of bills gets even higher.

You realize you won't be going back to school anytime soon.

You turn on the charm because it increases your tips. One night, a man with a designer suit and a Tag Hauer watch walks in. You make sure you're the one who takes care of him. When he leaves you a one hundred dollar bill for a twenty dollar scotch, you turn on the charm even more to show your appreciation.

He mistakes the appreciation for interest and invites you back to his hotel. You say you can't, that you have to get up early for work in the morning. As it stands, by the time you get home from this job, you'll maybe only get three hours of sleep, but you've trained your body to function on less than that.

Since this man's used to being able to buy anything he wants, he flashes his billfold, promising to make it worth your while.

You're offended at first, wanting to hold on to the small amount of pride you have left. Then you remember the property tax bill that's been taunting you. You'd never seen a bill with so many zeros before. Your mother tries to help. She's been looking for work, but she's being turned down left and right. Jobs she's overqualified for won't hire her because they want someone who won't quit after a few months for something better. Jobs she is qualified for won't go near her because word travels fast in her industry.

So, instead of declining the man's offer, you ask where he's staying. You almost turn back nearly a dozen times. You try to convince yourself you don't need to do this, that you'll find another way. But the fear of losing the house pushes you forward.

When you knock on his room in a hotel you'd never be able to afford, he answers with a smile that sends a chill through you. But you swallow down the bile and walk inside, officially out of options. That night, part of you dies.

When he's done, he leaves a stack of bills on the bed for you. It takes everything inside you not to break down and cry. You dress quickly and leave, not looking back.

You tell yourself you'll never do that again, that there's another way.

Then your mother's house is foreclosed on, despite all your efforts to keep it, and you move into a tiny studio apartment in an area of town where you're scared to fall asleep. But it's all you can afford at the moment.

So you turn on the charm once more. Some men are interested in more of a girlfriend experience, so that's what you give them. Some just want to have fun for a night, so you oblige. They bestow you with cash and gifts—jewels, shoes, purses. All things you can sell to pay your bills and hopefully save enough money to move into a better place, a nicer place...a safer place.

Finally, the clouds seem to part when you come home one day and learn your mother got a job. A good job. You want to burst out in tears at the relief of not having to sell your body anymore.

You go back to school. You quit your waitressing job. You move into your own place. You find out about a promotion at the magazine and put all your effort into that, even if it means doing a few questionable things in order to get it. The pay will be enough that you'll never have to sacrifice your dignity again.

Then you take your mother to her AA meeting and smell alcohol on her breath. So you put your life on hold again, withdrawing from school in an effort to keep a closer eye on her.

You somehow convince yourself it's all your fault. That you deserve everything life's handed you. That maybe you don't deserve to be happy, don't deserve to be loved.

Then a man comes into your life and makes you believe that maybe you are. That maybe you do have worth. Maybe you do have value. Maybe you can be loved.

But you're scared. What if he learns the truth of everything you've done? What if he learns of the lies you told? What if he's able to see past the walls you were forced to build all those years ago and no longer likes what he sees?

Yet, somehow, he does. When you hit your lowest point, he stands by your side and helps lift you up. He doesn't judge when he learns the truth. He doesn't look at you in disgust. Instead, he sees something you never thought anyone would — strength. He doesn't make you feel worthless. He calls you a survivor. Calls you strong. Calls you remarkable.

And those walls around you come crumbling down.

You let this amazing man in. You open up to him.

You fall in love.

Guardedly.

Timidly.

Hesitantly.

But you still do.

Then the bottom drops. Regardless, he tries to fight for you, says he'll go to battle for you.

But you know his love will never win the war. You've lived your entire life on a runaway train, desperately trying to get it back on its tracks. So you do the one thing you can to control this situation.

You lie.

It's not the first time. You've lied to everyone most of your life. About your mother. About where that designer purse you had days ago disappeared to. About the bruise on your arm where one of your new "friends" got a little too rough.

When your parent is an alcoholic, you become a master at deception, so much so that it's hard to remember what's real and what's part of the elaborate façade you built to hide the truth.

You convince yourself you don't need love, that love makes you weak, and you refuse to show even a hint of weakness.

You smile and tell your friends how thrilled you are when they find their own happily ever after that would rival even the cheesiest romantic comedy.

They joke and tell you that you're next. You brush it off, saying you're not interested in all the trappings of love, of finding your happily ever after.

But I did find my happily ever after.

Convincing myself I didn't, convincing him I didn't, is the biggest lie I've ever told.

I wipe my tired eyes, stretching my legs out in front of me as I read over what I spent the last several hours writing and rewriting, telling my story, not leaving out a single detail. Izzy was right. It's amazingly cathartic to get it all down on paper. And maybe it will help other people who are just as lost as me, who feel just as worthless as I do.

Content with my work, I sit back, contemplating what to do now that it's out there. But is it?

I'm not sure what comes over me, whether it's lack of sleep or the peaceful glow filtering into my apartment in the predawn hours, but I open up my email and attach the document, then type a message.

To: Evie Fitzgerald
From: Chloe Davenport
Subject: Maybe?

Hey, E. Think Viv would want to run this in next month's issue instead of the piece on the best celebrity Instagram accounts?

C

I hesitate, my finger about to click on the send button. Once I do, my friends will know all my secrets. After these past few hours of soul-searching, it doesn't seem the cataclysmic event I once thought it to be. So I click, listening to the whooshing sound as the email flies into cyberspace. A part of me regrets being so rash.

Until Evie and Nora appear on my doorstep before seven in the morning, tears in their eyes. When they wrap me in their arms without a single ounce of pity or judgment, I'm confident this is the right path. That this is what I need to do to move forward, to turn that page on a new chapter in my life.

Even if Lincoln's name doesn't appear on any of them.

Chapter Forty-Three

A SEA OF black robes fills the lobby of a state-of-the-art theater, a post-graduation reception underway. Of course, this wasn't the official ceremony, just one the journalism department puts on for its students. A more private affair honoring a few hundred graduates instead of the university graduation, which has several thousand.

I'd been uneasy about the prospect of attending. I'd planned on foregoing walking during my graduation ceremony altogether, not wanting to run into Lincoln. But my friends reminded me of all the obstacles I'd faced in getting to this point. I needed to do this.

That still didn't stop me from nearly turning around and leaving a dozen times as the graduation coordinator had lined us up, unsure whether I could enter the auditorium and face Lincoln. Thankfully, he wasn't among the rows of faculty members on stage.

With the ceremony over, I make my way through the lobby packed with people in the post-graduation celebration, searching for my friends and mother, which proves difficult due to my height. My path obstructed, I place my hand on the shoulder of a tall man in a suit in order to get his attention so I can squeeze through. He turns around, the jovial expression instantly falling from his face when those familiar green eyes lock with mine, cold and distant.

Despite the boisterous voices filling the space, a strained silence, tense and uncertain, echoes in my ears. I've spent the past few weeks doing everything in my power to make peace with my past and move forward. But I can't do that until I finally close this chapter in my life. And that includes apologizing and coming clean with this man.

"Lincoln," I begin, my eyes soft.

He shoots up a hand, cutting me off. His jaw tenses, lip curling. "It's Professor Moore," he states sternly.

"Please, I just wanted to—"

He leans toward me, his harsh voice no more than a whisper. "No. You graduated. You got what you wanted. Now I never want to see you again." He pulls back, straightening his tie. "Best of luck on all your future endeavors, Miss Davenport. But I doubt you'll need it. You'll do whatever it takes to get what you want."

His biting words sting as they linger between us. Then he turns, the crowd seeming to part to allow him passage. I want to call out, tell him I love him, that I did what I did to protect him, but I don't. He wouldn't believe me anyway. Every action has consequences. And these are the consequences of my own actions. Ones I'll have to live with the rest of my life.

Swallowing hard through the lump in my throat, I plaster a smile onto my face, continuing through the lobby, relieved when I see all my friends waiting.

"You did it!" Evie says, hugging me enthusiastically, Nora also getting in on the action before pulling back to allow my mother to embrace me and offer her congratulations.

I gaze upon my friends with a bit of envy as they stand beside the men in their life — Evie with Julian, and Nora with Jeremy. They both look so happy. I try to remind myself I never would have had what they do.

"Come on." Izzy slings her arm over my shoulder. "Let's go celebrate. I hear Camille's been busy back at Julian's making her famous chocolate soufflé."

I peer in his direction. "Is that right?"

"Evie's a sucker for it. And whatever Evie wants, Evie gets."

"Don't I know it." I roll my eyes, following my friends out of the building.

Once we're out of earshot, Izzy leans into me, whispering. "You okay?"

"Never better." I flash a smile, but when she narrows her gaze, I know she can tell I'm not myself. I exhale a long breath. "I just ran into him."

"Oh, Chloe…"

"It's okay. I'm okay." I shrug it off, pretending to be happy so no one else can pick up on my unease.

"No, you're not."

I meet her eyes. "I know. But I have to believe, in time, I will be."

After we've all stuffed ourselves with the delicious meal Julian's housekeeper, Camille, prepared, my mother clinks her fork against her glass, then stands from the table. At first, I was hesitant to agree to have any Champagne here, but she insisted she didn't want to ruin any more special moments in my life. I should be able to celebrate my college graduation with a glass of Champagne if I wanted. And to my surprise, she hasn't even looked twice at a glass, drinking club soda instead.

"It's not every day you can stand up in front of your daughter and all her wonderful friends to celebrate everything she did to overcome adversity and graduate college."

I smile, grateful there are no jokes about it taking me ten years, like there would be with my father. But my mom knows the truth now, knows I dropped out to try to keep a roof over her head, keep her from becoming a statistic.

"You are a remarkable young woman, Chloe. And I'm honored to be able to call you my daughter. You may think this isn't a big deal, that it's just a piece of paper, but it's so much more than that. You've proven you'll never give up on your dreams. That you'll fight for them and achieve them, regardless of how long it takes." She lifts her glass, everyone at the table following suit. "Congratulations."

Everyone repeats the word as we all clink glasses.

"On that note…," Nora begins excitedly. "Here…"

She withdraws a t-shirt-sized box from a hiding place under the table and shoves it toward me.

"Guys, I told you no presents."

"You should know by now that we are *horrible* at actually listening to you."

I tilt my head, pinching my lips together.

"Just open it, Chloe," Jeremy says, placing his arm around Nora's shoulders, his broad muscles dwarfing her slender frame. "You know how persistent Nora can be. You won't win with her."

Playfully sighing, I grab the box and tear the wrapping from it. When I open the lid, I'm not sure what I'm looking at. It's a couple pieces of paper. One containing an airline itinerary, the other with information on the hotel in Hawaii where we're all staying for Nora's upcoming wedding. My name is on both reservations, but the dates aren't what I'd originally booked.

"What is this?" I glance around the table, confused.

"I hope you don't mind," Evie begins, grabbing Julian's hand. "But we took a vote, and the consensus is that you need a vacation."

"I'm taking a vacation. For Nora's wedding."

Nora rolls her eyes. "You're flying in Friday and leaving Sunday. The wedding's Saturday. Doesn't give you much of a vacation."

I lower my eyes, not wanting to tell her it's all I can afford.

"So we took it upon ourselves to change your flight and your hotel," Evie explains. "All paid for. And don't worry. The entire staff at the magazine donated some of their paid leave so you won't have to use any of your accumulated time. You even have some extra days now, too. You leave Saturday."

"Saturday?" My eyes widen. "As in seven days from now?"

"Well, since it's Sunday, technically six," Nora interjects. "But who's counting?"

"You," Izzy quips. "If I'm not mistaken, you've been counting down to this wedding since you set the date over a year ago."

"What can I say?" She shrugs, tilting her head to meet Jeremy's dark eyes. "I'm so excited to have one penis for the rest of my life."

I watch as she kisses him. Normally, I would have joked and told them to get a room, but there's something about their love that's so sweet, so pure, so hopeful. It makes me optimistic that I'll find love again.

When Nora reluctantly tears her lips from Jeremy's, she looks at me. "It'll be great. We're flying there Friday. Izzy's flying in on Sunday, right?"

I look to Izzy, who nods.

"And Evie and Julian are arriving on Sunday, too. You were the only one who was flying in, doing the wedding, then leaving the next day. I want some time with my friend."

"You deserve this, sweetie," Mom says. "You've worked your tail off taking care of yourself and me for far too long. Enjoy it."

"I don't know what to say." I shake my head, knowing how much something like this must have cost. The rooms at the hotel alone are close to $400 a night. To pay for me to stay there eight nights? I tell myself it's too much, that I don't deserve it. But I'm trying to learn I deserve better than I've afforded myself.

"Just say you won't miss that plane, because the last thing I want to worry about is rebooking your damn flight. Again," Nora says.

"I'll be there." I reach across the table, grabbing both Nora's and Evie's hands in mine. Izzy covers one of mine and I look at all the incredible women who've supported me through everything, even if they haven't always agreed with some of my decisions. "Thank you."

The celebration continues for a while longer, all of us indulging in the ridiculously rich chocolate soufflé. I don't know how Julian stays in such great shape with Camille's cooking. Based on the way Evie can barely keep her hands off him, I surmise the workout she must give him in the bedroom helps in that department.

"You got a minute?" Evie asks as everyone lounges in the sitting area of Julian's penthouse condo, the breathtaking view of Central Park and Manhattan a stunning backdrop. It's still hard to picture Evie living here, to be in this life with Julian, a man she was just supposed to pretend to date for a summer. I guess we can't control who we fall in love with. The last few months have taught me that.

"Sure." I set my coffee on the marble table in front of me and get up from the couch, following her to a room she's revamped as her office.

A modern, white desk sits in the center, brightly colored chairs on either side of it. The walls are lined with framed photos of various important editions of *Blush*, including the first one that listed her as assistant editor. She's come a long way from being the sex and dating columnist we all read for a quick laugh. I suppose I have, too.

"What's up?" I ask as she walks to the desk and retrieves a large envelope.

She faces me, chewing on her lower lip. "Don't get mad."

I eye her skeptically. "When you start out like that, I have a feeling I might."

"I know. I just…" She blows out a breath. "I really think you need this." She hesitantly extends the envelope toward me.

I stare at her, unsure I want to know what's inside. But intrigue gets the better of me and I open it, pulling out what appears to be a proof of the July issue of *Time*. The cover has the signature red border, the image a single rocks glass filled a quarter of the way with an amber liquid.

"Wha—"

"Viv loved your piece. I mean *really* loved it."

"I know. She was going to make it the feature article in the July issue of *Blush*."

"And she was. Until she found out that *Time* was doing a feature on alcoholism in America. They're running stories from people who dealt with it themselves, as well as family members of alcoholics."

My pulse increases when I see a tab sticking out, marking a page. I open to it, the air sucked from my lungs when I read the title and byline.

The Biggest Lie
By Chloe Davenport, Contributor

I fling my eyes back to Evie, a dozen questions on the tip of my tongue.

"Viv thought your piece too important to run in *Blush*. So did the editor at *Time*."

I run my finger over my name, still feeling like this can't be real. I often imagined seeing my name in this magazine. I never thought it would happen. Thought all I'd ever do was write about the hottest celebrity gossip. But here it is… My story. In all its tragic, heart-wrenching beauty. Something that never would have been possible if Evie didn't believe in me.

Overwhelmed, I throw my arms around her, squeezing. "Thank you."

"You know I love you, Chloe. Cracks and all."

CHAPTER FORTY-FOUR

I ZIP UP my suitcase, then check my bathroom and bedroom one last time to make sure I'm not forgetting anything. As long as I remember my bridesmaid dress and shoes, everything else is replaceable.

At first, I was uncertain about spending a week in Hawaii when I could be working, but getting out of Manhattan is exactly what I need. Hopefully it will help clear my mind. And maybe I'll even meet some hot islander to make me forget, even if for a little while.

My buzzer sounds and I check the time, seeing it's not yet 5:30 in the morning. The driver Evie and Julian sent must be early.

I drag my bags into the foyer, then open the door without looking through the peephole, stopping short when my eyes fall on the familiar man standing on my doorstep.

"Dad? What are you—"

He brings his hand from his back, revealing a copy of the edition of *Time* my piece will appear in. It's not supposed to drop until next week, but I'm sure someone in the industry saw my name and sent him a copy, probably to do damage control.

With a sigh, I step back. "Would you like to come in?" I figure it's best for him to ream me out now instead of having this weigh on my mind during my vacation.

He doesn't say anything. Just nods and walks into my apartment. I follow him, finding it odd to see him here. I don't think he's ever actually been to my place. To be honest, I'm surprised he even knows where I live.

"Can we make this quick? I have a flight to catch." I cross my arms in front of my chest, not even asking why he thought it a good idea to come to my apartment so early on a Saturday. Based on the fact that he's dressed in a suit, his tie loosened, his eyes bloodshot, he's probably been at the office all night working. As always.

He parts his lips, but words don't come right away. I furrow my brow. I can't remember a time my father didn't have an opinion about something. When he held anything back. When he struggled to find the right words.

Then I notice tears forming in the corners of his eyes as he looks at me. I mean, *really* looks at me. Really sees me. There's not so much as a hint of disappointment in his gaze. Only sorrow. And regret.

"Is this true?" His low voice quivers, barely able to get his question out. It's a stark contrast to the man who always seemed so confident, who never cared much for people's feelings. At least not *my* feelings.

I nod slightly.

He slumps onto the couch, burying his head in his hands. I'm not sure what to make of this. Over the years, I've learned to remain guarded around this man, concerned he'd take advantage of any weakness. If I didn't know any better, I'd think this person were an imposter, his demeanor not resembling the man I thought to be my father.

He lifts his weary eyes to mine. He's always had a youthful appearance, and I've often heard some of the other students at the university refer to him as a "silver fox". But now, he looks to have aged immensely.

"You really did all these things just to keep the truth from me?"

I could sugarcoat it to protect his feelings, but he never did that with me. I'm trying to move on, trying to start over. I can't keep lying.

"You already had such a low opinion of me. I figured the truth wouldn't change that. It would probably only make it worse."

He hangs his head again, pinching the bridge of his nose. I don't move, simply observing him, trying to figure out the game he's playing. Then a sob cuts through the stillness of my minuscule apartment.

"God, Chloe…" He briefly looks to the ceiling. "What have I done?"

I remain silent, unsure how to answer that. Unsure I *can* answer that.

"I should have paid more attention to your mother. To you. I was so focused on fighting for a cause I believed in…" His eyes lock on mine. "When I should have been fighting for you. For your mother. For my family. How could I…" He draws in a deep breath. "How could I have been so blind?"

"We're all blind to things we're not equipped to deal with." I lower myself to the couch. I can't remember the last time I sat beside this man. I can't remember the last time we've talked without him belittling me.

"That sounds like something your mother would say." He laughs slightly, swiping at his tears before his expression turns serious. "I don't expect you to forgive me for this. I certainly wouldn't. I've been a horrible dad. When I was growing up, my father was always working, always pushed us to achieve more. Not that it's any excuse for how I treated you, but it's all I knew. And your poor mother…" He trails off as he looks into the distance.

"*I* was the one who begged to have a family with her, even though I knew how much she loved her career. Hell, we met at a rally in support of the Equal Rights Amendment. She was a firecracker back then, even though she was only a college freshman. I should have known she wouldn't be happy at home with kids. But I ignored her, too."

He grabs my hands in his, his grip firm. I peer at them, the feel of my father's skin against mine odd.

"I'm begging you to give me a chance to show you I can be a better person. To make up for…this." Dropping his hold on me, he lifts the magazine that's open to my article. His eyes skate over the words on the page… *My* words. "All of it. You never should have…" His voice catches and he swallows, squeezing his eyes shut. "You never should have had to go through this. To do these things."

Absorbing his heartfelt plea, I look away from him, drawing in a deep breath as I collect my thoughts. I never anticipated my father would show up on my doorstep, let alone apologize. If anything, I figured he'd chew me out for publicizing private matters, as ironic as that sounds for a lawyer who fights to ensure the public has access to important information.

I don't have to forgive him. Don't even have to give him a chance. But one of the things they talk about in the Al-Anon meetings I've made a point to attend is letting go and moving forward. Of accepting the things life has thrown at us and growing from those experiences.

When I look back at him, I respond the only way that makes sense. "I think I did."

His brows furrow. "Wha—"

"I think I did have to go through all of this." I wrap my fingers around his hand, squeezing reassuringly. "My past has shaped me into the person I am today. For the first time in my life, I like this person. That may have been a different story a few weeks ago, but I'm learning how to accept things and learn from them. If I didn't go through everything I did, I would never have written this." I grab the magazine out of his hands, holding it up. "I may never have seen my name in *Time*. *Time*! That's just… I don't even have the words."

He smiles, then wraps his arm around me, pulling me against him. I thought it would feel awkward, but it doesn't. I inhale, the familiar spicy scent reminding me of my childhood. "I think you would have found your way there eventually, sweetie." He kisses the top of my head.

"Thanks… Dad."

We have a long way to go to bury the past, and some days will be harder than others, just like with my mother. But it's nice to know he finally realizes his approach to parenting has been anything but healthy.

"I just want you to promise me something," I say, pulling out of his embrace.

"Anything."

I pinch my lips together, pausing. "Stop working so much and get to know Midge. She's a really great kid."

A smile covers his mouth, his eyes sparkling. "I can do that."

"And if she doesn't want to ride a horse, or learn archery, or do fencing, or any of the other ridiculously snooty sports you signed me up for, listen to her. Kids should be able to kick a ball up and down a field instead of stab a sword into their opponent."

"You got it. No snooty sports."

"Good."

"Good." It's silent for a moment before he speaks again. "I'm sorry for what I said to you the last time I saw you. The night—"

"It's okay. Like you said, it never would have worked. He would have always been my professor. He would have had to sacrifice too much to be with me."

He pulls me against him again, holding me like a father who really loves his daughter. Deep down, he probably always has, but just showed it in a…different way.

"If he's smart, he'll sacrifice it all. Just like I should have years ago."

CHAPTER FORTY-FIVE

I LEAN MY forearms against the railing of my ocean-front room, inhaling the fragrant Hawaiian air, the crash of waves sounding from mere yards away. A breeze picks up, blowing my hair in front of my face, and I relax, exhaling a satisfied sigh.

This is exactly what I needed. Fresh air. Ocean waves. Stunning scenery. I can't remember the last time I've taken a day off to enjoy myself. Now I have ten days to myself, having been ordered by my boss not to pick up my phone or answer an email until I'm back in the office. I'm not sure what to do with all this free time.

A knock on the door interrupts my moment of serenity, and I tear my attention away from a few well-built surfers, their glistening bodies bobbing up and down as they wait to catch a wave. I retreat into my home, leaving the sliding glass doors open to allow the ocean air inside.

When I pull back the door to my room, I'm instantly assaulted by an excited Nora, who practically tackles me to the floor. "You're here! This is really happening, isn't it?"

I hug her back, laughing. When I first landed at the airport less than an hour ago, I wondered if this was a mistake, if I would have been better off staying in New York a little longer. The entire baggage claim area seemed to be filled with couples on their honeymoon, fingers intertwined, a sparkle in their eyes as they struggled to keep their hands off each other.

But seeing Nora, being here for her, spending time with her, is more important than any longing or heartache I feel at the thought of wishing Lincoln were here with me. As I'd reminded myself time and again these past few weeks, he never would have been able to be here with me. Never would have been able to hold my hand in baggage claim. Never would have been able to kiss me as we watched one of the most magnificent sunsets in existence.

This is for the best.

Pulling out of her embrace, I glance from her to Jeremy. They've only been here a day, yet he looks like he's been on the island for a while. He's already acclimated to the tropical attire, wearing a neutral Hawaiian shirt with khaki shorts. His skin is sun-kissed, his sandy hair a little lighter at the ends.

"It is," I answer. "Unless one of you gets cold feet within the next few days."

"Not a chance in hell." Nora wraps her arm around Jeremy's waist, pulling him against her. She meets his eyes. "You're stuck with me."

"Sounds good to me, babe." He kisses her nose. Such a simple gesture, but it has me sighing.

"We'll let you get all settled. We're off to meet with our wedding coordinator anyway, but I wanted to stop by and say hi."

"Do you want me to come and help?" I ask, feeling like I've been a shitty maid of honor lately. Thankfully, Evie picked up the slack, considering she worked as a wedding planning assistant prior to getting the job at the magazine.

"You take it easy this afternoon. Go relax on the beach. Check out the local…flavor." She waggles her brows.

"I already have." I gesture toward the balcony. "This is certainly a room with a view." I force a smile, since that's something pre-Lincoln Chloe would do.

"Good." She grins, but it doesn't reach her eyes. I know she wishes the past several months had a different outcome, too, despite the fact I kept her in the dark until it all fell apart. Then she pulls a piece of cardstock from her purse, handing it to me. "Now, here's our itinerary for the week."

I grimace. "Itinerary?"

"This island is full of fun activities. Sightseeing. Volcanos. Helicopter rides. Snorkeling. Paddle boarding. Surfing."

I scan the sheet of paper. "You left out the waterfall picnic lunch," I jest, reading her plan for Wednesday.

"I know it's not your idea of a fun vacation, but when are we all going to be in Hawaii together again? We should take advantage of it."

I exhale, the idea of having to be somewhere at a certain time making my skin crawl. But if this is what Nora wants, I won't rain on her parade.

"Fine. But only because I love you and want you to have the wedding of your dreams."

"Thank you." She beams, then her expression falls. "On that note…" She pulls her bottom lip between her teeth, nervously shifting her gaze from me to Jeremy, then back again. "We have a favor to ask."

"Okay…," I reply in a drawn-out voice.

"You see…Jeremy's best man has a…" She looks to him, searching for her words. "Reputation."

I shift my eyes up to Jeremy's, hoping for a better explanation.

"He tries to screw anything with a pulse." He smirks.

"Ah."

"And since all our guests are spending a lot of money to be here," Nora continues, "we were hoping you'd—"

"Make sure he keeps his dick in his pants," I finish.

"More or less. You have a low tolerance for bullshit."

I squint, vaguely recalling a conversation I'd overheard recently about Jeremy's supposed best man.

"I thought your best man was no longer able to make the wedding." I place a hand on my hip, studying them. Their expressions exhibit a hint of nervousness. Nora doesn't maintain eye contact, looking anywhere but at me, an overly enthusiastic smile on her face. "That his wife, who's pregnant with twins, was ordered on bed rest so he's staying with her."

Jeremy laughs, sheepishly running a hand through his hair. "That's true."

"I thought you said you were going to go without one."

"He was, but…" She trails off.

"But I changed my mind," Jeremy interjects. "Nora didn't like the idea of things being uneven."

"So you added a completely new best man? Why not ask one of your groomsmen?" My suspicions grow, fearing this is a set-up. Nora's been on my case about meeting someone, thinking it would help me move on. But I have no interest in what I can only imagine is some elaborate scheme to set me up with a guy she thinks is perfect for me. There's only been one perfect.

"His brothers are his groomsmen. He didn't want to pick one over another, so he asked a buddy from college."

I form my lips into a tight line, having trouble believing this story.

"Please, Chloe," Nora begs, clasping her hands in prayer. "It would mean the world to me if you'd just do this." She peers at me with those sad puppy-dog eyes I can never say no to.

"Fine," I huff. "I'll babysit." If nothing else, it will allow me a chance to figure out what game Nora and Jeremy are playing.

"Thank you so much." She wraps her arms around me, squeezing me before releasing her hold. "We have to go. Take it easy. Go soak up some sun. And enjoy the view." She passes me a devilish grin, then grabs Jeremy's hand and tugs him down the hallway. "We'll see you tonight."

"Wait. Tonight?" I call after them. "What's tonight?"

"It's on the itinerary."

I glance down at the paper in my hand. Dinner with Nora, Jeremy, and this mysterious best man.

Great.

CHAPTER FORTY-SIX

I CHECK MY reflection one last time, smoothing a few strands of blonde hair behind my ear. I wasn't quite sure what to wear tonight. I hadn't exactly packed a dress that screamed emasculation. But since I'm in Hawaii, I figured I may as well attempt to fit in, deciding on a flowing floral sundress.

Content with my appearance, I run a bit more gloss over my lips, then head out, glancing at the blasted itinerary for the location of tonight's "dinner meeting", as Nora referred to it.

It takes me a minute to find my way around the large resort, but I eventually locate the waterfront restaurant. When I enter, I'm immersed in a laidback island vibe, the sound of a local trio entertaining the patrons with Hawaiian-style music filling the air. The entire perimeter of the restaurant is windows, apart from the areas where the sliding glass doors are open, allowing the gentle ocean breeze to fill the place.

I float my eyes around the dining room for any sign of Nora or Jeremy, not seeing them anywhere. Normally *I'm* the one who's late, not Nora.

I walk to the host stand and a woman, who's obviously a local, greets me warmly. She's dressed in a slim-fit floral dress that has an Asian influence, a lone flower pinned in her slick, black hair.

"Aloha, miss. Do you have a reservation?"

"Actually, I'm meeting a few people here. Nora Tremblay and Jeremy Boyd."

She looks at her computer screen. "Yes. I have their reservation right here. They haven't arrived yet, and we don't seat our parties until everyone is present." She gestures to the open-air bar and lounge to my right. "But if you'd like to have a drink while you wait, the view is beautiful."

"Thanks." I consider waiting in the foyer, knowing Nora won't be too long. But the view undoubtedly is stunning. So I head into the lounge, searching for an empty table, since the bar seems to be full.

"A table just opened up right next to the railing," a man wearing all black and carrying a tray of empty glasses instructs. "Grab it before someone else does." He winks, then continues past me.

Shifting my eyes in the direction he indicated, I see a small hightop table and walk toward it. Luckily, I'm able to reach it before anyone else and hoist myself into the chair. A gentle breeze comes off the ocean, and I smooth a few wayward locks behind my ear, listening to the trio play. The sky is an impressive mixture of orange, pink, and red, the hue unlike any I've seen. Couples walk hand-in-hand on the white sand, stealing a few kisses as dusk sets in. I can't help but sigh.

"Maybe one day," I say to myself.

"Here you go, miss," a voice cuts through. I tear my eyes to my right to see a petite woman wearing a crisp white shirt and black pants removing a martini from her tray, placing it in front of me.

I furrow my brow. "I haven't placed my order yet."

The similarities between this and that night in Vegas aren't lost on me. But Lincoln's not here. He's back in New York. Unless my father has him pulling an all-nighter because of some big deadline, he's probably sleeping in his bed.

I swallow past the lump in my throat at the thought that another woman may already be in that bed with him.

"Oh, I'm sorry," the server apologizes. "I'm all mixed up today. Let me go check the ticket, then I'll be back to take your order."

She hurries toward the bar, and I look back to the horizon. For a split second, there was a part of me that *did* think Lincoln was here. But he'd made it more than apparent when I attempted to talk to him at graduation that he wants absolutely nothing to do with me. I can't blame him. No one deserves to be treated the way I treated him.

"Um… Actually, miss…"

I turn to see the same server approaching with the same martini.

"This *is* for you. A gentleman saw you walk in and asked the bartender to send it your way."

"A gentleman?"

I look past her, searching the bar, holding out a twinge of hope that I'd see a familiar silhouette standing there when, in reality, it's probably just some overweight man wearing a gaudy floral shirt who's going through a midlife crisis.

Suddenly, her gaze widens and she backs away, leaving the martini.

"I took a guess at what kind of vodka you'd prefer," a deep rumble sounds.

Paralyzed, every muscle in my body stiffens, my pulse skyrocketing. I blink repeatedly, praying this isn't just a dream, a side effect of sitting by a couple of college students smoking pot during my afternoon on the beach.

"But something made me think you were a Belvedere girl." The heat of his breath closes in on my neck, sending a shiver down my spine. Then a finger runs the length of my arm. "Smooth. Layered. Sophisticated. And so fucking stubborn." He grasps my hand, stepping in front of me.

I stare into Lincoln's brilliant eyes and part my lips, struggling to say something, anything, but no words come. I don't know what to make of this, considering the animosity and pure hatred that covered his face the last time we saw each other. But it's no longer there. In its place is a look of unmatched devotion, complete admiration, and wanton desperation.

"I am so sorry." His voice is choked with emotion, everything about him exuding the same passion and intensity he has since the first time I felt his body against mine.

"Sorry? What are you—"

"That night I took you to dinner." His hands go to my face, gripping my cheeks. "Our first official-unofficial date. Do you remember what I promised you?"

I swallow hard. "That you'd always fight for me."

"No matter the battle. But I broke that promise."

"I didn't give you a choice. You just said it yourself." I laugh slightly. "I'm really stubborn. I'd already decided what I needed to do. No matter what you said, nothing would have made me change my mind. Not after…" I trail off.

"Not after your father saw us together and reminded you of everything I would lose if you didn't break it off with me."

I briefly close my eyes. "He told you."

"Yes, and so did you."

"Me?" I fling my gaze to his.

His lips curve up. "Your father left an early issue of *Time* on my desk this morning, along with a note that said if I didn't get on the first flight to Hawaii, I'm not as smart as he thought and he'd seriously reconsider his decision to hire me."

"Oh." I pull away, unsure how to react to Lincoln reading that article. I knew it was a possibility. I figured he wouldn't care anymore. That my words wouldn't matter. Judging by the anguish in his eyes, they still do.

He lifts his hand to my nape, not allowing me to escape him. "Every man in your life has disappointed you. It kills me that I'm one of them. So I'm here to make it up to you. To promise that I'll do my best to never disappoint you again. I can't promise I won't, but if you just give me a chance, I'll do everything in my power not to deliberately piss you off, like slurp my soup or leave my shoes in the middle of the floor so you trip on them. Hell, I'll even stop stealing your panties."

I playfully slap him. "Don't you dare. My panties will always belong to you."

A peaceful smile crosses his mouth as he closes the distance, his lips so close to mine. "And what about your heart?"

"That will always belong to you, too."

"I was hoping you'd say that." He goes to erase that last bit of space between us, but I put my hand on his chest, preventing him from doing so.

He pulls back, an eyebrow raised in question.

"That still doesn't mean this will work. Just because we want to be together doesn't mean we should. It still doesn't fix the fact that I was your student. That you lied for me. Intentionally kept our relationship a secret so no one would find out you violated the code of conduct. Not even the strongest love will fix this. I'm not sure I'm—"

"You're not sure you're worth it?" His tone is full of fire and zeal as he finishes my thought.

I simply shrug. I've done quite a bit of soul-searching these past few weeks. Have come to terms with my past and know I'm worthy of love. I just don't know if I'm worthy of Lincoln's love. Not with what's at stake.

He shakes his head, looking around, his expression wracked with indecision, as if frantically trying to come up with something…*anything* to make me reconsider. Then a devilish smile tilts his mouth and he leans toward me, kissing my temple.

"Wait right here."

Dropping his hold, he rushes from me, leaving me confused and a bit intrigued, which quickly changes to utterly horrified when he walks up to the stage where the small band has been serenading us. During a break in the music, he talks to the singer, who happily welcomes him up on stage, offering him the microphone.

I meet his eyes, vehemently shaking my head, a heat spreading from behind my ears to my face and chest.

"Aloha, friends." Lincoln's voice comes over the speakers, to which the audience replies with a polite "aloha". "I won't be long, because I'm sure you'd much rather listen to this beautiful island music than me. My name is Lincoln Moore. As you can tell, I'm not from around here." He gestures at his suit, looking incredibly out of place, especially when surrounded by people in casual island attire. Several patrons chuckle, nodding in agreement. "I work as an associate attorney at a little newspaper called *The New York Times.*"

My pulse steadily increases as I stare at him, wondering what he's doing, other than making a complete ass out of himself in front of the crowd, and eventually the entire world once someone decides to upload this to YouTube.

He loosens his tie, sweat forming on his brow, the combination of the June humidity and the lights on the stage beaming down on him. When he shrugs out of his jacket and rolls up the sleeves of his crisp shirt, a few women whistle.

"Thank you very much," he says in his best Elvis impersonation.

I laugh as I'm treated to this side of Lincoln, one I haven't seen in too long now.

"You see, almost five months ago, I met my boss' daughter, although I didn't realize it at the time. And I made the colossal mistake of falling in love with her."

A few *ooh's* sound from the crowd. I have no idea what game Lincoln's playing here, what he hopes to get out of telling our story, but I can't take my eyes off him. Either can anyone else.

"That's not even the worst of it. You see, in addition to being an attorney for the *Times*, I teach First Amendment Law in the journalism program of a local university. And my boss' daughter?"

Gasps echo from the crowd, and he points to the group of women who appear to be celebrating a bachelorette party.

"They guessed it. She walked into my class that first day as a student. Now, I know what you're thinking. How did I not know that not only was she my boss' daughter, but also set to be a student of mine when the semester began?" A devilish glint flashes in his eyes. "Suffice it to say, the early days in our relationship weren't exactly filled with philosophical questions about the meaning of life."

The entire audience erupts in cheers and whistles. It takes a lot to make me blush, but as his gaze catches mine and he winks, causing nearly everyone to turn in my direction, my cheeks heat even more. But it's one of the most fulfilling and satisfying feelings I've ever experienced.

"That's her, ladies and gentlemen." He jumps off the stage, heading toward me. "The woman I am madly in love with. I'd have to be if I'm telling a group of complete strangers about the fact that I've been sleeping with one of my students, which is a very big no-no. The truth is, I loved her before she was one of my students." His voice becomes sincere as he approaches, his eyes trained on mine. He smiles a small smile before addressing the crowd once more.

"But the problem is, she doesn't think this will ever work. In some respects, she's absolutely right. Our love was doomed from the beginning. Like Heathcliff and Catherine. Romeo and Juliet, except for the suicide part."

"Jack and Rose!" an enthusiastic young woman adds.

Lincoln turns around, finding her in the crowd. "We all know there was room on that plank, so that wasn't a doomed relationship. It was murder. Or, at the very least, negligent homicide."

The crowd's roar of laughter echoes against the still night air. When Lincoln turns back to me, his voice grows sincere. "Like Orpheus and Eurydice."

A small breath escapes my mouth.

"Do you remember what Orpheus' problem was?" he asks softly.

I nod, pulling my bottom lip between my teeth to stop my chin from quivering. "He looked back," I barely manage to say.

"He looked back," he repeats. "Something I refuse to do. Not where you're concerned. I only want to look forward. Nothing that happened before this moment matters."

"But—"

"But what? You still don't believe you're worth the risk?" He steps back, spreading an arm and turning in a slow circle. "What do you think I'm trying to prove to you? That you *are* worth the risk. Do you think I care about my job as much as I care about you?"

I wish I could give him the answer he wants to hear, but it's not that easy. Despite this incredible gesture — getting on a plane, flying halfway around the world, making a scene in front of all these people — it's hard for me to trust blindly, to put all my faith in someone's words. Nearly thirty years of experience has taught me otherwise.

He brings a hand to my face, and I melt into his touch. "What do you need me to do to prove it to you? That you're all that matters. That no matter what happens, my life will be full as long as you're by my side." He swipes a tear from my cheek. "I know what life's like without you. And I mean *really* know what it's like. I can survive without my job, without my apartment. Hell, I'd even give up my season tickets to the Mets."

"You can't do that," I sniffle. "You'd probably have to pay someone to take them off your hands instead of the other way around. It's a terrible business decision."

The crowd breaks out in laughter, and I join them, my emotions a wild pendulum. One minute I'm crying. The next I'm laughing through my tears.

"See, Chloe? We're still good together. We still make sense. That hasn't changed. What do I have to do to prove that you deserve that fairy tale? I've already declared my love in a way that would put any cheesy romantic comedy to shame. What more can I do?"

At that instant, the band begins playing the opening chords of "Hawaiian Wedding Song", apparently thinking this moment required background music.

"Please, Chloe," Lincoln murmurs over the opening verse of the classic Elvis song. "If I have to sing to get you to be mine, I will."

My eyes widen, horror crossing my expression. "You wouldn't."

"For you, I certainly would."

Before I can stop him, he takes over the vocals, his hand wrapping around mine. The crowd erupts in applause and cheers that would probably rival if the real Elvis had come back from the dead and were here singing to me. I'm surprised he even knows the lyrics to this song. It's not exactly one you hear on a daily basis, unless you watch *Blue Hawaii* on repeat.

I cover my mouth with my free hand, laughing, crying, then laughing again. This isn't the kind of thing that happens in the real world, is it? At least not in *my* world. I was never the type of girl who necessitated a call from a guy the next day. And here is this amazing, incredible, sophisticated man, singing horribly out of tune in front of dozens of people, passersby on the beach stopping to listen and watch the scene with interest.

"Just kiss him already!" a woman shouts over the melody.

"If you don't, I will," another voice calls out. I shift my eyes, shaking my head at the man toasting me with his mai tai.

Lincoln gives me a questioning look, but when I don't do anything, he only sings louder. While Lincoln Moore has many talents, singing certainly is not one of them. But that doesn't stop him.

As I listen to him sing the lyrics, begging me to promise to be his forever, my heart is on the brink of bursting. All I've ever wanted was to feel like I had value, had worth.

Maybe I do deserve the over-the-top romantic comedy ending.

Jumping off my barstool as he fumbles through the Hawaiian words, I clutch his cheeks, bringing his face toward mine. "Oh, just shut up and kiss me."

His lips kicking up in the corners, he allows the microphone to fall to the table. "With pleasure."

He yanks my body hard and firm against his as his mouth slams against mine. Thunderous applause erupts around us, but that only makes him kiss me deeper. He curves into me, dipping me slightly, his hand running along the contours of my frame as our bodies mold together. His tongue swipes against mine, exploring my mouth like it's the first time. And that's what this is. Our new beginning, one we both deserve.

When he slowly pulls back, I'm met with his breathtaking smile. "Did you kiss me just so I'd stop singing? Or because you want to give us another chance?"

Running my fingers through his hair, I relish in the sensation of his coarse locks, something I've craved so much over these past few weeks. "I never had a chance with you."

"And I never had a chance with you." He brings his lips back to mine.

"And I did want you to stop singing," I add with a smile. "I think I heard a few dogs howl on the other side of the island."

His deep chuckle echoes in the air, filling me with warmth. Before I know what's happening, his arms snake around me and he lifts me into a cradle hold.

"Lincoln!" I playfully swat at him as he makes his way through the lounge, people clapping and cheering as the band transitions into a Hawaiian version of "Over the Rainbow". "Put me down! I'm meeting Nora, Jeremy, and—"

"A best man who can't keep his dick in his pants?" He arches a single brow.

I gasp, putting the pieces together. "That was *you*?"

"What can I say?" He stops walking as his feet hit the sand of the beach, and he slowly lowers me, yet keeps a firm hold on me. "I figured if I was going to give you the cheesy happily ever after you claim you don't deserve, I needed backup. I was worried you wouldn't hear me out if I just showed up, especially with the way I treated you the last time I saw you."

"So you had my friend lie to me?" I give him a playful look of disapproval.

"It was Izzy's idea. Anyway, I'd like to consider it more like an alternate version of the truth." He circles his hips. "I do have trouble keeping my dick in my pants. At least when *you're* around."

I lift myself onto my toes, feathering my lips against his. "You lawyers. Always getting off on a technicality," I murmur.

"I haven't heard you complain." With a wink, he pulls back. "Now, let's go. I have plans for you." He grips my hand and tugs me along the beach.

"And what plans are those?"

A mischievous smile builds on his mouth as his eyes darken. "To finish what we started a few weeks ago before you stood me up. Don't think you can get off that easily."

I come to a stop, forcing him to face me. Then I hook my arms around his neck and touch my lips to his. "With you, it's all easy."

He breathes into the kiss, then meets my eyes. "I love you, Chloe Davenport."

"And I love you, Lincoln Moore."

"Say it again."

My lips curve as peace washes over me. "I love you."

"God, it's even better than I imagined it would be."

Then he kisses me…fully, completely, madly.

The best kiss in the history of kisses. Because finally, after everything, I know I'm worth this man's love. And there's no better feeling in the world.

CHAPTER FORTY-SEVEN

"IT'S STRANGE, ISN'T it?" Izzy asks, scanning my apartment, the last of my items officially boxed up. This place has been home for years now, has served as a meeting spot for our little circle of friends. It'll be a bit of a readjustment to not come home to this every day, but I now have a new place to call home.

"We've had some great memories in this shithole," I agree.

Izzy laughs, squeezing my arm. "We sure have. But now you'll make new memories. Happier memories. In an even better shithole, although I'm not so sure I'd consider Lincoln's apartment a shithole. I've seen that place. It's incredible."

I beam, considering the road ahead. For the longest time, I never thought much about the future. Now I look forward to every day I spend with Lincoln. So much so that when the lease on my apartment was up for renewal, I didn't hesitate when he suggested I move in with him, considering I spend every night at his place anyway.

"Well…" Izzy pulls away, her voice brightening. "I should get going."

"Do you want to order Chinese and eat on the floor like we did when I first moved in? One last memory?"

"I wish I could, but I have plans."

"Plans?" I tilt my head. "What kind of plans? You never have plans that don't involve us or work."

"I do have a life, Chloe," she retorts, avoiding my eyes.

"No, you don't. You've admitted you don't on a regular basis." I narrow my eyes, leaning into her. "Do you have a date?"

"Most certainly not," she answers quickly. Too quickly, which only serves to increase my suspicions.

"Who's the lucky guy?" I waggle my brows. "How did you meet? Is he a doctor at the hospital? Better yet, a patient whose life you saved who wants to…repay the favor? Or is it one of the guys I saw flirting with you at Evie and Julian's wedding?"

"Chloe!" She playfully punches me. "None of the above. First of all, I don't hook up at weddings. Second, most of the doctors I work with are married. Third, and most disturbing, I work in *pediatric* oncology. All my patients are minors."

"Then you'd better tell me who you're going out with or I'll keep making up ridiculous scenarios. You can't drop a bomb like that and expect me to leave it alone." I place my hand on my hip, tapping my foot in mock irritation. "You know how I can be. Soon, Evie will call you to ask why you've been dating a crowned prince and never told her."

She stares at me, then huffs out a breath. "Fine." Her expression turns severe as she shoves a finger in my face. "But you cannot mention this to anyone. I swear to god. Not one…fucking…soul. Not even Nora or Evie."

"Fine. You got it." I pretend to zip my lips and throw away the key. "Sealed tighter than Fort Knox."

She assesses me for a moment, then nods. "Okay." She draws in a deep breath. "Jessie York is in town and asked to see me." She cringes, stealing a glance at me to gauge my reaction.

"And you told him to go fuck himself, correct?" I place my hands on my hips, annoyed.

"Chloe…" Her tone is a cross between a warning and a plea.

"So… What? He calls and you drop everything? Need I remind you that the prick cheated on you? While you were engaged, no less."

"Thanks for the reminder, but I was there, remember? And I'm not dropping everything for him. He said he needed to speak to me."

I lower my voice. "Do you think he found out about Asher?"

Biting her lower lip, she slowly shakes her head. "I don't know how. I didn't tell him, and I doubt Asher would have said anything. Not to mention, with the way his music's been taking off, he probably doesn't have time to think about that night. Not with all the groupies hanging all over him." She averts her eyes, crossing her arms in front of her chest.

When I learned Lincoln was my professor and we could no longer be together, I struggled with the constant reminders of what I could never have. I can't imagine how it must be for Izzy to have a front row seat to Asher's rise to fame over these past few months. Once it was announced he was the musical genius behind Fallen Grace's new album, he was bombarded with offers. Within months, he'd signed with a label, released a solo album of his own, and is now opening for one of the top rock bands. It's only a matter of time until he's headlining and selling out stadiums, too.

But despite the longing I spy in her eyes whenever Asher's voice comes on the radio, Izzy insists it doesn't bother her, that nothing could ever come of their one night together. Not when he's her ex-fiancé's older brother.

"Izzy," I begin, about to voice my concerns.

"He said it was important."

"And you believe him?"

"It sounds crazy, but yeah." She shrugs. "I do. There was something in his voice that made me think he wouldn't reach out to me after all this time unless it were."

"I don't like this. I don't like *him*."

"I know you don't." She runs her hands up and down my arms, reassuring me. "He could be full of shit, but if I don't find out what's going on, I'll never be able to forgive myself. Especially if it has something to do with his family."

As much as I don't like the idea of her seeing that prick again, I know how she is. Izzy is one of the kindest, most sympathetic people I've ever met. And she *was* close to Jessie's entire family, until he broke her heart. Not only did she lose him, she also lost his family.

"Want me to be your out? What time are you meeting him? I can call you after fifteen minutes to give you an excuse to leave."

She smiles at the memory of our old ways whenever either one of us had a date. "Thanks, but I'll be okay." She wraps her arms around me, hugging me tightly. "I'm so happy for you, Chloe."

"Thanks, Iz."

"You bet." We hug each other a moment longer before she drops her hold on me, then walks out of my apartment.

Once I'm alone, I turn in a slow circle, taking one last look at the place I've called home for the past several years. These walls have seen a lot of laughter, tears, and everything in between. It's time I finally leave all that behind and start fresh.

"You ready?" Lincoln's deep voice cuts through, and I spin around to see him standing in the foyer.

"Are *you* ready?"

"You've been practically living at my place these past six months anyway." He smirks as he approaches.

"True. But now *all* my shoes will be at your place. You'll—"

He covers my mouth with his, interrupting me with a kiss. "*Our* place, Pixie." He holds my face in his hands, his eyes intense. "It's *our* place."

"I like the sound of that."

"Me, too."

I whisper my lips against his. "So why don't you take me back to *our* place so we can christen it. Then we can spend all weekend snuggled in bed and watch the snow fall." I pull back. "Unless you have work to do."

He slowly shakes his head. "I'm taking the weekend off. In fact, I'm taking the entire week off."

"You *are*?" I cock a brow, unable to mask my surprise.

Ever since my father retired back in September and tapped Lincoln to take his place as chief general counsel, Lincoln's been working his tail off. It doesn't bother me, since he still makes a point to spend time together. My new position as the current affairs editor at *Blush* has had me working a lot, too. At least now I no longer feel like I have to work myself to the bone to get the inside scoop on celebrity gossip before anyone else. And I get to write stories with substance.

"Yup. I didn't bring home a single file. And I spoke with Evie. She says you can take the week off, too." A devilish glint flashes in his eyes.

"We can have a lot of fun with that much time to ourselves," I say, recalling our time together in Hawaii.

"We sure can," he murmurs, his lips inching even closer.

"So why don't we go so we can get started."

"Always so eager, Miss Davenport," he croons in a sly voice.

"Always, Professor Moore. So take me back to your…*our* place."

"I'd love to." He abruptly pulls back. "But I have a better idea."

I grin deviously, knowing all too well where this is heading. At least once a month, Lincoln has sent a box of panties to the office, along with a card dictating a place and time for me to meet him, usually a swanky hotel bar. It doesn't matter that our relationship is now out in the open. We still go back to our roots, if for no other reason than to remember how far we've come.

"Role-play? What'll it be tonight? I can be a sweet Midwest girl who's never been to the big city, and you can be a mysterious stranger who will open her mind to her darkest desires."

"Tempting, but why don't we try something…different."

"Different? What did you have in mind? Something kinkier? I can do that. I love the kink."

"I know you do. But I was thinking of maybe getting away with you instead." He licks his lips, a nervous twitch in his eye.

"Getting away?"

He smiles, pulling my body against his. "Yeah. Vegas. After all, in just a few days, we'll be celebrating the one-year anniversary of that blackout. I thought maybe we can recreate our own little blackout."

When his lips meet mine, I moan, the idea of getting out of Manhattan and into a warmer climate exactly what I need, even if it is to Vegas, a city I once despised. But now, I don't mind it as much. In fact, I actually like the notion of revisiting the proverbial scene of the crime with Lincoln.

"And since I stole something of yours last time I was there, maybe I can convince you to come home with something of mine. A souvenir of sorts."

"A souvenir? What kind of souvenir? If it's panties, you're only going to steal them anyway."

"No, not panties." He leans in for another kiss. "I want to give you my last name."

My breath hitching, I stiffen, pressing my hand against his chest. "What did you say?"

A look of serenity washes over him. "I want to give you my last name,

Chloe. I want to spend the rest of my life with you." He reaches toward my ear and, with a magician's flourish, reveals a stunning round-cut solitaire, the band inlaid with diamonds. "I want to marry you."

"How did you do that?" I breathe.

His lips curve playfully. "A magician never reveals his secrets." He winks, then his expression turns serious, his green eyes peaceful and steady. "So, what do you say? Will you marry me? Let me show you how incredible you are every day for the rest of your life?"

"In Vegas?"

"If you'd rather something else, we can do that," he says quickly. "Whatever you want, it's yours. If you want a huge, elaborate wedding in the Hamptons, like Evie and Julian, we can. If you want to get married on a white sand beach in Hawaii, like Nora and Jeremy, I'll give you that, too." He gets down on one knee, taking my hand in his and bringing the ring up to my finger. "You deserve the fairy tale. So if your fairy tale ends in walking up the aisle while wearing a train that would rival any royal wedding, that's what you shall have."

I stare at him, words escaping me as I wrap my head around the fact that this man is kneeling before me, begging me marry him. I was never one of those girls who envisioned her own wedding, not like Evie, Nora, and even Izzy, although she'll never admit it. Until I met Lincoln, I didn't think I *wanted* to get married. Didn't think I *deserved* to find love. But he's taught me I do deserve that happily ever after.

In one swift move, I drop to my knees. He stares at me, worry evident in his gaze. Then I smile. "*You're* my fairy tale. And I can't think of a better place to start my life with you."

He exhales, his muscles relaxing as he slides the ring into place. The perfect fit.

"I know Vegas is a bit…unconventional, but—"

I curve into him, pressing my lips to his. The first kiss of the rest of our lives.

"It may be unconventional, but when have we ever played by the rules… *Professor*?"

THE END.

PLAYLIST

Wicked Love - Sara Bareilles
Hit and Run - LOLO
No Roots - Alice Merton
In My Head - Maisie Peters
Power Over Me - Dermot Kennedy
Anxiety - Julia Michaels
Natural - Maygen Lacey
Light as the Breeze - Billy Joel
Let You Love Me - Rita Ora
Be Scared with Me - Canyon City
If This is Love - Ruth B.
Devils Don't Fly - Natalia Kills
All This Love - JP Cooper
Symphony - Thomas Daniel
You & Me - James TW
Terrible Love - Birdy
Don't Wanna Think - Julia Michaels
Birthday - Maisie Peters
Bitter Pill - Gavin James
Let it all Go - Birdy
Rush - Lewis Capaldi feat. Jessie Reyez
Move Together - James Bay
Orpheus - Sara Bareilles
Human - Christina Perri
Marina del Rey - Lola Rhodes
Heaven - Julia Michaels
Bad guy - Billie Eilish
Ain't Gonna Lose You - Brett Dennen
Speechless - Dan + Shay
More Like Love - Ben Rector
The Greatest Bastard - Damien Rice
Break My Heart Right - James Bay
Our Story - Graham Colton
You and I - Jon McLaughlin
Hawaiian Wedding Song - Elvis Presley
Connection - OneRepublic
Passport Home - JP Cooper

Mind Games

USA TODAY BESTSELLING AUTHOR

T.K. LEIGH

Dear Reader,

Thank you so much for picking up a copy of Mind Games! This is a bit of a unique book, in that it serves as a companion novel to Wicked Games, as well as an optional prequel to Dangerous Games.

Wicked Games starts in Vegas, where there's a blackout. As you can expect, when the lights go out in the city of sin, all bets are off. The story in Wicked Games revolves around Chloe and Lincoln. But there's another couple as well - Izzy and Asher. This is that same Vegas blackout from Izzy's perspective.

I never intended to publish this book. It was simply something I needed to write in order to start working on Izzy and Asher's full story - Dangerous Games. Truthfully, I thought it would just be a short novelette I could give to my reader group. But what I thought would be a short story turned into a full-length novel, although it's short for one of my novels. So I decided to publish it.

Again, you don't have to read any of the prior books in order to read this one, but I hope you'll go back and check out the rest of this series of interconnected standalones. Each of these stories and characters hold a special place in my heart, and I hope they will in yours.

Thank you, and I hope you enjoy Mind Games!

~ T.K.

CHAPTER ONE

HAVE YOU EVER wondered what would have happened if Alice never saw the White Rabbit and followed him into Wonderland? If Cinderella never found the courage to walk into that ball all alone and dance with Prince Charming? If Ariel hadn't gone to the surface and saved Prince Eric from drowning, even though everyone warned her about humans?

One moment. One decision. One life forever changed because they opted for one path over another. It's remarkable to think our choices have this much power, this much ability to alter the course our lives had been on.

I've often imagined what my life would look like had I chosen differently. Different college. Different profession. Different love. It's one of those things that keeps us up in the wee hours of the night, contemplating deep thoughts we have no control over, since the likelihood of getting a second chance is doubtful.

At least that's what I've always thought… Until a trip to Las Vegas for a bachelorette party brought me back to that proverbial fork in the road. One I didn't know existed.

* * *

"Are you girls seriously not coming to the club with us tonight?" Bernadette whines over the loud, jarring noise of the busy casino. Her bright red lips form into a pout as she looks at Chloe and me.

When she'd first proposed celebrating Hannah's bachelorette party in Vegas, I looked forward to getting out of Manhattan for a weekend in Sin City, especially in January. But after only twenty-four hours, I longed for the sounds and smells of New York. Now that I've been here going on four nights, I'm all but counting down the minutes until I can board that plane. In a little more than twelve hours, I get to do just that.

"We have an early flight tomorrow," Chloe responds.

Out of the entire bridal party, we're the only two who seem to have commitments and obligations back home. Not only are we leaving a day earlier than everyone else, we're using it as an excuse not to have to suffer through yet another night at yet another club. A darkened room reeking of sweat, alcohol, and perfume. Ridiculously loud music. Barely any space to move or dance. It isn't my idea of a fun evening out.

"I thought your flight wasn't until one or two," Bernadette argues back.

"We still have to get to the airport on time. We don't have the luxury of sleeping in all day like you do."

Bernadette opens her mouth, presumably to continue stating her case, when Hannah steps forward, wrapping her arms around Chloe. "I'm so glad you took the time to come." Pulling back, she gives her a sincere smile before hugging me. "Don't worry. I get it," she whispers. "If I could, I'd be right there with you."

She drops her hold on me, and the three of us share a conspiratorial look, like we did as kids when we were up to something.

Growing up, we were three peas in a pod. We lived in the same neighborhood and were practically inseparable. Hell, I remember many summer days giggling about our dream weddings to our dream guys. Hannah always fantasized about marrying a successful doctor, one who loves kids as much as she does. Now, she's mere weeks away from marrying that successful doctor.

"Come on." She spins from us, looping her arm through Bernadette's. "I'm a bit parched."

Several of the other bridal party members whistle and cheer as they retreat from the lobby, on their way to one of the many clubs. As they're about to get swallowed up by the hectic casino atmosphere, Hannah glances over her shoulder, blowing both of us a kiss. We return it, as we always do.

Chloe and I wait until they disappear from view, then exhale simultaneously.

"Well, thank god that's over." She starts toward the bank of elevators, her strides purposeful. "I swear, if one more guy approaches me thinking I'm a prostitute because my hair's a different shade, I'm going to lose it. I'm not the first person to color my hair gray and lilac, for crying out loud." She gestures to her wavy locks that fall to her mid-back.

I must admit, it took me a while to get used to the color, knowing I'd never be so bold as to change my hair to such a unique tone. But that's Chloe. Daring and a bit reckless. Plus, her natural shade of blonde makes it easier to do something like that. There's not much I can do with my nearly jet-black hair. As far as our appearance goes, Chloe and I are as opposite as can be. She's short and petite, the picture of an all-American girl, aside from her choice in hair color. I'm on the taller side with curves and olive-toned skin, thanks to my Latina heritage.

"You know how this place can be," I respond when I catch up to her. "It's bachelorette party central. You saw how the girls behaved. They're away from home and responsibility so they decided to throw common sense out the window and flirt with anything with a pulse. Same goes for the men here for bachelor parties. And, as we all know, men aren't nearly as intelligent as women, so they say and do even dumber things."

Her laughter fills the elevator vestibule, overpowering the abrasive noise of the casino. "You've got that right." When a car arrives, she slings her arm over my shoulders, which proves slightly difficult due to our height difference, her five-two to my five-seven, but we manage. Like always.

"Lobby tomorrow at eleven?" I arch a brow at Chloe when the elevator stops on my floor.

Another reason I get along so well with her. While the rest of the bridal party insisted on cramming eight people into two rooms, we refused to take any part in that. The only thing that made this trip bearable was that I had my own space.

"Or maybe I should tell you 10:30 so you'll be on time."

She playfully jabs me in the side. "Don't worry. I'll be there. There's no way in hell I'm missing my flight out of this godforsaken town."

"Good. Or I'm leaving without you. Because there's no way in hell *I'm* missing my flight out of this godforsaken town."

"Goodnight, Izzy," she sings, pushing me out of the car before the doors close on me.

"Night, Chloe," I call back as I make my way toward my room.

Once inside, I take a minute to relish in the tranquility. My ears still ring from the constant barrage of noise in the casino, but other than a faint conversation I can make out from the room next door as the occupants get ready for a night out, it's peaceful, the whirring of the air conditioner the only sound.

An urgent need to wash off the remnants of tonight's festivities, namely the showgirl lessons that came complete with full makeup, overtakes me and I head for the bathroom, starting the shower.

A few minutes later, after scrubbing my face rigorously, I feel like myself again. Not this dress-wearing, club-going girl I've been the past few days so Hannah could have the bachelorette party she deserved. Though I suspect this was more the type of bachelorette party Bernadette, her older sister, would want. Hannah would have preferred a quiet weekend in Wine Country. Hell, knowing Hannah, she would have preferred a weekend where we all volunteered at the inner-city schools.

Emerging from the bathroom, I glance at the clock to see it's just after eleven. I should pack and get some sleep, but I'm not even close to being tired. As a nurse, I typically work the night shift. After staying out until the early hours of the morning all weekend, my body has remained on that schedule. So, instead of throwing on some pajamas, I slide on a pair of jeans and a black top, then leave my room to explore the Vegas nightlife on my own. And hopefully find a low-key bar. After a weekend of nothing but overpriced, pretentious clubs, I need a simple bar and a good beer.

Most other women my age probably wouldn't want to venture off on their own at night in Vegas, but I'm not most women. I like being alone. Like being able to do what I want when I want. Like not having to depend on anyone else for my own happiness. That's the benefit of being an only child. An *adopted* only child. I became fiercely independent at an early age.

I meander along the casino floor, the tables overflowing with people trying their hand at blackjack, poker, or roulette, probably gambling away their life savings in the hopes of winning big. Cocktail waitresses in skintight dresses that barely cover their ass carry trays holding drinks. Despite having one of the top air filtration systems available, a thin layer of smoke seems to fill the space, the stench of nicotine permanently ingrained in my nostrils. It's going to take days to get the stink out of my hair once I get home.

As I wander in search of a place where I can grab a decent beer, the sound of live music cuts through, a nice change from the typical thump of club music they blare all hours of the day. I look in its direction, spying what appears to be an Irish pub. I grin at the familiarity. My mother would admonish me for going to an Irish pub while in Vegas, considering I live in New York and we can't trip without falling on yet another pub just like this one. That's probably what calls me to this place. It reminds me of home.

I step inside, everything about my surroundings seeming to go against what Vegas stands for. Yes, it's still a bar and the music is loud, but it's not ostentatious. Not filled with women wearing as little clothing as they can get away with on the prowl for some poor schmuck to buy them overpriced drinks for the night. Not crawling with men dressed in suits who bathed in far too much cologne.

I walk toward a long bar that sits along the wall and find a vacant stool. My eyes are drawn to the ceiling, dozens of bills of every currency pinned to it. A bartender approaches and takes my order for a beer, returning with a pint within seconds. I take a sip of the hoppy ale, exhaling at the flavor that seems so foreign after the past few nights of only consuming mixed, saccharine drinks. This is exactly what I need to feel normal again.

I survey the darkened space, nothing flashy or unique about it. Just like every other bar I've been to in my adult life, the lounge is filled with heavy wood tables, patrons enjoying a variety of beers and bar food while they listen to live music. A large crowd fills the empty area in front of the stage, dancing to the band as they cover a Coldplay song. They're pretty good, much better than some of the artists I hear on the radio these days. I'll take rock music any day over the latest auto-tuned boy band who wouldn't know how to hold a guitar if their life depended on it.

The song ends and applause breaks out, a few girls cheering and clapping enthusiastically. Déjà vu washes over me, like I've been here before. In a way, I have. I was once one of those exuberant fans cheering for the local band, hoping they'd someday make it big. But that was a lifetime ago.

Shaking off the memories, I turn my attention back to my beer, perusing the menu the bartender left for me.

"Thanks all," the lead singer's voice carries over the loud chatter and clanging of ice against glass. "We're going to take a quick break, but before we do, we have a special guest who's agreed to get up on stage with us tonight. Remember this name because in the next few months, you won't be able to turn on your radios without hearing his music. Ladies and gentlemen, give it up for Asher York."

A gasp escapes, my eyes darting toward the stage. I freeze, my brain unable to tell my lungs to breathe, my heart to beat, my body to move. All I hear is that name. It can't be him, can it? How? I've never been great at statistics, but the likelihood of the two of us being in the same bar in Las Vegas has to be… What? One in a million? A billion? It must be someone else with the same name. Someone else who's also a musician. Someone else who's six-two, with dark hair and a smile that can melt panties.

I tell myself I'm imagining it, that I'm still stuck in the memories of my college days when my friends and I would go to whatever club Asher's band was playing and dance the night away. That must be it. The reality of being in the same room as him seems so far out of the realm of possibilities, especially considering the last I knew, he was a music teacher in the suburbs of Boston, playing the occasional gig on the weekends.

Then again, the last time I spoke to him was eight years ago.

A lot can change in that amount of time.

And when a figure jumps onto the stage and faces the crowd, I realize truer words have never been spoken, or thought. A lot *can* change in that amount of time. And Asher York has certainly changed.

I watch with a mixture of intrigue and surprise as he grabs an acoustic-electric guitar from a stand, plugging a cable into the end of the body. The man resembles the Asher York I once knew, but he's a far cry from the lanky man I remember. His broad chest pulls at the simple gray t-shirt, his biceps filling the sleeves quite nicely. His dark hair is no longer perfectly groomed. It's grown out and has a sexy, disheveled vibe, the perfect complement to the scruff along his jaw. But that's not the biggest change. Oh no. As if he weren't rock god personified with the longer hair and muscular physique, he has to add tattoos to the fantasy.

I've always found Asher York attractive. But now… He is all man. Manly man. And when his voice fills the bar, sending an involuntary shiver down my spine, it's somehow deeper and more enthralling than I remember. And I definitely remember him. Asher York isn't the kind of person anyone could forget.

I should leave. Pay for my beer. Head back to my room. The last thing I need is to reopen old wounds. And seeing Asher does just that. But like the first time my college roommate dragged me to a club to see a local band that was gaining in popularity, I'm drawn to the man's rough, emotion-filled voice.

I stare at my beer, concentrating on the melody. It sounds familiar, like a cloudy memory trying to return to the surface of my subconscious. The longer I listen, the more clear it becomes. By the time he sings the first chorus, it hits me. It's the same melody I'd heard him toil over endlessly during those late summer nights we stayed up together at his grandmother's lake house, while my boyfriend, then fiancé slept inside.

Who also happened to be Asher's brother.

During the two years I dated Jessie, I was welcomed into his family with open arms. That included spending a few weeks of the summer at the lake house. It was actually one of the things I missed most when we broke up. The card games. The smell of burgers on the grill. Spending the early morning hours listening to Asher pluck away at his guitar as he attempted to piece together a song.

This song.

Allowing my hair to cascade in front of my face in the hopes that Asher doesn't recognize me in the crowd, I risk a glance at him. He seems to have cast a spell on everyone here, just as he did all those years ago. People bob their heads in time with the song, one I've heard more times than I care to admit, the familiar chords akin to coming home after a long absence.

I'm transfixed as I listen to him sing about feeling like he was made for a particular woman, but she never saw him until it was too late. I don't realize my eyes are glued to his every move until deafening applause thunders around me. The girls who preened before the lead singer of the other band mere minutes ago now fawn over Asher.

He smiles that breathtaking smile of his as he thanks the audience, still as enigmatic a presence as always. His gaze floats over the crowd, coming to an abrupt stop when he locks eyes with mine. I try to look away, but the simple act of our gazes meeting has turned me to stone, apart from the fluttering in my chest. It shouldn't. I shouldn't have any reaction to him.

Just like I shouldn't have tried to kiss him mere hours after I ended things with his brother all those years ago.

Snapping out of my stupor, I refocus my attention on my beer and drain it. I grab a bill from my wallet and leave it on the counter, not caring about getting any change. The excessive tip is a price I'm willing to pay to avoid having to talk to Asher, considering the last time I saw him I pretended to have no memory of the previous night and our almost-kiss.

I'm about to jump down from the stool when a hand on the bar next to me stops me.

"Running off without saying hi?"

My eyes dart up, coming face-to-face with Asher York. His voice is even smoother than I remember. A low rumble that hits places on my body that haven't felt excitement in an eternity.

I part my lips, attempting to come up with a response, but I'm rendered speechless when I catch a glimpse of his arm leaning on the bar, the position causing his biceps to flex and push against the confines of his t-shirt, stretching the fabric.

A woodsy scent surrounds me as I stare, the smell reminding me of large family dinners, playing guitar on the dock overlooking the lake on his grandmother's property, roasting marshmallows. Reminds me of a girl I used to be. One I've tried to keep in the past.

Swallowing down the bittersweet memories, I push a strand of hair behind my ear, forcing a smile. "Asher. Good to see you." I hold my head high, looking anywhere but directly into his eyes. I can't. He has the same eyes as Jessie. Born eleven months apart, their appearance was always strikingly similar. But that was where their similarities ended, the two brothers as opposite as two people can be. Regardless, I've never met two siblings as close as they are. Or maybe I found it so foreign since I'm an only child.

"Phew." He blows out a breath, laughing shakily. "I wasn't positive it was you. I thought it was, but everyone in this town seems to look like someone else."

I shrug, finally meeting his gaze. "It's me."

"Good. That would have been awkward otherwise." A flirtatious smile curves up the corners of his lips. He even has the same smile as Jessie. But Asher's looks more natural, like he's actually happy. "What are you doing in Vegas?" he continues when I don't immediately say anything.

"I could ask you the same question."

He nods at the stage. "Music." He doesn't embellish. "Your turn."

"Bachelorette party. Hannah's getting married next month, and Bernadette was in charge of planning her bachelorette party."

A look of understanding crosses his face. "Say no more."

As uneasy as it should be to see Asher again, considering his connection to a time in my life I'd prefer to keep in my rearview mirror, it's refreshing to talk to someone who already knows me, scars and all. Someone I don't have to go into all the details of my life with because they already know.

"Cash you out, miss?" The bartender's voice cuts through.

I nod. "Thank you."

"Actually," Asher interrupts before the bartender can retreat with my money, "she'll have another. And I'll have an IPA." He places a finger on the cash I'd left on the bar and slides it back in front of me. "Put all her drinks on my tab."

"That's not necessary," I insist, attempting to push the bill back toward the bartender. "I really should be going. It's been a long night and I—"

The heat coming off him as his hand wraps around my arm stops me mid-sentence. I fling my wide eyes to his, my insides vibrating at his touch. Something that never happened when his brother touched me, caressed me, made love to me. That should have been a sign back then, but I was too young to realize it. Too smitten by the handsome college senior who noticed me. Or maybe I just didn't care. Maybe I'd wanted to feel like I was wanted, like I was cherished.

"Stay."

One word, and my mouth goes dry.

One word, and my heart pounds in my chest.

One word, and I forget all the reasons I should leave.

"Okay." I slowly slink back into my barstool.

What harm can one drink with an old friend do?

CHAPTER TWO

"SO YOU QUIT without a backup plan?" I ask several hours later as Asher and I sip on our beers, the bartender having just announced last call.

I'd told myself I'd only stay for one drink. One drink soon turned into three as I caught him up on everything that's been going on in my life. How I ended up getting my master's, something I never would have done if I'd married Jessie. Hell, before I broke off our engagement, I probably would have been happy working at a general practitioner's office where the hours were normal and the stress level low. But something about the breakup made me reevaluate my plans and think about what I really wanted. So I continued with my education, focusing on pediatric oncology. The hours are less than optimal, the mental strain of holding these precious young lives in my hands high, not to mention the heartbreak when I lose a patient, but I can't imagine doing anything else.

"If I wanted to pursue my dreams, I didn't want anything holding me back. My teaching job was a crutch. I turned down gigs because I couldn't take time off from work. *Good* gigs, too. A few opening up for Dave Matthews Band, Ed Sheeran, Jason Mraz. Granted, I would have been the first opener when everyone was waiting in line for beer, but it was still a great gig I had to miss because it was during the week and my headache of a principal refused to sign off on the time. Thought it was a waste. So about four years ago, when I needed to either start my master's so I could keep teaching or do something else, I decided to take the leap and do something else."

I drain the remainder of my drink, then sip on some water. "That takes some serious *cojones*. I don't know many people who would quit their job and move to Los Angeles to chase their dreams."

"What can I say? I'm not most people." He playfully nudges me. "You should realize that by now."

"I certainly do."

There's a warmth within his gaze when I lift my eyes to meet his. But there's something more, too. Something that's been missing from my life all these years.

I clear my throat, breaking through the mounting tension I'm convinced is one-sided. "Weren't you scared?"

"I was." He looks forward, staring into the distance, squinting. "But I was more scared of never pursuing my dreams. Of being content with a life that was just good enough. Don't get me wrong," he adds quickly. "I loved my job. Loved teaching kids about music and seeing the joy on their faces when they nailed that difficult passage for the first time. But I always looked at teaching as something I could do to pay the bills while I pursued my dreams. So when teaching got in the way of those dreams, I knew what I had to do."

I smile a genuine smile, one that reaches my eyes and warms my heart. "That's incredible. And inspiring."

"It hasn't all been easy. Sure, they call Los Angeles the city of dreams…" He shakes his head, sipping on his beer. "Believe me. It's not."

"But you made it work."

The corners of his mouth quirk up. "I have."

The lights snap on, the universal sign of the bartender saying, "You don't have to go home, but you can't stay here." I check my watch, surprised to see it's practically two and that we've been talking for nearly three hours. I can't remember the last time I've been so immersed in another person that I lost all concept of time. It was probably at the lake house when Asher and I would end up staying awake all night without either of us realizing it, too lost in the music he strummed.

"I guess that's our cue to leave," he remarks, finishing his beer.

"I suppose it is."

I slide off my barstool, but my heel catches on a leg, propelling me forward. Asher reacts quickly, wrapping an arm around my waist and pulling me upright…directly into his body.

His warm, firm body.

Every inch of me instantly buzzes to life as a thrilling sensation washes over me, leaving me nearly breathless. This isn't the first time Asher's held me. Hell, it's not the first time he's broken my fall, preventing me from making a complete fool out of myself. But it's never felt like this. Like my insides are ready to ignite from the electricity coursing through me.

I tilt my head back and peer into his eyes that glisten under the bright lights of the bar. His chest expands a little more with every inhale. The motion is subtle, but I notice it. Just like I notice the swipe of his tongue along his bottom lip, moistening them. The slight flaring of his nostrils. The awe and curiosity in his stare. Does he feel this, too?

"You okay?"

Eyes the shade of whiskey skate over my frame before returning to mine. He makes no immediate move to drop his hold on me. In fact, he seems to draw me even closer, his fingers thrumming against the exposed flesh between my jeans and top, his touch a ray of sun on that first spring-like day. So unexpected. So surprising. Yet still very welcome.

"Izzy?" he presses when I don't immediately respond, lost in the tremors the mere sensation of his arms wrapped around me kindles. His voice pulls me back to the present, reminding me who I am. Who he is.

Just like he reminded me all those years ago.

I push out of his embrace, increasing the distance. "Those beers must have caught up to me. I should have eaten something."

I smooth my hands over my shirt, pulling it down so no more skin shows around my waistband. Fidgeting with the hem, I rock on my heels, the way he's staring at me unnerving, like he can read my thoughts and is about to recite a list of reasons we can never be together. I am more than aware of those reasons. I don't need a recap of them.

"Well…" I scramble to push past him. "It was good seeing you. Thanks for the beers."

I hold my breath as I make my escape, about to ring the victory bell when I hear his voice call out, "Want to grab a bite to eat?"

I come to an abrupt stop, blinking. I slowly glance over my shoulder. "What was that?"

He averts his gaze, scraping a hand through his hair. Asher's never been the nervous type. More brooding, mysterious, aloof. I'd lost count of the number of girls I'd witnessed fawning over him whenever his band had a gig. But he never seemed to notice them.

"Sorry. I don't know what I was thinking. I just enjoyed spending time with you again and wasn't ready to say goodbye yet. But you're right. You probably should—"

"Yes," I interrupt before he can finish his statement.

His brows furrow. "Excuse me?"

I fully face him. "Yes, I'd like to grab a bite to eat. With you."

"Are you sure? You're not too tired?"

I pass him a sardonic look. "Were you not paying attention to a single word I said tonight? I'm a nurse. My body's used to staying up late."

A dazzling smile flashes across his features. "So you're still a night owl? Even all these years later?"

I shrug. "Guilty as charged."

"Well then…" Approaching, he extends his arm toward the exit. "Shall we?"

"We shall." I make my way onto the casino floor, which is even busier than it was earlier. It doesn't seem to faze these people that it's after two in the morning. They're still slamming back drinks, which causes them to be more reckless with their money.

I've never been a gambler. Hell, I don't think I've so much as put a single bill into a slot machine the entire time I've been here. Living in Manhattan with the high rent doesn't give me much wiggle room to throw away money on frivolities.

I allow Asher to take the lead through the casino, but make sure to keep some space between us. Regardless, there's still a buzz in the air. As we pass a group of men in their twenties dressed in dark shirts and jeans, their hair slicked back, their musky cologne overpowering, a few of them eye me up and down, lasciviously licking their lips.

Asher steps closer and rests his hand on my lower back, his protective nature flaring. "You really should be careful walking around this place at night. Especially alone." He narrows his disapproving gaze on me, which is riddled with concern.

"I can take care of myself." I roll my eyes. "And for the record… I walk around Manhattan at night all the time."

"I'm more than aware you can take care of yourself, Iz. If I remember correctly, there was an incident at one of the festivals our band played where you managed to bring some schmuck who attempted to hit on you to his knees. It was the highlight of the gig."

I laugh, surprised at his memory of one particular performance when he's played hundreds, maybe even thousands. Then again, he *is* an artist. He crafts beautiful melodies with heartfelt lyrics. He probably remembers everything about everyone, pulling inspiration from everywhere he can.

"You still remember that?"

"How could I forget? It was all anyone talked about for weeks. About how tiny Isabella Nolan took down the star quarterback."

"What can I say? My father refused to send me away to college unless I took self-defense classes. When that prick wouldn't take no for an answer and tried to make a move on me, I knew exactly how to send him to his knees. There's nothing as effective as an open palm to the nose and a knee in the groin to knock out your opponent." I playfully waggle my brows, following him outside to the valet stand, where he hands a ticket to an attendant.

The instant I step into the chilly night air, a shiver rolls through me. I rub my arms. While the temperature has been above average for January, according to several of the locals I've spoken to, nighttime is still on the cooler side. When I'd dressed earlier, I hadn't expected to go outside. I didn't expect to run into Asher York, either, yet here I am.

"Take this." He shrugs out of his leather jacket and places it over my shoulders, leaving himself in just a t-shirt. A few women in tight dresses whistle as they walk past, ogling him.

I'd like to say seeing his muscular arms doesn't have the same effect on me, but it would be a lie. His physique is one you can't help but admire. Not too bulky, yet not just skin and bones, either. His arms are ones you crave to have wrapped around you. Arms you hurry home to after a long day. Arms you subconsciously seek out in the middle of the night as you sleep peacefully.

"Thanks," I say in a small voice, tugging his jacket closer, savoring the warmth. I inhale deeply, the material smelling like Asher — a woodsy, citrus scent. It's refreshing to know some things never change.

"Only out in the desert does it go from eighty degrees during the day to the forties and fifties at night." He looks up to the sky, the stars barely visible against the bright lights of Vegas. On a long exhale, he returns his eyes to mine. "But it beats all the snowstorms back east."

"You've got that right. The last few winters have been rough. I've lost count of the number of times I slept at the hospital so I wouldn't miss my shift. Or so I wouldn't have to try to find my way home in the middle of a blizzard."

"It's been that bad?"

I nod. "We've had some big storms that dropped upwards of a foot, sometimes more. If it's only a few inches, it's not that bad. But when we get that much snow, the city has trouble keeping up with shoveling and plowing, especially where I live."

"And where's that?"

"Tribeca. It's—"

"I know where it is. Jessie…" He stops short, wide eyes flinging to mine.

It's the first time either of us have brought him up, our very own elephant in the room. I've thought of Jessie throughout the night. How could I not when spending time with Asher? But now that his name is out there, an awkward tension has made itself known, coiling around and squeezing the life out of what, mere minutes ago, was a fun, lighthearted evening.

"I mean…" He stammers, trying to recover, apprehensive about Jessie's presence between us. "I played a few gigs in the city before I moved out west."

A small ball of guilt lodges in my stomach. We've both moved on, both dated other people. But those other people weren't his older brother. His own flesh and blood. Granted, Asher and I *aren't* dating, nor will we ever, but I know how Jessie is. He'll grow suspicious if he learns Asher was with me, even if merely as a friend. Just like I know Asher's struggling with his own thoughts of betrayal.

"Here we are," Asher announces, his voice brightening. Perhaps out of relief.

I look up to see a classic red Mustang convertible rounding the corner. "Is that *yours*?" I blink repeatedly, gaping at the stunning vehicle rumbling our way, the beautiful purr of the engine like a siren's call.

"And if it is?"

"That car is…" I shake my head. "Wow. My dad would lose his shit if he learned you were driving one. And by lose his shit, I mean he'd try to con you out of it. It's… What? A sixty-five?"

"Sixty-four."

"Damn. My dad would *definitely* try to con you out of it."

I follow him toward the passenger side, my eyes soaking in the beauty before me. And I'm not the only one. Every male within the vicinity has stopped, their attention drawn to the sleek lines of the car instead of their dates. It's not something you see every day.

"He always did have a thing for old cars, didn't he?" Asher holds my elbow, helping me into the passenger seat before making his way around to the driver's side. "Want me to put the top up?"

"I'll be fine. I should take advantage of the fresh air while I can, even if it is a little chilly."

He slides into his seat with ease, pressing his foot against the clutch before shifting into first. I tug his jacket tighter around my body, the wind cutting against my face. But I wouldn't trade this moment for anything. Hair whipping in front of me. The Vegas lights blinking all around me. And Asher York sitting beside me. It's a completely unexpected turn of events. Then again, the best things in life often are.

"Are you sure you're okay?" Asher shouts over the noise of the wind and engine as he merges onto the interstate. "I can pull over and put up the top."

"I'm fine," I yell back. "But I thought we were going to get something to eat."

"We are." He flashes me a devious grin before returning his attention to the road.

"Where? The Strip is—"

"Do you think all this town has to offer is located on Las Vegas Boulevard?"

I shrug. "Pretty much."

"Trust me. There are a few hidden gems."

"Is that where you're taking me? To a hidden gem?"

"Absolutely. A hidden gem for a hidden gem."

CHAPTER THREE

"THEY HAVE RED velvet pancakes?" Excitement oozes from my voice as I scan the menu that seems to have everything someone looking for a post-bar snack could ask for.

I've been to my fair share of late-night diners. This place is like a late-night diner on steroids. Red velvet pancakes. Amaretto french toast. Hell, if you wanted to go big, you could get a filet mignon. Even the ambience is a far cry from the grungy diners I'm used to. It's more reminiscent of a trendy supper club from back in the day. In fact, it probably was. Booths line the walls, white cloth-covered tables filling the rest of the open space. The lighting is on the dark side, all the windows tinted, presumably to make everyone forget that dawn is slowly approaching. As would be expected in this town, the bar serves alcohol twenty-four/seven.

Viva Las Vegas.

"And they are delicious," Asher comments. "In fact, you can't go wrong here. Everything they serve is incredible."

"So you come here often?" I ask in a fake seductive voice, grateful we're back to the way things have always been with us. Light. Fun. Easy. No more talking about Jessie.

"Actually, I do."

His response piques my interest. "Do you play a lot of gigs out here?"

"You could say that," he answers after a moment of contemplation.

"How long of a drive is it from LA?"

He brushes his thumb along his chin, looking into the distance before shifting his eyes back to mine. "About four hours. Depending on traffic."

"Kind of like living in the Tri-state area."

"It's even worse in LA. At least in New York, the public transportation system is great. You could just hop on Metro-North."

"Which is what I do, since it only takes... What? An hour?"

"No such luck in LA. If you want to get anywhere in the area, you're stuck driving."

"There's no subway system at all?"

"There's the metro, but it's not convenient and doesn't go everywhere most people need it to. It's nowhere near as convenient and widespread as the subway in New York. Or the T up in Boston." A hint of his accent slips in when his mouth caresses the name of the city he once called home. It was never overpowering or annoying, as was the case with some of the guys I met when I moved to Boston for college. It's subtle, an acknowledgment of his roots. One I hope he never loses.

"Well…" I lean back into the booth. "At least you have an incredible car to be stuck in traffic in."

"I can't complain about that. Actually, I—"

"Here are your drinks," our petite blonde waitress interrupts, placing a Bloody Mary in front of me and a coffee in front of Asher.

I felt a little guilty ordering an alcoholic drink, since he's not drinking, but I needed something to take the edge off after the way my body reacted to his arms around me. And the Bloody Marys coming out of the bar looked too good to pass up. Shrimp. Bacon. Blue cheese-stuffed olives. It's a drink that was made for me.

"Are you ready to place your orders?"

"I am," Asher replies confidently, without even opening the menu to peruse the options. Then he looks at me. "Do you know what you'd like?"

I close my menu, holding it toward our waitress. "I can't resist. Red velvet pancakes."

"Good choice," she assures me before shifting her attention to Asher. "And for you?" She bats her lashes, her smile turning from polite to coquettish when she steals a glance at his tattoo-covered arms.

I never thought I'd be the type of girl who'd be interested in a guy with tattoos. I certainly shouldn't be interested in *this* one. But I can't dismiss the pang of jealousy rolling through me at the thought of this stranger ogling Asher. I try to tell myself it's because he's a friend, that I want what's best for him and this woman isn't it. But that didn't cause me to be jealous of anyone Asher dated while I was with Jessie. I'd even attempted to set him up with one of the girls in my dorm, thinking they'd be perfect for each other. She was a music major with a voice that was a combination of Adele and P!nk. I had listened to her go on about how great of a kisser he was, how much she loved his body. Not one flare of jealousy. But now, the mere idea of someone flirting with Asher has me glowering, judging everything about this complete stranger when I normally don't judge anyone.

He orders steak and eggs, which includes a filet mignon instead of a skirt steak, as is the case at most diners. The waitress lingers a few extra seconds, smiling coyly at Asher. Then she spins from us, and I can't help but think she's swaying her hips a little more than necessary.

"She wants you," I observe once she's a safe distance away. I take a much-needed sip of my Bloody Mary, which is as delicious as it looks.

"No, she doesn't." He pours a bit of milk into his coffee, skipping the sweetener altogether. Just like I remember. It's comforting to know some things haven't changed. "She was just being friendly. Probably hoping for a good tip."

"Right...," I say in a drawn-out voice, rolling my eyes. Speaking of things that never change...

It didn't matter how blatant the girls who fawned all over him were. He always brushed them off. He dated, but he never seemed to have the same passion about any of them as he did his music.

"Your girlfriend must hate going to your gigs, knowing the women in the audience will drool all over you." I swipe the condensation off the side of my glass.

He rests his forearms on the table between us, leaning toward me. His eyes darken, almost leering. The light, carefree atmosphere we've enjoyed since we arrived here vanishes. My gaze locks with his, meeting that same wanton stare he'd regarded me with as he held me in his arms. But this time it's even more pronounced. More shameless. More devious.

"What makes you say that?" he asks in a low tone, swiping his tongue along his bottom lip.

My core clenches, blood rushing to my cheeks. This reaction is so wrong. On so many levels. But there's no denying the hunger bubbling within me. The electricity sparking in the air between us. As much as I want to blame it on the lack of male companionship over the past few months, I can't. I know the truth. That my body has always acted this way around Asher. I just didn't want to acknowledge it for what it was. What it still is. A connection even the passing of years couldn't fracture. In fact, it's only made it stronger.

"I—" I stammer, fumbling for a response that doesn't give away how out of sorts I am.

"Oh, come now. I've never known you to be tongue-tied, Isabella," he remarks smoothly, a different side of Asher. "Tell me." His voice turns gruff, causing the hairs on my nape to stand on end. My heart rate increases. My head becomes foggy. The background noise fades away, like this is a dream. Maybe it is.

Maybe I fell asleep after showering and Asher York manifested in my dreams for some reason. Just like Ebenezer Scrooge was convinced his manifestation of Jacob Marley was due to something he ate, perhaps this fantasy of spending a night in Vegas with Asher York is the result of too much liquor and not enough food.

"Why do you think our waitress wants me?" he presses, his eyes focusing more intently on me.

I consider a viable response. I could list the obvious signs that would cause even a blind person to realize they're getting hit on. Instead, I test my limits. If this is a manifestation, a dream, what do I have to lose?

"Because if our situation were reversed, I'd act the same way," I admit, the words leaving me before I have a chance to evaluate the potential ramifications of being so truthful. My statement rings around us as I stare, seconds ticking by in a savage march. I feel like a contestant on one of those talent shows waiting to hear whether they'll continue on to the following week or be sent home, their dreams of stardom dashed. That's the power Asher holds over me at this very moment.

Hope seems to build in his gaze, his eye contact strong, his lips parting slightly. He leans closer, the corners of his mouth quirking up, as if struggling to reel it in but can't. As if he's waited years for me to say something like this.

Then, just as quickly as his bright expression appears, it fades, gaze distant and even. As stoic as a soldier. "Thankfully, that's not an issue."

"You're right." I swallow down the pain of disappointment rising through my body, forcing the most fabricated smile of my life. If Asher can tell it's fake, he doesn't bring it up. "It's not."

With a shaky hand, I grab my Bloody Mary, taking a long sip. The spicy drink tingles as it hits my tongue and throat, but I've had spicier food. Hell, my mother jokes she pureed jalapeños and spoon-fed them to me as a baby to toughen me up.

"Not that." When he grabs my free hand, I fling my eyes to his, loosening the desperate grip my lips have on my straw. I remain silent, awaiting further explanation. "I'm talking about my girlfriend coming to one of my gigs. *That's* not an issue."

I perk up. "Oh?"

A sexy smirk draws on his full mouth and he releases his hold on me, angling away. "No girlfriend."

I nod, pretending the information is inconsequential. Inwardly, my libido does a little victory dance. I attempt to settle her down, tell her this doesn't change anything, but the sex-starved nymph refuses to listen.

"And your boyfriend wouldn't like it if he learned you were here with me at, oh…" He looks at his watch, "three in the morning."

"That's not an issue, either."

He raises a single brow. "Oh?"

"No boyfriend."

He makes a subtle gesture of acknowledgment by pursing his lips. Otherwise, his expression is unreadable. I peer into his dark orbs, searching for any sort of positive reaction to this news. But there's nothing, my not having a boyfriend seemingly as mundane a detail as how I take my coffee.

"So…" I tear my eyes away before I do or say something else I'll regret. Something else to make this awkward. "How's Grams doing?"

That's all it takes for a brilliant smile to light up his face, as I knew it would. I always admired the bond Asher had with his grandmother. "Still as headstrong and crazy as ever." A deep chuckle vibrates through his chest, natural and unforced. "She recently took up kickboxing, a fact I have first-hand knowledge of after witnessing it this past Christmas."

"You were in Florida?" I ask, recalling how his parents typically spent the colder months down south. His father's job as a financial planner allowed him to work from wherever he was. And spending November through April in the south allowed him to have clients in multiple parts of the country.

"Boston," he corrects. "Since Grams is getting older, Mom and Dad have been staying up north. Of course, she tries to insist she's fine, that age is only a number, and she has no intention of dying anytime soon."

"That sounds like something Grams would say." Regret squeezes at my heart, the heaviness settling deep in my chest.

Despite everything that transpired between Jessie and myself, I should have made more of an effort to stay in touch with Grams. She'd reached out to me in the months following the breakup, but I'd made my decision. The only way to repair the splintered fragments of my heart was to walk away from the entire family. It hurt too much otherwise. Which is why I should have walked out of that bar tonight when I had the chance. I fear it will take another eight years to repair my heart again.

"So… Kickboxing?" I press, swallowing back the memories.

"Right." He brightens his sympathetic gaze. "I'd been home for no more than five minutes when Grams walked in wearing workout clothes. And not, like, old granny workout clothes."

"Oh god." I cover my mouth with my hand. "Was she wearing spandex?"

He rubs his eyes. "I still have the image ingrained in my memory. I mean, she's in great shape for being nearly ninety, but still. After a while, gravity does its thing. Grams has never been one who cares what people think of her, though. Anyway, I'd barely had time to unpack when she came barreling in and said she was dragging me to her kickboxing class. Claimed she'd been telling all the people in her class about my music, that they were all dying to meet me. I thought about blowing her off, but she's getting older, so I indulged her. I figured we were going to the Y or the senior center. You can imagine my surprise when she directed me to the parking lot of some industrial building. It was an actual MMA gym."

I burst out laughing. As ridiculous as the picture he's painted sounds, it's entirely believable. Grams never adhered to society's expectations. And she certainly wouldn't let her age get in the way of doing something she wanted.

"What did you do?" I ask, wiping the corners of my eyes.

"What *could* I do? I'd be lying if I said I wasn't curious about the entire scenario. So I went in with her, prepared to defend her against any asshole who tried to tell her she should go somewhere else. But the second she walked through those doors, everyone welcomed her. Hell, Grams even got into all the locker room talk, too. I will admit, she's got one hell of a round kick." He winces. "I found that out the hard way."

"How's that?"

"Let's just say I got a little too close and her leg hit me with such force that an ice pack was attached to my balls for the next twenty-four hours."

My laughter echoes in the restaurant, nostalgia filling me. Of all the people I lost when Jessie and I broke up, Grams was the hardest, more so than Jessie, or even Asher. She had this spirit, this vitality I felt drawn to the second I met her. Like she was a kindred spirit. Like she knew me and I her, even though she was a stranger to me at that point.

"Knowing Grams, she intentionally did that to prove she could take care of herself."

He lifts his coffee to his lips with a wink. "You're probably right."

"Here you go." Our waitress approaches, carrying two plates. "Red velvet pancakes." She sets the dish in front of me before turning toward Asher, her smile shifting from cordial to much more flirtatious. "And your steak and eggs." Her voice grows seductive as she places it in front of him, pushing her arms together to make her cleavage pop.

I take this opportunity to study her. Her appearance is similar to every other woman out here who's trying to catch their big break in modeling. Waif-thin. Blonde hair that's most likely not her natural color. Overdone makeup. Nothing about her stands out as remarkable. I'm not saying I'm supermodel material, but I hate the idea of Asher and this cookie-cutter blonde being together, as unlikely as that is. Or maybe it's the idea they *can* be together that irritates me. That she *can* flirt with him, and he her, with no consequences.

"Thank you. This looks delicious."

"Is there anything else I can get you?" Her voice becomes increasingly breathy. "Ketchup? Tabasco? More coffee? Or maybe something else?"

Asher waggles his brows at me before returning his attention to Waitress Barbie. "I believe I have everything I need right here." Eyes connecting with mine, he reaches across the table, grabbing my hand in his, gently brushing his thumb across my knuckles.

The subtle sensation causes me to inhale a sharp breath. I don't move. Don't blink. It's not the first time I've felt his hand on me. But this seems so much more charged than any of the other times he's touched me. Then again, that was *before*. When I was blind to everything and everyone other than Jessie York.

"Oh." Waitress Barbie straightens, her expression falling, but Asher doesn't seem to notice. If he does, he doesn't care, his stare still trained on me in a way that makes me think he's peeling back layer after layer, exposing every single one of my vulnerabilities. Or am I just imagining that, too?

One minute, I'm confident it's all in my head. The next, I feel something I didn't think possible, confident Asher does, too. This is why I've avoided dating for so long. It's too stressful.

"Well, if you change your mind, give me a shout."

She shoots her eyes to mine before spinning around. I'm about to pull my hand away, but Asher tightens his grasp.

I try not to read too much into it. We're just two friends holding hands. Hell, there were quite a few nights I'd dozed off on his shoulder as I listened to him strum his guitar at the lake house.

Each summer, I looked forward to spending time there. After dinner, we'd sit by the lake, a campfire burning, and actually talk to each other. No distractions. Spending time together in a way most people no longer do in this technology-driven society. Jessie would inevitably go inside early, complaining about the mosquitos, despite not having a single bite on his flesh. I should have known then we were incompatible. He hated everything to do with nature, preferring the pace of the city. While I love urban life, I enjoy getting away from it all, too. Something I haven't had the opportunity to do for too long now.

A squeeze on my hand brings me back from my memories, and I return my eyes to Asher as he releases his hold. "Sorry. I shouldn't have used you as a barrier, but I don't think she would have gotten the hint otherwise."

I smile weakly. "What are friends for?"

CHAPTER FOUR

"I CAN'T REMEMBER the last time I stayed out this late," I remark as Asher and I make our way across the nearly empty parking lot. It's now that in-between time of night. Most bar and clubgoers are passed out in their beds. The nine-to-fivers haven't started their day yet. The only people out and about are the insomniacs or the ones who seem to find inspiration in the romantic notion of being awake when the rest of the world sleeps. "Except the nights I work, but I don't consider that staying out late. It's not exactly voluntary, but something I do so I can pay my bills."

"I get it," he responds with a slight wink. "My body's hard-wired to stay up late, too. That was always the difficult part about teaching, and the part I don't miss. I could never adjust to the early hours. Grams always said it was because I inherited her non-conformist free spirit. It was hell waking up at six every morning after having gone to bed only a few hours earlier. Falling asleep by two was a good night."

I nod in understanding as we approach his car. He opens my door, and I slide into my seat. "That's why I don't mind working the night shift. I think it gives you a different perspective on things. Makes you see the world in a different light."

He ducks in behind the steering wheel, treating me to a small smile. "Glad to see there's still a little Holly Golightly in you."

I scrunch my brows.

"Holly Golightly," he repeats. "You know. *Breakfast at Tiffany's*."

"I know who she is, but I—"

"The opening scene. When she's strolling down Fifth Avenue in an evening gown and stops in front of Tiffany's to eat her breakfast. Something about that scene always spoke to me. Like it was the calm before the storm. Few people get the opportunity to see Manhattan, or any city, so peaceful. I think that's why I do my best work at night after the world's gone to sleep. There's no distraction. No constant buzzing of my cell phone. I can lock myself away in the studio and write."

"Are you working on something now? A new album?"

"You could say that." He sucks his bottom lip between his teeth, glancing at me in contemplation. "Actually, it's something pretty big.

Something that could change everything for me."

"That guy at the bar…," I begin, meeting Asher's gaze. "The one who said in a few months we wouldn't be able to turn on the radio without hearing your music."

"Wasn't lying," he states without me having to ask the question on the tip of my tongue. "As long as I meet this deadline. Honestly, I shouldn't have gone out tonight, but when Mark mentioned his band was in town, I figured taking a break and performing could be a good way to get the creative juices flowing again."

"Did it?"

He cranks the ignition, stealing a glance at me before reversing out of the parking spot. "I do believe it has."

He shifts into first and maneuvers the car through the lot, coming to a stop before merging onto the street. I focus on my surroundings, relishing in the chilly night air on my skin. The sky's no longer pitch-black as it was when we entered the restaurant. There's an almost purple-blue hue, a warning that daybreak is on the horizon.

We come to a stoplight, the lack of any noise unnerving, especially when I feel the heat of Asher's gaze on me. I glance his way, a flicker of something I can't explain in his expression. Yearning? Nostalgia perhaps? He parts his lips, peering at me as if my face holds the answer to whatever has him so conflicted.

Then his mouth quirks into a combination of a grin and a smirk. "Are you tired? Or do you think you can last a bit longer?"

A little voice in my brain warns me I've already spent more time with Asher than I should have. But just like those nights at Grams' lake house, I don't want tonight to end.

"Oh, baby, I can last all night long," I shoot back playfully. My smile falls quickly when I notice his grip on the steering wheel tighten. The vein in his neck throbs, his jaw ticks. I continue to stare, making sure I'm not imagining it. This time, I know I'm not. I see it. The quickening rise and fall of his chest. The constricting of his muscles. The flaring of his nostrils. All over what should have been a harmless sexual innuendo between friends, one I'd made several times with him in the past. But that was before. When it truly was harmless. I'm not sure I can say the same thing here.

Not saying a word, he pulls a quick U-turn, driving deeper into the night. The wind blows my hair as I observe the commercial buildings turn into more residential neighborhoods, the traffic becoming more and more sparse. I steal a glance into the rearview mirror to see the familiar silhouette of the Vegas Strip grow smaller and more distant behind me.

"Where are we going?" I break the cryptic silence.

"You'll see."

"So secretive."

"Trust me. If I told you, you wouldn't believe it. It's better if you see for yourself."

Desperate to cut through the stiff tension, I flash him a bright smile. "You've been moonlighting as an Elvis impersonator and have to perform a last-minute wedding for some celebrity A-listers."

He glances my way, his tight expression waning, his dimples popping. I remember looking through family photo albums from when Jessie and Asher were younger. Due to their proximity in age, it was often difficult to tell one from the other. Unless they were both smiling. Asher has these adorable dimples that have only made him more endearing with age. He can give off this tough, brooding persona of a tortured artist all he wants. But the second he smiles and those dimples pop, he looks like the boy next door.

Maybe the *bad* boy next door.

But he's not a bad boy, either. I'm not quite sure *how* to describe Asher York. I also wasn't sure back then.

"Nope. But good guess. Try again."

"Was I even remotely close?"

"The only thing I have in common with Elvis is that he could also play guitar and sing."

"Okay." I exhale dramatically, looking at the sky as I try to come up with yet another ridiculous scenario. When I return my eyes to Asher, I can't help but admire his carefree and relaxed demeanor. One hand rests on the steering wheel, the other on the gear shift. Something about how casual he is as he drives this beautiful classic car makes him appear even sexier than when he performs on stage.

"You have an audition for one of those all-male reviews and want me to give you a quick rundown from the striptease classes Bernadette made us attend a few days ago."

His wide eyes fling to mine, the vein in his neck pulsing once more. Maybe I shouldn't have mentioned those lessons.

"You took striptease classes?" His voice comes out as a low growl, heat and desire dripping from him. I can only imagine his reaction if I offered to give him a private show.

"And pole dance lessons."

"Fuck," he hisses, his hand sliding off the gear shift and onto my thigh, squeezing.

I remain still, unsure where to go from here. All I know is the way he's touching me has me wanting more, that spark returning with a vengeance.

He suddenly slams on the brakes, causing my body to jolt toward the windshield. The only things that keep me from crashing through it are the seatbelt and Asher's arm bracing me.

"Sorry." He clears his throat as he takes a quick left, the houses becoming more spread out and opulent. This isn't a regular residential neighborhood anymore. This is where the wealthy play when they're in Vegas. "Almost missed the turn."

"Did something distract you?" I tease.

"I'd have to surrender my man card if I *wasn't* distracted by that."

"I can see how that would be a problem with whoever sets the rules. Just like women are supposed to fawn over shirtless, well-built men as they dance on a stage, men are supposed to salivate over a woman on a pole."

"Not just any woman," he clarifies. "The idea of *you* pole dancing is, well… It's like every fantasy I've ever had." The flirtatious quality to his voice is gone, replaced with a truthfulness I didn't quite anticipate.

"Asher, I—"

"Here we are," he interrupts, his voice brightening. I study him for a moment, but his expression is even once again. Like he's flipped a switch, and any craving he exhibited mere seconds ago is nothing but a distant memory.

I look away, my brows drawing together when he pulls up to a gated driveway. He stops outside a box, inputting a four-digit code. The large, metal gates slowly open, granting us access.

"Who lives here?" I ask. "Do you have some wealthy benefactor, like Paul Varjak did in *Breakfast at Tiffany's*?"

He chuckles as he navigates up a winding driveway. The instant the sprawling mansion comes into view, my jaw drops. I have no idea what's going on, but my curiosity piques more and more with each beat of my heart.

"No wealthy benefactor. Well, not like that anyway. There's no rich older woman I'm sleeping with in order to bankroll my life while I write."

"Then—"

"Have you heard of Fallen Grace?"

I snort. "Who hasn't? You can't turn on the radio without hearing their music. Not to mention I work in pediatric oncology. I have several patients who are teenage girls. A few of them have even hung up posters of the band in their room."

Asher pulls the car into a detached garage off to the side of the main house and engages the parking brake, killing the ignition. I stare in awe at the row of sports cars. Tesla. Mercedes. BMW. Even a Maserati.

"They're patients long enough to decorate their rooms?" Asher's voice pulls me back from the myriad of questions swirling in my mind.

"Some of them will never walk out of that hospital again. Unless the family makes the decision to do home hospice care in their final days."

"But they're kids." He shakes his head, heartache etched in the lines of his face over this sad truth I confront daily.

"Cancer doesn't discriminate. Young. Old. Rich. Poor. It doesn't matter."

He stares deeper into my eyes. Then he reaches toward me, cupping my cheek, his long fingers burrowing into my thick hair. "You are an incredible woman, Izzy. I've never met anyone as compassionate and selfless as you. You deserve better than…" He trails off, stopping himself from finishing his sentence. He doesn't need to. I know what he was about to say. "Well, you deserve better."

"Thank you."

He keeps his hand on my cheek a heartbeat longer. For a second, I think he's about to kiss me, the way his gaze strays to my mouth and he licks his own lips in preparation. Kissing him would be wrong, would violate the unspoken rule against falling for a woman your friend — your *brother* — already dated. But it doesn't bother me like it should.

He closes his eyes and I tilt my head toward him, my breathing increasing in anticipation. Then his shoulders fall and he drops his hold on me, his expression pinched, as if reminding himself of who we are. Who we'll always be to one another.

"Come on." With shaky hands, he opens the door and steps out of the car, rushing around to help me. A stiff silence fills the air as he leads me out of the garage and down a path lined with succulents in a stone bed.

I glance up at the vast, two-story house that would rival some of the ones I grew up near in Greenwich, still having no answers about who lives in it and what we're doing here, other than it having to do with one of the most popular boy bands around today.

"Is this Fallen Grace's party house?" Chloe had mentioned several celebrities owned houses on the outskirts of the city for that exact purpose. Since she works as a celebrity news columnist, she would know.

"They bought it for that purpose a few years ago, but lately it has served as more of a recording studio."

I halt in my tracks, mouth agape, eyes wide. I didn't expect him to agree with my statement. "This is Fallen Grace's party house-slash-recording studio?"

He shrugs, as if he'd just told me he had to do laundry or some other mundane task. "Sure is."

I blink, gawking at him. Then the house. Then back at him. "Are they here? Am I going to meet Fallen Grace? Some of my teenage patients would lose their minds, especially if I'm able to get their autographs."

"They're home in London for a break before we hit it hard in a few weeks."

"We?"

His grin widens as he extends his hand toward me. "Come on. I'll explain everything."

I stare at his hand with skepticism before lifting my eyes to his. He arches a brow, tilting his head slightly. I wonder if this is how Alice felt when she noticed the White Rabbit scurrying past her. If she was torn between remaining in her normal life and experiencing something she'd never forget, even if it was fleeting. But that didn't stop her from following the White Rabbit. I don't let it stop me, either.

Blowing out a breath, I place my hand in his, following him deeper and deeper down my own rabbit hole.

But there's no place I'd rather be.

CHAPTER FIVE

"YOU LIVE HERE now?" I ask as I run my fingers along the cool ivory of a baby grand piano, floating my eyes to where Asher leans against the soundproof wall in a state-of-the-art recording studio. No more walls and ceiling covered with egg crate foam to prevent outside noise from filtering into the basement of his parents' house. This is all professionally constructed and designed. A musician's dream.

"It's more a temporary home out of convenience. The guys need to get a new album out, as well as prepare for an extended engagement at one of the casinos. I need to be somewhere I have access to whatever I require. Granted, when they first approached me to help with the new album, the plan *was* to record in LA."

I sit on the piano bench, lightly pressing the keys, the soft sound filling the room. It's been years since I've played, but it's like riding a bike. You may have a few slips and falls at first, but once muscle memory kicks in, you're cruising right along.

"And how *did* they approach you?"

"Pure dumb luck." He pushes off the wall and closes in on me in three long strides, sitting next to me. "Or maybe the big man upstairs decided to give me a break." He places his hands on the piano keys, playing a simple baseline to compliment the B-flat blues progression I'm fooling around with. "To be honest, I was ready to give up. I was months behind on rent and facing eviction."

"Was gigging your only source of income?" I play with a little more confidence, my transitions coming with greater ease.

"I taught private guitar and piano lessons in the afternoons, so that helped," he answers, looking at me instead of the keys. He could probably play it blindfolded.

Mmm… Asher in a blindfold.

I extinguish the thought, silently berating my libido for going there.

"I had enough money in savings to keep me afloat for a little while. But after a year, that savings had dwindled to practically nothing. I'd reached the point where I didn't see any other option but to go back home, tell my parents they were right and it was a crazy idea, then hope they'd let me move in with them while I got my master's degree so I could teach again."

"That sucks," I respond, hitting the wrong note, causing a dissonance. I cringe, but Asher smiles, shrugging it off. I'm sure he's heard much worse musicians than myself. Hell, he used to teach beginner strings. If there's any class requiring earplugs and sedatives, it's that one.

"So one day, my phone in my hand, about to call Mom to ask if she'd help me settle up my affairs in LA so I could leave this chapter of my life behind, it rang with a number I didn't recognize. I almost didn't answer. Figured it was another bill collector."

"But you did."

"I did." He sighs, his posture relaxing, his lips kicking up into a small smile. It's obvious how grateful he is for this opportunity, that he has no intention of taking it for granted. "And that was the phone call that changed my life. Changed everything. I was seconds away from quitting, Iz. *Seconds*," he emphasizes, his voice brimming with passion and intensity, the music he's playing matching it.

I steal a glance at the way his fingers move across the delicate ivory with ease. I could watch him play for hours and never tire of it. It's so hypnotizing. So captivating. So mesmerizing.

"I truly believe some bigger force intervened, saying 'not yet'. At first, I thought it was a prank."

"Why's that?"

"Think about it. If you were a struggling musician, months behind on your rent and living off Ramen noodles, something you never even had to do in college, how would you respond to getting a phone call from someone purporting to be the manager of one of the highest grossing musical acts of the past decade, offering you a job writing and producing their new album?"

I smile. "I'd think it was a joke, too."

"David, their manager, knew it would probably come as a surprise. He convinced me to meet him the following morning and judge for myself. When I walked into the luxurious office in Century City, I knew it wasn't a prank. Gold and platinum records hung on the wall. Posh furniture filled the space. Hell, I'm pretty sure even the receptionist's shoes cost more than my rent. Christian Lou-something."

"Louboutins," I interject. "They're Christian Louboutins. They have this signature red sole that all women foam at the mouth over."

He cocks a brow. "Including you?"

I pinch my lips together as I focus on the white and black keys in front of me, the melody coming easier now, even if I am sticking close to the chord progressions. Unlike Asher, who's riffing off the tune as if it's second nature to improvise a song on the spot.

"A girl can dream, can't she?" While I'm not one to spend a fortune on clothes or shoes, considering I spend most of my life wearing scrubs, I can still look. Can still pine. Can still fantasize.

A pair of Christian Louboutins is the female equivalent of a wet dream coming true.

"She certainly can."

"So, what happened next?"

"I was brought into this incredible corner office that was bigger than my entire apartment, the five members of Fallen Grace sitting on the two couches. If I hadn't gotten that phone call the previous night, I probably wouldn't have recognized them, but I did some research. I'd *heard* of Fallen Grace, but I'm not exactly a pre-pubescent girl, so I didn't know what they looked like."

"I could probably tell you which one has dimples, which one has the goatee, and which one has the 'adorable' birthmark right above his lip," I retort sarcastically. "They're just so *dreamy*." I bat my lashes, mimicking the way some of my patients fawn over their teen idols.

He chuckles. "Well, I couldn't. I'd never even listened to their music until I got that phone call. After doing so, I wasn't sure why they called me. Or how they even found me. My stuff isn't the pop music they typically perform."

"Right. So…"

"When I asked about it, their manager told me they were tired of the normal 'dog and pony show', as they called it. Wanted to go for a different, more mature sound now that they were in their mid-twenties. If they didn't want to die the same death every other boy band seemed to, they needed to do something to make themselves attractive to a broader audience."

"Take the 'boy' out of boy band," I offer.

"Exactly. They'd brought in some of the top songwriters to help with the transition, but no one 'got it'. They were all professionals who'd made a living writing melodies and lyrics that were popular. The band already knew what was popular. They didn't want that anymore. So they started hanging out in area bars in various cities, checking out the local music scene. Incognito, of course."

"And they just so happened to be at a bar in LA where you were performing?" I tilt my head at him, then quickly return my attention to the piano when I hit another wrong note. After looking at Asher's fingers to figure out where we were in the progression, I recenter my hands on an F-major-seven chord, regaining my confidence.

"They were. Well, one of them was anyway. Grabbed a postcard I was giving out containing free download codes of the songs I'd written. Played it for the rest of the guys, then their manager. And the rest, as they say, is history."

"So you're actually writing the songs for Fallen Grace's new album?" It seems so far-fetched, like something he'd tell a girl in a bar to get her to sleep with him.

"I am."

My fingers fall from the piano as it sinks in. Why didn't he mention anything earlier? Maybe he couldn't. Maybe he's under a non-disclosure agreement. That would make sense, considering the band probably hasn't gone public with this new direction yet.

"The way you made it sound, you were only here for the weekend."

"I never said anything like that." He shrugs. "You assumed."

"But you still didn't correct my assumption when it was obvious what I was thinking, especially when I asked how long it takes to get here from LA. Why?"

The music fades away as he stops playing, facing me. "I guess I wanted to make sure you were the same Isabella I remember. That you'd want to spend time with me for me. Not because of all this." He waves a hand around. Guitars of every brand hanging along the wall. A drum kit sitting in the corner that any serious drummer would drool over. Even a wet bar with top-shelf liquor so you don't have to venture into the house for a drink.

Resting my hand on his arm, I lock eyes with him, refusing to look at anything else. "I've always enjoyed spending time with you for you, Asher. Everything else has always just been…noise."

A tiny exhale of air escapes his lips as they part, a slow smile building. He scoops my hand off his arm, holding it in his, running his thumb along my skin. This time, he doesn't have an overly amorous waitress as an excuse for touching me. He doesn't have any excuse, other than he wants to, *needs* to. I try to tell myself it's a platonic gesture between two old friends, but the tenderness with which he brushes my knuckles, the darkening of his eyes, tell me that's not the case. Tell me we could very well be playing with fire.

An outside force pulls me toward him, a tether keeping our bodies bound to each other. As I lean closer, Asher shifts his eyes to my lips. His shoulders rise and fall in a quicker pattern, his grip on my hand tightening to the point of being nearly painful. A tumultuous tug-of-war plagues his expression. Desire, then guilt. Infatuation, then indifference. Hunger, then repulsion.

His conscience winning out, he jumps up from the bench, stalking toward the door. "It's almost sunrise." His voice trembles with the aftereffects of his internal battle.

I can't even pretend to be surprised by his abrupt retreat. That seems to be the game we're playing. One step forward. A giant leap backward. A promise to move ahead. Then a swift change of course. Or maybe change of heart.

"It's beautiful off the back patio. You should really see it. It'll be like old times."

I sigh, briefly closing my eyes before standing. "Like old times," I repeat, meeting him in the doorway.

He offers me an apologetic smile, which I return with a nod of understanding. Then he leads me out of the recording studio and down the long corridor lined with framed prints of some of the biggest names in the industry. When we emerge into the living area, he continues toward a set of French doors, opening one and allowing me to step outside before him.

"This way." He rests his hand on my lower back, steering me through a luxurious patio, complete with a fire pit, past what appears to be a regulation pool, and up to the edge of the property. A glow has already begun to sneak out behind the mountains in the distance.

I'd always thought Las Vegas to be flat. For the most part, it is, but this house sits on a parcel of land that's elevated enough so I can see the Strip with no obstruction.

"Not my favorite city in the world, but it's home to one hell of a sunrise."

"Even better than at the lake house?"

A smile radiates through his features. "Well, I wouldn't go that far." He rests his forearms on the steel fence surrounding the property, peering into the distance, deep in thought. I do the same, basking in what I know will be our last few minutes together. We've settled into our old routine. A few drinks. A bite to eat, although it used to be in the form of roasting marshmallows and hotdogs. Playing music. Watching the sunrise. Then going our separate ways.

"I hope it's not too bold of me to say…" He leans toward me, "but the reason I loved those sunrises was because of *who* I often had the pleasure of watching them with." The heat of his breath on my neck sends an involuntary tremble racing through me.

"Are you cold?" he asks, oblivious to the fact that my reaction was because of him. Because of his words. His honesty. His everything. "Let me grab a sweatshirt for you." He starts toward the house, but I wrap my hand around his bicep, stopping him.

"Don't." I quickly release my hold on him, increasing the space between us before I'll no longer be able to control myself. "I wouldn't want you to miss the sunrise."

I resume my position, subconsciously rubbing my arms to fight against the chill as I watch the glow make its gradual ascent over the peaks. It's unlike any sunrise I've seen. One side of the mountain is in light. The other still shrouded in relative darkness. Like an eclipse.

As I marvel at how beautiful this planet truly is, a presence approaches from behind. Asher wraps me in his embrace, pulling me into his strong body.

"Glad to see some things never change," he comments, running his calloused hands up and down my arms.

"What do you mean by that?"

"You're still as stubborn as you were all those years ago. When we sat and watched the sunrise together at the lake, you never let me run inside to grab you a sweatshirt. Why's that?"

I'm not sure what comes over me. Maybe it's the lack of sleep. Maybe it's feeling like this is a dream. Or maybe it's the idea that I've longed to be in this man's presence again for the past eight years. So instead of brushing off his question, I do something I normally wouldn't. I offer him a piece of the truth, regardless of how he'll respond. In a few hours, I'll be on a plane heading back to my life, and he'll return to his. May as well take a risk.

"I didn't want to lose the moment," I answer in a soft voice. "Didn't want it to disappear."

I don't have to turn around to feel the smile on his lips. He draws me closer, the sear of his breath on my nape spreading a glow within. "I won't disappear."

* * *

"Here we are," Asher announces as he pulls the car into the valet area under the awning leading to the lobby.

"Here we are," I repeat, pretending not to be as forlorn over the idea of saying goodbye as I am. The entire drive here, I wanted to tell him to take me back so we could have another day, another hour, another minute. But it's after seven in the morning. Chloe and I are supposed to leave for the airport at eleven. That only gives me a few hours to get a little sleep so I'm not a complete zombie.

But I'd gladly trade those few hours of sleep for more time with Asher. To recreate whatever I experienced the last several hours.

He holds my gaze, his expression making me think there's a question on the tip of his tongue. As seemed to be the case all night, he shakes it off, stepping out of the car and making his way around to my side, helping me to my feet.

"Promise you'll stay in touch." He brushes that same errant strand of hair behind my ear. "That you won't shut me out because—"

"I promise," I respond, saving him from having to bring up Jessie.

"Good."

I shift on my feet, uncertain of the protocol in saying goodbye to your ex-fiancé's brother, whom you fantasized about kissing on more than one occasion throughout the night. I doubt there is one.

"Well then…" I clear my throat, stepping back. "It was—"

Before I can utter another syllable, he advances and clutches my face in his hands. It steals my breath, a current pulsating through me. I swallow hard as I'm forced to stare into the fervor in his deep-set eyes, years' worth of longing swirling into a tidal pool of lust.

"Izzy." The way my name rolls off his tongue has my insides coiling and tightening. It's husky, yet still prayer-like. A wanton benediction. A sensual communion.

My virtuous sin.

His lips inch closer and closer as his grasp on my face becomes harsher, more punishing, more consuming. I can physically feel the battle waging, his mouth struggling to advance while the wounded pieces of him sound a retreat, yanking him back.

His chest heaves, muscles shaking, everything about this moment so surreal, so hypnotizing, so fucking perfect. I don't even care if he actually kisses me or not. The knowledge he *wants* to is enough.

With a growl, he tears his hands from me, anguish and turmoil covering his expression. A beat passes, then another as he hangs his head, attempting to collect himself. When he returns his eyes to mine, they're no longer inflamed, those of an untamed beast. They're even, albeit still flickering with want.

He expels a sigh and brushes his lips against my forehead. The touch is slight, yet profound. More profound than any act of intimacy I've experienced these last few years. Because with just the most subtle of touches, I feel the meaning behind it.

"Thanks for tonight. It was exactly what I needed."

"Me, too," I respond with a half-hearted smile when he pulls back.

"Go get some rest."

"You, too."

"I don't think I could sleep if I tried," he admits.

"No?"

He treats me to one last devilish grin, slowly shaking his head. "No. Can't waste this."

"Waste what?"

He grabs my hand in his, bringing my knuckles up to his lips. His eyes remain glued to mine as he feathers a soft kiss across the skin.

"You inspire me." He allows his words to linger in the air between us. Then he drops his hold on me, rushing to his car and jumping behind the wheel. He cranks the ignition, which roars to life, grabbing the attention of a few valet attendants and early-morning stragglers making their way to whatever hotel they're staying at.

As he's about to drive off, he glances back at me. "You've *always* inspired me."

CHAPTER SIX

I STARE OUT the windows of the airline lounge, watching airplanes prepare to depart. I've always found airports fascinating. It probably comes from my mother's background as a flight attendant and her love of flying, but something about air travel speaks to the romantic in me, even if it's nowhere as glamorous as it once was.

"Thank God for espresso." Chloe's voice cuts through my moment of peace. I shift my eyes forward as she plops onto the chair across from me. "It's good for what ails you. Like I always say…"

"I know, I know. When you need something stronger than coffee but weaker than cocaine."

"Precisely. So, back to work tomorrow?" She avoids my eyes, looking out at the runway.

"Don't think you're getting out of this so easily," I warn, then lean toward her, lowering my voice. "Who was that guy I saw you practically humping in the lobby?"

"Humping? Did you just say humping?"

I take a sip of my coffee, needing it to keep my eyelids open. Thankfully, my body has learned to function on minimal sleep so the few hours I had once I returned to my room is enough to trick my body into thinking it got more.

"You're deflecting. Just like you did the entire ride to the airport."

"Which lasted all of ten minutes."

"Still…" I raise my brows in expectation, a silent warning I have no intention of dropping the subject until she talks.

When I walked into the lobby to meet Chloe earlier, I was convinced my eyes were deceiving me. Or there was a Chloe doppelgänger roaming the streets of Vegas. The last thing I expected to encounter was my friend, who's always shunned any semblance of romance, wrapped in a man's embrace, about to kiss him. Until a group of rowdy guys, who didn't look old enough to drink, bumped into her, making her lose her balance. We'd been in Vegas for four days and she never mentioned meeting a guy. Based on the way he looked at her, this was not their first encounter.

Then again, I haven't told her about running into Asher. I'm not prepared for the barrage of questions she'll inevitably have. I'm still uncertain how to answer my own, especially after his admission that I've always inspired him.

"You can't avoid this forever. We do have a five-hour flight where I can continue to pester you until you tell me what I want to know. And I can be *very* annoying. You should know that by now."

Her mouth in a tight line, she studies me for a few moments, then sighs. "Fine." Uncrossing her arms, she brings her espresso back to her lips, taking a sip. "Remember the club we went to our first night here?"

I roll my eyes. "I'd rather forget it."

"Wouldn't we all." She mirrors my own sentiments on the ridiculousness of this weekend.

"So..." I arch an expectant brow.

"Remember when I excused myself to get a drink after Bernadette demanded blow job shots at the top of her lungs?"

I nod.

"Well, after I got my drink and was on my way back, some guy came up to me thinking I was a prostitute. I tried to tell him I wasn't, but I'm pretty sure he was dropped on his head too many times as a child because he refused to believe me."

"So... What? You see him in the lobby this morning and decide to kiss him?"

She scrunches up her face. "God no. If I ever run into him again, I'll knee him in the balls, like I should have the other night. But before I had the chance, an arm wrapped around me and pried me out of his grasp."

"An arm?" I give her a sideways glance.

A smile unlike any I've seen on my friend's face pulls on her mouth, serenity engulfing her. "A really muscular and defined arm dressed in a blazer." She stares into the distance for another beat before returning her eyes to mine. "He ended up sending the guy packing with his balls between his legs. Then I thought *he* was trying to pick me up because he called me 'Dick Girl'. In reality, he was calling me that because of the stupid penis necklace Bernadette insisted we all wear."

"I didn't think you were gone *that* long."

"I wasn't."

"Apparently long enough for him to leave an impression on you."

"That, and we kept bumping into each other all weekend. The other night, I went to the Italian restaurant off the casino floor to get something to eat before the striptease and pole dance classes. He was there. Sat next to me. Had this incredibly sensual conversation. Paid for my tab. Then this morning, as I was riding down to the lobby, the elevator stopped on the floor below mine. Wouldn't you know it? When the doors opened, he stood there, waiting to get on. So we walked to the lobby together, then he left."

"But—"

"He came back. Said he couldn't leave without kissing me." Her mouth crawls into a dreamy smile again, a blush blooming on her cheeks as she seems to glow from the memory.

I can't remember the last time Chloe has talked about a guy like this. Hell, I can't remember the last time she's talked about a guy…period. She has her reasons, the most prominent being an alcoholic mother she's been taking care of the past decade. She doesn't think she can manage both.

"And, considering you saw the rest, that brings you up to speed."

"So… Who is he?"

She sips her espresso. "Like I told you earlier, just some guy."

"His name would suffice."

She shrugs. "I don't know it."

My jaw slackens and I lean toward her. "You mean to tell me that, of the three times you've seen him—"

"Four, if you count him coming back to try to kiss me."

"Whatever…" I wave her off. "That's not the point. The point is that you never thought to ask him his name?"

"I *did* think of it."

"A name is usually the *first* thing I ask. You'd think with all the time you spent 'bumping' into each other this weekend, you would have gotten that much."

"It's just…" She exhales, visibly flustered. I want to ask who this imposter is and what she's done with my friend. The woman who doesn't let anyone or anything get to her. "Every time I saw him…" Her expression softens as she shakes her head, her tone contemplative. Her eyes shine with weightlessness. "It was quiet."

"Quiet? What do you mean?"

Setting her small cup on the coffee table between us, she angles toward me. "All the noise of my life…" Her voice is no louder than a whisper, as if worried someone she knows might overhear and announce to the world that underneath the hard outer shell is someone who wants the same thing we all do. "It was…gone."

I nod. Although Chloe and I aren't as close as we once were, there's something to be said about being around when the shit hits the fan, so to speak. And I was there when the shit hit the fan in Chloe's life. When her parents divorced. When she left the quaint, upper middle-class neighborhood in Connecticut and started a new life in New Jersey with her mother. When she tried to hide the fact that her mother was an alcoholic.

But I knew.

Chloe can hide from a lot of people. But she can't hide from me. I see through it all. Even the shit she doesn't think anyone knows.

"Sometimes you just need someone to quiet it for a minute," I respond thoughtfully, giving her a reassuring smile.

"Because of that, I didn't think a name was necessary."

Our eyes lock, my expression relaying complete understanding. Then her lips turn into a devious grin. "You *do* have to admit, the entire scenario is kind of hot. Not knowing his name, anything about him…"

"*Kind of* hot?" I giggle, fanning myself. "Try off the charts! I noticed the chemistry between you two right away, even if all he did was kiss your cheek. It was incredibly…sexy. I can't imagine how it made *you* feel."

"Like I could let go. For once, I didn't worry about the fact that we're polar opposites. That he's presumably this guy who has his shit together, whereas I'm lucky if I don't lock myself out of my apartment on a daily basis. But each time I saw him, I didn't think about any of that, didn't try to distance myself because of how it would play out. It's almost like we were in our own little bubble."

"Bubbles can be good," I respond, knowing all too well what she's going through. I felt the same way with Asher all evening. Like we were protected from the reality of who we were to each other, even if for a brief moment. "Especially a bubble that sexy." My voice brightens, and I hope Chloe can't see past *my* walls as easily as I can peer through hers.

She stares at me for a split second with her analytical eyes. I hold my breath, waiting for her to pounce. Then she breaks into a laugh, and I follow, sending up a silent prayer. I'm not sure how I'll ever be able to explain my night with Asher to anyone. I'm not sure I want to. I want to keep that memory mine. Hold it close and cherish it once I return to New York.

"So, what do you think the girls are up to today?" she asks once our laughter dies down.

"Knowing Bernadette, something cliché and inappropriate."

"If I ever get that lonely and desperate for attention, promise me you'll smack some sense into me and tell me I don't need to stay in a loveless marriage. That there's better out there for me."

"You know I will," I assure her just as a chiming echoes from her cell phone.

She glances to where it sits on the table, and I steal a peek, seeing her mother's name appear on the screen. With haste, she grabs the phone, firing off a quick text before placing it back down.

"She doing okay?" I ask, a touch of hesitation in my voice.

"Yeah." She reaches for her espresso, finishing it. "She's been dating this guy who works in the same building." She looks past me, a smile pulling on her lips. So uncharacteristic. "It's actually a sweet story. Somehow, they kept riding up to their floors in the same elevator. After about a week, he mentioned it to her. Said he couldn't ignore it anymore, that it was a sign."

"Hmm… A sign?" My lips quirk up.

"That's *not* the same thing," she snips back, fully aware I'm referring to her multiple encounters with her mystery man this weekend.

The same could be said about my chance encounter with Asher. Maybe it was a sign that I shouldn't have erased him from my life. But it's harder to call one random meeting a sign.

"Mom works in the same building as Aaron. There's a decent likelihood of running into him again. This thing with me and…whoever he is, well… It's different. I have a better chance of winning the lottery than seeing him again."

"You're probably right, but what if you do?"

"It'll never happen," she retorts. "I'm about to get on a flight back to New York. He was headed…" She waves her hand around, "wherever. So yeah. Not going to happen."

"But if it does?" I press, this time more out of curiosity. A part of me wants…*needs* to hear Chloe admit that maybe she'll consider pursuing something, despite all the obstacles in her life, even if many of them are self-imposed. Then I won't feel so mixed up about Asher. The way his fingers warmed my skin. The way his body felt against mine. The way his words filled me with hope.

"It won't," she insists.

"But if it does?"

"It won't."

"Yeah, but if it does?"

She groans, dramatically rolling her eyes. "Fine. If by some miracle I *do* see him again, maybe I'll admit there might be a reason for it all."

I nod, leaning back into my chair, content with her answer.

"But it won't happen," she adds.

I glare at her. "Always have to have the last word, don't you?"

"Always."

Her phone dings once more, probably another text from her mother, and she grabs it. "Shit," she mutters as my own phone chimes.

"What is it?" I reach into my bag, retrieving my cell. A part of me hopes it's a text from Asher. Instead, it's an alert from the airline. "Dammit."

"Yup. Flight to JFK is canceled."

I close my eyes, pinching the bridge of my nose. "Just how I want to spend my day. Stuck in the airport." Normally, a canceled flight wouldn't bother me. But I was looking forward to getting on that plane and catching up on my sleep. I hate the idea of sitting in this hellhole all day while we wait for another flight.

"And not any airport." She gestures in the direction of the terminal, past the doors of the serene lounge, the clanging of slot machines faint but still ever present. I have a feeling I'm going to hear that noise for the next few weeks. "McCarran Airport in *fabulous* Las Vegas. If the Strip is the tenth circle of hell, this place is purgatory."

"Glad to see all those literature classes paid off."

"What flight did they rebook you on?" She looks at her phone, and I do the same.

"Red-eye. Eleven PM. And here's the kicker. No seat assignment available." I hold out my cell toward her.

"Me, too."

"It looks like they're cramming everyone onto that flight. What are the chances of us actually getting on?" I ask rhetorically.

"I'd like to say they wouldn't rebook us just to tell us no in ten hours."

"My mother used to work for an airline," I remind her. "They absolutely *would* do such a thing. I'll be right back."

Without giving her a chance to ask what I'm up to, I jump from my chair and walk with determined strides toward the front desk of the lounge, where it appears several other people on the same flight are attempting to rebook.

As I wait, I come up with a plan. If we're able to get seats, I'll take that as a sign I'm supposed to leave my one night with Asher as just that — one night. But if we can't, maybe it's the universe's way of saying we weren't supposed to have left things the way we did. That we're supposed to explore what I'm confident he felt, too. The connection. The electricity. The passion. God, I've missed having this kind of passion in my life.

When it's my turn, the agent waves me over with a smile. "Let me guess. You're on the canceled flight to JFK."

"Yes. Both my friend and I were rebooked on the red-eye tonight without any seat assignment. What are the chances we'll actually get on that flight?"

"I'm sure—"

"I know how these things work," I interrupt. "My mother is a former airline employee. We suffered through all those standby employee trips for years. And I'd rather not have to do that again. So just tell me how far down the list we are. Unless you can get us seats now."

Blowing out a sigh, she taps at her keyboard for a moment. "What's your name?"

"Isabella Nolan. And my friend is Chloe Davenport."

She refocuses on the screen, a slight cringe crossing her expression. "It's oversold," she tells me, although I already knew that. "Doesn't mean you *won't* get on."

"But we're pretty far down on the request list, right?"

"Since you're a displaced traveler, you do have priority."

"But there's an entire flight of displaced travelers," I argue back.

"I can get you confirmed seats on the noon flight to JFK tomorrow if you'd prefer."

"Let me go check with my friend. I'll be right back."

"Certainly."

I spin around, hurrying back to tell Chloe the news. "I can get us guaranteed seats on the noon flight tomorrow. The red-eye is oversold and they'll most likely be forced to rebook again if they can't get enough people with confirmed seats to give them up. You in? Guaranteed seats or take a risk on the red-eye?"

She blows out a breath, rubbing her temples. It's more than apparent she's not too keen about being stuck in this town. Maybe I should have pushed harder to get us on the red-eye. But the truth remains. The instant I saw our flight was canceled, hope brimmed inside me. Grams always said, "*With every new day we're given a new chance.*" Maybe this is my new chance. For what? I'm not quite sure, but I can't shake the feeling there's a bigger reason for this.

"Guaranteed seats."

I brim with excitement, but do my best to hide it. "Give me your boarding pass and I'll get you rebooked." I hold out my hand. She places her phone into it, her boarding pass on the screen. "Thanks. Be right back."

I return to the desk and approach the same agent, handing her both our boarding passes. Within a few moments, we're rebooked. As I turn to head back to Chloe, my phone dings. I figure it's just my new flight information, but glance at the screen anyway. When I see Asher's name, my heart ricochets into my throat. Speaking of signs…

> **Asher:** *Safe travels today. Seeing you again was the highlight of my month. Hell, probably my year. I hope our paths cross again soon.*

I chew on my bottom lip as I read his text. I may regret what I'm about to do, may be trying to see something that's not there, but some other force is pulling the strings.

Drawing in a deep breath, I find Asher's contact in my phone and press it, listening to it ring.

"Izzy?" he answers almost immediately. All these years later and he still has the same number. Then again, so do I.

"Hey, Ash."

"Is everything okay?"

"I suppose…," I respond in a drawn-out voice before blurting, "My flight was canceled. Chloe and I are stuck in Vegas for another night. And—"

"Do you need a place to stay?" he offers without a moment's hesitation. "You're both more than welcome to come here."

"Are you sure? I wouldn't want to put you out. I know you're trying to write."

"An old college buddy is visiting today, so I won't get much writing done anyway." He lowers his voice. "And I'd love to have more time with you. I hated leaving you this morning with the thought that another eight years would go by without seeing you. Now I get one more chance."

A shiver rolls through me at the huskiness in his tone. I try to tell myself he doesn't mean anything by it, that his words don't carry the double meaning my sex-starved brain attributes to them. He's an old friend. Nothing more.

"We'll be there in about an hour," I say, not responding to his comment. "Maybe sooner. Is that okay?"

"Absolutely. I'll text you the address and gate code. Come on up once you get here."

"Sounds good."

"Perfect."

I stay on the line, almost waiting for him to back out, tell me this isn't a good idea. After the constant see-saw last night, it's not out of the realm of possibilities. But he doesn't.

"See you soon, Iz."

"See you soon, Ash."

I go to disconnect when he calls my name. "Izzy?"

"Yes?"

"I'm really glad your flight was canceled."

I exhale a tiny breath. "Me, too."

Chapter Seven

QUEASINESS SETTLES DEEP in my stomach as our Uber makes the turn onto Asher's street. My eyes are laser-focused out the window, avoiding Chloe's inquisitive stare crawling along my skin from across the back seat of the car. She hasn't pressed about this so-called "friend I knew in college" who we'd be crashing with. Now that we're driving past large estates that rival the size of those on all those celebrity lifestyle shows, I can sense her curiosity grow. I don't have to look at her to know her eyes are wide, her mouth agape, her brows pinched. It's how *I* looked a few hours ago.

"Right here," I tell the driver when I see the familiar gate come into view. He slows to a stop in front of the sprawling house, and I inhale a calming breath. This isn't a ludicrous idea, is it? God, I hope not. Only time will tell.

"Where the hell are we? David Copperfield's house?" Chloe quips.

"No." I make a show of collecting my purse and laptop bag. "But my sources say he lives around here somewhere."

"Sources? What sources? *I'm* your source for all things celebrity."

"Maybe there are some things about me you *don't* know."

More than she realizes.

My fingers on the handle, I pass her a conniving smile, then climb onto the sidewalk. It's strange not to be met with a barrage of cars or slot machines, as would have happened had we stayed at a hotel on the Strip. How does that saying go? "*Toto, I don't think we're in Kansas anymore.*" Well, we're certainly not in the Las Vegas Chloe was probably expecting. We've flown over the rainbow. At least I have.

I walk toward the trunk where our driver is retrieving our bags. When Chloe doesn't immediately appear, I head to her side, rapping on the window before opening the door.

"Are you coming? Or do you want to call Bernadette and see if you can crash with her tonight? Maybe stay up and do a makeover, then go to some Pure Romance party."

"I wouldn't mind going to a Pure Romance party." She scoots out of the car. "I'm all for women exploring their sexuality. But I'll pass on the Bernadette makeover. With the amount of makeup she'd cake on my face and the revealing outfit she'd stuff me in, I'd come out of there looking like a blowup doll." Collecting her bag from our driver, she smiles her thanks, then walks up to the gate with me.

I retrieve my phone to verify the code Asher texted earlier and punch it into the security box. Once the gate slides open, I continue up the elaborate driveway. When I don't sense Chloe following, I glance over my shoulder.

"Are you coming?" I huff once more, this time with irritation for good measure.

"I suppose…" She continues toward me with reluctant steps, neither one of us saying a word as she takes in the well-maintained grounds that make it appear as if a gardener comes daily.

But the second we round the corner and Chloe is treated to her first glimpse of the house, that silence comes to an end. As I knew it would. I'm not stupid enough to think I wouldn't have to tell her this "friend" is Asher York. I didn't want her to talk me out of this, to remind me of all the reasons this is a bad idea. I have enough of those on my own without her adding to them.

"Iz?" she says as we approach the front steps.

I face her, albeit with reservation.

"Who lives here?"

"Just an old friend from my undergrad days."

"A…friend? Does this 'friend' happen to be of the male persuasion?"

"Yes." I straighten my spine, but still don't look her directly in the eyes.

"Call me crazy—"

"You certainly are."

"But I get the feeling there's more to the story than this guy being just a 'friend'."

I worry my bottom lip. How do I explain I spent all night with my ex-fiancé's brother without her throwing a yellow flag on the play?

I can insist we're only friends, that we ran into each other last night and caught up, which *is* the truth. If I'd run into anyone else from my college days, that would be the story I'd tell. But I felt it the first time I saw Asher perform, before I'd even heard the name Jessie York. I felt it last night when I heard his voice after so many years. And I felt it this morning when we said what I thought would be goodbye to each other.

Asher will always be something more than simply a friend. He will always own a piece of my heart.

"What is it?" She rests her hand on my bicep, giving me a reassuring smile. "You can tell me anything."

"I know that. But this…" I shake my head, staring into the distance, as if the answer is there. I doubt there will ever be a solution to this jumbled puzzle I've trapped myself in by accepting Asher's invitation to stay at his house for the night. Drawing in a deep breath, I bring my eyes back to hers. "It's Asher York."

Everything seems to stop now that the truth is out there. Time. The earth's rotation. Hell, even the birds have grown silent, the breeze gone, everything still in the stagnant desert air.

"Asher York? As in Jessie York's older brother?" she asks calmly, her expression unreadable, which only heightens my edginess.

"It's not exactly a common name, is it?" I laugh, trying to cover my nerves, but it has the opposite effect.

"Asher York, the handsome, struggling musician?"

"Yup."

"The Asher York with a singing voice that makes you forget your name?"

"That's the one."

"The Asher York who looks like a fucking Adonis with a guitar strapped to him?"

"Yes, Chloe. *That* Asher York," I say louder as a blush blooms on my cheeks. If she only knew just how amazing Asher York looks now with a guitar slung over his chiseled body.

He's a far cry from the guy I knew all those years ago. Hell, if the band's lead singer hadn't introduced him by name last night, I probably wouldn't have recognized him. But I would have eventually figured it out. He still has the same raspy, soulful voice, still writes lyrics filled with so much passion and heartache.

"The Asher York who would have been your brother-in-law if you hadn't smartened up and called off your engagement to Jessie?"

"Exactly." I swallow hard, a pang squeezing my heart, my stomach churning. I shouldn't feel guilty about this. I haven't spoken to Jessie in years. But I still can't help but feel like I'm betraying him by being here, even if nothing untoward has happened between Asher and me.

She blinks once. Twice. Then she steps back, glancing around at the exquisite grounds, her voice chipper. "Well, it looks like Asher's not a struggling musician anymore, is he?"

"Oh, this isn't *his* place," I correct quickly. "He's just kind of…staying here."

"Like, house sitting?"

"Not exactly. He, uh…"

A motion catches my attention. I whip my eyes to the front door, Asher appearing. A wicked smile curls his lips as he crosses his arms over his chest, leaning against the doorjamb. It takes all my willpower not to ogle his biceps. Hell, it seems to take all Chloe's willpower, too. I can't blame her. He is really nice to look at.

"When I told you it was okay for you both to crash here, I meant *inside* the house. Not on the front stoop."

"Hey, Ash." My cheeks warm as my lips kick up in the corners, the response as innate as breathing. I avert my eyes, doing everything I can to hold on to the little composure I have left so as not to make it obvious there's something more going on between us. I keep reminding myself there isn't. We've never even kissed. Not like that. So why do I feel like a hormonally crazed teenager who's run into the object of her affection during a middle school dance? "Thanks for this."

"It's nothing, Iz. You know that." He uncrosses his arms, taking a step toward me. "I was thrilled to hear your voice, considering I thought you'd be 35,000 feet in the air by now."

I lift my eyes to his. "I guess the universe had different plans."

"I guess so." A beat passes as we stay in our bubble where it's just us. Then he remembers we're not alone and clears his throat, looking to my left. "Chloe. Good to see you again. I like the hair. It suits you."

"Thanks for letting us stay here."

"Anytime. I'd never turn away a friend in need." I notice the faintest hint of a wink as he gestures for us to come in.

"Hear that?" She leans into me as we pass him, entering the foyer. "He'll never turn away a *friend* in need, Iz."

"Oh, hush. It's not like that."

"You want it to be like that, though, right?"

"Maybe," I mumble in a barely audible voice, hoping she can't hear. But the devious expression on her face tells me she did.

"I'll show you around down here, then take you up to where you'll be staying," Asher announces.

"Great!" I respond brightly, spinning around to face him.

"Great...," he repeats, his voice full of uncertainty as he eyes me, my overly enthusiastic reaction presumably catching him off-guard. That's the downside of trying to hide things from someone you once knew so well. They'll know in a heartbeat when you're acting out of character. Just like I am now.

"So, the tour?" Chloe asks, stepping forward.

"Right. This way." He turns around, and I can't help but stare at his backside. It doesn't matter that he's wearing a white linen shirt and a pair of loose-fitting shorts. I can still make out the definition of his muscles through his clothes. I thought the dimples on his face were addictive. They have nothing on those right above his waistline.

"Come on, Izzy." Chloe grabs my arm, snapping me out of my mental undressing. I stumble, my face burning, but I push down any embarrassment from getting caught ogling him. We follow him into the spacious open living area that contains the kitchen, an informal dining space, as well as a sitting area, complete with large-screen TV and what I can only imagine is a state-of-the-art sound system.

The entire place boasts high ceilings, neutral walls and furniture, the space bathed in natural light. Based on the décor, I never would have guessed *who* owned this house. It's muted and understated. Apart from a glass display case in the corner of the living room containing a handful of Grammys that Chloe pays no attention to, nothing indicates this is home to Fallen Grace's recording studio.

Asher leads us down a long corridor, showing Chloe the game room, library, workout room, and the wine "cellar", even though I struggle to call it a cellar since it's on the ground floor. I feign interest in the tour, not wanting to make it too obvious I've been here before, although it's only a matter of time until I'm forced to come clean.

As we leave the theater room, I expect him to show her the one remaining space — the recording studio. Instead, he heads back toward the foyer. Grabbing our bags, he leads us up the stairs and down what he referred to as the guest wing.

After showing Chloe to her room, he turns to me, pulling my roll-aboard a little farther down the hallway, opening the door into a luxurious space that would rival even a five-star hotel. Lush, four-poster bed. Fireplace. Magnificent view. Ensuite bathroom I imagine contains a jetted tub.

"I hope these accommodations are up to your satisfaction." He enters behind me, setting my suitcase on an ottoman sitting below one of the windows overlooking the patio, the Las Vegas skyline on the horizon, majestic mountains stretching beyond it.

"I suppose it'll do," I joke, shifting on my feet. "At least it's only for one night."

"You're a resourceful girl. I'm sure you'll survive these inferior quarters." His eyes shine as they trace over my face with amusement, his smile wide. Then he steps back. "I'll let you get settled. I'm about to fire up the grill and make some burgers."

"Burgers? Are they—"

"Dad's recipe? You'd better believe it."

I place a hand on my hip, and his gaze floats to the sliver of exposed skin between my jeans and my shirt. "So he finally decided you were trustworthy enough to be given it?"

"Sure did," he replies boastfully, jutting out his chest. "Of course, it took quitting my decent-paying, respectable job, with great benefits and summers off, and moving out to California for him to share it. Said if things got bad, I could at least sell the recipe to make a bit of money." He winks, the gesture causing my knees to weaken.

"I'm glad you didn't have to resort to that. Your father's recipe should stay in the family." I pat my stomach. "Although I hope you have enough. It's been years since I've had one of your father's world-famous burgers. I may eat my weight in them."

"If I have to run to the store to get more ingredients, I'll do it. Can't have you leaving…unsatisfied."

My mouth grows dry at the innuendo, every cell in my body humming with the need to know all the ways Asher can satisfy me. I imagine he'd be able to do so in a manner no man before him has. In a manner no man after him will again. But that's all this can be. A fantasy. Nothing more.

With a smirk, he turns, his footsteps sounding his retreat. I go to my suitcase, about to unpack, when his deep voice fills the space. "Hey, Izzy?"

I whirl around, meeting his dark eyes swimming with deep indecision, the pendulum still swinging madly within. He licks his lips, squinting, searching for an answer that remains out of reach.

Then he exhales, his expression softening. "I'm glad you're here. *Really* glad."

He doesn't wait for me to reply, spinning around and disappearing down the hallway.

"I'm in so much trouble," I murmur to myself.

CHAPTER EIGHT

"WHEN WERE YOU going to tell me you've been getting all chummy with Asher York?" Chloe bites out the second I pull back the door to my room after changing into the only bathing suit I brought with me — a revealing black bikini that seems to make my already ample chest seem even more voluptuous. As if I'm doing it intentionally for Asher.

Maybe I am.

"Have you been waiting outside my room this entire time?"

"No." She grabs my arm, ushering me back into my room and closing the door. "But I figured twenty minutes would give you enough time to shave all your naughty bits to clear a landing strip." Dropping her grip on me, she sweeps her gaze over me, a smirk pulling on her mouth. "I was right."

I wrap my arms over my stomach, trying to hide my body, but my sheer, white coverup doesn't help much in that area. "Don't get your hopes up. There will be no landing."

"Why? I saw the way you looked at him."

"Chloe," I begin, but she doesn't let me say another word.

"And I saw the way he looked at you. How long has this been going on?"

Sighing, I collapse onto the bed. "Less than twenty-four hours." Although one could argue it's been going on since my freshman year of college.

"How?" She sits next to me, frowning, her brow wrinkled. "We've spent our entire weekend together. I'm pretty sure I would have noticed you talking to Asher. Hell, pretty sure Bernadette would have noticed, too. She would have included it in the gossip section of one of her daily 'Bachelorette News' emails she's been sending."

"Please tell me you don't actually read those."

She shrugs. "I may have fed her a fake story or two. But that's irrelevant. What's the deal with you and Asher?"

"No deal. We ran into each other last night," I explain, looking ahead with an unfocused gaze.

"Last night? When?"

"My body still thinks it's working the night shift, so I ended up going out and found an Irish pub with a live band. It was a nice change after the thumping club music we've been forced to endure this weekend."

"You mean you haven't been enjoying all that electronic crap?" she mocks in faux disbelief.

Brushing off her comment, I continue. "I went inside to have a beer and unwind. Imagine my surprise when the lead singer of the band performing announced a special guest by the name of Asher York. After he finished singing, he noticed me in the crowd and came up to me. We ended up hanging out."

"But you've been here before," she remarks, as I suspected she would.

Chloe has one of those analytical minds that doesn't miss much. It's what makes her one hell of a gossip columnist. She can smell a story before it even starts. I've lost count of the number of celebrity pregnancies she's accurately predicted before they've been announced to the public. Hell, there were a few she knew about before the celebrity's own publicist was made aware.

"After last call, we went to get a bite to eat." My lips tick up into a smile. "Then he wasn't ready for our night together to end, so he brought me back here."

"And what did you two do when you got here?" She waggles her brows.

"Played the piano," I answer.

"I bet you did."

"We did. Then we watched the sunrise before he drove me back to the hotel."

"So you mean to tell me you spent all night with Asher York… And not the Asher York you knew those years ago, but *that* Asher York." She points toward the closed door. "You're trying to tell me you spent all night with him, played piano, watched the sunrise, and nothing happened?"

"Precisely."

She pinches her lips together. "Did you *want* something to happen?"

"I don't know, Chloe." I get up from the bed, pacing as I attempt to make sense of my warring emotions. "The entire time I dated Jessie, I never once thought of Asher this way. Never looked at him this way." Until the day I realized the truth.

"I find that hard to believe," she mutters.

"Why?"

She rolls her eyes. "I may not have gone to college with you, but I saw how you guys were. Even back then. And I wasn't the only one. Hell, at your own engagement party, you spent most of the night hanging out with Asher."

"Because Jessie got drunk at the Sox game earlier in the day. Asher was only trying to make up for his brother's lack of self-control."

"Still…" Standing, she shrugs before crossing her arms in front of her.

"You guys have always been good together."

"We've always been friends."

She approaches. "What changed?"

I point toward the door, just as she did a few seconds ago. "Have you *seen* him? You just admitted you've noticed the changes."

"He's definitely got an incredible body now." She giggles. "And that hair… He's got that sexy Johnny Depp hair. And you know how much I love me some Johnny Depp. And so do you. Bet you'd love to tug on that. Am I right?" She nudges me, passing me a devious smirk that has me cracking a smile in less than a second.

"Maybe."

Her playfulness fades as she peers at me with all the sincerity I've come to expect from my lifelong friend. "So what's stopping you?"

"Oh, I don't know." I throw my hands up, my voice laden with sarcasm. "Maybe the fact I was once engaged to his brother. And not a brother he doesn't get along with. A brother who's also his best friend. He'd never betray Jessie like that. And even if he would…"

"You hate the idea of doing anything that would jeopardize their relationship," she finishes.

She knows me better than most people. She was the first person I went to when I found out I was adopted. She made me see it didn't change anything. That I still had a loving family, even if we didn't share DNA. Learning you're adopted makes you see family in a different light. Makes you treasure it more. My stomach roils at the idea of being the cause of any strife between Asher and Jessie. Which is why I cut ties with them all those years ago. My heart had splintered in two different directions. It was better to walk away before it was beyond repair.

"Do you blame me?"

On a long exhale, Chloe drapes an arm over my shoulders, pulling me back onto the bed. "I certainly don't. But you also don't need to sit here, making long-term plans for a future. Hell, you don't even have to make plans for tomorrow, since we're headed back home… God willing. Have fun and enjoy your time with Asher." The seriousness and compassion in her expression wanes, her mouth kicking up into a mischievous grin once more. "And if something should happen, you know what they say about this town, don't you?" She stands, heading toward the door. "What happens here…"

"I know. I know. Stays here," I finish, dragging myself to my feet.

"Exactly. Now, let's go enjoy one more day in the sun before we have to return to the frozen tundra of Manhattan." She loops her arm through mine, pulling me out of the room and down the stairs.

The instant we turn the corner into the open kitchen, my heart speeds up at the sight of Asher standing in front of the island. I can't stop my lips from parting, my eyes drawn to the flexing muscles in his forearms as he works the meat into patties. It's a simple act, one that shouldn't be considered erotic in any sense, but it sets my body aflame.

"All right, Asher," Chloe says, flashing me a sly grin, noticing my stare trained on him. "Whose house is this? Izzy said you're not house sitting, so what *are* you doing in a place like this?"

"Don't think I can afford it myself?" He catches my eye, winking, which only serves to turn me into a ball of putty. God, this man can wink.

"Last I heard, you were playing bars in LA, trying to make it big." This statement surprises me since *I* didn't even know he'd left Boston.

"Maybe I've made it big."

"Have you?"

It's silent for a moment while he considers Chloe's question. Then he returns his attention to the hamburger mixture, continuing to form the patties.

"Not yet, but I'm one step closer."

"What do you mean?" She looks from Asher to me, searching for some explanation. My gaze flashes to the display case in the corner of the living room containing the Grammy awards. Noticing my gesture, she turns, walking toward it. When she realizes who they belong to, her reaction mirrors what mine was. Mouth falling open. Dazed stare. Body stiffening.

"You're in Fallen Grace?" she all but shrieks, whirling around.

"Certainly not." A low chuckle rumbles through him. "They're not really my style."

With an unaffected attitude I find attractive, considering most men in his position would probably brag about their good fortune, Asher recounts the story of how he came to form a partnership with one of the most successful music acts in the world today, demonstrating the same humility he always exhibited toward everything.

"It goes to show that sometimes good things happen when we least expect it," he remarks thoughtfully once he finishes telling Chloe the story he relayed to me last night. Or this morning.

Heat washes over my face, and I lift my eyes to find the source. Has he always looked at me this way? Have his nostrils always flared as his gaze rakes over my body? Have his pupils always dilated with hunger as he steals a glimpse of my cleavage? Has this electricity always existed?

Maybe he acts this way around all women. Maybe he's behaving like this because he's been stuck in a house with a boy band for God knows how long and I'm the first relatively attractive female he's seen in ages. The reasons for his unabashed admiration of my body don't matter. All that does is that I've been given the gift of spending another day with him. Maybe Chloe's right. Maybe I need to stop worrying about the potential ramifications and just let the cards fall where they may.

"So…" Asher clears his throat, looking away. "What can I get you to drink?"

I exhale. A drink is exactly what I need to help settle these nervous butterflies flitting in my stomach.

Once we all have a beer in hand, he grabs the plate of burgers and leads us toward the open French doors. As I follow behind him, I can't help but admire his long, toned legs, the way his plaid swim trunks fall from his hips, the faint outline of more tattoos underneath his white, linen shirt.

"Lincoln!" he calls out once we emerge onto the pergola-covered patio, forcing me out of my thoughts. "Get off your phone and be social." He lowers his voice, addressing us. "He'll be done soon, I hope."

He sets the plate on a table beside the grill. I inhale the charcoal aroma, the combination of the smell and being here with Asher reminiscent of the summers at Grams' lake house. Now if only she were here, regaling us with yet another one of her outrageous stories, my heart would be full. Then again, it's best she's not. She'd probably force us all to do paddleboard yoga in the pool. Or she'd go skinny-dipping. Grams was never shy about the naked form, which served to embarrass Jessie and make Asher laugh.

"Who's *he*?" Chloe asks. Her eyes flame, presumably over the idea of one of the band members being here.

"Lincoln Moore," he explains as he places the burgers onto the grill, which causes my stomach to growl. My mouth salivates in anticipation of what I know will be one hell of a burger. "We went to college together. In fact, he was a workaholic back then, too. Constantly studying. He was one of those guys who lived according to the motto 'work hard, play hard'."

"I like to think that now it's 'work hard, play even harder'," a deep voice says, and I look in its direction, sucking in a sharp inhale of air when I see the figure approaching Chloe from behind.

I may have been a few yards away, but I'd be able to pick out the man who had my best friend in a passionate embrace in the hotel from a lineup. The mysterious, deep-set eyes with swirls of caramel and gold. The full lips that quirk up in amusement. And the tall, muscular physique that easily has a foot over Chloe. She was right. They appear to be as opposite as you can get. But does that matter?

Unable to move, Chloe stares at me with wide eyes, as if waiting for me to confirm that her suspicions are correct, that the enthralling voice belongs to the man she thinks it does.

This day just got *much* more interesting.

"Chloe, Izzy…," Asher begins, oblivious to the growing tension sizzling in the air. "This is my friend, Lincoln. Lincoln, this is Izzy and—"

"Dick Girl," Lincoln finishes, stepping in front of Chloe, his gaze glued to her.

"Dick Girl?" Asher furrows his brow, his stare ping-ponging between them. If Chloe hadn't told me about his nickname for her, I'd be just as confused. "Do you two know each other?"

"We've had the…pleasure."

I notice a shiver roll through Chloe's body, a strange response for someone who normally has no reaction to the opposite sex.

"Or perhaps I should say *I've* had the pleasure of experiencing her sharp tongue."

Damn. Now I can see what has Chloe acting so out of character. This guy is as smooth as a twenty-year-old scotch. And seemingly just as mature, which is what she needs.

"Yes." She holds her head high, thrusting her hand out toward him in a manner you'd expect to find in a business meeting, not a chance encounter between two people with off-the-charts chemistry. "It's nice to see you again, to *formally* meet you, Lincoln."

He takes her hand in his. Instead of shaking it, he brings it to his lips, not peeling his eyes off hers as he places a soft kiss on the skin. "Likewise, Chloe. I didn't think we'd see each other again."

"Either did I."

"Funny how that keeps happening, isn't it? How we keep…bumping into each other. If I didn't know any better, I'd think someone, some*thing* wants us to keep seeing each other."

I feel the heat of Asher's breath on my neck, followed by that low, husky voice. "I could say the same about you."

I turn to face him, the hair on my nape standing on end when I see the unyielding desire in his eyes. I bring my beer to my lips, taking a long sip. "Is that so?"

He slowly nods. "That's so." His expression changes, this one more curious than needy. He closes the distance between us. "Why do you think that is?"

"I don't know," I answer honestly, my chest rising and falling in a quicker rhythm.

"Me, either. But a part of me wants to find out."

"And the other part?" I barely manage to squeak out.

"Is so fucking torn." He rakes his hand through his hair, retreating into himself. Just as he did on more than one occasion last night.

"Me, too."

CHAPTER NINE

"SO, WHAT'S NEXT on the agenda for game night?" I ask in a bright voice after we cleaned up all the Jenga blocks that clattered to the ground, thanks to Lincoln getting cocky and not paying attention as he placed one, slightly skewed, on top of the tower.

The afternoon sped by in a fog of burgers, bachelorette party stories, and a fun game of Jenga, something I haven't played since my Introduction to Nursing Science class when my professor had us work together in groups to prevent the tower from toppling over, equating it to the teamwork necessary in the nursing profession.

"Game night?" Chloe scrunches her nose, her lip curled up.

"Yeah. Game night."

"Oh no." She quickly shakes her head, her reaction akin to one you might expect if accused of a horrific crime. "This isn't game night. That's something bored, married couples do to mask the fact that they have nothing in common with each other. The arrogant husband acts as if he's a know-it-all anytime his wife answers a question wrong in Trivial Pursuit. And during a rousing game of Taboo, she realizes exactly how little her husband listens to her. No thanks. Not interested."

I pass her a wry smile. "Not all games are boring."

Able to sense the wheels spinning, she narrows her eyes on me. "What did you have in mind?"

"You'll see." I jump up and walk into the house without a single look back.

Once inside, I head straight for the game room. I'm not sure how everyone will react to my idea, but we're all adults. If I hadn't consumed the number of beers I have, I probably wouldn't suggest this, but I need *something* to cut through the constant push and pull between Asher and me. An icebreaker of sorts. In my experience, this game has always been great at doing just that.

"I told you, Chloe," I say once I return to the patio, placing a box on the wicker coffee table. "Game night doesn't always have to be boring. What do you guys think? Want to take things up a notch?" I float my eyes around our little party sitting on a pair of couches placed on either side of the coffee table, girls on one side and guys on the other. When my gaze stops on Asher, he swallows hard, pulling his bottom lip between his teeth. "Or are you too chicken?"

"Never Have I Ever?" Chloe turns her nose up as she reads the words printed on the box.

"Why not? I thought you were an open book, that you had no shame."

"I don't."

"Then what's stopping you?" I steal a glimpse at Lincoln before looking back at her.

As day turned into night, their flirting has become a bit more obvious. The angst is killing me. I can only imagine how it's affecting Chloe.

"Fine." She pushes out a sigh, feigning annoyance, but I can tell she likes the idea. "But if we're going to play this, I'll need a fresh beer." She starts to stand, but Lincoln stops her with a gentle hand on her arm.

"I got it." His gaze lingers on her a beat longer than normal before shifting his attention to the rest of us. "I'll grab another round for everyone. I have a feeling we all may need it."

I watch as he disappears into the house. I probably should have told him I didn't want another beer, considering I'm already tipsy, but it's my last night in Vegas. Might as well have some fun while I still can.

"I'm going to take advantage of this break and go change." Chloe stands, her eyes averted as she walks away.

"Are you sure you're not planning to take advantage of something else?" I call after her, even though putting on something warmer sounds appealing now that the temperature has dipped significantly from earlier. Asher warned me it would happen. The second the sun disappeared beyond the horizon, it was like someone turned off a heating lamp, an instant chill setting in.

She waves me off, not even acknowledging me as she steps inside, closing the French doors behind her. I slowly shift my eyes back to Asher's, not sure what I'll see, whether it will be warmth and endearment or purposeful distance. When I peer into them, I see something else. Something I can't quite explain. He gazes upon me with affection, but it's so much more pronounced. More charged. More intense.

Standing from his position across the coffee table from me, he heads toward me, each step causing my pulse to kick up a little. He assumes the open spot beside me, draping his arm along the back of the couch. He leans toward me, his scent wafting into my nostrils, a natural aphrodisiac that has me wanting to burrow my nose into the crook of his neck.

"What do you know about those two?" he asks in a low voice.

"Not much." I fidget with my hands, the huskiness in his tone and lust in his eyes unnerving me. I hate not being able to read this man, one whom I once thought I knew as well as my own boyfriend at the time. Maybe even better. "Chloe mentioned she kept running into some guy all weekend. At the club. Then the restaurant bar. Then in the elevator this morning. Up until you introduced him to her, she didn't even know his name."

He lifts a single brow. "She didn't?"

"No. She didn't. Even though when I walked into the lobby to meet her, she was a breath away from kissing him."

He pulls back, tilting his head. "They've kissed?"

"*Almost.* But some drunk college kids bumped into her before they could seal the deal, so to speak."

"She was willing to kiss him without knowing his name?"

"Does a name really matter if you have a connection?" I push my hair behind my ear.

I should stop, knowing my words may very well spark Asher's guilt and pull him back. My guilt is pulling me back, too. But if I don't say it now, I'll always wonder *what if.* I've suffered through years of *what if.* No more.

"Does anything really matter if you feel a connection? Especially when finding someone you click with seems to be such a rarity these days. Maybe that's why so many relationships fail. They let all the outside noise cloud what they know can be an amazing thing. They let all the reasons they shouldn't be together overpower the one reason they should."

"And what would that be?"

"That they *feel* something."

He peers deep into my eyes. I physically feel the indecision, the contradicting desires tugging him in two different directions. One keeping him firmly in place, reminding him who I am. The other pushing him forward, imploring him to take a leap of faith. No matter what he chooses, he risks losing something. It's just a matter of what's more important.

When he tears his gaze from mine, his head hanging as he shakes it, I know the answer. In a sense, I've always known.

I'm about to excuse myself to find my own beer to drown myself in when his soft voice stops me.

"You're right."

I raise my eyes to his, my pulse gradually increasing as he reaches for my face. The seconds stretch to an eternity in anticipation of the touch of his hand against my skin. When I feel the subtle brush of his fingers, I sigh. It's such an innocent contact, but I love the roughness of his flesh on mine. The callouses on his fingertips from hours of playing guitar make me feel alive. More alive than I've ever been.

"I guess nothing else *should* matter." He pushes a tendril of hair behind my ear.

I lick my lips, eyes focused on his deep orbs. His gaze shifts to my mouth, pupils darkening. I notice the tightening of his muscles, his chest heaving a little more, jaw clenching and unclenching.

"But that's not the case, is it?" I squeak out as he closes the distance between us.

"One second, I tell myself it doesn't matter. That nothing else matters." He runs the pad of his thumb over my bottom lip. His caress is so soft, barely noticeable, but the way every inch of me ignites, you'd think he were touching the most intimate parts of my body, my mind, my soul.

"And the next?"

"The next, I'm reminded of what's at stake."

I expect him to pull away, but he doesn't. So I keep going. "And what *is* at stake?"

"Everything," he admits, his voice becoming harsher, almost like a growl. "But you know what they say, don't you?"

I shake my head. "I don't."

"The worse the odds, the bigger the reward."

"And what do you hope to be your reward?" Hypnotized, I inch closer, his breath dancing on my lips. Like Asher, I may regret this tomorrow. Hell, I may regret it in just a few minutes, but I need to stop worrying about the future. I need to just live in the moment. After all, I'm in Vegas, a city where everyone lives in the moment.

"Everything I never knew I always wanted." He pauses, then adds, "Actually, that's a lie."

He flashes his breathtaking smile. I push down the thought that it's so similar to Jessie's, apart from the dimples. Perfect white teeth framed with full, luscious lips.

His grip on my face tightening, he digs his fingers into my scalp, the raw need in the way he holds me making my hunger for him grow. "Deep down, a part of me always wanted this, but I just needed a reminder of what I'd lose if I let the chance slip away again."

"And what was that reminder?"

"Feeling you in my arms last night, Isabella." He runs a lithe finger down the curve of my face. I close my eyes, savoring the delicious tremor his touch causes. "Nothing ever felt so…perfect." He pinches my chin, bringing my lips closer to his. So close. So warm. So wanted. "*You* are perfect."

I hold my breath, bracing for him to consume every part of me.

One minute, he's on the cusp of kissing me. The next, there's a vacancy where he once was, his touch gone.

"Shit," he curses.

I fling my eyes open, disoriented. Everything seems darker than it was mere seconds ago. Asher jumps up from the couch, stalking away from me, and my heart sinks. I'm ready to berate him for all these fucked-up games he's been playing. Before I can, his distressed voice interrupts me.

"We must have blown a fuse."

My mouth snaps shut as I scan the back yard. Now I know why everything seems darker. It wasn't Asher's confusing mood that cast a shadow over us. It's because the power's off.

I stand to join him as he stares down at the pool, the lights illuminating the depths gone. As are all the lights on the patio, the entire back yard dark. Looking to the house, we realize it's also devoid of any light.

"How?"

"I don't know." He shakes his head. "I'll go check." He squeezes my arm, then places a soft kiss on my temple. It's a crappy consolation prize, considering I was hoping for more, but it'll have to do…for now.

"I'll come with you to make sure Chloe's okay." I catch up to his long strides with ease.

"Oh, I'm sure she's *more* than okay." He waggles his brows as he holds the door for me, allowing me to step into the darkened house first, the entire place eerily still.

Asher rests a protective hand on my lower back, ushering me toward the kitchen island. It's probably a good thing, considering the layout of the house is as foreign as the Palace of Versailles.

"Lincoln seems to have disappeared, too." He rummages through a drawer by the sink, finding a flashlight. "Think he's helping Chloe slip into something more…comfortable?" He flicks on the flashlight, which illuminates the devious grin on his face.

"It *is* Vegas after all." I spin from him, heading in the direction of the staircase I can barely make out in the stream of light. As I approach the bottom step, I glance over my shoulder. "If you can't sin a little here, where can you?"

He catches up to me as I ascend the staircase with timid steps. "Is that what you want?" His husky voice causes the hairs on my nape to stand on end, a rush of desire pooling in my core. "To sin a little?" He narrows his gaze on mine as we crest the top of the stairs.

Emboldened, I come to a stop, angling into him. I don't move for several long seconds, sensing his composure crack, that vein in his neck throbbing with suppressed want. "Play your cards right and maybe you'll find out." I allow my words to float around him for a beat before I continue down the hallway, Asher following. I can almost taste the lust in the air between us. Tonight is about to get a lot more interesting, especially if the lights don't come back on.

Approaching Chloe's room, I notice the door is ajar. I round the corner, figuring she would have closed it if she were getting it on with Lincoln.

"There you are!" I say, heading toward where she stands by the window, still in her bathing suit. Apparently, she *has* been too preoccupied to change. When Lincoln walks out of the ensuite bathroom, I stop in my tracks. "Both of you."

"Did we blow a fuse?" Chloe asks, averting her eyes, fidgeting with her hair. Which is the Chloe tell that she's been doing something, or some*one*, she'd rather I didn't find out about.

"I don't know." I cross my arms over my chest. "Did you?"

"I don't think it was a fuse," Lincoln interrupts, joining Chloe by the window.

Everyone looks in his direction, following his line of sight. After watching the sunrise with Asher last night, I'm more than aware of what the view out that window should be. Instead of seeing the bright lights of the Vegas Strip, there's nothing, the only lights that of cars meandering along the streets. Everything else is barren. Deserted. Empty.

"Like I said," Lincoln continues as we all congregate around him, staring at a scene that's reminiscent of a post-apocalyptic horror film, minus the zombies feeding on human brains. "I don't think it was a fuse."

CHAPTER TEN

"OKAY, SO WHAT are the rules here?" Chloe asks after we've all settled back outside.

With no power, it was the most logical place to congregate, considering we have the fire pit to offer us heat and light. It's another reminder of my few summers at Grams' lake house. While there was electricity, that's where the amenities ended. No cable. No internet. No cell service. Our only form of communication with the outside world was a landline Grams put in for emergencies. I'd often hated returning to civilization, wanting to go back to how simple things were at the lake. Jessie seemed to careen down the narrow roads at breakneck speed to get back to the point where our cell service would kick in.

"I've never played the board game version of this." Her expression instantly brightens. "There's one. Never have I ever played the board game version of Never Have I Ever! Do I get a point or something? Or maybe I just win game night outright and we can stop this torture?"

I roll my eyes. "You're having fun and you know it."

She bites her lower lip, looking from me to Lincoln. "Maybe."

"That's what I thought." I catch Asher's eyes as he sits beside me. There's a hint of amusement and curiosity in them while he observes me in silence. An artist studying his subject, unearthing every crevice, every valley, every subtle imperfection in order to paint her with painstaking detail. I wonder if that's what he's doing. If he's writing a song in his head. He has that look about him. Excitement. Concentration. Inspiration. I like the idea of being Asher's inspiration. His muse. The Marianne Faithful to his Mick Jagger. A much younger and more attractive Mick Jagger.

"So… The rules?" Chloe's voice cuts through.

I snap my attention back to her, ignoring the smirk drawn on her face. "It's pretty straightforward. You roll this die." I pick it up, showing it to everyone. "On each side is a symbol that corresponds to a category on the cards." I grab one from the stack to demonstrate. "Whatever you roll is what you have to say. So if I roll this male and female symbol, which is the sex and dating category, I have to say 'Never have I ever ditched a date after the first ten minutes.' If I haven't, I move my game piece forward. If I have, I take a drink. The first person to cross the finish line wins."

"Have you played this before?" she inquires.

"I didn't even know they'd made a board game out of it until I saw it in the game room."

"Then how did you know how to play?"

I grab the rule sheet out of the box and wave it in front of her. "I read the directions. Not exactly rocket science." I pass her a sardonic smile, then return my attention to our assembled group. "Okay. Who's first?"

"Since this was your lame idea, you should go first," Chloe suggests with playful arrogance.

Passing her a smug grin, I say, "Never have I ever ditched my date after the first ten minutes." I grab my beer and take a sip, indicating I have, in fact, done just that.

"You need to roll and pick a new card," Chloe insists.

"After you tell me all about the poor schmuck you ditched," Asher chimes in.

"Why? So you can tell me I should have given him a bit longer?"

"No." His gaze remains locked on me as he slowly shakes his head. "So I know what *not* to do." He clears his throat as he nervously glances around our little circle. "You know. Research. For a song maybe."

"Really?"

"Why not?" His lips quirk up into a mischievous grin. I don't think I'll ever tire of the sparkle in his dark eyes as they look upon me with wanton affection.

"Stop cheating and roll," Chloe admonishes.

"Fine." I grab the die and toss it onto the table. It lands on a symbol of the earth, which means the subject could be anything. Taking a card off the top of the pile, I read the corresponding phrase. "Never have I ever gone streaking." Rolling my eyes, I grab a red game piece and move it forward a square. "Well, that's an easy one because it's never happened. Who's next?"

"I'll go," Asher pipes up, reaching for the die.

Chloe whistles when it lands on the symbol for sex and dating. "I have a feeling this is going to get interesting fast."

"You and me both," I mutter.

Asher chuckles when he reads the phrase off the card. "Never have I ever kissed a celebrity. Yeah. Definitely haven't done that." He takes his green game piece and pushes it forward a spot.

"You mean you haven't gotten in on some of the orgies Fallen Grace is rumored to host?" Chloe jokes.

He looks up at her, brows scrunched. "Is that really a rumor?"

"Fallen Grace fans aren't our target audience, but I keep a finger on all celebrity gossip. Rumor is two of the guys are gay and in a relationship with each other."

"Do I want to ask which two?" He leans back, brushing his thumb against his bottom lip, which makes me salivate, remembering how he'd caressed my lip like that.

Chloe squints, trying to pull some names out of her memory. I have no idea how she keeps all these celebrities straight. How she remembers who's dating whom, who's in whatever band, who's starring in whatever movie. Then again, she says the same thing about my line of work, amazed at how much I do as a nurse.

"I think Mason and Ellis."

Asher chokes on his beer, coughing a few times. "Mason and Ellis?" he grinds out, clearing his throat. "Did you seriously say Mason and Ellis are rumored to be gay and into each other?"

"Again, this isn't my area of expertise, so—"

Asher chuckles. "They are not gay." His laughter grows, his face reddening, tears dotting the corners of his eyes. I can't remember the last time I've heard him laugh like this. "Actually, none of the guys are, but Mason and Ellis? They're so far from being gay, they're not even in the same hemisphere." He draws in a deep breath to get his laughter under control. "Not that being gay's a bad thing. In my opinion, love is love, no matter who it's between. Well, within reason. Those child brides being forced to marry some sixty-year-old dude is disconcerting, but that's beside the point. Trust me. With the number of women Mason and Ellis bring back here, you'd think they were considering starting their own brothel."

"So no wedding bells between them in the future?" Chloe presses.

"Certainly not. Now, who's next?" He looks around the circle.

"I think Chloe should go," I offer.

"This ought to be good," Lincoln interjects, having remained silent during the rest of our exchange.

His aloof attitude reminds me of Asher. They both have a mysteriousness about them. An analytical way they observe the world around them, carefully selecting their words before saying anything.

It's a stark contrast to most men I've had the unfortunate displeasure of dating. Men who felt the need to impress me with so much bravado, constantly talking themselves up, not once asking me a single question. I didn't think it bothered me. I don't like talking about myself, especially considering the normal questions most people ask on a date — What do you like to do? What's your family like? How many brothers and sisters? The instant I tell someone I'm adopted, things change. There's a look of sympathy on their faces. I hate that.

The next few hours pass in a mixture of laughter, increasing sexual tension, and consumption of more beers than we should, but what choice do we have? The power is out, so those beers will only go bad. We're simply doing our civic duty of saving the beers from meeting an unfortunate demise.

At first, I was unsure how everyone would react to this game. To my surprise, it's gone over well, so much so that even when Lincoln is the first to cross the finish line, we continue, throwing the die and going around the circle, drinking if we've done whatever is on the card. We've even reverted to some of the original rules from when we played in college, requiring others to drink if they've done whatever was said, even if it's not their turn.

Once our laughter dies down after Lincoln told everyone how his ex cockblocked him by using her cat to curse him, I look at the coffee table, frowning. "We're out of cards."

I hate the idea of our game ending. While there's still some tension between Asher and me, the constant push and pull has evaporated. Like he's decided to just let go, allow the night to take us where it's meant to. We've returned to the way things have always been. Easy conversation. Laughing at ridiculous stories. Not wanting the night to end. Of course, the things we've talked about have been much more personal, but that's the nature of the game. And something I was hoping for anyway.

"Maybe it's time we go off-script," Chloe suggests. I whip my eyes toward her, a single brow cocked. "We stopped with the board game part of this a while back." She gestures at the discarded board. "Maybe it's time to make things more interesting and ask different kinds of questions."

"What kinds of questions did you have in mind?" I ask.

"I don't know. Something deeper. A little more…personal."

"*Therapist* personal or *sexy* personal?"

"Therapist personal." She holds her head high, then shifts her eyes to Lincoln before adding, "And sexy personal."

In a heartbeat, a charge is sparked. It's no longer an easygoing, albeit slightly risqué game among friends, both old and new. We don't have to share our thoughts with one another to know we're all thinking the same thing — this has the possibility to change everything.

"I'm okay with that," Asher states. "We're all adults. Not much makes me uncomfortable." His demeanor is calm, maybe even a little intrigued. He's not pulling away like I thought he would.

"We *are* all adults, aren't we?" I muse.

"What's going through that brain of yours?" Chloe asks, able to sense the wheels spinning in my head.

I look into the distance where the skyline of Las Vegas should be illuminated, but it's not, the entire world shrouding us in relative darkness, as if we're in a bubble where the events of tonight won't matter when the lights come back on. Where we can give in to our deepest desires with no consequences.

I grab a flashlight off the table and proceed into the house without saying a single word. Chloe wants to take our game to the next level. Well, we still need a pair of dice.

Making my way to my room, I open the bachelorette goody bag Bernadette put together, which contained mostly inappropriate items, including a vibrator. Apparently marrying the guy who knocked you up in college doesn't always equal sexual satisfaction, as was evident by her constant flirting with anything with a pulse. I toss butt plugs, eye masks, and body paint into my suitcase, finally finding what I'm looking for. Wrapping my fingers around them, I hurry down the stairs and return to the patio, three sets of expectant eyes meeting mine.

"What's going on?" Chloe asks.

"Like Asher said…" I hold my head high, despite the small ball of doubt forming in my stomach at the possibility no one will want to go along with this. But if we can't throw caution to the wind, can't take a risk during a blackout in Sin City, when can we? "We're all adults, correct?"

"Yes…," everyone answers, their voices laced with curiosity.

"I'm declaring a circle of trust…a bubble, so to speak." I wave my arms in a circle, drawing an invisible dome around us. "I submit for your consideration a new take on Never Have I Ever."

"I'm not sure I want to know what this new take is." Asher's voice is playful as he crosses his arms in front of his broad chest.

"You probably don't, considering it's how I met your brother…" The second I see his face blanch, I regret saying that. We hadn't brought up Jessie all evening. It's been as if there never was a Jessie. Regardless, I continue, recovering quickly. "But circle of trust." I waver on my legs, thanks to all the beers I consumed throughout the afternoon and evening.

When I'm met with more blank stares, I explain the rules. "We'll go around in a circle, saying something we've never done. If someone says they've never done something and you have, you drink. The changed rules apply to the person speaking. For example, if I say 'Never have I ever shot Abraham Lincoln', obviously no one here will drink. In that case, we go to the penalty round."

I extend my hand, revealing a pair of dice. But they're not your traditional dice. Considering our goody bags were filled with nothing but sex toys, these dice are sexy, too, one die containing an action, the other a body part.

Chloe looks at the dice in my hands. "How do we know whose thigh we have to bite?"

I swipe my nearly empty beer off the table, finishing it. "That's what this is for. Whoever the bottle lands on is the lucky, or perhaps *unlucky*, winner…"

"I am *not* biting Asher's thigh," Lincoln bellows, his voice deep.

"And I am not…" Asher grabs the dice and rolls them, "sucking his finger."

With an over-exaggerated sigh, I fall back onto the couch beside Asher. "Men. This game is much more fun with only girls. They don't care about this shit. We have no problem licking each other's tongues."

Asher and Lincoln simultaneously dart their wide eyes to mine, their bodies growing rigid at the mention of two women kissing. Just as I suspected would happen. Boys will always be boys.

"But fine," I continue, doing my best not to pay attention to Asher as he adjusts his shorts. "How about this? Everyone gets one free pass. Of course, just say something you know at least one other person sitting here has already done and you won't have to worry about spinning the bottle. Unless you *want* to…" I retrieve the dice and roll them, "blow on someone's neck." Lifting my bottle, I glance around our circle expectantly. "Are you all in?"

"Blackout Club," Chloe mutters.

"What?" I tilt my head.

"The first rule of Blackout Club…"

"You don't talk about Blackout Club," the guys finish in unison, and the lightbulb goes off over my head. Every guy knows a *Fight Club* reference when they hear one. They'd probably get their man card revoked if they didn't.

"Exactly." Chloe floats her eyes back to mine, raising her own beer. "Like you said, this is a bubble. We're all consenting adults… *Single* consenting adults. I'm in."

"Me, too." When Asher lifts his bottle, I exhale a tiny breath. I wouldn't have put money on him agreeing to this. I just worry when the see-saw he's riding hits the ground, it will be with so much force and velocity everything will come crumbling down.

We shift our attention to Lincoln. He raises his beer and we all clink bottles, sealing the deal. "Let the games begin."

CHAPTER ELEVEN

"WHAT ARE YOU doing? Contemplating the meaning of life?" Lincoln quips as Asher stares into the distance, brows scrunched in deep concentration.

The evening took a curious turn once we started playing our own version of Never Have I Ever. While there's no rule we say something personal or risqué, it didn't matter. It was assumed we'd go in that direction. Add in all the alcohol we've consumed, and it's become increasingly difficult to think of things we're certain someone else has done. My only saving grace has been the fact that Chloe and I are childhood friends. We have an advantage over everyone else. Correction… *I* have an advantage over everyone else, considering I also know Asher pretty well.

"I'm thinking," he answers. "Everything I come up with has been said."

"At the rate you're going, my buzz will be gone by the time you finally say something," I joke, taking another sip of my beer. "Hell, I may even have gray hair by then."

"I thought you already did," Chloe jabs. "Pretty sure I saw one the other day when I was helping you curl your hair. You are less than a year away from turning thirty."

"Oh, hush. It was merely sun-kissed." I wink.

"That's the story you're sticking with?"

"Damn straight it is."

Our laughter echoes in the stillness of the night as we turn our attention back to Asher, who's tapping a finger against his bottom lip.

"Okay, that's it." I grab the dice and shove them at him. "New rule. If you fail to say anything in the time allotted…say, a minute…it's an automatic roll of the dice and spin of the bottle. So let 'em roll, Ash."

"That's not fair." He glances toward Lincoln. "Isn't it unconstitutional or illegal for laws to be applied retroactively?"

"Generally speaking, yes."

"See." He smirks, crossing his arms in front of his chest, an air of superiority about him. "So that rule doesn't apply to me."

"Although, due to the grievous nature of your offense, I'd be inclined to agree with Izzy in this instance," Lincoln continues.

I smile at him. "Thank you. I knew there was something I liked about you."

"You bet."

"Traitor," Asher quips.

"Can you blame me?" Lincoln shoots back. "You're messing with the flow of the game. And like Izzy pointed out…" He lifts his beer. "I'm *also* losing my buzz. There should be some sort of punishment for that."

I face Asher, grinning. "You definitely deserve to be punished."

He twists toward me, his hungry eyes skating over my chest before meeting my gaze. "Is that right?"

My voice is husky as I lean closer, my breath dancing against his mouth. "Oh, that's right."

His jaw clenches so hard I'm confident it'll lock in place. I edge closer still, his body growing more and more rigid with each painful second that passes. When I'm a whisper away from his lips, I pause. All it would take would be a flick of the tongue and I'd have my first taste. But as much as I want that, I want this more. The knowledge that I drive this man to the brink of all reason.

Abruptly pulling back, I extend my hand toward him, grinning. "Better roll the dice."

His eyes are a pool of desire and lust as they bore holes into the fiber of my being. He's never looked at me with such unabashed desperation. Such primal craving. It's the way every woman wants a man to look at her. Like he can't go another minute without crushing my body to his, our souls intertwining, never to separate again.

"Very well." Not looking anywhere else, he slowly reaches toward my outstretched hand. His fingers tease the flesh of my palm, tracing a light circle against it before scooping up the dice.

I exhale the breath I was holding, my teeth chattering as I sink back into the couch, needing it to support me. Then he abruptly erases the distance between us. My heart catches in my throat, swallowing my gasp.

"But if this bottle lands on you, I'd be hard-pressed to call that a punishment." He's shameless as he drinks me in, starting with my dark eyes, along my lips, down my neck, settling for several long beats on my chest. "More like a reward." I grow lightheaded as he nears, breath by excruciating breath. "A very…" He brings his finger up to my mouth, and I plump out my bottom lip. "Very…" His touch skims my jawline and toward my ear, pushing my hair over one shoulder.

When he dips toward me, his heat skates along my neck and I fist the cushion below me, needing something, anything, to keep me grounded when I'm certain I'm about to blast off into oblivion. I don't even care that Chloe and Lincoln are witnessing this very public, very erotic exchange. We're in a bubble. There are no rules. No tomorrow. Just right now. And right now, I want more of Asher's words.

"Welcome reward," he finishes, pausing before retreating. I shoot my wide eyes to his, my chest heaving in labored pants like I'd just run a marathon in under two hours, setting a world record. "Two can play this game, Izzy."

Acting as unaffected as always, he refocuses his attention on the game, shifting empty beer bottles off the coffee table to make room for the dice. I attempt to fight the blush warming my cheeks, but I fear, even in the relative darkness, it's obvious. Chloe catches my eye, grinning slyly. I return her raised brow with one of my own, the two of us holding an entire conversation without saying a single word.

When Asher rolls, I turn my attention to him, unusually invested in the outcome. A part of me wants the dice to land on KISS and LIPS, then the bottle to stop on me so he can finish what he started. But I have a feeling even a kiss won't be enough to extinguish the fire burning inside me. Seeing him last night sparked the embers that had been crackling for years. Not even the most skilled of firefighters could extinguish this flame.

The dice come to a stop, and we all lean forward to peer in the darkness, cheers and whistles erupting when we see BITE and EAR displayed prominently.

"I bet Asher really knows how to bite an ear." Chloe playfully nudges Lincoln.

Maintaining his air of mystery, his expression remains even as he curves toward her. He brushes her hair behind her ear and whispers something. What I wouldn't give to be a fly circling them. But the raw electricity coming off their bodies would zap it in a heartbeat.

I can't quite figure out what it is about him that has Chloe turning into putty when she's spent the past decade remaining detached from every man who showed even a modicum of interest. All I know about him is he's a lawyer, and surprisingly also lives in Manhattan. Oh, and that a cat put a cockblocking curse on him.

But the fact that she knows so little about him doesn't seem to matter to her. Maybe all that stuff is inconsequential. Maybe the past doesn't matter. Maybe all that does is the connection. The chemistry. The electricity. Like I told Asher earlier.

"Well, let's see who the winner is." Asher swipes the bottle off the table and spins. It slides and skitters before slowing, our eyes following its journey until it finally comes to a stop.

On me.

I stare at the bottle, trying to silence my libido, who's shaking her pom-poms and doing a victory lap around the field.

"Well then. I guess it's time I serve my sentence."

Heat blooms on my cheeks as I slowly face him. "I guess it is." I pick at the label on my beer bottle, failing miserably at keeping my cool now that

I'm seconds away from feeling Asher's mouth on my skin in something much more intimate than a chaste kiss on my forehead.

"I'll take that." The throaty timbre of his voice causes my stomach to clench, my thighs involuntarily squeezing together. A puppet to whatever he commands, I allow him to take the bottle from me and place it on the table. "Now, where were we?"

When he curves toward me, every muscle tightens, my body turning to stone. I can't remember how to breathe, the promise of this man nibbling on my ear sending lust shooting through my veins. I try to tell myself it's due to the lack of intimacy in my life lately. Or the beers I've consumed. Or because we're stuck in a blackout in a city notorious for encouraging people to sin. But deep down, those things are completely inconsequential. I'd be this desperate for Asher regardless of the circumstances. I've *been* this desperate for Asher since the first time I heard his raspy voice come over the speakers at a club in Boston.

"Oh yes. I believe I was about to serve my sentence." His breath tickles my skin, every excruciatingly long second torturing me even more. I'm so on edge. So delirious. So hungry. "But can it really be considered a punishment when I'm getting so much pleasure out of this?"

Before I can utter a response, his teeth lightly clamp onto my earlobe. Sparks shoot through me and I arch my back. I do everything to fight back a moan, losing the battle the second he swipes his tongue along my flesh. If this is how I react to a slight nibble of my ear, I fear what his kiss would do to me.

Then again, I have a feeling I already know that answer.

His kiss will ruin me in all the ways I want to be ruined.

And in all the ways I'm scared of, too.

CHAPTER TWELVE

MAYBE INSTITUTING A time limit wasn't as great an idea as I originally thought. With our heads becoming foggy…apart from Chloe, who's only had a couple of beers over the course of the afternoon and evening…it's been increasingly difficult to come up with something no one's said in the time allotted. Which has resulted in more throwing of the dice and spinning of the bottle.

"Never have I ever gotten so drunk I had to be carried out of a bar," Asher announces, shooting me a sly glance. It was only a matter of time before he used this little nugget. He was probably waiting until he had a little more to drink, considering the story behind it.

With a smirk, I bring the beer to my lips, indicating I have, in fact, been carried out of a bar.

"Okay." Chloe's gaze flickers between Asher and me, able to sense he played a role in the incident. "There's obviously a story here. I need to hear it."

"Fine." I shrug, acting as if the night isn't permanently etched in my mind…and my heart. I'd never told Chloe the exact details of the night my relationship with Jessie ended. It was just easier to let everyone draw their own conclusions based on the few tidbits I provided, pretending to be too distraught to discuss it at length. By the time the dust settled, our breakup was old news.

My shoulders squared, I face her, steeling myself to get through this without giving too much away. "It was Christmas break my junior year of college. I was spending it in Connecticut with my family. Jessie was in Massachusetts. I had planned to visit him, but decided to surprise him and go early."

"Jessie? Your brother?" Lincoln asks, looking at Asher.

"Yes. They were, well…" Stammering, he rubs his hands over his shorts. "They were—"

"Engaged," I blurt out, not caring if he knows. It was years ago. Jessie doesn't matter. Or he shouldn't. But it's impossible to write him off, especially when my past and present have collided the past twenty-four hours. "Until that night." I swallow hard before my expression brightens, continuing the story. "Their parents are snowbirds who flee the cold north for the south every winter. The guys usually went down to Florida for Christmas. Well, Jessie was getting back into town that day. Asher was already back, since he was a music teacher and school had resumed. Anyway, I told Asher my plan to surprise Jessie when he got home that day."

I steal a glimpse at Asher, who stares at me furtively, brows bunched together. Not wanting to raise anyone's suspicions, I embellish the story a little.

"I had this entire scenario in my head. At first, it all *did* go according to plan. I even made Jessie the lasagna he loved, thinking he'd be hungry after traveling all day. When I heard the car pull into the driveway, I went into the dining room, taking a page from Julia Roberts' character in *Pretty Woman.* You know, when she surprised Edward wearing a tie…and that's it. Sexy, right?" My expression falls. "Until Jessie walked into the house and I could hear moans and giggles."

"Oh, Iz," Chloe exhales.

"He tried to apologize, promise it was just a one-time thing, but in my heart, I knew that wasn't the case, that it had probably been going on a lot longer, especially considering *she* was the one he ran to the second he landed in Boston, not me. So I stormed out of there. After getting dressed, of course. I was a mess and not thinking clearly. I was so convinced he was the perfect man for me," I lie, not wanting Chloe to poke holes in my story. It's not a complete fabrication. At one point, I *did* think he was the perfect man for me. Just not at that time. "As I tried to figure out what to do, I passed a bar."

"Which just so happened to be where my band was performing that night," Asher interjects, flashing me a smile, although it doesn't reach his eyes. I can feel his unspoken question about why I'm leaving out one rather important detail about our breakup. Maybe it's easier to put the blame on Jessie than myself. Or maybe I've told this version of the story so many times I can't be sure *what* the truth is. "Around the time we finished our first set, I looked up to see her sitting at the bar, some punk putting his hands all over her. But she was too drunk to realize what was going on."

"Not one of my finer moments."

"I knew some kind of shit had to go down for her to be there when she was supposed to be with Jessie. So I hauled her out of there before something untoward happened. Canceled the rest of our gig that night, much to the displeasure of the bar's owner, and took her to my place to sober up."

He swallows hard, and I can tell he's thinking of what happened next. How he comforted me, told me everything happens for a reason. How I took that advice to heart, thinking maybe there was a reason I'd ended up in that bar. Then how I almost kissed him, but he stopped me, telling me

I was drunk and upset, that he refused to take advantage of me.

"The next morning, as he helped me nurse one of the worst hangovers of all time, I told him what happened," I explain. "To which he said…" I trail off, blinking as the words come rushing back, words I'd forgotten in the haze of everything.

"You deserve to be with someone who looks at you every day as if they won the lottery." His eyes lock with mine, a dozen emotions swirling in his mahogany depths. Sympathy. Admiration. Devotion. All things I shouldn't see from him. But I do. They were there when he uttered those words to me the first time, too, but I'd refused to acknowledge them, his rejection from the previous night still stinging. Or maybe I wasn't supposed to see them yet. Maybe it wasn't our time yet.

Is it our time now?

I quickly look away, snapping out of whatever trance Asher's mere presence places over me. "So that's how I was carried out of a bar. Who's next? It's your turn, isn't it, Chloe?"

She doesn't say anything at first, simply gapes at me. I can see the questions in her stare. I narrow my eyes, an unspoken warning not to press the topic.

"Okay then." She straightens as Lincoln sets the timer. "Never have I ever given or received a lap dance."

"Try again," I taunt, thankful for the distraction. "Already asked."

"Crap. That's right." She pulls her bottom lip between her teeth, staring into the distance as she searches the recesses of her mind for something that hasn't been said and at least one person has done. I'm glad she's in the proverbial hot seat, because my mind's coming up blank, too. All the beers I've consumed tonight certainly haven't helped.

"Ten seconds, Chloe," Lincoln warns, waving his phone in front of her.

"Okay, okay." She passes him a wry smile, the wheels spinning in her head. "Never have I ever gotten freaky in an elevator." She brings her beer to her mouth, taking a small sip, although I doubt she's actually drinking. She refuses to admit it, but Chloe's biggest fear is turning into her alcoholic mother.

I lean back into the couch, not drinking. Either does Asher. I take solace in this, the jealous monster who's flashed her teeth a few times during the game remaining in check. For now.

"Remember, we're in a bubble. Circle of trust. Blackout Club and all that. It's okay if you have."

I glance around the circle, everyone shaking their heads. "Looks like you earned a penalty round."

Chloe reaches for the dice, acting as if it's no big deal. She tosses them onto the coffee table. When they land on SUCK and TONGUE, Asher and Lincoln whistle, their devious grins floating between Chloe and me, as

I suspected they would. They've been itching for us to make out all night.

Men.

"Looks like things are about to get *very* interesting." I waggle my brows.

"I suppose they are." She takes the bottle and spins it. Her sly glances at Lincoln every few seconds don't escape my notice.

As the bottle slows on Asher, I tense, the mere idea of Chloe kissing him making my stomach churn, even though there's no doubt in my mind she'd use her pass, regardless of the fact that Asher and I aren't a couple. There's still an interest there. A spark. Plus, it's girl code. Never mess around with the object of your friend's affection.

Can't the same be said for Asher, though? But in his case, it's even worse. I was once his brother's fiancée. If we were to kiss, we'd break the bro code in every way possible.

Then again, I'm pretty sure we've already broken it.

I exhale a breath when the bottle continues past him, landing on Lincoln. I whistle, passing her a playful smirk, as he casually leans back into the couch, his dark, devilish eyes trained on Chloe.

"You can use your pass if you want." His deep voice has a teasing quality to it. "I'll understand."

"Rules are rules. Plus, I'd rather save my pass for when I have to suck on Izzy's chest."

"Please don't," Asher begs, groaning. "Use your pass if you have to touch her ear, but not that. *Anything* but that." With a wink, he flashes me a boyish grin, his playfulness endearing another piece of my heart to him.

I love how one minute, he can be so sensual, so erotic, whispering how pleasurable biting my ear is. The next, he's the same Asher, whose full-bellied laughter surrounded me with comfort when I flipped over the boat we were trying to paddle in the lake. I thought he'd be pissed he got wet, but it didn't seem to bother him. Nothing ever did.

"We'll cross that bridge *if* we get to it," Chloe says, crawling toward Lincoln, straddling him, bringing her lips toward his. Apparently, this isn't going to be just a chaste kiss. "I believe the dice have spoken."

I avert my eyes, feeling like I'm snooping in on a private moment between them. If what Chloe told me earlier is true, they *haven't* kissed. They almost did, but then the lights snapped off, ruining their chance. Witnessing their first kiss feels invasive. And makes me a little jealous, wishing I were experiencing that same spark, same electricity, same excitement with Asher. There's nothing like a first kiss. The buildup. The angst. The hunger for more.

A finger brushes against my nape. I tilt my head to Asher as he rests his arm along the back of the couch, wrapping a tendril of my dark hair around a finger.

"So, when are you going to roll those dice and have the bottle land on me?" he whispers in a gruff voice. The hairs on my nape stand on end, every synapse in my body firing.

"There's no guarantee the bottle will land on you," I respond in a breathy voice. "And wouldn't it be a shame if I rolled those dice for them to land on KISS and LIPS only to spin and have to do that to Lincoln?"

"It certainly would." He licks his lips, inching closer to me, but I angle away, staying slightly out of reach, taunting and teasing him. "Then perhaps I'll just have to sabotage the bottle somehow. Use magnets so there's no way it *won't* land on me."

I give him a playful look of disapproval. "But that would be breaking the rules."

He continues to close the distance until I have nowhere to escape. "I've already broken the rules where you're concerned."

"How so?" I know the answer. I just need to hear him say it.

"I shouldn't be thinking about you this way." He traces a finger along the curve of my face, swiping my bottom lip.

"What way?"

"Like I've been starved for months, years, and have finally found a source of sustenance." He nuzzles into the crook of my neck, inhaling. "Like I've been wandering the desert, and you're the mirage promising to quench this unyielding thirst."

He takes my earlobe between his teeth, nibbling. This time, the sensation is much more charged, much more electric, the idea that he's doing this because he wants to, not because the game requires him to, flaming the embers burning within.

He locks his gaze with mine. "Like I've been searching my entire life for something when it's been right in front of me all along."

A slight rustling cuts through the still night air, and he floats his attention across the coffee table. I follow his line of sight as Chloe breaks apart from Lincoln. I'd almost forgotten about them, too consumed by the spell Asher cast over me.

He pulls away, helping me back to a sitting position. Just as Chloe crawls off Lincoln's lap, Asher curves into me once more. "Regardless of whether that bottle eventually lands on me, I *will* be kissing you tonight, Isabella. That's a promise. Just like I should have let you kiss me all those years ago."

Gasping, I shoot my wide eyes to his, feigning confusion. "I don't know wha—"

"Yes, you do. And I'll be damned if I make that same mistake again."

CHAPTER THIRTEEN

"THIS GAME IS rigged," Lincoln states over Chloe's feigned moans of ecstasy, her chest heaving dramatically as I blow a light stream of air onto her finger.

"We've been waiting for one of you to spin the other all night," Asher adds.

I stand and scoot around the coffee table, smirking as I return to my position next to him on the couch.

"When you finally *do*, all you have to do is blow on her finger? I feel short-changed." He casually drapes his arm along my shoulders. This feels right, like no time at all has passed since this was a natural occurrence for us.

"Rules are rules," I sing, giving him a knowing look. "We can't just make out because you want us to, hornball." I jab him in the stomach. "If you want to see girls make out, go watch a porno."

His eyes darken as they rake over me, narrowing in on my chest. "Want to join me?"

"Maybe later." I lean closer, my lips skimming against his. He sucks in a breath, his muscles tightening. "Too bad there's no power." I abruptly pull back, pretending to be unaffected when, deep down, I don't know how much longer I can last without tossing out the rules and kissing him like I want to. "It's your turn." I hit the START button on the timer app on Lincoln's phone. "Go."

Asher's Adam's apple bobs up and down in a hard swallow as he scrubs a hand over his face, attempting to compose himself. Expelling a long breath, he tilts his head from side to side, putting his game face on.

"Never have I ever taken a sexy selfie."

"Nope!" I imitate a buzzer. "Already asked. Try again."

His head falls on the back of the couch, looking to the sky. This is my first trip to Vegas, but in the short time I've been here, I've never seen the evening sky so clear, even last night. Now that there's no other light to fight with the stars, I can appreciate their brilliance.

"Never have I ever slept with someone whose name I couldn't remember the next morning."

"Try again."

"Shit."

He squeezes his eyes shut, and I can't help but admire the concentration. It's identical to how he looks when he's in the middle of writing a song. The focus. The intensity. The passion. I can only imagine his expression when doing other…things that require concentration.

"Tick-tock," I tease.

"Never have I ever…"

"Five seconds," Lincoln taunts.

"Never have I ever…" He brings his eyes to mine, his lips parting as he struggles to come up with something. As his gaze leisurely travels down my face, his mouth curves into a sly smile.

"Four… Three…" Lincoln continues his countdown as Asher's smirk grows, his eyes lighting up with promise.

One look, and I know he has no intention of saying anything that would keep him safe from rolling those dice, regardless of the risk of the bottle landing on someone else. It's a risk he's willing to take just to have the chance to kiss me.

But I'd let him kiss me even if it's not part of our game.

"Never have I ever…," he repeats once more, his stare never leaving mine.

Chloe joins in with Lincoln's countdown, their shouts reminding me I'm not alone. I force my gaze from his, counting along with them. "Two… One…"

Swiping up the bottle, I shove it into Asher's willing hands. "Spin it, baby."

He flashes me a devious smile as he returns the bottle to the table. Remembering the order we've been doing things all evening, he retrieves the dice and rolls. When they land on KISS and LIPS, I whistle, trying to mask the butterflies flapping in my stomach.

"I'm so looking forward to watching you two make out." Chloe jabs Lincoln in the side. He wraps his arm around her shoulders, pulling her close and whispering something into her ear. Judging by the blush building on her cheeks, I doubt it was something as mundane as the weather forecast for the week.

"Time to spin, Asher," I instruct, hoping my voice drowns out the thunderous pounding of my heart.

"With pleasure." Grabbing the bottle, he places it on its side and spins.

I scoot to the edge of my seat, watching as it goes around. And around. And around. Over. And over. And over. No other spin felt like it took this long, like it's on a perpetual roulette wheel. Now I know what gamblers go through as they watch that tiny ball travel in an excruciatingly slow circle, bouncing from number to number. It could mean the difference between going home with everything they've dreamed of or walking away empty-handed.

The bottle begins to slow and my body tenses, teeth tugging at my bottom lip. My breathing increasing, the seconds stretch until it finally comes to a stop. Right in front of me. I expel my nervous energy with a laugh.

"Well then…" Asher leans toward me, scanning me up and down. "I suppose it's time we finally kiss." Indecision flashes across his expression, the see-saw of his emotions returning now that we're about to cross the proverbial point of no return. "Unless…"

Not wanting him to retreat when we've finally made it here, I clutch his cheeks, forcing him to only see me. Nothing else. "I suppose it is."

I lower myself onto my back, bringing him on top of me. The instant his body presses to mine, all the reasons we shouldn't be playing this dangerous game disappear, only raw need and desire consuming his entire being.

"I suppose it is," he repeats in a seductive tone. His lips scrape against mine, sending a delicious tremble through me. Then he nibbles on the bottom one, the unexpected jolt of pain serving to intensify the ache in my core.

"The dice say *kiss* my lips, not *bite* them."

"I know." He pulls back, his gaze locking with mine so I can see the truth in his words. "But I've imagined this for years now. I need to take advantage of it while I can, while we're still in the bubble."

I inhale a sharp breath. "*Years*?" That's all I hear, not his insinuation that once the blackout bubble vanishes, so will whatever this is. That doesn't matter right now. All that does is this moment that's been almost a decade in the making.

"Yes, Iz." He nuzzles his nose against mine, the simple gesture making my heart expand so much it's ready to combust. "Years."

"What are you waiting for?"

He smooths a tendril of hair behind my ear, the seconds agonizingly slow as his lips descend. My breaths come in pants and I brace for my first taste. So help me, nothing better interrupt this from happening, not after hours of unbearable foreplay.

When his mouth lands on mine, all the tension leaves me in a moan, my body fusing into the couch. The joining of our lips is light at first, neither one of us pushing forward. As much as I want to succumb to the swiping of his tongue against mine, his breath giving me life, his taste on my lips, I want to savor in this. It may be the only time I get to know if he's gentle or dominating, sweet or savory, desperate or hopeful. I don't want it to end. Not yet.

"God, Izzy," he groans, pressing his mouth more firmly against mine. I don't wait for him to demand entry, parting my lips for him to explore me fully, to have all of me.

His tongue swipes against mine, penetrating, devouring, needy. I tighten my hold on him, losing myself in this moment. I wasn't sure what to expect. A part of me worried he'd kiss like his brother. Jessie's kisses weren't *bad*, so to speak, but it felt…wrong. Like there was no emotion behind them. Like he was kissing me as a precursor to getting laid. Like he was going through the motions, reading an instruction manual, inserting part A into slot B, then moving on to the next set of directions.

But it's different with Asher. I can physically feel the passion brimming inside him as he takes his time exploring, discovering everything I have to offer. He consumes every inch of me with his kiss, leaving no part unaffected. I pull him closer, wrapping my legs tighter around him and pulsing. Another groan falls from his throat as he concedes to my unspoken demand, kissing me with more urgency, more ardor, more everything.

He threads his fingers into my hair, tugging, pulling, making me burn for him even more. I try not to think about the fact that I'm kissing Asher York. That we've obliterated any line between friendship and…whatever this is. That I've put him in the difficult position of betraying his brother. For brothers as close as Asher and Jessie, this *is* the ultimate betrayal.

His desperate rhythm wanes, turning into something sweeter, yet still as deep. "If I don't stop now, I'll never be able to," he murmurs against my lips, his voice raspy and heady, evidencing how much he hungers for just a taste of me. He nibbles on my lower lip one last time, which causes a nervous giggle to escape.

He gradually pulls back, helping me into a sitting position. A movement out of the corner of my eye reminds me we're not alone.

"Well, that was unexpected," I say breathlessly, trying to downplay the electric currents still pulsing through me, my skin unusually sensitive to even the light breeze caressing it.

"Hopefully in a good way." Asher wraps an arm around me, folding me into him. It's not like before when he brushed his fingers along my skin. Now his hold on me is firm and purposeful, leaving no question in my mind, in anyone's mind, that I belong to him, and vice versa. But for how much longer?

"In an amazing way." I flash him a wide smile, then quickly turn my attention back to Chloe. "Now, I believe it's Lincoln's turn. Or is it Chloe's?"

They share a look before Chloe stands. "Actually, I hate to be the one to put an end to game night, but I'm beat. It's been a long day. And tomorrow will be another long one with heading home, provided the power comes back on."

"Always the responsible one, aren't you?" I retort.

"Always."

I steal a glance at my watch to see it's only a little after midnight. Chloe's sleep schedule is almost as out of whack as mine. She often pulls all-nighters on the weekends, since that seems to be when a great deal of celebrity gossip occurs. I highly doubt she's going to her room to sleep, a suspicion that's confirmed when Lincoln offers to walk her to her room.

The second they disappear into the darkened house, an awkward silence stretches between Asher and me. He drops his arm, increasing the distance between us.

"Sorry." He runs a hand through his hair, at complete odds with the confident man whose kiss consumed me mere seconds ago. "I know this..." He trails off, licking his lips, collecting his thoughts. "Well, I guess I could have used my pass. *Should* have used my pass." A subtle laugh escapes his throat before his eyes darken, his voice coming out a potent growl. "But I've been wondering how your lips tasted for years, and I couldn't resist the temptation anymore, to hell with the consequences."

Leaning toward him, I hover my mouth over his. "And how do they taste?"

"Like the sweetest drug."

I pause before asking my next question, unsure how he'll respond. Unsure if I'm prepared for him to reject me now that it's not part of the game. "Do you want another hit?"

Groaning, his fingers circle my nape, locking me in place. "I thought you'd never ask."

I crash my lips against his, thrusting my tongue into his mouth in one quick motion. If our last kiss was an explosive culmination of years of unrequited need, this one is like a bomb going off, leveling everything in sight, just leaving him, me, and this insane craving filling my blood.

Determined hands grip my waist, yanking me on top of him. My legs fall on either side of his, a gasp sucked from my lungs when I feel how much he aches for me. I circle my hips, and he tugs me harder against him. Chest to heaving chest. Heart to racing heart. His tongue penetrates me with more frenzy, more violence, more conviction to kiss me in a way that would ruin me for all kisses to come after this one.

A fire to submit to *all* of him burns deep, the myriad of reasons this is a bad idea going up in smoke. My hands go to his chest, finding the buttons of his shirt, fumbling with them as I desperately try to rid him of his clothes. He moans when my fingers dig into his chest, nails scraping before I reach for the hem of my shirt.

"Shit. Wait." He tears away and grabs my wrists, preventing me from going any further. Conflicted eyes search mine, as if I hold the answer he so desperately needs. I suppose I do. A second passes. Then another. And another. Then he exhales, shaking his head, his shoulders falling. "We can't do this."

Those four words are the equivalent of a bucket of cold water being tossed over me. Actually, it's worse. I did the Ice Bucket Challenge all those years ago. The chill that covered me then was nothing compared to this.

I scramble off him, shooting to my feet. "We can't do this?" I shriek, hugging my arms around my stomach. "You have no problem feeling me up and practically tongue fucking my mouth, but the second I try to take things to the next level, you decide you want nothing to do with me?"

"It's not like that, Izzy." He stands, advancing toward me, but I back up, my heart squeezing, my cheeks burning with a mixture of anger and embarrassment.

"It's not like what?" I've officially reached my breaking point of the internal tug-of-war he's been playing. "You've been hot and cold all afternoon. Hell, even last night. One second, you admire me like no man in my life ever has. The next, you push me away. It's fucked with my mind."

He parts his lips to argue, but I hold up my hand, preventing him from uttering a single syllable.

"Believe me, I understand your trepidation. Don't you think I have that little ball of guilt in my stomach, too? Because I do. But this feeling in my heart is so much stronger." I draw in a deep breath, struggling to speak through the lump in my throat. "I thought it wasn't one-sided. Apparently I was wrong."

"You know that's not true." He advances, brows creased, eyes still clouded with turmoil. "I just—"

"Don't." I step back. "I don't need you to placate me with excuses. I misread the signs. I *always*—"

"You've been drinking," he interrupts.

"So have you," I accuse.

He narrows his gaze, his expression borderline condescending. At least it seems that way after his rejection. "Not as much as you. My judgment isn't compromised."

"And you think mine is?"

He shrugs. "I don't know. But I can't have that on my conscience. I refuse to take advantage of you."

I blow out a sarcastic laugh. "Sure. You had no problem 'taking advantage' of me when you were kissing me."

"Izzy, that's not the same thing and you know it. It was just a kiss, nothing more."

That bucket of cold water he threw on me earlier has now turned to ice, his words shattering my heart. "I see," I struggle to say.

"I didn't mean it like that. I—"

"It's okay. You don't need to explain. It *was* just a kiss." I swallow hard. "Nothing more." Doing my best to make it appear as if his rejection has little effect on me, I turn from him, heading toward the house.

"Izzy, wait."

I glance over my shoulder, his eyes pleading with me to understand. And I do. From the beginning, I knew we were playing with fire. I didn't realize how much it would burn.

"Thanks for letting us crash here. Hopefully the power comes back on soon and we'll be out of your hair." I offer him a tight-lipped smile. "Good luck. I have no doubt all your dreams will come true."

Ignoring his further pleas, I continue into the house, shining the flashlight of my phone in front of me, illuminating the path. I don't even raise my eyes to acknowledge Lincoln as he passes me on his way back outside, much to my surprise.

Safe in my room, I release a breath, falling onto the bed. I lay awake for hours, listening to the gentle sound of Asher playing guitar on the patio, holding out hope he'll come rap on my door and tell me he's willing to take a risk.

He never does.

CHAPTER FOURTEEN

I SHOULD HAVE no problem sleeping. I'm now going on almost forty-eight hours with minimal rest. While my body may be exhausted, my mind is not, too preoccupied with the wild swings of Asher's attitude toward me, culminating in his final rejection. I had plenty of warning it would end like this, given the constant push and pull. I just thought we were past that. Or I hoped we were.

In an attempt to shake off this spell Asher seems to have cast over me, I toss the covers off and step out of bed. I grab a pair of yoga pants out of my bag, slide them up my legs, adjust my tank, then walk out of my room.

The flashlight of my phone illuminating the path in front of me, I pad down the corridor, descending the stairs to the main level. The house is still, peaceful, as it should be at three in the morning.

I just wish my mind could rest, too.

As I walk toward the refrigerator to grab a bottle of water, I make out the faint sound of a piano playing a beautiful melody. Drawn to it, I'm on autopilot as my legs carry me away from the kitchen and down the hallway, the music growing louder the closer I get to the recording studio. It's haunting, the top note remaining the same despite the underlying chord changing in an even rhythm of quarter notes.

I turn off the light on my phone so as to not alert Asher, allowing his music to lead me to him, each measure sounding more heartachingly beautiful than the one preceding it. As I reach the threshold of the open door to the studio, Asher's voice carries into the hallway, stopping me in my tracks. I peer inside, the room dark, apart from a handful of candles distributed throughout. The reflection of the flames dancing on the walls makes the song even more hypnotic and heartbreaking. With no distractions typically afforded us through technology, all my attention is fully drawn to the man sitting at the piano. I listen, unable to leave if I wanted to. But I don't, not when I hear him sing of unrequited love, of never being enough, of finally giving up and moving forward. Not moving on. Not getting over it. But understanding when enough is enough.

A fitting story for the situation we find ourselves in. Or at least the situation *I* find myself in.

The intensity and passion grow as he belts out the bridge, the raspiness of his voice addicting and soul-wrenching. I know why so many females flocked to whatever bar his band played in. There's something incredibly sexy about his voice, the way his fingers caress the ivory keys of the piano with such expertise. I started playing piano when I was young myself, so I know how difficult it is. But Asher plays it as if he were born to do just that. To write music. Share his talent with the world.

The song comes to an end, his voice ringing out against the perfect acoustics of the room. I debate trying to slip away without him knowing I eavesdropped on this private moment, but there's a vulnerability in him, evidenced by the way he sits at the piano — head hung low, shoulders hunched, fingers still clinging onto the keys as if it's the only thing keeping him afloat.

"That was beautiful," I say quietly.

He shoots to his feet and whirls around, his eyes wide as they search for me in the darkness. I step out of the shadows, a candle shining a flickering light against my face.

"Izzy, what are you—"

"Is that for Fallen Grace's new album?"

He doesn't move for several long moments, simply stares at me, torn. I keep my eyes glued to his, unwavering, silently pleading with him not to push me away.

"No," he finally says, his voice low. "It's one of mine."

With a nod, I continue into the dark room. It's warmer than the rest of the house, due to the lack of ventilation and windows.

"It sounds personal," I remark, studying his expression for a reaction. But there isn't one. His face stays placid, giving nothing away, peering at me with disinterest. "Is there a story behind the lyrics?"

That gets his attention, his stance becoming rigid, the vein in his neck making an appearance, as it often does when he's at an extreme of one of his emotions. "You weren't supposed to hear that. It's still a work in progress." His mouth forming into a tight line, he scoots past me. "I should go."

I whirl around, my mouth agape. Why does he keep pushing me away? I try to understand it, try to rationalize it's because of the sticky situation between his brother and me, but my relationship with Jessie didn't stop us from being friends. In fact, it was *because* of my relationship with his brother we became such good friends. Why can't we go back to that? I have a feeling I know the reason. I need to hear him finally admit it. To me. And to himself.

"Why don't you want me?" I call out as he's about to turn the corner and disappear into the hallway. My voice echoes, the desperation in my tone surrounding me. Mocking me. Exposing me.

He stills, stopping in his tracks. His fists clenched, he shakes his head as the battle wages within, pushing him to the breaking point. He wants to face me, but he doesn't. He wants to respond, but is afraid of what his words will reveal. He wants to wrap me in his arms, but knows with every embrace, it will become more and more difficult to walk away.

"What is so wrong with me that you can't even stomach the sight of me now?" I choke out, not holding anything back. Not anymore. "So what? We kissed. Like you said, it was just a kiss. It doesn't—"

"Is that seriously what you think?" he growls, turning to face me in one swift move. My heart rate spikes, the hairs on my nape standing on end. "That it was just a kiss?"

My mouth grows dry as a jolt of adrenaline shoots through me. When he stalks toward me, I back up on instinct, the power in his gaze, in his stride, in his aura startling me.

"I—"

He clutches my cheeks, stealing my protest. "Impossible, Izzy. Fucking impossible."

"What is?" I try to look away from his stormy eyes, but I can't, a force bigger than me keeping my stare locked on his.

"That it was just a kiss. It could never be just a kiss. Not with you. Hell, I told you I'd wanted to kiss you for years. That's true. I have. I'd lost track of the number of times I went to sleep after staying up all night with you and fantasized about how your lips would taste. Grew jealous whenever I had to watch my brother kiss you. God, Izzy."

His grip on me tightens as he brings his head closer to mine, a whisper between us. My breath quickens as I bask in his spicy, sweet scent, the aroma of citrus and wood wrapping me in comfort. The only comfort I've ever known.

"Every time I saw him kiss you, all I could think was how I should have been the one doing that."

I open my mouth, not wanting to bring Jessie into our bubble. That would cause it to burst, to implode into a fiery mess. He cuts me off before I can say anything.

"Every time I saw him place his hand on your leg and run his finger along your exposed flesh, all I could think about was how cavalier he was about it. How he should have appreciated you for the fucking gift you were."

He loosens his hold on my face, one hand going to my nape, the other sliding down my frame. When he lifts the hem of my tank top and caresses the exposed flesh, a shiver runs through my body.

"And every time I said good night to you, only for you to go to bed, to *his* bed…" His nostrils flare, a tick in his jaw. "All I could think about was that it should have been *my* bed. *My* arms that held you. *My* body that worshipped yours."

No words come. How can I respond? Tell him I always craved his company but assumed he'd never be interested in me, not when so many girls who were more mature and experienced than me sought him out? That every time I heard him perform a new song, a part of me wished he were singing about me?

That the real reason I ended things with Jessie was because I realized I'd also fallen in love with Asher?

"I don't have the same competitive nature as my brother," he continues when I don't say anything. "I don't need to prove I can be the best at everything I do. I never wanted to graduate at the top of my class. Be class president. Run the world. The only person I care about being better than is the person I am today." He chuckles, a momentary break in the tension. "Although, after tonight, you could probably argue I haven't exactly been a good person."

My chest squeezes at the reminder of the position I put him in. I told myself I wouldn't allow him to put his relationship with his brother at risk. But that was before I was cast under his spell again. Before I was reminded of why I'd allowed him to possess a piece of my heart. Before I had a taste of him after years of fantasizing. It's left me desperate for more.

"I've never wanted something he had, never wanted to be him." He returns his hands to my face, leaning toward me. "Until you." His hold on me tightens as he erases the last bit of space between us, sealing my mouth with his.

He leaves me no room to protest, his kiss touching every part of me, stealing my breath, invading my soul as I succumb to what this man does to me with just a simple meeting of our mouths. But nothing with us has ever been simple. His kiss isn't, either. In it is a piece of his heart. And mine. Fusing together in this beautiful connection most people search for their entire lives.

I wrap my arms around his broad shoulders, curving into him, even a heartbeat between our bodies too much space. He moans, a surge of electricity reawakening me. His hands roam my body, his sensual touch making me feel wanted. Not like so many other men who just wanted to cop a quick feel of my chest before pulling out their dick. But not Asher. Hell, he hasn't even brushed a single finger against my breasts, which only increases my need, moisture pooling between my thighs at the thought.

A hand grips my hip, and he backs me across the room until my legs hit the baby grand piano. Grasping my ass, he lifts me onto the surface with ease, as if I weigh no more than a speck of dust. I try to stay in shape, but I'm not a waif. My five-seven frame is leggy, my Mexican heritage giving me an ample chest and curvy hips.

When I part my thighs and pull his body between them, he groans, his lips leaving mine for the first time. A man starved, he runs his tongue along my jawline, the scruff of his unshaven face causing a delicious ache to settle in my core. I've never been so aroused, so ready to toss aside reason for one moment of ecstasy.

"Fuck, Izzy," he growls as I tighten the grip my legs have around his waist. When his erection throbs against me, I whimper, my body trembling from the sensation of him through our fully clothed bodies. If I'm on the cusp of coming undone from this, I can only imagine what it'll be like when it's flesh against flesh. I refuse to wait any longer to find out.

I fist his shirt in my hand, tugging him into me, my fingers fumbling for the buttons. He straightens, abruptly stepping back. My heart drops to the pit of my stomach as my eyes lock with his. I swallow hard, unsure if I can handle him rejecting me yet again.

Then a lazy smirk crawls across his lips as he leisurely unfastens the top button of his shirt, making a show of it. My shoulders falling out of relief, I place my hands behind me on the piano, sucking in my bottom lip.

"If you're trying to audition for one of those all-male reviews, I'll have you know they're quick with taking off their shirts. Hell, most of the time they're not wearing a shirt at all."

He pauses, mid-unbutton, a single brow cocked. "Is that right?"

"That's right."

"Well then…" He smiles deviously. "Maybe you should give me a lesson."

"In what?" I straighten, my voice rising in pitch. "Stripping?"

His eyes flicker with mischief as he closes the distance between us, leering at me in a way that strips me bare. In the most tantalizing of ways. "Didn't you say Bernadette made you all go to striptease and pole dance lessons?"

"She did, but…"

He leans into me and his teeth capture my earlobe, tugging on it, erasing any objection from my mind. I'll do whatever he asks if it means I'll be rewarded with his tongue on me. On every inch of me.

"Please, Izzy. Dance for me. Just like you used to whenever our band played 'Amante'."

All it takes is hearing the title of one of his earlier songs to be transported back to my college days. To my roommate dragging me to a club where a hot, local band was playing. To falling in love with the music and making a point of returning week after week. To being unable to stop from swaying my hips whenever they played that particular song, a sensual, Latin-inspired rhythm that spoke to me the first time I heard the opening measures.

He extends a hand to me. Does the idea of stripping for Asher turn me on? Hell yes. But to this song? One I always felt he wrote for me after he noticed me in the audience that first night. After his earlier confession that he's been wanting to kiss me for years, it's not that far out of the realm of possibility.

My eyes focused on his dark pools, I place my hand in his. In one quick movement, he pulls me off the piano, spinning me around so my back is pressed against his front. The sudden motion steals my breath, a gasp escaping. My surprise turns into a burning need when he sensually circles his hips against me.

"When I wrote it, I always imagined you stripping to it. Even though I didn't even know your name." He runs a calloused hand along my collarbone before easing his way up to my throat, wrapping his fingers around it. I crane my head, my breath coming in pants, a surge of hunger filling me from his possessive hold. His mouth skates near my earlobe, teeth nipping at my flesh. "Never thought that fantasy would come true."

He drops his hold on me, stepping back. I remain still, a bundle of sensation. How the hell did we get here? How did I go from wanting to clear my head to considering giving Asher a striptease in the span of mere minutes? As is always the case with us, some things just can't be explained.

The opening lines sound from Asher's cell phone, and I close my eyes. My body still tingling, I'm on the brink of unraveling, a slave to Asher's touch. And I'll do whatever it takes to have his touch again.

I glance over my shoulder, flashing him a seductive smile. My tongue skates across my bottom lip in an elaborate show, as if I'm about to feast on the finest of delicacies. That's exactly what this man is. Six-foot-two. Broad shoulders. Defined muscles. And that perfect V disappearing into the waistband of his shorts. I could overindulge on him for hours and still not get my fill.

With slow motions, I face him, swaying my hips in time with the music as I advance toward him. My hands resting against the hard planes of his tattooed-covered chest, I push him into a chair in the corner of the room. He doesn't protest, simply obeys my unspoken command, his eyes never leaving mine.

I take several steps back, increasing the distance between us. One of the things I'd learned in my striptease lessons is that it's important not to give it all away at first. Stay out of reach. Make them want you. Beg for you. That's what I do.

The music comes to an abrupt stop, and I dart my eyes to Asher.

"I'm going to start the song over." There's a flash in his gaze. A heat. A warning. "If this is the only time I'll ever experience this, I need to milk it for every damn second. Every chord. Every eighth note. I need it all."

"God, I love a man who can talk music to me," I joke in a sensual tone, although my words hold a great deal of truth. Music has always been a turn-on for me. And a man who plays a musical instrument? One who appreciates the patience and practice essential to master it? That's the kind of man I want to be with.

"Well, you can blow my horn any day, baby."

I giggle, then quickly cover my mouth. "Sorry."

"What are you sorry about? I love your laugh."

"I know. It's just… I'm supposed to be doing this whole seductive temptress act here."

"Well, tempt away." He starts the song again before setting his phone on a nearby table, freeing his hands.

I close my eyes, taking a moment to allow the provocative rhythm to invade my soul as it did all those years ago when I couldn't help but move with the melody. It has a more mature sound now, evidence he must have re-recorded it. When his voice sings about spotting a beautiful woman in a bar who ends up infiltrating his every thought, it's deeper, more raspy, more soulful. The way Asher is today.

Shaking off my nerves, I fix my expression in front of me, emboldened by the fire I can make out in Asher's gaze. The few flickering candles create the perfect ambience for this, the darkness a blanket protecting me, allowing me to pretend I'm all alone, dancing for no one. It's not the first time I've danced to this song. This is no different from dancing to it when his band played it during my college days.

Except this time, I'll end up naked when the dance is over.

I sway my hips, subtly at first, allowing my soul to feel the music. Muscle memory kicks in, my body forgetting about the years that have passed since I've danced. I move with more confidence, tuning everything else out as I lose myself in the erotic sound of Asher's voice filling the room.

Approaching him, I run a lithe finger along his chest and collarbone before moving behind his chair. He attempts to glance over his shoulder, but I force his head forward. When I scrape my nails against his firm chest from behind, he throws his head back, a moan escaping his lips. Carnal. Wanton. Igniting.

As desperate as I am to keep feeling the warmth of his body on my fingertips, I remove my hands and circle to the front of his chair. I can see the raw need emanating from every pore, the fire in his eyes enough to light all of Las Vegas.

He reaches out, gripping my hip, pulling me closer. Giving him a playful look of admonishment, I take his hand, removing it. "No touching," I murmur breathlessly.

"God, you're going to kill me," he groans as I straddle him, pulsing my hips against his waist. I jut out my chest, leaning closer so I'm a breath away.

His body tightens beneath me in all the right places, giving me an added boost of confidence, knowing I do this to him. That the sight and feel of me, even fully clothed, pushes him to the point of oblivion. There's nothing so addictive. I now understand why some girls love stripping. I'd rolled my eyes when the woman teaching our class told us how powerful it made her feel, even when she felt she was losing control of everything else in her life. But the second she stepped into the club, she'd felt in charge, in control.

I hoist myself higher, my long, dark hair forming a curtain around us as I continue teasing and torturing. The frustration builds in his expression, and I can tell it's taking every ounce of resolve he possesses not to touch me, not to grip my hips or squeeze my ass as he takes charge of my seduction.

My lips skim against his, and he cranes his head toward mine, chasing my kiss, but I don't allow him to capture it just yet. Desperation blooms and grows, and I know he won't be able to hold off much longer. I don't think I will, either, the restraint I've had to exhibit until this point nearly making me combust.

Playfully waggling my brows, I pull back, climbing off him in measured movements. My eyes locked on his, I slip my fingers into the waistband of my yoga pants, teasing him by exposing a flash of skin on my hip before retreating, dancing around him once more. When he groans, I inwardly smile. I've been with my fair share of men over the past several years. Not one of them had ever been so unabashedly shameless in his need for me. So many men, at least in New York, have a "take it or leave it" attitude, thinking if it doesn't work out, there's always someone else who'd give them a piece of ass. But Asher has no qualms about showing me just how much he needs me.

Moving in front of him, I turn around, facing away. I pause for a beat, drawing in a breath. Once I do this, there's no going back. Then again, there was no going back the second we kissed. We both knew what we were getting into, yet did it anyway.

Hooking my fingers into my waistband, I slowly slide my pants down my legs, praying those years of ballet classes will pay off and keep me upright. I lean over, my legs remaining straight as I tease Asher, my ass dangling in front of him like a delicious treat.

A hiss echoes in the room. "You're killing me, Izzy." The unquenchable thirst in his voice nearly pushes me over the edge. I don't want to rush this. Don't want this to end.

Straightening, I step out of my yoga pants, sauntering back up to him, clad only in my tank top and panties. When I draw near this time, he cups my ass, tugging me toward him.

"Tsk, tsk, tsk." I curve into him, my lips hovering over his. "Didn't I already have to warn you once about touching?"

"I've never been one to listen to directions. You should know that about me."

"I do. But you were the one who asked me to strip."

"I changed my mind." He brings a hand to the back of my neck, his hold firm, unwavering, demanding. "If I don't have you right now, I'll lose my fucking head." He crushes his mouth against mine, his kiss stealing my breath with its ferocity. He thrusts his tongue past my lips, his loss of all control like the most addictive drug. Growing dizzy from the kiss, I manage to push away, panting.

"I can't deprive you of your fantasy."

"Don't you realize? *You* are my fantasy." This time when he kisses me, it's not as frenzied, but still brimming with want. Maybe more so. It's slower. Heavier. Sharper.

His hands go beneath my tank, skimming against my abdomen, deliberately making their way up to my chest. When he cups my breasts, I succumb to his touch, needing more. The tips of his fingers skim against my nipples, which harden instantly, eliciting a moan.

"Take off your top," Asher murmurs against my lips before burying his head in the crook of my neck, licking and sucking before pulling back.

Unable to deny him anything, I grab the hem of my shirt, yanking it over my head in one quick move, tossing it onto the floor.

He takes a minute to look at me. But unlike every other guy I've been with in the past, he doesn't stare at my chest. Instead, his eyes stay on mine. A finger traces the curve of my face before he threads his fingers through my hair, drawing my lips back to his.

"You are so fucking beautiful, Isabella." He eliminates the last breath between our mouths, but I retreat.

"I don't want to give it all up so soon. Not when you were hoping to get the most out of this seduction."

"Trust me. I have."

"How? I only danced for half a song."

He clutches my cheeks with both hands. "You seduced me the first time I saw you. Maybe not physically, but in here." He releases me, tapping the side of his head. His Adam's apple bobs up and down when he brings that same hand to his heart. "And here. The more time I spent with you, the more I got to know you, the more you seduced my soul." He grips my nape, pulling me back toward him. "Every fiber of my being."

His words are so choked with emotion, my brain refuses to fire. What can I say to that? A voice inside tells me he doesn't mean it, that this is just part of *his* seduction. After all, he *is* a writer. A musician. A poet. These words are second nature for him, as easy and natural as jotting down his grocery list. But I can't ignore the truth in his eyes. It's vibrant. Real. Spellbinding. Even the most practiced of actors couldn't fake that.

"So, to address your concerns, you needn't feel like you're short-changing me." He nibbles on my lower lip. A moan rattles from my throat at the perfect contact. "I've been able to enjoy a decade worth of your dance of seduction. Now I can finally join you. Let me join you."

I slam my lips to his, pressing my body as far into his as possible, needing to feel every strained muscle, every hard surface, every drum of his heart that only beats for me.

He runs his hands along the lines of my stomach, brushing the swell of my breasts before retreating once more. I don't want him to retreat. Only want him to push forward. Grabbing his hands, I press them against my chest, throwing my head back when he rolls my nipples between his thumb and forefinger.

He leaves a trail of desperate kisses along my jawline, his scruff rough but achingly pleasurable as it scrapes against my skin. Cupping my breasts tighter, he lowers his mouth. I curve back as best I can in our awkward position, my breathing increasing at the promise of feeling his lips on me.

Suddenly, I'm lifted, and I fling my eyes open. "Hold on," he rasps.

I do as he commands, tightening my grip around his neck as he transitions me into a cradle carry. Shoving his phone into his pocket, he walks with purposeful strides out of the studio, practically running up the stairs and into my bedroom, kicking the door shut behind him. I want to ask why he didn't take me back to his room, but before I have a chance to worry about that, he places me onto the mattress, slithering up my frame.

A whimper falls from my throat when his tongue traces delicate circles around my belly button. The touch is light, but hits me so deep, the way he worships me pushing my body higher and higher.

"Please, Asher," I beg, gripping the sheets as I writhe below him.

He cranes his head up, a salacious smirk forming on his lips. "Something I can help you with?"

Chest heaving, I clutch his face in my hands, tugging him toward me. "If I don't feel you in the next two seconds, I'm going to get myself off. And I'd much rather *you* do that."

"Now *that* sounds fucking hot." He seals his mouth over mine, his tongue sweeping against mine as he caresses the contours of my frame, inching farther south. When a finger swipes under the material of my panties, I circle my legs around his waist, pulsing, needing, wanting.

"Please." My word comes out a desperate plea, my eyes rolling into the back of my head as his hand grows closer and closer to my center.

Breaking our kiss, he hooks his fingers into the band of my panties. Pausing, his eyes lock with mine, giving me one last chance to back out. When I nod, he crushes his lips to mine, his kiss too short for my liking. Then again, I get the feeling his kisses will always seem too short. The way they seem to devour my soul has increased my appetite for him to a nearly incomprehensible level. I can take and take and take, yet fear I'll always need more of him.

His motions are slow as he lowers my panties down my legs, his eyes not breaking from mine, as if waiting for me to change course. But I can't. Tonight was the perfect storm. The canceled flight. The invitation to stay here. The blackout. All the pieces snapped into place for this to happen. There's no reason to deprive ourselves of this.

After tossing my panties onto the floor, he runs a hand up my leg, his tongue following. I throw my head back, the ecstasy from his soft touch more than I can handle. With every inch, my core tightens in promise of what's to come. When a finger ghosts against my center, I moan, my pulse skyrocketing.

"God, you're so wet."

"Because you're driving me crazy. I told you I needed to get off."

"Well then," he begins coyly. "Allow me the…pleasure." He waggles his brows, then brings his mouth to me, his tongue lapping up my juices.

I melt into the mattress, all the tension rolling off my body at how expertly he tastes me, then inserts a finger, stretching and exploring. "I believe the pleasure is all mine," I murmur as if having an out-of-body experience.

"Oh no, baby. This is all mine."

"Yours…" I run my hand through his locks as he inserts another finger, pushing me higher and higher, my body flooding with warmth in places I didn't even think existed. I've never felt so full. So complete. So beautiful.

"All mine," he growls, picking up speed.

It takes no time at all for me to succumb to his ministrations, the combination of his erotic touch and the amount of time since I've been with a man sending me over the edge. Lights flash before my eyes, despite the darkness shrouding the room, my body convulsing as one of the most intense orgasms I've experienced rolls through me. But that doesn't make Asher stop. He keeps licking, tasting, devouring, wanting every last drop, every last shake, every last tremor until I have nothing left to give, my cries echoing into the Las Vegas night through the open window in my bedroom.

Sated, I flutter my eyes open, meeting Asher's lazy smile that's coated in my desire. "I hope that was as enjoyable for you as it was for me."

Cheeks clutched in my hands, I drag him toward me, kissing him fully, tasting me and him in one incredibly erotic combination. "I need you inside me," I murmur, nibbling on his lower lip.

"And I need to be inside you." His expression falls. "But I don't have any condoms. I wasn't exactly planning on this happening, so I—"

"It's okay. I'm on the pill. I trust you."

Asher was never the type to sleep around. Granted, it's been years since we've seen each other. In some respects, he's not the same Asher. I don't think he's changed *that* much.

"Are you sure? I don't want you to feel like you have to if you're not comfortable without protection."

I flip him onto his back in one swift move. His eyes flame before darkening. I sensually grind my hips against his, my hair falling around us.

"I need you." I reach down, palming the erection straining to be released. "And I can feel how much you need me. I want this, Asher. More than I've wanted anything I can remember in years." I bring my lips to his, skimming them. "I want *you*."

He delicately pushes a curl out of my eyes. I expect him to treat me to a beautiful kiss. Instead, his gaze becomes clouded with lust as he grips my hair forcefully, passion surging through me. "And I want you." He yanks my head to the side, his teeth clamping onto my neck. I release a noiseless gasp. I didn't think this kind of pleasure was possible. "So fucking much."

"Then have me."

With a growl, he flips me onto my back, climbing off me to undress. A sliver of moonlight illuminates him as he shrugs his shirt off his shoulders, revealing even more ink on his back. He's not fully covered, but the few tattoos that spread from his shoulder blades onto his arms are tasteful. They're the perfect accent to his broad shoulders, not obscuring his sculpted pecs or defined abs.

His eyes remain steady on mine as he unbuttons his shorts and pushes them down his legs, his arousal springing free. It takes every ounce of resolve I possess not to compare Jessie to Asher. One thing is certain. There is one area where Jessie will never be able to outshine his brother. While Jessie was pretty well-endowed, and the inexperienced girl I was when we first had sex thought he used it quite well, it's no match for Asher.

He crawls onto the bed, slithering up my body. When he settles between my thighs, I enclose my legs around his waist, the feel of flesh against flesh causing my stomach to clench in anticipation.

Pulling back, he lifts his erection to me, spreading my wetness around. Neither one of us looks away as he pushes into me, inch by incredible inch, stretching and filling before retreating, then sliding back in again. He continues acclimating my body to his, every motion deliberately sensual, giving me a taste of how amazing it could be before pulling back.

I dig my hands into his scalp, tugging him against me, chest to chest, heart to heart. I cover his mouth with mine, tightening my hold around his waist, matching his rhythm. He moans, the vibration in his chest hitting the deepest parts of my soul.

I rake my nails up his back and he tears his lips from mine, arching into the contact, his chest heaving, sweat forming on his brow. "You're driving me fucking crazy."

I crane toward him, taking his earlobe between my teeth. "That's the point."

With a groan, he increases his sensual rhythm, each thrust deeper and more fulfilling. I fall back onto the mattress as his lips kiss every part of me he can get to. My mouth. My neck. My chest. His frenzied hands explore every inch of my body, squeezing and bruising. When his finger rubs against my clit, I moan, my breathing growing ragged.

"I want you to come again."

I'm about to tell him I don't think I can, that it's never happened, when that familiar tingling sensation bubbles deep inside, becoming brighter and stronger until I scream out, waves of mind-erasing pleasure washing over me.

An animalistic growl rips from Asher's lungs, the sensual, seductive lover turning into a man obsessed, desperate, hungry. He brings my legs onto his shoulders, increasing his rhythm to an almost punishing level as he drives into me, harder, deeper, faster, eyes dark, frantic, pained.

He stills, emitting a strangled cry as his warmth spreads through me, his motions jerky. Tremors overtake him and he releases his hold on my legs, allowing them to fall to the mattress before he covers my body with his. Our labored breathing fills the room, stark against the silence, which is even more pronounced due to the lack of power.

"Damn," he breathes, nuzzling my chest. "I knew sex with you would be good. I just never could have imagined it would be so…electric."

I smirk. "You imagined?"

He lifts his eyes to mine, a salacious grin crossing his mouth. "You better believe it. Let's just say, for quite a few years, you were the leading lady of my spank bank."

With a laugh, I push him off me. "Gross." I attempt to scoot away, but he wraps an arm around my waist, pulling me back into him, thwarting my lackluster escape plan. When he brushes my hair over my shoulder and peppers soft kisses along my shoulder blades, I can't help but melt into him.

"You can't tell me you've never thought of someone else when you touched yourself."

"Maybe," I muse.

He nuzzles his nose into my neck. "And who would that lucky bastard be?"

I shift my position, turning to face him. "What would you say if I told you I've thought of you?"

Impassioned, he covers my mouth with his, his kiss brief but still full. "I'd say that's one of the hottest things I've heard in a long time." He grabs my knee, hooking my leg over his waist, thrusting to demonstrate his reawakening arousal. "And when was this?"

Leaning toward him, I scrape my teeth along his pec. "This morning." My answer comes out breathy. "I get really horny first thing in the morning."

He groans, smashing my body against his, his arms enveloping me.

"You're going to be my undoing. Do you know that?"

"That's what I'm hoping for."

CHAPTER FIFTEEN

THE SOFT TICKLE of chest hair against my back stirs me from a restful sleep. One of the most restful nights I've had in a while. I exhale a contented sigh, not wanting to open my eyes, able to sense the sun is already bathing the room in light. I don't want it to be day. Not yet. Not when that means I'll have to come to terms with what Asher and I did last night.

He tightens his arm around my waist, pulling me into his body, a raspy moan reverberating through his chest. "Mmm." He subtly thrusts against me, jumpstarting my libido, as if she needs any help. Just being near this man skyrockets my sex drive. "I can get used to waking up like this."

"What? With some naked chick in your bed?"

"Not just any naked chick." His hand travels along my stomach, making the laborious journey south. I adjust my legs, parting them, an unspoken invitation to continue his exploration of my body. "Only you. I can get used to waking up next to you."

When he toys with my folds, I succumb to his touch, ignoring the voice of reason telling me to put a stop to this, to find out what time it is, if the power's come back on. By the whirring fan kicking on from the central air and heating system, I surmise it is. I don't want to do anything to interrupt this moment.

"I can get used to this, too," I whimper as he inserts a finger, then another, massaging me in the most delicious of ways.

He pulses against me, and I part my thighs even more, allowing him better access. "Prop your leg up with your foot," he orders. "With your knee bent."

I do as he asks, which spreads my legs wider. He grips the underside of my thigh, pulling it to the other side of his body, leaving me sprawled out and at the mercy of his fingers.

"God, Izzy…" He scrapes his teeth along my neck, the pleasurable pain almost more than I can bear. "I need you one more time."

I moan, lost in the sensation, unable to form a single coherent thought.

"Do you want me?" He pushes his finger deeper, tantalizing and teasing. I couldn't tell him no if I wanted to, my mind devoid of reason.

"Y-yes."

"I was hoping you'd say that." He withdraws his fingers, the lack of his touch causing an unwelcome chill to wash over me. But before I can beg for more, his length thrusts against me from behind, sliding into me.

We exhale simultaneously and he pauses, filling me before retreating, continuing his same sensual motion. Over. And over. And over. My jaw falls slack, a noiseless whimper escaping at the utter bliss invading me. Last night was incredible. I'd never been with any man as selfless and passionate as Asher. But this position, lying on my side with my back to his front, my leg propped up, he's able to hit parts of me no other man ever has.

"Asher," I manage to say, my veins throbbing with the electric current burning through me. "I don't—"

"Touch yourself," he orders gruffly, cutting me off. "I want to feel your pussy clench around me."

A slave to his demand, I lower my hand between my legs, toying with my clit. My teeth clench with the unmatched desire seizing me. The idea of touching myself while Asher fucks me is all I need to come undone, my world crumbling into a thousand pieces of the most brilliant light.

"Yes," he hisses. "Like that." He picks up his pace, his hand squeezing my thigh, spreading me more, his punishing grip only serving to increase my pleasure. "So. Damn. Good." Each word is punctured with another thrust until he climaxes, a suppressed roar ripping through the room.

The tremors overtaking his body match my own in intensity. I can't remember sex ever being like this. I'm not naïve by any stretch of the imagination. I've had my fair share of a variety of relationships, from committed to one-night stands and everything in between. But it's never been like this. This powerful. This inspiring. This explosive. I wonder if Asher feels the same way. By the way he struggles to catch his breath, the way his heart pounds against my back, the way he seems to be speechless, I imagine he probably does.

A ringtone cuts through our heavy breaths, and I sigh at the confirmation that the blackout is over. I glance at my watch on the nightstand to see it's after nine. As much as I'd love to stay in this bed all day, I need to pack my things and get to the airport. I have to get home today.

"Aren't you going to answer that?" I ask when Asher doesn't make any move.

"I wasn't planning on it. I'd hoped to stay right here with my cock inside you as long as I can. Then when my happy warrior snaps to attention, I'll already be in position."

I laugh, wiggling my butt against him as the ringing stops. "Well, maybe I should help him along."

"He's a little spent right now, but I'm sure he can be coaxed into playing again very soon." He nips at my shoulder blade. "Maybe in the shower."

"Mmm. I can get on board with that."

When his phone rings again, he groans.

"You should get that. Whoever it is must have an important reason to try you twice in a row."

"They should know better than to call me in the morning."

"True." I shimmy away as he slides out of me. Facing him, I feather my lips against his. "But I'll make you a deal. You answer your phone, then come join me in the shower where you can wash every inch of me clean. And I do mean every…" I drag my tongue along his jawline. "Single." I dig my fingers into his chest. "Inch." My mouth covers his before I scoot off the bed and pad toward the bathroom.

Just before I disappear behind the door, I glance over my shoulder, giving myself a mental high-five when I see his erection spring back to life.

CHAPTER SIXTEEN

"YOU'RE INSATIABLE, IZZY," Asher struggles to say, our breathing even more ragged after the strenuous effort it takes to have sex in a shower. It's not as easy as romance novels make it seem. You need to be in damn good shape to keep your body upright. Thankfully, Asher is in amazing shape, his flexing muscles able to support my sated frame with ease.

"You're not so bad yourself," I reply, kissing him, my skin still tingling.

He practically has to peel my legs from around his waist as he steps away, helping me find my footing. My balance is a little unsteady from the amount of sex we've had the last several hours. In the past six months, I don't think I've had sex the number of times I have these past six hours. A girl could get used to this.

After rinsing off one last time, he places a soft kiss on my forehead. "I'll let you finish showering on your own."

"Oh really?" I pout dramatically. "You really want to leave this?" I step under the stream, allowing it to cascade over my breasts.

Asher's in front of me in a heartbeat, yanking my body against his. He seals his mouth over mine, water falling over him, me, and our kiss before he pulls away, chest heaving. "I don't want to leave you, but if I don't walk away now, I won't be able to keep my hands off you. Then I'll have to kidnap you and keep you here forever."

"You won't hear any complaints from me."

"Me, either." Leaving me with a delicate kiss on my temple, he opens the shower door and grabs a towel, securing it around his waist.

God, there's nothing sexier than Asher York wearing only a towel, droplets of water gleaming on his body.

I steal a glance as he pauses in front of the long vanity, briefly leaning his arms against the counter. He closes his eyes, blowing out a long breath. It's a fleeting expression of remorse, but it still hits me, reminds me of the reality of what we've done.

Once he walks out of the bathroom, I finish showering as quickly as possible. I don't have much time left before I need to get to the airport to catch my flight. When I checked the status, it showed on time, much to my surprise.

As I towel off my hair, Asher reappears in the doorway of the bathroom, dressed in a pair of jeans and t-shirt. "Hey." He crosses his arms in front of his chest, leaning on the doorjamb.

"Hey."

"So, I need to tell you something, but I don't want you to freak out."

"Okay..." My response is drawn-out as I straighten my spine, re-securing the towel wrapped around my body.

He pushes off the wall, his eyes averted. From this alone, I can sense I'm not going to like what he's about to say. He runs his hands through his hair that's still damp from our sex-filled shower. On a long exhale, he slowly lifts his gaze to meet mine.

"That was Jessie on the phone."

My pulse increases slightly. Since I stepped foot into the studio last night, I haven't thought of Jessie more than a fleeting comparison in size. Based on the expression on Asher's face, I have a feeling that's about to end.

"And?" I ask, my voice trembling.

He doesn't say anything right away, simply stares at me. Then he sighs. "He's downstairs."

"What?"

My heart plummets to the pit of my stomach, frantic eyes searching his for an indication that this is a joke. That this isn't real. But all I see is the same honesty I always have from Asher. He wouldn't lie to me, not about this.

"How?" I push past him, darting toward my suitcase. I hastily throw all my items back into it, a need to get out of this house overtaking me. "Do you think he knows?"

"Of course not. Pretty sure he would have greeted me with a broken nose instead of a hug."

"Then why—"

He places his hands on my biceps in an attempt to placate me, but nothing can. This all just got real. A little too real. I knew what I was getting into last night. Knew the ramifications, but ignored them. The blackout bubble seduced me into thinking we wouldn't suffer the consequences of our actions. At least not anytime soon. For once, I chose to live in the moment. And now we'll both have to pay the price.

"He heard about the blackout and came out to check on me."

"From Boston? How did he get a flight if the airport just reopened?"

He licks his lips, his gaze steady, expression calm. "Because he doesn't live in Boston anymore." He swallows hard. "He lives in Los Angeles. He's..." He hesitates. "He's my manager."

My body freezes, his words a punch to the gut. "Your manager?" I squeak out, blindsided.

Granted, I never asked who his manager was, or if he even had one, but considering my history with Jessie, you'd think Asher would have mentioned that little tidbit of information. It's not just a familial relationship I'm dealing with here. Asher and Jessie have a professional relationship, too. It's like learning the guy I just had amazing sex with is my ex's new boss. But it's worse with us, because I should have known better. Now, there's so much more at stake than I ever could have imagined.

"Yes." He doesn't embellish any further, but he doesn't need to. It makes sense. Jessie was a business major, a natural salesman. He could charm the squirrels out of the trees in the dead of winter, even though they knew it was their only means of protection against the elements. Not to mention, right after college, Jessie worked as a client specialist for a talent agency in Boston. He understands the business side of the music industry. There's no one else Asher would trust with his career. It was always their plan.

I shake off his touch, shrinking into myself. "Why didn't you tell me?"

"It didn't seem like it mattered."

"Didn't seem like it mattered?" I repeat, my voice rising in pitch. I quickly lower it, unsure where Jessie is. For all I know, he could be eavesdropping outside the door. "It matters. It matters a lot. So… What? You let Jessie in and then came up to fuck me one last time before dropping this bomb?" My disbelief at this situation growing, I grab the first pair of pants I find in my disheveled suitcase and yank them on, not caring I'm not wearing any underwear.

"It's not like that, Iz. I'm as surprised as you are. I bought us a little time and have him in the studio, listening to some demos I've written for a solo album I have in the works."

I slow my motions, finding solace in the fact that Jessie's locked away in the opposite end of the house. Then memories from last night float back and my eyes widen.

"Asher! My pants and tank top are in there! They have my perfume all over them. The same perfume I wore back in college. The same perfume he bought me repeatedly. If he picks them up and—"

"Relax," he soothes, running his hands down my arms. "I grabbed them and brought them back up here before letting him in." He nods at the pants I just tugged on. "You're wearing them."

"That still doesn't make this okay." I push out of his hold, grabbing a bra and slipping it on, facing away from Asher. It's not like he hasn't seen me naked. For the past several hours, that's the *only* way he's seen me. But I feel exposed, especially now that we've been propelled into the real world, facing the consequences of sleeping together. After tugging on a shirt, I add, "You should have told me."

"Would that have changed anything?"

I whirl around to face him, my mouth agape. How do I answer that? *Would* it have changed anything? Would I have wanted Asher any less than I did last night?

When he reaches for my face and brushes his fingers against my skin, I can't help but melt into the contact. One touch is all I need to reassure me that his intentions were noble, even if the outcome was less than desirable. Maybe I'm just overreacting. Did his omission really do any harm? I can't see how.

"I understand I should have mentioned it. But I didn't want to burst our bubble. Wanted to prevent you from enduring any heartache." He brings his lips toward mine, and I sigh at the promise of his kiss. "Just like I hoped to do all those years ago."

I melt into him, digging my hands into his hair, his words wrapping around me like a blanket. But as the meaning in his statement sank in, I stiffen, pushing against him.

"What did you say?"

Disoriented, he blinks repeatedly. This time, *he's* at a loss for words. "I—"

"What heartache did you want to prevent all those years ago?" I step back, eyeing him with suspicion, a knot tightening in my stomach.

"I…," he stammers, his breathing quickening.

"What heartache did you want to prevent?" I ask again through clenched teeth, my temper flaming. He doesn't say anything. He doesn't have to. The answer is etched in the worry lines on his face. In his pleading eyes. In the hard bob of his Adam's apple.

I back up. It makes perfect sense. I always wondered why Asher argued vehemently against my decision to surprise Jessie. Now I know why.

"Oh, my god. You knew. That's what you mean, right? When you said you hoped to prevent my heartache, you're talking about that night, aren't you?"

Again, he remains silent. What *is* there to say?

"How could you keep that from me? You knew what I was walking into, yet—"

"No." He darts his eyes to mine, that vein in his neck throbbing. His fists clench, every muscle in his body vibrating with a passion I've yet to see in another person. Even him. "I had no idea what you were walking into."

"But—"

"Maybe you've forgotten, because the story you told last night left out quite a few things."

"I didn't think it was necessary to go into all the gory details."

"Really?" Defensive, he folds his arms across his chest. "Is that why Chloe didn't even seem to know what happened? Why she appeared just as interested in the story as someone who'd never heard it? Because you didn't think it was necessary to go into 'all the gory details' with one of your dearest friends when it happened? Don't you always say that keeping the truth is as bad as lying?"

"That's not the same, and you know it. The details didn't involve Chloe."

What can I say to him? That the reason I left out so many details was because of what I feared it would finally reveal. That the real reason I ran out on Jessie wasn't because he sought comfort in another woman's embrace. After all, I did play a part in pushing him there. It was because, as I sat waiting for him, I found myself staring at a photo of Asher and me together, my mother's words ringing around me.

"How will I know if he owns my heart?"
"You'll just…know."
"How?"
"You'll see it in his eyes. You'll see a piece of yourself staring back at you."

That was when I realized I'd allowed myself to fall in love with two men. While I saw a piece of myself staring back at me from Jessie's eyes, it was no match to the giant piece looking back from Asher's penetrating gaze.

"You kept something from me that affected *me* directly," I continue.

"How was I supposed to know you wanted to reconcile with him? According to what both you and Jessie told me about the fight you had before Christmas break, it seemed you'd written him off. Hell, he said you tried to give back the ring, but he begged you to keep it."

"All the more reason he shouldn't have sought out his ex," I snip back.

"Agreed, but you also can't stand there and blame me for this. I figured you were so adamant about seeing Jessie so you could officially end this chapter, not start a new one." He shakes his head, swallowing hard. "I didn't even stop to consider you might still want to be with him after refusing to talk to him all of Christmas break."

"Maybe you should have," I say in a shaky voice. "Like you should have thought about telling me what you knew about Jessie."

"I *did* think about it, goddammit!" He slams his hand into the wall, frustration radiating from his fist, spreading up his tense arm and through the rest of his body. "I'm not saying what Jessie did was right, but he was in a really bad place. I wanted to tell you Candace had started circling like a hawk again." His head hangs as he expels a breath.

"Then why didn't you?"

It's not the fact that he kept this from me that has betrayal flowing through my body. Once I'd realized my feelings for Asher, I knew I could never be with Jessie again. It's the realization of the truth that's been screaming at me ever since I first felt myself falling victim to Asher's hypnotic spell. Since I realized I'd fallen in love with him all those years ago.

He will *always* choose Jessie. I shouldn't be surprised. And I can't blame him for it. They're brothers. Family. I'm no one.

"Jessie's my brother." His voice is choked as he brings his eyes back to mine. "I couldn't betray him like that."

All I can do is nod at his confirmation of my suspicion, the lump in my throat bordering on painful, cutting off my oxygen. This is the reason I walked away all those years ago. And the reason I should have walked away the other night at the bar. There is no possible way for us to have a happy ending. Not when it means hurting someone we both love. And despite it all, I do still love Jessie. At least the Jessie he was when we dated.

A loud chiming cuts through the tension, causing Asher to flinch. I have no reason to believe it, other than a feeling in my gut, but I know the alert is a text from Jessie. I don't say a word, just glance at the outline of a cellphone in Asher's pocket. I can tell he's struggling between staying in the moment with me and seeing what his brother wants. When it chimes again, he groans, yanking it out.

"You should go," I say softly, turning from him. "Distract him. I'll finish packing and be out of your way so you don't have to keep him hidden."

"Please, Izzy. I don't want to leave you like this. What can I do to make up for it? I'll do anything."

I glance over my shoulder as I'm about to disappear into the bathroom. "We both know there's nothing you can do. Jessie will always come between us. We were fooling ourselves to hope otherwise."

"He doesn't have to. We don't have to let him."

I force a smile, although my heart is breaking. I step toward him, a breath away. "I think you already have."

He parts his lips, but I place a finger over his mouth, silencing him. Then I hoist myself onto my toes, kissing him one last time. A lone tear slides down my cheek at the finality of it all. He senses it, too, his chin quivering.

"Goodbye, Asher." Lowering myself to my heels, I walk into the bathroom, closing the door behind me. It's silent for a moment, not so much as the rustling of his clothes or shuffling of his feet across the carpet.

Then his phone chimes again, the sound striking against the stillness.

"Fuck," he groans, his footsteps loud as he storms out of the room, slamming the door. I remain still for several long moments, unsure if Asher's frustration is aimed at me or Jessie. I get the feeling it's the latter.

Just when I'm about to head back into the bedroom to finish packing, I hear the door open once more. I freeze, barely breathing. Soft footsteps pad into the room and stop for a moment. Maybe two. Then they retreat, the door opening and closing again.

I wait a few minutes to see if he returns. When he doesn't, I peek into the room. Confirming I'm alone, I hurry to the bedroom door and lock it before heading to my suitcase to finish packing. As I approach, I stop in my tracks. On top of my haphazardly packed clothes sits an origami dove.

A soft smile pulls on my lips as I pick it up, examining it. It's something we did whenever we got into an argument, which usually revolved around Jessie. It was our way of apologizing to each other. Our way of reconciling.

I don't think that's in the cards anymore.

Once I'm dressed and all my things are shoved into my suitcase, I request an Uber, praying the service isn't down as an aftereffect of the blackout. Thankfully, it goes through. I fire off a quick text to Chloe to let her know.

Me: *Requested an Uber. Will be here in ten. Meet me by the front gate.*

All I can do is hope she's awake. Worst-case scenario, she can find her own way to the airport.

When my phone buzzes, I glance at the screen.

Izzy: *Okay. Just packing up.*

Shoving it into my purse, I do one last check of the room. Apart from the mussed-up sheets, it looks exactly as it did yesterday when I first stepped over the threshold, blown away by the posh surroundings. Longing fills me at everything I lost in the past twenty-four hours. Then again, two days ago, I never expected to see Asher York. I'll just forget I saw him. Leave whatever happened in this godforsaken city.

My bags in hand, I open the door and step into the hallway, pausing to listen for any indication that Jessie may be in one of the common areas. Thankfully, I don't hear him. I don't hear anything.

With quick steps, I make my way to the lower level as quietly as possible, keeping my eyes forward as I dash toward the front door. The second I'm outside, I exhale, my muscles relaxing. This scenario reminds me of having to sneak out of my high school boyfriend's house when his parents unexpectedly returned from a weekend trip before either of us anticipated. But this is worse. I knew who I was running from then. Now, I'm not sure.

I head down the walkway, slipping out of the open gate, and peer down the street for our car. Within moments, I sense Chloe approach.

"Hey, Iz."

"Hey, Chloe." I shift my eyes to hers, smiling a small smile. She doesn't have to say a word. I can tell things between Lincoln and her ended as spectacularly as between Asher and me. And she can probably sense there were quite a few fireworks on our end this morning.

We both shrug at the same time and say, "Vegas."

Our laughter surrounds us as we hug each other. This is what I need right now. To laugh with one of my oldest friends. To feel her understanding. To give her the comfort she needs, too.

"So you're not going to see him again," I state.

She pulls away. "What choice do I have?"

I nod, more than aware of her reasoning for not wanting to see Lincoln again, even if they do live in the same city. She's so used to people disappointing her, she assumes no one would want to be with her if they knew about her mother.

"You're not going to see him again?" she asks after a beat.

I face her, my eyes brimming with tears. I could finally tell her the truth of what really happened all those years ago and get her opinion. But would any of that matter? Regardless of whether Jessie actually did cheat on me, as I led everyone to believe, nothing could ever come from this thing with Asher. I'll always be his brother's ex-fiancée. As he just demonstrated, he will always choose Jessie over me. As he should. After all, I'm just someone he knew once upon a time.

"What choice do *I* have?"

TO BE CONTINUED . . .

ABOUT THE AUTHOR

T.K. Leigh, otherwise known as Tracy Leigh Kellam, is the *USA Today* Bestselling author of the Beautiful Mess series, in addition to several other works ranging from sexy and sinful to fun and flirty. Originally from New England, she now resides in sunny Southern California with her husband, beautiful daughter, and three cats. When she's not planted in front of her computer, writing away, she can be found training for her next marathon (of which she has run over twenty fulls and far too many halfs to recall) or chasing her daughter around the house.

T.K. Leigh is represented by Jane Dystel of Dystel, Goderich & Bourret Literary Management. All publishing inquiries, including audio, foreign, and film rights, should be directed to her.

www.ingramcontent.com/pod-product-compliance
Lightning Source LLC
Chambersburg PA
CBHW020349310726
48979CB00015B/2553/J

* 9 7 8 1 7 3 3 7 3 6 2 9 9 *